THE LINDISFARNE SERIES

Books 1 - 3

BY THE SAME AUTHOR

THE WEST COUNTRY TRILOGY
Moonshine (Prequel)
Bridles Lane (Book 1)
Hills of Silver (Book 2)
Wild Light (Book 3)

FAR FROM MY NATIVE SHORE: A COLLECTION OF
AUSTRALIAN HISTORICAL NOVELS
One of Us Buried
Forgotten Places
Playing the Ghost

STANDALONE TITLES
The Devil and the Deep Blue Sea

THE LINDISFARNE SERIES

BOOKS 1 - 3

JOHANNA CRAVEN

Book One:

Firelight Rising

HOLY ISLAND OF LINDISFARNE, ENGLAND

AUGUST 1715

CHAPTER ONE

It's a fisherman's cottage grown wild. Rolling grassland on two sides and sea on two others, leathery and purple in the late-afternoon light. A house at the end of the world.

There are hints of its Tudor beginnings in the gabled roof and oriel windows, the forest of chimneys pegged against the sky. Walls are cobbled together in a mismatch of stone and faded brick, the red tiles of the roof washed to the colour of earth. Vines are scrawled across the house, the grass so long in places it tickles the grimy windows. Eerily beautiful in its own devastated way.

Eva waits for a prick of recognition, for some sense that this house, this island, is not as foreign as it seems. Lindisfarne had been home for the first four years of her life. But no part of it strikes a familiar chord. Whatever connection she might have had to the place has been frayed by two decades of London life.

She reaches for her niece's hand, and with their duffel bags slung over one shoulder, they slink towards the front door. Eva rehearses her speech to her older brother in her head. An explanation. An apology for her failures.

Before she can ready herself, Nathan appears from inside one of the dilapidated out-buildings. He is clearly knee-deep in his restoration work, wearing rolled-up shirtsleeves and a tatty brown vest in place of his usual embroidered waistcoat and justacorps. His coffee-coloured hair is unpowdered and tied back messily, a few stray coils plastered to his neck. His eyes widen at the sight of his daughter and sister, here where they were never supposed to be.

Theodora calls to him excitedly. She lurches forward but stops inches from her father, as though registering his look of bewilderment.

Nathan had been adamant that London was the best place for Theodora, away from the broken beams and shadows of Highfield House. He had left his daughter under Eva's supervision, back in the neat sea-less confines of Knightsbridge, while he restores the shell of their family's house into something sellable.

He will not be pleased to see them. But it is not as though they have a choice. In the right moments, Eva can convince herself that none of this is her fault. But that doesn't change the fact that she and Thea have nowhere to go but out to this Holy Island of Lindisfarne to face Nathan's disappointment.

He drops the hammer he is holding and it thuds dully on the grass. "Why are you here?"

"Are you not happy to see me, Papa?" Theodora is theatrically pitiful.

"Of course I'm happy to see you, my love. I just…" He looks searchingly at Eva. "You can't be here," he says, voice low. "This is no place for a child to be running around. The house is in a state. It's dangerous."

Eva drops the bags. "She's seven years old, Nathan. She's not an infant."

Something she dimly recognises as anger flickers across his eyes. She can count on one hand the number of times she has seen her brother angry. Usually his rage is hidden behind a façade of warmth and cordiality. Today is no different—when he speaks, there's a thin control to his voice.

"Why are you here?" he asks again, slowly, as though reining in his displeasure.

Eva lets out a deep sigh. The story was devastatingly shameful when she was tossing it around in her head. Telling it to her older brother makes her wish the earth would swallow her. She had spent the long coach journey from London trying to piece the right words together.

"Mr Walton no longer wishes to marry me. He says it's for the best that Thea and I leave the townhouse." Despite how quickly she blurts them out, the words are bitter on her tongue. This is the first time she has spoken of the thing out loud, apart from the brisk, smooth-edged version she had fed her niece in the carriage as an explanation for their trek across the country.

She ought to have known better than to move to her betrothed's townhouse before they were married. Of course, Walton had not been there at the time—no, he was tucked away in his private lodgings in North London, the bachelor's hideout he used between endless business trips and pleasure jaunts across the Channel.

A year earlier, Nathan had been forced to sell the family house in Chelsea to repay the debts his merchant business had racked up, and they'd had no choice but to rent on the edge of the city. When Nathan had made his plans to head to Holy Island last month, he had welcomed Walton's offer to put a roof over the head of his wife-to-be.

All in good faith, I can assure you, Nate. I'm never at the townhouse myself. There shall be nothing improper about it.

The offer of the townhouse, Eva had discovered, after Walton had sat her down in his office of all places—as if their betrothal had not felt business-like enough—had turned out to be a fickle one.

I'm afraid this match will not be suitable for me after all…

Two days later, Eva was rattling up the coast of England with her every plan for life unravelling.

Nathan frowns. "Are you certain?"

"Of course I'm certain."

"I've heard nothing of this."

"Well," she says sharply, "perhaps your dear friend Mr Walton is not the fine upstanding fellow you imagined him to be." She gives him a wry, thin-lipped smile. "Although he was kind enough to pay for our passage up here."

Nathan scrubs a hand across his forehead. What is he thinking? Is he cursing Matthew Walton's name, Eva wonders? Or is he cursing hers?

"I'm sorry," he says finally. "I imagine this is my fault."

Eva doesn't speak. Nathan is nothing if not predictable, and she had known he would attribute the breaking of the betrothal to the recent failures of his business. Eighteen months ago, he had signed a deal with a smooth-tongued watch manufacturer whose products had not lived up to expectation. Nathan had discovered far too late that the pieces he was selling his wealthy clients were not of the quality they were used to. Word had spread and business had dried up, leading to the sale of the family home in London. No doubt he assumes Matthew Walton had changed his mind about marrying into a family in such a fragile financial state.

She ought to tell Nathan the truth, of course. Tell him the real reason Walton had ended the betrothal. She can practically see the weight of his guilt pressing down on his shoulders. But right now, all she wants is for this conversation to be over.

"I know you don't want us here," she tells her brother, "but there really is nowhere else." She meets his eyes pointedly. "We've been travelling for days. And Thea… She missed you terribly."

Nathan looks down at his daughter and his smile is suddenly genuine. "I've missed you terribly too, my love." He looks up at Eva, nodding faintly. A resignation. He looks exhausted, she realises. Older than his twenty-eight years, with dark circles beneath his eyes and grey at his temples. Flecks of blood scarring his knuckles. The restoration is clearly taking its toll on him. Perhaps having his daughter here will be good for him. Even if he doesn't know it himself yet.

"The housekeeper, Mrs Brodie, will find you somewhere to sleep," he says finally. "Tell her to put Thea in my room."

Eva manages a faint smile. "Thank you." She swings the bags onto her shoulders again.

"Leave those," says Nathan. "I shall bring them in for you."

"I can manage." And she is off before her brother can protest.

The house is a wreck. All broken beams and faded walls, like a foundered ship that has been lying on the ocean floor for decades. While the housekeeper makes up rooms for the unexpected arrivals, Eva walks the passages, breathing in the place. A large seascape hangs in the entrance hall, its colours faded, turning the landscape dull and wintery. Some long-buried ancestor looks down from the wall beside them, candlelight flickering on his cracked cheeks.

The vast dining room on the ground floor is swathed with dark wood panelling, bare smoke-coloured stone on the back wall. A long table fills most of the room, and a half-attended fire simmers in the grate. Next door she finds a sitting room with a worn settle and a bookshelf standing empty, the volumes piled up on the floor beside it. The room smells of dust and damp, and the faint breath of the sea. There is a vague sense of familiarity here, perhaps. But nothing solid. Nothing that tells her for certain that she belongs in this house.

Though Nathan has been at work here for close to a month, it still looks forgotten, with its bowed stairs and grime-thickened windows, and exhalations of dust from between the worn stones of the walls. Unloved and abandoned. Eva supposes that's exactly what it is. Twenty years since her family had last lived here. To the best of her knowledge, it has been empty for all that time.

For years, Nathan had shown no interest in the property. With the family in London, Highfield House had been little more than a name, a neglected and nostalgic shadow. Occasionally, he would toss in mentions of selling it, or tearing it down, or at the very least finding a tenant willing to take on such a ruin, but there was never any urgency to his plans.

And then that day a month and a half ago when he had announced with feverish enthusiasm that he was to travel to Holy Island and bring Highfield House back from the dead. Restore her to her former glory and sell it for what he hoped would be a sizeable profit. Bring the wealth he had squandered back to the family.

The thought of selling the house feels almost blasphemous. Eva wonders what their parents would think of it. It matters little, of course. They have both been dead for years. Their father had taken his last breath right here in Highfield House when Eva was a child, their mother succumbing to consumption five years ago. She supposes Nathan is right to sell the place. The family needs money far more than they need a sentimental shadow hanging in the background of their lives.

Nathan had convinced their brother-in-law Edwin to help him with the restoration. In London, Edwin has a reputation as a fine craftsman, whittling sought-after furniture for the wealthy upper classes. The hastily patched holes in the sitting room ceiling suggest he has not worked his magic on Highfield House just yet.

Edwin had brought Eva's sister Harriet and their infant son Thomas with him. Now she is walking the dust-laden halls of the house, Eva can only imagine the displeasure with which her polished younger sister has been doing the same this past month.

The stairs creak loudly as she climbs to the second storey. The staircase opens out into a wide corridor with rooms on either side. The door to what she assumes is Nathan's bedroom is slightly ajar; several others looked unused. She can hear the sound of hammering coming from a room at the end of the hallway. She walks down the passage and peeks inside. Edwin is kneeling on the floor with his back to her, hammering new boards into place. He looks as ragged and dirt-streaked as Nathan; dust-worn and wigless, with sleeves rolled to his elbows and his dark hair in a loose queue. He doesn't notice her.

"Your room is ready, Miss Blake." Eva turns at the sound of Mrs Brodie's voice. The housekeeper is a tall woman with a thin but friendly face, and a thick Northumberland accent. Greying hair peeks out from beneath a cloth cap. As far as Eva can tell, Mrs Brodie is the only member of staff here, beside Thomas's nurse, who she knows made the journey up from London with Harriet and Edwin.

She follows Mrs Brodie down the hall to her bedroom. The room is sparse and cavernous, with a narrow, childlike bed along one wall, and a washstand and chipped chest of drawers in the corner. A tiny fire is spitting in the grate, the mantel topped by a cracked gold-rimmed mirror. It smells of dust and woodsmoke; of the past.

"I'm afraid it's a little bare," says Mrs Brodie. "And I've only just now lit the fire, so there's still a chill in the air. Summer takes its time arriving up here."

Eva offers her a smile. After a week and a half of travel, she would happily sleep on the floor of a cart shed. "It's quite all right. I know I was not expected. Thank you."

Mrs Brodie bobs her head and disappears back down the hall, leaving Eva to the faint echoes of the house. She peers out the cracked window at the sea; at the shadows of the Farne Islands dotting the horizon. An arrowhead of birds glides past the glass.

Exhausted, she sinks onto the edge of the bed. It creaks loudly; an old, hard relic, not so far removed from the floor of a cart shed. She closes her eyes, her body weighted with exhaustion and swaying slightly, as though she were still in the carriage.

When she hears delicate footsteps making their way down the passage, somehow managing to avoid the squeaking boards, she knows they can only belong to Harriet. Her sister taps on the door, then steps inside without waiting to be invited.

"I thought I was imagining things when I heard your voice outside." She reaches down and pulls Eva into an embrace that barely manages to touch her.

Even after a month in the grime of Highfield House, Harriet is still polished and golden, with blonde curls twisted high on her head, and her embroidered pink and green stomacher far too fine for a place like this. In her dark, mud-streaked travelling dress, Eva feels positively dour.

Harriet's gaze travels to the duffel bag tossed on the floor beside the bed. "Is that all you've brought with you? Where are the rest of your things?"

"I've all I need," Eva says tightly. She had abandoned most of her belongings at Walton's townhouse. Her former betrothed had offered to send her things on to the island, but she had told him such a thing was not necessary. Surely there was little point carting all her worldly goods up to the end of the earth when her family would only be here for a short time. She will simply send her brother to collect them once they are back in London.

She had shoved a few of her favourite books into the bottom of the duffel bag, along with a single change of clothes—enough to make herself vaguely presentable. She cannot find the energy for much more than that. Besides, there is something freeing about carrying only the duffel bag with her. A pleasant simplicity to this one-cloak, one-bonnet existence against the chaos the rest of her life has become.

Harriet perches on the edge of the bed beside her. "I overheard your conversation with Nathan. What happened between you and Mr Walton?"

Eva shakes her head. She does not want to speak of it to anyone. Least of all to Harriet.

To her relief, her sister doesn't pry.

"How has it been here at the house?" Eva asks. "Is Thomas well?"

Harriet huffs. "It's been dreadfully dull. The town is almost non-existent. And all I hear inside the house is the thudding of hammers all day long." She shakes her head. "It's a foolish idea, every bit of it. Nathan ought to have just sold the place and moved on. Surely it would have been far less trouble for everyone concerned." She stands and peers into the mirror. Tucks a stray strand of hair back into place. "Edwin had a coachload of timber brought in the other day and it was nearly swept away by the tide. The villagers watching had a fine time of it. They're not fond of us, you know."

"I gathered." When Eva had asked a woman in the village for directions to Highfield House earlier that afternoon, she had been gifted with cold and critical eyes. A look that told her in no uncertain terms she was an outsider. "But you know Nathan," she continues. "He blames himself for the trouble our family is in. If he thinks he can make the lost money back by restoring the house, he's going to do all he can to make that happen."

Harriet hums. "It was all rather sudden though, wasn't it. He'd hardly made mention of this house in years. And now he's planning to restore the place? It's a little strange, don't you think?"

Eva gets up from the bed and tosses a log into the grate. Sparks fly up the chimney. "Well," she says, "maybe he needed something to put his mind to. Something to stop him dwelling on all he's lost. If this madness with the house is what he needs to find himself again, we ought to let him do it."

"Tell us about the journey, Thea," Nathan says, too cheerfully. "Did you see the ocean? And did you have some lovely horses?"

Theodora's cheeks are flushed, no doubt with the thrill of sitting among her entire family at this ridiculous banquet hall table. She ignores her bowl of stew and barrels into a breathless recollection of everything they saw in the coach between London and the island, oblivious to her father's displeasure at her being here.

"And four big black horses," she is saying, "just like from a story book. It was so wonderful"—neatly avoiding the rain and the mud, and the ten days of complaining she'd subjected her aunt to.

Nathan winds the handle of the pepper mill, a muscle tightening in his jaw. "I'm glad the journey was not too trying for you," he says stiffly.

Eva forces down a mouthful of stew and dares a glance at her brother. There's anger behind his eyes, but she can't tell if it's anger at himself or her. If he is to be furious at anyone, it ought to be Matthew Walton.

Edwin nods along to Theodora's story for a while, before growing bored and rattling off a list of the improvements he and Nathan have made to the house. They seem to be few and far between.

"Yes, it's coming along," Nathan puts in. "Although rather slowly, I'm afraid."

"Well," Edwin says, "you can hardly be surprised at that. Takes an age to get any of the building materials carted out here. Ordered some timber to be brought out to Lindisfarne and the fellow carried on as though I had asked for it to be taken to the moon." He snorts. "Mind you, I suppose we can't be surprised. The Jacobites have this part of the country in disarray. The troublemaking bastards." He gives a short chuckle, tucking a strand of limp charcoal hair behind his ear. "It's chaos up here, Eva. You shan't know what you've wandered into."

"Come on now," says Nathan tensely. "I think that's something of an exaggeration."

Edwin waves a dismissive hand. "It's no exaggeration at all. Can't go two minutes without hearing of another Jacobite protest. And have you not heard the rumours? Government spies on the island? Sent to hunt down those who want the Old Pretender on the throne."

Harriet rolls her eyes. "Tell us about London, Evie." She sighs wistfully, as though it has been years since she was there, and not mere weeks. "Is it just as inspiring and wonderful as ever?"

Eva smiles wryly to herself. Her last week in London had been anything but inspiring. "I'm sure you'll find it just as you left it," she tells her sister.

Harriet directs an overt sigh in Edwin's direction. "I do hope I'll see it again soon." She gives Eva large, mournful eyes. "You must be terribly disappointed to be here."

Theodora reaches for the plate of bread and knocks over her glass of ale. Nathan swoops in with a napkin.

"Indeed." Edwin takes a mouthful of wine. "I do hope old Matthew has a good explanation for all this."

Nathan's attention snaps away from the pool of ale at his elbow. "I think we all know Matthew's reasons for doing as he did."

"Nonsense," says Edwin. "He knew what he was getting himself into. Financially, I mean. Matthew has known for months about the trouble with the business, Nate. If that was the reason for his change of heart, you'd have thought he'd have reached the decision sooner."

Eva's cheeks burn. She wills Edwin to stop talking. She had not imagined she might be able to keep the breaking of her betrothal a secret, but nor had she expected it to become dinnertime conversation.

She feels an uncomfortable prickling beneath her skin. A sense of rising panic she is barely able to contain. In the shadow of Harriet's impossible charm, Eva has always prided herself on being the sister with her head on straight, the *sensible choice* with her life under control. She had been engaged to Matthew Walton for almost a year and a half; had never seen fit to complain when his cross-Channel jaunts and business trips had continuously delayed their marriage. She had used the time to set out her plans; to determine which rooms in the townhouse would be their parlour, their dining room, their children's nursery. She planned which gown she would be married in. Devised the names of their future sons and daughters. Planning gave her a sense of purpose. A feeling of faint control over this life that had been laid out for her by expectation—and her older brother. Now she is almost halfway through her twenties, and completely without prospects. Those plans—those orderly and sensible plans, of sky-blue sack gowns and sons named for their grandfathers—are trailing through her fingers like seawater, leaving nothing in their place.

She tears at her bread with far too much aggression. Harriet places long consoling fingers over her wrist.

Eva grits her teeth. A part of her had been looking forward to seeing her family. But she feels like an utter failure. And the sight of perfect Harriet, with her perfectly styled melancholia and her perfectly sympathetic eyes, is not helping matters.

Eva excuses herself, taking a candle from the mantel and carrying it up the groaning staircase. Her body is aching from days in the carriage, and from the tension she had carried in her shoulders in anticipation of her brother's disappointment. She is ready for the day to be over. Ready for morning light to make the shadows lying over the house a little lighter.

She kicks off her shoes and unlaces her stays. Wipes her body down with the lukewarm water Mrs Brodie had placed in the washstand in the corner of the room. She rolls onto the bed and closes her eyes, listening to muffled remnants of the dinner conversation floating their way up the staircase. Outside the window, the sea sighs and shifts the shoreline.

Eva pulls the blankets up towards her chin. Though she can tell from the heady smell of lye that the sheets are clean, the woollen blanket smells musty and disused. She wonders if it had been tucked away in some forgotten cupboard since her family had last slept under this roof.

And with that thought comes a sudden, searing pull of dread. She sits up in bed, gasping down a breath. Because as she lies here in the cradle of Highfield House, with gulls wheeling and the German Ocean rising to lock them onto the island, a solid memory digs itself up from somewhere deep within her. Pieces of the past come out of the dark, seeping from the walls and jostling their way to the front of her mind.

She is a child; screaming, crying; water on all sides and thick, impenetrable dark. She is wrapped in her mother's arms as she runs through the shallow sea connecting Lindisfarne to the mainland. And they flee Highfield House without looking back.

CHAPTER TWO

Nathan is awake when the first light finds its way through the window, unsure if he was ever asleep. He remembers long hours of lying awake, listening to Theodora's deep breathing as she lay in the truckle bed on the far side of the room. Remembers the creak of the floorboards when Eva had got up in the night.

His sister has ended up in the same room she had slept in as a child. So has he. It had been an almost unconscious thing. On his return to the house, he had gravitated to his childhood bedroom without a second thought. Memory had pulled him back onto a hazy but well-worn path, between his father's old study and the bedroom once belonging to his older brother Oliver.

There is something odd about sleeping down the passage from Eva again, crammed into his childhood bed. Something that is at once both comforting and unsettling, as though time has twisted in on itself. The house is just as full now as it was back then, in that time before Harriet, before Theodora. Many of the same bedrooms are filled, the hallways again alive with footsteps. The house ought to feel warm and inhabited. But there are shadows in corners that refuse to be swept away.

Theodora murmurs in her sleep, and the sound makes Nathan start. Since her mother's death three years ago, his daughter has been prone to nightmares. But this morning, mercifully, she seems calm. Nathan is surprised by it. He had imagined the gloomy halls of Highfield House would find their way into her dreams.

He knows he has not always been like this, so rigid and fearful. He remembers a life with soft edges; a life with Sarah in it. A life in which he did not have to try so hard to keep a smile on his face. But the last three years have been almost intolerably difficult: first the death of his wife, and then his foolish choices that led to the collapse of his business. His characteristic brightness has become more forced; he knows these days his smile rarely reaches his eyes.

He watches Theodora sleep, her pale blonde hair fanned out upon the pillow. He had been protective of Thea back when Sarah was alive too, of course. But not like this. Now there is this crushing fear that something might take his daughter from him, the way it had taken his wife. With Thea in London, away from Highfield House—away from *him*—it had been easier. He had trusted that Thea would be in safe hands with Eva, and that he did not have to watch her as though she might crumble with the next gust of wind. He knew, too, that his daughter would be far happier in London with her aunt than she would be here with him poring over her every move. Infecting her with his poorly hidden panic.

He sits up, knowing there's no chance of sleeping. Best he get an early start on the seemingly endless undertaking before him. Every day, Highfield House seems to get bigger, and he becomes more overwhelmed by the task he has taken on. There are floorboards to replace, walls to paint and polish. Broken steps and windows to repair. Edwin, thankfully, has taken the reins of the restoration, giving Nathan the most mindless and mundane of tasks. This new life on Lindisfarne is far more physically demanding than his pen-and-paper-filled workdays in London. But there is something faintly comforting about ending each night with aching arms and a shirt damp with sweat. It keeps him from losing himself in an ocean of worrisome thoughts. He dresses silently and creeps out of the bedroom, shooting his daughter one final glance before he leaves.

He is surprised to find Eva sitting in front of the fire in the dining room, a teapot on the table beside her. He had not heard her get up. Dull, dish-related crashes come from the kitchen, along with the comforting smell of baking bread. Blue early-morning light filters in through the high windows, making dust motes whirl as he passes.

"Tea?" Eva asks, gesturing to the pot. "Mrs Brodie just brought it out."

Nathan nods. He sits beside her as she fills his cup.

She looks tired this morning, her blue eyes underlined in shadow. But she is tidily dressed as always, with her mousy hair pinned at her neck and her dark blue woollen skirts sponged clean.

Nathan feels a fresh pull of irritation. He had worked hard to secure her marriage to Matthew Walton. He knew it his duty to find his sisters the best matches possible, and a connection to a well-respected family like the Waltons would have done no end of good to his ailing status. Would have gone some way to restoring the Blake name to their rightful place among London's upper middle class. What had gone awry? Such a disaster he would have expected from Harriet. But not staid and reliable Eva.

He is bitterly disappointed. In her. In himself. In Matthew, who he had considered a good friend—or at least a good enough friend to come to him with his changed decision, rather than packing his former betrothed onto a coach to Holy Island. But he has trained himself not to show such things.

He reaches for the poker and jabs at the fire in an attempt to avoid eye contact. "I know you're reluctant to speak of it," he begins carefully, "but I need to know exactly what happened between you and Mr Walton." He keeps his voice steady, even. Perhaps it is not too late to fix this. But he cannot do that without knowing details. He has always been close to Eva—at least, far closer than he is to Harriet, who often seems like an entirely different species. With the right words, he is sure he can nudge the truth from her. But he senses this is a delicate subject, and the right words seem to evade him. He clears his throat. "It's important that—"

Before he can finish, gunfire splits the sky. Eva jerks, slopping tea onto the flagstones. Nathan strides outside to find two of the villagers standing close to the house with muskets in hand. Donald Macauley is standing atop the highest dune, his son Martin close behind. The two men are identically dressed in faded slops and grimy woollen caps, broad hands wrapped around their weapons. Their blue corduroy jackets are flapping in the wind.

Nathan inhales, trying to harness his anger. "I've told you before, Macauley. This is my land. I'd appreciate it if you refrained from hunting upon it."

Donald Macauley lifts the musket to his shoulder and sends another shot into the cool morning air. Birds screech and hurtle into the sky.

"We've been hunting here for years, Mr Blake. Long before you showed up. Roe deer like this part of the island."

Nathan knows Donald Macauley has lived on Lindisfarne forever. Knows he is well respected among the islanders. A man with plenty of influence. He does not want to get on the wrong side of him. Nonetheless, he cannot have bullets flying all over the property, especially now Theodora is here. "I understand that," he says, trying to level his voice, "but my family is here now. So please find somewhere else to hunt. There are children in the house."

Donald Macauley chuckles to himself and trudges across the dune to stand eye to eye with Nathan. "Well," he says. "Seeing you went and asked so nicely…"

Heat prickles Nathan's neck. But he does not step away. After a moment, Macauley strides off to retrieve the fallen roe deer. He slings the small brown body over his shoulders. Blood beads on the grass. "Come on then, Martin," he says, though his son has already fallen into step beside him, "let's leave Mr Blake to all these fine acres."

Nathan watches until they have disappeared back towards the village. When he returns to the dining room, he finds Eva standing at the window, watching in the direction the men had disappeared.

"Who was that?" she asks.

"Name's Donald Macauley. One of the village elders." Nathan grabs his tea and gulps it down, trying not to let the run-in shake him. It's lukewarm now, and anything but settling.

He remembers Donald Macauley from their time on the island when he was a child. He'd been just as much of a bastard then as he is now. Nathan remembers being scolded by the man for venturing too close to his fishing boat. Remembers being afraid to sit close to him at church. When Oliver had dared him to steal an apple from the tree from outside Macauley's cottage, he had refused, even knowing the ridicule his brother would inflict on him. Even as a boy, Nathan had had a strong sense that Donald Macauley was to be kept away from.

"Don't let him worry you," he tells Eva anyway. "He's just hunting."

But he is certain the Macauleys' near-daily appearance has less to do with the deer on this part of the island, and more to do with intimidation. After all, these are unsettled times. He knows this part of the country to have more than a dash of Jacobite support. And with the placing of Hanoverian King George on the British throne last year, the Jacobite movement, which has lain dormant for close to a decade, is beginning to rear its head again. With an unpopular foreign king at the helm, the Jacobites are seizing their chance to return the crown to the Stuarts.

Nathan had managed to keep his distance from the riots in London, but the movement is on its feet here in northern England, so close to Scotland and the Jacobite heartland. No doubt the people of Holy Island have little trust for outsiders from London who might be harbouring Hanoverian sympathies. Nathan has seen Donald Macauley striding around the village with the Jacobite cockade pinned to his cap. Surely a man bold enough to risk arrest by doing so would have little reluctance to scare those he distrusted. And Nathan is fairly sure he and his family fall into that category.

Eva gives him a shrewd look over the top of her teacup. "Hunting? It sounded more like they were trying to scare us."

Nathan looks at her for a long second. "Perhaps now you're beginning to understand why I did not want my daughter here."

She turns away from him and edges a little closer to the fire. "Well," she says tautly, "I'm sorry, Nathan. But we've nowhere else to go."

CHAPTER THREE

Eva is distracted as she rattles through Theodora's lessons later that morning. Her first night back in Highfield House had been restless. As she had lain in the dark, listening to the sea rattle the shore, she had tried to piece together her fragmented memories of the night they had left Holy Island.

She has no thought of why they had fled. Her mother had never spoken of that night when Eva had been growing up; the memories had sat untouched within her until she had set foot back in Highfield House.

She stares out the window as Theodora's quill scratches across the paper. Looks out at the bleak gunmetal sea, as though it might provide answers. She thinks of Donald Macauley and his son with muskets in their hands. They had done little to calm her unease. Nathan can tell her they were hunting all he likes, but she knows there is more to it. She had seen the faces of the villagers when she and Theodora had passed through the streets yesterday. Had felt the animosity coming from every look that was sent her way. She misses the blissful anonymity of London.

The Blakes are well known here. Highfield House has been in her family for generations. Her great-great-grandfather had been the one to lay the foundations; to find that slice of buildable land among the hummocks and dunes at the top of Holy Island. The story goes that it had been nothing but a fisherman's cottage back then, added to generation by generation as the family's wealth expanded. Now those riches are all but gone, thanks to decades of bad business decisions by the men in her family. But she is sure her family's reputation as wealthy landowners has done little to endear them to the villagers. The Macauleys, she feels certain, were either trying to scare them, or watch them. For what purpose, she cannot imagine.

"Auntie Eva?" She snaps out of her daze. How long has Theodora been calling her? "I've finished."

Eva clears her throat and tries to focus. She takes the book from Theodora and skims through her sums. "All right. Good. Let's do one more page."

Theodora puts down her quill. "Can't we finish now? Please? Can't we go exploring?"

Eva has vague memories of promising her niece some grand explorations once the interminable carriage ride had deposited them on Lindisfarne. "Where do you wish to go? You know your papa doesn't want you exploring the house."

Theodora sighs like a tired, widowed mother. "I *know*. He's told me *so* many times. I'm not a *child*."

Eva smiles. "You are, actually."

Theodora huffs. "Can we go and see the village?"

"All right. Tidy your things and fetch your bonnet and cloak. It looks as though it might rain."

Theodora slams her book closed and is out of the room before Eva is even on her feet. Shawled and bonneted, with cloaks tossed over their arms, they make their way out of the house and over the grassy embankment that leads toward the village. The tide is out, revealing the planes of sand that tie Holy Island to the mainland. In the late afternoon, the sea birds are a chorus, swooping down in graceful arcs to pluck squirming creatures from the mudflats. Soon, the ocean will return, cutting Lindisfarne off from the mainland and ringing them in sea.

Wind whips up off the water and Eva slings her cloak over her shoulders. Red-coated guards peer down at them as they skirt the castle. Theodora reaches for her hand.

Lindisfarne is a grey stone shadow of a village, watched over by the ghostly ruins of the monastery that tower behind the church. There is an odd stillness to the place. It's an almost absence of sound; wind rustles the grass that lines the harbour, and ratlines knock and chime against the thin forest of masts in the anchorage. But there's an emptiness, a quiet, that feels almost otherworldly after the rattling chaos of London. This scrap of land at the top of England has seen bloodshed and miracles. Viking raids, the slaughter of monks, and inexplicable marvels at the hands of men who would become saints. In the bleak summer light, it feels as though the past is blowing in through each weatherworn stone.

Eva feels the muscles in her shoulders tighten as they step into the warren of lanes that make up the village. Two women pass, darting glances at her, then quickly look away and murmur to one another. Eva presses her shoulders back and lifts her chin, trying to conjure up confidence she doesn't feel. She refuses to let these people faze her. Her family has owned Highfield House since Elizabeth was on the throne. This is her home, at least for now.

"Auntie Eva. Look at this place." Theodora points to a shop on the corner of Church Lane. Eva peers through the window. Shelf after shelf is overflowing with old books, with painted teacups, with tarnished tobacco boxes and dust-covered toys. Theodora's eyes light. "Can we go inside?" she begs. "Please?"

"Of course. But you're not to touch anything."

Theodora shoves open the door, a bell at the entrance announcing their arrival. They are accosted with the smell of the dusty past, mildew and grime clinging to the mad clutter of objects crammed onto the shelves.

A woman stands up from behind the counter, two old books in the crook of her arm. A pale pink kerchief is wrapped around her shoulders, clashing violently with the shock of red hair escaping out the sides of her cap.

"Good afternoon." She gives them a bright smile, one that is far more genuine and welcoming than anything Eva has seen on Holy Island so far. The woman waves a hand, gesturing to the shop. "Look as you please." Eva nods her thanks and the woman goes to one of the shelves, shoving aside a faded toy drum to make room for the books.

Theodora floats from shelf to shelf, lips parted and eyes wide as she scans the disordered display. "Look," she breathes, pointing at a doll staring down from between an old vase and what Eva guesses is some kind of navigational tool. It is draped in a silky green dress, with wide painted eyes and long, dark lashes. Theodora steps closer, until her fingertip is an inch from the porcelain face. "Can I have it?" she begs, tugging at Eva's arm with her free hand. "Please? I've been ever so good."

Eva raises her eyebrows, gives her a playful smile. "Have you just? I seem to remember an awful lot of whining during your arithmetic this morning."

"But arithmetic is just so awful. And I've not touched anything. Not a single thing." She takes a step back from the doll, as if to emphasise her point. "*Please?*"

Eva reaches into her pocket, but finds it empty. "I've not brought a penny with me. You'll have to speak nicely to your father."

Theodora's shoulders sink. "We'll be back," she tells the shopkeeper solemnly.

The woman grins. "I'll look forward to it."

They head towards the path that slices down the middle of the island. "Did you see her dress?" Theodora is saying. "All silky, like a queen."

Eva smiles. "Yes, it was beautiful." She puts a hand to Theodora's shoulder, guiding her down a narrow lane.

A wrong turn.

The moment she steps into the alley, she can feel it. That sense that they are not where they are supposed to be. That sense that they are trespassers.

At the bottom of the lane is a large outbuilding she guesses to be a barn or shed. She cannot see the house beyond, but the thick stench of animal waste suggests a nearby farm. Through the ajar door, she can see men moving about inside the shed.

Eva is about to turn on her heel when Theodora darts forward. "Look! There's a big horse inside!"

"Thea," she hisses. "Come back at once." The last thing Eva wants is to anger the villagers further by trespassing onto their land.

The door to the shed creaks open and a bristly head pokes out. Eva recognises the older man she had seen hunting outside the house that morning. Donald Macauley. Up close, his eyes are flinty and cold. Something in them makes Eva wary.

At the sight of him, Theodora scurries out of the lane and around the corner, disappearing from sight.

"I'm sorry," Eva tells Macauley. "I did not mean to trespass. I'm new in town. I lost my way, is all."

His eyes narrow. "You're one of them, then are you? The Blakes. I heard there was more of you arrived yesterday."

Eva presses her shoulders back. "Yes," she says, forcing steadiness into her voice. "Eva Blake. Pleased to meet you." She holds out a hand in greeting. This is the best way forward, surely, to try and create some amicability between her family and the villagers. Show them they mean no harm.

Macauley looks down at her outstretched hand. She can tell from the cold look in his eyes that there is to be no amicability between her family and his. She can't begin to imagine what might have caused such hatred. Had Nathan done something untoward when he had first arrived back on the island? Something he is refusing to share? Or does this animosity go back to the days when her father owned Highfield House?

She lets her hand fall. Swallows hard. She hates conflict, hates confrontation; hates the dithering mess it turns her into. "My family means you no trouble," she says, hearing her voice rattle.

"Is that so?" Macauley's eyes are cold.

Instinctively, Eva stumbles back, but he takes a step forward, forcing her against the stone wall of the alley. She can smell earth and sweat on his skin. The faint hint of liquor on his breath. He looks deep into her eyes as though he is searching for secrets. He can sense her fear now, surely. Can sense it pouring off her in waves.

A younger man emerges from the barn, wearing a long dark coat and riding boots. He is leading the horse behind him. He nods to Macauley without speaking, then disappears down the alley without so much as a glance Eva's way.

"You are not welcome here, Miss Blake," Macauley says, voice low. "Not on this island, and especially not on my property."

Footsteps crunch towards the lane and he takes a sudden step back, allowing her to dart past him. She rushes from the alley before he can manage another word.

CHAPTER FOUR

Harriet stands in front of the easel with her paintbrush in hand. She tilts her head to examine her painting. Too much light. Or is it too much dark? The sky on her canvas is swirling, murky, and too unreadable.

The falling dusk is not helping matters. She puts down her brush and lights the lamp on the mantel.

This little room on the ground floor of the house was once servants' quarters. These days, with just Mrs Brodie and Thomas's nurse Jenny in their employ, Harriet has turned it into a workroom of sorts, with her easel in one corner and her paints cast out across the table.

Edwin enters without knocking. He stands behind her and peers over her shoulder at the canvas. She is challenging herself with this piece. A landscape—bleak and windblown, with pale sunlight pouring over a shadowed sea and forest at its edges. Inspired by the view from her workroom window, perhaps. Along with a need to paint more than the still-lifes that are expected of her as a female artist.

"That's coming together nicely," says her husband.

Harriet gives him a thin smile. He has an infant's understanding of art, but she is grateful he has allowed her to continue painting now they are married. She had been fearful he might forbid her from doing so, ever since Nathan had engineered their betrothal a year and a half ago.

He kisses the side of her neck, clearly hoping for a little attention. But the muddy sky needs far more attention than her husband does. She hopes he takes the hint and leaves.

He doesn't. He sinks into the worn armchair in the corner of the room and stretches his arms up over his head. He is still wearing the stained shirt he was working in today, and wood shavings have ended up in his dark hair. She smells ash soap on him, and a faint hint of sweat. He looks as though he's not seen a razor in days. In London, he had been careful to present himself as a professional and well-groomed tradesman, befitting of the lavish houses of his clients he spent so much time in. Doused in rosewater and fine silk shirts. Here, he and Nathan have begun to look like a pair of vagrants.

Harriet dips her brush back into the paint and returns to the troublesome sky, doing her best to ignore him.

"Well then," he says in a conspiratorial tone, "have you managed to get anything out of Eva yet? Any word on what happened between her and Matthew?"

Harriet sighs and puts down her brush. "She wouldn't say," she tells him. "Whatever it is, it's embarrassed her. She doesn't like it when things don't go to plan."

Eva's sudden appearance—and the news of her broken engagement—is the most excitement this place has seen in weeks. Harriet is determined to get the truth out of her. Though she supposes that truth will be nothing more interesting than Mr Walton's unwillingness to marry into a family with such empty coffers. A rather dull outcome, Harriet thinks, just like Eva herself. She allows herself the faintest of smiles, but chides herself for her cruelty. She can't imagine being in Eva's position, with a life of spinsterhood laid out before her.

Nonetheless, she is glad Eva is here. Theodora too. They will add a little life to this house that seems completely devoid of it. The past four weeks have felt almost interminable. An endless cycle of inept childrearing, stolen moments with her easel and paints, and peering out of windows in search of something other than sea. Dinnertime conversation has largely consisted of Edwin listing the improvements he has made to the house each day, and Nathan saying, *Yes, it's coming along,* before the three of them run out of things to say.

When she had first arrived on the island, Harriet had told herself she would not bother making friends. There seemed to be little point. After all, this was just a temporary inconvenience. Besides, the choice of potential friends was woefully small. Most of the islanders are too rigid to accept new people into their lives—especially people from Highfield House. She is no fool; she knows the villagers would rather be rid of them. Not that she truly understands why.

She told herself she didn't care. Told herself she had no desire to be friends with these islanders anyway. What would she talk about? Horseshoes and herrings?

The loneliness didn't matter. Soon she would be back in London, among people she truly did count as friends. But it wasn't long before the boredom, and the painfully dry dinner conversations, ran her to the end of her patience. Since then, she has made a half-hearted attempt at building acquaintances, staying for conversation after church services and grinding out small talk at the market, but the villagers seem determined to keep their distance.

Edwin crosses one leg over the other and rubs his dark stubble. "This whole business is a damn shame if you ask me. I was looking forward to Matthew being part of this family."

"I'm sure you were."

Edwin, Nathan and Matthew Walton have been friends for years, the three of them serial frequenters of London's coffee houses. Harriet can't imagine how much wrangling it must have taken Nathan to betroth both his sisters to his best friends. Little wonder he's so bent out of shape now Eva has put her foot squarely in his plans.

Harriet rinses her brush. Perhaps she can sneak back down here later tonight. But best make it look as though she is finishing for the day. A wail comes from the nursery on the floor above them and she feels her shoulders tighten. She had hoped for at least a few hours' respite before having to tend to Thomas again.

Edwin pauses. "Will you go to him?"

"No," Harriet says tautly. "He cannot possibly need feeding again. Jenny can go." Her eyes drift upwards, listening for the nurse's footsteps. She is infinitely grateful that Edwin had agreed to bring Jenny along on this foolish little jaunt—and that Jenny had accepted. Harriet is sure she has only survived the first five months of Thomas's life because she has his nurse to share the load. Or shoulder it. It is not that she doesn't love her son—of course she does. She just loves him a little more when he is fast asleep in his crib.

She goes to the window and yanks the flimsy muslin curtains closed. The sun has almost disappeared and long shadows are lying across the room.

She will hear them again tonight, she is sure; the footsteps that sound outside the window of her workroom. They come regularly, several times each week, late at night when the rest of the house is sleeping. At first she had thought it just her imagination, that rhythmic slap of feet on the path that winds around the house. Had put it down to a racing mind, or remnants of a dream, or the unmoored feeling of being out here on the edge of the ocean.

But no. The footsteps are far too regular and far too real to be imagination, or a leftover dream.

She knows, of course, she ought to pull back the curtains and catch a glimpse of whoever is out there. But she cannot find the nerve to do so. Who knows what she might come face to face with?

Edwin stands behind her at the window and squeezes her shoulders gently. "What's bothering you?"

She shakes her head. She has said nothing to her husband about the footsteps. She knows he would just scold her for her overactive imagination. Or far worse—forbid her from visiting her workroom at night. And Harriet cannot have him take her painting away. Right now, it's the only thing that makes her feel alive.

CHAPTER FIVE

Rain settles over the island the next day, drizzling in threads down the sea-stained windows of the house. After breakfast, Harriet locks herself away with her easel and paintbrushes, while Eva drags Theodora through her Latin lessons.

Hammer blows and splintering boards echo through the house. Eva has little idea what Nathan and Edwin are up to—since Theodora's arrival, her brother has ensured that the rooms they are working in are kept locked at all times. For his daughter's safety, he claims, but Eva can't help but wonder if perhaps he wishes to hide the dreadful job he's doing—and the fact that he really ought to have hired someone experienced to do the job. Not that he could have afforded it.

When the sun finally breaks through the clouds after dinner, Eva and Theodora head out for a walk. Nathan chases them down the stairs. He is dressed tidily, in bone-coloured breeches and an embroidered woollen justacorps, the dark waves of his hair tied back and powdered neatly.

Theodora bounds towards him, but stops short of taking his hand. "Will you come for a walk with us, Papa? We're going to the rock pools to look for mermaids."

He winks at her. "I'm a little too big to fit in the rock pools, don't you think?"

Theodora giggles.

"Shall I walk to the village turnoff with you? Then you and Auntie Eva can go searching for mermaids, and I can call on Mr Holland."

Theodora nods enthusiastically.

"Who is Mr Holland?" asks Eva as they step out the front door.

"From the fishing fleet," Nathan tells her. "We got speaking of the restorations at church on Sunday. He's offered me use of his frame saw."

She gives him a crooked half-smile. "I'm glad we've not managed to estrange ourselves from all the villagers."

Nathan chuckles. "Give it time."

"Do you have any idea how to use a frame saw?"

"That's what I have Edwin for." He nods towards his daughter, who is galloping ahead down the path. "Was she sleeping in London? Have her nightmares been bad?"

"Regular," says Eva. "Once a week at least. But she seems to remember little of them when she wakes."

Nathan nods. "It's a small mercy. Although I have to say, she seems more settled here than I expected."

They walk in silence for several paces, their footsteps sighing against the damp grass.

"Do you remember the house?" Eva blurts. "From when we were children?"

"Of course."

"What do you remember?"

Nathan folds his hands behind his back. "I remember plenty. Playing on the beach with Oliver. Eating at that enormous table. I remember Father taking me to look at the stars on the Heugh."

"What else?" Eva glances at Theodora. Drops her voice slightly. "What happened here? Why did we leave?"

Nathan doesn't look at her. "Nothing happened. We left after Father died because this wasn't the right place for Mother to raise us on her own. That's all."

Eva cannot tell if he is lying. "Why do the villagers hate our family so much?" Wind whips up off the water and she wishes she had brought her cloak. She tugs her shawl tighter around her shoulders. "Donald Macauley threatened me yesterday. I took a wrong turn down the alley behind his property and he behaved as if he'd caught me with my hands in his life savings."

Nathan gives her apologetic eyes. "I'm sorry you had to deal with that.

But it's just that they don't trust us yet. That's all. The prospect of another Jacobite Rising has people on edge. The country could be at war again any day now." He shakes his head. "That Donald Macauley... He's a good man to stay away from."

Eva snorts. "I am doing my best."

"Father's death was awful on Mother," Nathan says after a moment. "The smallpox took him horribly quickly. You likely don't remember. And then all the worry Mother went through, terrified we would all take ill too. Can you blame her for wanting to leave the house where it happened?"

Nathan is right—Eva remembers almost nothing of her father. She was not even four when he died. These days, he is little more than a name and a half-remembered story.

Theodora rushes back to them with a fistful of sea thrift. "Look!" She waves the pink flowers under Nathan's nose. "Isn't it pretty?"

"Beautiful, my love."

Theodora hands one stem to Nathan, and one to Eva, before darting back off down the path again. Eva twirls the stem between her fingers.

"But we left with such urgency. Didn't we?" She looks up at Nathan for confirmation. The memory of that night is fragile, but there are parts of it she is beginning to recall with clarity. It seems as though the longer she stays in the house, the more memories resurface.

She remembers her mother waking her from a deep sleep. Remembers being carried from Highfield House in her nightgown, a blanket around her shoulders. And she remembers the darkness; pools of it. Cold, ink-black air against her cheeks. Why would they have raced from the house in the middle of the night if their mother had only wished to escape her memories?

Nathan watches his feet for several paces. "Grief can make a person do strange things," he says finally. There's a thickness to his voice.

"You're right. I suppose I'm just...adjusting to the way of things."

Nathan meets her eyes with a look of sympathy that manages to sting. "I mean to write to Matthew Walton," he says. "Ask him to reconsider."

"No," Eva says hurriedly. "Please don't." She can't bear the embarrassment of it.

"Do you not wish for the security that will come with marrying a man like Matthew?"

She bristles. "Security for me, or for the rest of the family?"

Nathan shrugs, oblivious to her bitter tone. "Both."

Eva wraps her arms around herself, suddenly craving space. There is plenty of it here, and yet, since arriving on Holy Island, she has felt hemmed in and stifled. By Nathan's disappointment. By her own failures and the unravelling of her plans. She had spent so long preparing to be Matthew Walton's wife that without it, she feels as though she has little purpose. She needs space to breathe.

"Thea," she says suddenly, "why don't you go with Papa to visit Mr Holland? We'll explore the rockpools another time."

She waves away Nathan's queries and is marching off towards the coast before either of them can protest. Wind skims across the water, rippling the inky surfaces of the rockpools. Already, the days are pulling towards autumn; each evening arriving with a little more haste.

Eva holds up her skirts as she strides over the uneven ground. She tries to concentrate on balancing over the rocks at the edge of the water, but thoughts about the house keep tugging her back.

Is Nathan telling the truth about the night they left Holy Island? She has never known him to lie to her. But she can't shake the thought that he was not being entirely truthful. Had they really left the house so impulsively, all because their mother was consumed by grief? The mother Eva remembers was reserved and insular, not one to take risks. But was it possible their time in Highfield House had made her that way?

As she approaches Emmanuel Head, Eva sees a small wooden dinghy sitting at the edge of the water. Donald Macauley is pacing the beach, his boots crunching against the shingle.

Eva's stomach dives and she changes direction quickly.

He calls her name. Calls again, louder, when she does not answer.

Finally, she dares to turn around. Macauley is striding up the grassy embankment towards her. Heat floods her body and she fights the urge to run.

He lurches forward and grabs her arm. "You and I, we need to speak, lass." His face is close to hers, and she can smell liquor on his breath. His cap is pulled down low, thick brows poking out from beneath the grimy blue wool. He starts to walk back towards the dinghy, his fingers digging painfully into her upper arm. She tries to pull away, but his grip tightens.

"Get in the boat," he says.

"Do you think me mad?" Eva's voice shakes. Because this side of the island, wild and ocean-bound, is almost painfully empty. The curve of the dunes mean she is hidden even from the topmost windows of Highfield House. And she knows that if Donald Macauley, with his iron grip and unforgiving eyes, wants her in his boat, she has little choice but to obey.

He shoves her forward, her shins knocking hard against the bulwark. Eva stumbles and drops the sea thrift Theodora had given her, its delicate petals mashing beneath her shoe. Macauley reaches into the boat for his musket. "Get in."

Eva hears herself murmur with fear. She steps over the gunwale, legs shaking. Macauley shoves the dinghy into the water then leaps in after her. He sits opposite Eva, placing the musket under his seat. He reaches for the oars and begins to pull the boat away from the island. The oarlocks creak and groan; one looks to be held together by little more than a thread.

Eva watches the house get smaller. Watches the smoke from the chimneys melt into cloud. Her knuckles whiten around the edge of the bench seat. "Were you waiting for me?" she asks shakily. "How did you know where to find me?"

Macauley pulls hard on the oars. They are heading away from the mainland, out into the German Ocean. The boat tilts across the swell. "This is a small island, Miss Blake. Anyone can be found with a little effort."

Eva grits her teeth, trying to bury her panic. Surely this can't be merely because she trespassed onto Macauley's land. There's more to it, of course. She just cannot determine what that might be.

"I know you're not fond of my family," she says. "But trying to scare me like this is not going to achieve anything. I don't see why we cannot just get along. We mean you no trouble."

Macauley snorts. "Get along?" He keeps rowing. "I know what you are, Miss Blake. The lot of you. I know why you're here."

She frowns. "What are you talking about?"

"I know you've been sent out here by the Hanoverian pig and his men. To weed out those of us who support the true king. Report back to the government on when we're about to strike."

Eva stares at him. "You think we're government spies? Reporting on the Jacobites' plans?"

"I don't think it. I know it. I'm no fool. Your father was outspoken against the Jacobites. And your ma, well, we all know where her alliances lay."

Eva's lips part. "What do you mean?"

"That house has sat empty for two decades," Macauley says, pushing past her question. "And you all turn up now, just as our movement is finding its legs?"

Eva lets out her breath. Suddenly, the islanders' treatment of her family makes glaring sense. Ludicrous as the accusation is, she understands how they might have reached such a conclusion.

"You're mistaken," she says, with as much calmness as she can muster. "We've come to Highfield House to restore it. Sell it. Let us do that in peace and Holy Island will be free of us. Is that not what you want?"

"What I want, Miss Blake, is to see our rightful king upon the throne. And I am willing to do whatever it takes to make sure that happens."

There is no changing his mind, she realises. He has her and her family pegged as government spies, and she knows nothing she says will convince him otherwise. "Do you truly think this is what your king wants?" she asks. "For you to make such threats against young women without proof of the accusations you are throwing?"

He laughs humourlessly. "Don't pretend you're innocent. I know it's the lasses we ought to be most wary of. 'The ones they least expect,' they say. Well, I've seen enough skirts in the Jacobite cause to know you young women like to poke your noses into men's business." He shifts forward slightly on the seat, his grey eyes spearing hers. "I saw you outside my cart shed. With your eyes on the messenger."

The messenger? Eva thinks of the man in the dark greatcoat, leading his horse from Macauley's barn. Had he been passing word between the Jacobites?

She shakes her head. "You're mistaken," she says again, with as much firmness as she can muster. "My family and I are not spies. I saw nothing yesterday." She clenches her hands to stop them shaking. She cannot even begin to think about what Macauley might be planning to do with her. But she does know that, as of now, out here on the ocean, with no one else around, she has little to lose. She looks him squarely in the eye. Holds his gaze, despite the sweat prickling the back of her neck. "And you are also a fool." She hears a strange, cold clarity enter her voice, as though she has gone past fear to something else entirely. "Because if I truly were a spy, you would just have given me the very information about your rendezvous point I was seeking."

She sees Macauley's bristly jaw harden as that realisation falls over him. In his rage, he has said too much. Of course, so has she. Right now, Donald Macauley has two choices: either he believes her when she tells him she is not a spy. Or he makes sure she is silenced.

He lifts his right hand from the oar. Moves it towards the musket. And Eva is suddenly on her feet, making the boat lurch wildly on the swell. Instinctively, blindly, she reaches for the oar and wrestles it from the splintering oarlock. Macauley stands, and she stumbles backwards, the oar teetering in her fist. All she sees is the musket. He is raising it, stepping back.

Without thought, she swings. The oar misses the musket and strikes the side of Macauley's head. It's a cold, dead sound; at once both dull and sharp. His body tumbles into the sea with an almost-silent splash. The musket teeters on the gunwale for a second, before following his body into the water.

Eva drops the oar, her cry of shock dying in her throat. She lurches across the boat and reaches into the ocean, grappling after his body. The dinghy lurches violently and her hand comes up empty. And there is not a single blemish on the sea that might hint at where a man has just disappeared.

CHAPTER SIX

Sound distorts, leaving her in a sea of twisted silence. Her heart is drumming in her ears and she feels bile rising up her throat. She huddles in the bottom of the boat, clutching either side of the gunwale. The sea rocks her in its inescapable cradle. She feels the weight of the oar pressing against her thigh.

A killer.

Murderer.

No. An accident. Self-defence.

Donald Macauley had been about to shoot her. Send her to the bottom so she could not share her spy's secrets.

Hadn't he?

In truth, she does not know. It had all happened too quickly to make sense of. All she knows is that Macauley is gone. And she is alone with his death on her hands.

She tears her eyes from the patch of ocean where his body had disappeared. Thick cloud hides Holy Island from sight. She is surrounded by sea and a soupy, opaque sky. She has little idea which direction they had come from—she had been far too terrified to pay attention to where she was being taken. And even if she could row all the way back to Holy Island, how could she turn up alone in Macauley's boat? The villagers would string her up before she managed a word in defence.

And perhaps, Eva thinks, they would be right to do so.

Wind whips across the water and she shivers hard. Her bare forearms prickle with goosebumps and she picks up her shawl from the bottom of the boat, where it had fallen during the altercation. She pulls it tight around her body, feeling patches of dampness on the wool.

The boat is drifting. In which direction? Is she being dragged back to Holy Island, or away from it?

Perhaps she ought to try for the mainland, and the anonymity that will come with it. And do what? She has not a thing with her but the clothes on her back.

All her mind can make sense of is that she cannot stay in this horrifying limbo. Tentatively, she picks up the oar with which she had struck Macauley. She cannot look at it too closely. Cannot inspect it for blood, or hair, or any other hint of what she has done. She settles it into the broken oarlock, careful not to lose it over the side. Without releasing her grip on the handle, she shuffles around on the bench and begins to row.

The oar slides and groans in its broken casing, but the boat begins to move. She has no idea which direction she is going, but the movement steadies her a little. Perhaps she may still die, but she will not sit here waiting to do so.

She rows until her arms are screaming. The pain is a welcome distraction. The haze is thick and close, but when she turns to look over her shoulder, nuggets of land are peeking through the cloud bank. She hears herself murmur in relief.

These jagged jewels of rock, they must be the Farne Islands. She must have drifted south from Lindisfarne. South from that unplaceable circle of ocean where Donald Macauley's body had been swallowed.

She tugs harder on the oars, guiding herself towards the closest island. Mist is threaded over the rocky outcrops, but as she draws closer, a dark shape emerges from within the cloud. A cottage—as impossible as that seems out here. A small stone tower stands beside it, an unlit iron brazier hanging from it. A shipping beacon, perhaps? It is the only sign of human life she can see on any of these islets.

She pulls towards the cottage. The boat moves in a jagged path and she trains herself to guide it this way, that way, slowly growing familiar with the workings of the oars. The sea knocks the dinghy into protruding rocks; she hears it grind against undersea stone. Sucking in a breath, Eva leaps from the boat and scrabbles up the edge of the island. Pain shoots through her shin as it slams against rock. She pitches forward, making flecks of blood appear on her palm. She drags the boat higher up onto the island, its flat bottom scraping noisily.

The land around her is nothing but rock, glittering with pools and flecked with green and yellow moss. A purple curtain of dusk is beginning to fall across the island, and she hears the wild squall of sea birds from somewhere within the cloud.

Eva stumbles towards the cottage, wet skirts tangling around her shins. The house is made from the same dark stone as the island, and almost looks part of the landscape. Both the cottage and the crooked outbuilding beside it are built on high stone foundations. Half-towers, with two large rainwater barrels beside them. The firebasket swings slightly in the wind, the chain groaning, a thin stream of ash skittering out between the gaps in the brazier.

In the fading light, she cannot see any sign of the lightkeepers, though a larger boat is roped to a mooring post not far from the cottage. For a moment, she thinks to call out, to announce her arrival. But something stops her. She does not want to break the strange stillness that hangs over this place. It feels the right kind of stillness, given she has just sent a man to his death.

She climbs the stone stairs at the front of the house and peeks through the salt-speckled window. Through the grime she can just make out a narrow bed with blankets thrown over it haphazardly. A single plate and tin cup sit on the table. The remains of a fire glow in the grate.

The place is clearly inhabited. It is also clearly a house for one. Even with her limited knowledge, Eva knows keeping the light is not a job for just one man. At least, it shouldn't be. What kind of person would agree to such a life? To such isolation, such responsibility? She doesn't know. But in her rattled, fearful state, she knows she does not wish to meet him. Surely it's no sane person that lives out here alone like this.

She hurries down the stairs and slips into the shed beside the house. Inside the thick stone walls, the shrieking wind is muted, and there is a close earthy smell to the air that Eva feels in her throat. In the long shadows, she can make out mountains of chopped wood, and great heaps of what she assumes to be coal and peat. She finds a lightless corner at the back of the shed and sinks to the ground between two enormous woodpiles. Sudden tears escape down her cheeks. She cannot tell if they are tears of grief over all that has happened, or vicious relief that she is still alive. Perhaps a little of both.

As the darkness thickens, footsteps emerge from within the constant sigh of the sea. Closer they come, rhythmic and sharp over the rocky ground. The door of the shed creaks open, letting in a shaft of dusk. Eva holds her breath. Half-hidden behind the woodpile, the lightkeeper is no more than a dark shape. A tall man, broad shouldered. She sees the outline of a short and rugged beard. A long greatcoat and woollen cap. He digs a shovel into the mound of coal and disappears from the shed.

Eva lets herself breathe.

His footsteps fade slightly and she hears the groaning of the firebasket chain. She smells the chalky odour of the flames, sees orange firelight squeezing through the gap beneath the shed door.

The footsteps return. Eva sits up straight, grips her knees with frozen fingers. The door groans open and the lightkeeper steps into the shed, tossing the shovel back against the wall. Then he freezes. Listens. Eva presses a hand over her mouth to silence her noisy breathing.

"That you, Macauley, you bastard?" The man's voice is rough and northern. He snatches his shovel again and comes striding towards the woodpile. He raises his makeshift weapon.

Eva scrambles to her feet. Holds up her hands to shield her face. "Please, no."

The man drops the shovel. "Jesus Christ. Who in hell are you?"

"No one. I'm no one." She tries to shuffle past him, but he grabs her arm roughly.

"What are you doing in my shed?"

"I'm sorry. I'll leave at once. I—"

"How d'you get here?"

"The boat…" she manages. She hears her breathing get faster, louder. She gulps down breath, swamped in fear.

"You came in a boat? Alone?"

"No. I mean, yes. Yes. Alone." Her voice rattles.

He frowns, eyes shadowed in the half light. "Is there someone else out there?"

Eva opens her mouth to speak, but freezes. It feels as though his eyes are boring into her. Piercing her.

He shakes her arm, as though trying to yank her from her mania. "I said, is there someone else out there? Has your vessel gone down? Are there people that need help?"

"No," she coughs. "No. There's no one else. I…" She hunches over, gasping for breath. Fresh tears spill down her cheeks.

"You what?" he pushes.

"There's no one else," she sobs. "He's dead. He's dead because of me."

CHAPTER SEVEN

The man lets his hand fall from her arm. "Right, then. I see."

Eva turns her back, hunching, hiding her tear-streaked face. What in hell had she been thinking, confessing to such a thing?

"It was an accident," she blurts. "I swear it. I thought he was going to hurt me. I swung the oar to defend myself. I didn't mean to knock him over."

Dread pulls at her stomach. What will he do with her now, this killer who has arrived on his island? Strike her with his shovel? Shoot her? Turn her in to face the hangman?

He scratches his beard, shadowed in the dancing light of the shipping beacon. "Is anyone after you?"

"No." Eva shivers. "No one knows what I did. Except you." She tries to edge past him but he blocks her way.

"Where's your boat?"

"What?"

"Your boat," he says impatiently. "Where d'you land?"

"I…" Eva's thoughts knock together. "I don't know. I just… I saw the cottage…"

"Where d'you come from?"

She hesitates. Surely it can do her no good for him to know where she is from.

He looks at her expectantly. "Do you not know that either?"

"Holy Island," she murmurs.

He strides out of the shed. Eva races after him. He grabs a lamp from the table inside the cottage and hurries back down the stairs.

"What do you want with the boat?" she asks desperately. That flimsy little dinghy is her way off the island. Her way out of this man's life.

He lifts the lamp, panning it in a wide arc. Light falls on the sorry shape of the dinghy beached against the rocks. He marches towards it and shoves it out into the sea.

Eva panics. "What are you doing?"

"Can't have a dead man's dinghy on my island, aye? What will people think?"

Eva stares transfixed as the boat is tugged into darkness. She closes her eyes, forcing herself to breathe.

"I can't take you back to Holy Island tonight," he says. "Not in the dark. We'll strike the reef."

Eva nods faintly. She cannot bear to think how worried her family will be.

Now he has sent her boat away, he has her as trapped as a rabbit in a snare. And what will happen when people find out Donald Macauley is missing? Will there be a reward on her head? Is the lightkeeper thinking of making his fortune by turning her over to the hangman?

He glances at her bare arms, and the wet skirts clinging to her ankles. "I've a fire going in the cottage," he says. "You'd best come inside."

She does not want to be in this man's company. She has told him far too much, and she has no idea how to navigate his brusque, unpolished words. But she knows she has no choice. The night is growing cold, and her way off this island has just floated out towards Donald Macauley's grave.

She follows the lightkeeper into his cottage, finding thick, smoke-scented warmth, and flames dancing in the grate. The place is at once both sparse and messy, with blankets bunched at the bottom of the bed and breadcrumbs littering the table. The mantel is cluttered with candle stumps and rolls of twine, and old brassy shapes she assumes are navigation tools. A worn sideboard leans against one wall, partially blocking what she assumes is the back door of the cottage. Light from the firebasket blazes through the window, making shadows dance across the walls. Heavy wooden shutters are folded open against the windows.

"You keep the light alone?" Eva asks shakily.

"Aye."

She hovers by the door, waiting for further explanation. Nothing comes.

The lightkeeper throws another log on the fire. Jabs it with the poker. "Warm yourself. You're shivering." It sounds like an order.

Eva edges closer to the hearth, eyes drifting to the firebasket and the reams of black sea beyond. How can a man commit to a life of such solitude, such responsibility?

"Why?" she blurts. She wants some rational explanation, like a colleague's illness, or a fellow lightkeeper flitted off to the mainland for supplies.

He looks back at her. "What?" He slides off his coat and tosses it over a chair.

"Why do you keep the light alone?"

He gives a single, humourless chuckle. "D'you really think yourself in a position to be asking questions? After all you just told me?" There is no darkness to his words, but she senses the veiled threat beneath. And she sees her own foolishness. Of course, she is no place to do anything other than keep her mouth shut and make herself as small and unimposing as possible.

Especially now she is relying on this man to get her off this island.

She swallows. "I'm sorry. I didn't mean to pry."

For a fleeting second, she meets his eyes. There is something magnetic about his gaze that makes her oddly reluctant to look away. His walnut-coloured hair is tied back in an attempt at a tail, but most of it hangs loose, tangled on his shoulders. His thick beard is unevenly trimmed to his chin, his skin tanned and weatherworn. But there's a youthfulness to his brown eyes, to the ropey muscles in his forearms that show beneath his rolled-up shirtsleeves. He is older than her, yes. But not by as much as she had first imagined when she had seen him stalking towards her in the coal shed. Perhaps close to Nathan's age.

He clears his throat, pulling his eyes away. "You can use the bed. I'll not need it."

"No," Eva says quickly. "No, I couldn't." Spending the night in this stranger's house is bad enough. Climbing into his bed is unthinkable.

He shrugs. "Suit yourself. There's bread on the table if you're hungry."

Her stomach is churning far too violently to eat. All she wants is to curl up in a corner and disappear. Hopes that when the light comes it might shine on something other than this bleak corner of reality.

Harriet paces the nursery with Thomas on her shoulder. She knows there is no chance of sleeping tonight, not with Eva missing.

When she had not returned by dusk, they had told themselves not to worry. She needed the space, they'd said, turned upside down as she has been by Mr Walton's rejection of her. At nightfall, Nathan and Edwin had gone into the village asking after her. And now, with midnight long past, Harriet is finding it hard not to imagine the worst.

Thomas is restless, as though sensing his mother's unease. Somehow, the house seems to sense it too, creaking and groaning like a ship upon the rocks. Harriet rubs the baby's back, the way his nurse had shown her. He's faintly sticky, the sleeve of his nightshirt inexplicably wet. He wriggles in her arms like a fish plucked from the water. Harriet's shoulders tighten as he paws at her neck and whines.

"I know," she says, "I hate this place too."

Unlike Nathan and Eva, she was not born in this house; their mother had left the island not long after her husband's death, with her youngest child growing inside her. There is not a single thing about Highfield House that makes it feel like home. Nor does she have any desire to make it so.

She decides to ignore the stickiness and the wet sleeve. This child seems to be eternally damp and filthy, so there seems to be little point in rectifying the situation. She paces across the nursery, trying to coax Thomas towards sleep. Finally, she settles him into the crib in the corner of the room. For a moment, she considers going downstairs to paint, but her mind is too cluttered, churning through all the terrible possibilities of what might have happened to her sister. She finds herself standing at the window, a corner of the curtain pulled back in wait. Tonight, with Eva missing, Harriet feels unsettled and reckless. Too bold for her own good. Tonight, when the footsteps come, she will catch the prowler in the act.

She had waited for him last night in her workroom. After Edwin had fallen asleep, she had slipped out of bed and locked herself away with her easel, painting until long after midnight, with her ears open for the footsteps. But there had been only silence, and Thomas's early-morning shrieking. Tonight though—she hears it. Footsteps on earth as the prowler emerges from the dunes onto the path surrounding Highfield House.

Harriet blows out the candle flickering on the mantel. She returns to the window and pulls the curtain back an inch.

She sees a man, lit only by the faint glow of the moon. He is dressed in long boots and breeches, a large greatcoat pulled over his shoulders. Harriet's heart jolts, scared of her own bravery.

She squints, trying to catch hold of any distinguishing features. But the figure's face is hidden beneath a cocked hat. Shielded by the darkness.

She knows she ought to fetch her husband, or her brother. Have them confront the intruder and demand an explanation. But she cannot do that. Nathan will fret, and Edwin will fold his arms and announce she is to stay locked up safely in their bedchamber at night.

It's selfish, of course, to gamble with her family's safety for her own gain. Once, Harriet had assumed motherhood would whittle that selfishness out of her. But it seems to only have made it worse. Well, she thinks, she can blame her husband for that.

She presses her forehead to the glass, watching as the figure moves past her window. And then he turns the corner of the house and is swallowed by the night.

CHAPTER EIGHT

Eva wakes in a corner of the lightkeeper's cottage, curled up on her side in front of the hearth. Morning light is filtering through the dirty window. Outside, a thin line of smoke rises from the extinguished fire basket.

The lightkeeper is snoring lightly in his bed. He lies on top of the blankets, still fully dressed in his ash-streaked shirt and breeches, sleeves rolled to his elbows and one hand tucked beneath his head. His boots lie tipped over beside the bed.

Throughout the night, they had barely spoken. In spite of all Eva had confessed, the lightkeeper had had no questions. Was he simply not fazed by the foolish admission she had dropped at his feet? Or was he staying as far away from it as possible?

He had moved around the cottage like a ghost, tending the fire, darning a shirt, scrawling in a notebook, and heading out to restoke the firebasket each time the flames began to dwindle. Eva had curled up in a corner of the cottage in an attempt to disengage herself from the lightkeeper's strange world. She had done her best to stay awake, stay watchful, but her physical and mental exhaustion had finally pulled her down. She has vague memories of the lightkeeper climbing into bed with the dawn, as the beacon burned itself out.

She sits, rolling the stiffness out of her neck and shoulders. Her skin feels sticky, her woollen skirts streaked with salt. The muscles in her back and arms are aching after an eternity with oars in her hands.

Now her thoughts have settled slightly, she sees she must get back to

Holy Island as soon as possible. She knows her family will have gone into the village asking after her. And she does not dare think on the conclusions the islanders will reach when they learn her disappearance aligns with Donald Macauley's.

Eva finds herself staring at the lightkeeper as his chest rises and falls with breath. She is completely at his mercy. Will he take her back to Lindisfarne this morning? Or does he plan to turn her in? Either way, there is nowhere to run.

He opens his eyes, catching her watching him. She turns away suddenly, her cheeks flushing. She busies herself folding the worn blanket he had given her and setting it on the table. He sits up and rubs his eyes. Swings himself out of bed and pulls on his boots. "Come on, then. Let's get you out of here."

Her shoulders sink in relief.

He grabs his greatcoat from the back of the chair and tugs it on over his broad shoulders. His slides his hair back from his face in one swift movement, tying it at his neck with a leather band pulled from his pocket. He cocks his head, gesturing to her to follow him. Eva pulls on her damp shoes and grabs her bonnet from the floor.

She steps outside. Gasps. Much of the island has vanished beneath the sea, leaving only a small circle of rock around the cottage and firebasket.

"The water," she breathes, "it's so close to your house." At once, the raised foundations of the cottage and shed make perfect sense. With the high tide, the sea is impossibly close.

The lightkeeper turns up the collar of his coat, nonchalant. "Tide won't get much higher than this."

In the early morning, the sea birds are a chorus, great gusts of them flocking around the nuggets of land not swallowed by the sea. The other Farne Islands dot the ocean ahead, sitting similarly low in the water. There's a bleak beauty to the place, a sense of otherworldliness and intense isolation. "Does it not frighten you? Being so remote? So vulnerable to the sea?"

He gives a short chuckle. "I've not been swept away yet." He steps onto the jetty. His boat is a much more solid thing than the battered dinghy Eva had arrived in, with a single mast and neatly furled sail. It knocks against the moorings with each inhalation of the sea.

The lightkeeper climbs aboard with a large stride, and takes up the oars from beneath the bench seats.

He can have had no more than a couple of hours' sleep, but his movements are brisk and energetic, while Eva's legs ache with exhaustion. Perhaps his body is accustomed to the lack of sleep. She wonders how long he has been living out here.

"Which island is this?" she finds herself asking.

"It's Longstone."

"I thought Longstone was uninhabited," she says.

"It's not." He nods towards the boat. "Get in."

Eva waits for him to offer his hand to help her climb inside. When it is not forthcoming, she bundles up her skirts and clambers ungracefully into the boat. He waits as she staggers onto the bench seat opposite him, then unties the mooring rope and uses the oars to push away from the jetty.

"Last night in the shed," says Eva, "you thought I was one of the Macauleys. Do they come here?"

"No one comes here." He looks at her with sharp brown eyes. "Where am I taking you then? Back to Lindisfarne? Or are you a woman on the run?"

Eva hesitates. She does not know which is more foolish—to step onto Holy Island with Donald Macauley's blood on her hands, or to abandon the only place in the world she can right now call home. Either way, she needs to tell her family she is safe. Or alive, at least.

"Take me back to Holy Island," she says. "Please."

He reaches up to release the sail, then tugs hard on a line, opening it to the wind. Neither of them speak as they begin to fly across the water. Sea spray flies across the bow and Eva wraps her arms around herself, shivering.

The shapes of Lindisfarne emerge from the cloud within minutes.

"Will you land on the north side of the island?" she asks. "At Emmanuel Head?"

She does not dare to show her face in town. Who knows what questions are being asked, what stories are being told? But she imagines that appearing in a boat with this strange man from Longstone will only raise more questions. Make her look more guilty.

His lips part. "Emmanuel Head. Near Highfield House."

Eva swallows, surprised at his knowledge of the manor. She nods faintly, but doesn't reply.

The lightkeeper skirts the island on its ocean side and eases the boat around the rugged north coast. There is Highfield House, dark and dominant, smoke rising steadily out of two chimneys. Eva is relieved to see it. But when she glances at the man in the boat beside her, she sees a hint of unease in his face.

In the high tide, the sea is knocking up against the embankment. The lightkeeper jumps into the shallows and shoves the skiff over the thin line of pebbles at the water's edge. Eva lurches over the bow, not waiting for his hand this time. Seawater sloshes into her shoes.

The lightkeeper steps out of the water and looks up at the smoke puffing from the chimneys. A frown creases his forehead. "Someone living there now, then? Is it you?"

"I…" Eva's words fade at the sight of a figure on the dunes. She can make out his face as the sun washes him with golden light. Donald Macauley's son, a hunting musket in his hand.

Her stomach dives. Is it just coincidence that he has appeared here now, at the very moment she is stepping back onto Holy Island?

It does not feel coincidental. It feels as though he has been watching, waiting for her. It feels as though he *knows*.

How could he know?

Hunting, she tells herself. He is just out here hunting.

He sees her—she has no doubt. Because his gaze is suddenly trained on her, and he lifts his musket to his shoulder.

The lightkeeper shoves her forward, out of Macauley's eyeline. "Run," he hisses. "Get away from him."

Eva lurches over the embankment. She hears the crack of the musket and a cry of shock escapes her. She tears across the rocks and uneven grass without looking back, waiting for the pain to hit, for her legs to give way beneath her.

She fumbles with her key, then flies through the front door of Highfield House, slamming it behind her. There is no pain, she realises. Somehow, she has made it inside without being hit.

Footsteps patter down the staircase and Harriet rushes at her. "Evie.

We were so worried."

Eva lets out her breath and sinks to the ground, her dirty skirts pooling around her. Harriet kneels beside her, gripping her hand.

"What happened? Where have you been?"

"I…" Her words tangle. Heart racing, she reaches for her sister, pulls her into an embrace.

"You're safe now," says Harriet. "You're home."

Right now, Highfield House feels neither safe, nor like home, but she doesn't say it. She leaps to her feet and rushes into the dining room. Looks out the windows to the sea. Donald Macauley's son is no longer visible, but there is that handkerchief of a sail, growing smaller as the man from Longstone disappears back towards his island.

Nathan's footsteps thunder down the staircase, Edwin and Theodora close behind. Theodora flies at her, throwing skinny arms around Eva's waist. Nathan lets out a breath of relief.

"Eva. Thank God. Are you all right?"

She nods faintly.

Nathan looks at his daughter. "Upstairs, Thea. Finish your letters." Clearly rattled by the gravity of the situation, Theodora disappears upstairs without a word of complaint. Nathan turns back to Eva. "I heard a gunshot."

She glances towards the window. "He didn't hit me."

"He," Nathan repeats. "One of the Macauleys."

She nods. "Donald's son."

"Harriet, have Mrs Brodie bring us a pot of tea." Nathan looks at Eva. "Come and sit down. Tell us what happened."

With a teacup in trembling hands and her shoes drying by the fire, Eva sinks into the settle in the parlour and tells them everything—from Donald Macauley's accusations and his swift and sickening death, to her night on Longstone and the lightkeeper who had brought her home. Nathan paces in front of the hearth as she speaks, rubbing his shorn cheek.

Eva grips her teacup. She can smell the night on her skin; woodsmoke and sweat and sea. "I know what everyone will think. They'll believe I knocked him overboard on purpose."

"That's not true."

"He accused us of being spies, Nathan. They think we're reporting on Jacobite plans. Who knows how many of the other villagers think the same?"

"Spies," Edwin snorts. He is leaning against the wall in the corner of the room. "The damn fools. She's right though, Nate. We asked after Eva all around the village last night. Once people realise Donald Macauley went missing that same night…" He trails off.

Nathan paces, paces, scrubbing a hand across his forehead. Eva has never felt like more of a burden. And she has never felt more guilty.

"If the villagers ask, we'll tell them you crossed off the island in the low tide yesterday afternoon," Nathan says at last, "and got caught out by the rising water. You were forced to spend the night lodging at the tavern in Beal."

Eva rubs her eyes. "Mr Macauley's son saw me return with the lightkeeper."

"So we'll simply say you met him in Beal and he offered to bring you home."

Eva says nothing. The story is far too easy to poke holes in, of course. Anyone who saw the Longstone beacon brightening the horizon last night would know the lightkeeper had not spent the night in Beal. But she knows she has little choice. A story with holes in it is still preferable to the truth.

She picks listlessly at the dirt beneath her fingernails. "I fear Donald Macauley's son already knows what I did. When the lightkeeper brought me back to Lindisfarne, he was there waiting. He was quick to raise his musket."

"How could he possibly know?" says Nathan. "You were out at sea when it happened. Surely Martin was just hunting. You were frightened. It must have felt like he was shooting at you."

Edwin raises his dark eyebrows. "Or he was shooting at you because they believe you a spy."

Eva nods faintly. She knows Edwin's is the most likely explanation. She had seen the way Martin Macauley had aimed his musket so carefully in her direction.

Nathan goes to the window. Does he see Macauley's son prowling? Does he see that sail disappearing towards Longstone?

"We say nothing," he says, turning back to face his family. "But if anyone asks, we tell them Eva was simply caught out by the tide. Agreed?"

Edwin folds his arms across his chest. "Agreed."

Harriet nods, echoing her husband.

"Eva?"

She sighs inwardly. "All right," she murmurs finally. She stares into her cup. Doesn't drink.

"Perhaps it's best if you leave the island, Evie," Harriet speaks up suddenly. "I can come with you. We can—"

"I can't run," says Eva. "It will make me look even more guilty." Her words are followed by silence. No one argues. Harriet's shoulders sink.

When the men head back upstairs to work, she gets up from the armchair and comes to sit beside Eva on the settle. She flicks her long blonde plait over her shoulder. "So. You met that strange fellow that lives on Longstone." She refills the teacups with a new light in her eyes. "I've heard talk of him. At church. They all say he's rather mad. Out there keeping the light all on his lonesome."

"That does not sound like a particularly Christian thing to say." Eva shuffles forward in her seat, reaching towards the fire. A violent shiver goes through her. It feels as though not an ounce of summer warmth has made it through the thick stone walls of Highfield House.

Harriet ignores her comment. "His name is Finn Murray. They say he's not set foot on the mainland in his whole life."

"I'm sure that's not true."

"Why do you say that?"

"That island is nothing but a rock, Harriet. No one could survive out there without going to the mainland for food. Coal and peat for the firebasket…"

Harriet's lips break into a crooked smile. "I did not expect you to take his side. I thought a night out there with him would have terrified you."

"It did," she says. "But it was the situation that terrified me. Not the lightkeeper. Not really."

Harriet hums to herself. "How interesting."

"What is that supposed to mean?"

She shrugs airily. "Nothing."

Finn Murray. They all say he's rather mad. Eva feels oddly indignant on his behalf. And oddly irritated at her sister. She finishes her tea in silence.

CHAPTER NINE

The bells of Saint Mary's echo across the island, calling the village to Evensong. Nathan's instinct had told him to keep his family locked within the walls of Highfield House and refuse to show their faces at church. But he knows all too well how that will look.

It has been two days since Eva's return. Three since Donald Macauley's death. No doubt his son will be concerned. People will be asking questions. They need to show their faces and pretend nothing is wrong. Provide an explanation for Eva's night away from Holy Island.

He had known from the beginning it would be a risk coming to Lindisfarne. Had suspected the locals would not trust the arrival of Londoners during a time of such political and social unrest. But he had not imagined things would take such a turn as this.

Nathan can count on one hand the number of times he had heard his mother speak of Highfield House after they'd left. Once they had arrived in London, it was as though the place had ceased to exist. For Nathan, eight years old when they'd left the island, their former life had begun to feel like a dream. But there has always been a bitter taste in his mouth at the thought of this place. That bitterness is not helped by the half-truths he had told Eva when she had asked why they had left the house.

He had hoped she had no recollection of the night they had fled. She'd been barely four, clinging to their mother's neck and wailing as they had traipsed across the sand back to the mainland, the rising sea licking at their ankles. Still, the story he had fed her—that their mother had left the house out of grief—is not a lie. And how on earth would Eva benefit from knowing the whole truth of the matter? Especially now, after the horror of Donald Macauley?

When he'd first returned to Highfield House, he had found it drenched in evidence of their hurried escape. Tables and chairs and sideboards and desks just as his mother had left them. The same worn cushions tossed across the settle, the same blankets now faded over the beds. Long-cold ash in the grates and unopened jam jars in the kitchen. Dusty cloths and plates in the pantry had hinted at food that had long disintegrated. Everything had been covered in grime and earth and crumbling mortar, and an unplaceable heaviness had thickened the air.

They walk to church in near silence, beneath a weighted sky that looks closer to winter than the midsummer not long passed. Edwin is leading them down the path, a hand pressed to Harriet's back as she walks with the baby in the crook of her arm. Nathan is at the back of the group, Theodora by his side. Unspoken, they have surrounded Eva like pack animals, and she walks with her eyes down and her cloak pulled tight. Walking as though she is guilty.

None of them had suggested that they not attend Evensong. A wordless agreement that pretending nothing is wrong is the best way forward. Since their hushed conversation the morning Eva had returned, none of them have spoken Donald Macauley's name, even within the impenetrable walls of the house.

Nathan knows he needs to be aware at all times. If Donald Macauley was willing to kill Eva on account of his belief she is a spy, there is nothing to say his son will not have the same idea about the rest of them. Nathan does not even want to consider what might happen if Martin Macauley discovers what happened to his father. Having Theodora here among such uncertainty fills him with dread.

People are filing steadily into the church, a dour parade of sea-stained greatcoats and patched cloaks. Nathan's shoulders tighten at the sight of Martin approaching the gate. He feels a sizeable amount of guilt over the secrets and lies he has goaded his family into. But he also feels anger. Because although he had tried to convince Eva that she had just dodged a wayward hunting shot, he can't quite make himself believe it. Had it been a warning shot? Or had she evaded a bullet intended to kill her?

As much as he wants to avoid Martin Macauley for fear of his questions, he knows he cannot do so. Only a man with something to hide would let another fellow fire his weapon across his doorstep without consequence. Nathan is all too aware that this is a game. One that must be played with care.

Edwin hangs back from Harriet to fall into step beside him. "You need to confront Martin about the shooting. Before he comes to you."

Nathan nods faintly. "I know." Edwin is right, of course, but he has never been one for confrontation.

Edwin catches his eye. "Perhaps I ought to speak to him."

Nathan bristles. "I'm more than capable of defending my family."

Edwin lowers his voice when Theodora looks up at them curiously. "Of course you are. I just mean… You need to be firm with him, Nate. And I know firmness is not your strong suit. The man's a bastard. Whatever else has happened, he—"

"I said I shall speak to him," Nathan says irritably. "I do not need you to fight my battles."

But perhaps he has lost this game already. Because Martin Macauley is approaching. Weaving through the crowd to seek him out.

Nathan nudges his daughter in Eva and Harriet's direction.

"My father been hunting out your way lately, Blake?" Martin asks without greeting.

Nathan looks at him squarely. "No. Not for days." He feels a line of sweat run down his back. Feels Edwin's eyes on him. "And I'd appreciate it if you stayed off our property too." There's a sourness in his voice, but Nathan knows he sounds far from intimidating.

Edwin steps suddenly in front of him, menacingly close to Martin. "Come near our house again and we'll have the authorities after you," he hisses. Several churchgoers stop to watch the confrontation. "My sister-in-law could have been killed the other morning."

Something passes over Martin's eyes. What is he thinking, Nathan wonders sickly? Have they just put Eva in his line of fire again?

Martin looks between Nathan and Edwin, hesitating. Finally, he says, "Your sister ought to learn to keep better company. Wouldn't trust that lightkeeper further than I can spit." He turns and walks into the church, without looking at them again.

Thomas is grizzling determinedly as the priest rattles through his sermon. It's as though he's aware of it, this grand deception his family has taken on. Harriet rubs his back, coos to him, but he just cries harder. She feels like a fool, with her mindless jabbering and pointless lullabies. Poisonous looks fly her way.

Edwin leans over to whisper in her ear: "Take him outside."

Harriet grits her teeth. She hates when her husband gives her advice on mothering. She shuffles out of the pew and slips from the candlelit church, feeling heads turn as she passes.

A part of her is glad to be out of there; that damp, righteous building with a smell of earth that reminds her of the grave. Divine eyes staring down at her, reminding her of the lies and secrets her family has agreed to.

Outside is just as gloomy, the late-afternoon sun drowned in banks of cloud. Lamps in the churchyard cast long shadows into the ruins of the monastery. She paces the churchyard with Thomas wailing on her shoulder; past worn and crooked headstones, between the pillars and towers of the crumbling priory.

Footsteps sigh through the grass and Harriet turns to see a young woman in striped blue and white skirts. Red curls are escaping out the sides of her bonnet. She offers Harriet a sympathetic smile.

"When my son was a little one, he used to stop if I hummed to him. I think he liked feeling the vibrations in my chest. Perhaps you've not tried that?"

Harriet is grateful for the assistance. When it comes to Thomas, she welcomes advice from everyone other than her husband. Unable to grasp at a melody, she hums a broken collection of notes, holding the baby close to her chest. To her unfathomable relief, Thomas's howling begins to ease. She lets out a breath. "Thank you." She shakes her head. "Sometimes I've no thought of what to do with this child."

The woman grins. "I gave up trying to get my son through church years ago." She nods towards the back of the churchyard where a dark-haired boy is balancing on the low stone wall. "Although I figure at least one of us ought to make an appearance."

Harriet shifts Thomas to her other hip. "I'm sorry to disturb the service."

The woman shrugs. "No bother to me. Just thought you could use some help."

"You came out just to stop my baby crying?"

"Well. That and the fact that I downed three cups of tea before the service and I'm absolutely bursting." She hoicks up her skirts and squats beside one of the gravestones, not a hint of embarrassment on her face. Harriet can't hold back a smile.

The woman stands and smooths her skirts. "Your family means to sell the house, I hear?"

Harriet raises her eyebrows, caught off guard by the abrupt change of subject.

The woman flaps a hand as though waving away her own discourtesy. "I'm sorry. Didn't mean to poke my nose in where it's not wanted. I'm Julia Mitchell. I run the curiosity shop on Church Lane."

Harriet accepts her outstretched hand; introduces herself.

"I think I met your sister earlier in the week," says Julia. "And her daughter."

"My brother's daughter," Harriet tells her. "Theodora has been talking endlessly about your shop."

Julia smiles. "Aye, she liked the doll in the silk dress."

"She's been begging her father for it for days." Harriet bats Thomas's hand away from the strings of her bonnet. "You're right," she says. "My brother means to sell the house. He and my husband are restoring it, but I can't see much of an improvement yet. I feel as though we'll be here for an eternity."

"There are worse places to be," says Julia.

"I suppose." Harriet shrugs. "It's just that we've not been made to feel particularly welcome."

A look of regret passes over Julia's face. "The people here are suspicious of outsiders. That's all. And poor old Donald Macauley's vanishing has people in a twist."

"What do you think happened to him?" Harriet asks, trying to keep her voice level.

Julia shrugs. "An old drunk like him? Probably took himself out to sea and couldn't find his way back."

Harriet hopes the rest of the village has come to the same conclusion.

Julia heads towards her son at the back of the churchyard, making it clear she has no intention of returning to the service. "You're welcome to come and see me at the shop anytime you need a little company," she tells Harriet. "And I'll put that doll aside for your niece. In case her da decides to spoil her."

Eva flies out of the church the moment the service is finished. Harriet is waiting by the gate, Thomas now angelic in the crook of her arm. Eva takes her sister's free elbow and hurtles away from the village.

"That was unbearable," she hisses. "It felt as though everyone knows what I've done. Felt as though God were staring down at me, cursing me for my lies. And for…well…" *Killing a man.* Speaking it makes it far too real.

"What choice did you have but to lie?" asks Harriet, sidestepping a mound of sheep dung. "What else were you to have done? Stand up in front of the congregation and confess to Donald Macauley's murder?"

Eva wraps her arms around herself. "It wasn't murder."

"Of course it wasn't. But you know that's how the villagers will see it."

Eva says nothing. Harriet is right, of course, and the weight of that knowledge presses down on her, making it hard to breathe. Over and over, she hears the dull thud of the oar striking Donald Macauley's head. Hears the faint sigh of water as his body disappeared below the surface. Guilt pulls at her chest.

She takes the baby from Harriet and squeezes him to her, needing the comfort of his warm body pressed close to her heart.

For a while they walk in a heavy silence, broken only by the slosh of their footsteps and Thomas's sporadic babbling. When they reach the path that cuts through the dunes towards the house, Eva keeps walking. She is not ready to venture back into the darkwood world of Highfield House. The manor is stifling in the weight of the secrets they are keeping. Stifling with the weight of a past she can't quite make out.

She steps out onto the beach and closes her eyes. Lifts her face to the wind. Harriet slips an arm around her shoulder and squeezes. Though Harriet's presence is rarely a calming one, Eva is glad she is here now. In spite of everything, she had missed her sister in the month they were apart. And there had been more than one moment while she was stranded on Longstone when she imagined they might never see each other again.

She opens her eyes. Trudges back to the top of the beach, her shoes sliding over the pebbles. And she sees it then: that rusty splatter across the white shingle at the top of the embankment. Blood. There can be no mistaking it.

Her mouth goes dry.

"Eva?" she hears Harriet say. "What is it? What have you found?"

It's the blood of a sea bird, she tells herself. A fish, or a seal. Or some poor roe deer Martin Macauley has blasted from the dunes. These, she knows, are all likely explanations. But she can't shake that possibility that is making her heart pound and the sounds in her ears feel distant.

That when Martin Macauley raised his musket on her, his bullet struck Finn Murray.

Impossible, she tells herself. She would have heard him cry out. Perhaps seen him fall. But when she thinks back to those terrifying moments, she remembers screaming, remembers running, remembers not looking back at Finn until his boat was moving towards the horizon. It is possible, she knows, that Martin Macauley's bullet found him without her being aware of it. It is more than possible. She presses the baby back into Harriet's arms, unable to tear her eyes from those darkened petals of blood.

And she knows she must return to Longstone.

CHAPTER TEN

Eva rushes back to the house. She shoves spare skirts and stockings and petticoats into her duffel bag, along with her shawl and gloves and a small pouch of coins.

Harriet ploughs into her bedroom with Thomas under her arm, a barrage of questions. What is she doing? Where is she going?

"I have to go back to Longstone. Finn Murray… He may be hurt." She is off down the stairs before Harriet can gather a response. She blusters towards the kitchen, passing Mrs Brodie in the hallway as she returns from Evensong.

"All right, Miss Blake?" asks the housekeeper, following her into the kitchen.

Eva flings open the pantry. "I need to go to Longstone. I'm afraid Mr Murray has been hurt."

"Mr Murray? The lightkeeper?" Mrs Brodie frowns. "What do you need?"

Eva rifles past jam jars and potted meat and baskets of potatoes. "Food. Tea. I don't know, I…" She has no idea what she will find when she steps back onto Longstone, and no idea what she will do if the lightkeeper truly is hurt—all she knows is she must go. What if Finn Murray has bled to death in that lonely cottage? Or what if he never made it back to the island at all? What if he is lying dead in that little boat, his body at the mercy of the waves? Dread squeezes her chest. She cannot live with another death on her conscience.

She scrubs a hand across her eyes, trying to tamp down her panic. She has no idea how she will even get back to the island.

Mrs Brodie goads her out of the cupboard and produces a block of cheese and a loaf of bread from the shelf, along with a jar of potted meat and a tin of tea. She wraps the bread in a cloth and hands the food to Eva. "These should last you a few days. How long will you be gone?"

She shakes her head. "I've no idea."

The door cracks open and Harriet appears in the kitchen. "Evie. This is madness. You cannot seriously be going back there."

"I have to."

Mrs Brodie emerges from the pantry with another small jar. She hands it to Eva. "Here. It's figwort ointment. If the fellow is hurt, this will help it heal. It will keep the wound from festering."

Eva shoves it in her bag and nods her thanks. She flies past Harriet before she can stop her.

Out the front door she runs. There are Nathan and Edwin, deep in conversation as they walk the inland path back from the village. Theodora is just ahead of them, skipping backwards and chatting animatedly.

Eva darts towards the coast path, hoping she will not be seen. Harriet will tell Nathan everything, no doubt. Right now, Eva has neither the time nor the inclination to explain things to her brother.

She hurries onto the wharf, praying she will not see Martin Macauley. A young fisherman, barely older than a boy, is kneeling on the jetty, wrestling with a tangled fishing net.

Eva holds out a handful of coins. "I need to get to Longstone. Will you take me?"

Confusion crosses his freckled face. "There's nothing on Longstone. Nothing except the firebasket."

She holds his gaze. "Will you take me?"

The young man stands. He looks out to sea, then down to the money in her outstretched palm. "You're one of them, aren't you. The Blakes."

Eva grits her teeth. "That has nothing to do with anything. Will you take me or not?"

The fisherman grabs the coins and shoves them into his pocket. He nods towards his boat. "Get in."

Eva sits at the bow, eyes fixed to the dark shape of Longstone. The fisherman's boat pitches over the swell, sea spray stinging her eyes. She can make out the shape of the cottage on its distended foundations, the coal shed behind it. Can make out the stone tower of the firebasket, unlit in the pink twilight. She grips the gunwale. "Can you not go faster?"

"I'm sorry, Miss," says the fisherman. "Big swell today. Got to be careful around the reef."

She clenches her hands until her nails dig into her palms. The need to get to the cottage is overwhelming.

After what feels an eternity, the fisherman draws close to the jetty. The sight of Finn's boat knocking against its mooring eases a little of Eva's panic. At the very least, he has made it back to the island.

The moment the fisherman's boat touches the jetty, she leaps out, clutching her duffel bag to her chest.

"I can't wait for you," the fisherman calls. "I've to get back…"

Eva nods. She casts a single glance back over her shoulder and sees the boat moving away from the jetty. She rushes towards the cottage, stumbling through a shallow pool beside the staircase.

She is breathless when she pounds on the door. Throws it open without waiting for a response. And there is the lightkeeper, yanked from sleep as she clatters into the cottage.

An unreadable expression passes across his face as he sits up in bed. Anger or amusement? Maybe somewhere between the two. "You. What in hell are you doing here?"

Eva swallows. Water drips from her wet skirts and pools at her feet. "Martin Macauley," she garbles, "I thought he hit you. I passed the beach on the way back to the house today. And I saw blood on the rocks, and I thought…"

He raises his eyebrows as he shoves back the bedclothes. Tangled brown hair hangs loose on his shoulders, dishevelled and flattened on one side. "You thought you'd come fleeing back here to see if I was dead?"

"Yes." Why does it sound so foolish when he says it? Eva swallows, her fingers tightening around the strap of her bag. "I may have overreacted."

A faint smile quirks his lips. "You think?"

Eva hesitates. "The firebasket is not lit."

"No." He looks down, away from her eyes. "It's not."

And she sees it then—that pile of bloodied cloths in the chamber pot beside the bed. Sees the discoloured strapping around his calf, peeking out from beneath his woollen slops.

"He did hit you." She rushes towards him.

He jerks away, holding out a hand to keep her at a distance. "What do you think you're doing?"

Eva straightens indignantly. "I'm checking to make sure you're not bleeding to death."

He snorts. "I'm not bleeding to death. It's just a scratch."

Up close, she sees his cheeks are flushed beneath his beard. Sees the sweat glistening on his forehead. She thinks of him sailing back to Longstone with Martin Macauley's bullet in his calf. Thinks of him tending to his own wounds, alone on this island with the sea closing in. It makes her chest ache. But she takes a step back, suddenly aware of how close she is standing to him.

"You don't need to be here," he says. "I'm fine."

Eva looks at him squarely. "You are clearly not. I am not leaving you on your own like this."

His lips part at her directness. No doubt he thought her capable of nothing more than panic-stricken tears and snivelling. "I don't need a house guest," he snaps. "I don't know what you were thinking, charging in here uninvited." As if to prove his point, his hand tightens around the bed head and he attempts to stand, swallowing a grunt of pain. Eva puts a firm hand to his shoulder, forcing him back onto the mattress.

"Don't be so damn foolish. You need to rest." The conflict is making her whole body hot, but she refuses to back down. "You can be as angry at me as you wish, Mr Murray. But I am not going anywhere until you are healed. So you may as well accept it."

His eyebrows rise; she knows his name—she has clearly been discussing him. But her outburst seems to have shocked him into silence.

Flustered, Eva looks around. Now she has made her grand proclamation, she has no idea what to do. "I need to see the wound," she says, trying to conjure up confidence she doesn't feel.

He gives a short, humourless laugh. "Nah you don't."

She rifles through her bag for the jar of figwort. "Please. This will help fight off the fever."

"No need for that," he says dryly. He picks up a bottle of whisky from beside the bed and lets it dangle in his fist. "Already cleaned it out with a little moonshine."

Eva hesitates, debating whether to argue. She senses pressing the issue will only cause him to push back even harder. She puts the jar of figwort on the mantel beside a burnt-out candle stump and sets her bonnet on the table. The cottage is in disarray. Finn's greatcoat has been flung over a chair, bloodstained breeches on the floor beside the bed. A half-eaten loaf of bread sits in the middle of the table, a knife poking out of a jam jar beside it. The place smells of whisky, of sweat, of sea. Eva shivers hard. The cottage is freezing.

She spots the kettle sitting beside the unlit fire. Tea, she decides. She will make tea. At the very least, it will calm her, order her mind a little. And perhaps settle a little of Finn's anger.

She can feel his eyes boring into the back of her as she crouches by the blackened bricks of the hearth and carefully arranges the kindling from the basket beside the grate.

"D'you know how to do that?" he asks with a hint of mockery.

Her cheeks flush, but she does not give him the satisfaction of seeing it. "You think I cannot lay a fire?" she asks, keeping her back to him.

"I think a lass who dresses like you and speaks like you has always had these things done for her."

Eva hates how true his words are. Hates that she only knows how to lay a fire from having watched her housekeepers do it. And she hates how terrified she is that this fire won't take. Asking for help, after she has appeared here so impulsively—and after she has made such a scene about caring for him—would be close to the worst thing she can imagine. She strikes the tinderbox once, twice, before it sparks. After several minutes, the tiny flames licking the kindling have grown into something warming and bright. She fights the urge to give Finn a self-satisfied look.

Finding the kettle still half full of water, she hangs it on the hook and rummages in her bag for the tea Mrs Brodie had given her. In the back of the sideboard, she finds a cracked floral teapot. A single tin cup and plate sit abandoned on the table. She wipes the thick layer of dust from the pot and cracks open the lid, startling a spider out from its depths. She uses a little of the water from the kettle to rinse it. Her wet shoes leave footprints across the floor as she paces between the hearth and the table.

When steam is curling from the nose of the kettle, she fills the pot and pours the tea carefully into the cup. She cuts a little of the bread and cheese and sets them on the plate. Holds the food out to Finn.

He eyes it, before looking up at her. "I'm not hungry," he says dryly. "And I don't like tea. But well done. On managing the fire and all."

Eva presses her lips into a thin line. She dumps the cup and plate on the table, cursing under her breath as hot liquid splashes onto her finger.

Finn tilts his head, taking her in. "What would you have done if I were dead? Stood waving on the shore until a ship passed?"

Her cheeks flush. "I don't know," she admits. "It was foolish. I just… I saw the blood on the rocks and I panicked. I knew I had to come and see if you needed help."

She waits for his taunt, but it doesn't come. He lowers his eyes.

"Is there anything else you need?" Eva asks.

Finn opens his mouth, but says nothing.

"What?" she presses.

When he speaks again, a little of the mockery is gone from his voice. "The firebasket. I've not managed to light it."

"The firebasket," Eva repeats. "Of course." She looks out the window at the brazier swaying gently on the end of the chain. The dusk is thick now and the jagged shards of the Farnes are being swallowed by the night.

Building the fire was one thing, but lighting the beacon with the wind whipping up off the ocean feels like something else entirely. Finn makes to stand, but she holds out a hand to stop him. "No. I can manage. Just tell me what I need to do."

She waits for that ridicule; that comment that a well-to-do lady like her will never spark that basket to life. But Finn says:

"Unhook the chain and use the pulley to lower the brazier. The fuel is in the shed. Use the kindling to get it started, then bank it up with coal. The same way you lit the fire in the hearth."

Eva nods. She takes the tinderbox from the mantel and shoves it in her pocket, then goes out to the shed. Her wet shoes squelch loudly as she carries armfuls of wood towards the firebasket. Wind is swirling off the ocean, and she sees dark planes of sea rising and falling against the edge of the island. Slowly, carefully, she unhooks the chain from its moorings and lowers the brazier down to the earth, the rusty metal leaving orange streaks on her palms. Carefully, she arranges the wood in the firebasket and strikes the tinderbox, sending a spark into the kindling. Wind whips off the water and snatches the tiny flame.

Eva grits her teeth. She rearranges the kindling and snaps the tinderbox again. This time, the fire sparks, and with a little coaxing, it spreads. Orange light blossoms, illuminating the night. For a moment, she stares into it, feeling the warmth against her cheeks. Her arms strain as she heaves on the chain, sending the brazier into the sky. Using all her strength, she secures the chain to its hook. Light arcs out across the sea.

Inexplicably, Eva feels tears prick her eyes. After Walton's rejection, after Nathan's disappointment, and worst of all, after Donald Macauley, being capable of this felt like the air she needed to survive. She blinks her tears away quickly. She cannot let Finn Murray see them.

When she comes back inside, the cottage is bathed in orange light from both inside and out. The fire in the grate is starting to warm the frozen corners. She feels a soft sense of accomplishment.

She goes to a corner of the room and pulls off her wet shoes and stockings, replacing them with a dry pair from her bag. Her damp skirts and petticoats soak through the dry wool quickly, but she will have to wait until Finn is asleep before she can change her clothes. She shoves her wet stockings back into her duffel bag, then goes to the table and begins to eat the bread and cheese she had cut for Finn. She is famished, she realises. She has barely eaten a thing since Donald Macauley's death, and now, in the relief of finding Finn alive, her hunger has returned with force. She can't help but glance at him as she eats. He is watching her with a look of open curiosity.

"Who are you?" he asks. "What's your name?"

He knows not a thing about her either, Eva realises. Beyond the fact that she killed a man, and took Finn back to Holy Island to face Martin Macauley's musket. Little wonder he had looked so unimpressed when she had barrelled back through his door. "Eva," she says finally. "Eva Blake."

Something passes across his eyes. "Blake. Your family owns Highfield House."

She nods faintly. And she feels a strange heaviness in her chest that, even out here in such vast isolation, the shadow of the house might still manage to reach her.

CHAPTER ELEVEN

Finn's chest is heaving.

Eva Blake, of Highfield House.

She cannot stay here. Of all the people in the world, *she* cannot stay here.

But what are the choices? He is in far too much pain to take the skiff back to Holy Island tonight. And no one else is coming for her.

Besides, as much as he can't bear the thought of having one of the Blakes under his roof—and as much as he doesn't want to admit it—he needs her help.

The wound to his lower leg could have been far worse—Macauley's ball had made both a clean entry and exit, neatly finding the stripe of flesh between his breeches and his boots. But even a few steps is enough to have sweat beading on his forehead. He can feel a fever closing in.

This life is a physically challenging one, even without such an injury. Last night, he had made it as far as the coal shed, but carrying shovelfuls to the firebasket had been a step too far. He had lain in bed in thick, unsettling blackness, kept from sleep by pulsing pain.

He looks through the salt-speckled window at the bloom of orange light in the sky. He's surprised to see the fire roaring in the basket. Was sure he'd be hobbling out there himself to tell her where to find the coal. He has to admit, he's a little impressed.

Eva sits at his table, chewing through bread and cheese like she hasn't eaten for a week. She is oddly fascinating, with her stockinged feet and the thick blue cloak still wrapped around her shoulders. Is she cold? Or too enthralled by her supper to realise she is still wearing it? Strands of brown hair have come loose from the knot at the back of her neck, spidery against the white skin above her collar. Something about her is impossible to look away from. Maybe it's just the novelty of having another person in the cottage with him. He was a child the last time that happened.

When she has finished her food, she looks around, he supposes for a trough or washcloth. She'll find neither—the bucket he uses for washing his dishes is lying on its side behind the coal shed. He barely uses it at the best of times.

She leaves the plate on the table and looks over at him, wrapping her arms around her body.

"You ought to try and sleep," she says. "I can watch the light."

He shakes his head. "I'll not sleep til dawn." He nods towards the door half-blocked by the sideboard. "You can sleep in there."

Eva goes to the sideboard with a curious frown on her face. She throws her weight against it and it groans along the floor. She opens the door and peeks inside curiously.

The room is dark, the shutters fastened over the windows to keep the sea from finding its way through the glass. Finn can't remember the last time the room saw sunlight. An orange glow from the lamp on the table reaches inside, and he can see the shape of the narrow wooden bed in the centre of the room. No blankets or pillows, but a cotton-stuffed mattress, which he hopes is still intact. He can tell the room is shadowed and cold, the chill of unused decades trapped in its rugged stone walls. He has vivid memories of lying awake on that narrow bed, listening to his parents chatter, tracking his father's footsteps across the cottage and out towards the beacon. How many nights had he lain awake in that room, making up stories about the shadows the firebasket cast on the wall?

He is sure the room is filthy, filled with the sour breath of forgotten years and sea. A part of him is embarrassed to offer it to a lady like Eva Blake.

She turns to him with raised eyebrows. "You have another room? Why did you not tell me that last time I was here?"

"I offered you the bed," Finn says tautly.

"Who did it belong to?" she asks. "It looks like it's not been used for years."

He swallows. "D'you want it or not?" He desperately hopes she will take the room. Disappear into it for a few hours. He needs the space—especially now he knows who she is.

He's become too used to being kept company by only the light and the tides. These days, he needs to prepare himself for any disruption to his solitary existence. And he most certainly was not prepared for Eva Blake to appear at his door with panic in her eyes and figwort in her hands.

"Yes," she says. "Of course I want it. Thank you." She dumps her duffel bag inside the door, then looks at him with intent blue eyes. "But not tonight. Tonight you need to rest. And I will watch the light." Her words are thin and he can tell her confidence is forced.

Finn reaches down for the bottle of whisky beside the bed. Takes a long gulp. The liquor is awful, but he swallows it smoothly. His body has grown far too used to it over the last few days. The alcohol dulls the pain in his calf, but does nothing for the fierce thumping behind his eyes.

He opens his mouth to argue, but can't quite form the words. He is exhausted, from two sleepless, pain-filled nights—and from five years of keeping the light alone. He has trained himself to sleep in short spurts; a few hours at dawn, a few before dusk. But he is not immune to the rhythms of nature, and his body's inherent need to sleep in the darkness. There have been far too many times that he's woken at the table to find himself in blackness, with the firebasket spitting ash. Still, he supposes a sporadic light on the shore is better than no light at all.

Tonight, though, with a second person to keep the flames alive, he finds himself closing his eyes.

It's a broken, fevered sleep, though it's far more than he's managed in the past two nights. Eva is constantly there on the edge of his awareness, pouring water down his throat, pressing a damp cloth to his forehead, trudging out into the night to restoke the basket.

Sometime before dawn, he opens his eyes and watches her in the firelight. She puts the jam jar in the sideboard and wipes crumbs from the table with a cloth she has magicked from somewhere unknown. She lets out an enormous yawn; doesn't bother to cover it. There is something oddly thrilling about watching her without her being aware of it. Like observing a swan through a bird hide. Her black leather shoes are drying by the hearth, lined up neatly with their buckles side by side. Her feet are soundless on the floorboards as she moves back and forth across the cottage.

In spite of everything Eva's presence has stirred up in him, he can't deny there's something faintly comforting about having another soul on the island tonight. Even if that person does come from Highfield House. In spite of everything, as he had stitched and bound his wound, dousing it in whisky to fight off the fever, he had been unable to shake the fear that he might die alone on this island.

What would happen to his body? Would he disappear back into the earth or the sea, with no living soul any the wiser? There is a certain beauty to that, he supposes. But it is more than a little unnerving. The thought of it, just like Eva's presence, reminds him of things he would rather forget.

It's been years since anyone else has set foot on Longstone. Even the churchmen who own this land never venture out here. His willingness to keep the firebasket lit, even without a real commission, keeps them from venturing his way; keeps them from demanding payment for the land. An arrangement that has been in place since his father was alive.

Eva Blake, a child of Highfield House. Eva Blake, who had knocked a man into the sea and watched him drown. There is something faintly settling about the terrible deed she had confessed to. She is carrying her own crime, so she is unlikely to dig too deeply into his.

An accident, she had told him. Who was the sorry soul? And why was she out at sea with him so close to dark? The question has been swirling through his mind unbidden since he had plucked her from his coal shed three nights ago. But he can't ask. Won't ask. He cannot set a precedent of them being open with each other. Nonetheless, he's achingly curious about her. What brought her back to Holy Island? Because that polished London accent tells him it's been years since she last set foot in Northumberland.

She turns her head, catches him watching her. "I'm sorry," she says, "I did not mean to wake you." She takes the waterskin from the table and strides purposefully towards him. "Here. You ought to drink a little while you're awake."

The rainwater tastes of the sky, and faintly, somehow of the sea. Everything out here comes to taste like the sea. A stray drop slides through his beard, cooling his heated skin. He nods his thanks, then turns away quickly, to prevent conversation.

He shakes his curiosity about her away. It doesn't matter why she's here. All that matters is that she does not stay under his roof for a minute longer than necessary.

CHAPTER TWELVE

In the lamplight of her workroom, ripples of painted sunshine are coming alive. Harriet's brush moves across the canvas, and she is dimly aware of a smile on her face. Around her, the rest of the house is silent. Has been for hours.

She has been painting for what feels like her entire life. Does not dare to imagine what she would be without it. She remembers the friend of her mother who had taught her her craft: Madame Octavia—self-styled, of course—with her loose-flowing grey hair and silk robes that billowed out behind her like windblown clouds. Madame Octavia used to brag she had studied with Sirani; would toss Italian phrases into Harriet's lessons, all for the purpose of the exotic.

They would not be constrained, Madame Octavia would say, by the limitations the art world placed upon their sex. They would not be content to paint meagre still-lifes and visions of the home—*we are far better than that, are we not, Harriet, dear?*

How she craved those lessons, when the madame would flounce around the sitting room of her townhouse on the Strand, her bare, paint-speckled feet pattering against the floorboards. They would paint with their easels side by side, and with the madame's careful tutelage, Harriet brought to life grand seascapes and portraits and imagined visions of worlds she had never seen. Those lessons had been full of inspiration, of freedom. They had been some of the happiest days of Harriet's life. They feel impossibly distant.

Before she had died, Octavia had introduced Harriet to her fellow artists across the city. Men and women with whom she could lose herself in conversation, spending hours in discussion over this painter's use of shadow, the drama captured in this artist's work. People who understood her. Passionate, single-minded people she felt she could relate to. She misses them with an ache that seems to reach her bones.

"Harriet. What are you doing?"

She doesn't turn. "I am sure you can work that out for yourself, Edwin."

Her husband sighs loudly from the doorway. "It's far too late for this."

She does not tell him she has been creeping down here at midnight almost every night since they arrived in this place. Does not tell him how irritated she is that he has finally woken up and caught her. Instead, she says, "I like this time of night. It inspires me."

These nights in front of her easel have begun to feel like her saviour. The only time she can live something close to the life she wants to live. Never mind the figure creeping around outside the window, perhaps seeking to punish her family for their spying ways.

Two days ago, Harriet had ventured to Julia Mitchell's curiosity shop for tea and conversation, and had left with the sense that she might actually have something close to a friend in this place.

As she and Julia had chatted easily over their teacups, Harriet considered telling her about the figure she had seen around the house at night. But something had held her back. Perhaps a fear of being ridiculed. Or perhaps a reluctance to share the goings on of Highfield House with a village that seems fixated on her family.

Edwin steps through the doorway, glancing around the shadowed, lamplit room. "It's dreadfully dreary down here. How can a place like this inspire you?"

Harriet looks back at the canvas. In a way, he is right. The light is far too poor to allow for any great accuracy. But this gloomy hovel has become her saving grace. "You're a craftsman," she says. "I thought you considered yourself an artist. I would have thought you understood the way inspiration works."

Edwin takes her wrist, lifting the paintbrush from the canvas. "Come to bed." There is a firmness to his tone now, and Harriet can tell his words are not merely a suggestion. She hesitates. She knows she cannot push back too hard, or she risks her husband taking her painting away from her. But this impossible streak of sunlight cannot wait. She steps closer to the canvas, examining the arc of her brushstrokes.

"I will be there shortly," she says.

"No." His fingers tighten around her wrist. "You will come upstairs now. We've barely spent time together all week."

"Because you're too exhausted to keep your eyes open at the end of every day."

"Yes," he says pointedly. "Securing our future. Our son's future."

Nathan has offered Edwin a handsome cut of the profits once the house is sold, in addition, of course to a return of all the funds her husband has invested in the project. Harriet does not even dare imagine when that might happen. Lindisfarne feels like a purgatory she will never escape.

She does not miss the undertone in Edwin's comment, the words that go unsaid. The warning that in order to be permitted to keep a brush in her hand, she must remember she is first and foremost a wife. A mother.

She must remember that her husband is not to be neglected.

She sighs heavily, defeated. She places her palette into the water tray she has set up on the table beside her. And she trails Edwin back down the hallway to their bedroom, deliberate in not cleaning the paint from her hands. The streaks of light and dark staining her wrists and fingers serve to keep her mind focused on her work, rather than the task that lies ahead. Specks of sunlight on her palms to take her attention away from reality.

Edwin is brisk, efficient as he sifts through layers of clothing and eases her back on the wide curtained bed. Harriet looks up at the canopy; forces her mind to other places.

It is not that she is repulsed by her husband. Edwin is fine-looking enough, with dark hair that has not yet begun to thin, and a narrow, unblemished face that could almost be described as handsome. And yet it does nothing to warm her, or to persuade her closer. In the first days and weeks of their marriage, he had been attentive to her needs—or had at least attempted to be. These days, he seems to have given up the pretence entirely. Harriet is glad of it.

Nonetheless, it is not the act itself that she dreads so desperately, but the fear of finding herself with child again. Such a thing would be worse than having her painting taken from her. Being Thomas's mother is already far too big a weight to carry. Having another child in tow is a horror she cannot even begin to contemplate.

Before she sleeps tonight, she will pray for a reprieve. Reacquaint herself with a God she only speaks to while lying on her back beneath the bed curtains, with her husband's scent on her skin.

CHAPTER THIRTEEN

By dawn, Eva's eyes are heavy. She sits wearily at the table, staring out the window as the last threads of firelight are sucked away by the morning. There's an allure to this beautiful solitude, she realises. Out here on Longstone, with the rest of the world feeling far away, that weighted regret over Donald Macauley's death is sitting a little lighter on her shoulders.

Thanks to her efforts during the night, the cottage is in slightly better order, with the table cleaned of food scraps and jars tucked away in cupboards. Today, she will scrub down the plates and cups that don't seem to have seen a wash cloth in decades. Soak Finn's bloodstained clothes and air out the bedroom.

She yawns. Hopefully she will manage a few hours of sleep this morning too.

She looks over at Finn. His chest is rising and falling with sleep, his breath slower and steadier than it had been throughout the night. She hopes it means his fever is beginning to pass.

"If I die," he'd mumbled at her during the night, "take the skiff back to Lindisfarne."

And avoiding the prospect of being back on that ocean alone, Eva thinks, is as good a reason as any to keep this man alive.

She knows that, as impulsive as this journey to Longstone was, it was the right thing to do. Whether Finn Murray plans to admit it or not, she knows she is needed here, and after the devastation of the past few weeks, it feels good to be of service.

She is fairly certain he is not going to admit it.

Eva takes the knife from the table and begins to slice through the bread Mrs Brodie had given her. Decides to leave the brick-like remains of Finn's loaf to the birds.

The bed creaks and she turns to see him open his eyes. His gaze drifts to the hearth, where her wet stockings hang drying over the fireguard. Eva leaps to her feet and snatches them hurriedly, cheeks flushing with embarrassment.

"Good morning," she says guardedly, stockings in one hand and knife in the other. "How are you feeling?"

"Grand," he says wryly. "Just grand." He looks bleary-eyed and disoriented at having slept through the darkness. But in spite of his saltiness, he seems a little better this morning, his eyes somewhat brighter and the shadows in his cheeks less pronounced.

Eva shoves the stockings into her pocket, hovering in front of the bed. This is a far more awkward thing now Finn is not half vacant with whisky and sleep. She is all too aware of the impropriety of their situation.

She fills two plates with slices of bread and cheese. "Here. You ought to eat something." She attempts a smile. "The cheese is good. I think you will like it." Finn takes the plate. Says nothing. His complete lack of gratitude—and manners—stings. "Or do you dislike cheese as well as tea?" She is unable to keep the sharpness out of her voice.

Finn studies her for a moment before taking a bite. "It's good," he says. His words sound somewhat begrudging.

Eva sits at the table, the chair creaking loudly beneath her. For long moments, they eat in silence. Wind pushes against the glass, making the window frames creak.

This stiltedness, Eva realises, it's new. When she had first blown onto Longstone and disrupted Finn Murray's solitude, he had been brusque and rough spoken. But he had not been reluctant to talk to her. Now, getting a word out of him is like trying to squeeze blood from a stone.

It's the pain, she tells herself. No doubt he's in little mood for conversation.

Or perhaps there is more to it.

Because this coldness, she realises, it started the moment Finn learned her name.

"You know my family's house," she says.

He keeps his eyes on his plate. "Everyone knows your family's house."

"Well," she says, "it won't be ours for much longer."

He looks up in interest.

"My brother is restoring it. He means to sell it."

Finn takes another bite of bread. Chews slowly. "You live there with your husband?"

She smiles wryly. Does he really imagine a husband might allow her to come out here alone like this? "My brother. And sister. And their families." She tears the crust off her bread and breaks it into pieces. "We are not government spies. If that's what you think." Because that's what this new coldness is about, isn't it? Is that not why Finn Murray closed down the moment he heard her name? Because he knows Highfield House, and he knows the rumours surrounding the Blakes, and perhaps he has his own involvement in the Jacobite cause he wishes to hide from her and her fictitious contacts within King George's government.

"What I think?" he repeats. "What does it matter what I think? What your family does is of no concern to me."

Eva grits her teeth. She had tried to nudge the conversation towards some semblance of openness; lay their cards on the table so they might get through this ordeal without blood being spilt—at least no more than it has already. But she can tell there is to be no such thing.

"Well," she says tautly, "it concerns you to the degree of Martin Macauley putting a bullet in your calf."

Finn looks at her squarely then, and it catches her off guard. His brown eyes seem to bore into hers, making her feel suddenly exposed. He opens his mouth to speak, then seems to change his mind. He turns back to his plate and shifts on the bed, tries to hide a grimace.

Eva forgets the need to exonerate her family. "Please," she says tentatively. "Will you let me see the wound? I'm sure the figwort ointment will do it good. Our housekeeper says it will help it heal." She takes the jar from the mantel and holds it out to him. "Please?"

Resignedly, Finn pushes back the blanket and tugs his woollen slops above his knee. He unwraps the strapping he has tied around his calf. The wound has been jaggedly stitched closed, tracking the path Martin

Macauley's bullet had carved through his flesh. Though the skin around the wound is pink and swollen, and still flecked with blood, Eva is relieved to find it looks somewhat clean. Not that she really has any damn idea what she is looking for.

She swallows heavily and takes a step closer to the bed. She can smell the salt and woodsmoke on Finn's skin. Can feel the heat rising from his body. Her heart begins to quicken.

When she had thrown herself into the fisherman's boat, desperate to return to Longstone, she had not stopped to consider the intimacy, the indecency, of being out here alone with Finn Murray. She had not thought beyond his survival. But she had become aware of it the moment she had stepped back into his cottage and found him in bed. Had been aware of it as she had sat at the table in the thick stillness of night, listening to his heavy breathing. And she is acutely, painfully aware of it now.

She uncorks the jar. Hesitates for a moment. She reaches for the washcloth sitting in the basin and dips the corner into the ointment. She edges closer to Finn, fingers tight around the cloth. He swoops a hand out suddenly and snatches the jar. "Let me do it." His voice is husky.

Eva nods and backs away.

Finn doesn't look at her as he tentatively applies the ointment with his fingers. His shoulders round, as though he is trying to close in on himself. He turns away from her slightly, as if he too is feeling exposed.

He rips another strip of linen from the torn shirt hanging on the end of the bed. Ties it around his calf and pulls down the leg of his slops.

Eva hovers by the table. "I'm sorry," she says.

"For what?"

"It was all my fault."

He sets the jar on the floor beside the bed. "It was Martin Macauley's fault."

"You would not have been there if it weren't for me." She glances down at his wound. "Did you pull the ball out yourself?"

"The ball passed through. I told you, it's just a scratch."

She raises her eyebrows. "I think we both know that to be a lie."

One corner of his lips turns upwards into a hint of a smile. It takes Eva by surprise. "Well. I'm sure I will survive."

She catches his eye. "I am not leaving until I know that for certain."

CHAPTER FOURTEEN

"*Please,* Papa." Theodora is standing as close as possible to the doorway without actually being inside the bedroom. It's this room, his brother Oliver's room, that Nathan cannot bear to have his daughter in. He has just begun tearing up the stained and timeworn floorboards that are in desperate need of replacing. Already, he can't wait for the task to be over.

"Can I please have the doll? It's so beautiful, you just have to see it. It looks like an *actual* person. She has real, honest eyelashes."

Nathan looks over his shoulder at her. "Theodora, I've told you before—"

"I'm not *in* the room, Papa. I'm just outside it. Look where my toes are."

He can't hold back a smile.

"Auntie Harriet says the lady in the shop is keeping the doll for me and I just have to convince you to buy it."

Nathan raises his eyebrows. "Does she now?"

"Just this one doll, please. Then I'll never, ever come into the rooms you're working in again."

He comes towards her, blocking the doorway and ushering her from the room. Instinctively, she takes a step back, to avoid making contact with him. The gesture fills him with regret.

Physical contact—even with his daughter—has always been hard for him. An intense discomfort bordering on fear. It's a crawling beneath his skin. A hot swirling in his belly. When someone touches him without consent, he feels the ghost of the contact lingering for days.

Somehow, with Sarah, it had been easy. Nathan had always assumed he would never be a husband; never be a father. Had assumed he would live out his life in his self-imposed isolation—a strange, peopled loneliness. But when he had met Sarah, he had felt something inside him shift. For the first time in his life, he had craved her. Craved the feel of her hair beneath his fingers, her hand intertwined with his. Longed to have her body pressed against his own. She had been endlessly patient as he navigated his way through his fear, one graze of the fingers at a time. Sitting motionless as he explored her almost experimentally. A finger traced around her jawline. A hand pressed to her arm. And then, finally, slowly, a kiss; his skin to hers; his body moving inside her.

When Sarah had passed away three years ago, there had been another sensation alongside the grief. A sense of him closing up, stepping back into the shell of solitude he had existed in for so much of his life. A need to keep everyone—even his child—at a distance.

He knows, of course, what that distance could do to Theodora, especially after the loss of her mother. And so, he tries. Tries for Thea, and for everyone else around him. Tries to be as warm and affable as possible, to prove the distance he is keeping is nothing to do with them.

He hates how acutely aware Theodora is of his fear. Hates that his affectionate daughter changes her behaviour to appease him.

He gives her his brightest smile to make up for it. "You'll never come into the rooms I'm working in again? That does sound like a fine deal."

"It is," she tells him solemnly. "It's a very fine deal."

He laughs. "Very well. The deal is made. Just let me tidy myself." He locks the door behind him and shoves the ring of keys into his pocket.

"And at this house," Theodora says as they walk towards the village half an hour later, "there are two sheep. I call them Peter and Pigsy, but I don't know what their real names are."

Nathan chuckles. "Pigsy is a rather strange name for a sheep, don't you think?"

Theodora shrugs. "Not really. I think it suits him." She runs ahead towards the alley that leads to the back of the Macauleys' farm. "And I saw a beautiful big horse in here once."

Nathan calls her back hurriedly. "Don't go down there, my love."

She gives him knowing eyes. "The man who lives there is not very friendly."

"Something like that, yes."

Theodora skips away from the alley. She turns to look back at Nathan, stray pieces of blonde hair blowing over her eyes. Sometimes he adores how much she looks like her mother. Other times, he can't bear the ache of it. "On the way home," she says, "can we go and look for mermaids in the rockpools again? I wonder if they were all hiding last time because they saw us coming."

Nathan smiles. "You like it here, don't you." He is surprised. Had not imagined his city-born child would ever feel at home with earth-caked shoes and her hair blown wild with sea. Perhaps a little of his concern about her is unwarranted.

"Of course I do. I wish you had brought me with you when you first came."

He feels a pang of guilt. "You did not like being in London with Auntie Eva?"

Theodora balances across a log next to the road, her arms held out to the side. "Well, yes. But I'd rather be here with you." She leaps off the log and shoves open the door of the curiosity shop, making the bell above the door jangle.

Nathan follows her inside. He looks around the cluttered shop with a mixture of interest and horror. It feels as though the overloaded shelves might come crashing down at any moment and pin him and Theodora beneath them. At least that would be a memorable ending.

"Good day, there."

Nathan recognises the copper-haired shopkeeper from church. Julia Mitchell, Harriet tells him. She must know who he is—everyone here does—but her smile is warm and bright. It seems to light the dingy corners of the shop. He finds himself smiling in response.

"My daughter saw a doll in here last week. I hear you put it aside for her."

"In a green dress," Theodora puts in. "With eyelashes."

"Of course." Julia bends down behind the counter and reappears with the doll in her hands. Theodora's eyes light as she hands it over.

"Thea," murmurs Nathan. "What do you say?"

"Thank you," she gushes, turning the doll around carefully and smoothing its creased skirts. "Look, Papa. Eyelashes."

"So I see."

Julia watches her with a smile, before looking back at Nathan. "So you're the famous Mr Blake."

He lets out a laugh he doesn't really feel. "I would have thought infamous was more fitting."

Her green eyes are apologetic. "I'm sorry you haven't been made to feel so welcome. Like I said to your sister, the people here can be rather stuck in their ways."

"Well. I don't suppose I can blame them for that. Especially not at a time like this."

She tilts her head. "I don't suppose you can. Trust is rather hard to come by these days, with war on the horizon."

Nathan jumps at the feel of something downy brushing past his ankle. He looks down to see a ginger cat sidling past, tail in the air.

Julia gives a short laugh. "She likes you. Usually she'll not go near strangers."

Nathan's smile twists into a grimace. He hates cats with a passion bordering on the unnatural. "The doll," he says throatily. "How much do you want for it?"

"It's yours," Julia tells him. "Consider it a welcome gift. I'm sure you could use one."

The gesture brings an unexpected rush of emotion to Nathan's chest. He swallows heavily. Shakes his head and pulls out his coin pouch. "I couldn't." The last thing he wants is a reputation of accepting charity.

Julia's lips part, and for a moment of horror, he wonders if he has offended her. "A shilling, then," she says finally.

Nathan shakes the money from the pouch and places it on the counter.

Julia sweeps up the coins in one swift movement and tucks them in the pocket of her apron. "If you find any treasures in that old house of yours that need a new home, this is the place to come. I'll give you a good price for them."

Nathan nods. "I shall keep that in mind." Warmth returns to Julia's smile, making him realise how much he had missed it. "Thank you, Mrs

Mitchell," he says, bobbing his head to her.

"It's Miss. I've never been married."

"Oh," Nathan splutters. "Forgive me. I thought Harriet mentioned you had a son."

"I do, aye. His father didn't even stay around til the morning. Bobby and I are better off without him." Her bluntness makes Nathan's cheeks colour with something he can't quite identify. He garbles out a flustered response, then flies out the door, praying Theodora is following.

Eva pulls a basket of sorry-looking vegetables out from the bottom cupboard of the sideboard. Potatoes are growing sprouts, the onions are curling, and the carrots have the consistency of twine. Still, she is sure Finn will benefit from eating something more than bread and cheese— never mind that the bread is finished and she has no thought of how to make more.

She rifles through the chaos of the sideboard in search of anything else to throw into her soup. If there is any kind of order to the cupboards, she cannot make it out; jars of potted meat are crammed in beside old ink pots and chapbooks, an enormous sack of flour shares space with fresh candlesticks. Shoved in a drawer beside the pepper mill, she finds a large leather-bound book.

Peeking over her shoulder to check Finn is still asleep, she opens it curiously. Page after page is filled with scrawled dates and times and notes; a logbook, she realises, tracking the tides and the weather, the sunrise and sunset, ships that have passed the island.

She turns back through the pages, following the dates. How long has Finn been out here? Has he been alone all this time? She has so many questions, and she feels quite certain none of them will be welcome.

The bed creaks and she shoves the book back in the drawer, retrieving the pepper mill and dumping it on the table with the vegetables.

"You're cooking?"

Eva whirls around. "Why?" she demands. "Did you not think me capable?"

An amused smile flickers on Finn's lips as he sits up in bed. "Your words. Not mine." He squints in the early-afternoon sunlight pouring in through the window.

Eva's cheeks flush. She hates how easily she is rattled by him. "How are you feeling?"

"All right." He rubs his eyes, rakes fingers through his dishevelled brown hair. "You can read the log," he says. "I don't mind. Although I don't imagine you'll find anything too thrilling in there."

The burning in her cheeks intensifies. She says nothing. Just goes to the table and begins to slice the vegetables. She can count on one hand the number of times she has cooked in the past—and those were just childish games in which she had helped their family's cook by mixing dough and peeling potatoes. Without instruction, she feels completely lost.

Not that she has any intention of letting Finn Murray know that.

The soup, predictably, is terrible. Far too much pepper, and too little of anything else. Eva forces down a few mouthfuls at the table, while Finn sits up in bed, bringing reluctant spoonfuls to his mouth.

"You ought to check the lobster pots tomorrow," he says after a moment. "By the jetty. If there's anything in there, I'll show you how to cook them."

Eva smiles faintly. She had been expecting a far blunter assessment of her cooking skills. Buoyed by his attempt at conversation, she asks, "How long have you—"

"There's a box of cards somewhere," Finn cuts in. "Top drawer maybe. Do you play?"

"Do *you*? You seem to be rather lacking in opponents."

He gives a short chuckle. "Well, there's the ghosts of the old lightkeepers, of course."

Eva smiles. She forces down the last of her soup and rifles through the drawer for the box of cards. She hands them to Finn and pulls a chair up towards the bed.

"Cribbage?" he asks, pulling them from the box and beginning to shuffle.

Eva nods. Her curiosity and questions, she supposes, will have to wait. But she is glad they will not spend the day in silence.

There he is. The figure in the garden. The sight of him sends a bolt of shock through Harriet's body, though she does not know why she is surprised. For days she has been watching out the window of her workroom, waiting for him to appear.

What does he want with her family's house?

Spies. The thought is so ridiculous she almost laughs. What does she care who sits on the throne?

Perhaps, she thinks suddenly, recklessly, she will go out there and confront this intruder, and tell him just that. Demand to know what he thinks he is doing, trying to scare her family from their home like this.

Somewhere in the back of her mind, she is dimly aware that she ought to be afraid. Since they have arrived on this island, danger and death have seemed far too close at hand. But she can't quite make herself feel that fear. These days, she struggles to feel anything beyond a dull hollowness.

Is this man truly trying to scare her family from the island? If so, he is doing a rather terrible job of it. As far as Harriet knows, she is the only one who is aware of his presence. Surely if he intended to scare them, he would have come creeping about the shadows much closer to supper time.

The realisation makes her even more curious. And even more determined to confront him.

She hurries out of her workroom and glides towards the front door. When she pulls it open, a cool, salty breeze touches her skin. There's a faraway, haunting sound on the wind that could be seals howling, or could be imagination.

She steps outside. Rounds the house towards its ocean side, where she had seen the figure outside her workroom. Through the thin curtains, she can still see the faint glow of her candle.

But there is nothing else. No movement, no figure, no hint that anyone has been here. For a second, Harriet's mind goes to ghosts and otherworlds. But another part of her fights this explanation. Perhaps, many years ago, she would have believed the man a ghost. But now the world feels too cold and rigid for this to be the explanation, even out here on Holy Island with sea mist closing in.

Pulling her robe and nightshift up to her calves, she strides through the darkness and circles the building. Highfield House feels monstrous, with row after row of lightless windows staring down on her. The shed and unused stables behind the manor loom in the dark. Fine places to be hiding, if they weren't padlocked tight. For a second, she thinks to call out. Demand whoever is there show themselves. But she cannot be so bold, not when she is standing here unarmed and unaccompanied, in nothing but her nightshift and shawl. Not that there is any point in calling out. She knows for certain that no one will answer. The emptiness feels almost tangible. And doubtful of ghosts or not, Harriet can't deny the fact she is now alone.

CHAPTER FIFTEEN

The worst part of all this, Finn thinks, is that he likes having her around.

She has been here a week, and though he thinks himself capable of managing the skiff, he has not yet made the offer to take her back to Holy Island. Nor has she asked to be taken.

It's foolish. He had told himself he would get her off Longstone the moment he could make it into the boat. But he is yet to tell her she is leaving. He doesn't know why. All he knows is it's far too dangerous to be keeping her here.

All week she has been a vicious gatekeeper, refusing to let him leave the bed for anything more than a hurried piss. Now his fever has broken, she seems satisfied he is not going to die quite yet, and has been content to let him hobble about the place, leaning on the fire poker as a makeshift cane. The fresh air outside is a welcome relief after the stifling days and nights in the cottage, the prospect of death hanging a little too close at hand.

It's almost dark now, with slate-coloured clouds clogging the horizon, and the chill of autumn on the wind. Finn smells the rain before he feels it, and when the sky opens, he lifts his face upwards, enjoying the coolness of the water in his beard.

Eva appears from behind the cottage, lugging the trough she has filled from the rainwater barrels behind the house. Finn reaches out a hand to help her, but she pulls away.

"I can manage." Water slops down the front of her skirts as she climbs the steps. "Ought to have just left the trough out here to catch the rain." She shoulders open the door. "It almost feels like winter."

Finn smiles crookedly. "There's nought of a summer out here."

The night Eva had appeared on his island, terrified out of her mind, she had barely said a word beyond frantic, incoherent stammering. But with each day of her stay, she has become more chatty. There are stories about brothers and sisters and nieces and nephews, and a long carriage journey from London in a week and a half of rain. She seems oblivious to his forced coldness—or at least determined to ignore it.

He had told himself the best way through this was to remain tight-lipped. Offer her little more than a terse good morning and goodnight, and instructions where necessary.

But that is turning out to be much harder than he imagined. *Look at all these beautiful birds*, says Eva Blake, and he finds himself telling her about nesting patterns and mating calls, and asking her if she's seen the nightingales on Lindisfarne yet. Because against every grain of sense in his body, he is curious about her, eager to know more. And that curiosity is far too risky.

Finn limps up the stairs and pulls the door closed behind him. Eva is standing at the window watching streams of water roll down the glass. The trough sits on the floor beside the table, and she has left a trail of wet footprints in her wake.

The cottage is cleaner than it has ever been. Finn has never bothered much for tidiness, but since his injury, the place had seen a new kind of chaos. Eva has spent the last week bringing some order to the sideboard and mantel, dusting and scrubbing surfaces that have not been attended to in years. Jars of jam and potted meat are now tucked away in the cupboards, instead of being spread out across the table, and he can actually see through the windows. He can't deny there's much to be said for being able to stumble around the place without fear of tripping over a stray washbin or a greatcoat fallen to the floor.

"I suppose there's to be no beacon in weather like this." Eva sounds despondent.

Finn takes a jar of potted meat from the sideboard and uncorks it. "We can try. The fuel is dry at the minute, so if the rain eases a little we may have a chance, as long as we keep the fire fed. It's on nights like this that the sailors need the beacon the most."

"Of course." There is a seriousness in her eyes as she turns to look at him. "Then we will try."

Her words make something shift in his chest. When was this last a task for *we*? Not since he was a child, and his parents had kept the light together. He can't deny there is something achingly pleasant about it. But this cannot be a task for *we*, not when the second person is a member of the Blake family.

He feels suddenly restless, like he wants to walk the whole island. Of course, that's impossible. All he can do is stay here in the cottage, trapped like a bear in a cage of Martin Macauley's making.

"A big fire, then. Make sure it's burning well on the ground before raising the brazier." As she instructs herself, Eva goes to the hearth and pulls on the wet shoes she had only moments ago discarded.

"I can manage," says Finn. "I—"

"No. You need to rest. You've already been on your feet far too long today."

He has learnt there is little point in arguing. Eva Blake, he has also learnt, has something to prove. To herself or him, he is not quite sure. Perhaps both.

This well-mannered lady of the manor has immersed herself in the role of lightkeeper. Each night she is studious in watching the beacon; keeping flames reaching skyward, and watching the purple shapes of the shore in case a wayward vessel should come careening towards them.

She has fallen into a meticulous routine, of retiring to bed a few hours before dusk, and rousing herself in time to light the basket. Each time she appears in the living area, her expression business-like and serious, Finn feels a tug in his chest. There is a part of him that dreads the sight of her. And there's a part of him that craves it.

He tells himself there is no need for the dread. Out here on this thread of rock, there is no past and no future. Soon Eva will leave, and will be none the wiser to the things he has done. Why does that thought make him feel so hollow?

He swallows down a spoonful of potted meat, then pulls on his coat and follows Eva outside. He shuffles to the beacon and lowers the brazier, while she hurries to the shed to gather the fuel. Rain swirls and whips against his cheeks, pelting hard against his greatcoat.

Eva dumps a pile of wood at his feet, then hurries back to the shed for a shovelful of coal. Finn resists the urge to take over. Instead, he hovers over the basket, shielding it as best he can from the rain, while Eva shovels out the last of yesterday's ash and carefully stacks the fuel.

"Build it a little higher tonight," he tells her, turning up the collar of his coat against the wind. "The more established we can make the fire, the more of a chance it will have against the weather."

She snaps the tinderbox, cupping the fragile flame with her hand until it begins to take. Finn huddles close to the fire, protecting the basket from the wind and rain. He takes Eva's elbow, tugging her forward to do the same.

"Stand close. Use your body to shield the flames. We need to let the fire take." Smoke coils upwards, meeting rain and a spray of sea. "Now bank up the fire with as much coal as you can."

The fire is a roar when Eva tugs on the chain and sends it into the sky, but the fierce rain attacks it in seconds. Steam hisses and curls. Finn catches the look of disappointment on her face. Hair whips around her cheeks as she stares at the dwindling flames. He puts a hand to her shoulder, urging her back inside.

Condensation is clouding the windows, and the cottage smells of woodsmoke and the misshapen bread loaf Eva had made that afternoon. She leaves a trail of water in her wake as she disappears into the bedroom, pulling the door closed behind her. She returns moments later in her dry blue skirts and shawl, her wet things over her arms and her damp hair dark and thready as it falls down her back. She slings her sodden skirts over the fire rail and hangs the kettle on its rusty hook. Lines her wet shoes up on the hearth.

As he lowers himself into a chair, Finn can't help but follow her with his eyes. He tells himself it's the strangeness of having another person here, inhabiting his space. But he knows it's more than that. There's a warmth to her, an inherent kindness. When Eva had first crashed onto his island, she had felt like an imposition. Now, padding around his cottage in her stockinged feet, her clothes dangling over his fire guard, she feels strangely like a comfort.

She pours the boiling water into the teapot, the rich, smoky smell of tea seeping out the cracked spout. She fills the tin mug she has made her own, and carries it back to the fire.

Finn pulls his chair a little closer to the hearth. A little closer to her. For the warmth, he tells himself. To bring life back to his frozen fingers. Nothing more.

He watches her sip from the cup. He doesn't know why he told her he doesn't like tea. It's far too inoffensive a drink to dislike. He supposes he had just been trying to rile her; to warn her not to make herself comfortable in this solitary life he has made for himself.

He eyes the teapot. He's longing for a cup, but doesn't want to embarrass himself by asking for one. He knows he's been a bastard to Eva, and she has every right to hurl the same sharpness straight back at him. "Your tea smells good," he says finally.

She gives him a lopsided smile. A smile that says she knows she has won. "Would you like a cup?" There's a mocking sweetness in her words, one Finn knows he deserves.

"Maybe just a small one."

Eva doesn't bother to hide her gloating smile as she takes a second cup from the sideboard and wipes it out with the cloth. She fills it and passes it to Finn.

"Careful. It's hot." Her fingers brush his as she hands him the cup. The feel of her bare skin sends a jolt through him he was not expecting.

Once the cup is firmly in his hand, she pulls away quickly and returns to her seat in front of the fire. He can feel her eyes on him, watching as he brings the cup to his lips.

"Well?" she asks.

"It's all right. I suppose."

She laughs, and the sound of it fills the room. When, Finn thinks distantly, was the last time this cottage heard laughter?

Eva doesn't speak, just sips from her own cup again, not taking her eyes from him.

Wind hurls itself against the house, sucking the last of the flames from the firebasket. The cottage fills suddenly with shadows, lit only by the dim flicker in the hearth. Eva gets to her feet instinctively.

"Don't bother," says Finn. He knows this wind, this rain; they can do no more than what they've done already. "There's no point." He reaches into the darkness and lights the lamp.

Eva nods faintly and sits back down, her face half-lit in the firelight. Is she closer to him now? Perhaps it's just his imagination.

He feels utterly trapped. He knows he needs to keep his distance from her, and yet he is craving her nearness with every inch of his being. Can feel energy coursing through him where his fingertips touched hers.

He gets suddenly to his feet, slopping tea across his breeches as he stumbles on his injured leg. He curses, dumps the cup on the table.

Eva looks up in surprise. "What's the matter?"

"Go to bed," he says shortly. "The light will stay dark tonight. I don't need you here." He turns his back to her, unable to bear the look of shock on her face. He's not so removed from the rest of the world that he can't see how his words might sting her. But he cannot let himself get close to her. Not any closer than he has already. And so he says, "I don't want you here."

He hears the rustle of her skirts as she stands, but she doesn't leave the room. His knuckles whiten as he grips the top of the chair.

There's a moment of silence. A horrible, deep silence in which he can feel Eva's eyes spearing him, demanding an explanation for this sudden cruelty. But when he hears the floorboards creak and the bedroom door thump closed, he knows he will have the solitude he has demanded. And that solitude has never made him feel more wretched.

CHAPTER SIXTEEN

Eva is still asleep when he wakes the next morning; at least, she is still locked away in his childhood bedroom. He doesn't blame her. He'd keep away from himself too if he had a choice in the matter.

The rain has blown over and the air smells fresh and clean. Lobsters are squirming in the pots beside the jetty. Finn leans heavily on the fire poker, testing the strength in his leg. After his foolish behaviour last night, it feels crucial that he gets Eva back to Holy Island and puts a large amount of sea between them.

The tide is low, and this morning Longstone feels vast and expansive. If he had it in his legs, he could walk to the southern tip of the island, a spit of rock so often under the veil of the tide, and look out towards the mainland.

He does not have it in his legs, of course. But he starts to walk in that direction anyway. Because there's a ship on the horizon. A three-masted barque, bigger than the fishing vessels he usually sees in these waters. Smaller than the passenger ships that shift silently by on their way to Edinburgh. Rebels from down south, perhaps, sailing to Auld Reekie to join the Earl of Mar's Jacobite army.

Finn shades his eyes from the morning sun. He squints at the hazy shape of the ship. As it glides past his island, he tries to make out the shape of the figurehead. From this distance, it looks to be an eagle with wide wooden wings.

His stomach twists.

Impossible.

What would the *Eagle* be doing in these waters?

He limps back to the cottage and grabs the spying glass from the mantel. And out he goes across the island, south, and south again, over plains of moss-streaked rock. The wound in his calf screams at him to stop, but he knows he can do no such thing. He needs a good look at that ship.

Impossible, he tells himself again. But he knows he can try and convince himself all he wishes, but that does not make it any less plausible that this ship might have returned to Northumbria. The *Eagle's* captain is a native of these parts.

Then again, he's surprised to see the ship at all. The last he knew, the *Eagle* was a licensed privateer, set against the French. But there has been a tentative peace with France for some months, and the Jacobite Rising is yet to begin.

He is out at the tip of the island now, with sea licking his boots. From here, the cottage and shed look like twin fortresses, buttressed against the sea.

His calf is throbbing in time with his heart. Birds are lined up along the green-tinged rocks out here, in this place so rarely intruded upon by humans. Finn skirts the colony, careful not to disrupt them.

The wind has picked up, and he sees it swell the sails of the vessel. With a silent prayer that he might be wrong about the ship, he raises the spying glass.

He is not wrong. There is the barque he knows too well, with its eagle figurehead, silent and graceful on the sea. Moving north towards Holy Island, and then, with any luck, up into Scotland with no thought to the tiny spit of Longstone.

Finn tries to tell himself he is well hidden. No one will find him all the way out here. But he can't quite believe it. Not when he sets a fire blazing on his shore each night, showing the world the island is inhabited. Still, the *Eagle* is from a past that is distant enough to be forgotten. Distant enough for her captain to sail right on by the Farnes, with no thought to who might be lighting that beacon.

But he can't quite believe that either. Because with Eva Blake sleeping in his childhood bedroom and scrubbing the grime from his windows, that past is feeling less distant every day.

Nathan throws his weight against the pry bar, forcing up another floorboard in Oliver's room. Rotting wood splinters at his feet, exhaling a cloud of century-old dust.

He hates this room, with its hiding place within the wall.

The priest hole, Nathan's mother had told them, had been built into the house in the late sixteenth century when religious persecution was at its peak. Those were the days, she said, before the Catholic faith had been bred out of their family through fear and hasty marriages.

In spite of himself, Nathan's curiosity gets the better of him. He puts down the pry bar and pushes against the wooden panel on the wall beside the fireplace. It pivots open, revealing the tiny brick enclosure behind. It's a horrible cramped and dusty place. He cannot imagine the horror of being forced to hide in there with a priest hunter on your tail. He has no thought of whether it had ever been used to save a Catholic priest from being burned alive by the Protestants.

Nathan has vivid memories of playing in the priest hole with Oliver.

"Come out and face your maker." He can still hear Oliver's voice in his head, cracking and growling on the cusp of adulthood.

Nathan closes the priest hole hurriedly and shoves the pry bar beneath the floorboards again. The old wood splinters with a satisfying crack.

So much of this house feels on the verge of collapse. Boards hang loose and windows rattle, stairs groan as though they are about to spill open. Perhaps it really would be best for everyone if he let it crumble. Let the dunes swallow the place. He wishes he had that option.

He hears a bright peel of laughter float up the staircase. The sound catches him off guard. Laughter is not something this house has heard a lot of, of late, at least beyond the childish giggles of Thomas and Thea. He opens the door a crack; finds himself listening.

He recognises the bell-like voice of Julia Mitchell. She is chatting with Harriet in the entrance hall. Julia's laughter is oddly jarring against the coldness, the sadness, this room around him carries.

Harriet looks up the staircase, catching him poking his head out of Oliver's bedroom. "You can come out and say good morning, Nathan," she scolds lightly, "instead of hovering there like some creeper."

He feels colour rush to his cheeks, but Julia catches his eye and gives him a smile that looks almost conspiratorial.

He quickly wipes his dirty hands on the cloth tucked into his breeches and wrangles his hair behind his ears. He knows he looks a sight, and he does not like the thought of guests seeing him in such a state. But something makes him walk down the staircase anyway. There is something about Julia Mitchell's warmth that he finds himself craving.

"Come to scour the house for treasures?" he asks her. "I'm afraid you'll leave wanting. I can confirm there's nothing here except rotting wood."

Julia laughs. "Nothing like that. Harriet invited me for tea, is all. I've been longing to see what you've been doing to the place." She runs her hand along the intricately carved rosettes on the newel post. "Although I do think you're wrong about there being nothing of value in here. The paintings in the foyer are stunning. And these carvings are wonderful."

He nods towards the newel post. "It's not an original feature. Our father carved the post to suit the rest of the house," he tells her with a smile. "A hundred years too late for his work to be worth much."

"Well. It's beautiful in any case."

He looks again at the delicate woodwork, its finer features worn away by time. Perhaps it is beautiful. It's been a long time since he looked at things with such an eye. Life has felt too rushed and desperate for such a luxury.

"Nathan," Harriet says, sickly sweet. He had forgotten she was there. "Would you like to join us for tea?"

"Oh no," he says quickly. "I'd hate to impose. I only came down to wish Miss Mitchell a good morning."

"Is that so?" says Harriet, in her infuriatingly haughty way. He can hear the implication in her voice; the suggestion that he might have come downstairs with a little more in mind. That he might see more in Julia Mitchell than a visitor passing through. It's a foolish notion of course; these days, he can barely hold his daughter's hand without his stomach tying itself in knots. Building any kind of connection with a woman is completely out of the question. That part of him had died with Sarah.

He offers his sister a smile as forced and syrupy as her own. "Yes, Harriet, that is so." He turns back to Julia. "If you'll excuse me, Miss Mitchell, I'd best get back to work. This house seems to grow bigger every day."

He curses himself for his inane comment, but Julia laughs anyway. "Good luck," she tells him, as Harriet waves her towards the parlour.

Nathan is distracted as he returns to his work, pulling away the boards, sifting through the layers of the past and peering at what hides beneath. He can still hear Oliver's words in his head. It has been years since he had given his brother more than a passing thought, but here in Highfield House, Oliver seems to hide in every corner.

He is still working on the floorboards when he hears Harriet walk Julia to the door sometime later. He finds himself balancing across the exposed beams of the floor towards the window, watching as they embrace on the front doorstep. Watching as Julia begins to walk back across the dunes. She stops for a second and looks back up at the house, and for a moment Nathan worries he has been seen. But her gaze is beyond him, looking up at the peak of the roof, as though she is trying to see beyond the clouds.

CHAPTER SEVENTEEN

Eva stares up at the rugged wooden beams across the ceiling and listens to waves throw themselves against the edges of the island. A pale thread of sunlight shines through the gaps in the shutters and she turns her back to it, closing her eyes and pulling her knees to her chest. She has been lying awake in this lumpy old bed for what feels like hours, but can't bring herself to leave the safety of the bedroom.

Of all the unmooring, clouded parts of life on Longstone, navigating Finn Murray is the most difficult thing of all.

This life of firelight and tides is so different from the life she had lived in London; the life she thought she would live as Matthew Walton's wife. A few weeks ago, she would never have imagined herself with callused palms or coal-streaked hands. But a part of her feels oddly drawn to the hectic simplicity of lightkeeping on Longstone. The physicality of this life is completely foreign to her, and yet she welcomes the ache in her arms and legs each night. Welcomes the feel of rain in her hair and the smell of woodsmoke that has seeped deep into her clothes.

But then there is Finn and his painful changeability. His words last night had stung her deeply. She cannot begin to make sense of it. They had been getting on better than they ever had before he had turned on her like a rabid dog.

Eva tugs the blanket to her chin. Wounded leg or not, Finn can make his own damn breakfast this morning.

It's foolish, she knows, to let a near stranger make her feel so worthless. But Finn's coldness, his mockery, his fickle-mindedness, only reminds her of how unwanted she is. Reminds her of the way Matthew Walton had thrown her from his townhouse and declared her unworthy of being his wife.

Eva had found out early in her betrothal that Walton had wanted Harriet instead. Had overheard a conversation between him and her brother when they had assumed her out of the house. It had come as no surprise—Harriet was the princess and she was the lady-in-waiting. But by the time Walton had made his intentions clear, Harriet was already promised to Edwin.

Eva knew she was something of a consolation prize; how could she be anything else beside Harriet's impossible beauty? But she had done her best to show her betrothed she would make a fine wife nonetheless—a well-mannered, educated lady who would always put her husband's needs before her own. It had not been enough. Eva had not appreciated the intensity of Matthew Walton's feelings for her sister. Had assumed they went no deeper than infatuation. But when Walton had sat her down in his office, he had spoken carefully and ashamedly about his unrequited love for Harriet and how, with further consideration, it made marrying Eva an impossible thing. And yes, Eva saw that too. How could she sit with her husband at a family dinner and know he was pining after her sister? She had not tried to argue, or convince him otherwise. She had just smoothed her skirts and packed her things, and requested enough money to see her and Thea to Holy Island.

Eva tries not to blame Harriet. She knows none of it is her fault. But sometimes she is unable to hold back her bitterness. At just nineteen, Harriet's life is in fine order: a handsome, wealthy husband, and a beautiful, healthy son. Meanwhile, Eva is shovelling coal with no prospects, despite being almost five years older.

She sits up in bed. The cottage is still oddly quiet. Since his fever burnt away, Finn has returned to his old fractured sleeping pattern, and she knows he would have retired late, despite the washed-out light. Nonetheless, she is surprised not to hear him clattering around the cottage by now.

She dresses, and, drawing in her courage, steps out of the bedroom.

Finn's bed is empty, his coat and boots gone. A half-eaten slice of bread sits abandoned on the table. She will not go after him, she tells herself. She will not chase him like some devoted puppy, determined to prove her worth.

She sits at the table beside the burnt-out fire and eats the remains of Finn's breakfast. Today, she will ask him how much longer he imagines he will need her. She will make it clear that she does not wish to be here any more than he wishes to have her. Perhaps up until last night that was not true. But it certainly is now.

She swallows the last of the bread, unable to shake the irritating voice in the back of her head, nudging her to find out where Finn is, what he is doing. It's a flicker of worry, in spite of herself. She hates that it is there.

She goes outside and lifts a hand to shield her eyes from the sun. The tide is rising beneath a fierce blue sky, and licking at the edges of the island. Seals flit through the shallows and rock pools glitter in new places.

She hears him call her name.

She squints. And she sees the tiny figure of him out towards the southern end of the island. She hurries towards him, but her path is blocked by a blue-grey ribbon of sea. Finn is hobbling over the rocks, face contorted in pain. Has the fool been walking all morning?

"What do you think you're doing?" she demands. "The tide's far too high to be out here!"

Across the water, he gives her a sardonic smile. "It wasn't too high when I got here." He hunches, leaning on the fire poker and catching his breath. "I need your help, Eva. I shouldn't have come out this far."

Eva folds her arms, half wishing she had the nerve to leave him to his own devices. He'd deserve such a thing, she tells herself. Both for his callousness last night, and for being stupid enough to go off on this one-legged jaunt around the island.

"What do you need me to do?" she snaps.

Finn nods towards the river of seawater blocking his path. "It's shallow here at the edge," he says. "Come across. I need you to help me get back."

In case he hadn't registered her displeasure, Eva narrows her eyes and yanks off her shoes and stockings. She dumps them out of reach of the rising tide, then knots her skirts above her knees and steps into the water. The cold steals her breath and she bites back a curse.

"You'd best have a good reason for being out here," she snaps, balancing across the slippery rock beneath her feet. When she stumbles onto dry land, inches from Finn, an infuriating half-smile appears on his lips. "Did you do this on purpose?" she demands. "To see if I'd be mad enough to come after you?"

His smile disappears. "Of course not. I…"

"You what?" She glances at the spying glass in his fist. "What were you doing out there?"

"Nothing. I just saw a vessel passing and wanted a closer look. Seems I'm not quite as well healed as I'd hoped."

Eva glances down, glimpsing a fresh bloom of blood on the strapping around his calf. "You're a fool," she snaps.

"So it would seem."

She plants her hands on her hips. "Take your damn boots off then. And quickly. I don't fancy getting any wetter than I am already."

"My boots are already soaked. It's no matter. Just help me get across, aye?"

Eva grips his arm with both hands, digging her fingers into his flesh a little tighter than necessary. She doesn't miss his sharp intake of breath.

She helps him into the shallow pool. Finn swallows a curse as the seawater covers his wound. Step by step, they stumble through the water and back to the cottage.

Finn sinks onto the bed, pulling off his wet boots and dumping the spying glass on the mattress beside him. He leans against the wall, looking at Eva as she yanks her stockings back on.

"Let me see the wound," she says. "You've obviously done some damage to it, walking as far as you did." She snatches the jar of figwort from the mantel. Has half a mind to douse his calf in whisky instead. That would teach him to be so careless and hurtful.

She steps close to the bed, expecting Finn to protest. He stays motionless, waiting. And Eva's anger shifts, replaced with nerves. Nerves at his sudden nearness. And nerves over the task at hand. Slowly, carefully, she unbinds the wet strapping, tinged pink with blood and water. She is relieved to see that, though the wound has opened again in several places, it seems to be healing well. She dips the washcloth into the bowl and gently wipes away the blood. Then she dips the dry end of the cloth into the figwort ointment and touches it to the wound. Finn flinches.

"I'm sorry," she murmurs, her other hand sliding instinctively over his bare shin to keep him from moving again. She applies a little more ointment.

She can feel his eyes on her as she works, and it makes her feel intensely exposed. Vulnerable. She hates that he has the power to make her feel this way. Hates that all she can think about is how he had told her to leave last night.

"You don't think much of me, do you," she says after a moment.

He catches her glance, and there's a sincerity in his eyes she has not seen before. "I'm sorry if I gave you that impression."

Eva swallows heavily. An answer she was not expecting. She presses the lid back on the jar. "I know you want me out of your way. But how could I not help you? You got in the way of a bullet intended for me." Finn reaches for the torn shirt that hangs on the edge of the bed. He yanks off another strip of fabric and hands it to her. She wraps it around his calf and knots it tightly.

Finn tugs the hem of his slops down below his knee. "Martin Macauley wasn't shooting at you, Eva," he says. "He was shooting at me."

Her lips part. "What? Why would he shoot at you?"

He shakes his head. "It doesn't matter. It's nothing."

"Truly? Nothing? He could have killed you. He could have killed both of us."

Finn looks a little taken aback by her outburst. His fingers graze her elbow. "Will you hang the kettle?"

Eva finds herself giving him a half-smile. "Tea?"

He returns the gesture. "Aye. I like your tea."

Eva sets the jar of figwort on the mantel and hangs the kettle on the hook, tossing a log onto the fire and jabbing it to life with the poker. Finn reaches for her arm, tugging her back down to sit on the edge of the bed.

He is close to her now, less than a foot between them. She can see the golden flecks in his eyes. Can smell the woodsmoke and sea on his skin. And the look her gives her, it is not one of annoyance, or pity, but something else entirely. Something she can't quite read. There is something almost apologetic in his eyes, as though he is aware of how much his changeability has stung her.

"I stole some coal from the Macauleys," he says simply. "For the firebasket. Actually, I've stolen coal from them more than once."

"Why am I not surprised to learn you're a thief?" But there is no heat to her words. She supposes there's something almost noble about stealing coal to keep the firebasket burning. Almost. "They shot you for a little coal?"

He shrugs. "They're bastards." He gives a short chuckle. "Also, it was quite a lot of coal. Martin came out here a few months ago, seeking to take some of it back. I caught him before he got his hands to it. That's why I thought you were him when I heard you in the coal shed that night. My family has been feuding with the Macauleys since before I was born." He snorts. "Me and Martin are just carrying on a fine tradition started by our fathers."

So Martin Macauley had not been firing at her. He did not know she had knocked his father into the sea. The knowledge ought to settle her. But it doesn't. Perhaps it is because the thought of Martin shooting at Finn is no less unnerving than him shooting at her.

Or perhaps it's because none of this changes the fact that she is hiding the truth about what happened to Martin's father. And nothing will change the fact that she has killed a man.

"It was very brazen of him to shoot at you out in the open like that," she says.

Finn shrugs. "Who would notice if I disappeared?"

Eva shifts uncomfortably at the truth of it. How easily Martin would have escaped justice if his ball had hit Finn's chest. His crime would have been hidden away at the wild top end of Holy Island, no one to miss the unsociable man from Longstone. And the only witness a suspected government spy. A perfect crime, at least until a ship rammed into the unlit Farne Islands.

"In any case," Finn says, too easily, "I don't think he meant to kill me. Just give me a bit of a scare."

Eva shakes her head, unsure if his blasé attitude is real, or just a cover for how much the incident had shaken him. "And you will just let him get away with it?" She knows the answer before she finishes the question. Why would Finn draw attention to his own crimes by going to the authorities?

He doesn't bother to respond. "Why did you think Martin was shooting at you?" he asks. "I thought you would have assumed I was the target."

His question feels pointed. It reminds Eva that nothing she can tell Finn is worse than what he already knows her to have done. But something stops her from admitting it was Donald Macauley's body she had sent tumbling into the ocean. She has already told him far too much.

"We're unwanted on Lindisfarne," she says. "There are Jacobites on the island who suspect us of being government spies."

"But you're not."

"No."

Finn nods faintly, and she can tell he believes her.

"So that's where the coal comes from," says Eva. "The Macauleys' sheds."

"Some of it, aye. But most of it was paid for honestly, believe it or not."

"How do you pay for it?"

He chuckles. "I have money. I've not been here my entire life, you know. Despite what people like to say about me. I do a few days' farm work here and there when I need to. There are a few farmers on the mainland who hire me during the harvest and planting seasons. Sometimes they pay me with peat from their land. My da built up a nice collection too. Some of the fuel has been there for years."

"You've sacrificed a lot," says Eva. "To run the light. It shouldn't be your responsibility."

"Aye, well Trinity House couldn't get the funds together to pay a proper keeper. And this is a dangerous patch of sea. My father lost two brothers out here on the Knavestone reef. Da was among the men who petitioned to have the light on Inner Farne built. When he realised they didn't have the money to light it, he built the beacon out here himself. And the cottage." He chuckles. "He liked to harp on about all the trouble he went to getting the stone out here."

"I can only imagine."

Finn shrugs. "We're only a few miles from shore. Plenty of people are willing to sail goods out here if you pay them enough. Mind you, my da never thought to tell no one he was building the place. When the church found out, they were wild about it. Da managed to talk them round. Made them see he was doing a good thing."

Eva smiles, surprised by his openness. It feels almost like he has forgotten himself, and the wall he is trying to maintain between them. "That's why you do this?" she asks. "Because your uncles drowned out here?"

"That's why my da did it. I'm just doing as he would have wanted." There's a sudden thinness to his words, and he shifts back on the bed, as though regretting his brief moment of candidness.

Eva stands, putting space back between them. She takes the teapot from the mantel and begins to fill it with tea leaves.

"Shall I take you back tomorrow morning?" asks Finn. "I think I can manage the skiff."

Eva puts down the spoon, feeling a jolt in her chest. "Is that what you want?" She forces herself to look at him.

He holds her gaze. "I asked you first."

She hesitates. Draws in a breath. "No," she says. "That's not what I want. I want to stay until you're healed."

He nods. "All right." Looks away. "Good."

Eva hides her smile. It feels like a small victory. Or perhaps even a large one. She takes a step towards him, planting a hand on her hip. "If you want me to stay," she says, emboldened by his unexpected admission, "perhaps you ought to show a little gratitude."

"What?"

She looks down at him challengingly. "You've never thanked me. Not once. Not for coming to make sure you were all right, or for helping you keep the light. Not even for a damn cup of tea."

Finn stands, suddenly towering over her. He takes a step closer, his warm breath tickling her nose. Eva feels something twist in her stomach. "You've never thanked me either."

She swallows, but doesn't look away. "For what?"

"For taking you back to Lindisfarne after you washed up on my doorstep. And for not telling anyone you knocked a man into the sea."

He is right, of course. And the reminder of what she has done releases a fresh wave of guilt. But she refuses to show it. Refuses to back down. "Well," she says, challenge in her eyes, "who are you going to tell?"

CHAPTER EIGHTEEN

"There are baby seals, Papa." Theodora trots past the churchyard, and Nathan has to quicken his stride to keep up with her. "I can't wait for you to see them." Her cheeks are pink, her blonde hair spidery beneath her bonnet. And Nathan sees something in her eyes; a brightness, a glow of aliveness that has not been there since her mother's death. Holy Island has brought an energy to her she had not had in London. Since she has arrived, her nightmares have been almost non-existent. It will be harder than he had first imagined to take her back to the city when all this is done. He is glad at least one positive thing has come out of this whole debacle.

"Listen." She stops abruptly, bumping into his hip and darting away. "Can you hear them?"

The honking of the seals makes him smile. "I loved coming to see them when I was your age too," he tells Theodora. "Your Auntie Eva was terrified of them."

Theodora giggles. "Why would you be afraid of seals?" Skirts in her fist, she races down the hill towards the tiny outcrop of Saint Cuthbert's Island. In the low tide, the islet is linked to Lindisfarne by a chain of flat rocks and shingle.

They are not alone on the beach. Nathan stops at the edge of the embankment, recognising Julia Mitchell on the edge of the mudflats. She is teetering over the rocks with a dark-haired boy he assumes is her son. She is not wearing a bonnet or cap, and her fiery hair is coming loose from its knot, blowing wildly around her pale cheeks.

She looks up, flashing him a smile. Nathan approaches with a hint of reluctance. Harriet's behaviour the other morning had been far from subtle, and he does not want Julia to be misled. As appealing as he finds her, he would hate her to think he is offering more than he is capable of. Not, he is sure, that she would have any interest in someone as awkward and clumsy as him.

He smiles at Thea, who is already tearing across the beach with Julia's son. If only it were as easy to make new acquaintances as an adult as it was during childhood.

"Your son looks around the same age as Theodora," he says to Julia, cursing himself for the abrupt entrance into the conversation.

"Bobby is eight," Julia tells him easily. "Although sometimes I think him more like eighteen. He can be rather protective."

Nathan smiles. "A good man to have around."

"He is, aye." She brushes her hair from her eyes. "How is the restoration coming along?"

"Slowly," Nathan admits. "There's much to do. I'm thankful for my brother-in-law's expertise."

She nods. "Why did you decide to restore the house without outside help?"

"Because I couldn't trust anyone else to do it." The moment the words are out, Nathan can't believe he has spoken them. He barely knows this woman. How could he have admitted to such a thing? What must she think of him? "I'm sorry," he blurts. "I did not mean to suggest that the people here are not trustworthy…" His thoughts flash to Donald Macauley forcing Eva into his boat. Raising his musket on her. Perhaps he is right to be distrusting of the islanders. But in the back of his mind is the dull knowledge that he has likely offended Julia Mitchell again.

She gives a faint nod, but doesn't speak. Ought he take that as confirmation that the islanders are not to be trusted? Or is he reading too much into things?

Julia gestures to the beach where Bobby and Theodora are clambering over the wet rocks towards Saint Cuthbert's Island. Nathan hears Thea's giggles rising up in the cool air.

"You daughter seems to be enjoying herself here, at least."

Nathan smiles. "She is, yes." In another life, perhaps, he and Thea could be happy on Lindisfarne. But far too much has happened here for him to feel any sense of peace.

"You ought to send her to the dame school," says Julia. "With Bobby. The woman who takes the lessons is wonderful. A dear friend of mine. And a fine teacher at that."

Nathan hums noncommittally. He can't deny that, with Eva away, Theodora's lessons have fallen somewhat by the wayside. But settling her into school feels like far too permanent an arrangement.

"I don't know," he tells Julia. "I'm not sure how long we will be here. I would hate to put Thea into school only to take her back to London the moment she has settled in."

Julia eyes him. "That's a shame," she says, and he can't tell if she is referring to the school, or his plans to return to London. Heat prickles the back of his neck.

"I remember you, you know," she says suddenly. "From when you were a lad."

Nathan raises his eyebrows. "You do?"

"Of course. Every knew who you were; the family from the big house on the head."

He doesn't reply. What did people think of the Blakes back then, before they became Londoners? He suspects they were always something of outsiders, bundled away in their manor at the top of the island.

She eyes him. "You don't remember me, do you."

He hesitates. He wishes he did. Wishes he knew what this sunny woman was like as a child. He wonders how he might have missed her explosion of red curls running around the island.

She laughs at his lack of response. "Didn't think so. We're forgettable, us penniless types."

There is light in her voice and Nathan knows she is playing with him. Nonetheless, he says, "I'm sorry."

She shakes her head dismissively. "Truth be told, I remember more of your brother than you."

Nathan smiles wryly to himself. This is no surprise. Oliver was a far more memorable child; tall and lanky, with a shock of bright blond hair and tongue that could slice a grown man to pieces.

"He was always hovering about the harbour," says Julia, "watching over the fishermen's catches."

Nathan snorts. Stealing from them, more likely. "Have you been on the island all this time?" he asks, keen to change the subject.

"Lived here my entire life," says Julia. "Never once thought to leave. I'm sure there's not a place on earth as beautiful as this."

"And the rest of your family?"

"After Bobby arrived, my father wanted nothing to do with me. Couldn't handle the shame of me having a child outside of wedlock. Made a life for himself over in Bamburgh. Barely knew my ma. And my brothers are off training with the rebels in the West Country."

Nathan raises his eyebrows, caught off guard at her brazen admission. Though a new Rising seems to be gaining momentum by the day, there are few people who speak so openly about supporting the Jacobites, even in this part of the country.

"Careful now," he says lightly. "Have you not heard we're a pack of government spies?"

Julia laughs. "I have heard that, aye. And what a load of rubbish it is too. If you were, I hardly think you'd be so obvious as to set yourselves up in the biggest house on the island."

"I wish the rest of the village had your sense."

Julia's gaze drifts past him and Nathan turns to see a small army of men appearing over the hill above the beach. Martin Macauley is among them. He catches sight of Nathan, and gestures to the others to change course towards him. Nathan's heart thuds, but he holds his ground. He darts a frantic look over his shoulder at Theodora. She and Bobby are splashing about in ankle-deep water. He doesn't wave her in. Wet shoes are far preferable to her being in earshot of these men.

Martin nods at Julia in greeting, then turns hard eyes to Nathan. "We're going out looking for my father."

"I see."

"We could use another pair of eyes."

Nathan blinks, caught off guard. What is this? A threat? A challenge? Or is Martin simply after all the help he can get?

Either way, he has only one option. "Of course," he says. Refuse and he will raise further suspicion.

Martin nods towards the harbour, where the fishing boats are bobbing on the rising tide. "Can you sail?"

"I can follow instructions."

Nathan feels Julia's eyes on him; a look of concern he cannot bring himself to acknowledge. He needs to believe these men don't want to harm him, or he will never climb into that boat. He glances at Theodora, then back at Julia. "Will you—"

"I'll see her home safely." She looks at him pointedly. "You be careful."

He nods. The thought of leaving Thea in the hands of a near stranger is almost as unsettling as sailing under Martin Macauley. But he realises he trusts Julia Mitchell. And he also knows he has little choice but to help the men with their search. He is following them towards the harbour before he can change his mind.

The sea is choppy, grey. Fine weather, Nathan thinks, for tossing a man overboard. He forces the thought away. Think guilty and he will look guilty.

Or at least, look as though he is hiding a secret for his guilty sister.

Nathan is sailing with Martin Macauley and Joseph Holland, from the fishing fleet. Martin had been deliberate in directing Nathan onto the same boat as himself. It is hard not to imagine he knows what he is hiding. After all, Martin had been there the moment Eva had returned to Holy Island after knocking his father into the sea. Surely he has his suspicions.

Three fishing boats have left the harbour. One is moving towards the mainland, another out into open water. Holland's boat heads towards the Farnes.

Nathan feels the urge to speak; to convince Martin he and his family are not working for the government. But he stops himself. Donald had told his suspicions to Eva moments before he had ended up in the water. There is no way Nathan ought to know about them. He has no choice but to keep quiet. To let Martin and the other villagers sit with their suspicions, with his family in their firing line.

For far too long, there is silence, broken only by the rhythmic hiss of sea against the fishing boat's hull. The two other boats are tiny shapes on the horizon. Nathan hears his heart thudding in his ears. His stomach turns over at the constant roll of the sea and he prays he can keep his breakfast down. He despises boats at the best of times.

Holland glances at Nathan; at his white-knuckled fingers gripping the gunwale. He chuckles. "Not got your sea legs then, Blake?"

Nathan forces a smile. "Far from it."

"Typical Londoners."

While Holland's words are predictable, there's warmth in his tone. Is it designed to lull him into a false sense of security? Or is he seeing conflict where there is none to be found? His dealings with Joseph Holland so far have been civil; friendly even. When he had visited the man to borrow the frame saw, they had spent much of the evening chatting over whisky glasses, while Theodora chased Holland's dog around his house. Nathan would almost consider him a friend. But Martin Macauley's presence makes him nervous.

"I'm afraid you're right," Nathan says to Holland. If the man truly is attempting a little geniality, he does not want to destroy it with suspicion. "Us city folk have plenty to learn about island life."

"Did you tell that to your sister when she got caught out by the tide?" asks Martin.

Nathan's stomach dives. "Indeed. Though I suspect she has learnt her lesson."

"Heard about that, Joseph?" Martin keeps his eyes on the sea. "Miss Blake stranding herself on the mainland for the night? Same night Da disappeared."

The back of Nathan's neck prickles. Joseph Holland stands suddenly; points. "Up ahead. What's that?"

Nathan squints. There's a small shape ahead, bobbing on the water. From this distance, he cannot make out what it is.

Martin leans on the tiller. "We need to get closer."

Nathan's heart quickens. He is not sure why. He already knows of Donald Macauley's fate. And surely nothing they find out here is going to implicate Eva. How could it? All the villagers can possibly have on her is suspicion.

None of them speak as the fishing boat skims over the water. It's a small dinghy ahead of them, Nathan realises. Its oars lie in the bottom of the boat.

"This belong to Donald?" asks Holland.

Martin nods, not speaking.

At the sight of the boat, Nathan thinks of Donald Macauley forcing Eva aboard. Taking her out to sea and raising his musket. He swallows down a swell of rage. He is not sorry Donald Macauley is gone.

But when he glances sideways at Martin, he sees the man's face twisted in grief.

"I'm sorry," he finds himself saying. And he means it. He knows the pain of losing a father, and he would not wish it upon anyone—even if that father is Donald Macauley. He hates the weight of this secret, this guilt he is helping Eva carry. Hates the weight of this silence he has insisted upon.

Will it happen now, he wonders? Will Martin Macauley, in the throes of grief, hurl Nathan from his boat, to sink to the bottom as his father has clearly done? He hears his own breath coming hard and fast, a counterpoint to the rhythmic clapping of the sea against the two boats.

"Tie the dinghy to us," Martin says finally. "We'll take it back to shore."

CHAPTER NINETEEN

Donald Macauley's memorial service is predictably awful. What seems to be the entire village crams into the churchyard to pray over the wooden cross erected in his memory. Nathan bats away poisonous looks and accusing eyes—real or imagined, he cannot tell. He stands stoically beside Edwin on the edge of the gathering, the two of them twin figures in their grey coats and breeches, as though doing their best to disappear into the morning mist.

Harriet had made her excuses in the name of mothering, though Nathan supposes it had far more to do with a need to paint—or sleep. In any case, one sister's absence seems to sufficiently explain the other's, or perhaps the gossip of Eva's journey to Longstone has already filtered through the village. Either way, Nathan is not asked questions about her whereabouts. And he is more than a little grateful.

The sky opens as the crowd begins to file out of the churchyard. Great sacks of cloud hang over the ruins of the monastery, raindrops bouncing off the headstones.

As he steps out of the gate, Nathan sees Julia on the edge of his vision.

"Go on ahead," he tells Edwin impulsively. "I shall catch you up."

Edwin gives him a curious half-smile, but thankfully, says nothing.

Nathan falls into step beside Julia. Bright curls are escaping out her bonnet, a stark contrast to the gloom that has swallowed the rest of the village.

"Good of you to come," she tells him.

Nathan allows himself a wry smile. Not for a second had it felt like a choice. "Well. We are a part of the village now. Ought to pay our respects."

"I see Harriet has no such concerns."

"Well. Harriet is a special case."

Julia laughs. "She is indeed." She stops outside the door of her curiosity shop. "Will you come in out of the rain? I can make us some tea?"

"Oh…" Nathan falters. "I would hate for people to think badly of you. If they were to see us alone together, I mean."

She laughs. "Don't concern yourself with that. This village made their mind up about my decency years ago." She gives him a pointed smile. "And I'd say they've made their mind up about you too."

Rain runs down the back of Nathan's neck. "Yes," he admits. "I suspect they have."

He steps into the shop. It is stuffy inside, holding the warmth of the smoking logs in the grate. Rain patters softly against the windows.

"Wait here if you like," says Julia. "I'll bring some tea down."

As she disappears up the staircase, Nathan lets out a breath he had not realised he was holding. This is easier, of course, floating around here in the wilds of the curiosity shop, than the uncomfortable intimacy of venturing into Julia's living quarters. This way he can tell himself he is nothing more than a customer; can remind himself there is nothing of note between the two of them. And how could there be? Everything of note is an impossibility.

Nathan wanders through the shop, neatly avoiding the cat, who is curled up asleep on the hearth. In the far corner, he spots a telescope sitting on a wrought iron stand. He inspects it curiously, running a hand along the shaft. It's an old six-draw piece, with a tarnished brass barrel and wood at one end. Much like the telescope his father had given him when he was a child. Nathan hunches, holding his eye to the lens. He sees nothing but a blur, of course, with the glass pointed into the corner of the shop, but there is some odd comfort in the action itself. Something that reminds him of simpler times.

"Where do all your wares come from?" he asks Julia when she reappears in the doorway. She has a teapot in one hand and two mismatched porcelain cups in the other. She sets them on the counter and drags two chairs out from the corner of the shop.

"I collected things at first," she says. "Went around the village gathering up the treasures that people no longer wanted. Bought cheap pieces from curiosity shops on the mainland." She lets out a private laugh. "Before I opened the shop, Bobby and I were living with my brother. He was not all that happy when I started filling his kitchen with my treasures."

Nathan smiles.

"Most of the things I have now come from my customers. They bring me their unwanted pieces and I give them a few pennies for them." She nods towards a large brass candleholder on the top of the nearest shelf. "That one belonged to Donald Macauley. He weren't impressed when I only gave him a shilling for it. Told me it was worth two pounds at least. He always was a bit mad, the poor old fellow." She fills the cups and slides one across the counter to Nathan. "Still, I imagine he would have liked to know there was so much mystery around his passing. Suspicious old bastard that he was."

Nathan swallows heavily. "Did you know him well?"

"He was a good friend of my da's. He always had a liking for me. At least, he was less grumpy around me than he was around most." She smiles crookedly. "I suppose he liked that we had a similar alliance."

"Are you not afraid to speak of your Jacobite alliance so openly?" asks Nathan, sipping his tea.

"I'm not speaking of it openly. I'm only speaking of it to you. I trust it will not go further than this room."

Her words are light, but Nathan feels the gravity of them. He is painfully aware of all he is keeping from Julia. It feels like the greatest abuse of her trust.

"In any case," she says, "I'm doing my best to stay out of the Jacobite cause. My brothers wished me to be more involved. Running messages and the like. I told them I'd not do it. My and Bobby's safety is far too important."

"Very wise of you," says Nathan. "If you were caught running messages, you'd be arrested at once." He is not sure why the thought of Julia being involved in the Jacobite cause makes him feel so unsettled. Is it the thought that she might put herself in danger? Or the uncomfortable notion that, if forced to choose sides, they would clearly not be allies?

"Do you miss London?" she asks suddenly. "As Harriet does?"

"No," says Nathan. His thoughtless response catches him off guard. London is home—a place to be returned to once Highfield House is finally off his hands. But: "There's little to miss, really." And he finds himself telling her about the dire business decisions he had made of late; of the clients who, one by one, had taken their money elsewhere. Tells her of the shame he had felt at being forced to sell the family's London home.

"I am sorry to hear it," Julia says. Her eyes are warm. "Your wife?" she asks tentatively.

"Sarah passed three years ago," he says. "Influenza." He cannot remember the last time he spoke aloud about Sarah, even to his daughter. Speaking her name has become a forgotten thing, and doing so makes something warm in his chest.

"It sounds as though you've had a difficult few years." Julia tops up the teacups. "I'm sure such things are not so easy to speak of." She looks up, fixing him with vivid green eyes. "Thank you for being so open with me."

Guilt seizes him. Because he has not been open with her. Not at all. She had clearly cared for Donald Macauley, and here he is hiding the truth of his death. The secrets he is carrying have never felt more weighted.

"I ought to go," he says suddenly, despite the freshly filled teacup. He will offend her again, of course, but what does that matter? What point is there in staying here, when all he can offer are secrets and lies? He gets to his feet before she can protest.

CHAPTER TWENTY

"I need to go to the mainland," says Finn. He is digging last night's ash from the firebasket and depositing it into a bucket for Eva to dump into the sea. "For food. And peat." He glances at her. "You've no problem digging up a little peat, have you? Carting it back to the boat?"

A look of horror flashes across her eyes, but she blinks it away quickly. "Oh… Yes… I mean, no… I'm sure…"

Finn chuckles and her face flushes scarlet. Sometimes this is too easy.

"We've enough fuel to keep us going for a while longer," he says with a grin. "But I appreciate your commitment." He dumps another shovelful into the bucket, sending a grey cloud rising into the air. "There's no need for you to come ashore. I can manage on my own."

Eva looks at him with raised eyebrows. He supposes he can't blame her. His little misadventure with the tide a week and a half ago certainly suggests otherwise.

As does the fact that he has not yet asked her to leave.

"I'm coming with you," she says, her tone leaving no room for argument. "I know you don't like it, but you need my help. At least for a little while longer. I'll not let you traipse around the market with blood running into your boots."

I know you don't like it. She has it wrong, of course. Not that he can blame her for thinking such things. A part of him wants to tell her everything, every piece of it. Tell her he likes it too much, and that that is far too dangerous. Tell her the thought of taking her back to Lindisfarne leaves him hollow. But he just taps the bucket with the shovel. "It's full. Dump it over by the jetty."

"How often do you leave Longstone?" Eva asks as they make their way to the skiff in the early afternoon. She brushes a streak of ash from her skirts.

The fire poker Finn is leaning on crunches against the rocky ground. "Once a fortnight, perhaps. Sometimes more often, when there's work on the farms."

"Do you not get lonely out here? Do you not miss human interaction?"

He considers the questions. "Sometimes." He has acquaintances. Men he works with on the farms, takes a drink with at the end of the workday. Familiar faces around the markets of Bamburgh. But it has been a long time since he has had someone he could call a friend. Someone with whom he can be open and honest and say what is on his mind. He reminds himself hurriedly that he does not have that luxury with Eva either. "But what's to miss really?" he says instead. "Most humans are bastards."

Eva shifts the basket she is carrying to her other arm. "Is that so?"

"Most humans, aye." He glances sideways at her. "Is that not your impression too?"

He sees a small smile. Wonders what she is thinking. "Perhaps not most humans," she says. "But some, yes." She eyes the skiff. "Can you get into boat?" she asks, a frown creasing the bridge of her nose.

Finn gives her a half-smile; a look that tells her she is worrying too much. "I'll be fine." He nods to the boat. "Get in."

Eva gathers her skirts and steps onto the jetty, then into the boat with a single step. She stumbles as the skiff rocks on the water, and lurches forward to grab the gunwale. He sees her eyes drift over the wine-dark blood staining the bottom of the boat. He climbs in quickly, nudging her towards the bench seat in an attempt to distract her. He grits his teeth at a jolt of pain, then unloops the moorings and sits. The skiff seesaws over the swell as he pulls away from the jetty.

Once they have cleared the island, he nods towards the furled sail. "Open it up," he tells Eva. "It's a fine day for sailing."

She looks at him in alarm. "You want me to sail the boat?"

"You're here to help me, aren't you?"

She presses her lips together. She knows he is testing her, surely, finding out how far she will go before admitting she is incapable. And he can tell that, above all things, she does not want to be incapable.

She gets tentatively to her feet and approaches the furled sail as though it's a wild animal she does not want to provoke. Finn chuckles. "Untie it. It won't bite."

Eva flashes him a look, then turns back to the knotted bindings, frowning in concentration as she unties them. The sail spills open, thwacking against the wind.

Finn pats the seat beside him. "Now sit down and take up the halyard."

Eva stumbles back towards the bench. He takes her arm to steady her; helps her sit. He hands her the sheet and she pulls. Her eyes light as the sail comes to life.

Finn helps her secure the line. He tears his gaze from her to guide the boat past the edges of the archipelago. "Let me get free of the islands, then you can take the tiller."

Eva lifts her face to the sky. Wind tousles the spidery strands of hair poking loose from her bonnet. Her blue eyes are glowing. "It's very beautiful here," she says.

Finn looks out across the water, and for a moment it is as though he is seeing the place for the first time. Clouds are banking steadily, and the ocean is a patchwork of colour; green on the fringes of the island and blackening in its depths. Castles of rock reach up out of the water, guarded by armies of birds. As they pass Inner Farne, he looks up to see the crumbling walls of St Cuthbert's Chapel. A reminder of the holy men who had once made these islands home. He feels like the most unholy of replacements.

But Eva is right; there's an eerie beauty here; bleak and windblown with barely a speck of human scarring. A beauty he forgets all too often to see.

Bamburgh village is swarming. People jostle through the narrow streets, and Eva can hear shouting coming from within the cobbled alleyways. The beach is dotted with dinghies pushed high up on the sand, and there are several larger vessels in the deeper water beyond the shore.

"Is it always so busy?" asks Eva. She had not expected the place to be such a wash of activity. The air feels restless and charged.

"No." A frown darkens Finn's face. "It's not."

Eva glances at him. She guesses it a decent walk from the beach to the market, and she does not want a repeat of the tide incident. "I can go to the market alone," she tells him. "There's no need for you to come traipsing around the village."

He shakes his head. "It's best I come with you. Something is going on." He takes a step towards her, closing the space between them.

Since running into trouble, he has clearly resigned himself to her company. But it does not seem to be reluctantly. This morning, as they had sat at the table drinking their tea together, there was a look in his eyes she would almost describe as warmth, if she had not learnt better. Whatever it is, it is a welcome relief. If more than a little disorienting.

The crowd, Eva realises, is gathering close to the castle, and funnelling into the narrow streets. Most are men, several dressed in tartans, though she sees a few women among them. Many of them are waving flags, and among them she sees both the Stuart coat of arms and the White Horse of Hanover, signalling support for King George. Many in the crowd have the white cockade of the Jacobites pinned to their cloaks and bonnets. Men are pushing through the crowd, shoving tracts into the hands of passers-by.

"A protest?" she asks Finn.

"Looks that way. Let's get what we need and leave."

Eva doesn't take her eyes from the crowd. "Do they not know of the new riot act?"

Finn chuckles. "I'm sure they'll find out about it soon enough."

"Is it likely to get violent?"

"There's a chance of it, aye."

Eva glances at him. "Do you support them? The Jacobites?"

"Nah." He wraps his hand around her bare forearm, tugging her close. "Not that I support Geordie. I just don't want to see this country at war again."

Eva walks with her shoulder pressed to Finn's. Though England has been at war for most of her life, conflict has never felt as close as it does here, with Donald Macauley's death on her shoulders and the shouts of protesters echoing through the streets.

The noise of the riot dims as they get further from the castle. "Do the Jacobites truly imagine they have a chance this time?" she says, keeping her voice low. "The last time they tried to rise, they were defeated before their troops even managed to land."

"Things are different for them now," Finn reasons. "They feel they've more of a chance with a foreigner on the throne."

Eva nods. In London, too, displeasure at the new king had been widespread. Ever since Queen Anne's death last year, pamphleteers and protests had been rife throughout the capital. Up here, so close to Scotland, the energy of the riots is magnified. "Still," she says, "what chance do these rebels have against the army?"

"Perhaps nought," says Finn. "But they believe God put the Stuarts on the throne. And they will fight for that to the death."

Eva glances back at the crowd of protesters. She cannot think of anything she would risk her own life for. Cannot think of anything she would even bother protesting over.

She suddenly feels empty. With her life laid out in front of her for long, with her townhouse mentally decorated and her children pre-emptively named, there had seemed little else to put her mind to. Yes, she has always kept up with the turnings of the world around her, but this had come from a need to maintain the intellect she had sold herself to Matthew Walton with, rather than a desire to bring about any sense of change.

But look at those men and women beyond the castle, putting themselves in the path of the redcoats out of love for their exiled king. Look at Finn Murray, resigning himself to a lonely life on Longstone so the firebasket might come to life each night. Even Harriet, when she stands in front of her easel, comes alive with a passion that Eva craves. She has never known anything worth fighting for. Nothing that is worth challenging the neatly ordered life that is expected of her.

Finn does not release his grip on her arm until they reach the market. They make their way from stall to stall, filling the basket—carrots and potatoes, flour and apples. A seed cake, and a bottle of whisky from a still in the back of a wagon.

The staccato rap of horse hooves echoes through the marketplace and a raft of dragoons thunders past. Eva feels the air shift against her cheek. A shout goes up as they clash with the rioters at the end of the street. Gunfire splinters the sky.

Finn puts a hand to her shoulder, guiding her quickly towards the tavern at the end of the alley. "Let's get out of the street. Hopefully they'll bore themselves soon enough."

Eva stops walking. "In the tavern?" she says. "No, Finn, I can't."

"Why not?"

"Because it is not the done thing. I'm an unmarried woman. I cannot be seen alone with you in such a place."

He grins. "I promise I'll be the most decent gentleman you ever did see." He nudges her towards the doorway. "Come on, now. It's dangerous out here. You'll just have to find a way to resist my charms."

Eva hesitates. She glances back over her shoulder as gunfire breaks over the castle. And she steps through the door that Finn is holding open for her.

The air inside the tavern is thick with pipe smoke and drink. Sunlight struggles through grimy windows, is drowned by dark stone walls. The pale light from a single lantern spills from the beamed roof. Eva glances around, wary of being recognised. She is glad to find the place quiet. A few men lean up against the bar and another sleeps on a bench in front of an unlit grate, but it seems most of Bamburgh is out in the street.

Finn gestures to a table in the back corner of the tavern. "Here. Sit down. Hopefully we'll not be here long."

Eva slides onto a stool and takes off her bonnet and cloak. She sits her hat in her lap and winds its ribbons around her hands edgily. What if word gets back to Nathan that she is prancing around a tavern in the company of a man? Still, she can't deny she feels safer inside solid walls than she had in the midst of the protest.

Finn shuffles to the bar and Eva turns to look out the window. Fat drops of rain are pocking the glass. Though she can't see much through the grimy pane, she can hear shouting in the street. Can hear the dull clatter of wood striking wood. The sharp echo of gunfire.

Finn returns with two tankards and sets one in front of Eva. She takes a sip, not caring what's inside. Lukewarm ale slides down her throat.

Finn sits opposite her. "All right?" he asks.

She nods. Takes another mouthful. A little of the tension begins to ease from her body. "Has it been like this for long up here?" she asks. "So unsettled, I mean."

Finn sips his drink. "Aye. A while. Riots and the like, since the Hanoverian took the throne. Big protests on Restoration Day, of course. And on the anniversary of Geordie coming to power."

"In London, there was talk of the king fleeing," says Eva. "Can you imagine it?" She shakes her head. "And then my family appears on the island among all this unrest… It is no surprise they distrust us. We are outsiders."

"It's not just because you're outsiders," says Finn. "It's because you own Highfield House."

Eva frowns. "What do you mean?"

"Before you lot turned up, it was used as a meeting place for the Jacobites on Lindisfarne. I daresay they weren't happy when they found out your family'd returned. They'll be back to holding their meetings in cellars and cart houses again now."

"Why would the Jacobites need to hide away in Highfield House? The islanders are sympathetic to them."

"Some of them," Finn agrees. "But not all. Word is there really are government spies on Holy Island."

"Who are they?"

He smiles. "I've no idea."

She tilts her head, taking him in. A strand of hair has come loose from its queue and hangs across his eye. "How do you know all this when you spend all your time on Longstone?"

"I don't spend all my time on Longstone. I told you, I come to the mainland at least once a fortnight. And I make it a point to go to Lindisfarne from time to time too. Keep an eye on things there." He gives a short chuckle. "Not that that worked out so grand for me last time."

"Everyone there seems to know who you are," Eva tells him. "Is that because you're so light-fingered?"

He returns her half-smile. "Probably. I've not made too many friends over there. But I need to keep an eye on the place. It may feel isolated out on Longstone, but I'd like to know about it if we're to go to war again."

"Is that what you believe will happen?" Eva asks. "War?"

Finn scratches his bristly chin. "Only a matter of time before the Rising kicks off proper, I'd say."

Eva turns her tankard around. If the Jacobites do take up arms again, she hopes her family will be back in London. Holy Island feels far too exposed, a stone's throw from Scotland, with escape at the mercy of the tides.

"What is so special about Highfield House?" she asks. "Why were the Jacobites using it? Holy Island is full of places to hide away."

"It's hidden in the dunes," says Finn. "Private. Hard to see from the land. And it has easy access to and from the sea. Easy to make an escape."

Eva takes a long mouthful of ale. Twenty years ago, her mother had made an escape from Holy Island. And she cannot make sense of why.

She sits back in her chair, cradling her tankard. Rain is pelting against the windows now, and much of the daylight has been obscured by cloud. In the half light of the tavern, it feels as though nightfall is approaching, though she knows it can be no later than four or five.

Finn looks up suddenly and curses under his breath. A man is striding towards them; Eva recognises him as one of the Lindisfarne fisherman. She grapples for his name. Cordwell, perhaps? He's a bear of a man, with a long white beard and broad, meaty shoulders. From Finn's reaction she can only gather they know each other, and do not get along. She wonders if Finn has been stealing from him too.

Cordwell hovers over their table, arms folded across his thick chest. His greatcoat smells sour, like old salt and herrings. His eyes shift between Eva and Finn.

"Aren't you too much of a lady to be gallivanting around the place with this scoundrel, Miss Blake?"

Eva feels her cheeks flush, hiding her tankard of ale beneath the table. She prays Cordwell does not tell Nathan about having seen her. "Leave us be," she says tightly.

The fisherman turns to Finn. "You been out Donald Macauley's way lately, Murray?"

Eva's heart quickens.

"Nah." Finn gives him a thin smile. "I've enough coal to see me through til winter."

Cordwell snorts. "We ought to send the constable after you."

"You should," Finn agrees. "But then you'd have no one to keep you from getting wrecked when you go out after those herrings so late at night."

A muscle ticks in Cordwell's jaw. "Maybe we ought to be asking you about Donald's disappearance."

Finn's lips part beneath his beard. "Donald Macauley is missing?"

"Aye. No one's seen him in almost a month. Everyone's saying he's dead. They found his boat floating out your way. You know anything about that?"

Eva feels a jolt in her chest. Her heart is thumping so loudly she is sure the men can hear it.

Finn stares Cordwell down. "Why would I know anything about that?" He shakes his head. "Leave us alone, man. You know I had nothing to do with poor old Macauley."

Cordwell hesitates for a moment, then makes his way across the tavern without looking at them again.

Finn glances at Eva; a pointed look, full of questions. But he says nothing.

The door creaks open, letting in an explosion of noise. Rioters bluster into the tavern, dripping trails of rainwater. One has a sodden Jacobite flag slung over his shoulder. The downpour blows in through the open doorway.

"Out of here, you lot," the barkeep calls, pointing a fat finger towards the door. "Don't want none of this trouble in my tavern."

"Looks as though the redcoats have broken up the protest," says Finn. "Hopefully they'll—" He stops abruptly, his eyes following a man who steps into the tavern behind the Jacobites. He is tall and broad-shouldered, fair hair tied back in a long queue. He removes his cocked hat and shakes the rain from it, then makes his way towards the bar, weaving neatly through the protesters.

Eva frowns. "Who is that?"

Finn pulls his eyes away. "No one. I thought I knew the man. But I was mistaken." He tosses back the last of his drink and gets awkwardly to his feet. "Let's go. It's getting madder in here than it was outside."

Though the riots around the castle have broken up, the narrow streets are still teeming with people. Two men are dragged past the tavern by dragoons and shoved into a wagon at the end of the lane. Rain is bouncing off the cobbles and wind tears through the alleys. Eva tucks the food basket under her cloak in an attempt to keep it dry. Her heart is still hard and fast with the knowledge that Donald Macauley's boat has been found. Do people suspect her involvement, given she had been missing from the island the night of Macauley's disappearance? Cordwell's questions had suggested not, but she cannot find much comfort in them—especially since his suspicions were squarely aimed at Finn.

She glances sideways at him. Now they are alone, she is certain he is going to ask. Because surely now he has come to suspect that Donald Macauley was the man she had sent to the bottom of the sea.

They emerge from the tangle of streets to find a wild grey ocean folding out ahead of them. Waves are stirring the beach, tugging at the dinghies lined up along the sand. The Farnes have vanished behind a thick wall of cloud. A few hundred yards from shore, a larger vessel rocks at anchor, the wings of its large eagle figurehead tilting in the rain.

Eva hears Finn curse under his breath. "This weather's only going to get worse," he says. "We never should have stayed this long." Water drips from the ends of his hair. "It's a bad idea to try and get back to Longstone tonight."

Eva pulls her wet cloak tight around her body. Water has soaked through her shoes, and she can barely feel her toes. She longs to curl up in front of the fire in the cottage on Longstone. But she trusts Finn's knowledge of the sea. "What about the firebasket?" she asks.

He rubs a hand over his jaw. "It'll do no one any good if we drown trying to get back out there."

Eva nods. Shivers. "Is there an inn here in town?"

"Aye. Of course." He leads her back into the village, a hand pressed lightly to her shoulder. The feel of him goes someway to steadying her unease.

The lodging house is a sorry-looking building not far from the tavern, with a crooked front door and sagging wooden awnings. But Eva can see the glow of a fire through the windows; can smell cooking spices. She marches towards the door. Finn holds her back.

"I think…" He swallows. Tries again. "I think we ought to take a room together. It doesn't feel safe here tonight." He rubs the back of his neck. "I don't mean… Rather, I'd keep my distance… I…"

Eva can't help a slight smile.

A part of her wants to agree to his suggestion. But the thought feels suddenly overwhelming. It's foolish, she knows, to be feeling this way. She and Finn have spent three weeks keeping the light together. She has spent nights hunched over his bed, a damp cloth held to his forehead as he slept. Has tended his wound like the most devoted of physicians. There is no reason why she ought to be so unmoored by this suggestion. But something about this feels different.

Something about *him* feels different.

With the world rioting around them, Finn is caring and protective. Unable, or unwilling, to keep her at a distance.

And that new warmth is a little terrifying. Because it has made Eva strikingly aware of the way his closeness has her heart thumping in her chest. Strikingly aware of how much she wants to be near him. And strikingly aware of how impossible that might be. No doubt Nathan is already knee-deep in another plan to secure her a husband. And she feels quite certain that plan does not involve the thieving lightkeeper from Longstone.

She pulls a handful of coins from her pouch and strides inside out of the rain. "I will be quite all right in the dormitories."

CHAPTER TWENTY-ONE

Nathan has far too much to do to be sitting here at his desk staring blankly at his inkpot. There are business proposals to compose, in an attempt to rebuild his enterprise after the disastrous decisions he had made last year. And then there is the letter to Matthew Walton he has been putting off for far too long. It ought to be a strongly worded letter, of course. One in which he professes his utter dissatisfaction at the way his friend had treated both Eva and the family as a whole. But strongly worded letters have never been his strength. He can't quite find space for it.

Really, what he wants is to sleep. To curl up beneath his blankets and listen to the weather throwing itself against the house. But his thoughts are charging far too rapidly for that.

He fears that, at any moment, Martin Macauley might appear on his doorstep to string him up for his lies. To hunt down Eva for her role in his father's death.

Nathan uncorks a bottle of gin and refills the empty glass beside his inkpot. He wishes Eva was here. He has always enjoyed his sister's company, and tonight, he could use her level-headedness to keep his thoughts from venturing into dark places. Not that he supposes her own thoughts might be any less troubled. Still, perhaps they could steady each other somewhat, remind each other that, though they are teetering, nothing has toppled yet.

Since Sarah's death, Nathan has come to value Eva's place in his life even more. The two of them are strikingly similar, with a bone-deep hatred of conflict and a need to see everything in its rightful place. Logical and undistinguished middle children, against the terrifying brilliance of Oliver and the flightiness of Harriet.

He thinks of her out on that tiny speck of rock. Fleeing to Longstone is not the kind of impulsive thing he has ever known her to do. When Harriet had told him of Eva's leaving, he had had half a mind to go after her and demand she do nothing so reckless and improper. But he knows Eva, and he knows she is doing it for the right reasons. Knows how heavily her conscience must be weighing on her heart.

He can also only imagine how inordinately dreadful a boat trip out to Longstone would be. And he'll quite willingly leave his sister to her own devices if it means avoiding such a horror.

Thunder stirs out over the ocean and he finds himself glancing through the half-open curtains. Most nights, he can see the shipping beacon on Longstone winking in the darkness. Tonight, though, the horizon is black. Of course, there can be no firelight in weather such as this.

Nathan brings his glass to his lips, listening to the storm rattling the shutters. He has given up on the idea of writing tonight, but he knows that sleep is still far away. In the wild wind, the house shifts around him, not quite alive, and not quite still. He can hear footsteps in the passage downstairs, no doubt belonging to Harriet. The ceiling creaks loudly above his head.

If he is honest with himself, it is not the letters, or Eva's absence, or even Donald Macauley's death that has him so rattled tonight. It is thoughts of Oliver and the bedroom with the priest hole tucked into its walls.

Nathan had looked up to his older brother. Revered him, been blind to his flaws. His cruelty. All too often, Oliver had shunned his brother's company, preferring to explore the island alone, or lock himself away in his bedroom, doing heaven only knew what. Anytime he could grab a scrap of his older brother's attention, Nathan took it.

Come out and face your maker.

Oliver had always been obsessed with the dark history of Holy Island. The stories of the Viking raids had fascinated him. He would walk the ruins of the priory, telling Nathan tales of monks murdered in their monastery by the wild men from across the seas; stories of the villagers slaughtered in their homes.

They had been walking the rocks around St Cuthbert's Island when Oliver had pulled the knife from the water. Barely six inches long, it was tarnished with time, but its blade was still sharp enough to inflict plenty of damage.

"A Viking knife," Oliver had told him. "From the raids."

At seven years old, Nathan had believed him.

Oliver had taken the knife home, tucked into his pocket to hide it from their mother. "Let's play a game."

Nathan had agreed at once. A game, yes. When was the last time Oliver had sought his company?

Go and hide in the house. Don't make a sound. Imagine the Vikings are coming for you.

And Nathan would run, thrilled and terrified, craving his brother's attention and fearing it too. He knew, of course, to hide out of sight of his mother, and the housekeepers, and anyone else who might catch sight of what they were doing. Knew to hide in the cupboards and wardrobes and under the beds where no one would find them.

His brother, three years older, was sharper, stronger, wiser. Would uncover Nathan's hiding places in minutes.

Come out and face your maker. Always spoken in the same low, taunting voice, letting Nathan know he had been found.

And Nathan would find himself frozen in place, terrified of facing his brother and the punishment he would suffer for having his hiding place uncovered. Hands around his ankles or wrists, Oliver would drag him from the cupboard, the wardrobe, from the beneath the bed. Hold the knife to his throat.

And now you will die like the monks did.

Hard enough to cause a murmur of pain. Hard enough to fear the knife would break the skin.

Once, Nathan had hidden in the priest hole. Oliver had not appeared within minutes to drag him from his hiding place, and at first Nathan had been proud of himself for tricking his brother. He sat there in the tiny darkness with his heart thumping hard, half exhilarated, half terrified as he waited for that moment when the priest hole would flood with light again. That moment when his brother would drag him out into the bedroom and press the knife to his throat.

More time passed. Minutes—or was it hours? Perhaps Oliver was not coming. Perhaps the hiding place was too good. Nathan could not bear much longer in this airless, lightless space. He shoved against the panel that opened out into the bedroom. It did not move. And he knew at once that he had not tricked his brother at all. Because there was no tricking Oliver. His mind was too sharp. Too wicked. Nathan did not know what his brother had pushed in front of the priest hole to prevent it from opening. All he knew was that, once again, he was at his older brother's mercy.

Nathan had no idea how long he stayed prisoner in the hole. Time was distorted by the dark, and by fear of that moment when Oliver would come for him. He did not cry out. Did not call for his mother. He knew that would only make things worse.

Finally, he heard the scrape of wood on wood as Oliver shoved—*what?* His bed? Wardrobe?—away from the door of the priest hole. "Come out and face your maker."

Nathan's muscles stiffened as his brother reached for him, yanking him out into the light. His legs ached from being held to his chest for so long, and he could do little more than spill out across the floor. Oliver loomed over him, obscuring his vision of the tree-trunk beams across the ceiling. "Show a little imagination next time, Nathan. I think you need to be punished for choosing such a dreadful hiding place."

Nathan tried to scramble away from his brother's grip, but Oliver held him down. And then the knife. His chest. His stomach. His throat. The pain intensified and he felt a thin line of blood run onto his collar.

Nathan cannot say for certain that Oliver's game had led to his fear of human touch. He cannot determine when such a thing had begun. All he knows is that he does not remember having such a fear in the days before his brother had found the knife in the ocean.

"There are rats in the roof, Nathan," says Harriet, appearing in the doorway of the study. Paint is streaked along one cheek, and her blonde curls are spilling loose over her shoulders. Though it is well past midnight, she is still dressed in her pale blue day dress, as though she has no intention of sleeping. "I can hear them moving around up there. Big ones. I can hear them over all this rain. Can smell them too. The filthy beasts."

Lightning jags, filling the room with sudden white light.

"What would you like me to do?" Nathan asks. "Climb up to the attic and kill them all?"

"That would be nice," she says. "It's dreadfully hard to concentrate with all that scrabbling."

Nathan bites back a retort. He knows Harriet is only trying to get a reaction out of him. "What does Edwin think about you staying up so late?"

"Edwin is fast asleep," she says. "As he is most nights. He probably assumes I'm asleep too." She pins Nathan with hard eyes. "Do not even think of telling him."

He hesitates. "He is your husband, Harriet. I think he ought to know what you're up to."

"Do not even think of it," she repeats, jabbing a long finger in his direction. "It's your fault we're up here in this dreadful wilderness. My painting is all that's keeping me sane."

Nathan sighs. He'll not think of telling Edwin, no. As far as he is concerned, Harriet's theatrics are for her husband to deal with now, and he has no desire to get involved. The rats, however, are a different story.

He leaves his study and makes his way down the passage. He looks upward, listening. Perhaps there is a rustling. And definitely a foul smell. Little wonder. After twenty years of abandonment, the place is probably crawling with far more than rats. But as far as he knows, the space inside the roof is inaccessible. He has no thought of how he might find his way inside.

As he is pondering that unpleasant prospect, a shriek comes from his bedroom.

He rushes down the passage and throws open the door to find Theodora huddled on the floor next to her truckle bed. He drops to his knees beside her. "What's happened, my love?"

She replies only with a loud sob. Nathan grits his teeth and scoops her from the floor. She throws her arms around his neck and clings to him as he carries her to his bed. His heart hammers against his ribs at the feel of her little body wrapped around his.

"Were you sleepwalking again?" he asks gently. "Did you have a bad dream?"

Her reply is muffled against his neck.

Nathan smooths her hair. Feels sweat prickling his skin. His instincts war with each other; half desperate to comfort his daughter, half desperate to put space between their bodies. He forces himself to breathe. To keep a hold of her.

"Men in the walls," Theodora manages.

He eases her back so he can see her face in the lamplight spilling in from the passage. "What?"

"Men in the walls," she says again.

"Where?"

She bursts into a fresh rush of tears. Buries her head in his shoulder. Nathan eases her under the covers, forcing himself to keep his fingers tucked around hers. *Just a dream*, he hears himself say. Can't make sense of why he is finding it so hard to believe his own words.

CHAPTER TWENTY-TWO

Something wakes Eva from a broken sleep. The dark is thick, and for a moment, she is disoriented, until she makes out the outlines of the dormitory's three other beds. The smell of roast meat and cold grease drifts in from the nearby kitchen, joining the fug of wet clothes and shoes. Rain is still loud against the windows, punctuated by a rattle of thunder.

Eva hears yelling in the street. The words are thick with a Scottish drawl and she can't make them out. But the pistol shot that follows is clear enough.

She sits up, heart jolting.

"Bloody animals," says the older woman in the bed beside her. "Thought the redcoats cleared this place out." She slides out from under her blanket and goes to the window. She pulls back the curtain, letting a spear of light from the streetlamps into the room. Through the wash of rain on the glass, Eva can just make out the shapes of men brawling in the street. She hears drink on their voices. Knots of shouted Gaelic.

The barrel of a musket comes flying through the window. Glass sprays out between the curtains and the older woman lets out a shriek. Eva scrambles out of bed and hurries to her side. On the other side of the room, someone lights a lamp.

"Are you all right?"

The woman looks down at her arms and hands, inspecting them for damage. "I think so." The curtains bloom in the wind and rain blows in through the broken window, along with a gust of cold, sea-scented air.

There is a pounding on the door. Eva hears Finn calling her name. She hurries across the room and pulls open the door, poking her head into the passage to obscure his view into the dormitory. He is dressed in only his breeches and shirtsleeves, the neck of his shirt hanging open, revealing sparse curls of hair.

"What are you doing?" Eva hisses. "You can't be in here."

The older woman shoves her way past them, shoes in one hand and shawl in the other. She disappears down the passage.

"There's a fight in the street," says Finn. "I thought I heard glass breaking." He peers over her shoulder to the shattered window. When he looks back at her, there's an intensity to his eyes that she hasn't seen before. "Please, Eva. Come upstairs with me. I just want to make sure you're safe. I'll sleep outside the door if you wish it. But I don't want you in here."

And it's bare instinct that makes her nod. She wraps her arms around herself, suddenly aware of the thinness of her shift. "Just give me a moment to dress."

What in hell is he doing? The *Eagle* is moored in the harbour, his former captain is here in Bamburgh, and now Eva Blake is about to curl up to sleep in his room. Having her in such close quarters would be a brainless idea at the best of times, but having caught sight of the captain in the tavern earlier—and having glimpsed his barque anchored off the beach—only emphasises the stupidity of this. The impossibility of his desire for Eva. She cannot know any of it, of course. Not of the *Eagle*, or his past with Captain Ward. He wonders if she had believed him when he had fibbed about recognising Ward in the tavern. He had hated the lie. But what is one tiny fib amongst everything else he is keeping from her?

The wooden stairs of the inn creak beneath his weight. He did not for a second imagine Eva might agree to this. But he hears her steady footsteps behind him and his heart is thunder in his ears. This is clearly inviting trouble. But what else can he do? Letting her stay in the women's dormitory is not an option, not with bullets flying across the street and men brawling outside the window. He knows Eva can look after herself in many ways—but he also feels fairly certain that her life in London has not thrown her in too many situations like this one.

He tries not to let her nearness rattle him. After all, he has spent almost a month in her company. But something about this feels different. Is it the fact that tonight, when he sleeps, there will be no wall between them? Or because, in his concern for her safety, he has let her glimpse the way he really feels about her?

He turns the key in the lock and steps aside, gesturing to her to enter. She turns to look back at him. "Are you not coming in?"

He shakes his head stiffly. It's a bad idea. "Just bring me my coat. I'll stay out here."

"Finn. Don't be foolish. You're still hurt. I'd rather go back to the dormitories than have you sleeping in the hallway on account of me." She meets his eyes. "No one need know of this. No one will judge us. Besides, we've been sharing the cottage for weeks." It sounds as though she is trying to convince herself more than him.

Reluctantly, he steps inside. Locks the door behind him. The glow of a street lamp fills the room and Finn pulls the curtain closed. Now Eva is safely with him, he has no desire to watch what's going on out there. Though he can still hear voices in the street, mingled with the steady slap of rain, the violence seems to have eased. A single candle flickers on the side table, and a fire simmers steadily in the grate, making shadows dance across the walls. His wet coat and vest hang drying on a chair beside it.

Eva hovers on the opposite side of the room, her cloak and bonnet clutched to her chest. Her hair hangs over one shoulder in a dishevelled brown plait, the ends curling slightly.

Finn nods towards the basket sitting on the table, filled with the food they had bought from the market. "Are you hungry?" His voice comes out stiff and strained.

Eva goes to the table and rifles through the basket. She considers the loaf of bread and the seedcake, then pulls out an apple. Her eyes drift towards the narrow bed pressed up against one wall, its blankets undisturbed. "Have you slept?" she asks. Smiles faintly. "I suppose not."

"I'll sleep when we get back tomorrow morning."

He can hear the faint sigh of the sea beneath the storm. Thinks of waves breaking on the Knavestone reef. And tonight, the firebasket will not be lit. Still, he knows he has made the right decision. Trying to get back to Longstone in this weather would have been far too treacherous. After all, he never has a beacon to guide himself home. Tonight, he knows, the waves will break against the walls of the cottage. He has not closed the shutters over the windows, and he hopes he will not return to broken glass and a flooded home.

But there is little point dwelling on that dark firebasket. He just has to hope that tonight, no wayward ships will be passing the Farne Islands.

Finn takes the poker and stirs the fire. Clears his throat. "You ought to try and sleep. Take the bed."

"I'm far too awake to sleep any more. Those men firing their pistols outside my window made sure of that." She takes a bite of the apple that echoes in the stillness of the room. The sound shatters the tension and makes Finn laugh.

"So you decided you'd wake the rest of the inn too?"

Eva jabs him in the ribs with her elbow. She takes another thunderous bite, and gives him a defiant smile.

With his wet clothes occupying the only chair, Finn lowers himself awkwardly to the floor. Eva sits beside him.

"Do you think you will do it forever?" she asks, once she's swallowed down the last of her food. "Keep the light, all on your own?" She tosses the apple core into the fire.

Finn shrugs. Usually, he tries not to think too far into the future. There does not seem to be much in it except the Longstone light. "Someone needs to do it," he says. "So I suppose I will be out there until Trinity House puts up a real beacon in the Farnes."

"They never thought to pay you?"

He shifts his injured leg, trying to dull the ache of it. "The church that owns the islands is letting me live out here without paying a penny."

Eva catches his eye. "They're getting a fine deal. It is not a job for one man."

"Good thing I've got you then, aye?" The comment comes out sounding far more intimate than he intended. Eva looks down at her clasped hands. Doesn't speak.

Longstone had been Finn's first home. His uncles had drowned on the Knavestone more than a decade before he was born, and his father had petitioned heavily for the beacon to be raised on Inner Farne. When that proposed light had remained dark, the Newcastle merchants unwilling to pay for its upkeep, he had taken it upon himself to change that. Near single-handedly, he had gone about building the cottage and the firebasket on the island closest to the reef that had taken his brothers' lives.

Finn's childhood had been spent fishing and sailing, and learning to light the firebasket, taking turns with his parents to keep watch over the light.

But he and his father had never got along. Had never seen eye to eye. Finn was eight when his mother passed, and after that, the island had felt particularly stifling.

But it wasn't just his relationship with his father that made him want to leave the place. As a child, that inkblot of rock was just not enough. Each night, as he helped his father light the basket, he would look out to sea and watch the lights of passing ships. Imagine where they might be heading; where they might have come from. He longed to see more of the world than this stifling, sea-drenched corner. For the first decade of his life, his world was unbearably tiny, made up only of Longstone and the small mainland villages nearby that kept them fed.

He felt resentment towards his father too. Didn't understand his need to make the firebasket his life. Why did his da feel the need to do what no one else was willing to do? The Farne Islands had been dark for centuries. Why should it be their job to change that?

Yes, his father's brothers had succumbed to the sea. But sacrificing his life like this would not bring his brothers back. It would only worsen his already strained relationship with his son.

Finn was nine years old when he met Henry Ward. He had taken the skiff over to the mainland, leaving his father with no way off Longstone except the leaky dinghy they saved for emergencies. He'd fought with his father the night before; can't remember why—barely a night went by without them bickering about the watch or the supper, or anything else as inconsequential. They had both flown into a rage, as usual, and had spent the night in silence.

When he had arrived in Beadle Bay, he had found Ward's barque in the middle of the harbour, effortlessly attracting attention. The ship was beautiful, its intricate eagle figurehead looking out over the water and daring passers-by to ask questions. Finn rarely saw vessels like that here—usually the harbour was cluttered with fishing ketches and the barnacled hulls of single-masted dories. Curious, he circled the ship in his skiff, eyes on the barque as he leant on the tiller. He guessed it too small to be a ship of the line. A merchant, perhaps? Privateer? Perhaps even a pirate. What would it be like to climb aboard a ship like that and see the world?

Finn had not expected anyone to be aboard, but Henry Ward appeared on deck and called down to him.

"You like the ship, lad?"

He nodded, squinting into the sun. "Aye, sir. It's a beauty."

Ward watched him ease the skiff around the bow. "You look as though you can handle a vessel. How old are you?"

"Nine years, sir."

Ward raised his eyebrows. "You're big for your age. Would you like to come aboard a moment? Have yourself a look at my ship?"

That moment aboard the *Eagle* had led to the invitation Finn could not refuse. He needed a cabin boy, said Henry Ward, to ferry messages across the ship and run the captain's errands as they fired broadsides at the French, under the title of legal privateers. A letter of marque signed by the king himself.

A life as a cabin boy fighting the French was far more than Finn could have imagined. Far more excitement, more fear, more exhilaration. A life far more expansive than he had lived so far.

For two years, he had sailed with Ward and the *Eagle*, prowling the Channel, tracing the seas of Europe, in search of French prey. Two years of hammocks and hardtack and smoke in his lungs.

Henry Ward was a good captain. Strict but fair, with a constant eye out for his cabin boy. Finn ate his meals in the officers' ward-robe. Learned to scramble up the rigging in seconds to trim the sails. Ran messages across the ship while gunfire roared around his ears.

But everything had changed in an instant. A single moment, a single mistake. Two years after he had first climbed aboard the *Eagle,* Finn had had no choice but to run from Henry Ward and his crew.

For years he roamed the country, a moving target in case Ward saw fit to come after him for the crime he had committed. Fishing and farming in whichever part of England the work led him. Sometimes even up into

Scotland, hauling ancient wooden ploughs through muddy fields. Anything to put pennies in his pocket and keep him from thinking about his time on the *Eagle*.

Finally, seventeen years after he had left Longstone, guilt brought him back. Guilt and a long-buried need to be a decent son. It had taken adulthood for Finn to see the odd nobility in what his father had made his life; made him see the utter decency in keeping the light and protecting strangers' lives at the cost of his own freedom. And it had taken adulthood for him to realise just how terribly he had treated his father. How much worry and regret the man must have felt for him, out there alone on his island.

When Finn had stepped back onto Longstone for the first time, an odd stillness had hung over the place. It had always been a place of unsilent silence. But now it felt different. Otherworldly. The firebasket swung in the wind, old, cold ash skittering over the surface of the rock pools. The candles in the cottage had burnt down to stumps. A loaf of bread sat in the middle of the table, gathering mould.

He found the body the next morning when the tide fell. Dark and swollen, a mat of grey hair half-obscuring the face. Finn stared at it for a long time. He tried to imagine what his father's last moments had been like. Had his heart seized and taken him suddenly? Or had he suffered slowly, unable to move from the grasp of the rising tide? The grotesque, discoloured body was impossible to look away from. Barely recognisable as his father. It seemed to highlight all the terrible mistakes Finn had made.

He wrapped his father's remains in sailcloth and rowed out into deeper sea. Slipped the body into the water, murmuring a prayer cobbled together from distant childhood memories. Eighteen years ago, he and his father had buried his mother out here like this too. At least his parents would be together now, at the bottom of the lightless sea.

Regret hung heavy on his shoulders as he rowed back to Longstone. He and his father were all each other had had in the world. And Finn had left him to die a lonely death; left his body to disappear beneath the tide.

He is only dimly aware of having spoken aloud to Eva. Of having told her of his return to Longstone, and the discovery of his father's body. Of course, he had said nothing to her of the barque with the eagle figurehead.

I'm sorry, say her eyes, but she doesn't speak. He is glad of it. Speaking will not change anything. And he does not want her pity.

He knows he should not have told her. Knows no good can come of getting close to her, of allowing these feelings he has for her to turn into anything at all. Because what he does not tell her, is how, from the moment he returned to Longstone, he has always been aware of that vast house on the edge of Holy Island, a stone's throw across the water.

The silence between them is weighted. She is leaning forward slightly, as if waiting for him to speak again. No. There will be no more. There can be no more. It would send her running into the street to be caught up in the remnants of the protest.

"You are doing a good thing, Finn," she says finally. "I am sorry people don't see that."

"Well, I've stolen from people on Holy Island. Other places too. I can hardly expect them to look past that." And his mind goes to a vanished man, a vanished boat; to the accusation Tom Cordwell had made against him in the tavern. He looks at Eva. He wants to ask; can't ask. But what what what was she doing at sea with Donald Macauley? Because surely this vanished man is now lying at the bottom of the German Ocean.

He and the Macauleys have never gotten along. He and Martin had been born into a feud between their fathers, a petty thing over some long-forgotten dispute that he'd foolishly felt the need to continue. Stormy years, he thinks. The years of his father; of Donald Macauley; of Eva's mother. Kind and foolish Abigail Blake. He tries not to follow that thought too far.

He glances at Eva again, willing her to speak unprompted of Macauley's drowning. She won't, of course. She has kept that information close to her chest for three weeks. Finally, he says, "Why were you at sea with Donald Macauley?"

Eva stares into the fire for a long time, glassy-eyed. She does not look surprised at his question. No doubt she has been waiting for him to ask ever since Cordwell planted the idea at his feet.

She draws in a long breath. "He believed I witnessed an exchange of information between him and a Jacobite messenger. He thought to be rid of me before I could report back to the government. He forced me into his boat, and when we were far enough out to sea, he raised his musket. I swung the oar at him before I even knew what I was doing."

"So you were defending yourself."

"I don't think his son will see it like that, do you?"

"No," Finn says finally. "Probably not."

Eva covers her eyes with her hands. "Martin deserves to know what happened to his father. I cannot just keep the truth from him. I need to tell him."

Finn presses an impulsive hand to her knee, forcing her to look at him. Her skirts are still damp beneath his fingers. "If you do that, they'll string you up. If they truly believe you a spy, they'll be looking for a reason to be rid of you. They'll see you on the scaffold for murder."

Eva sucks in a breath, and for a moment, Finn regrets his harshness. But she needs to know where truth-telling will lead her.

She gets to her feet suddenly and begins to pace across the room. "How can I ever go back to Holy Island?" she is saying. "Knowing what I know? How can I pass Martin Macauley in the street, or sit by him in church?"

He can hear the guilt rearing up inside her. Guilt she has clearly been pushing down for weeks. He stands, ignoring the sharp pain that shoots up his leg. He catches her arm as she paces past. Pulls her to a gentle halt. "The man was trying to kill you," he says. "What were you to have done? Let him shoot you?"

Eva says nothing. She closes her eyes and her tears spill. As though on impulse, she wraps her arms around his waist. Finn pulls her close. Swallows hard. He is dimly aware of just how hard his heart is pounding.

He wants this. Desperately. Wants to be the one to hold Eva Blake, to comfort her when she falls apart. But how can that ever be when his past has the power to break her?

He runs his palm over her damp hair. Feels her shiver slightly. After a moment, she steps back and wipes her eyes with the heel of her hand. In the coppery lamplight, Finn can see the faint sprinkle of freckles across her nose. Sees the dark flecks in her blue eyes. Before he can stop himself, his hand rises to cup her cheek. And she lifts her hand to cover his.

"You won't…tell anyone, will you? About Donald Macauley?" She lets out her breath. "No," she says, before he can speak. "Of course you won't." Her fingers slide between his, erasing any chance he had of pulling away. She looks into his eyes, and his other hand slides to the back of her neck. Before he can think, can stop himself, his lips find hers. She tenses for a moment, then her mouth opens beneath his, seeking more. He feels her sink against him. Grips a fistful of her hair as he deepens the kiss.

It is intoxicating, seamless. And the most dazzling of mistakes.

He pulls away suddenly. "I'm sorry," he mumbles. "I'm sorry." He turns so he cannot see her. Steps back, forcing himself to put space between them. "You take the bed," he says throatily. His boots thud dully, unrhythmic, as he goes for the chair in the corner. "You ought to try and sleep."

CHAPTER TWENTY-THREE

Eva manages a far more broken sleep than if she was keeping the light out on Longstone. She stares into the blackness, feeling Finn's kiss on her lips, and sensing the coldness that had fallen over the room the minute he had pulled away. She cannot make sense of it. Cannot make sense of his regret. His changeability. Cannot make sense of anything more than the hollow, sinking feeling in the pit of her stomach.

All she knows is that it is time for her to leave him.

She is glad when blue morning light finally pushes through the curtains. The room is chilly and thick with the smell of cold ash and tallow. She can hear the faint patter of rain against the glass, but the wind has calmed and the storm blown over.

She hears the chair creak and dares to glance at Finn. He is already pulling his vest and coat on. Eva slides out from under the blankets and reaches for her shoes.

"I'm going back to Holy Island," she says brusquely.

Some foolish part of her wants him to protest. Instead, he just nods. "I'll take you."

"No." She gathers her cloak from the table. It is still slightly damp, but she slings it over her shoulders anyway. "I don't want you anywhere near the place. Not after what happened last time." Her voice is clipped. "I can make my own way there."

"Don't be daft. It will take you hours."

"I have the time."

Finn sighs. "At least let me walk with you. I can manage."

Eva lets out a cold laugh. "Can you now?" She shakes her head. "I can manage just fine without you." She hopes he knows she is referring to far more than just the walk to Holy Island.

He reaches for her suddenly, his coarse fingers wrapping around her bare forearm. The sudden feel of him makes her breath catch. "Eva." She looks up at him, expectant. His lips part but he doesn't speak. He gives her wrist an almost imperceptible squeeze, then shakes his head. Lets his hand fall. "I'm sorry."

So it is to be like this. Is he not even to offer an explanation? Perhaps it's best this way. She does not need an explanation. Everything in Finn's eyes tells her that last night was a mistake. It will do her no good to hear the words spoken.

She yanks on her bonnet and marches out of the lodging house, not waiting for him to follow.

He manages to catch up with her in the street outside the inn. The cobbles are littered with footprinted banners and sodden tracts, smeared with running ink.

"Let me at least walk with you as far as the beach."

"For what purpose, Finn?" She feels her anger rising. "You've made it very clear that what happened between us was a mistake. This morning you can barely even look at me. How am I supposed to take that?"

He scrubs a hand over his face. "I know. I should never have…"

"You ought to have slept outside the door," she snaps.

"Aye. I should have."

He turns suddenly, looking past her. There is man they had seen in the tavern yesterday, the man who had caught Finn's attention. He is striding purposefully towards the beach, hands dug into the pockets of his greatcoat. Three other men are following a few paces behind.

"Who is that?" Eva asks tautly.

"No one. It's no one. It doesn't matter."

She shakes her head. Let him be tight-lipped with his secrets. They are no business of hers. "You're right," she says. "It doesn't matter."

She turns and strides away from him without another word.

The walk, of course, is utter stupidity. Ten miles at least. It will take her most of the day. But she had stuffed half of the bread they had bought in her cloak pocket and she is sure it will be sustenance enough to see her home. Hours of walking is preferable to climbing back in that boat with Finn.

The air smells of rain, but blue sky is beginning to break through the clouds, suggesting summer might linger a little longer yet. The golden light feels like a stark contrast to her mood.

Eva blinks back tears as she walks. Every inch of her body feels weighted with sadness. Nothing about this makes sense. Not Finn's abrupt coldness, or his evasiveness, or his hungry kiss.

She hates that she can still conjure up the feeling of his lips against hers. Hates that she craves it. Hates the way her body longs for his in a way she could never have imagined wanting Matthew Walton.

The miles pass slowly. Exhaustion tugs at her legs, and her feet begin to rub inside her shoes. But she doesn't care. It gives her something to focus on beyond the hollow ache inside her. She knows, of course, that there is no more foolish thing she could have done than allow herself to grow feelings for Finn Murray.

The tide is still draining when she reaches the sands that lead across to Lindisfarne. A thin pane of sea blocks her way onto the island. She ought to wait until the path is dry, of course, but all she wants is to be back home. She takes off her shoes and stockings and steps into the shallow water.

The sea is glassy, the deep stillness both welcome and disconcerting after the chaos of last night. Water licks at her ankles and she bundles her skirts up in her free hand. What must she look like, striding barefooted through the water like this? Before her time on Longstone, she would never have considered doing such a thing. Now, it almost feels normal.

The sea is breathtakingly cold against her aching feet, but the chill brings with it a sense of clarity. She reaches down and splashes her face with seawater, washing away the last of her tears. She tells herself she has cried all she is going to cry for Finn Murray. He is worth no more than that.

CHAPTER TWENTY-FOUR

"I'm glad you're home," says Nathan. "And I'm glad you're safe. Although I do wish you had waited for the tide before crossing back."

Eva gives him a pale smile and brings her teacup to her lips. She looks exhausted, her eyes underlined with shadow and her body sinking against the settle. Her cheeks are pink from sun, and if he didn't know her better, he would have said she had been crying. Her dark hair hangs loose over her shoulders, and though she has changed out of the damp clothes she arrived in—into one of Harriet's dresses, he thinks—she still looks like a windblown islander. Alarmingly out of character for the sister he knows.

"How have you been faring here?" she asks. "I heard Donald Macauley's boat was found…"

Nathan nods. He tells her, succinct and undetailed, about the discovery of the dinghy; about the memorial cross that now stands behind St Mary's.

For long moments, Eva doesn't speak. She stares blankly ahead, toying with the lacing on her bodice. "Does anyone suspect…"

"No," says Nathan. But he is not convinced. He cannot help but feel as though Martin Macauley is biding his time, searching for proof, waiting for the right time to confront them.

"Heard about that, Joseph? Miss Blake stranding herself on the mainland for the night? Same night Da disappeared…"

But this he will keep to himself.

Eva's gaze drifts out the window as she takes another sip of tea. "There was a Jacobite protest in Bamburgh yesterday," she says after a moment.

"I was there helping Mr Murray buy food. It turned rather violent."

Nathan nods. "I can't say I'm surprised. The Rising is gaining momentum. Sounds as though the new riot act is having little effect."

"They were using this place, you know," says Eva. "The Jacobites. They used to meet here, out of sight of the authorities."

Nathan raises his eyebrows. "Well. I suppose we cannot be surprised. Given how long the house has been empty." The thought is more than a little unsettling. For not the first time, he regrets leaving Highfield House unguarded for so long. He sips his tea. "You weren't in danger, I hope? In Bamburgh?"

Eva keeps her eyes down. "I was safe."

"And this Mr Murray. I trust he behaved in a gentlemanly manner while you were taking care of him?"

Eva wraps her arms around herself. Her jaw tightens. "He did nothing untoward," she says tautly. "If that is what you're asking."

Nathan frowns. She is not usually one to show her emotions so openly. "Eva? Is there something else?"

"No," she says. "Nothing else."

Nathan lets the silence settle for a moment, hoping to nudge her into speaking further. But she just sips her tea with a faraway expression.

"I mean to write to Matthew Walton today," he says.

Eva looks up, finally drawn away from the contents of her teacup. "You've still not written to him?"

"I know I ought to have done it sooner. But I was rather upset by his behaviour. I feared my words might come across too harshly."

She scoffs. "Do you not think he deserves a little harshness?"

Nathan bristles. She is right, of course. But he still has faint hope of rescuing the betrothal, and he knows harshness will not help the situation.

"It would do you good to be angry every now and then, Nathan," Eva tells him, before he can speak. "Surely it cannot be healthy to be so agreeable all the time."

"I'm an agreeable person," he says. "Is there something so wrong with that?"

Eva lets out a harsh breath, but does not bother dignifying his question with a response. "There's little point writing to Walton," she says instead. "Especially now, after so long. What can it possibly achieve?"

"Well. At the very least, he owes me an explanation."

"What were you expecting would happen?" she demands. "You betrothed me to a man who preferred my sister over me."

Her words catch him off guard. "You knew of that?"

She nods. "I overheard the two of you speaking of it."

Nathan lets out a breath, hit with a pang of regret. He and Matthew had spoken of Harriet twice: once when Walton had expressed his initial interest in her, and a second time…when? At the rented house in Islington, he realises. Matthew had come to him airing his concern over marrying Eva when he had such feelings for her sister. Nathan had had no idea Eva had been in the house at the time. He had gone on to list her many positive qualities. Had convinced Matthew she would be a far more suitable wife than prickly, quick-tempered Harriet. He had left the conversation certain Matthew was more than happy to become Eva's husband.

"Is that why he changed his mind about marrying you?" he asks.

Eva nods, her cheeks colouring slightly. The glassiness in her eyes seems to have magnified, and Nathan regrets raising the issue.

"I'm sorry," he says. "I wish you had not overheard that conversation. But when I told Matthew you would make a fine wife in Harriet's place, I truly believed it. He would have been immensely lucky to have you."

After supper, he writes the letter.

It is brief and curt. Hurried words expressing his displeasure at the breaking of their agreement, and his treatment of Eva. And then a carefully worded urging to him to reconsider. He doubts it will make any difference. And he knows it is probably for the best. But now, on top of all the stresses of the house, he must set out to find Eva a more suitable match. A near impossible thing to do from Holy Island, of course. He knows there is little hope of them returning to London by year's end. But hopefully by the spring, this whole sorry episode will be behind them and Eva will be happily married. He finds it hard to remain optimistic. To be a woman of almost twenty-five and without prospects is hardly an enviable position. Nathan knows he ought to have pushed Matthew to marry her sooner. Their drawn-out engagement has done no one any favours.

Nathan slides the pounce pot into the drawer and peers through the window into the night. A thin moon is tossing its light off the water.

He has always had a fascination with the sky, at times even bordering on obsession. As a child, he had spent countless hours poring over star maps and tracking glittering trails of light across the night sky. The vastness of the universe has always calmed him; always made his problems seem a little less pressing. But with adulthood, that fascination had faded away, as life's challenges had refused to be relegated to unimportance. The telescope his father had given him had sat unused for years, and he had sold it before coming to Holy Island. It had not even crossed his mind to bring it with him. Nonetheless, leaving his curtains open for the starlight to spill inside is a habit he has not attempted to shake.

Sarah had always encouraged him to go back to astronomy, his childhood love. She had claimed it would be good for him, and he knows she was probably right. But without her nudging him in that direction, he feels even less likely to do so.

He had been more open-minded before Sarah had died. More willing to spend time in the stars, to see the magic in the everyday. It had been easy to do in the presence of his ethereal, blue-eyed wife. But with Sarah gone, the world feels far more stern and rigid. A difficult place to navigate with his ethereal, blue-eyed daughter.

Men in the walls.

Theodora has always been an imaginative child, prone to sleepwalking and nightmares. But something about this chills him. Perhaps it's because he remembers people in the walls in this place too. Remembers them all too vividly.

I think you need to be punished for choosing such a dreadful hiding place.

There is no way Theodora ought to know about the priest hole. Nathan has been painfully deliberate in keeping her out of Oliver's old room. Indeed, that room had been one of the main reasons he had not wanted her in the house in the first place. And he is certain none of the others know of the priest hole's existence. Still, Theodora is no angel. If she has sneaked into Oliver's room for a little exploration, it would certainly not be the first time she had deliberately disobeyed him.

He takes the ring of keys from his desk drawer and the lamp from the mantel. Heads out into the hallway. Faint light is glowing under the door of Eva's bedroom. They are becoming a family of nocturnal creatures. Nathan is careful not to make a sound as he passes. He does not want his sister to catch him. Does not want to admit he is going looking for the shadows from Thea's nightmares.

He rattles the door of Oliver's room, finding it locked tight, as he had left it. Would Theodora have stolen the keys from his desk drawer? He does not want to believe it. But he can't deny it's a possibility. He unlocks the door and steps inside.

He shines the lamp around the room, golden light arcing over the walls. Everything is just as he had left it, with half the floorboards replaced, and a large gap in the floor by the window, revealing the beams beneath.

He presses on the panel to open the priest hole. With a pounding heart, he shines his lamp inside. Empty, of course. Was he truly expecting otherwise?

He shakes his head, trying to expel his racing imagination. What is he thinking? Of course Thea has not ventured in here. *Men in the walls* is nothing more than a nightmare—and hunting through the house in the dark like this is no way to allay his daughter's nocturnal fears.

He leaves the room, locking the door behind him, cursing the house for upturning his ordered thoughts.

Eva lies on her back, staring up at the ceiling. It feels like hours since she had blown out her lamp, but sleep continues to evade her. She supposes she can't be surprised. Three weeks of lightkeeping have wreaked havoc on her sleeping habits.

In spite of herself, she slips out of bed and goes to the window. She sees the faint flicker on the horizon; the glow of the Longstone light. She lets the curtain fall.

She hates that there is something comforting about the sight of the firebasket. It assures her of Finn's safety—and she hates that she cares so much. Hates that she can't push him from her mind like she ought to.

She grabs her shawl from the end of the bed and makes her way down into the kitchen. The lamp in her hand lights a faint path in front of her.

A mouse scuttles past her feet and disappears down the staircase. Eva pushes open the kitchen door, finding her sister taking a cup from the shelf.

Harriet whirls around. "Evie. You scared me. What are you doing awake?"

"I couldn't sleep. Are you working?"

"I am." She hands Eva the cup and takes down another.

"I don't suppose you'd like a little company?"

Harriet makes her way out of the kitchen, nodding for Eva to join her. "I've a bottle of Edwin's whisky in my workroom. Sneaked it in there when no one was looking."

Eva follows her into the workroom. Despite the lamp blazing on the side table, a chill has settled into the walls. Harriet has come prepared, she notices, dressed in thick winter skirts and a heavy green shawl. She takes a blanket from the chair in the corner and tosses it to Eva, then uncorks the bottle.

Eva accepts a cup and wraps the blanket around her shoulders. She tilts her head to inspect Harriet's painting. Pale streams of sunlight pour across the sea, its light reflected in a row of waves. Shadowed forest crams the edges of the foreground.

"It's beautiful," she says.

Harriet's nose wrinkles. "Is it? I can't tell anymore. I've been staring at it so long it's ceased to make sense to me. Perhaps I ought to just return to still-lifes. But they just feel so empty. I need to go further than that. Although I'm starting to feel as though I don't have the skill to do so." It sounds as though she is speaking to herself.

"I see." Eva feels completely adrift. Completely devoid of culture and beauty. She sinks into the chair in the corner and takes a gulp of whisky.

Harriet stays at the easel, examining her painting as she sips from her cup. "It's too bleak," she says finally. "The trees are almost indistinguishable from the water. That is not the effect I was trying for at all. It's all wrong." She laughs humourlessly. "Perhaps that will teach me to paint by lamplight in the middle of the night."

"Is that how you're feeling?" Eva asks curiously. "Bleak?"

Harriet shrugs. She looks surprised by the question. "Sometimes, I suppose."

Eva turns her cup around in her hands. Her encounter with Finn Murray has left her feeling utterly colourless too, but over the years, she has learnt better than to drop her problems at Harriet's feet. Her sister has a way of making things all about her.

"Do you truly hate it here so?" she asks instead. "I think the island is beautiful."

Harriet snorts. "Isn't it. Impossibly, disgustingly beautiful." She sips her drink, leaning back against the table. "It's the quiet I don't like. Too much space to think. In London, I've my circle of other artists, and I don't have to pause and look too closely at the way of things."

"What do you mean? What things?"

Harriet stares towards the window, though the drawn curtains prevent her from looking out. "Do you ever feel as though you were made for entirely the wrong thing?"

"I'm not sure what I was made for. I seem to be of little use to anyone." The moment she has spoken the words, Eva regrets her self-indulgence. Harriet glides right past it.

"I'm a terrible wife. A terrible mother. And yet those are the things the world sees me as."

"You are not a terrible mother," says Eva.

Harriet lets out a cold laugh. She tosses back the last of the liquor and refills her glass. "I thought when Thomas was born, I would be drawn to him," she says. "But I wasn't. I'm not. He feels like someone else's child. Like a stranger. Edwin too, sometimes." Too lightly, she says, "It's terribly lonely."

Eva hesitates. Harriet is rarely so open with her, and she knows she cannot let the moment pass without comment. But what can she offer beyond empty platitudes and consolation? She knows nothing of being a wife. Nothing of being a mother. And nothing of being as capricious and flighty as Harriet.

Before she can open her mouth, faint footfalls sound outside the house.

Harriet darts to the window. She peeks through the curtain and gasps. "He's here."

"Who's here?" Eva is on her feet, jostling her sister at the window. Through the glass, she sees nothing but darkness.

"The prowler," says Harriet. "He's been coming for weeks now." She sounds oddly close to excitement. "I've gone out to try and catch him once or twice, but he always manages to disappear. It's the strangest thing."

Eva's eyes widen. "Are you mad? There has been a prowler coming to the house for weeks? Did you not think to tell anyone?"

Harriet rolls her eyes. "Don't be so dramatic."

Eva snatches her arm as she darts towards the door. "You can't go out there. We have no idea who they are, or how dangerous they might be." She shakes her head, hardly able to believe her sister's apathy. Does she truly not understand the danger this family is in? She squeezes her wrist. "Please, Harriet."

As though catching hold of the seriousness in her eyes, Harriet gives a resigned nod. "Very well. I'll fetch Edwin. Tell him to get his pistol."

CHAPTER TWENTY-FIVE

Nathan has just climbed into bed when he hears the thud of footsteps down the passage. He hears Harriet open the door across the hall and hiss her husband's name.

"Come quickly," says Eva.

Nathan slides out of bed and snatches his breeches from the chair in the corner of the room. He steps out into the passage. "Is something the matter?" Eva is barefooted, with a blanket wrapped around her body and her dark hair hanging loose. Harriet is still dressed, a heavy shawl at her shoulders and a look of excitement in her eyes.

"There's a man outside the house," says Eva. "Creeping around in the dark."

Edwin emerges from the bedroom tugging on his jacket, his pistol in his hand.

The two men are out of the house in moments. The night is clear and still, an explosion of stars. The sea sighs steadily against the invisible beach.

Nathan looks back at his sisters, huddled in the doorway. "Which way did he go?"

"Harriet saw him pass her workroom," says Eva. "I've no idea where he went after that."

He grips the pistol he had taken from the bottom drawer of his desk. A lantern sways in his other fist. The moon is bright, lighting the arc of the dunes. He moves around the house to the left; Edwin to the right.

Nathan strides past Harriet's workroom. "Who's there?" he calls. "Show yourself." The knot in his stomach tightens.

Movement in the dunes, but the light catches only the fleeing shape of a deer. Nathan completes his circle of the house, meeting Edwin back at the front door. He shakes his head in response to the wordless question.

"Perhaps you were imagining things," Nathan tells Harriet.

She lets out her breath indignantly. "Is that really what you think?"

"It's not the first time she's seen him," Eva puts in.

"What?" Edwin demands.

Harriet glares at her sister. She sighs, folding her arms across her chest. "He's been coming regularly. Ever since we moved in."

"And you did not think to tell us earlier?"

"Perhaps we might save the lecture for later, Edwin? He must be around here somewhere. Perhaps you ought to find him."

The pool of light from Nathan's lantern skims across the dirt path in front of the house. It's flecked with footsteps; his and Edwin's yes, but perhaps another set as well. He follows the faint trail around the corner. It leads up to the wall of the house, he realises. No, not to the wall. To the drain leading out from the kitchen.

He crouches, pulling away the grate blocking the mouth of the drain. It's impossible. Although the drain is wide here, at its other end it is nothing but a narrow pipe leading out from the trough in the kitchen. Certainly not big enough for anyone to fit inside.

Edwin crouches beside him. Leans forward to shine his lamp into the hole. "This is big enough for someone to get inside, Nate," he says.

"No. It's just the drain. Leading down from the trough. No one could—"

"Just look."

And so he does. Kneels forward, eyes to the ground, hot light scorching his cheek as he shines the lamp into the dark opening. There is the narrow pipe leading up towards the kitchen. But branching off from it in the other direction is a wider tunnel, big enough for a man to fit through. Leading—where? Somewhere inside the house?

Nathan's stomach rolls. He thinks of his daughter, asleep upstairs with a prowler on the loose. His eyes drift upward. He is right beneath his bedroom window, he realises. Right below where Theodora is sleeping.

Men in the walls…

Had she seen the prowler slip in through the grate? Disappear into the walls of Highfield House?

"I'm going in," says Edwin. "Are you coming?"

The thought of it is horrifying, of course. It's every vile piece of Oliver's twisted games. But the alternative—doing nothing—is far worse.

He glances over his shoulder. His sisters have followed them to the grate. Eva wears a deep frown, while Harriet watches with a look of detached fascination.

"You go first," Nathan tells Edwin. "I'll follow."

On hands and knees, Nathan shuffles into the tunnel, clinging to his lamp as though it might save him from drowning in the darkness. The pistol in his pocket presses against his hip.

He sees at once that this tunnel is not new. Nor has it been hastily built by whoever has been creeping into their house these past weeks. Worn wood panelling shores the walls, interspersed with smooth stone to keep the earth at bay. It is a part of the house, he realises; has always been a part of the house. Built, perhaps, by whoever had created the priest hole.

Nathan shuffles deeper into the passage, loose earth grazing his palms. Is he under the ground? Or within the walls of the house? He is not sure which is more disconcerting. After what could be no more than ten or fifteen yards, Nathan hears:

"There's a ladder."

Ahead of him, he sees Edwin wriggle out of the tunnel, his feet disappearing upwards. The ladder is narrow, rough-hewn wood. It leads up between the outer stone wall of the house, and the wooden panelling of the internal walls. Nathan steps onto it tentatively, hearing it groan beneath his weight.

The ladder stops on the second storey. He and Edwin are crammed into a narrow space, with a stone wall on one side and wood panelling on three others. A sour stench thickens the air. Beneath their feet are the same worn floorboards Nathan recognises from Oliver's room. But this is not the priest hole. This space is tall enough to stand in. And even as a terrified child, Nathan knows he would have remembered seeing a ladder that led down into the walls of the house.

Edwin shines his lamp up to one of the internal walls. "Look at this."

The panelling is slightly crooked. He pushes against it. The wall groans and shifts beneath his weight. And it swings open, revealing the priest hole beside it.

"A double-barrel priest hole," Nathan murmurs. He has heard of such things before; a hiding place within a hiding place; an extra layer of protection against the priest hunters. And in this elaborate system: a way to escape the confines of the house. He would almost be fascinated if he had not just followed a prowler up here.

Nathan crawls into the priest hole, then out into Oliver's room, fingers tightening around the pistol. He tries the door. Locked from the outside, as he had left it earlier that night.

"The prowler," he says, "he must be in this room. There's no way for him to get out into the house."

"He's not in that room, Nate," Edwin calls to him from within the hole. "He's up here."

He is shining the lamp up towards the thick beams of the attic. Faint footholds have been scraped into the stone wall, and in the pale light of the lantern, Nathan sees the loose boards in the ceiling, allowing access to the roof space.

He sets the lamp at his feet and grabs at the footholds. The stones are worn enough to give him purchase, and he hauls himself up towards the attic.

He realises then that he is not climbing into blackness. Not entirely. There is a faint, fragile light up here, as though from a single candle. And that smell; that acrid, animal stench he had sensed the night of the storm, it's more potent with every step.

He heaves his body through the gap in the roof, the splintered boards scraping his arms through his shirt. And as he spills out onto the floor, he freezes. Crammed into the attic space are two men. And one woman, her coils of red hair spilling out the side of the scarf tied around her head.

Julia Mitchell.

She is dressed in breeches and a man's greatcoat that hangs ridiculously from her narrow shoulders. Their prowler.

At the sight of Nathan, she backs away, as far from him as she can get, before the pitch of the roof prevents her from going further.

Nathan stares in disbelief. In the light of the candle spluttering in one corner, he sees two blankets laid out across the floor, a large waterskin and a loaf of bread beside them.

The two men have the same shock of red hair as Julia. Their beards are long and unkempt, and the stench of human waste rises from a wooden bucket in the corner.

Nathan looks from Julia to the men, then down to the food and water sitting between the blankets. She has been making regular visits, he realises, to keep her brothers fed and watered while they hide away in Highfield House. Anger stirs inside him. He feels utterly betrayed.

The boards creak as Edwin emerges into the attic. Nathan hears him curse under his breath.

"I'm so sorry, Mr Blake," Julia gushes. "Please let me explain."

Nathan swallows heavily. "How long…?"

"A few months," Julia says, her voice low. "My brothers, they're in trouble with the law. They needed somewhere to hide. When we first came here, the house was empty. We had no idea your family was coming back."

A few months…

"Leave," he grinds out. "This second."

"Please, Mr Blake," says one of her brothers, "we've nowhere to go."

Nathan laughs coldly. "Nowhere to go? Your sister has a fine shopfront on Church Lane that I'm sure she could cram you into."

"No," Julia says. "They can't. They—" She stops speaking suddenly, then gives a nod of resignation, half directed at Nathan, half at her brothers. The two men begin to gather up the waterskin and bread.

"Leave it all," hisses Nathan. "Just get the hell out of my house."

Neither man argues. With their blankets tucked under their arms, they head for the hole in the roof, stepping past Nathan with looks of wordless apology. Nathan watches them disappear into the blackness below. "Go after them," he tells Edwin. "See that they leave."

As though taken aback by Nathan's uncharacteristic sharpness, Edwin doesn't argue. He follows the two men to the hole in the roof and climbs back down into the tunnel.

When Nathan tears his gaze away, Julia is watching him with wide mournful eyes.

"I meant for you to leave too," he tells her sharply. His heart is thudding and his skin is hot with anger. To think he had let his guard down around her. And to think he had felt guilty over the secrets he is keeping from her. How laughable that seems now.

"The passage," he says tautly. "How did you know of it?"

"The Jacobites have been using the house as a meeting place for years," she murmurs. "We know every inch of it."

Nathan lets out a cold laugh. How fitting, he thinks, that the people of Holy Island might know this house better than he does. He doesn't look at her. "And your brothers?"

Julia lets out a breath. "They left for the West Country a few months ago to join the Duke of Ormonde's Jacobite army. I begged them not to go." She starts pacing across the attic, tugging at the hem of her oversized coat. "The fools barely made it out of Northumberland before they got themselves in trouble. Got into a fight with the redcoats at a protest in York. One of the soldiers was shot. My brothers only just got away."

Nathan's anger flares. Rage spills out; rage he has always forced himself to keep inside. It tears through him, making him unable to see straight. "How dare you? Do you have any idea… There are children in this house!" He snatches the waterskin from the floor and hurls it across the room. "Not only do you dare to bring violent men into my home, you have the audacity to befriend us in the process?" It's not just rage at Julia now, he realises. It's rage at the manufacturer who had deceived him; rage at damn Matthew Walton for the way he has treated this family; rage at God for taking his wife. He feels it pour off his body in waves. Letting it out feels oddly cathartic.

"My brothers would never hurt you!" Julia cries. "They are not violent men! They're just fools who got caught up in all this madness." Her tears spill suddenly and she shoves them away with the back of her hand. "They thought they were doing the right thing. They swear the soldier's death was an accident. They were just defending themselves. If they're caught, they'll hang. And you saw the way they look—they are hardly capable of blending into a crowd.

"The house was empty when we moved them in here," she says. "I never expected you and your family to come back. You've been away from the place for twenty years." She begins to pace. "Do you truly think I liked creeping into your house night after night, bringing enough food to keep them alive? All the while, making friends with Harriet? And... coming to know you too?"

Nathan turns away uncomfortably. Her words just remind him of how much of a fool he has been. "Your brothers are easy targets here in the house," he snaps. "Anyone comes looking and they'll be found at once."

She looks at him pointedly. "It took you more than two months to find them."

Nathan smacks an angry hand against the wall. He hates that she is right. "If you want them to be safe, they need to get off Holy Island. It's far too small a place to hide. They'll be safer hidden away in London." There is no warmth in his voice. None of the compassion he is so used to forcing.

"Do you truly think I don't know that?" Julia wraps her arms around herself and stares at her muddy boots. "I have a third brother," she says, voice low. "Hugh. He was with Michael and Angus at the protest. In the fight. They got split up when the dragoons came after them. The two of them made it back to Holy Island. But they've no idea what happened to Hugh." She draws in a breath. "They refuse to go to London without him. Once they leave, I know we'll not be able to write each other. Not while things are so unsettled at least." Her voice wavers slightly. "It's too dangerous. If the letters were intercepted, my son and I would be in danger. Michael and Angus know that if they leave for London now, they'll likely never see Hugh again."

Nathan folds his arms. The story would be far more pitiable if she hadn't been deceiving him all this time. "They cannot stay here," he says firmly. "I'm sorry."

Julia looks up at him with pleading eyes. "Might they at least stay until I find somewhere else for them? I swear to you they'll do no harm to any of your family."

"Are you truly asking me such a thing?" Nathan demands. "After the way you deceived me? Deceived all of us?"

"I know it's wrong," she says. "I really do. But I'm desperate. Please, Mr Blake. I'm begging you."

For a moment, the rage falters. For a moment, he wavers. But no. He can't. Cannot let this woman take another inch. "I want you out of the house immediately."

CHAPTER TWENTY-SIX

Harriet lifts her face to the sky. It is a pleasure to be out of the house, away from Thomas's tears and Eva's sulkiness and the background dread that has settled over the place since they discovered Julia's brothers hiding in the attic.

Edwin had had firm words for her after learning she had kept the prowler's visits to herself for so long. And Nathan, well, he seems to be carrying around decades of repressed anger in his eyes, skulking around the place with barely more than a grunt for anyone. This morning he had yelled at Theodora for knocking over the milk jug. She had sat silent and tearful through the rest of breakfast, that eerie beast of a doll in her lap.

Harriet has been waiting for Edwin and Nathan to leave for the mainland all morning, so she might slip away to visit Julia at the curiosity shop.

She supposes she ought to be outraged at Julia too. But in truth, she had imagined far worse things for that prowler to be. Had imagined it might be Martin Macauley, or an armed Jacobite, or—when she is at her most sleepless—a ghost vanishing into the dunes.

She pushes open the door of the shop. The bell tinkles and Julia looks up from behind the counter. When she sees Harriet, she flashes a desperately apologetic half-smile.

"Have you come here to tear me to pieces?" she asks. "I know I deserve it."

Harriet shrugs. "I've come for tea. If you're making it."

Surprise passes over Julia's face. "I can make tea. Will you watch the shop a moment? Just make sure no one comes in and pockets anything."

Harriet nods and Julia disappears upstairs into the living quarters. Harriet glides through the shop, scanning the cluttered shelves, without taking anything in. Julia's cat brushes against her legs and she bends down to scratch its ears.

Julia returns with a teacup in each hand. She sets them on the counter and pulls up the chairs.

"I saw you from my workroom," says Harriet. "I wondered if perhaps you were a ghost."

Julia gives a short laugh, then her eyes grow serious. "How angry is your family?" she asks, hands interlaced around her cup.

Harriet shrugs. "Nathan is steaming. But it will pass."

Julia nods, eyes down.

"Don't look so sad," says Harriet. "It could well be the best thing that's ever happened to him. Will do him good to get a little of that anger out of his blood."

Julia smiles half-heartedly. "Must be something right special about me to have been the one to get the anger out of him."

Harriet smiles to herself. Julia is right, of course. Nathan clearly does see something special in her. Not that he would ever admit it.

"What about your husband?" asks Julia. "Is he wild with rage too?"

"More at me than you," Harriet says. "And Eva, well, I think the only thing she has on her mind is that rogue from Longstone."

"Longstone?" Julia repeats. "Finn Murray?"

Harriet nods, rattling swiftly through the drama that is Eva's tryst with the lightkeeper. She is surprised Julia had not heard of it earlier.

Julia raises her eyebrows. "Interesting. From what I know of Mr Murray, I didn't imagine he'd welcome anyone onto his island."

Harriet drops her voice, though they are the only ones in the shop. "Are your brothers here with you?" She's had enough of Eva's woes of late; has no desire to rehash them with Julia.

"They're down in the cellar. But they can't stay here. It's not safe. We know there are spies on the island. But we've no idea who they are. If the wrong people were to find out Michael and Angus are here…" She trails off. "Their only choice may be to go to London. Lose themselves in the city."

"Nathan tells me they are waiting for your other brother to return."

She sighs heavily. "It's no good them waiting for Hugh if they're caught in the process." She picks at something beneath her fingernail. "And honestly, with every day that passes, I feel less and less confident that Hugh is going to return home at all. It's been months. I know there's a chance he may have gone on to the West Country alone. When he left, he was determined to fight with the rebels. But surely if that were the case, we would have heard from him by now. He would have written to let me know he is safe." Her voice wavers.

Harriet reaches over and squeezes her wrist. "Let me speak to Nathan. He—"

"No," Julia cuts in. "Please don't. It's far too much to ask."

"He's fond of you. I can tell."

Julia smiles wryly. "I doubt he is any longer."

They sit in silence for several moments. The cat leaps onto the counter and circles the teacups.

Julia sighs. "Harriet… I truly am sorry for what I did. I never meant to hurt you or your family."

Harriet shakes her head airily. "You did what you had to do."

"You're not angry with me?"

Somewhere in the back of her mind, Harriet knows she ought to be. Knows that, in many ways, what Julia has done could—should—be considered a betrayal. But she can't find the energy to be angry. Or really, to care.

Has she always felt like this? So empty and detached? She can't seem to make herself care about anything except her art these days, not even her child. Or strangers walking within the walls of her house. That will change, she tells herself. When she returns to London and her artist friends. When her life is bigger than this thread of an island and she leaves the house behind.

Longstone feels empty without her. Particularly now he knows she'll likely never set foot on this island again.

The duffel bag Eva had arrived with is still tucked away in a corner of the cottage. Her tin of tea is still on the mantel. Her skirts hanging over the end of her bed.

Every time he sees them, Finn is back at the inn in Bamburgh, feeling her lips against his own. Seeing the hurt in her eyes when he had pulled away.

Taking a room with her was bound to lead to trouble, of course. There had not been a second that he'd doubted that. But letting her stay in the dormitory had not felt like an option. Not with armed men brawling outside and a shattered window littering the floor.

He has never felt like this about anyone before. Why did it have to be a woman from that cursed house? That cursed family? Fate certainly has a way of playing tricks.

The daylight is beginning to drain away. He can hear seals barking on a nearby island. He trudges outside to light the firebasket. Tonight, it feels like a chore. Tonight, he is feeling the weight of the responsibility he has shouldered. Tonight, he would rather be anywhere else.

The shovel in his hand, he glances out to sea, then looks away quickly. He keeps his back to the water as he builds the fire in the basket and strikes the tinderbox.

It's not just Eva that is making him so unsettled. It's the knowledge that Henry Ward is back in Northumbria, sailing the *Eagle* far too close to Longstone. For reasons that Finn does not dare think about.

There has always been a part of him that has been afraid of Ward returning. Afraid of being dealt a long-overdue punishment for the mistakes he had made as a young and foolish cabin boy.

A big part of him wants nothing more than to leave Longstone. Climb into his skiff and disappear to some place where Henry Ward won't find him. But he can't do that.

Thanks to him, his father had died alone. Had not even had the dignity of a real burial. Lighting the firebasket feels like the least he can do for the father he had abandoned. The least he can do to make up for the time he had spent under Ward's tutelage. And for the terrible mistakes it had led to.

Finn heaves on the firebasket chain, sending the spitting brazier into the sky. He keeps his eyes on the flames, avoids looking out to sea.

What is Ward doing in these parts? Yes, he had always had an affinity with Holy Island, but that was back when Abigail Blake had owned Highfield House. Finn had been surprised to see him still sailing the *Eagle*. The fragile peace against the French means there is little cause for privateers in these waters. Perhaps it's the Rising that has brought him north; perhaps he imagines there will be a place for privateers if the Jacobite army takes up arms.

Finn's logical side knows, of course, that Ward is not here looking for him. It does not make sense for him to do that after so many years. Besides, there is no way, surely, that his old captain would have recognised him in the tavern, or in the street in Bamburgh. Finn had been a child the last time they had seen each other. He tells himself again, trying to make himself believe it. Because that morning at the beach, he had seen a glimmer in Ward's eye that had looked far too close to recognition.

He looks out to sea, daring to scan the horizon for the *Eagle*.

There is no sign of Ward's ship. But the ocean is not empty. A small fishing dory is headed directly for Longstone, as if drawn towards the light.

For a brief, foolish moment, his heart leaps at the possibility. Eva. He quashes it quickly. Even if Eva did have any desire to see him, which he is sure she does not, she would never find someone willing to undertake this treacherous sailing so close to dark.

He stands on the jetty with his arms folded, watching the boat approach. Two men and a woman. Not Eva.

One of the men brings the vessel up alongside the jetty. The woman gathers her skirts and leaps out, without waiting for assistance. Her face is pink with cold, and loose red curls blow around her cheeks.

"I'm a friend of the Blakes," she says. "And my brothers need a place to hide."

CHAPTER TWENTY-SEVEN

Eva narrows her eyes at her reflection as she runs a comb through her hair. In the morning light, the shadows under her eyes are horribly pronounced. She tells herself her sleeplessness is simply her body readjusting after three weeks of nocturnal life. But she knows it has more to do with the thoughts of Finn Murray that have been circling around her head without pause since she returned from Longstone. She does not like who this ordeal has turned her into. Since when is she the kind of woman who lets herself be so upturned by a man?

Had she looked into this mirror as a child too? Stood on the bed to see her tiny self, sharp-eyed and serious beyond her years? And had she had stood at the window and looked out towards the Farne Islands? Watched that flame come to life on the horizon as the sun slid into the water?

She tries to shake the thought away, but it lingers. She flings the comb onto her bed and marches across the room to yank closed the curtains. Can't help but pause there for a second, squinting into the hazy light. The crack in the window seems to have widened, and the view of the Farnes feels oddly distorted.

"I must say, Evie," says Harriet, appearing in the doorway, "you've been spending an awful lot of time at that window."

Eva lets the curtain fall hurriedly, her cheeks colouring. She turns to face Harriet's smug expression. Eva opens her mouth to speak, but decides against it. She has no desire to explain herself to her little sister. She feels like enough of a fool as it is.

"The lightkeeper?" says Harriet with a smirk. "Truly?" She is still dressed in her robe and nightgown.

Eva plants her hands on her hips. "And what do you know of him, Harriet?" she snaps.

Harriet's self-satisfied expression doesn't falter. "I know that Nathan will never allow it."

Eva looks down. "There's nothing to allow. Believe me."

Harriet perches on the edge of the bed, placing the discarded comb on the nightstand. "You ought to have gone over there with Julia. Paid him a visit."

Eva frowns. "What do you mean?"

"I thought you knew," Harriet says airily, in a tone that suggests she knew Eva was completely unaware. "I told her of your little dalliance with the lightkeeper, and she decided Longstone was the perfect place for her brothers to hide while they wait for Hugh to show himself."

As she races into the village, Eva's anger burns away her hatred of conflict. She will confront Julia Mitchell for her deviousness, and she will demand she go back to Longstone to collect her brothers, and she will do it all without getting so damn shaky and flustered.

Eva has had a crawling sensation under her skin ever they had discovered Julia's brothers hiding in the attic. The thought of those men creeping around their house had been bad enough. And now Julia has the nerve to foist them onto Longstone?

"Ah," says Julia, when Eva blusters through the front door of the curiosity shop. "I suppose Harriet told you of my plans. And I suppose you don't approve of them." Her eyes are lowered with shame, but somehow that makes it worse. As though she is well aware of the damage she is doing, but has decided to do it anyway.

"Plans?" Eva spits. "It sounds as though they're already well in motion."

Julia comes out from behind the counter and looks up to meet Eva's eyes. "I'm sorry. Truly."

Eva folds her arms. "Is that how you always operate? Do as you wish, then beg forgiveness afterwards?"

Julia glances over Eva's shoulder, as if to check there are no customers approaching. "I had no choice but to take my brothers to Longstone." Her voice is a murmur. "They are in grave danger."

"Yes," Eva hisses. "I gathered that when we found them hiding in our roof." She feels her skin growing hot. Ignores it. "What if the authorities had found them in the house? We would have been implicated. You put my family in danger. And now you're putting Mr Murray in danger too."

Julia nods. "You're right, of course. And I truly am sorry. But would you not do the same for your brother and sister?"

Eva grits her teeth. She has no idea what she would do if she were in such a situation. But she knows it is of little consequence. "Do you know how to sail?" she asks Julia instead.

"Yes, but—"

"Take me to Longstone," she demands. "I need to see Finn."

CHAPTER TWENTY-EIGHT

Julia doesn't argue. At Eva's demand, she locks up the shop and heads wordlessly for the harbour.

Eva's heart is quick as she follows close behind. She is nervous about seeing Finn. They had parted on such bitter terms, and her anger at him has not faded. Nor has her desire for him. But that is not what this is about, she reminds herself. Somehow, Finn has got caught up in business that was not his; business that could put him in danger. She needs to apologise; on Julia's behalf, and on her own. And she needs to convince Julia and her brothers to get the hell away from Longstone. She knows it is only because of her dealings with Finn that Julia even thought to dump her brothers on his island. Once again, she feels horribly responsible for the danger he is in.

When they reach the water, Julia nods to a tiny dinghy tied up to the jetty. "Get in. My brothers' fishing boat is out there." She points to a small sailboat in the middle of the anchorage.

She rows them out to it and ropes the dinghy to the stern. She knots her skirts at her calves, then climbs expertly onto the larger boat. Eva clambers up the ladder, ignoring Julia's offer of assistance.

They don't speak again until Longstone is in sight.

"I asked his permission, you know," says Julia, handing in the sail as they approach the island. "I did not just dump them there."

Eva doesn't respond. She has no idea whether Julia is telling the truth. Her eyes are fixed to the thin silhouette of the unlit firebasket and she is hit with a pang of longing. Perhaps coming here was a mistake. She knows she has little chance of convincing the Mitchells to leave the island. In the back of her mind, she knows it is her desperately missing Finn that has brought her here. And her hollow hope that things might be different. That this time he might beg her forgiveness and ask her to stay. She shoves the thoughts away.

They have not come unnoticed. As Julia eases the boat towards the jetty, Finn is already striding towards them, reminding Eva that little that happens here escapes his notice. But he halts in his step as he gets closer, perhaps noticing her for the first time. His pale brown hair is loose on his shoulders and blows across his cheek in the wind.

Eva swallows heavily. Tries to ignore the way her stomach flips at the sight of him. She climbs out of the boat and strides deliberately in his direction. "Julia Mitchell's brothers are here?" she asks.

A look of surprise flickers over Finn's face. "Aye. They're inside. Is that why you're here? I…" His face softens slightly, and she sees that same gentle look of concern she had seen the day of the riots in Bamburgh. Behind her, she hears Julia's footsteps disappearing towards the cottage. Eva is grateful for the privacy.

"I'm sorry, Finn," she says, her voice low. "I had no idea she was going to do this. But it's my fault. She only thought to come here because she knew I'd spent time with you."

Finn tilts his head, looking at her intently. "You blame yourself for a lot of things, Eva. Very few of them are your fault."

She feels his eyes on her, searching her face. She looks down, gaze fixed on her feet.

After a moment of silence, Finn says, "Don't worry yourself over the Mitchells. If they need to stay here a while to keep their necks unbroken, they can do so."

"What if the authorities come looking? You'll be seen to be harbouring Jacobite criminals."

"No one will come looking out here. Besides," he smiles crookedly, "I've got them taking the midnight watch while I'm sleeping away the night in your room." He falters. "The bedroom, rather."

Eva swallows hard. "Did she ask your permission at the very least?"

He shrugs. "In a way, I suppose. At least, she thanked me once they were here."

She lets out an angry breath. "That woman. I can hardly believe her insolence."

Finn chuckles. "Watch that vulgar tongue of yours, Miss Blake. It will get you into trouble."

Eva finds herself smiling slightly. In a strange sort of way, she has missed his mockery. "How are you?" she asks finally. "Has your wound healed?"

"Almost. The figwort is good for it. Turns out you were right. Imagine that." Finn holds her gaze for a long second, and she feels her chest tighten. He shifts slightly; moves towards her, then stops, as though thinking better of it. "Take care, aye?" he says thickly. "Things are only going to get more unsettled. Especially in this part of the country."

She nods. Tugs her cloak around herself as cold wind whips up off the water. She glances at the cottage. Julia and her brothers are speaking in the doorway. "We ought to leave. That is, if you are all right with all this…"

Finn nods shortly. "Thank you. For everything. I know I've never said that before."

Eva closes her eyes. How can he show such kindness to her in one breath, and be so cold and dismissive the next? She swallows a lump in her throat. Turns and marches back to the boat so she doesn't have to respond.

Finn goes back to the cottage, unable to watch her leave. He can't shake the thought that he will never see her again. For the best, he tells himself. Even if there wasn't this great secret keeping them apart, he knows a man like him does not belong with a woman like her. Eva Blake is an educated, genteel lady; and him, well he's like something the tide dragged in.

The Mitchells have been into the whisky; have pulled three tin mugs from the sideboard that Finn hasn't seen in years. Michael fills a cup for him and nudges it across the table. "Drink up, man. You look as though you need it."

And yes, he does need it, because there on the floor beside the sideboard is Eva's duffel bag. He ought to have reminded her of it. What will he do with it now? He cannot throw her things away. But nor can he bear the sight of it. He tosses the whisky back in a single gulp. Holds the cup out to Michael for another.

When dusk falls over the island, he goes out to the firebasket and sets the beacon simmering. He sits on the rock beside it for a long time, staring out over the leathery water, feeling the warmth of the flames on the back of his neck.

He can hear dull chatter coming from inside the cottage. Can hear the clatter of dishes, the thud of the sideboard door. It's far too crowded in the house with these strangers.

He stays on the edge of the island until the dark is thick and stars are glittering between clouds. And there is more light, out on the water. Moving; another vessel, but bigger this time, than the fishing boat Eva and the Mitchells' sister had arrived in. Finn stands, squinting out at the light. It's close; too close. No vessels come this close to the Farnes unless they are in trouble.

Finn watches the wooden eagle emerge from the dark. His blood pumps hard, hot with whisky and dread. And he knows the time has arrived when he can no longer outrun the past.

CHAPTER TWENTY-NINE

It is long dark when the rap of the knocker echoes through Highfield House. Nathan hears Mrs Brodie's footsteps clicking down the passage.

Eva looks at him from where she is seated on the other side of the parlour. "Are you expecting someone?"

Nathan can see the apprehension in her eyes. He is also well aware that the book in her lap has been open to the same page for at least twenty minutes. "No," he says, getting to his feet. "I'm not expecting anyone."

He finds Joseph Holland at the door, hands dug into the pockets of his greatcoat and a woollen cap covering his bristled head. When she sees Nathan approach, Mrs Brodie bobs her head and disappears back towards her living quarters.

"May I come in?" asks Holland.

Nathan swallows. Tries for a friendly smile. "Of course." He steps back, allowing the man into the house.

Holland's eyes roam the foyer, taking in the faded paintings with curiosity. "Is your sister here? Miss Eva?"

The knot in Nathan's stomach grows a little tighter. "She is. May I ask what you wish to speak with her about?"

"I imagine you know the answer to that question."

Nathan keeps his expression level. "No. I'm not sure I do." Has Holland come on Martin Macauley's bidding? What conclusions have they drawn? Sweat prickles his neck as he gestures down the hallway. "We can speak in the parlour."

Holland follows him down the passage, his boots clicking loudly on the flagstones. Nathan feels like a prisoner walking to the gallows. Deny everything, he thinks. Surely they have no proof of Eva's involvement in Donald Macauley's death. How could they?

When they arrive in the parlour, Eva is already on her feet. Her hands are knotted and her face is pale. She looks painfully guilty.

Nathan clears his throat. "Eva. This is Joseph Holland. I'm not sure the two of you have met."

Holland nods a greeting, and Nathan ushers him towards the armchair in the corner of the room. He ought to offer tea, of course, or whisky. But he just wants this man gone.

"I'll be frank, Mr Blake," Holland begins. "There are suspicions. Regarding your sister and the night of Donald Macauley's death."

Nathan glances at Eva. She is perched back on the edge of her armchair, her hands folded tightly in her lap. Her face is stony, but she does not speak. Nathan looks squarely at Holland, hoping he cannot hear how hard his heart is thudding.

"The night of Mr Macauley's death, Eva was in Beal, caught by the tide."

"Aye, I know the story." Holland slides forward in his chair and pulls a folded page from the pocket of his coat. He shifts his attention to Eva. "It is not up to me to judge you, Miss Blake. But the matter stands that Donald's son, and many of the other villagers, believe you had something to do with the man's disappearance."

Eva's knuckles whiten. "Is that so?"

Holland places the page on the tea table in front of them.

Nathan frowns. "What is that?"

"It's a written statement from the innkeeper at the tavern in Beal, stating Miss Blake was indeed lodging at his tavern on the night in question. Along with a copy of his ledgers containing her name."

Eva flinches, catches Nathan's eye. This statement, it's a lie, of course. Is Holland aware of this?

Clearly aware of his confusion, Holland spears Nathan's gaze with his own. "The innkeeper in Beal is a staunch supporter of King George and the government," he says. "He is determined to quell another Jacobite Rising. As are many of us on this island."

Nathan raises his eyebrows. He had expected Holland's sympathies to align with Martin Macauley and the other Jacobites.

"I went to him and told him of the situation," Holland continues, "and he agreed to provide this document. A document which, if presented to the authorities—and Martin Macauley—will clear Miss Blake of all wrongdoing."

Nathan swaps glances with Eva. Why does this feel like a trap?

"What do you want for it?" Eva blurts.

Holland turns to her. He does not look surprised by her outburst. "We want use of Highfield House," he says bluntly. "As a delivery point for messages between the government spies across Northumbria. We know Lindisfarne is an important site for the Jacobites. It's a fine vantage point to see vessels approaching from Scotland. We suspect they have eyes on the castle, and we need a secure rendezvous point on the island." He glances at Eva, before looking back at Nathan. "With the restoration of the house taking place, no one will be suspicious of people coming and going. The messengers can disguise themselves as workers."

Nathan's skin feels hot. The last thing he wants to do is get involved with the chaos that is beginning to sweep the country again. He has far too much to concern himself with, without entangling himself in these poisonous politics. But what choice do they have? The islanders have been suspicious of this family since they set foot back on Holy Island. He knows it is only a matter of time before the net closes completely around Eva. Agree to this and they will—rightly or wrongly—clear her name.

"This house is well known to the Jacobites," Nathan tells Holland. "They were using it for their own purposes until very recently." He does not dare speak Julia Mitchell's name. In spite of all she has done, he cannot risk putting her and her son in the line of enquiry of Holland and the other government spies.

"We are well aware of that," says Holland. "But I trust that activity ended when your family returned."

"Yes," Nathan says thinly. "Of course it did."

He sees the irony of this. It was the villagers' belief that his family were government spies that had led them to this position in the first place. And now here is an actual spy providing them with a way out. Or perhaps it is a way in—to a place Nathan never wanted to go.

He can feel Eva trying to catch his eye. She knows, of course, of the stress he has been carrying. Of the huge weight that has been pressing down on him since they arrived on Holy Island. No doubt she has been feeling no less strain herself. And no doubt she is aware of the extra pressure it will place on him to have Highfield House used by government spies. He knows there is every chance she will refuse this way out, for his benefit.

"Mr Holland," she begins.

"You may use the house as you wish," Nathan cuts in, before Eva can finish. He snatches the innkeeper's statement from the table, his fist tightening around it. If he cannot see his sister into a secure and comfortable marriage, he will at least keep her from the scaffold. No matter what it costs him. He does not dare think about what would happen if Martin Macauley and the other staunch Jacobites discovered he is about to open his door to government spies. He tells himself Holland will not let that happen. It is in his best interests, of course, to ensure the secret is kept.

Unbidden, Nathan finds himself thinking of Julia. What would she, an active Jacobite, think if she discovered what Highfield House was about to be used for?

And then Nathan wonders why he cares.

He stands, ushering Holland towards the door. "I assume I shall be hearing from you?"

Holland nods once, briskly. "You shall."

And as the door closes behind him, Nathan is overwhelmed by something that is either relief or dread.

Holland has barely been gone ten minutes when there is a second knock at the door. Eva's shoulders tense. She knows she ought to feel relief that she might have escaped punishment over Donald Macauley's death. But she knows the last thing in the world Nathan wanted to do was get caught in the riptide of the Rising. Using Highfield House as a rendezvous point will plant them firmly against Martin Macauley and the other Jacobites on Holy Island.

Not that they weren't firmly planted against them already.

Nathan has not returned to the parlour since showing Holland out, and she hears his footsteps sound down the passage towards the door. Hears him murmur to whoever is on the other side. When he returns to the parlour, the frown on his face has deepened.

"Eva? Miss Mitchell's brothers are here. They need to speak with you. They say something has happened on Longstone."

CHAPTER THIRTY

Part of Henry Ward's game, Finn is sure, is to make him wait. Agonise. He must have been sitting here in the great cabin of the *Eagle* for at least an hour. Three of Ward's men had rowed their longboat up to the jetty on Longstone and ordered him aboard, pistols waving.

Ward's great cabin is painfully familiar, with its polished oak panelling and the ornate black lantern swaying above his head. A large wooden desk is tucked into a corner close to the curtained-off bed, books crammed into the shelf above. At the far end of the room, large windows look out over ink-black sea.

Ward's great cabin had always had a certain mystique about it—or perhaps that was the captain himself. In those days, Finn had seen him as a hero. He had sat beside Ward at this table many times, learning to decipher maps and navigate by starlight; smoothing his clumsy reading and writing into something more fluent. He was forever in awe of him. Always desperate to do his best; to prove to Ward he had done the right thing by making him a part of his crew. His captain had filled a gap left by the father Finn had abandoned.

Finally, the door clicks open.

Henry Ward is just as Finn remembers him: wolf-eyed, clean-shaven and impossibly neat. His black justacorps is trimmed with silver, a row of matching buttons down his chest. A white cravat is knotted at his throat, his greying hair tied back and powdered neatly. Though twenty years have passed since they last stood face to face, Ward barely seems to have aged.

Of course, Finn cannot say the same for himself. He had been a child of eleven when he'd last seen the captain, on that fateful night in Highfield House. He had not for a second imagined he might be recognised. Perhaps the panicked glance he'd sent Ward's way in the Bamburgh tavern had been his undoing.

Ward's boots click rhythmically as he makes his way across the cabin. He opens a cupboard beneath his desk and produces a bottle of claret and two tin cups. He carries them to the table and sits opposite Finn. Looks him up and down, curious, taking in his adult form. Finn shifts uncomfortably under his scrutiny. He knows that, to Henry Ward, he is a source of great disappointment.

"You don't look surprised to see me." Ward uncorks the bottle and fills the cups. His voice is deep, smooth, just as Finn remembers.

"Why should I be surprised? You've been following me for days."

"I've not been following you. I came to these parts for other reasons. Though I must say, I was surprised to find you still here. I thought you would have fled Northumberland long ago." He nudges Finn's cup towards him. "You always said keeping the Longstone light was not enough for you. Was that not why you came to me in the first place?"

"Aye," says Finn. "I was a fool."

The corner of Ward's lips turn up. "I'm glad there's something we can both agree upon."

Finn's eyes drift around the great cabin. How many times had he knocked on the door with a message for Ward from one of the other officers, waiting breathlessly to be invited inside? "I'm surprised this ship is still sailing," he says. "It's peacetime. Just. The king has no cause for privateers. I never imagined you as a merchant captain."

"There is no cause for privateers," Ward agrees. "But a man can make his own fortune if he is bold enough. Willing to bend the rules a little."

Finn snorts. "Piracy. I thought you had more decency than that." The knowledge is uncomfortable. It suggests Henry Ward has given up on a little of his morality. And Finn knows that does not bode well for him.

Ward tilts his head. "Sometimes a man has no choice but to do things he never imagined himself doing."

A knock at the door interrupts and Ward's steward enters, carrying two plates. He sets one down in front of Finn. It is loaded with roast beef and gravy-slathered vegetables. He looks up at Ward with raised eyebrows. "Am I truly to eat with you?"

Ward lifts his cup towards Finn's. "It's been many years. Perhaps for old time's sake?"

"Before you hang me from your yardarm? That's why I'm here, aye? So you can hand out the punishment you think I deserve?"

Ward takes a sip and sets his cup back down. "Even the worst of men deserve to go out with a good meal in their belly." He nods at the steaming food. "I'm sure this is far better than most of the swill you make for yourself on Longstone." He slices his meat and pops a piece in his mouth. "Or have you a wife out there? Children?"

Finn turns his eyes downward. "No." He slices into the meat, but doesn't eat. "What are you doing back in Northumberland?"

"That's no business of yours."

He gives a short laugh. "You're to kill me, aren't you? Surely you can at least tell me why you've come back. Who am I going to tell? The devil?"

A second knock at the door makes Ward turn. "I'm sorry to interrupt you, Captain," says the steward. "The lookout has sighted another vessel. Looks to be a small dory. Two or three people aboard."

Ward gets to his feet and strides from the cabin, abandoning his meal. Finn hurries after him, the steward at his shoulder. The steward is familiar, Finn realises. Now grey-haired and narrow-faced, he has been serving the captain for two decades or more. He shows no sign of recognising Finn.

They follow Ward through the lamplit passages of the ship, Finn trailing a hand along the bulwark to steady himself. They break onto deck. Several men are clustered at the gunwale.

"Watch him," Ward murmurs to them. One of the crewmen grabs Finn's arms, wrenching them behind his back.

He glances down into the dark sea. The skiff is close to Ward's ship now, its lantern casting a faint pool of light over the water. This is his boat, Finn realises, taken from the jetty at Longstone. The realisation turns his stomach. Because there are the two Mitchell brothers, each pulling hard on an oar. And there is Eva with her jaw clenched in fear, taking in the barque with the eagle figurehead. Henry Ward looks down on her with blatant interest in his eyes.

This, Eva has no doubt, is by far the most foolish thing she has ever done in her life.

When the Mitchells had come to Highfield House, they had only come seeking information.

The men in the ship. Do you know who they are?

And Eva thought at once of the vessel in Bamburgh harbour with the eagle figurehead. The man in the tavern that Finn had refused to speak of. She knew it had to be the ship the Mitchells were speaking of. But what other information could she offer? Whatever his connection to the ship, Finn had been determined to keep it to himself.

The Mitchells had made to leave, promising to search for him.

"I'm coming with you." Eva had had no intention of not being involved. Apart from anything else, she has no idea whether Michael and Angus Mitchell are any more trustworthy than their sister. She had run upstairs to grab her cloak, then slipped out the door before Nathan could ask questions.

The ship had been easy enough to find, lamps aglow just a few miles east of Holy Island. The sailor who had taken Finn clearly has no interest in hiding. Perhaps he imagined no one would care enough to come after Finn. Eva knows that, a few weeks ago, he would have been right.

She looks up at the ship now; at the shadowed faces of the men staring down at them. Their only flimsy plan had been to approach in the dark and somehow make it aboard without being noticed. With the brightly lit vessel looming over them and men lined up at the rail, Eva sees now how fragile and foolish such a plan was. But the sight of Finn, alive and unharmed, steadies her a little.

The man she had seen in Bamburgh watches with folded arms as their skiff approaches. Whatever manner of ship this is, he is clearly the captain. And from the way he had taken Finn against his will, she doubts he is operating legally.

"Eva!" Finn shouts down at her. "What in hell are you doing? Get away from here!" One of the crewmen shoves him away from the gunwale.

The captain's eyes shift to Finn, then back down to her. In the lamplight shining down from the mast, she sees curiosity in his eyes. "Eva? Eva Blake?"

Her heart thunders. How does he know her name?

She does not respond. But her silence seems to tell the captain everything he needs to know. He turns to speak to a crewmate beside him, then a rope ladder appears over the side of the ship.

"Come aboard, Miss Blake," he says smoothly.

"Row away, Eva," yells Finn. "Don't come anywhere near him!"

"Closer," Eva tells the Mitchells. "Let me get aboard."

"Are you certain?"

"Yes."

Michael and Angus pull through the water. The skiff knocks against the side of the ship, close enough for Eva to grapple with the ladder. Angus passes her his pistol and she tucks it into the pocket inside her cloak. She reaches for the first rung. Her skirts tangling around her legs, she climbs carefully up the ladder. Feels it sway beneath her. She takes another step, feet grappling clumsily against the slippery hull of the ship. When she reaches the top, the captain holds out a hand to help her over the gunwale. Reluctantly, she takes it, scrambling onto the deck and hurriedly straightening her skirts.

Finn pins her with hard eyes. "I told you to leave," he says thickly. She meets his eyes, but doesn't speak.

The captain looks her up and down. "Eva Blake. You were a child last time I saw you." He takes a lamp from above the door of the forecastle and holds it to her face. The light is hot against her cheek. There's a faint smile on the captain's lips—an expression that almost seems warm. "You look just like your mother."

Eva darts a horrified glance at Finn, but his jaw is still set grimly, his face giving nothing away. She looks back at the captain. Up close he is painfully handsome, with a square, clean-shaven jaw and fierce blue eyes. There is something unsettling about his rugged, unnatural beauty. "How do you know my mother?" She hears the faint waver in her voice.

"Abigail was an acquaintance of mine. We met on Lindisfarne one day when she was in need of some assistance. I spent much time in these parts back when you were a lass." He gives her sympathetic eyes. "I was very sorry to hear of her passing."

"How do you know of that?"

"News travels." He glances over the gunwale at the Mitchells in the skiff, then turns to back to Eva. "Tell them to leave."

Her stomach tightens. They were her way back to safety. But the only other option is leaving Finn here alone. She cannot do that. Nor can she just walk away without learning what this man knows of her mother.

She leans over the gunwale. Calls down to the men, with instructions to leave. Yes, she is sure.

She turns away. Can't watch them go.

The captain nods to one of the crew, and without speaking, the man steps up to Eva and begins patting her down.

She stumbles back. "What do you think you're doing?"

"Calm yourself," says the captain. "No offense intended. It's merely a formality."

The crewman's roaming hands find the pistol in her cloak. He pulls it out, handing it to the captain.

"Why are you here, Miss Blake?" he asks, tucking the weapon into the pocket of his coat. "Surely you haven't come for Mr Murray."

Eva's eyes dart to Finn, then back to the captain. "What do you want with him?" She hears her voice rattle.

The captain gestures towards the forecastle. "We've a fine dinner on the table and it's getting cold. May I suggest we continue this conversation inside?" He puts a hand to the small of Eva's back, guiding her inside without waiting for a response. Finn follows close behind, a crewman at his shoulder.

The captain leads her down a lamplit passage towards the cabin in the stern of the ship. Filled wine glasses and two plates of food sit on the table in the centre of the room. They have barely been touched.

"Please." The captain gestures to the table. "Sit." His voice is warm. Unsettlingly so. He looks to his steward. "Have the cook bring a third plate." He turns back to Eva. "Forgive me. Henry Ward." He offers her his hand.

Eva accepts it warily, her eyes darting between the two men. She slides onto the bench at one side of the table. Finn sits opposite, not taking his eyes from her.

Ward takes a third cup from a cupboard below his desk and fills it for

Eva before taking his seat at the head of the table. He lifts his wine. "Well. To this unexpected pleasure."

Eva raises her glass uncertainly. She brings it to her lips and takes a miniscule sip. Finn's hand tightens around his cup. He doesn't drink.

"It's an honour to have you at my table, Miss Blake," says Ward. "The last time I saw you, you were a little lass running the hallways of Highfield House."

Eva hears her inhalation. "Why were you in my house?"

"Your mother invited me. Invited us."

"Us?" Eva coughs. Who is he referring to? Surely not to Finn. No, she tells herself. Impossible. She had left Highfield House at four years old; Finn could have hardly been older than ten or eleven. But when she looks back at Ward, and to the lowered, shameful eyes Finn is hiding, she sees all she needs to know. Her stomach rolls.

"Why?" she asks, her voice thin.

Ward sips his wine. "Abigail was a good woman. A kind woman. She was good enough to offer my crew hospitality whenever our voyages brought us back to Northumbria." He smiles. "She knew how much a sailor values a night on dry land every now and then. The comforts of a warm house."

Eva shakes her head. "My mother would not have let pirates into the house."

"I assure you, Miss Blake, the *Eagle* was operating completely legally. Under a letter of marque authorising us to attack the French. I'm sure Mr Murray will attest to that if you doubt me. He was a valuable member of my crew for a number of years." Ward smiles thinly. "I suppose I cannot be surprised that he has not told you any of this. I must say, I think your loyalty is somewhat misplaced, given you have come traipsing all the way out here to find him."

Finn looks at Ward, eyes blazing.

"Mr Murray is not one to speak of his past," Eva says thinly.

A plate of roast meat appears in front of her, making her stomach turn. Ward nods his thanks to the steward, then turns back to Eva. "Well. I'm sure his silence is understandable, given the circumstances of that night."

Eva's heart quickens. She hears her breathing come loud through her nose, disoriented by the captain's words, and the swaying light of the lantern above her head. She knows instinctively which night he is referring to. Can there be any other night than when her mother had pulled her children from their beds and they had gone tearing out across Holy Island?

But whatever Finn's role in their fleeing, she does not want to hear it from this self-important sea captain. She wants to hear it from Finn himself. And she wants him to look into her eyes as he tells her, so she knows he is telling her the truth.

"What do you want with me?" she asks the captain.

Ward smiles. "You came aboard my ship voluntarily, Miss Blake. I invited you here on account of our shared past. Our shared affection for your mother."

"So you will let me leave when I wish?"

"Of course."

"What about Finn?"

"That matter is more complicated."

"I see." Eva stares into her plate, trying to order her thoughts. She feels completely overwhelmed, unmoored by this new information. She cannot trust Ward; of that she is certain. As for Finn, she has no idea. She wants to trust him, desperately. But how can she do so when he has clearly been keeping so much from her?

"You were in Highfield House," she says to him, voice low. "With his crew."

Finn's knuckles whiten around his cup. "I was, aye."

She forces herself to breathe deeply. Glances between the two men. "Something made my mother flee the house. Did she leave that night?"

"That I do not know, Miss Blake," says Ward. "All I can tell you is that after that night, I never saw Abigail again."

"Why?" Eva pushes. "What happened?"

Ward glances at Finn. When he gets no reaction, he says, "Your brother died rather violently in the house, Miss Blake."

Eva frowns. "No. Oliver died of smallpox. That's what my mother always told me."

"Your mother was lying to you," says Ward. "To protect you, I suppose. That—"

"Stop," Finn says suddenly. "I need to be the one to tell her." His hands make fists, then he looks up at her squarely. "Your brother didn't die of smallpox, Eva. He died the night I was in the house with Ward's crew." He draws in a shaky breath. "He died by my hand."

CHAPTER THIRTY-ONE

Finn's words fall heavily into the silence, and for long moments, Eva doesn't speak.

He thinks of her tearing onto Longstone and confessing to her part in the death of Donald Macauley. He had not judged her then, and he does not judge her for it now. After all, how could he? He is carrying the same guilt on his shoulders.

Highfield House was like a myth. A fable Ward disappeared into from time to time, when there was no action to be had a sea. Warm beds, good food, fine wine, and even better company.

The house of Abigail Blake. Ward spoke her name almost reverently.

Sometimes, he would go to the house alone. Other times he would take his officers with him, loaded with liquor, and in their finest clothes. Even as a child, Finn wondered whether Ward was truly as welcome at Highfield House as he believed himself to be. Or perhaps that simply didn't matter to him.

And then the night Ward came to Finn and told him he was to join him at the house. Finn had been racked with a vicious head cold, and couldn't be sure he wasn't imagining the invitation.

"You want me to join you, sir? At the house? At the gathering?"

Ward laughed. "At the gathering, no. You're too young for that yet, lad. But I'll see to it that you get a comfortable night's rest. Sleep off the last of your illness."

Highfield House was everything he imagined it to be. Vast and shadowed and elaborately beautiful, with a sense of the otherworldly, wrought by salt-splattered windows and candlelit halls. This place had always fascinated him. How many times had he stood on the deck of the *Eagle* while Ward was at the house, staring across the water at the forest of chimneys, wondering what might lie inside? He couldn't believe he was standing in its foyer.

The woman who had let them inside inspected the group with shrewd, narrowed eyes. She was fine-boned and slight, dwarfed by Henry Ward and the five other men he had brought with him. She had clearly dressed for the occasion, in a lace-trimmed blue gown, and jewels at her throat, her dark hair piled high on her head.

Her eyes fell to Finn. "He's one of yours?" Surprise in her voice.

"He is. A hardworking cabin boy, fighting the last of a fever. He's in need of a warm bed for the night. "

The woman managed a smile, but it didn't reach her eyes. "Of course," she told Finn. "You can have my eldest son's room. He can share with his brother for the night. Wait down here a moment." She turned to Ward. Gave him a faint smile. "Make yourselves comfortable."

Ward gripped Finn's shoulder, told him to behave. Then the men were off deep into the house, bottles swinging in their fists.

Finn hovered awkwardly in the foyer. In the flickering lamplight, the paintings on the walls seemed to be shifting; the sea on the canvas rolling, the eyes of the portraits looking his way. He glanced up the wide wooden staircase that led to the second storey, the steps at the top swallowed by darkness.

Finally, the woman appeared from the gloom of the stairs. She walked halfway down, holding a lamp out to guide Finn's path. "This way."

He followed her upstairs and down the passage. The woman brought a finger to her lips, gesturing for silence, and Finn tiptoed, guessing there were sleeping children behind those doors.

She pushed open the door of a room at the end of the passage. An enormous black fireplace filled most of one wall, dark wood panels on either side of it. The bed in the centre of the room was piled with blankets, and even a pillow. Finn was not sure he had ever slept on something that looked so comfortable.

He thanked the woman. Waited until she had closed the door behind her before pulling off his boots and climbing into bed. He was on the edge of sleep when he heard the door groan open again. Heard footsteps sounding across the room. Saw a globe of lamplight through his closed eyelids.

Finn scrambled into sitting. Came face to face with a boy about his age. Tall and thin, with white-blond hair tickling his shoulders. His eyes glittered in the lamplight.

"Who are you?" asked Finn.

"This is my room," said the boy. "I'm Oliver Blake. And I ought to be asking you that question."

Eva is staring at him, eyes full of questions. But it is Ward she speaks to first. "Do you mean to kill Finn? As punishment? Is that why you brought him here?"

He looks at her squarely. "Do you not think that is what he deserves?"

Eva's lips part. Ward must know, surely, that she is in no place to answer such a question. Not with only the barest fragments of the story. Or maybe those fragments are enough to condemn him.

When Eva doesn't speak, Ward turns to Finn. "You were a member of my crew when Oliver Blake was killed. Therefore you are bound by the articles of the ship. Articles that claim a slaying outside of battle or duel is punishable by death."

"Ward, please." Finn scrubs a hand across his eyes. "Let's not have this discussion in front of Eva."

"No," she cuts in, looking at him squarely. "I wish to hear what you have to say."

Finn holds her gaze for a moment. What can he possibly say that will make this any less horrific? He knows nothing can save his relations with Eva. They were doomed before they even began. But perhaps he can find a way to save his own life. He knows punishment is what he deserves. Death, if that is what Ward has planned for him. But his survival instinct makes him speak: "Oliver's death did not happen on your ship."

The captain leans back. "No," he concedes. "It did not. Therefore I know it could be argued that you were not bound by the ship's articles at the time. If one was looking for a loophole. But is that really what you feel you ought to be doing, while you are sitting face to face with Oliver's sister?"

Henry Ward had always been a strict captain. Finn had watched men hanged from the yardarm, and keel-hauled beneath the hull of ship, for breaking the laws set out in the articles. He knows he deserves no less.

But he does not want to die. And he also knows that, killer or not, he has a valuable job to do. He likes to think that the light he has set burning almost every night for five years might have saved the lives of countless sailors. And perhaps, in some small way, that might begin to atone for Oliver Blake's death.

So perhaps he is looking for a loophole. But he is doing it because surely, he is worth more alive than dead.

"You'll not kill me," he tells Ward. "Because it's not your place to do so, and you know it. I did not kill Oliver aboard your ship. And you have always been fair and rigid when it comes to your ship's articles."

Ward doesn't speak. Finn knows he is considering his words. He stands and looks squarely at his former captain. Tries to invoke a confidence he doesn't feel. "Take me back to Longstone. I've to light the firebasket to make sure men like you don't end up at the bottom of the sea."

Ward reaches over and refills Finn's wine glass, though he has barely touched the first. "Sit down, lad. You're not going anywhere."

Finn clenches his jaw. He knows he has no choice. Even if he were to shove his way past Ward and break out onto deck, his only option of escape would be to swim. Out here, the German Ocean would steal his breath in seconds. And he has no thought of how far he is from Longstone. Of course, none of that matters. Even if he could find his way off the ship, he cannot leave Eva here alone.

Can it truly be a coincidence that Ward has returned to Northumberland at the same time as Eva and her family? It does not feel like it. But he has no thought of what Ward might want with the Blakes.

He sits. Brings his cup to his lips to appease the captain, but he doesn't drink. He needs to keep as clear a head as possible.

"What?" laughs Ward. "You think I've laced it with nightshade? You know I've more decency than that. Or more creativity at least." He reaches over and spears a piece of meat from Finn's plate. Swallows it in one mouthful. "You ought to try a little. Good quality stuff. Fresh from shore."

Finn pushes his plate away. "I think this dinner is over, Ward." He turns. "Eva?" Dares to look at her.

She nods, her eyes unreadable.

"Very well." Ward tosses back the last of his wine and stands. He goes to the cabin door and calls for his steward. Murmurs to him with instructions, Finn is sure, to imprison him somewhere on the ship.

Ward turns to Eva. "I cannot let Mr Murray go. I'm sorry. What of you, Miss Blake? Do you wish to leave? If you do, I shall have one of my officers take you back to Holy Island."

Finn's stomach knots at the thought of Eva climbing into a longboat with a member of Ward's crew. But it is better than the alternative.

"No," she says. "I wish to stay."

Ward merely nods, as though expecting such an answer. "I shall have my crew find you comfortable quarters."

Finn grabs her arm before she can follow the steward down the passage. "She stays with me." He expects a protest from her. It doesn't come.

"Miss Blake?" says Ward. "Is that what you want?"

She glances at Finn. "Yes."

The steward leads Finn and Eva out of the great cabin and down the narrow, lamplit passage. He pulls a key from the pocket of his coat and unlocks a door at the far end of the corridor. Nods wordlessly for them to enter. The cabin is an airless tomb, thick with the stink of tallow and bodies. Two hammocks are strung across the bulkheads at the back of the room.

The crewman hangs the lamp on the hook beside the door. Then he steps back out into the passage, the lock clicking loudly in the stillness. His footsteps disappear. And they are alone.

CHAPTER THIRTY-TWO

Eva stands with her back to the door, but does not attempt to put space between the two of them. She is inches away from him, her eyes full of questions she doesn't ask.

Unable to bear the silence, Finn says, "Why are you here? Why didn't you leave?"

She lets out her breath. "How could I leave?"

"How could you have stayed?"

She closes her eyes; leans her head back against the door. "I need to hear it all, Finn. Every word."

Of course she does. The thing is brutal, but surely it can be no worse than whatever images are clattering around her head right now.

And so he tells her. Every piece of it, just as he remembers. Tells her of Abigail Blake opening her door to Ward and his crew; tells her of her mother being kind enough to offer him a bed for the night, to sleep off the last of his fever.

And he tells her about her eldest brother: blond-haired, sharp-eyed Oliver, who had pulled him from sleep with a spear of lamplight in his eyes.

"Why are you in my house?" Oliver asked. "Are you with them? The sailors?"

Finn slid from the bed, his bare feet soundless on the wooden floor.

He said nothing. He had learnt by now that in situations like this, silence was best. For all Ward liked to play up the honour of what they did, Finn knew one wrong turn would lead them all to the hangman. The line between privateering and piracy was a flimsy one.

Oliver took a step towards him, holding the lamp close to his face. Finn was inches taller, and Oliver had to look up to meet his eyes. "Why won't you speak to me? Are you a half-wit? Or are you scared?"

"Leave me alone," said Finn. "I just want to sleep. Your mother gave me this room." His body was still aching from the remnants of his illness; his throat on fire. The door sighed open and a second boy slipped into the room. Smaller, with wide blue eyes and dark waves of hair around his shoulders. He stood with his back pressed against the door, as though desperate to keep his distance, but too curious to stay away. Oliver glanced over his shoulder at him, then turned back to Finn. He lifted his hand, revealing a small tarnished blade that had been hidden by the sleeve of his nightshirt.

"Look at this," he said to Finn. "It's a Viking dagger. From the days when they raided this island."

Finn snorted. "A Viking dagger?" Was the boy trying to impress him? Intimidate him? "It is not."

Oliver's nostrils flared. "Are you calling me a liar?"

"You're lying, aye? Or are you just stupid?"

Oliver took a step towards him and Finn flinched, expecting retaliation. But he stopped coolly, turning the blade over in his fist. Finn felt the hair on the back of his neck prickle.

Oliver looked over his shoulder at his brother. "Tell him, Nathan. Tell him it's from the Viking raids."

They both turned to look at the younger boy. He hesitated, mouth hanging half open. Finally, he said, "I think it's just a fishing knife. But there's a real priest hole in this room. Behind the panel by the fireplace. Over here—"

Oliver shoved him away. "Get out."

Nathan looked up at his brother. Finn saw fear in his eyes. There was a part of him that was feeling it too. But he refused to let himself be intimidated by this boy. How could he be afraid of a child after he had stood on the deck of the *Eagle* and sailed into French gunfire? But there was something about Oliver Blake that made him wary. Made his fists clench instinctively. Made his heart quicken in readiness for a fight.

The door clicked closed again, leaving the two of them alone.

"Leave me be," Finn said again. "I'm not afraid of you." He wondered if the boy could tell he was lying.

A smile flickered in the corner of Oliver's lips. "Have you heard what the Vikings did to the monks on this island?"

Finn gritted his teeth, forcing away the urge to throw a fist into the side of Oliver's head. He could not fight this boy. Not Abigail Blake's son. Ward would never forgive him. And how many times had the captain lectured him about controlling his temper? About not flying into a rage at every provocation, like he had done with his father?

But Ward had also taught him not to let himself be pushed around.

What was this about, he wondered? Was Oliver Blake marking his territory? Or did he just like the power of inflicting fear? Surely this could not be a personal attack. Oliver Blake had no idea who he was.

"They cut them to pieces," said Oliver. "Ransacked the church and sliced their throats like they were pigs." He lifted the blade to Finn's neck. Instinctively, Finn shoved him away. Oliver stumbled backwards, his eyes widening in surprise for a moment, before a faint smile tilted his lips. He took another step towards Finn and pressed the tip of the blade into his stomach. "Left them all to die."

Finn's chest tightened. It was not fear he was feeling. Not anymore. Now it was anger; hot and sharp. Heart rapping against his ribs, skin prickling. This anger, he had felt it before, in those suffocating nights on Longstone when he and his father would spur each other into rage. Back then, he had let his anger out unbridled. But he knew his actions had to be calculated if he was to come out of this on top. He stood frozen against the silver tip of the knife. He had no idea what this boy was capable of. He only knew he had to act. Disarm him somehow. Run downstairs to find Ward. The other officers would mock him, of course. But he didn't care.

The floorboards in the hallway creaked.

"I can hear you out there, Nathan," said Oliver, not turning away from Finn. "Go to bed." There was silence in the passage. No movement. Oliver raised his voice slightly, turning back over his shoulder to speak to his brother. "Do you want to spend another night in the walls?"

Finn seized the distraction. He shoved Oliver backwards and lurched towards the door. Oliver grabbed a fistful of Finn's shirt, yanking him back. Lashed at him with the knife. Finn saw the stripe of blood appear on his forearm before he registered the pain. He swung a fist. Hard—too hard—into the side of Oliver's head. He fell sideways, skull cracking against the foot of the bed. His body slid to the floorboards, almost silent but for the soft clatter of the knife against the floor. Cold blue eyes stared up at Finn, but there was no light behind them. A thick seam of blood crept out from beneath Oliver's head, edging towards the blade of the knife.

Finn's lungs seized. He gulped for air. His legs wavered beneath him and he grappled with the bed head, trying to stay upright. His vision swam and vomit rushed up his throat.

Outside the door, he heard the younger boy cry out. And then there were footsteps moving up the staircase. Steady, growing louder. He rushed to the window; shook wildly at the sash, but it refused to open. He looked around for something with which to smash the glass. He was two storeys off the ground, yes, but surely the fall would be better than whatever Henry Ward would do to him once he found out what he had done.

The footsteps came closer. Finn thought suddenly of the younger boy's words. A priest hole in the panelling beside the fireplace. It would be no escape, but it would be a place to hide. He raced to the far wall, throwing his weight against the worn wooden panels, searching for the hidden compartment. Finally, he felt it give way. The priest hole opened up before him and he dived inside. He yanked the panelling closed, enclosing himself in blackness.

He hugged his knees, pressing his face to his thigh to silence his breathing. He could feel the warm wetness of the blood on his forearm. The cut pulsed in time with his racing heart. He heard footsteps thunder into the room; heard the screams of the boys' mother. And muffled words he knew came from Henry Ward.

He heard the captain call his name.

Finn pressed his hands to the wall on either side of him. Above his head was the same thick stone that made up the fireplace. It felt as though the tiny space was closing in on him, draining the last of the air. His breath came fast and loud. Loud enough to hear, surely, on the other side of the wall.

He shuffled backwards, his shoulder pressing hard against the corner of the priest hole. And he felt the wall shift. Felt the wooden panel twist and open, revealing a second narrow space. Below it, a passage yawning into blackness.

On hands and knees, Finn scrambled forward in the darkness, his fingers finding the coarse rungs of a ladder. He scrambled down it, ignoring the splinters that bit into his palms. On every side of him were thick slabs of stone. A passage built into the wall, he realised. It felt almost as if it had been put there for him. For this very moment. Perhaps this mysterious, mythical house might find a way to save his life.

When he landed heavily at the bottom of the ladder, he followed the passage on his hands and knees. It smelt of earth, of wood. Smelt like he was being buried alive.

He would deserve such a fate, he thought distantly. He had killed someone. Run away instead of facing up to his actions. He did not deserve the freedom that Highfield House had inexplicably granted.

But then there was moonlight. The sigh of the sea. Finn scrambled towards the pale, hatched light that marked the end of the tunnel. Perhaps he did not deserve freedom, but he would seize it with both hands anyway.

A rusty grate blocked his path. Wriggling onto his back, he shoved at it with his bare feet until it gave way. And out he scrambled, gulping down the salty air.

He didn't look back as he charged onto the beach. Didn't glance back to see if he had been followed. Wind tore at his shirtsleeves, but his body was blazing. Footsteps drummed in his ears, the sound distorted by fear and fever. He couldn't tell if the soft pounding of feet against earth were his alone.

He slid through the pebbles on the edge of the water. A lamp glowed not far from shore. Ward's barque.

The ship would not save him. The ship would only lead him to the gallows. He ran around the curve of the island, seeking the place where the mainland was closest. Moonlight guided him, but not well enough; he stumbled over rugged dunes and tussocks of grass, slipped into puddles that reached the hems of his breeches.

The tide was high. Tonight Lindisfarne was an island again, and his only way off was to battle the rising German Ocean.

He was in the water before his thoughts caught up to him. The sea closed in over his head and he kicked hard against the current. He thrashed through the water, through the cold and the dark, towards the vague shapes of the mainland.

Finally, the sea grew shallower and he stumbled up the beach. He knew this part of the world well. There were houses here in Beal; a tavern. Surely someone would offer him dry clothes and a little food. Enough to see him out of Northumberland and into a life where Henry Ward would not find him.

Finn stumbled to his feet, turning to look back at the dark mass of Holy Island. Lamps from the village broke the blackness, and beyond them, a pale glow that marked Highfield House. And far beyond that, so distant he was not sure if he was imagining it, was the flickering eye of the firebasket warning ships away from Longstone.

For several moments, the silence is thick, punctuated by the irregular breath of the flame inside the lantern. The hull of the ship groans.

"He was like that," Eva says finally. "Terrifying. I barely remember him. I can't recall what he looked like. Or sounded like. All I remember is that he frightened me."

But this comment, Finn knows well, from the hardness of her eyes and arms held stiffly across her chest, it is no absolution. And why should it be?

"I'm sorry," he says. It feels like a foolish thing to say. Foolish, but achingly necessary.

Eva looks up. "I know." Her eyes are glistening. "You would never have told me, would you," she says. "If I had not come out here looking for you, I never would have known."

He shakes his head. He feels like a coward. But the least he can do is tell her the truth. "No," he says. "I never would have told you."

He tries to catch her eye. Tries to read her. But he cannot do it. She has taken on a sudden blankness.

"Ward will kill you for this, won't he." Her voice is strangely level, hollow.

"Probably. I'm sure he wishes to avenge your mother."

"And is that what you believe you deserve?"

Finn thinks of that airless priest hole, of that tarnished blade pressed to his throat. He thinks of the crack of Oliver's head striking the bed, a sound that has stayed with him for the past twenty years. It might be what he deserves, but that survival instinct in him has not faltered. "Perhaps it is," he says. "But I want to live."

Eva raps on the door of the cabin she and Finn are locked in. "I wish to see the captain," she calls. "I need to speak with him."

The door clicks open at once, reminding her she is not the prisoner. Ward's steward nods at her to exit the cabin, then locks the door behind her. Without speaking, he leads her back through the passage towards the great cabin. Their footsteps click rhythmically and Eva focuses on the sound, to keep her thoughts from running away.

Oliver, the brother never spoken of. Oliver, who she believed had succumbed to smallpox like her father, a swift and unremarkable death. Why had her mother lied? To hide her shame over inviting Ward and his crew into the house? Her shame over inviting Finn into the house? Or was an unremarkable death just easier than the truth?

On one hand, there is clarity. This, of course, is why Finn had pulled away from her in Bamburgh. Why he had erected the walls around himself the moment he had learnt her name. How she longs for her old ignorance; ignorance in which his coldness came only from believing her a government spy. Now that seems far too easy.

When they reach the great cabin, the steward knocks loudly. "Captain. Miss Blake wishes to speak with you."

Footsteps sound across the boards and Ward pulls open the door. He gives her what looks to be a genuine smile. "Please come in."

She does. Their dinner has been cleared away, but the smell of roast meat lingers, mingling with the remnants of wine and the ever-present breath of the sea. Ward closes the logbook on his desk and gestures for her to return to the table. He sits opposite her.

"What is it you wish to speak about, Eva?"

She stiffens at his familiarity, both his informality and the genial way he is looking at her. Like he knows her. Knew her. Like he was walking the halls of Highfield House for far longer than just one night.

She senses that Ward feels his own guilt for his part in Oliver's death. After all, it had been because of him that Finn was in Highfield House in the first place. And while he cannot hope to make it up to Abigail, perhaps treating her daughter well is the least he can do.

Or perhaps she is being naïve. She knows nothing of this world of pirates and privateers that Ward and Finn are so entangled in. Before coming to Holy Island, she had known no world but the rigid life laid out before her in London. But she knows she should not trust a man like Henry Ward easily. And she knows she must act if she is to get what she needs. She cannot just stay locked in that cabin like a rabbit in a trap. How long might it be until Ward's kindness runs out?

She folds her hands in front of her on the table. Squeezes them together to steady herself. "I should like to be taken back to Holy Island. I've heard what I needed to hear from Mr Murray."

Ward nods slowly. "I see." A smile flickers in the corner of his lips. "You sound just like your mother, you know. She used to speak in the same detached manner as that when she sought to hide her emotions."

Eva tries to quell her irritation at the ease with which he has read her. "I'm nothing like my mother."

Ward's smile broadens, warms. "You're more like her than you know. She could be reckless too. And here you are putting yourself in danger by following the man you love out here."

Something flips in Eva's stomach. "You think I love Finn Murray?"

"Loved, perhaps. At least until you discovered what he was keeping from you. Why else would you risk your own safety by coming all the way out here?"

Eva looks at her tightly clasped hands. Ward's claim is one she cannot allow herself to bring to the light. At least, not now. "Well. It's as you say. He has been keeping things from me."

Ward nods. "Yes. And it's a damn shame. He had such potential, that lad. I believed he had the makings of a fine and decent man. I was sorry to see him throw it all away on one foolish mistake."

Eva squeezes her eyes shut. She cannot allow her thoughts to venture near Finn's decency, or his mistakes. All she can do right now is focus on the conversation at hand. Focus on remaining in Henry Ward's good graces.

"You are leaving Mr Murray to his own devices, then," says Ward.

Eva meets his eyes. "He killed my brother. And thought to keep it from me. I owe him no loyalty."

"I'm glad to hear that. I cannot imagine what it would have done to Abigail if she knew you were spending your time with him."

Eva says nothing. Her mother, too, is another thought she cannot go near. "What will you do to him?" she asks finally.

"I'm undecided. My ship's code says he is to die." He picks at a fleck of dirt beneath his fingernail. "I have no doubt that young Oliver's death was an accident. But that does not change the fact that Finn ran away that night. Refused to face up to what he did. Nor does it change that fact that he took a young man's life."

"No," says Eva. "It does not." Her thoughts drift towards Donald Macauley; the death she herself had run away from. For the first time since she had killed him, there is no emotion attached to the thought. She feels numb, detached. The only way, she knows, she will make it through this. Allow herself to feel anything and she will crumble. "Finn says the articles do not apply as he was not aboard your ship when Oliver was killed."

Ward nods slowly. "Yes. And that, Eva, is the only reason he is still alive. I know I've a decision to make. What do you think?"

Eva feels the knife she had tucked into her sleeve before she had left the dining table. The blade is cold against her arm. She swallows hard and looks into Ward's arctic-blue eyes. "He killed my brother," she says. "I think he deserves to die."

CHAPTER THIRTY-THREE

Ward's men come for him without speaking. One at each arm, dragging him from the cabin, up onto deck. The night is starlit, clear and cold. Finn finds himself looking out towards the horizon. Out towards Longstone. Tonight, no beacon breaks the blackness. Have the Mitchells failed to make it back without the firebasket to guide them?

It's a thought he does not have room for. Because he knows, from the way the men shove him onto deck, and from the emotionless eyes his former captain is watching with, that Ward has come to his decision. Tonight, he is to die.

His eyes drift upward to the yardarm above his head. Is he to hang by the neck with the ocean shifting beneath him?

No. He sees the pulley hanging from the yardarm in place of the noose. Sees the weights at Ward's feet.

So his captain plans to keel-haul him. Toss him into the sea and drag him beneath the hull of the ship. In a way, he sees the beauty of such a punishment. Death is not a certainty, but nor is survival. Let fate judge him. If he survives being dragged along the barnacled outer hull of the ship and the long minutes without air, then so be it.

But Finn knows that is far from likely. He thinks of the keel-haulings he had witnessed in the past. Thinks of the battered, bleeding bodies drawn out of the water after the punishment. Only one of the three men had still been breathing.

Eva is standing a few yards back from the captain, her cloak wrapped tightly around her body. Her face is pale, but her eyes give nothing away.

Ward nods to his crewmen. They shove Finn towards the gunwale, ripping off his jacket and tying the rope attached to the pulley tight around his shoulders and waist. Lead weights are fastened around his ankles. Rope wrapped around his wrists, binding them together.

Ward looks at him squarely. "I'm sorry, Finn."

Finn nods slightly. He knows his apology is genuine.

Somewhere at the back of his mind, behind his fear-tangled thoughts, he wonders what Henry Ward would have done to him if he had not run away that night. Would he have tied weights to the ankles of an eleven-year-old boy?

He supposes it is of little matter. Had he been caught standing over Oliver's lifeless body, Abigail Blake would have sent him to the scaffold long before Ward got his hands on him.

"Let me speak to him," says Eva. Ward nods shortly.

She steps close to Finn, body inches from his. She looks up into his face with a look of wide-eyed fear. A look that tells him that, for all he has done, she still cares deeply whether he lives or dies. And with her cloak held close to his bound hands, she slips a knife into his fist.

"Ward wanted to hang you," she murmurs. "I convinced him to do this."

He nods faintly. Grips the knife. Manages to brush his thumb over her knuckles. "Thank you."

The blade is close enough, sharp enough, to slice through the ropes securing his wrists, but the weights will pull him down fast. And if he does not slice the bindings before the men begin to drag him under the keel…well, he cannot bear to think that far.

This could well be death for him, and if Ward has any inkling of what Eva is doing, it could be death for her too. Finn hates that he has put her in such danger. Hates that he has agreed to this reckless plan of hers. But it is far too late to change tack now.

Eva backs away, her jaw clenched tight. She stands beside Ward in a false display of solidarity. Ward nods to the men.

They heave on the ropes attached to the pulley and Finn's feet leave the ground. Two men shove him towards the gunwale. Sea and air hang beneath him. His body is hot, pulsing, his heart in his ears. And then the men release their grip on the rope and he is falling, falling, until the icy black water closes in around him.

Eva turns away from the sea and looks up at Ward. "May I go to your cabin? I wish to be alone."

Her entire body is hot, trembling. She is sure Ward can hear the panic in her voice. Sickness rises in her throat at the thought of Finn being pulled beneath the surface.

I want to live, he had said. And no matter what else he has done, Eva knew she had to help him do so. Had to take this precarious fondness Henry Ward seems to have for her, and use it to their advantage.

The plan is dangerous, desperate. Could well end in both their deaths. But it is their only chance of leaving this ship together.

"You do not wish to watch the punishment?" asks Ward.

"No." The tears that spill are not an act. But the captain eyes her, and for a moment, Eva's panic intensifies. Perhaps his trust in her is not as secure as she had imagined. But then he turns to his steward. Hands him a key.

"Take her to the great cabin. And pour her a drink. She looks as though she needs it." He turns to Eva. "I shall have one of the men take you ashore once the punishment is complete." He gestures to the men at the pulley. "Drag him under."

The crewman leads her down the passage with excruciating slowness. Eva thinks of Finn below the surface; thinks of the weights at his feet pulling him down; the men on deck with ropes in their hands, dragging him beneath the razor-sharp hull of the ship. Her breath becomes even more ragged. She forces herself to breathe steadily so as not to give herself away.

He has the knife, she tells herself. A way to cut himself free. Desperate, dangerous—but a way nonetheless.

The steward unlocks the door of the great cabin and gestures for Eva to enter. She steps inside, her eyes moving instinctively to the bank of windows at the stern of the ship. The steward walks to the sideboard and uncorks the half-drunk bottle of wine. Fills a shallow cup and sits it on the table. Eva nods her thanks.

"Anything else you need, Miss?"

"No. Thank you." She wills him to leave. If they are to manage this escape, they cannot waste seconds. The moment the men at the pulley feel the ropes lose their tension, they will know Finn has cut himself free. And they will come looking.

After what feels an eternity, the steward steps out of the cabin, locking the door behind him. Eva grabs a chair by the legs and rushes to the window. Swings wildly. Glass explodes into the ocean and the sound seems to echo across the ship. Surely it will be only seconds before Ward comes for her. Terror weakens her legs. She has never swum in her life. And the moment she leaps from this window, she will start sinking to the ocean floor.

She cannot allow this thought to take hold. She pulls her cloak from her shoulders and flings it onto the floor. And she leaps out into the sea.

Dark water closes in over her head, the shock of the cold seizing her chest and snatching her breath. *Keep kicking,* Finn had told her, as they had planned their escape while locked in the cabin. *Just keep kicking. I will come to you.* She surfaces briefly, gulping down air, catching a glimpse of a slivered moon. And she kicks and she kicks, her skirts tangling around her legs. The water pulls her down, sucking the last of the moonlight away.

CHAPTER THIRTY-FOUR

Finn slices through the last of the rope and kicks towards the surface. He opens his eyes, but the water is like ink around him. A part of him is grateful for the darkness; by now, the men will know he has freed himself, and they will not hesitate to shoot. He bursts through the surface. He is close to the great cabin. Through stinging eyes, he can see the windows are shattered. Eva is in the water with him, somewhere. But he can see no sign of her.

Frantically, he dives below the surface again, eyes open, though he sees nothing but black. This, of all outcomes, would be by far the worst—if he is to survive only to have her drown. He longs to call out to her, but he knows he can do no such thing. And then the water shifts around him. He feel the ripples of her kicking and flailing. And he thrashes towards her, reaching, straining into the darkness.

He dives below the surface and his fingertips brush her body. Feels her grab a fistful of his shirt. He pulls at her, wraps an arm tight around her waist. And he kicks hard. His lungs and legs are burning, her heavy skirts dragging them towards the bottom. At last they break through the surface, gasping down lungfuls of the cold night air.

In the faint light of the ship's lamps, he meets her eyes. Sees a wordless mix of terror and relief. She wraps her arms around his shoulders, breathless.

Finn digs his fingers into her collar and kicks towards the longboat trailing behind Ward's barque. It's a dangerous ploy; deadly. He knows the moment Ward sees them, he will start shooting. More than anything, Henry Ward hates being deceived. Especially by those he has put his trust in.

Finn pushes Eva towards the boat. "Grab the side," her tells her breathlessly. "I'll climb in and pull you up."

Reluctantly, she relinquishes her grip on his shirt and grapples at the gunwale. Her eyes dart up at the lamplit shape of the barque. Finn pulls on the gunwale, causing the boat to rock, rock enough for him to haul himself from the water and scramble aboard.

As his knees hit the bottom of the longboat, the first shot comes. He hears Eva's murmur of shock. He grabs her arms and pulls her from the water. Lurches forward and unties the rope latching the longboat to the ship. "Get down," he hisses.

But the shooting has stopped. Suddenly, the night is quiet, eerily still. Finn wraps his hands around the oars, but does not dare lower them into the water. Not yet. He knows there is every chance Ward is trying to lull them into a false sense of security.

"Go," Eva whispers after a moment. "Go."

And he does. He lowers the oars into the sea and begins to pull away from the ship.

He knows he ought to feel relief. But he doesn't.

Ward is watching. Calm and still at the stern of the ship. And Finn knows then, with certainty, that they have only escaped because Ward has allowed it.

He looks up to meet his captain's eyes. There's a look there that he knows all too well. A look that tells Finn this is not a pardon. This is a game.

He has let him go now because he wants him to fret. To suffer, to watch the horizon as he lights the firebasket each night, and wonder when the lamps of the *Eagle* will again shine over Longstone.

He has let him go because he knows Finn has trapped himself out there on his shard of an island. Tied himself to the firebasket to atone for his mistakes.

And perhaps he has also let him go because Abigail Blake's daughter is sitting in the longboat beside him. Perhaps he will not risk another of her children losing their life on account of his crew.

But Finn is certain that once Eva is no longer at his side, Ward will come again. This is who he is: shrewd and calculating. He will see this as a fitting punishment: a life of watching, of waiting, of wondering when he might next appear. Wondering when his desire to avenge Abigail Blake and her son might finally drive him to pull the trigger.

Eva can know none of this. He does not want her to know it is likely her presence that has kept Ward from firing. Does not want to put her in the middle of this poisonous thing between himself and his former captain.

Besides, he can't quite find a way to feel that fear he knows Ward is trying to instil in him. Because somehow, against all reason, Eva is here beside him with an oar in her hand. She shuffles along the bench until her shoulder presses hard against his, as though unable to believe that they have both lived to see the morning.

CHAPTER THIRTY-FIVE

The sun has risen by the time they return to Longstone. The morning is clear and the sea is glass, pink light pushing through the thin layer of clouds on the horizon. Birds are wheeling around the far end of the island.

They had found Angus and Michael Mitchell waiting in the skiff, not far from Ward's ship. In the rising sun, the *Eagle* is still visible. A watching silhouette, but motionless. At least for now.

The two boats bump against the jetty on Longstone, and Finn ties Ward's longboat up beside the skiff. He climbs out ahead of Eva and offers her his hand. She holds tight to him as she steps from the boat. And then, after a moment of hesitation, she lets her fingers slide from his.

Shivering in her wet clothes, Eva goes to the bedroom and finds the dry skirts and petticoats she had flung over the end of the bed before they had gone to Bamburgh. They have been folded clumsily and placed on a chair in the corner of the room. With frozen fingers, she hurries out of her sodden clothing and climbs into her dry things.

She is still straightening her neckerchief when Finn comes barrelling through the door. There is a look of urgency in his eyes that says he does not care that he has caught her in a state of near undress.

He closes the door behind him. And he comes at her suddenly, pulling her close. For a moment, Eva lets herself sink against him. His dry clothes smell faintly of woodsmoke, and the linen of his shirt is rough against her cheek.

After a moment, he pulls back to look her in the eyes. "That was madness. You could have died."

"As could you." With a little distance, she can see the insanity of the plan she had set in motion. Sees how fortunate they had been to survive. And she sees how impossibly grateful she is that Finn is standing here in front of her. Alive and unharmed.

She brings a hand to his bristly cheek. "I don't blame you for what happened, Finn. I know Oliver's death was an accident. Just like Donald Macauley's." And for now, perhaps, the two of them have escaped punishment. But she has no thought of how long their reprieves might last. The shadow of the *Eagle* is still imprinted on the horizon. And government spies are about to descend on Highfield House, covering for her crime.

She lets out a breath. "How do you do it? Live with another's death on your shoulders?"

Finn doesn't speak at once. He rests his forehead against hers, tucking coils of wet hair behind her ear.

"You just carry on," he says finally. "You just carry on and hope that you might be able to do some good. Something that might pay for your mistakes in some small way."

And Eva sees then that the firebasket, and this teetering cottage in the sea is not just about Finn's father and his uncles lost on the Knavestone. It is also about her own brother; faceless and half-forgotten to her, but always at the forefront of Finn's mind.

Impulsively, she pulls him into a kiss. His fingers slide through her wet, tangled hair, making her sigh against his lips. And she sees things as they are. Sees that this is a kiss goodbye.

Because surely this is too big to ever climb over. How could she take Finn to her family, knowing what she knows? Nathan had seen him with Oliver that night. Is there a chance he might recognise him? Unlikely as it seems, she could never take that risk. Could never keep the truth from him and Harriet, or expect them to forgive Finn as she has done. And how could she ever expect Finn to set foot in Highfield House again, after the horrors he had experienced there?

She steps away and meets his eyes. "I'm sorry," she says. "I need to leave." And he gives a faint nod; one of understanding. She blinks away the tears that threaten to escape. And she says, "Take me home."

Finn guides the skiff towards the beach at Emmanuel Head. The same place Martin Macauley had raised his musket on him and splattered his blood across the shingle at the top of the beach. Today there is only stillness.

Eva looks up at the house. A thin line of smoke is rising from the chimney above the kitchen.

She swallows hard. Stands. Finn shifts, readying himself to climb from the boat and help her ashore.

"No," she says. "I can manage."

And as she climbs over the gunwale, she cannot muster more than a tiny smile goodbye.

Nathan is waiting for her at the front door. No doubt he had seen her coming.

She pauses on the front path for a moment to steel herself. To cobble together an explanation for the way she had fled the house so impulsively last night.

She meets her brother's eyes challengingly as she approaches the door. She will not allow herself to be scolded by him, or made to feel guilty. Because Nathan has been lying to her from the beginning. He knows the truth about Oliver's death; has always known. He had been outside the door when it had happened. Had deliberately kept it from her when she had asked about their past in the house.

Before she can open her mouth, he says, "Go and tidy yourself, Eva. You've a visitor."

She frowns. "Who?"

"In the parlour," he says. He eyes her bird's nest of wet hair. "Make yourself presentable first."

She goes upstairs to her room, dumping her wet clothes on a chair beside her bed. She has nothing else to change into, so she quickly combs her wet hair and re-pins it at her neck. Sponges the grime of the ship from her skin.

When she opens the door of the parlour, she finds Matthew Walton waiting.

Eva freezes in the doorway. She had never expected to see him again.

He stands at the sight of her, a rueful smile on his lips. "Miss Blake." He is a polished piece of London in a striped justacorps and dark blue breeches, lace at his throat and wrists. The dark curls of his wig are tied back with a length of black ribbon. He smells strongly of orange flower.

The sight of him here in Highfield House, with sea wind thumping the shutters, feels oddly disjointed.

Eva stays planted in the doorway. "Why are you here?" She does not attempt to inject any warmth into her voice. This thing between them has always been one of formality. Walton swallows visibly and gestures to the armchair across from him. He wrings his hands together and tugs at the hem of his coat. "Will you sit? Please?"

Hesitantly, she perches on the edge of the chair. Folds her hands neatly. "Nathan's letter reached you already?"

"No. He told me he had written. But I've not yet received it. Although I can imagine what it might say. I'm here on my own accord." Walton shifts forward in his seat. "I acted foolishly. Rashly. Once you had left London, I had much time to think. And I came to see that with great clarity." He pauses for a moment, as though waiting for her response. When it doesn't come, he says, "I'm truly sorry, Miss Blake. And if you are still willing, I would very much like to make you my wife."

Eva waits for the relief. The sense that things might be returning to the path they were supposed to follow. It doesn't come. She presses her lips into a thin line. "You are in love with my sister," she says matter-of-factly.

Walton lowers his eyes for a moment. "Of what consequence is that? You and I both know ours will be a marriage of practicality." His eyes meet hers. "But it will be strong one. A wise one." He reaches forward and tentatively takes her hand. "Eva. I agreed to marry you because I can see what a bright and promising young woman you are. I admit that I lost sight of that for a time. And I'm sorry. You deserved better. And you shall have it."

Eva lets out her breath. Walton is like an actor on a stage. Polished and perfect, with these fine words rolling off his tongue. Over and over, on that interminable journey from London to Holy Island, she had longed for Matthew Walton to see his mistakes like this. To see the value of what he was giving up. Now his words just feel empty.

A marriage of practicality. She supposes that is what she has always been destined for.

He squeezes her fingers. "I could make a good life for you, Eva. A secure life. One that would be of great benefit to your family too. Is that not what you want."

Eva gets to her feet and goes to the window. The wind through the grass is making the dunes breathe. She hears Walton's footsteps behind her.

"I need a good, respectable wife," he says. "And you need the security of a husband. It seems to me that this is an arrangement that will benefit us both. Is that not why we agreed to it in the first place?"

"I would not have agreed to it if I had known the way you feel about Harriet."

"Harriet is of no concern to me. And nor should she be to you." He puts a gentle hand to her shoulder, turning her to face him. "My loyalty will be to you, Eva. I know I cannot expect you to believe that now, after the way I treated you. But I hope you will come to see that in time. And I hope the fact that I have come all the way up here to see you in person might show you how much I regret sending you away."

Eva closes her eyes for a moment. Everything he has said is right, of course. This marriage is what this family needs. It will ease the pressure of selling the house. Ease the pressure on Nathan. Perhaps allow him to regain a little of his warm and easeful self.

In spite of everything, her marriage to Matthew Walton feels inevitable.

She hates that her life might be considered as such. But this is who she is, isn't it? As Samuel Blake's oldest daughter, her role has always been this. To marry a man whose wealth will dig this family out of poverty.

She hates the inevitability. And she hates the ache in her chest that comes when she thinks of that towering cottage on Longstone.

But she and Finn are an impossibility.

She thinks of the arrangement with Joseph Holland that Nathan has agreed to in order to protect her. She owes her brother this, she realises. Owes him a little peace of mind. Owes him the connections that will come with linking her family to the wealthy, well-respected Waltons.

She cannot find the words to accept Matthew's renewed proposal. But she finds herself nodding in agreement.

CHAPTER THIRTY-SIX

Eva shoves her wet clothes into the bottom of her duffel bag. They will likely be ruined when she gets to London, but she cannot bring herself to care. The rest of her wardrobe is waiting at Walton's townhouse, almost as though it has been expecting her return.

She knows she should not feel so empty. Things have been righted, and she will have the life she had always planned to have. Matthew's apology had seemed genuine, and she knows she is doing the right thing by Nathan and the rest of the family. The sooner she and Matthew return to London and begin their life together, the better.

She hates the thought of leaving without so much as a goodbye to Finn. She knows she has no hope of making it out to Longstone to see him, but perhaps she might at least pen a letter. Have Harriet take it to Julia to deliver when she next calls on her brothers.

Of course, things are better this way. Even though it does not feel like it. At all.

She looks up at a knock on the door. Nathan is standing in the doorway.

"Matthew tells me you have agreed to return to London with him."

She nods. Doesn't look at him. "It's the right thing to do."

He comes towards her. "Thank you, Eva. I'm grateful. Very grateful." He puts a hand to her shoulder. She manages a short smile, knowing how hard the gesture is for him. The look of gratitude, of relief in Nathan's eyes convinces her she is doing the right thing.

He pulls away and perches on the edge of the bed. "What happened last night?" he asks.

"Finn Murray was in trouble," she says shortly. "He needed my help."

Nathan frowns. "What kind of trouble?"

She shakes her head.

"You've been putting yourself out a lot for this Mr Murray," says Nathan. "Doing things I never imagined you doing. Is there anything I ought to know?"

Eva grabs the books from her nightstand and shoves them into her duffel bag. "I have agreed to marry Mr Walton. That is all you need to know."

But the moment she speaks, she realises she is wrong. There is far more she needs to share with her brother. She has no idea how a privateer like Henry Ward might have met their mother, and what would have driven her to invite him into their home. But somehow, this man is inexorably linked to their past on Holy Island. And she needs to know how much of this Nathan is aware of.

"Finn was taken by his old privateering captain," she tells him. "He tried to force him back into his crew." She winces at the lie. "But we managed to escape the ship." This is dangerous, of course, speaking of Ward and Finn in the same breath. Eva cannot bear for Nathan to know it was Finn who had caused Oliver's death. "The captain," she says carefully. "Henry Ward. He told me what happened to Oliver." Something almost imperceptible flickers across Nathan's eyes. "He was here at the house with his crew the night Oliver died."

For a moment, Nathan doesn't speak.

"You know all this, don't you," says Eva.

Finally, he faces her. "Yes. I was watching through the keyhole. Oliver fought with a cabin boy from Ward's crew. Oliver attacked him and the boy retaliated."

Eva's stomach twists. "That was why we left the house, wasn't it. Mother was mad with grief over Oliver. She was desperate to leave."

"I believe so," Nathan says after a moment. "We stayed to bury Oliver, of course. But after that… I've always believed that was why we left. I don't think she could handle being here any longer."

Eva stares into her knotted hands. Is that really all there is to it? They had torn out into a freezing night, without so much as a horse. Had her mother truly been so addled by loss she would be that reckless? Put her children in such danger? Or is there a part of the story they are missing?

"Why did you not tell me about Oliver when I asked why we left the house?"

Nathan sighs. "I'm sorry. I thought it for the best. What good would it have done if I'd told you?"

Eva doesn't respond. She supposes he is right. But she cannot help feeling betrayed.

She thinks of that night; herself tucked into the very bed she is sitting on now, oblivious to all that was taking place three doors down the hall. She thinks of Finn, of Nathan, of her mother. Thinks of Oliver, an almost mythical figure on the fringes of her memory.

For long moments, she and Nathan sit in silence. She can tell her brother's thoughts are back in that night too. Eva is almost glad to be leaving this house, and the poisonous air the past has left in its passages. But that life in London she had planned out so carefully, it feels so hollow. It seems like such a banal and empty existence to live a life not lit by the Longstone firebasket.

She stands suddenly and smooths her skirts. "I ought to go. I don't want to keep Matthew waiting."

Nathan nods. He stands; follows her to the door. "Take care, Eva. Be sure to write once the wedding plans are in place. We will do our best to attend."

She nods. Swallows heavily, forcing away tears. She picks up her bag and walks deliberately from the room, refusing the pull to look back at the islands behind the glass.

She makes her way downstairs, searching for Theodora and Harriet to make her goodbyes. Through the window she sees her niece rolling a hoop outside the house. Eva passes the kitchen, looking for her sister.

The door to Harriet's workroom is open a crack. Eva knocks lightly. When there is no response, she pushes open the door and tiptoes inside.

She finds her sister asleep in the old chair in the corner of the room. She is dressed in her nightshift and robe, her hair hanging loose over her shoulders. Paint flecks her hands, her arm draped over the chair, fingers reaching towards the half-drunk glass of whisky on the floor.

Eva turns to the painting that sits on the easel. A dark stripe has been slashed across the middle, blocking out the fine lines of sunlight Harriet had spent so long crafting.

Eva's heart lurches. Pristine and polished Harriet. How far has she fallen that she might allow herself to be seen like this? Is it the oppressive smallness of Holy Island that has poisoned her? Perhaps a little. But Eva knows Harriet had shown glimpses of this even while she had been flitting around London with a champagne glass in her hand. The light had begun to be sucked out of her once she had become a wife, a mother.

Eva kneels beside her sister, placing a hand over Harriet's thin white wrist. She does not want to wake her. But nor does she want to leave without saying goodbye.

She can't pull her eyes from the painting. From the anger and grief it expresses.

And in that dark and tainted artwork, Eva sees her own future. Sees this life that Harriet has taken on, at their brother's behest. Sees what being a dutiful sister, wife, mother has done to her. And this life she has agreed to, this life that has been laid out before her for as long as she can remember, Eva sees now that it will lead her to her own ruined canvas.

Suddenly there is not a sensible thought in her head—only this: that she cannot live the life she has spent an eternity planning. This polished life with the polished man in the parlour who smells of orange flower and loves her sister.

It is a betrayal to Nathan. A betrayal to her mother. To Oliver. To her whole family. She sees that, and it pains her. But for the first time in her life, she also sees something that she wants. Desperately. Passionately. For the first time in her life, she wants to break the rules.

She goes for the door, avoiding Matthew in the sitting room. As she passes the cart house, she hears Theodora call to her. She keeps walking, avoiding the questions, pretending not to hear.

She walks with a new sense of deliberateness, down the narrow path that cuts through the middle of the island.

She goes to the harbour, pulls her pouch from her pocket and puts coins in the hand of the first fisherman who agrees to take her to Longstone.

CHAPTER THIRTY-SEVEN

She is a mess when he sees her; windblown and frantic. Her cheeks are pink and she is twisting her bonnet in her hands. Finn loops the skiff's hawser around its moorings and leaps onto the jetty.

He has been on the mainland, asking after work. A need to distract himself from Henry Ward's presence—and, he had assumed, Eva's absence. How long has she been waiting?

She rushes at him, throws her arms around his neck. Her being here feels impossible. He can hardly make sense of it. And the torrent of garbling she throws at him sheds little light on the situation.

"Nathan will never forgive me," she is saying. "He will never speak to me again. I should never have… But I couldn't… I'm being so foolish…"

Finn takes her arms to steady her. Stop. Calm down. Tell me why you're here.

Her words are tangled with emotion, but he makes them out. A proposal. An ordered, respectable life in London. And: "But I want to be here with you, Finn."

Her hands are cold as he squeezes them in his. How can she be here after all he has told her, all the danger he has put her in? How is she seeking a life of such brutal isolation?

He ought to tell her, *yes Eva, you are being foolish. You ought to go to London with this toff who can give you a home that is not lashed by sea.* But this windblown cottage with the ocean at its edges, it feels like where she belongs.

He puts his hands to her shoulders and gives her a smile. "I'll make us some tea."

He is on edge as he hangs the kettle, fills the pot from her tin. The news from the mainland is unsurprising, but unsettling nonetheless. The Earl of Mar has arrived in Scotland and has held the first council of war. Two days ago, he had raised the standard of his would-be king James, signalling the beginning of the Rising. He knows it will not be long until the Jacobite rebels make their first attack. With Henry Ward's ship in these waters, war feels far too close at hand.

He and Eva sit on the rocks not far from the jetty, listening to the sea clop against the rim of the island. He will tell her, soon, of the Rising's beginning. Is certain she would want to know of it. But not now, while she is so unsettled. She sips her tea. She is calmer now, but there is still a bewildered look in her eyes, as though she cannot believe what she has done.

"All right?" asks Finn.

She nods. Covers his free hand with hers.

"Do you want me to take you back?" he asks.

"No." She does not hesitate. "Not yet, at least. I know I need to explain myself to Nathan. But…" She inhales. "This is where I want to be, Finn. If you'll have me." She shakes her head. "It's improper, I know, to be here with you like this. And I know there's no room. The Mitchells—"

"Eva." He squeezes her hand. "The Mitchells can sleep in the coal shed for all I care. The bedroom is yours for as long as you wish it." He wants more, of course, wants her in his arms. Wants to wake from his broken, cobbled sleeps with her in bed beside him. But having her here feels like enough of a miracle.

He kisses her. He is nervous. Because now this thing between them— this unlikely, impossible thing—it has a chance of being real.

He is wary of her being here, with the *Eagle* on the horizon. Knows there is every chance Henry Ward will come for him again. But he also knows it is no coincidence that Ward has returned to Northumberland at the same time as the Blakes. And whatever he wants with Eva's family, Finn is glad she will be here by his side.

They both have guilt to carry. Both have dreams, he is sure, that are haunted by the face of the life they had taken. Both hear the sound of his death ringing in their ears when the world is at its most silent. But these things, he knows, will be easier to carry when brought out into the firelight.

Book Two:

Moonlight Rising

HOLY ISLAND OF LINDISFARNE

OCTOBER 1715

CHAPTER ONE

It's a dream she has often, both asleep and awake. A dream of taking flight and finding a life beyond this. In sleep, it's a fractured, unfollowable dream, with indistinct colours like paint swirled on a canvas. When she is awake, it's a thing with edges; a tangible but distant hope of vanishing over the water like her sister has.

Harriet throws her pencil onto the blank page of her notebook and reaches for the whisky beside her, dark and oily in the bottom of the glass. Vivid and violent though these dreams of escape are, they are bringing her little in the way of inspiration. In the hours she has been tucked down here in her workroom, she has managed just a few sorry sketches—of the candleholder and the scattered pencils, and once, in desperation, her old house in London—each scribbled out with aggression, the page turned over quickly to hide her failures.

She empties the whisky glass, squinting in the muted light of late evening. The liquor makes her frustration soft around the edges—heightened by the thrill of having stolen it from her husband's liquor cabinet—but the taste is too familiar now for it to really make an impact. Perhaps that's the problem with this workroom too, with its worn armchair and bowed mantel and the table she has crammed half her notebook beneath to keep from wobbling: it has all become too familiar. Too uncomfortably comfortable. This room, this house, this island; it has all become so predictable she could scream.

Harriet reaches down for the whisky bottle she has hidden behind the table leg. She refills her glass to the top and carries it to the window. The sky is a rich cobalt blue, and in the last threads of daylight she can she see the inky outlines of a ship in the water beyond the house. Faint light blooms from the firebasket on the island of Longstone, where her sister Eva has made her escape. Building her unconstrained life.

Harriet closes her eyes. It's an ache inside her, that unreachable dream.

There is a knock at the door of her workroom. She hurriedly dumps her glass on the floor beside the whisky bottle.

Her husband Edwin does not wait to be invited inside. He steps through the door, eyes scanning the notebook and pencils strewn across the table. "Ah," he says, "you're working?"

Harriet presses her lips into a thin smile. She is fairly certain the blank pages of the notebook make it screamingly obvious she is not working, but so be it. "I am," she says tunefully. "Yes."

The thud of the door knocker echoes through the house. She hears footsteps, muffled voices in the entrance hall. Watches Edwin try to disguise his annoyance that she is downstairs to hear the knocking, rather than being tucked away in her bedchamber like an obedient wife.

"Please come in, gentlemen." Harriet hears her brother Nathan in the hallway, muttering greetings in his polite and stilted way. Welcoming men that are most unwelcome.

She knows who is at the door. She knows why they are here. And she takes some twisted pleasure in the fact that her husband and brother believe her ignorant to the whole damn thing.

No one had bothered to tell Harriet that Highfield House is being used by government spies in the fight against the Jacobites. Messengers come here regularly, posing as workmen in the manor's restoration. Tonight, she guesses, they are here for more than just an exchange of messages. Tonight, perhaps, the spies are meeting.

Had Nathan and Edwin assumed she would not notice that these so-called workmen appear and disappear without so much as picking up a hammer? Or did they just assume she would not care? She supposes that's a fair enough assumption—she has never had the slightest interest in politics. But disinterest is hard to maintain with spies creeping about their hallways.

Edwin spares a quick glimpse over his shoulder in the direction of the front door. "I assume you will be down here for another few hours?" he asks stiffly. He is uncomfortable at having the spies in the house, Harriet can tell. Possibly even more uncomfortable at the thought of his wife knowing anything about it.

She keeps her face deliberately empty. "I will, yes. I'm right in the middle of what I hope will be a very fine piece." Edwin glances back at the blank notebook, but her sarcasm remains unregistered. Or at least unacknowledged.

"All right." Another surreptitious glance in the direction of the hallway. "Good. Stay in here for a while, do you understand?"

She nods. Edwin comes towards her; leans in, in a rigid, practised motion. Harriet turns her head, offering him her cheek, but she knows it is not enough for him to miss the sear of whisky on her breath. His eyes narrow and he looks past her, collecting the bottle and half-drunk glass from the floor. He opens his mouth to scold her, then seems to remember he has more pressing concerns. Such as closing her away in her workroom and keeping her blind to all that is going on in the house.

He is out the door without a word.

Harriet waits for his footsteps to fade. Then she opens the door a crack and listens. She can hear a dull murmur of voices coming from the parlour.

Harriet knows Nathan had agreed to the spies' use of the house to clear Eva's name over the death of Donald Macauley some weeks ago. She had overheard Edwin and Nathan speaking of it not long after Eva had absconded to Longstone. Low, secretive voices, of course. There's suspicion everywhere these days. Since the Jacobites took up arms last month, distrust and rumours fill every alleyway on Holy Island. There are spies on both sides of the conflict in the village, they say. And Harriet knows her family is at the top of the list of those who are suspected to be working for the government.

She cannot blame the villagers for their suspicions. For reasons she knows nothing of, her mother and siblings had fled Lindisfarne twenty years ago. And they had reappeared on Holy Island, so close to Scotland and the Jacobite heartland, just as the Rising was beginning. But her family are not working for the government; they are just sorry fools coerced into letting the spies gather between their walls. Though she is fairly certain that will provide them with little leniency if the Jacobites in town discover what is taking place at Highfield House.

Harriet slips out of her shoes and makes her way silently down the passage. Rusty lamplight dances over the faded seascape and portraits hung on the walls of the entrance hall. The rich smell of pipe smoke drifts beneath the closed door of the parlour.

She waits, motionless, in case Nathan or Edwin show themselves. But beyond the hum of voices in the parlour, the ground floor of the house is quiet.

She presses an ear to the door.

Cotesworth, she hears. Yes, she knows this name. Knows this is the Newcastle merchant who has set these government spies into action. The man tasked with gathering the information that will quell the Rising in this part of the country. The man tasked with finding the leading Jacobites with warrants to their names—and making sure men like her friend Julia's wayward brothers are strung up by the neck to keep King George upon the throne.

Harriet knows this name because she listens. At the dinner table. At church. As she walks through the gossip-filled streets. Listens, with the practised art of a blank expression. A look of stark disinterest. Let them think her head is empty. Let them think her as blank and unintelligent as the unfilled pages of her notebook.

It is a powerful thing to be underestimated.

Meanwhile, she observes the world with the eye of an artist, trained to capture every nuance of the complicated life around her. *Listen*, she thinks. *Observe. Gather the pieces.*

Because she senses that each fragment, each word she collects might one day become useful. Perhaps they will come together to inspire a great piece of art. Or perhaps she will cobble together these fragments of knowledge and use them to build her own unconstrained life. Because knowledge, she knows, is power. Knowledge allows you to manipulate. Coerce. Build something from nothing.

There are more pieces: *Lesbury Common* and *an army gathering*, and *troops active*.

The stairs creak and she darts away from the door.

"Harriet?" Edwin's voice. She curses under her breath. "I told you to stay in your workroom," he says in a fierce whisper.

She is after a cup of water, she will tell him. Or an extra shawl against the evening chill.

And with her excuses forming on her lips, she hurries back towards her workroom, these new pieces of knowledge held close, like scraps that will keep her from starving.

CHAPTER TWO

Eva pauses on the path leading to Highfield House, smoothing her skirts and tucking windblown hair beneath her bonnet. The manor looms over her, gloomy and grey, even now, with the sun at its highest.

She feels like a child on her way to face the headmaster's wrath. Nathan is just four years older than her; why does she feel so damn scared? She tells herself she is being foolish. Tells herself it does not matter what her brother thinks of her, or the choices she has made.

But she knows this is a lie. Knows it is precisely because Nathan's opinion matters so much to her that her stomach is rolling and her heart is fast. She does not want to lose him. And she knows she is on the verge of doing so.

This is just her second visit to Highfield House since escaping to Longstone last month. She had first had Finn take her back to see her family two days after she had left Holy Island. Enough time, she had hoped, for her brother's anger at her leaving to have settled somewhat. And for her former betrothed, Matthew Walton, to have skulked back to London without her.

Eva had planned a long, drawn-out apology to Nathan; for disappearing without explanation, for shunning the marriage he had cultivated for her, and for leaving Walton standing alone in the parlour of Highfield House.

Nathan had refused to see her.

Perhaps it was for the best. Because she does not regret leaving Matthew Walton, or choosing this life with Finn on Longstone. But she does regret hurting her brother. She knows how much Nathan had been relying on her marriage to Walton. Aligning their family with the wealthy Waltons would have done much to restore the good standing of the Blake name, after the collapse of Nathan's merchant business last year. But the pull of life on Longstone had been too strong to resist.

This time, she does not announce her arrival. When Mrs Brodie, the housekeeper, lets her inside, she follows the sound of hammering towards the staircase. She guesses her brother is up on the second storey, working on his perpetual restorations.

"Auntie Eva!" Nathan's seven-year-old daughter Theodora bursts from the parlour, throwing her arms around Eva's waist. Eva gives her niece a squeeze. Thea looks up at her, her blonde hair spidery around her face and a fat blob of porridge on the front of her smock. "Are you back for good? Papa and Uncle Edwin said it was only a matter of time."

Eva smiles wryly to herself. "Where's your father?" she asks, sidestepping the question. "And your Auntie Harriet?"

Theodora points up the staircase. "Papa is up there, working. And Auntie Harriet is… I don't know… Not here. She went out."

"All right." She kisses Theodora on her forehead. "I missed you."

"Papa says we're not to disturb him when he's working," says Thea, fluttering up the stairs behind Eva, then pausing on the landing.

"I shall consider myself warned." Eva feels quite certain that, whether she interrupts Nathan's work or not, she will get the same brusque reaction.

She follows the sound of indistinct crashing to the room at the end of the hallway. The room beside Edwin and Harriet's that she thinks was once her mother's dressing room.

She knocks. But steps inside without being invited.

The room is chaos. The fireplace is in pieces, bricks strewn across the floor in a sea of dust and crumbled mortar. Several floorboards are missing, revealing the weighty beams beneath. A gaping hole in the wood panelling looks through to the worn stone of the outer wall of the house. Eva is not sure if Nathan is restoring the place or trying to destroy it.

Her brother has his back to her as he pries the last of the loose bricks from the fireplace and lets them thunder to the floor.

"Good afternoon, Nathan," she says.

He whirls around in surprise. His cheeks are pink with exertion, his sleeves rolled to his elbows and the brown waves of his hair tied at his neck. Patches of sweat darken the linen beneath his arms, his shirt discoloured with dust. A complicated look falls over his face at the sight of her. It's a look of irritation and profound anger, but there is something softer beneath. Something faint, that gives her the courage to get out what she has come here to say. He looks at her expectantly, the pry bar dangling from one hand and a hammer in the other.

Eva's mouth is suddenly dry. Whether from nerves or the dust-thick air, she cannot tell. "Thank you for not sending me away."

Nathan leans the tools up against the wall. "That would be rather petty, don't you think?"

No more petty than refusing to see me, she wants to say. But she bites her tongue. "What happened to the fireplace?" she asks instead. "Was it in such a state when you arrived back at the house?"

Her brother folds his arms, a hard look in his eyes telling her he does not appreciate the question.

"Mr Holland and the other government spies have been using the house?" Eva asks.

"Yes. They have." His voice is crisp and cold. Matter of fact.

"Has there been any suspicion from the villagers? From Martin Macauley and the other Jacobites?"

"Nothing more than usual. As far as I can tell, they are unaware of what the house is being used for."

Eva nods. Though it is hardly an assurance of her family's safety, it goes some way to allaying her concern for them. Not to mention her guilt. If it weren't for her, Nathan would never have had to agree to something so dangerous. And she has hardly gone out of her way to repay him. "I'm glad to hear it," she says.

"Is that why you came?" Nathan lops off the conversation before she can take it further. "To discuss the spies' use of the house?"

"No." Eva clears her throat. Inhales. "I came to tell you that Finn and I are to be married."

Nathan's lips twitch. "I see." He picks up the pry bar again and pretends to examine the broken fireplace.

"I know you're angry," says Eva. "And I know I've disappointed you. Let you down. And I'm sorry. Truly."

"But that does not change what you are about to do," Nathan finishes. She swallows. "No. It doesn't."

Finally, he turns back to face her. Despite his attempt at nonchalance, Eva can tell her news has surprised him. He rubs his free hand across the back of his neck, as though trying to find the right words. Perhaps he really had expected her to return home any day, meek and full of apologies. "And Mr Murray," he says finally, tapping the pry bar mindlessly against his thigh, "he did not see fit to discuss this with me first? To seek my permission?"

"Would you have given it?"

Nathan doesn't reply. He clenches his jaw—a gesture Eva knows well. A gesture that tells her he is doing his best to keep his anger from escaping. Although for what purpose, she can hardly tell. She is already well aware of how he feels towards her.

This role of patriarch, this role Nathan had grown into after the death of their father and elder brother, is one that was never supposed to be his. He is not a natural leader: too compliant, too affable, too averse to any kind of conflict. And yet the task of finding his sisters a husband is one he had approached with the utmost gravity. Eva knows that, by flitting in here with her scandalous news, she has stomped all over his carefully laid plans.

She thinks of Finn, waiting for her on the beach in front of the house. He had been adamant that he come with her, let Nathan know of his intentions. But she does not want him stepping into these rooms. Does not want him drawn back into the memories they will no doubt unearth, the shadows they will cast. This bleak weight that is always there; that she has come, perhaps too easily, to ignore. The night when Finn had come to Highfield House with Henry Ward, the privateer he had sailed with as a cabin boy. Tucked away in a bedroom upstairs, Finn had fought with Eva's eldest brother, resulting in Oliver's death.

She and Finn never speak of it—what is there to say? It had been a terrible accident that he has carried on his shoulders for the past twenty years. Eva knows stepping into Highfield House will paint those memories in fresh colours again. She cannot bear to put him through such a thing. Nor can she stand the thought of her family ever finding out the truth. Harriet and Nathan would never forgive her if they knew she was to marry the man who had killed their brother.

"Finn did wish to speak with you," Eva tells Nathan. "Very much."

He shifts the pry bar to his other hand.

"Will you put that damn thing down?" Eva reaches out and snatches it. "I told him I needed to speak with you first," she says. "To explain myself. And to apologise. I know I've treated you terribly. And I'm sorry."

Nathan tilts his head, studying her, as though trying to determine if her apology is genuine. His critical eye stings, though she knows she can expect little else. However close she and Nathan had once been, she had destroyed that the day she had run away to Longstone without a word of explanation. He is looking at her as though she is a stranger, and she supposes she cannot blame him.

"Well," he says finally, arms folded across his chest, "if nothing else, I'm glad you'll not be living in sin any longer."

Eva grits her teeth. "Finn has been a perfect gentleman," she says stiffly.

"I should hope so."

She sighs. She had hoped for more than brusque, obligatory conversation. Forgiveness, perhaps, had always been a step too far, but she had hoped for the chance to explain herself properly. But at least, she supposes, she was able to get a word out this time. She misses her warm and gentle brother. But perhaps it is too late for that. Too late to fix things. She sets the pry bar down with the rest of Nathan's tools and turns for the door.

"When?" he says suddenly. "And where?"

The words catch her off guard. "You wish to attend?"

"I'm your brother," he says, without warmth. "Of course I wish to attend."

Eva hesitates. She had not expected this. Had assumed she would marry Finn Murray away from the eyes of her family. And while there is a big part of her that is happy at the thought of her siblings attending, there is also a faint pull of dread. Because Nathan, at eight years old, had watched through the keyhole as Finn had struck the blow that had ended

Oliver's life. And though twenty years have passed, there is still a part of her that is terrified of her brother recognising the man she is to marry. There would be no worse place for him to do so than while they stand at the altar.

Still, keeping secrets is a price she is willing to pay to become Finn Murray's wife. And she knows forbidding her family to attend her wedding will put an end to any hope she might have had of reconciling with Nathan.

"St Aidan's Church in Bamburgh," she says. "Next Thursday at four."

"St Aidan's," says Nathan. "Where Father is buried."

"Yes." Half of her had chosen the church for that reason. The other half had wanted to stay as far away as possible from the gossip on Lindisfarne. Eva knows that if there's one thing the villagers love to prattle about more than the Blakes' fictitious ties to the government, it's her tryst with the Longstone lightkeeper.

Then, of course, there is the reason she is trying hard not to acknowledge: that marriage at St Aidan's will also keep them away from the grave of her eldest brother, who lies in the churchyard on Lindisfarne.

Nathan picks up his tools and returns to attacking the fireplace. "We shall be there," he says, somehow managing to sound both scathing and completely disinterested. Eva supposes that takes a special kind of talent.

CHAPTER THREE

This business with her brother has Eva distracted, Finn can tell. As they had sailed up to Highfield House, they had come within two hundred yards of the barque lying at anchor beyond Emmanuel Head. With her eyes fixed on the manor, Eva had not even noticed it.

Finn had not said a word to her about it. The last thing she needed before she faced her brother was to see Henry Ward's ship in the sea beyond her family home.

Five weeks ago, Finn's former privateering captain had taken him aboard his ship, seeking to punish him for the death of Oliver Blake. He and Eva had managed to escape, but both knew they had only done so because Ward had allowed it. The weeks since have been a waiting game, in which Finn's heart jumps at every light on the sea, expecting Ward to return for him. Ward and the *Eagle* have been on the edge of his consciousness for twenty years, but never more acutely than in the past five weeks.

Each time he sails to the mainland, to earn a little coin with days of farm work, he finds himself restlessly combing the sea. Out on Longstone, they spend days and nights with their eyes on the ocean, waiting for the masts of Ward's barque to cut through the cloud. But it's no surprise they have not seen him if Ward has been hiding away on the north side of Holy Island, Finn thinks. He and Eva have had little cause to come out here of late.

There is something painfully familiar about the sight of the *Eagle* in the sea beyond Highfield House, dark and skeletal and faintly threatening. It's a scene from Finn's childhood; a scene from haunted memories he can't push away. And a scene he is about to tie himself to forever, by making Eva Blake his wife.

Finn digs his hands into the pockets of his greatcoat and stares up at the ship, colourless and still in the afternoon haze. The furled sails tell him Ward has no plans to leave any time soon.

Eva's footsteps crunch across the embankment, pulling Finn's thoughts away from Henry Ward. Her face is hard to read beneath the shadow of her bonnet, but there is no anger there, or tears, so he dares to hope things have gone better than they did the last time she tried to explain herself to her brother.

"All right?" he asks, reaching for her hand. He turns her slightly, so her back is to the sea, Ward's ship hidden from her view. She will see it soon enough, of course. But one problem at a time.

She slides her arms around his waist. Rests her head against his chest at the place his heart is beating. "Well. He allowed me through the door this time. So I believe we're making progress."

"And? What'd he think of your news?"

Finn regrets leaving it to her to tell her family of their betrothal. As little as he knows about social decency, he is well aware he ought to have gone to her brother first, or at least been the one to tell him of their plans to marry. Still, Eva had been adamant that she go alone—and Finn has come to recognise that steely look in her eyes that tells him there is no room for argument. In any case, Nathan Blake's anger at his failure to follow convention is the least of his problems.

She looks up at him, catches his eye with a faint smile. "He's a stubborn bastard. But he will come around. I'm sure of it." She takes a step back, looks down at their interlaced fingers. "He wishes to attend the wedding."

"And you're not pleased by that?"

She hesitates a moment too long. "Of course I am." He can see behind her eyes. Can read the unease hiding there. A fear of what her brother might see when he looks at the man she is to marry. Finn doesn't blame her. It's a fear he has too.

Though he had not said a word of it to Eva, he is relieved that he had not had to step inside that house today. The memories the place conjures up are already vivid enough. Even now, he can feel his glance being pulled back to the ivy-covered walls of the manor. Trying to remember—or perhaps trying to forget—which room had belonged to Oliver Blake. Which of those rooms on the second floor had he been sleeping in when Oliver had appeared and held a knife to his throat? Which of those windows had he considered jumping from after Oliver's head had cracked against the bedpost? Which of those walls held the priest hole he had hidden in, and the passage that had allowed him to escape?

He pulls his gaze away from the row of dark glass. With luck, Eva's brother will finish the restoration of the house soon and sell it to some wealthy nobleman with a love for remote and windblown places.

"And you've not… changed your mind?" Finn asks, feeling his heart quicken slightly.

"Changed my mind?" Eva snorts. "Of course not. Don't be mad." Her sudden indignance makes him smile. That ship in the bay, the secret they are keeping from her family, it all feels easier to carry with Eva at his side. Strange that it might feel that way when her presence makes the stakes that much higher.

There's an impossible faultlessness to her place in their firelit cottage. A sense of her belonging, in spite of every piece of logic and reason. One night, with firelight pouring through the window, and her latest attempt at a bread loaf sitting charred and fragrant on the table between them, he'd looked up from his soup bowl and been almost surprised to find her sitting there opposite him. Had been overcome with a need to make this forever. With his soup spoon still in his hand, he'd spluttered out a request for her to become his wife, before he lost his nerve. Eva had given him a smile that said she'd been waiting an eternity for him to do it.

He bends his head to find her lips. Knows he ought to tell her of the ship beyond the house. She will see it, no doubt, when they head back to Longstone. And she will panic at Henry Ward's nearness to her family; will panic at the thought of what he might be planning.

Is his former captain here merely to mete out the punishment he feels Finn has escaped? As much as he wishes things were that simple, Finn can't quite make himself believe it. Henry Ward had returned to

Northumberland at the same time as the Blakes. He had been well acquainted with Eva's late mother, Abigail. Henry Ward is intertwined with Eva's family in a way Finn can't quite make out.

And then, of course, there is the slightly sickening fact that if all Ward wanted was to see him dead, it would be an easy enough thing to achieve.

And so just for now, he says nothing to Eva. Lets them have this fleeting moment, eye to eye, before they return to being hunted.

CHAPTER FOUR

Nathan's headache is not helped by the wailing of the baby coming from the nursery upstairs. He rubs his eyes and gulps his wine. Winces at its harshness.

On the other side of the dining table, his brother-in-law's eyes drift upwards. "No doubt the poor lad's due a feeding," Edwin says irritably. "I'll have strong words with his mother when she dares show herself."

Nathan puts his glass down a little too heavily. Crimson droplets slosh over the side and bead on the surface of the table. This is far from the first time Harriet has disappeared from the house for hours on end. These days, his sister seems to always be either locked away in her workroom, or wandering around the island on her own private journeys. Lost in thoughts she has no mind to share. Harriet's eyes have taken on a distant look of late; sometimes Nathan guesses she is merely lost in thoughts of her paintings. Other times, it is as though her mind has landed somewhere impossibly far away. His youngest sister has always been something of a mystery to him, but Lindisfarne seems to have drawn her further into herself. He knows how much she misses London; how much she had railed against coming here. He worries for her sometimes. And he knows she would not welcome his concerns.

Nathan glances at Theodora beside him, to gauge whether she has registered the conversation. She has a pencil in one hand and a piece of bread in the other, and is hunched over the table, scribbling furiously on crumb-covered paper. He catches a handful of words: *fairies* and *moon* and, inexplicably, *big furry seal suit*. He can tell from the faraway look in her eyes that her imagination has taken her far away. Good.

"I've a good mind to go and fetch her," Edwin says tersely, slicing his meat into slivers. "That Miss Mitchell, she's a bad influence."

Nathan feels something flip in his chest. He had not realised Harriet was with Julia Mitchell. Not that he can pretend to be surprised. As far as he knows, Julia is Harriet's only friend in this place. "You ought to forbid Harriet from seeing her," he tells Edwin stiffly. "She's not to be trusted."

Several weeks ago, Nathan had discovered Julia's two brothers hiding in the roof of Highfield House. Men on the run after their bloody clash with dragoons at a Jacobite protest in York. After Nathan had thrown them from the house, Julia had sent them to hide away on Longstone, out of sight of the authorities. Nathan has been painfully deliberate in staying away from her ever since. He wonders distantly if the men are still on Longstone. He had been tempted to ask Eva about it, but had not wanted her to think his talkativeness meant she was forgiven.

Some treacherous part of him misses being around Julia. He misses the brightness of her, the way her smile lights the dark corners of a room. But those things mean nothing when she had found it so easy to deceive him and his family.

He tosses back another mouthful of wine. Coughs as it sears his throat. "Thea," he says. "Eat your dinner."

Theodora glances up from the page, her blue eyes wide. She looks slightly bewildered at having found herself at the dinner table.

She spears a piece of roast beef with her fork and brings it to her mouth, without relinquishing her pencil. "Oh," she says around a mouthful, "I didn't get to read Auntie Eva my story."

Nathan slices his potatoes. "You can read it to me later. And please don't speak with your mouth full."

"You might have asked Eva to stay for dinner," says Edwin, not looking up from his plate.

Nathan hums noncommittally. He knows it was rude to send his sister away, especially with the smell of roasting meat floating up the staircase. But his anger is still far too raw to sit down to a meal with her. "Well. I was not quite yet in the mood to celebrate with her and her husband-to-be."

Edwin raises his eyebrows. "Husband-to-be? Is that so?" He chuckles, chasing down his meat with a mouthful of wine. "I have to say, I expected her to turn up back here with her tail between her legs and go chasing after Walton for forgiveness." He puts down his glass. "Probably for the best you didn't ask them to stay. That heathen of hers probably has no idea how to use a fork."

Nathan lowers his eyes. Says nothing.

In spite of himself, there's a tucked-away part of him that is happy for Eva. As much as he did not want to admit it, he had seen the grief in her eyes when she told him she had agreed to marry Matthew Walton. He had done his best to ignore it, knowing the marriage was what the family needed. And while Eva latching herself to Longstone and the lightkeeper is not the life he had imagined—or hoped for—for his sister, he cannot deny that when he saw her today, there was a glow in her eyes he is not sure he has ever seen before.

A thunderous knock at the door echoes into the dining room. Knowing Mrs Brodie is busy in the kitchen, Nathan pushes back his chair and gets to his feet. Strides down the hall.

He opens the door, heart jolting. There is Julia Mitchell, arm wrapped around Harriet as though keeping her afloat. Harriet's cheeks are pink, blonde snarls of hair clinging to her face and her bonnet swinging in one hand. Nathan can smell liquor on her.

"I lost my key," she says. She laughs, but there is no humour in it.

"I see," Nathan says tautly. His gaze is drawn to Julia, to her copper-green eyes and the unruly red curls escaping from beneath her cap. She looks away quickly, as though scorched by his scrutiny.

"Nathan," says Harriet, her voice syrupy, "are you not going to thank Julia for seeing me home?"

"Your son needs you, Harriet," Nathan snaps. "And dinner is on the table. Although I'd suggest tidying yourself first."

Julia nudges Harriet over the doorstep and she sidles past Nathan, heading precariously for the staircase. Nathan looks back at Julia. Meets her eyes for a moment.

"I'm sorry," Julia says. "She came to see me as I was closing the curiosity shop. We went upstairs and I offered her a drink. She must have refilled her glass when I wasn't looking. I didn't realise how much she'd had until she got up to leave."

Nathan wants to berate her. Wants to blame her for depositing his sister on his doorstep in such a state. But he can see the concern in Julia's eyes. And though he struggles to see beneath Harriet's brittle shell sometimes, he knows her well enough to be sure this was all her own doing.

But there is nothing else to say. He gives a terse nod and closes the door, ignoring the way his heart is hammering.

CHAPTER FIVE

This morning, the blank canvas feels as though it is mocking her. It has been more than a month since Harriet has even dipped her brush in paint.

The last piece she had begun, she had destroyed. Barely recalls doing it. She remembers little beyond anger, frustration, her thoughts distorted by one too many glasses of Edwin's whisky. When she had looked back at her canvas, it had been covered in angry whorls of black paint that had buried the sunlit scene she had spent so many hours crafting. She had stared at it for a long time with an odd sense of detachment, trying to make sense of why she had done it. And the answers, well, they are a little too frightening to look at in great detail. There are pieces of herself she would rather keep out of the light.

For five weeks, Harriet has let the frustration of the blank canvas swallow her. Has let herself be consumed by it, morbidly content in her inaction, her inability to conjure up any image worth realising. But today, things have changed. A letter. Arrived from London, from her dearest friend Isabelle. Harriet has read the excitable, curling script so many times she knows it by heart.

My patrons, Lord and Lady Baillieu were visiting from Paris last week and I told them about you and your work. They were most curious, and I took the liberty of showing them your seascape I so proudly hang in my workroom. Needless to say, the Lord and Lady were most impressed and they have expressed a wish to see more of your pieces. They would very much like to meet you.

And then, the letters becoming rounder and more elaborate, as though

Isabelle carried as much excitement at the prospect as Harriet did:

I would so love you to accompany me to Paris when I attend the Baillieus' next salon in April. Do say you will be back from the wilds of Northumberland by then and will be able to join me!

Harriet's childhood painting tutor, Madame Octavia, had introduced her to Isabelle and the other artists in her circle. Though Harriet had been barely sixteen at the time, they had taken her under their wings, welcomed her into their clique. Given her the praise and encouragement she needed to begin to believe in herself as an artist.

Once a fortnight, the group would gather in each other's homes—in chandeliered drawing rooms and garden sheds, and dank kitchens that reeked of old ale and tallow. Wherever they met, it did not matter. The group straddled class and gender lines, drawn together by a shared passion for their art. Peering over wine glasses and through clouds of pipe smoke, they would share their work, critique each other's paintings, discuss their inspiration.

When Harriet was among the group, it did not matter that she was a woman, or that she was not yet even twenty. Or that Edwin never allowed them to gather beneath his roof—and would grumble endlessly when she returned home with smoke on her clothes, light-headed with wine and ideas. All that mattered were the brushstrokes, the colours, the tools, the plans. And the sense of freedom that came with it all.

In the company of Isabelle—beautiful, talented Isabelle; all dark hair and curves, who painted portraits as though she were looking into another's soul—Harriet felt able to voice pieces of the things that lingered in the dark recesses of her mind. Her anger at Nathan for wrangling her into the marriage that suited him best. Anger at herself for blindly accepting. The way her husband and son so often feel like strangers. And the way there was not a single cell in her body that had ever wanted a husband at all.

Isabelle, eight years older than Harriet, was never fazed by her scandalous admissions. She just listened and nodded and let a moment of silence pass to craft her answers before she opened her mouth.

I know how it feels to be different, Isabelle would say. *I know what it is to feel as though you do not fit in.*

Isabelle had turned not fitting in into an artform. After several years of unhappy marriage, she was now living apart from her husband, spared the marriage market on account of her promise to support herself. And what a dazzling job she was doing at that, with a paint-filled garret in Lambeth and her portraits hung in the salons of one of the wealthiest families in France.

Isabelle is everything Harriet aspires to be. She misses her with an intensity so deep it almost feels like a physical thing.

This opportunity she has dangled in front of her, it's a piece of that dream, that unconstrained life. It feels too impossible, like it belongs to someone else.

Harriet knows the journey to Paris will not be cheap. The cost is well within her husband's reach, she is sure. But she knows Edwin despises her artists' group, with their disdain for social norms and their elaborate, outlandish ambitions. Knows he believes he deserves a sainthood for allowing her to attend their gatherings. How she will convince him to part with the money and let her flit off to Paris with Isabelle, she has no thought. Not that that is as pressing an issue as the blank canvas in front of her. The sum will matter little if she has nothing new to show the Baillieus.

She closes her eyes. Imagines her work on display at Lady Baillieu's salon. Sees people discussing, admiring. *Such fine use of colour. An intriguing perspective.* Sees a life in which she is more than just mother, wife, trapped on an island.

Perhaps, she thinks, she will have to paint under an assumed name, pretend a man had done the work. The letter from Isabelle had not discussed such details. Harriet knows her evocative landscapes are far outside the scope of the still lifes and domestic scenes expected of a female artist. But if she is to paint under a man's name, so be it. Having her work on display would still be the greatest of thrills.

She reaches for her notebook and pencil.

In a room above her head, her son Thomas wails. She feels instinctive dread tighten her muscles. Does her best to block out the sound. She puts the pencil to the page. Tries to let her imagination, her inspiration, guide her. The baby shrieks. The sketch refuses to find its shape.

Footsteps creak across the upstairs passage. Down the staircase. Thomas's howling gets louder, and there is a knock at the door of her workroom.

Harriet supposes it was inevitable. But she knows that, as she pulls open the door, the look she gives Thomas's nurse is sour and unwelcoming.

"I'm sorry to disturb you, Mrs Whitley," says Jenny, eyes lowered. "He's ready for a feed."

Of course he is. Harriet's hand tightens around the pencil. She can't help the tug of resentment. Has she not given enough of her body to this child?

She takes the baby, giving Jenny a brusque nod. There's an apologetic look in the nurse's eyes that makes Harriet faintly guilty. Quiet and loyal Jenny, who had long ago buried her own son and husband, has been with them since Thomas's birth six months ago. Harriet knows she would never have survived this long without Jenny's knowledge, her support, her patient encouragement. But that does nothing to quell her irritation at being disturbed. Every now and then, she sees a look in Jenny's eyes that suggests she is afraid of her. And what an odd thing that is, Harriet thinks, given the woman is more than twice her age, with endlessly more wisdom. An odd thing, but strangely thrilling nonetheless.

She carries the baby upstairs. Not once has she ever brought Thomas into her workroom. And she never plans to do so. She wishes she could keep her husband out too, but that is far more difficult, given he has control of his own two legs.

She sits in the chair in the corner of her bedroom with Thomas at her breast. Hears footsteps down the passage. The door creaks open. Edwin goes to the washstand and empties the jug into the basin. His shirtsleeves are rolled up and his coal-coloured hair clings to his neck. He splashes his face, sloughing away the dust of the renovations.

Harriet watches him curiously, trying to read his mood. It's a difficult thing, given how little she knows him, even after a year and half of marriage. Sometimes—often—he feels more like a headmaster than a husband. And they seem to have come to a wordless agreement that things will run more smoothly between them if they keep the more jagged parts of their personalities hidden from each other. But right now, she needs him. Or rather, she needs his money.

"Have you finished fixing that broken window in Eva's room?" she asks, with as much sweetness as she can muster.

Edwin turns to face her, eyebrows raised in surprise. Water drips off his sharp chin and he reaches for the cloth beside the basin to dry his cheeks. "Yes," he says. "I've put a second coat of paint on the dining room wall too."

"You've been busy this morning."

He looks at her, something tentative in his eyes. He seems caught off guard by her sudden interest in his work. Faintly suspicious. No doubt he suspects she is trying to make up for appearing on the doorstep like a vagrant last night. Which, she supposes, she is.

"You ought to come and see it once Thomas is fed," Edwin says, as though agreeing to take part in this game she has begun to play. "The colour is quite lovely. I think you will like it."

"All right." She lifts the baby onto her shoulder and uses her free hand to lace her stays.

Edwin looks down at their son, rubbing a hand across his downy blond hair. "That's quite a mop he's growing."

Thomas opens his mouth and fountains a trail of vomit down Harriet's shoulder. Edwin wipes at it with the cloth. "You were not at breakfast this morning," he says to her. "Have you eaten today?"

Harriet bites back an irritated retort. She knows Edwin, twelve years her senior, looks upon her as little more than a girl. A fragile, delicate thing in desperate need of guidance. But perhaps he might trust her enough to determine on her own when she is hungry. "I shall eat later."

He gives a murmur of displeasure. "What's in your hand?"

Harriet had not realised she was still carrying Isabelle's letter. It is crumpled in her clenched fist, tucked in behind the baby's back as though it has become a part of herself she is unable to detach from. "A letter," she tells Edwin. "From London." She knows there is no need to say more. She has few acquaintances in the capital beyond the members of her artists' circle. Certainly none that would write to her.

"Ah," says Edwin, that single half-grunted syllable enough to convey his every thought about whichever peculiar soul had written her the letter, and whatever it is they might want.

Harriet stands, planting Thomas on her hip. She will not speak of Paris yet. She needs time to wrangle herself back into her husband's good graces after plundering Julia's liquor stores last night. She gives him the girlish smile she knows appeases him. "Why not show me the dining room?"

CHAPTER SIX

"North-westerly wind," says Finn, climbing down the steps at the front of the cottage. The sea is restless and gunmetal grey, the afternoon air cold and briny. "Perfect conditions for learning to tack."

"As long as you're not in any hurry to get to Lindisfarne." Eva gathers her skirts in her fist as she passes the rockpools in front of the house. "And you don't mind me sailing around in circles."

"I'm never in any hurry to get to Lindisfarne." Finn chuckles. "In a hurry to leave, usually, so welcoming are the villagers."

Eva grins. Looks over her shoulder at him as she navigates over the rocks towards the jetty. "Well, that is what you get for stealing their coal. And for betrothing yourself to a suspected government spy."

He laughs. Then nods towards the empty mooring post on one side of the jetty. "I see Michael has left again. Thought the bloody fool was out here to hide."

Eva knows Julia Mitchell's brother Michael has been making regular visits to either the mainland or Holy Island—these days, the longboat is gone more often than it is here. For what purpose she does not know for certain, though she can guess well enough. She has little doubt that Michael is still deeply entrenched in the Jacobite cause, despite the hangman's noose already having been tied for him.

"Seems two months in the attic at my family's house and he's had enough of hiding," says Eva.

"I don't like it." Finn turns up the collar of his greatcoat against the wind. "It's dangerous. Feels like it's only a matter of time before the redcoats are at our door."

Eva shares his annoyance. Harbouring Jacobite criminals is risky. Every time Michael leaves the sanctuary of Longstone, he is putting them in greater danger. Still, she knows selflessness is not high on the Mitchells' list of qualities.

"I heard the Jacobites are going south," Finn tells her. "Planning to take Newcastle."

Eva feels a pull of unease. With the exception of Michael and his brother being crammed around their supper table, they have so far managed to avoid entangling themselves in the Jacobite Rising. At the thought of the conflict coming as close as Newcastle, Eva feels distinctly on edge. "Do you think that's where Michael is headed?" she asks.

"Could be," says Finn. "But they're saying the militia's close to securing the town. If he's on his way down there to fight, I don't think he's much to look forward to."

Michael and his brother Angus have been on Longstone for more than a month, and have not yet made any mention of leaving. Eva knows they are waiting for news of their elder brother, Hugh, before they head to London to hide away in the city. She doesn't begrudge them that. But it has felt far too crowded in the Longstone cottage, with sleeping pallets rolled up in corners and empty crates crammed around the table to compensate for the lack of chairs. A single bedroom for them all to navigate as they take turns keeping the light.

Nonetheless, there has been something thrilling about sneaking around Longstone with Finn, trying to snatch a scrap of privacy. A kiss without witnesses, a moment alone in the overcrowded cottage. A mouthful of wine in the dim light of the shed, hidden between piles of earth-fragrant peat.

Eva appreciates the irony that it might feel so congested in a place of such dazzling remoteness. But her courtship with Finn has always been a slightly backwards thing. They had been keeping the light as near strangers, had spent the night on Longstone together before they even knew each other's name.

Finn steps into the skiff. "Right then," he says, offering her his hand, "get in the boat, lass." He unties the mooring rope as she climbs aboard. "I'll row her clear of the island and then she's all yours. You can take us into this wind over to Lindisfarne."

Eva looks back at the island as Finn rows out into the sea. It's a sight she still struggles to believe is real: their stone cottage rising from the rock as if it had always been a part of it; the towering needle of the firebasket just beyond. Mirrored planes of rockpools, whorls of white water, and then sea, and sea, and sea. To the north-west lies Lindisfarne; and beyond the black rock crenelations of the other Farne Islands is the mainland village of Bamburgh, the silhouette of its castle like stacked dice on the horizon.

Finn slides the oars from the oarlocks and settles them at his feet, the boat tilting rhythmically on the swell. He nods towards the lines. "Haul in the sheets to get her moving, then we'll bring her close to the wind."

Eva frowns in concentration as she tugs on the ropes, opening the sloop's mainsail. It thwacks noisily before tightening. The boat begins to fly out in the direction of the open ocean.

"Good." Finn nods. "Now bring her into the wind."

Eva leans carefully on the tiller, feeling the boat shift beneath her. Wind tears into the sail, making it drum and flutter loudly. She grits her teeth in frustration. "This always seems far easier when we're talking it through at the supper table."

Finn chuckles, leaning back against the gunwale to watch her. "Aye, but it's quite useless information at the supper table, I've found." He nods towards the thundering sail. "How do we fix it?"

"We're too close to the wind," Eva says. "We need to fall off a little. Back the way we came."

He grins. "Seems there's hope for you after all."

Tentatively, she guides the boat off the wind, feeling it fall into a gentle rhythm. And she lets herself breathe.

The life she is building here is at once overwhelming and impossibly simple; a life of callused palms and wet skirt hems, and arms turned muscular from hauling the firebasket into the sky. A life in which she has learnt to bake bread, to pull bones from fish, to drink water straight from the sky. A life far beyond the one she imagined she would live.

A life which, if she is able to look past the fear of Henry Ward, has made her desperately happy.

As they skirt the south-eastern tip of Holy Island, Eva sees Finn's eyes pull northward. She knows he is looking towards Emmanuel Head. Looking for that dark outline of Ward's ship.

Despite the shock that had rattled through her when she had caught sight of the *Eagle* on their way back to Longstone earlier in the week, she knows she cannot be surprised that Ward is here. She has been waiting for more than a month for him to show himself. Glimpsing his ship had almost been a relief—had taken away the element of surprise. Still, knowing where the ship is, and knowing exactly what Ward plans to do to her and Finn—and her family—is another thing entirely.

Eva shuffles across the bench and lets Finn take the tiller as they make their way towards the Lindisfarne anchorage. A thick bank of clouds billows across the sun, turning the water to ink. A large brigantine lies at anchor on the edge of the bay, a single longboat cutting a steady line from its hull towards the shore.

Finn eases the skiff up to the rickety wooden jetty. It thuds softly against the moorings between an armada of tiny fishing boats. He secures the mooring ropes and climbs out of the boat. Offers Eva his hand. She keeps a hold of it as she walks down the jetty and across the beach. Her shoes crunch over the dried rafts of seaweed as they pass the tiny wooden fishermen's huts. A waft of seaweed and herrings hangs on the air.

She feels the heads turn, eyes pulled away from the brig in the bay. Eva knows she is not imagining the whispers, the murmurs, the gossip. She hears her name, half-whispered. Knows everyone is aware of her sinful life, living out on Longstone with Finn Murray.

"Something I can do for you?" Finn calls to an older woman who is passing with a basket on her hip. She is watching them openly, her expression wavering between curiosity and derision.

She puts her head down and hurries away. Eva hides a smile.

Finn puts a protective hand to the back of her neck. "Shall I see you to the house?" he asks.

"No. It's all right. You go to the market. I'll meet you back here later this afternoon."

While Eva has little hope of resurrecting things with Nathan right now, she is determined not to drift apart from her sister. Harriet had been in such a terrible state when Eva had left for Longstone, and now that Nathan has permitted her back through the door of Highfield House—however reluctantly—she plans to make up for lost time with her.

Finn meets her eyes. "Be careful."

"And you." She hates the thought of letting him out of her sight while they are so close to Ward and the *Eagle*. Nonetheless, she knows they are in far less danger here in the village than they are in the deep isolation of Longstone.

Finn kisses her cheek—for the benefit of the onlookers, Eva is sure—then she turns and follows the coast path through rolling dunes towards the house.

"Well now." Harriet looks up from her plate of toast as Eva appears in the dining room. "Look what the tide dragged in." She is alone at the vast expanse of the table, picking at her breakfast, though it is well past noon. Today she is back to her usual polished self, in a pale pink woollen dress, her blonde curls held high on her head with a fine pearl-studded comb. She lifts a teacup to her lips with delicate fingers.

Eva tries to flatten her windblown hair with her palm. As she slides into the chair opposite her sister, she glimpses the streak of ash on her skirts. How had she not noticed that on the way here? She tries ineffectually to scrub it away with her thumb.

A chaos of hammering spills down from upstairs, making the lamp above the table sway. The dining room, Eva realises, has been painted the colour of eggshells, the large fireplace blackened and polished. The piney scent of paint still hangs faintly on the air. It's one of the few improvements she has seen to the house since the restorations had begun. She nods towards the freshly painted walls. "The colour is nice."

Harriet smiles wryly. "Edwin thinks so too. I hoped he might have managed something a little more interesting."

Eva lets her comment slide. "I'm sorry I've not come more often." She raises her voice to be heard over the thumping. "It's just—"

"Oh I know," says Harriet airily. "Nathan's being an utter beast. I don't blame you." She lifts the lid of the teapot to inspect its contents. "I'll have Mrs Brodie fetch you a cup."

"No, it's all right. Perhaps a walk instead?"

Harriet laughs. "You wish to leave before Nathan catches you here?" She nibbles at her toast, then places her half-eaten slice back on the plate. "Very well. This racket is driving me mad anyway."

Wrapped in cloaks against the bracing autumn air, they follow the winding coast towards the village. Wind bends the grass of the dunes, catching the wings of a flock of pintails and carrying them back into the sky. Eva finds herself glancing sideways at her sister, trying to see behind her eyes. She can see no hint of the despair she saw in Harriet the day she had fled to Longstone. But she knows better than to believe it is not there. Knows Harriet is adept at quashing the chaos down under a pristine and polished surface.

She wants to ask her outright how she is faring. If she is happy. If life on Lindisfarne has become bearable. Uncomfortably, Eva realises she knows the answers to these questions. And she has no thought of how to make them otherwise.

"Are you painting?" she asks instead.

Harriet doesn't look at her. "Why would I not be painting?"

Eva debates whether to mention the ruined canvas. Decides against it. Instead, she asks, "What are you working on?"

Harriet is silent for a moment and Eva wonders what she is thinking. "I'm in between pieces," she says finally. "Waiting for inspiration to strike, I suppose."

"I'm sure it will come if you give it time." Eva wonders if Nathan has said anything to Harriet about her betrothal to Finn. Harriet has always been lost in her own existence, but Eva is still surprised they have made it through a scrap of toast, a cup of tea, and a mile of walking without her sister mentioning such life-changing news.

As Eva opens her mouth to speak, Harriet says, "I hear you shan't be skulking back to Highfield House with your tail between your legs."

Eva smiles to herself. She knows this is as close to a word of congratulations as she is ever likely to get from her sister. "No," she says. "I shan't."

Harriet watches her feet for several paces. She gathers her skirts in her fist and tiptoes around a mud puddle. "I was glad you went, you know."

Eva looks up at her. "You were?"

"Yes. Well. Not for me. I would have much preferred to have you around." Her voice is suddenly thin. "But for your sake, I'm glad you went."

Eva gives her a short smile. "I'm glad I went too. Rather, I'm glad I found the courage to go."

Harriet hums, yanking at her cloak as it entangles itself on a withered hunk of gorse. "Are you certain about it though?" she asks, keeping her eyes down. "Living that way for the rest of your days? It's not… well, it is hardly the kind of life you are accustomed to, is it."

Eva feels a flicker of irritation. "I am not sure the life I am accustomed to has ever made me happy."

"Still. Are you going to be any happier condemning yourself to a penniless life on an island the size of a rock?" Eva glares, but her icy look seems to barely penetrate Harriet's cool exterior. "And I'm sorry, Evie, but I know for a fact that you would rather die than wash your own bedclothes. And I also know you can barely cook a piece of toast. Are you really going to—"

"I can see what you are trying to do, Harriet," Eva snaps. "And you shan't talk me out of it. I have made my decision and I could not be happier about it. If Finn and I are to spend our lives penniless and eating burnt toast, then so be it."

"I am not trying to talk you out of anything. I already told you I was glad you went." Harriet shrugs. "I thought they were quite reasonable questions."

Eva grabs her arm to silence her as they step into the village. People are gathering around the hill at the bottom of the castle, eyes on the ramparts, chatter in the air. A pistol shot sounds from within the castle grounds.

Eva feels suddenly hot. The panic that has been at her edges since finding the *Eagle* threatens to rise. But this is not Henry Ward's doing, at least as far as she can tell. She hurries towards the water, trying to get a glimpse of the castle. A steady stream of onlookers is filtering in from the village. Two dragoons burst through the castle gates, a woman among them she guesses is one of their wives. Another pistol shot echoes in the cold air.

Eva catches sight of Joseph Holland on the edge of the water. She knows him a friend of her brother's—and she also knows him to be one of the government spies who are using Highfield House. She elbows her way towards him, tugging Harriet along behind her. A woman tears past, thumping into her shoulder.

"What happened?" Eva asks Holland.

"Jacobites," he says, folding his arms across his thick chest. "Taken the castle." He keeps his voice low. "They're saying it was the master of that brig out in the bay. Errington. I reckon Forster sent him over from Bamburgh."

Eva nods. She knows much of the village of Bamburgh, just across the water, is owned by Thomas Forster, a Jacobite commander.

"The guard's saying he let the fellow in to see the barber and Errington pulled his pistol," Holland tells her. "Seems he and his mate have taken charge of the place." He nods in the direction of the two soldiers who are hurrying towards the water. "Threw the redcoats out."

Eva looks up at the ramparts. "There were only two soldiers in the castle?"

"Aye. Looks like the rest of the garrison was off duty."

"Why?" she demands. "With all that's happening in Newcastle, how could they not have been expecting an attack?"

Holland smiles wryly, but doesn't respond. Eva glances out across the water, half expecting to see the anchorage filling with ships carrying Jacobite reinforcements. But beyond the large brig she had seen on their arrival—Errington's vessel, she realises now—there is little in the water beyond fishing boats and Finn's small skiff.

She feels distinctly uneasy. And painfully aware of the Jacobite criminals hidden away in her cottage. She finds herself glancing around the thickening crowd in search of Finn, needing the reassurance of his presence. She sees no sign of him.

"We ought to go back to the house," she tells Harriet.

"Don't be mad. This is the most excitement the place has seen in weeks." There's a shine in Harriet's eyes, a crooked half-smile on her lips. She lets out a private laugh. "I thought you were the adventurous type now."

"There's a difference between adventurousness and foolishness."

"Honestly, Evie, you do have a way of making everything so dismal. What are you afraid is going to happen? Some bloodthirsty Scotsman is going to come tearing out of the castle and throw you over his shoulder?" She laughs to herself. "That would be a thing to witness."

Eva grits her teeth. Turns away before she's tempted to wish such a fate upon her sister.

Harriet sees him on the edge of the crowd; a man who should not be here.

He is the brother of Julia Mitchell, and a known Jacobite with the shooting of a soldier to his name. Harriet had assumed he and his brother were hiding away on Longstone, in an attempt to keep their necks unbroken.

His head is down and a large cocked hat is pulled low over his face, but she has no difficulty recognising him, with a flame-coloured queue hanging down his neck, and coppery bristles covering his cheeks and chin. Little wonder Julia had shipped her brothers out to Longstone to hide them from the authorities. The Mitchells have about as much hope of blending into a crowd as a man with two heads.

Julia's brother makes his way through the throng, heading towards the water, as though trying to find a better vantage point. Curious, Harriet finds herself following him. She fancies seeing the look on Julia's face when she tells her her criminal of a brother is strolling about Lindisfarne in sight of the castle guards. Harriet has always had a desire to stir things up. Life is far more interesting that way.

As though feeling Harriet's eyes on him, he turns. His eyes catch hers. It's a knowing look, somehow. Does he remember her from the night he was dragged out of Highfield House by her husband? Perhaps. Either way, that look tells her he knows he has been recognised. It is a powerful feeling. Because Harriet knows he will not soon forget her.

"Where did you go?" Eva demands when she returns.

"Nowhere." She could tell her, of course, that one of her Longstone hideaways is strolling around the village, just to see her lose her mind. But Harriet is more interested in the man who is standing at her sister's side now, a protective hand to the back of her neck. He's tall, broad shouldered, towers over Eva. And though there is a gaping disparity between his colourless sailor's slops and her neat wool skirts, there's a strange compatibility to them that takes Harriet by surprise. Eva's fingers brush lightly against his, the motion seeming so instinctive she is almost unaware of it. She takes a step closer to him, as though steadied by his presence. There's a practised ease between Eva and her lightkeeper, Harriet realises, as though they have already lived their entire lives together. The sight of them strikes her with a violent and unexpected stab of jealousy.

It's Harriet's own presence that flusters Eva, clearly ruffled at this colliding of the two disparate parts of her life. Pink cheeked, she garbles out introductions, accompanied by an over-enthusiastic wave of her hand.

Harriet looks Finn Murray up and down, inspecting him openly. In spite of his slops and tarred greatcoat, and apparent inability to use a razor, he is not quite as wild and unkempt as she had imagined. His beard is trimmed close to his chin, light brown hair pulled back neatly, a faded blue neck cloth tied at his throat. There's a half-smile on his face, as though he is well aware of the examination she is subjecting him to. "A pleasure to meet you, Mr Murray," Harriet says smoothly. "You've come just in time. It seems Evie is rather concerned about wayward Scotsmen whisking her away to their lair."

The lightkeeper chuckles. "Is she just?" He catches Eva's eye and gives her a private smile.

"We'll see you back to the house, Harriet," she says crisply. "You shouldn't be on your own. Not with all that's going on."

"I hardly think any Jacobite rebels will be blockading the path to Emmanuel Head," says Harriet with a dull laugh. But her mind is racing with thoughts of Julia's escaped brother, with the castle siege, with the man who is to be her sister's husband, and she realises suddenly that she does not wish to be alone with her own thoughts. A stolen glass of Edwin's whisky and a few hours in front of her notebook are what she needs to calm her jealousy; calm her desperate need to appear on Julia's doorstep and create drama for the sake of something to do. Julia is her only friend in this place, and Harriet does not want to lose her out of her own petty need to cause trouble. She closes her eyes, hit with a pang of self-loathing. Perhaps when she returns home, she can funnel these unwelcome emotions into a piece of art that is actually worth looking at. Or at least more than a scribbled-out sketch. And so she capitulates to

Eva's motherly objections and allows herself to be escorted back to Highfield House.

CHAPTER SEVEN

Rain is thumping steadily against the windows of Harriet's workroom. She has given up on trying to paint, and is standing with her forehead to the pane, watching trails of water carve their crooked path down the glass. Beyond the window, the sea slaps hard against the embankment.

It's during the high tide that escape feels the most unobtainable. It's a foolish notion, Harriet knows, because she is just as trapped here whether the tide is high or low. But somehow, when the steppingstones of the Pilgrims' Way vanish beneath the water, cutting Holy Island off from the mainland, it heightens her sense of hopelessness. As though her paintings—and her dreams—will sooner be washed away than make it to a salon in Paris.

She takes her cloak from the back of her chair and slides it on over her shoulders. Never mind the rain. Yesterday, Edwin had forbidden her from leaving the house, convinced more Jacobites were about to land on Lindisfarne with guns ablaze. Now word has come that the redcoats have taken back the castle, he has unbolted the doors. And Harriet is not about to be constrained by a little filthy weather. She pulls up the hood of her cloak and slips out the front door before anyone can stop her. Cold air blasts away her sluggishness.

Wind is howling across the island, gathering the rain into a squall and tossing the high tide up over the beach. Harriet presses a hand to her hood, trying ineffectually to hold it in place. After a moment, she gives up. Allows herself to enjoy the feel of the wind making chaos of her hair. Sea spray mixes with rain on her cheeks.

She looks about her as she walks; at the hazy pall of the sea, the blown yellow tussocks of grass that cover the dunes. She tries to commit this silvery, windswept landscape to memory. It's the natural world she wants to paint; wants to capture the infuriating beauty of this island, her prison. But everything she has sketched or imagined so far feels so derivative and commonplace. Meagre attempts at matching Lorrain's perfection of nature. Godly images that feel hollow and inauthentic. Even the seascape she had gifted to Isabelle, the piece that had captured the attention of her friend's wealthy French sponsors, is full of other people's ideas.

How proud Harriet had been when she had first seen her piece hanging in Isabelle's workroom. She had told herself she was special; that it meant she held pride of place in Isabelle's heart. Perilous thoughts. She chases them away before they lead her into dangerous places.

Harriet's skirts are soaked by the time she reaches the curiosity shop, her waterlogged cloak heavy on her shoulders. Half the island is caked to her shoes.

Julia is unlocking the front door as she approaches. "What are you doing out in this weather, you madwoman?" She holds the door open with one arm.

Harriet stands in the doorway and steps out of her muddy shoes. Rain drips from her hair and trickles down the back of her neck.

"I'm surprised your keepers let you visit me after your little effort last week," says Julia. Her ginger cat peeks past Harriet, contemplating a dash out into the rain. Julia scoops it under her arm.

Harriet smiles crookedly. "I'm sorry. You know I can't hold my liquor."

"I do now, aye."

She's a little embarrassed, yes. Knows working her way through Julia's whisky and turning up back at the house without her key had not been her finest moment. But Harriet has seen her husband and brother in their cups on far more than one occasion. And she is fairly certain it has never caused the sky to fall in.

"May I stay?" she asks with a coy smile.

"What do you think, Minerva?" Julia says to the cat. "Shall we give her another chance?” The cat squirms out of her arms and stalks off across the shop with its tail in the air. Julia snorts. “Hideous thing.” She looks back at Harriet. “Stay. But you’re only having tea this time.” She pulls her pocketbook out of her apron and empties the coins onto the counter.

Harriet slings off her sodden cloak and hangs it over a chair that’s sitting in the corner of the shop, pushed up against an overflowing bookshelf. She stands in front of the newly lit fire. Holds her hands close to the flames for a moment, then pulls the pins out of her windblown hair and sets them on the mantel. She rakes her fingers through the wet tangles. “I think Nathan was a little pleased to see you the other evening.”

Julia doesn’t look up from the coins she is counting. “I’m sure. He looked simply overjoyed at my turning up on your doorstep.”

Harriet ignores her sarcasm. She wrangles her thick blonde curls into a fresh plait. “You ought to come for a visit.”

“Why, exactly? To anger your brother again? I don’t think so.”

“Don’t let his foul mood bother you,” Harriet says, pinning up her hair. “He’s just bent out of shape because Evie’s gone flitting off with the lightkeeper instead of marrying the fop he picked out for her.”

Julia snorts. “I think there’s a little more to his anger at me than that. It’s slightly more than a *foul mood*, wouldn’t you say?”

Harriet turns towards a loud creak coming from the cellar. She plants her hands on her hips in mock outrage. “Julia Mitchell. Do you have a gentleman visitor down there?”

Julia smiles wryly. “I think my creaky old shop has your imagination running. Nothing more scandalous than that.”

“I thought perhaps that was why you did not wish to visit Nathan,” Harriet teases. “Because your interests had turned elsewhere.”

“Ha. I wish it were that—” Julia slams down the coins and rushes towards the door. She throws it open and reaches out to grab the arm of the man who is approaching. It’s Julia’s brother, Harriet realises with a jolt. The man she had seen skulking through the crowd the day of the castle siege. She is almost glad he is here. The temptation to tell Julia she had seen him would have been too great for her to resist. Besides, this way she will get to see the ensuing confrontation. Because while Harriet is pleased the man is here, she can tell Julia is anything but.

She yanks her brother into the shop and locks the door behind them.

"What in hell are you doing?" she hisses, ushering him away from the window. "You know you can't be here! What if someone sees you?"

"Calm yourself," her brother says coolly. He takes off his cocked black hat and shakes the water from it. "This weather's far too hideous for anyone to be out. No one saw me."

"People have windows," Julia snaps.

Her brother glides past her comment. "I've just come to make sure you and Bobby are safe."

Julia folds her arms. "We were safe until my criminal of a brother decided to grace us with his presence."

His eyes shift to Harriet, catching the amused half-smile on her lips. "I recognise you."

"I should think so," she says. "Given I saw you being led out of my house in disgrace."

"Ah yes. You're one of them. The Blakes." Harriet had expected him to look ashamed, but he studies her with something close to fascination. He turns to his sister. "Didn't know you were friends with their kind, Jul."

Julia narrows her eyes in response.

"How about a drink then?" he asks.

Julia hesitates for a moment, and Harriet can tell she is debating whether to throw her brother straight back out into the rain. "Upstairs," she says finally.

Harriet is not sure whether the invitation is extended to her as well, but she has no intention of leaving. This is the most interesting thing to have happened here in weeks. Far more interesting than the siege of the castle that had barely lasted long enough for those two useless Jacobites to get through the door. She follows Julia and her brother up the creaking wooden staircase, leaving damp footprints in her wake.

Julia's tiny living quarters are marginally neater than the shop, with two narrow beds shoved up against a wall, the table at the other end of the space still filled with teacups and half-eaten bowls of porridge. The air is thick and warm with woodsmoke.

Julia's brother sinks into a chair at the table, long legs splayed. "Where's Bobby?" he asks, taking the spoon from one of the porridge bowls and scooping up the cold leftovers.

"He's at the dame school," Julia snaps. "Thank God." She throws a log on the simmering fire and pokes it back to life. "I've spent long enough explaining why you're hiding away. I don't fancy telling him why you've decided to behave like such a fool." She bends down for the kettle and hangs it on the hook above the flames.

"How about something stronger?" says her brother.

"At ten in the morning?" Julia shrugs resignedly. "Do as you wish." She takes out two fresh teacups, spearing Harriet with a sharp look. "*You're* only having tea."

Harriet smiles in amusement. "Yes ma'am."

A loud knock sounds at the door of the shop. "Anyone there?" calls an irritated male voice. "You open or not?"

Julia huffs, clearly flustered. She tosses a cloth at Harriet. "Make the tea," she orders. "And don't touch any more of my damn whisky." She charges down into the shop, the tinkle of the bell above the door echoing up the staircase.

Her brother watches after her with the faintest of smiles on his face. He turns back to Harriet. "Highfield House. It's not where I recognise you from. I saw you here on Lindisfarne the day of the siege."

Harriet spoons tea into the pot. "Which one are you?"

He chuckles. "I'm Michael."

"Shouldn't you be hiding away on Longstone with my sister?"

"I should, aye."

"But?"

"But there are pressing matters here on Lindisfarne."

She snorts. "The siege at the castle? Sounds like it all came to nothing."

"Aye." Something dark falls over Michael's eyes. "Should never have happened like that. Communication between the English Jacobites… it's not what it ought to be. Errington clearly expected reinforcements. But not a single soul came to support him, even with Forster just across the water. Now the poor bastard's locked up in Berwick."

Listen, thinks Harriet. *Observe. Gather the pieces.* "Is that why you were on Holy Island the day of the siege?" she asks. "Because you thought support was coming too? And you wished to join them?"

He hesitates, as though debating whether to trust her. Then he seems to remember that she already knows exactly who he is and what he has done, and that there is little point being so slippery. "I saw Errington's brig approaching from Longstone," he says. "Could hardly sit back and not find out what was happening, could I?"

"Seems like that's exactly what you ought to have done."

"And am I to hide away on Longstone and not do my part to help the Rising succeed?"

Harriet puts a hand to her hip, taking him in. He's a flat-faced bear of a man, with wide shoulders and cheeks sprayed with freckles. The same shrewd green eyes as his sister. He's a fool, certainly, to be strolling about here where anyone could see him. But there is something almost admirable about his passion. It's a cause she cares little about—at least beyond the information she can gather for her own hazy purposes—but she likes his determination to succeed in the face of the odds stacked against him. In a strange way, he reminds her of herself. Or at least the person she wants to be.

"Sounds to me like you've already done plenty," she says. "Is that not why you're hiding away on Longstone in the first place?"

Michael doesn't answer, and Harriet wonders if the stories about him shooting a dragoon are true. He reaches down to pet Julia's cat, but it stalks away from his reach and leaps up onto one of the beds. Turns in a circle before settling down among the blankets.

Rain patters softly against the narrow window. Harriet thinks of the fragments that had spilled out from the spies' meeting the night she had stood with her ear pressed to the parlour door. "If you want to do your part, you're in the wrong place," she tells Michael. "The Jacobites are mustering on Lesbury Common." Somewhere at the back of her mind, she knows she ought not have let this information out. Of course, he will demand to know where she heard such things. But inexplicably, the passion with which he speaks makes her want to help him. And the look of faint surprise on his face makes it worth it. It's a look beyond Edwin's condescension, beyond the thinly veiled pity she had seen in Eva's eyes when they had last met. A look that suggests she has something of value to impart. When, Harriet wonders, did anyone last look at her like that? Certainly not since she had left London and her artists' circle.

"Lesbury Common," Michael repeats. "And how exactly do you know that?"

"I hear things. Just like everyone else does." She doesn't look at him as she takes the boiling kettle from the hook and fills the teapot.

Michael chuckles. "I see." He goes to the cupboard and pours himself a cannikin of whisky. Holds the bottle up to Harriet in offering.

"I'm under strict instructions to only have tea."

"So I hear. But you don't strike me as a woman who takes orders."

Harriet smiles to herself. She wants to be that woman, of course. That woman who doesn't take orders, she has her paintings hung in French salons and does not bend to the will of her husband. But that woman feels impossibly far away. "Well," she says, "in any case, it's a little early for me."

"Is it?" Michael empties his cup in one mouthful and refills it. "Your sister and her dearly beloved have Angus and me keeping the light at all hours. Hardly know if I'm coming or going. Or what the hell time it is."

"Seems a fair trade," says Harriet. "Given they're risking their own backsides by hiding you from the redcoats."

Michael peers at her over the top of his cup. "How do you know where the Jacobites are mustering?" There's a faint look of suspicion in his eyes, and Harriet begins to regret her comment. "Is it because your family is spying for the government like everyone says?"

She snorts. "Don't be foolish. If we were, do you really think I would tell you what I know? More to the point, do you really think a woman would be privy to that information?"

Michael shrugs. "Plenty of the Jacobite spies and informants are women. Why should the government side be any different?"

Harriet lets out a laugh that sounds faintly hysterical. "I told you, I just hear things. I listen. It's a valuable skill—one you ought to try sometime." Michael chuckles, but Harriet is saved by Julia's footsteps striding back up the stairs.

"Just sold that dress sword for a small fortune," she tells them. "Told the fool it once belonged to the Earl of Carlisle. He's decided it will make a fine wedding gift for his son."

Michael empties his cannikin. "I'm glad to see your morals as a businesswoman have not gone begging."

Julia takes the teacup Harriet has filled for her and sinks into a chair opposite her brother. "Why are you here?" she asks him.

"I told you, I came to see that you and Bobby are safe."

She shakes her head. "Don't lie to me, Michael. Tell me what you're up to. Are there Jacobites meeting on Lindisfarne? Or have you come from another meeting in Bamburgh?"

Michael turns his empty cannikin around between his fingers. Harriet can tell he is reluctant to speak—but is it because he doesn't trust her? Or because he wishes to keep his plans from his sister?

He nods towards Harriet. "You ought to watch yourself around this one, Jul. Don't you know there's talk of her lot spying for Geordie?" There's a teasing tone to his voice, but Harriet knows not to take his words lightly. Her heart begins to quicken. She knows she should not have mentioned Lesbury. Knows that in her own need for validation, she has added fuel to the rumours about her family. If only she were as good at thinking as she is at listening.

"And don't you know better than to believe gossip, Michael?" Julia gives Harriet apologetic eyes. "Do you really think if Harriet's family were spies, they'd be mad enough to set themselves up on the biggest house on the island?" She gets to her feet and begins to gather up the breakfast dishes. Tosses them into the trough beside the hearth. "Besides, I've better judgement than that." Harriet can tell she is on edge. "I'd not be friends with her if I thought there was an inch of truth to the rumours."

"You know he can't truly believe them, Julia," says Harriet, peering sidelong at Michael. "If he did, he would not be hiding out on Longstone in my sister's company."

"Well. Perhaps that was not my wisest of choices." Michael gives Harriet a look that seems almost conspiratorial. And perhaps he had not previously believed the rumours about the Blakes. But perhaps her comments have given him pause. Made him wonder if there is truth to what everyone says about her family.

Harriet prays he does not tell Julia of her comment about Lesbury Common. Her family are not spies, of course. But that would be a difficult thing to explain if Julia was to ask questions. The Mitchells can never know what Highfield House is being used for. Even if she could trust them not to reveal such a thing to the rest of the village, it would put an end to Harriet's friendship with Julia. Would remove the last threads of trust between the two families.

"That's enough, Michael," Julia snaps. "Not only do you put me and

Bobby in danger by showing up at our door, you also have the nerve to make accusations against my friend?" She plants a hand on her hip and glares at him. "It's time for you to leave."

Harriet expects a retaliation, but Michael just stands and kisses his sister's cheek. "Take care, Jul. Tell Bobby I'm thinking of him." He glances back at Harriet, then seems to decide against speaking. He is down the stairs and out the door without another word.

CHAPTER EIGHT

Eva opens her eyes to flickering darkness. The light of the firebasket seeps through the gap in the shutters, casting a dim gold thread across the bedroom. She feels restless. Achy with the sleeplessness that has plagued her since she spotted Henry Ward's ship beyond Highfield House. She can tell she has not been asleep for long. Guesses it close to midnight. A few hours before she and Finn will take the watch from the Mitchells.

They had returned from Holy Island two days ago to find Michael back in the cottage, refusing to speak of where he had been. Finn had dished out a warning for him to stay hidden or leave; Eva doubts it will have an effect. But now the redcoats have reclaimed Lindisfarne Castle, and put a stop to the attack on Newcastle, her concerns over harbouring the two Jacobites have lessened. Or rather, they have been overtaken by her ever-present fear of Henry Ward.

She slips out of the blankets and navigates around the edges of the crowded room. With the Mitchells here, they have moved Finn's bed from the living area into the bedroom, beside the creaking old mattress he had slept on as a child. He is snoring lightly in the old sagging bed, and Eva is careful not to wake him as she passes.

She peeks through the gap in the shutters, needing a glimpse at the sea. She sees little but the blaze of the basket and the deep darkness beyond, and the absence of ships' lights goes some way to steadying her unease.

It's the anticipation, she thinks, that is hardest to carry. The knowledge that Ward had deliberately let them escape his ship so they might suffer through this almost unbearable uncertainty. He had wanted them to worry, to live each moment with one eye on the sea—and he has succeeded.

There is a part of her that wants to see Henry Ward again. Wants answers to the questions he had planted in her mind the night she had been aboard his ship. How had he known her mother? Why has he come back to Northumberland now? And what part—if any—had he played in her family fleeing Lindisfarne?

Nathan had claimed Abigail had taken them from the island out of grief over Oliver's death. But Eva is certain there are pieces she is missing. They had left Holy Island on foot in the middle of the night, taking nothing but the clothes on their backs. Abigail was logical, clear-headed; not the kind of woman to tear her children from their beds and race into the rising tide of the Pilgrims' Way without the most pressing of reasons.

Then again, the mother Eva knew would never have invited a man like Henry Ward into her home, so perhaps the woman she remembers is only a fragment of who Abigail Blake really was.

She creeps back across the room. Muffled voices come from the other side of the door.

"…to fight," she hears. Her curiosity piqued, she tiptoes towards the door and presses her ear against it. "I've heard word," she hears Michael say, "that the Jacobite army is gathering on Lesbury Common."

"Word from who?" Angus sounds doubtful.

"It doesn't matter. But I trust it's more than a rumour." A chair squeaks noisily. "We can make it to Lesbury in a day."

"Don't be mad," says Angus. "If we're caught, we'll swing."

"Once we re-join the army, we'll be protected. A day's ride," Michael is saying. "If that."

"That's a day too long," Angus snaps. "We know the redcoats are active up in these parts. I've not spent this long hiding just to do something foolish like this."

"You're a bloody coward. Hiding away when the cause needs you." There is silence, then the groaning of floorboards, a pacing back and forth. "We can't just sit back and do nothing," Michael snaps. "Look what happened on Lindisfarne. A prime opportunity lost."

Angus scoffs. "All the more reason to stay away from the rebel army. The English Jacobites are a bloody shambles. I can tell that even from out here."

"Do you truly imagine the two of us are so desperately wanted by the redcoats that they'll recognise and hunt us down the minute we set foot on the mainland?"

"It's not a risk I'm willing to take."

The pacing stops, punctuated by the crack of a log breaking in the grate. "I've heard other rumours," Michael says after a moment.

"About what?"

His voice drops, and Eva can barely make out his words. "We can't stay here. I don't know if we can trust her. This talk about her family… Maybe we were too quick to dismiss it."

Something tightens in Eva's stomach.

"We've been here weeks, man," Angus hisses. "Do you not think if she planned to turn us in, she might have done so already?" He laughs humourlessly. "I'm sure the two of them can't wait to be rid of us."

"What if she's already sent word to the authorities?" Michael's voice is an angry hiss. "What if it's just a matter of time before dragoons turn up on the doorstep?"

Angus snorts. "You're far too distrusting. Besides, Julia would never have brought us out here if she thought it would put us in danger."

"I don't think Julia knows as much as she thinks she does. Or else she's damn good at pretending otherwise."

"You're mad," Angus says again. "If you want to risk your life by re-joining the rebels, I can't stop you. But don't expect me to join you."

The men fall silent, and Eva tiptoes back towards the bed. Just what, she wonders, has Michael Mitchell heard? Rumours of her family spying for the government have been circulating since they returned to Holy Island almost four months ago. Surely Michael has heard them before now, given how often he is away from Longstone. There must be something else that has sparked his suspicions. Has someone discovered Highfield House is being used by government spies? Eva wishes she had managed to get a little more out of Nathan the last time they had spoken.

The smaller bed creaks.

"Evie," says Finn, leaning up on his elbow. "Is something the matter?"

She lets out a breath she hadn't realised she was holding, and slips into bed beside him.

"Careful now," he says lightly, "you know I'm not to be trusted."

Eva smiles into the darkness. "Yes you are."

He chuckles. "Well. You've been warned. If you don't make it to your wedding day with your good name intact, I can't be held responsible."

Eva laughs softly, sinking into the warmth of his body. "Two minutes," she says. "I'll just stay for two minutes." With his arm wrapped around her and his breath in her hair, she feels her heartbeat slow. Feels a little of the tension drain from her shoulders. "Michael has decided he doesn't trust me," she murmurs. "He seems convinced my family are spies, and that I'm planning to turn him in at any moment."

"Is that so?" Finn chuckles against her shoulder. He pushes aside her hair and kisses the back of her neck. "Hopefully that will inspire him to get the hell out of our house."

CHAPTER NINE

Watching her sister marry the lightkeeper makes Harriet feel as though she's drowning. Perhaps it's the close, fragrant church air; a smell of old, cold stone and earth. Perhaps the cloying presence of her own husband, his long legs stretched out in front of him as though to prevent her from escaping. Perhaps Nathan's surliness that is souring the air.

Harriet is surprised he had not changed his mind about attending. She had assumed his pride and anger would get the better of him. After all the effort he had put into securing Matthew Walton as Eva's husband, it must be a real slap in the face to see her marrying a man who has decided to attend his own wedding wearing a mud-coloured coat with mismatching buttons.

For a while, it had been refreshing to see some true emotion beneath Nathan's forced congeniality. But his saltiness is beginning to grow thin.

Eva looks impossibly happy. Standing at the altar with her lightkeeper and his chaotic buttons has made her blissfully ignorant to the look of displeasure on Nathan's face.

Harriet could not for a second have imagined Eva agreeing to a life like this; a man like this. During her long engagement to Matthew Walton, she had planned out every inch of her wedding ceremony: her lace-trimmed sack gown, the bride's pie and wedding cake, the flowers the attendants would wear in their hair. And here she is wearing nothing more elaborate than her blue woollen day dress and a ribbon at her throat, speaking her vows in a near-empty church, with the German Ocean thrashing beyond salt-speckled windows.

Harriet supposes stranger things have happened. Although she can't think of many.

She's happy for her sister. Of course she is; of course she is. But she can't shake the disappointment that Eva won't be there around the dinner table to save her when Nathan, Edwin and Matthew Walton launch into their next tobacco-fuelled diatribe. Then again, Harriet is fairly certain that Eva's marriage to this man the sea washed up has put an end to Walton joining Nathan and Edwin around the dinner table at all.

But the thing is done. Eva has pledged to honour, serve and obey, and live a life lit by the Longstone light.

Harriet feels hollow. Cold. She is glad when Theodora leaps to her feet and accosts the newlyweds, giving her space to sneak out into the churchyard. Heartfelt congratulations feel a little difficult to conjure up right now.

She finds herself wandering between the crooked teeth of the graves behind the church, desperate for a distraction. Her father lies somewhere in these grounds; the churchyard closest to where he had grown up. She walks the rows of weather-worn headstones, taking in the names; one tragic story of loss after another. Her father was in the earth before she was born, and he feels suitably distant and unknown. Throughout her life, Harriet has made her own image of him, cobbled together from the stories told to her by Nathan, by their mother. She wonders if there is any accuracy to the image of him she has in her head.

She finds him in the far corner of the churchyard, behind a veil of long grass.

Samuel Blake, beloved husband and father, departed this life December 8th, 1694.

Harriet's chest clenches like a fist. She feels suddenly breathless. Unmoored, like the earth is falling out from under her.

"Harriet?" Edwin's voice seems to pull her from the edge of a chasm. He is standing outside the church, an expectant look on his face. "Are you not going to come inside and congratulate your sister?"

The earth feels unsteady as she crosses the damp grass back to the church. She feels oddly outside herself as she pulls Eva into an embrace, kissing one cheek, then the other. Holding out a polite hand for her new brother-in-law. She hears herself murmur well-wishes in a voice that does not sound like her own.

"Are you all right, Harriet?" asks Eva, frowning.

"Yes, of course." She forces a smile. Wraps a hand around the top of the pew to steady herself.

She is barely watching as Eva and Finn make their goodbyes and head into the village. Barely listening as Edwin urges them towards the wagon, in order to make the low tide.

"Nathan," she says. "Come with me."

Her brother frowns in question, but follows her into the churchyard.

"The tide…" says Edwin again.

Harriet ignores him. She stares back down at Samuel Blake's headstone, eyes on the carved words as though she might somehow find a way to alter them.

Nathan bends down, yanking out the long tussocks of grass that obscure the grave.

"Did you know?" Harriet asks him.

"Know what? That Father was buried here? Yes, of course. I—"

"The date," she snaps. "Look at the date."

Nathan turns back to the headstone, his inhalation audible as the realisation swings at him. "It's a mistake, surely."

"How could it be a mistake? Mother would never have let that happen." But in that instant, Harriet realises she knows nothing of what her mother would have allowed. Her mother had spent Harriet's entire life peddling lies.

Because Samuel Blake, beloved husband and father, was lying in the earth a year and half before she was born.

CHAPTER TEN

"There are church records, perhaps," Nathan is saying as the wagon sighs across the sand back towards Holy Island. Sea licks and sloshes at the wheels, making Edwin tut with impatience. "They may be able to confirm Father's date of death."

Harriet is barely listening. She feels completely unravelled, like she has no idea of who she is. But has she ever? She has never wanted to look too deeply at her own inner workings, for fear of what she might uncover. And now, with this knowledge—or rather, lack thereof—she feels even more afraid to examine who she truly is.

"Nathan is right," says Edwin, his eyes drawn away from the water as the coach rattles onto the island. "This could be an error…"

Harriet smiles wryly. Shakes her head. She knows deep within herself that this is no error. As bewildering as this realisation is, there is also a sense of things falling into place.

Because she has always felt as though she was on the fringe of this family. Though, as children, Eva and Nathan had both doted on her, she has never felt truly able to connect with them. She and Eva are so strikingly different that their conversations rarely do more than scratch the surface. When she had seen her sister the day of the siege, it had not even crossed Harriet's mind to tell her about the Paris salon. And she is fairly certain Nathan has never seen her as anything more than a bothersome child, to be married off as briskly as possible, and turned into someone else's problem.

"It's no error," she says finally. She feels it with a certainty that reaches her bones. She looks out the window at the spiralling mound of Lindisfarne Castle, her eyes blurring over at the too-familiar sight. "Do not bother hunting down the records, Nathan. They will tell you the same thing."

They sit in silence for the rest of the journey. And when the hired wagon deposits them outside Highfield House, Harriet is quick to make her way inside and down towards her workroom.

She hears footsteps behind her and silently wills Edwin to leave. She cannot find room to entertain him right now. She knows she will say something she will regret. And she also knows she will not regret it much.

She is surprised to hear Nathan call her name. She cannot remember the last time her brother had sought her out like this. She and Nathan have never had any great need for one another's company. She looks up at him, sure her surprise is showing in her eyes.

"I just…" He clears his throat. "I just wanted to say… None of this matters, Harriet." He shakes his head. Rubs the back of his neck. "I mean… Of course it matters. But it does not change who you are to us."

His words are so painfully awkward and genuine that they make Harriet's throat tighten. Tears gather behind her eyes, catching her by surprise. She cannot remember the last time she cried. She blinks them away hurriedly, unwilling to let her brother see them.

Nathan is right; this does not change who she is because she has always felt like an outsider. But she appreciates this from her brother. Half-brother. The reality of it stings. She flashes him a short smile. A faint nod. And then she disappears into the sanctuary of her workroom to prevent her tears from spilling.

Nathan knows he ought to have realised this earlier. Ought to have been old enough to recognise the canyon of months between his father's death and his sister's birth.

He remembers his father's death vividly. Remembers him taking to his bed with a sudden illness; remembers his mother's fear that the smallpox would spread through the household. He remembers the burning clothes and the heady smell of smoking herbs billowing at every window. And he remembers watching that lonely coffin being lowered into the ground behind St Aidan's, in the town where Samuel had grown up. More than anything, he remembers the painful hollow that had taken root inside him when he had seen the empty chair at the head of the table. He had assumed it had all happened not long before Oliver's death. Not long before they had made their hurried escape from Holy Island.

Harriet was born mere months after they arrived in London. Nathan has clear memories of her as an infant. Of building a new life in the capital with his mother and sisters. But youth had made his memories run into each other. Made time distort. The lie his mother had told the world, of Harriet being Samuel Blake's daughter, was one he had never stopped to question.

He sinks into the chair in his study. Stares out the window and lets his eyes lose focus as they take in the ink-dark sea. He pulls off his wig and tosses it on the desk beside the pounce pot. Unties his hair and rakes his fingers through it. It feels limp and oily beneath his touch.

He had woken up dreading the day, fearing he might poison Eva's wedding with this anger he is unable to shake. Nowhere in his wildest of thoughts had he imagined it might turn out like this.

But with the knowledge that Harriet's father is not his own, it feels strangely obvious. He feels foolish for having overlooked such a thing for the past two decades.

A knock at the door startles him.

"Who is it?"

"You've a visitor, Mr Blake," says Mrs Brodie from the hallway. "Mr Holland is waiting for you downstairs."

Something tightens in Nathan's stomach. Joseph Holland comes to the house for one reason alone these days: to deliver messages that will be passed between the government spies. Nathan knows he can expect visits from men posing as workers over the next few days. They will collect the messages Holland has left behind, and Nathan will spend the rest of the week drowning in worry, terrified that someone from the village has caught wind of what is taking place at Highfield House.

He wonders if Mrs Brodie is beginning to get suspicious of all these visitors. Beginning to recognise that these so-called workers never do so much as lift a hammer. He realises he has no idea where his housekeeper's alliances lie, and what she would do if she did have any suspicions. Perhaps she, like many Northumbrians, is hedging her bets; lending support to whichever side appears to be on top.

He wonders, for not the first time, if it is too dangerous to have outside help in the house. The thought is chased by the one that always follows it: that letting Mrs Brodie go would likely raise even more distrust among the villagers. And, perhaps more pressingly, that they would be utterly at sea without her, given his family can barely boil water with all their cooking skills combined.

Tying his hair off his shoulders but ignoring the wig, Nathan makes his way down to the parlour.

Holland is still dressed in an enormous tarred greatcoat, a knitted cap pulled down low on his round head. His chin is covered in grey bristles, cheeks red with cold. A folded page is tucked into one of his meaty hands. At the sight of Nathan, he nods in greeting and hands over the missive. Nathan tucks it into the pocket of his waistcoat. The letter is sealed to prevent prying eyes, but even if it wasn't, he has never had an ounce of interest in what is inside the spies' intelligence. The Jacobite Rising is a calamity he wants to stay as far away from as possible.

Not that that has turned out so well for him thus far.

"You look exhausted, Blake," says Holland. "I hope all this business isn't getting to you. You know my men are as discreet as possible. The last thing I want is to put your family in danger."

"I know. And I appreciate it." Nathan chuckles dryly. "My exhaustion's not your doing, Holland. It's just been… quite a day."

"Don't suppose there'd be a glass of that fine brandy of yours on offer?"

Nathan goes to the liquor cabinet. "That's the best idea I've heard in ages." He pulls out two glasses and fills them generously.

Holland shrugs off his greatcoat and tosses it over the back of the armchair, sending a mildly unpleasant smell of herrings into the air. He takes a glass with a nod of thanks. Smiles at Nathan. "You know this good stuff is the only reason I seek out your company." He gulps down a mouthful. "Far better than the swill on offer among the fishing fleet."

Despite his tatty, unrefined appearance, Nathan knows Joseph Holland is not a man to be underestimated. When he had first arrived back on Lindisfarne, Nathan had foolishly assumed Holland to be a simple fisherman. But of course, he now knows him to be deeply entrenched in the anti-Jacobite cause, with contacts high up in the government.

Nathan sinks into an armchair and gestures for Holland to sit opposite. For a moment, the two men drink in silence, the fire popping steadily between them. Holland says, "I saw your sister in town with Julia Mitchell."

Nathan swallows another mouthful. "Yes."

"You know the Mitchells have Jacobite leanings," says Holland. "Julia's father fought at Dunkeld. And word is her brothers went to fight for the Duke of Ormonde."

Nathan keeps his gaze level. He knows all too well about the Mitchells' Jacobite leanings. He had heard it from Julia's own mouth, even before they had found her brothers hiding in the roof. To Holland, he says, "I've heard the rumours. They are hardly newsworthy, are they? There are plenty of families in this part of the country with Jacobite sympathies."

Holland hums to himself, clearly irritated at Nathan's apparent apathy. "I don't want her anywhere near this house," he says. "It's too dangerous." From his tone of voice, Nathan can tell this is not merely a suggestion.

"Why?" he pushes. "What do you know of her?" He is suddenly afraid of the answer. He has heard countless stories about the terror Cotesworth and his men have inflicted on Jacobites in other parts of Northumbria: houses raided and people interrogated. Catholics, and anyone else suspected of Jacobite sympathies, thrown behind bars. He couldn't bear to see that happen to Julia and her son.

He peers at Holland, trying to see behind his eyes. Is he simply conscious of the Mitchells' Jacobite leanings, or does he suspect Julia's direct involvement in the cause?

"I'd keep Miss Mitchell away from your sister too, if I were you," says Holland, sidestepping Nathan's question. He stretches tree-trunk legs out in front of him. "You know she has quite the reputation." He chuckles. "Seems she's not too fussy about who she lets warm her bedclothes. It don't look so good for your sister to be seen in her company."

Nathan feels the back of his neck heat. It's part anger, he realises—both timeworn rage at Julia, and at Holland for speaking about her so freely, so crassly. And it's part something else entirely. Something far more primal, that catches him by surprise.

Since he was a child, he has struggled with physical contact, and his aversion to human touch means such visceral thoughts are few and far between. The only other woman he had ever desired like this had been his late wife, Sarah. There is something more than a little unwelcome about deceitful Julia triggering these same extraordinary feelings.

The chaos of thoughts roils up inside him and he gulps hurriedly at his brandy. Narrowly avoids a coughing fit. "Believe me," he tells Holland, "keeping Julia Mitchell away from this family is very much my intention."

CHAPTER ELEVEN

"So tell me," says Finn, "was this fine establishment where you always dreamt of spending your wedding night?"

Eva laughs. "Since I was a girl." She shuffles her chair closer to the table so her thigh is pressed against his. He smells the sea on her. Feels the warmth of her body.

It's a sorry looking place as far as lodging houses go, with crooked tables and liquor on the air, though Finn has been in plenty worse. If he'd ever given any thought to the matter in the past, he would never have imagined bringing his bride to such a place, but the tiny village of Bamburgh has few better options. Nonetheless, there's a fire roaring in the grate in the corner of the dining room, and dishes of beef stew floating out from the kitchen that are making his mouth water.

This is a place he knows well. And a place he's sure Eva has not forgotten. He'd first kissed her in a room upstairs. Had made a mess of things then; let her go to protect his secrets. And he never plans on doing that again.

Two dishes of food land on the table in front of them. Eva nods her thanks to the barmaid. Her eyes are shining in the glow of the candle in the centre of the table, wine and firelight colouring her cheeks pink. She looks happy, Finn thinks. Impossibly, fiercely happy. There's still a part of him that's afraid she might disappear. That he might wake alone in his cottage after a doze he had not meant to fall into, and find she was nothing but a liquor-fuelled dream.

Eva leans close, her lips to his ear so he can hear her over the raucous chatter in the dining room. It's busy tonight, with cloaked travellers and sailors in tarred greatcoats marching in and out of the door. Blasts of cold air make the flames in the grate dance. "In any case," she says, a shiver going through him at the feel of her breath on his skin, "I'm just glad not to be spending my wedding night elbow to elbow with Michael and Angus."

Finn chuckles as he picks up his spoon. "I don't think I'll be missing them too much either." He slides his free hand over her knee. Two months of having her in the cottage beside him and it's taken the restraint of a monk not to crawl into her bed. Getting through their supper with their bodies pressed against each other like this is a supreme exercise in self-control. But after all she has given up to become his wife, the least he can do is let her finish her food before he carts her off upstairs.

He knows she's relieved that her brother did not recognise him today. Finn is relieved too, a little, though he knows his worry is unfounded. Too much time has passed, surely, for Nathan Blake to have any inkling of who he is.

"What in hell are you doing here, Finn?" He looks up to see two of the farmhands he had been working with in Berwick last week. "Thought you only showed your face off Longstone in the daylight," says Arthur, the older of the two men.

Finn chuckles. Gives them what he's sure is a ridiculously large grin. "Aye well. Special circumstances. This fine lass has just let me make her my wife."

Arthur belts a fat palm into the table, and Eva grabs at her cup of wine before it's upended in her lap. "Well then!" He bellows at the barmaid, "Another round over here, lass. Quick now." Arthur and his friend pull up stools and plonk themselves at the table. Finn wraps an arm around Eva's shoulder and mouths a silent apology. She smiles.

"I hope you know what you've got yourself into, lass," says Arthur. "They say he's a right troublemaker. Got no manners neither."

Eva sips her wine and gives Finn a smile over the top of her cup. "I shall consider myself warned."

Arthur looks up at the barmaid as she deposits four cannikins of whisky on the table.

"Tuppence." She holds her palm out flat towards him.

"No, no," he says, "no charge for these, all right, my love? Finn has just made this lovely lass his wife."

The barmaid snorts. Plants her free hand on her hip. She looks worn through with annoyance. "When you bring a bride in here, Arthur, you can have your drinks for free." She holds her outstretched hand under his nose. "Tuppence."

Arthur grumbles to himself and hunts around in his coat for his coin pouch.

Finn chuckles. "You're a right generous soul, Arthur."

"Don't mind her," Arthur tells him, nodding after the barmaid as she disappears with his coins in her fist. "She's just churned up cos of them ships in the bay. She reckons the rebels are going to storm the castle like they did on Lindisfarne. I told her she ought to expect such things in a Jacobite town like this."

The smile disappears from Eva's face. "What ships in the bay?"

Arthur shrugs as he tosses back his whisky. "Don't know who they belong to. Came in an hour or so ago. Probably here on Forster's bidding." He grins at her. "Or pirates, maybe."

Eva pushes back her chair. "Excuse me," she says. "I need a little air."

Finn catches up to her as she reaches the door. He takes her hand. "Ward has no idea we're here."

"You don't know that. He could have followed us." Eva steps out into the narrow lamplit street and hurries towards the bay, tugging him along beside her. The sea is sighing gently against the sand, lines of white water shimmering in the moonlight. Eva charges out onto the beach, squinting into the darkness. Several smaller boats, theirs among them, sit on the sand high above the waterline, the outline of two large brigs visible in the deeper ocean. Lamps glow atop their masts, casting silvery circles on the sea.

Finn joins Eva at the water's edge, pressing a hand to the small of her back. "Neither of those ships are Ward's," he says.

Eva scrubs a hand across her eyes. Nods. Finn watches her shoulders sink forward as she lets out a long breath in relief. "Your friend was probably right about them being Forster's ships." She looks up at him, her face shadowed in the moonlight. "I'm sorry. I did not mean to run off like a madwoman. I just… I worry for you. I worry about whatever it is he is planning."

Finn wraps his arms around her waist and pulls her close. "I think we're both entitled to a little madness." He tucks a strand of hair behind her ear and grins. "Besides, any excuse to get rid of Arthur."

It is late, thick dark, when he wakes. He sees her at the window, peeking through the curtains, the shape of her lit only by moonlight. She has her cloak tugged around her body, her dark hair hanging loose and tangled down her back. He's struck almost breathless by love for her, fresh need for her. Most of all, by a longing to protect her from Henry Ward, and the threat he has come to represent.

"Eva," he says. She turns. "Don't. Not tonight. Please."

For a brief moment, she hesitates, then makes her way back towards the bed. She lets her cloak fall to the floor and climbs beneath the blanket. Shuffles in so her body is pressed to his. Skin to skin, his lips find hers, and he pulls her close.

"It's all right," says Finn, breaking the kiss and finding her eyes in the darkness. "Everything will be all right. You know that, aye?"

Eva nods, entangling her legs with his, as though attempting to tether him to her. "Yes," she murmurs. "Of course. Everything will be all right."

But she has left the curtains open a crack, Finn realises, as if keeping a constant eye out for that danger he is unable to take away.

CHAPTER TWELVE

"How are you?" Edwin asks. It's early morning; Harriet can tell from the pale blue light creeping through the gap in the curtains. She had come to bed just a few hours ago. Has barely slept. A dawn chorus of birds is bawling outside the window.

She can tell from the expression on her husband's face that he is surprised to see her awake. Usually, she is only roused with some difficulty by Jenny when Thomas wakes and begins screeching to be fed. Last night, though, her thoughts had been racing far too violently to sleep.

She feels completely unmoored. Feels more out of place here than she ever has; lying in bed beside a husband she barely knows, in this house that belonged to a man who is not her father.

Edwin is propped up on one elbow, looking down at her with a frown of concentration, as though he is studying a new specimen of plant life. His face looks sharper than usual, thanks to the dark hair hanging loose on his shoulders. It's beginning to thin, Harriet notices, with a vague sense of detachment.

"I'm fine," she says. Before she can roll over, putting her back to him, he reaches out and presses a hand to her bare wrist. It's a tentative move, uncertain. There is rarely any incidental touching between them—Edwin had put an end to any attempt at romance in the early days of their marriage when it became clear his stilted affection was not going to be reciprocated.

"Harriet," he says gently. "Please. Do not shut me out."

Though she rarely enjoys his touch, there is something strangely comforting about his nearness right now. Something steadying about the feel of his rough craftsman's skin against her own. Something that reminds her of the way life used to be, back when she was still Samuel Blake's daughter.

Instead of rolling over, she sits up in bed. Allows him to keep a hold of her. "I am not shutting you out," she says. "There is just nothing to say."

"Nothing to say?" He sounds incredulous. But why, she wonders? Because between the two of them, there is always nothing to say. How can she tell Edwin how she feels, and who she is, when she barely knows that herself?

"I imagine you feel cheated," Harriet says finally.

Edwin raises his thin black eyebrows. "Cheated?"

"Yes. You married me thinking I was the daughter of a wealthy English merchant. And now your son could have any bastard's blood in his veins."

Edwin sits up and leans back against the bed head, releasing his grip on Harriet's wrist. He examines his thumbnail. "Well. That is not something anyone needs to know, is it." His voice is clipped.

Harriet nods silently. She knows this comment is meant for her benefit as much as his own. A promise that this shameful piece of her heritage might be kept away from gossiping ears.

She would confess such a thing to her artist friends, Harriet thinks distantly. They would not judge her. Isabelle would tell her to pour the pain and uncertainty into her paintings, commit them to her canvas. Harriet had tried to do such a thing last night, but had found herself paralysed with the mounting pressure of her lack of inspiration. She has become too adept at pushing things to the back of her mind to take any value from her pain.

"When do you imagine we might be back in London?" she asks suddenly.

She catches a flicker of irritation in Edwin's eyes at the change of subject. But he says, "There's still much to do on the house. But perhaps by the spring."

The spring feels impossibly distant; an entire north-England winter to crawl through first. But this is the first time she has ever succeeded in chiselling a possible date out of her husband. Spring—with luck she will be back in time to join Isabelle on her trip to Paris.

"I should like to be gone as soon as possible," Edwin says, "given the unrest up here. But I cannot leave Nathan to finish the restorations on his own. And he seems hell-bent on making the work far harder than it needs to be. He seems completely unable to finish one job before beginning the next."

"He does, yes." This is her chance now, Harriet realises. Now she has Edwin's sympathy, and they have come to rest in agreement of the futility of Nathan's restoration project. "My friend Isabelle showed one of my paintings to her sponsors," she blurts. "They wish to meet with me. In Paris. In April."

Her heart has struck up suddenly in a rapid cadence, and what a joy that is. A long-forgotten thing. How can it be, she wonders distantly, that she might have made it through spies and sieges, and the knowledge that she is not her father's daughter, with barely a ghost of a reaction. How cold and empty she must be. But this; speaking of this dream—and doing so to her husband, who could shatter it with a single word—this is where she feels alive.

"I see," Edwin murmurs. He hates the idea, Harriet can tell. But he has not yet shut it down completely. Whether out of mere sympathy for her, or whether he is truly considering it, she cannot be certain. "I do not think this the right time or place to discuss this, do you?"

"Why not?" she demands. But he is saved from answering by the shriek of their son, as though the two of them have been conspiring for it to be exactly this way all along.

Nathan finds himself pacing his study.

He is worried for Harriet. Since learning the news of her father three days ago, she has been more withdrawn than usual. Has spent even more time in her workroom, and even less time with her family. Though she is doing her best to pretend she is unaffected by her discovery, Nathan can tell the knowledge, or rather, the uncertainty, has cut her deeply.

He needs to tell Eva. He knows Harriet would benefit from a visit from her sister. And in any case, the news of Harriet's parentage is something Eva ought to know.

But getting the news to her is something of a challenge.

An irritating voice at the back of his head tells him it is no challenge at all; tells him that Julia will no doubt happily sail over to Longstone and bring Eva back to see Harriet.

No. There must be another option.

Perhaps he could go to the harbour and pay a fisherman to visit Longstone. And then what? Is he to expect Eva to climb into a boat with a near stranger? He can hardly expect that of her after all that happened with Donald Macauley. No doubt if he were to make the journey over alongside the fisherman, she would be more inclined to come back with them. But a boat trip to Longstone is top of the list of things he desperately wishes to avoid—narrowly beating out a visit to Julia Mitchell.

Perhaps he could wait until Eva comes to Highfield House of her own accord. But he can hardly hold his breath waiting for that to happen. He had made it through her entire wedding without cracking a smile. She is hardly going to be rushing back here for more brotherly kindness. And Harriet could use Eva's company sooner rather than later.

Dammit to hell, he knows Julia is his only option.

He pushes open the door of the curiosity shop. Julia is standing by the shelves, hunting through a collection of books while she chats to the elderly couple beside her. She is a chaos of colour, in striped green and white skirts and a pink neckerchief, her red hair bundled in a knot high on her head. She looks over and meets Nathan's eye for a second, before turning back to the customers. Nathan hovers by the door, watching as she pulls a book from the shelf.

He finds his gaze darting around the shop. Searching for what, he wonders? Jacobite pamphlets pinned to the wall? A rebel soldier hiding behind the bookshelf? He knows he is being ridiculous. But Joseph Holland's words have got under his skin.

"Ah. Here it is. I knew it was there somewhere." Julia smiles warmly as she passes the book to the older woman. Her husband hands over the payment and Julia thanks them as they make their way out the door.

Nathan shuffles awkwardly aside to let them by.

Julia's smile evaporates as she turns to look at him. "I'm surprised to see you here."

"Yes. Well." He clears his throat. "I need your help."

She folds her arms. "Do you just?"

Nathan hesitates. Each of the fifty-seven times he had played this conversation out in his head during the walk into the village, Julia had been far more acquiescing than this. Far less terse. He had imagined she would leap at the opportunity to help him, in an attempt to make up for the way she had betrayed him and his family. He realises he has made something of a miscalculation.

He ploughs on. "I need to get a message to my sister on Longstone. Something has happened with Harriet. And I think Eva ought to know about it."

Julia's eyes soften. She unfolds her arms. "With Harriet? Is she all right?"

From her words, Nathan guesses Harriet has said nothing to Julia about her recent discovery. And of course, he will not be the one to tell her. "She has not been herself of late," he says instead. "And I think she would benefit from a visit from her sister." He looks Julia square in the eyes, ignoring the treacherous fishtailing in his chest. "Will you take word to Eva? Ask her to come back to Lindisfarne with you?"

Julia gives him the faintest of smiles. "Of course."

Eva is checking the lobster pots at the edge of the jetty when she sees the boat cutting towards Longstone. She stands quickly, blind to the wave that recoils off the edge of the island and soaks the hem of her skirts. But it is not one of Ward's longboats.

It is the little fishing dory that belongs to Julia Mitchell.

Eva lowers the lobster pots back into the water and watches with folded arms as Julia approaches the moorings.

"Your brothers are inside," she says brusquely.

Julia stays aboard the dory, one hand pressed to the post of the jetty. "Nathan sent me," she says, ignoring Eva's sharpness. "He's asked me to bring you back to Holy Island. Something has happened with Harriet."

Eva knocks on the door of her sister's workroom. Steps inside tentatively.

Harriet glances up from her notebook. She looks pale, her blue eyes underlined in shadow. A teacup sits on the table beside her, along with an untouched plate of bread and cheese.

"Shouldn't you be galivanting around Longstone with your new husband?" she asks.

Eva hovers just inside the door. From where she stands, she can glimpse the scribbled-out sketches on the pages of the book. They remind her of the angry scrawls Harriet had left across her last painting. "Nathan told me what happened. I'm worried about you."

"Why?" Harriet turns back to her notebook.

"What do you mean, why?" When her sister doesn't reply, Eva walks up to the table in frustration. "Can we at least have a conversation?"

"What is there to say?" Harriet puts the pencil down anyway. Her eyes stay fixed to the page.

What is there to say, Eva realises? Nothing will change this. And she is sure nothing is going to make it any easier for Harriet. She goes to the window and pushes on the sash to let a little fresh air into the stuffy room.

"Leave that," Harriet barks.

Eva steps away obediently. She perches on the edge of the faded armchair. "I am glad you're working," she says, nodding towards the notebook.

"Why would I not be working?"

Eva picks at a loose thread on her shortjacket. "I saw what you did to your last piece."

"Oh. That."

Eva waits, but nothing more is forthcoming. "What made you do it?"

Harriet shrugs, without looking at her. "It was no good. The colours were all wrong. Unfixable. Best to just start again." Her words are thin.

"And this piece?" Eva asks. "Are you happier with it?"

"There is no piece yet," Harriet says tautly.

Eva swallows a sigh. She can practically feel the wall of ice her sister has erected around herself. Harriet picks her pencil back up and begins to sketch lightly. Eva follows the movement of the pencil. Watches the faint outline of a willow tree appear on the page. It's an enchanting ability that Harriet has, she thinks; to make images come to life on the page like this. A gift no one else in the family shares. Eva finds herself wondering if she had inherited it from her father.

"How is your little island?" Harriet asks after a moment.

"It's beautiful," says Eva. "The way the sea changes colour with the light, and the way the tide reshapes the place… It's magical." She smiles to herself. "And the sound of the birds is like nothing you've ever heard before. I think it would inspire you. Perhaps I can take you back with me one day. I would like you to see it."

"Yes. Perhaps." Harriet shades a faint shadow beneath the willow. After a moment, she says, "It is just… the not knowing." Her words are so airy and insubstantial that it takes Eva a moment to realise she is finally speaking of her father. "Having no thought of where I really come from. Of who my father might be. How can I have any sense of who I am?"

And Eva's chest squeezes with dread. She feels hot and she feels cold at once, and she forces herself to keep the gasp of her understanding silent. Because it is no mystery, she realises then. It's sickening and inevitable. And it is no mystery at all.

CHAPTER THIRTEEN

Eva says nothing to Harriet. She says nothing to Julia when she takes her back to Longstone that evening. But as Finn is shovelling coal into the firebasket, she is pacing, pacing in front of him, her stomach in knots and the words she has kept in all day spilling out without pause.

"I ought to have known it the moment I heard about Harriet's discovery," she says, her fingers entangled in the fine wool of her shawl. "How could I have been so blind?" She thinks of the night she had spent on Henry Ward's ship. Thinks of how fondly Ward had spoken of her mother. Thinks of the look in his eyes when he had mentioned Abigail Blake's name. "And the way he looks, Finn. His eyes. His hair. That unnatural beauty. That is all Harriet." She stops pacing. "I'm right, aren't I."

Finn secures the chain to the hook. "I would imagine so, aye."

Eva looks up at the flickering light, feeling it warm her cheeks. The sea clops against the edge of the island, a constant rush in her ears.

The realisation is turning her stomach. The realisation that Henry Ward had shared her mother's bed. That her sister has his blood running through her.

"Do you think…" She fades out, unable to finish the sentence. Tries again. "Do you think he forced her?" The words are bitter on her tongue.

Finn tilts his head; doesn't speak at once. Perhaps he is debating which would be worse: for her mother to have been forced into Ward's bed, or for her to have gone there willingly.

"The truth, Finn," she says.

He sighs. Looks up at the dancing light. "I was just a lad. So I don't know for sure. But when I saw Ward and your mother together, they seemed… Well. It seemed as though she enjoyed his company. She welcomed him into the house. Dressed up when he came to see her."

Eva nods faintly. She sits on the edge of the island, warmed by the glow of the firebasket. The sea reaches for the toes of her shoes. Somewhere in the darkness she can hear the throaty wail of a seal.

Finn sits beside her, reaches an arm around her shoulder. "All right?"

Eva hugs her knees. "When I was aboard Ward's ship, he told me I was just like my mother. I denied it, but I knew he was right. At least, I thought he was. I always believed Mother and I were so alike. Rigid. Followers of the rules." She shakes her head. "But for her to have invited a man like Henry Ward into our home… For her to have had a child with him… It's as though there was a completely different side to her that I never knew about."

Finn catches her eye and smiles crookedly. "I've never known you to be one to follow the rules."

"Perhaps I am like my mother after all." She leans her head against his shoulder, feeling it rise and fall with breath.

"Will you tell Harriet?" he asks.

For long moments, she doesn't speak. "No," she says finally. "I can't. No one can know. What if I told her and she decided to seek Ward out? There is so much he could tell her. About Oliver…" The words leave a dull ache in her chest. Around Finn, she never speaks her brother's name.

He nods slowly, not looking at her. "Aye, he could. But do you really think it's something you ought to keep from her?"

Eva stares out across the dark sea. On the edge of her vision, a volley of sparks flutter down from the firebasket and disappear on the water. Somewhere in the back of her mind, she knows Finn is right. But the thought of her family finding out what he did to Oliver is unthinkable.

"She cannot know," she says finally. "We cannot take that risk." She closes her eyes, trying to push away the nagging of her conscience. "Besides, I am doing her a favour. If I were Henry Ward's daughter, there is no way I would want to know about it."

Theodora is staring out the window, not paying the slightest bit of attention to her Latin text. Nathan can't quite find the energy to pull her back to the task at hand. At least when she is looking out the window, he is saved from hearing about how much she hates Latin.

Suddenly, she gasps with delight. "Bobby's here!" She flings down her quill, splattering ink across the page. She leaps up from Nathan's desk and presses her forehead against the glass.

"Theodora—" he begins, but she is already off down the stairs. And, he realises when he gets to the entrance hall, she has already opened the front door to Bobby and Julia. Before he can get a word out, she and Bobby tear into the dunes.

Nathan sighs. It's time he had strong words with his daughter about acting like less of a wildling, especially when he is attempting to teach her his questionable Latin grammar. Begrudgingly, he tries to remember when she has ever looked quite so free and happy. Certainly not since her mother died.

Steeling himself, he looks back at Julia. She is holding a large wooden box in her arms. "Why are you here?" he asks. The words come out cold and unfeeling, and he is unsure if he furiously regrets them, or if he is proud of himself for managing them.

Julia holds out the box. "This is for you. An apology of sorts. I've been wanting to give it to you for some time, but I figured I had best wait until your anger at me had settled somewhat." There's a faint glimmer in her eyes, the freckles on her pale cheeks pronounced in the sunlight.

"I see," says Nathan. "And you think my anger at you has settled?"

Julia doesn't falter. "I think I did you a favour by sailing out to Longstone to fetch Eva in the middle of my workday. So the least you can do is take the box."

Holland's warning echoes in Nathan's head. He knows the spies working for the government have little trust for Julia Mitchell—for reasons he does not want to explore. What he does not know, is what they will do if they catch sight of her at Highfield House.

Nathan takes the box, half out of curiosity, and half out of a need to get her off the property—both for her sake and his own. He lifts the lid and peers inside. And he feels something shift in his chest. Inside is a telescope, a six-draw piece of brass and wood, just like the one his father had given him when he was a child. He had seen it in Julia's curiosity shop last month. A metal stand is folded up beneath it.

"You seemed fond of it when you saw it in my shop that day," she says. "I would like you to have it."

Nathan swallows heavily. He'd had no idea Julia had even seen him looking at the thing. He holds it back out to her. "That's kind of you. But I cannot take it."

"Why not?" she asks, before he can get a hand to the door to close it.

"Because I really think it best that you have nothing to do with this family going forward." The words are hard to get out.

"You needn't have anything to do with me. You just need take the telescope."

"No. I can't." He pushes the box back into her arms, careful not to make contact with her.

She flashes him a smile, as though the words he has been grinding out have not even registered. "Bobby and I will leave you be. And I will put the telescope out by the cart shed. Best you take it inside before the weather turns and ruins it."

Nathan goes back upstairs, churning out a rote scolding to Theodora about not running off like a rabbit, and letting Mrs Brodie answer the door. His heart is not really in it. He sends her off to finish her Latin and returns to the dressing room to begin putting the fireplace back together. The damn thing has been in pieces for more than a fortnight. After a few minutes, he climbs to his feet and goes to the window. Looks down at the cart shed.

Julia has done as she promised. There is the telescope, the box leaning up against the padlocked door. The sight of it makes Nathan shake his head in frustration, but he can't deny there's some small part of him that is pleased to see it.

He goes out to the cart shed and collects the box, then tucks it beneath the desk in his study. It will rain tonight, he thinks. And there's no point letting a fine piece of equipment like this get destroyed.

CHAPTER FOURTEEN

It has become a game, Harriet realises. A sickening, pointless game of letting her eyes drift over every man in the congregation and wondering if he might be her father. Perhaps it's that grizzly fisherman in the corner, with the cap pulled low and a devious look in his eyes. Perhaps the too-righteous husband of the woman who owns the fruit stall, sitting front and centre, nodding along to the pastor's dreary words.

She forces herself to stop. Nothing good can come of this. She knows the chance of her father—whoever he may be—sitting in this church with her is impossibly small. And even if it wasn't, she could hardly just approach the man and accost him with such news.

Still, she wonders. More about her mother than her father. Had she let him willingly into her bed? Had she done so in some twisted act of grief over her husband, dead for less than a year before Harriet was conceived? Or had she welcomed Samuel Blake's death? Her mother suddenly feels like as much of a stranger as her father.

Harriet glances at Edwin beside her. He is nodding along routinely to the sermon, but the glazed look in his eyes tells her his thoughts are far away. Ought she prod at the issue of Paris? Instinctively, she feels that this will make him even less likely to agree to it. No doubt he is waiting for the news of her parentage to become old, and then he can turn her down without looking like too much of a bastard.

Harriet closes her eyes. Tries to breathe deeply. She hates sitting here among these cold, unyielding walls, with the frozen stone eyes of saints bearing down on her. It feels as though they can read her every sinful thought. Something that feels like dread rolls around inside her.

When the service finishes, she makes her way out of the church, her hand pressed dutifully into the crook of Edwin's arm. Jenny trails them silently, Thomas asleep on her shoulder. The morning is grey and cold, with just a thin rim of gold lining the bank of cloud above the ocean. Gulls swarm low, in perfect synchronicity, over the crumbling stone walls at the back of the churchyard.

Movement in the ruins of the monastery behind the church catches Harriet's eye. Michael Mitchell is standing in one corner of the old priory, his cocked hat pulled low. It's the most brazen of moves—almost as though he is daring the people of Holy Island to catch him and turn him in, just to find out where their alliances lie. Michael is deliberate in catching Harriet's eye. She tries to turn away, but his intense gaze spears her. With a brisk nod, he gestures to her to join him.

He's mad, surely. Does he truly expect she can just disengage herself from her husband and sidle into conversation with a wanted man? And does he not realise his own damn sister is here among this crowd? Still, Harriet supposes, for all this foolishness, whatever he wants must be important.

She murmurs to Edwin about hanging back to speak with the priest. Her husband releases her arm without a word.

Harriet waits until the crowd has dispersed and the door of the church has closed. Then she steps into the long shadows of the priory. Old stone towers rise up on either side of them, swallowing the meagre threads of sunlight. "Julia is right," she snorts. "You're a fool. Do you not know there are government spies on the island?"

He smiles faintly. "You would know." Harriet snorts. She turns to leave, but Michael snatches her wrist. "Wait. I've been thinking about you."

She raises her eyebrows. "Have you just?"

"Not in that manner," Michael says witheringly. "I've been thinking about why you told me about Lesbury Common. It was a dangerous thing to do. You're either a fool, or you have little loyalty to your family."

The words strike her. Because she realises they are true. How can she claim to have loyalty to her family when she had so carelessly revealed a secret that could put them in danger? Almost as though a part of her had known all along that she was the ill-fitting piece. The curly-haired blonde child of a man who is not Samuel Blake.

"Either way," Michael continues, not waiting for her to speak, "I could use your services."

"What do you mean, my services?"

He slips a piece of paper into her hand. "Read it," he says. "And think about it. I'll make it worth your while."

Harriet waits until she is safely tucked away in her workroom that evening before opening Michael's letter. It's little more than a scrawled note, containing a time and a place. One o'clock tomorrow morning, at an address she does not recognise. She ought to feed the note into the lamp, of course; see this foolishness burn to ash. But instead she crushes it between her fingers, indecision swaying inside her.

Something urges her to go. To hear what Michael Mitchell has to say— and why, of all things, he needs to say it to her. *I will make it worth your while;* what had he meant by that?

It's madness, of course, to even be thinking of traipsing across the island in the middle of the night, especially at the bidding of someone she barely knows. Michael is a known Jacobite; there is every chance he is leading her into a trap. But she has always found it hard to conjure up the fear she knows she ought to feel. When Julia had been sneaking around Highfield House to visit her brothers, Harriet had had no qualms about venturing into the night to confront the intruder. She had been far more intrigued at the prospect of some excitement than fearful of what might happen to her. Sometimes she finds it difficult to place any great value on her own life.

By midnight, the house is quiet. Harriet opens the door of her workroom and listens. No sound of movement, beyond a clock ticking steadily in the parlour and the shift of wood as the fire in the kitchen dies away. She pulls on the cloak she had hung over the back of her chair and takes the lamp from the mantel.

The night is clear and cold, with a dinted moon rippling its light off the water. Lamps glow atop the masts of the ship that has been moored beyond the house for the past weeks.

Harriet walks carefully over the uneven grass, the lantern held out in front of her. She feels a dull swirling in her belly, something that hints at a thrill, at excitement. A thrill at what, she wonders? The prospect of being caught? Of defying her husband? Of taking a step closer to that woman who does not follow orders?

The address on Michael's note is at the other end of the village to Julia's curiosity shop. Harriet keeps to the edges of the town, careful to avoid the anchorage and tavern. She knows that if any of the villagers saw her creeping around by lamplight, they would be even more inclined to believe her family were spies. A group of fishermen pass, laughing loudly, and Harriet darts into an alley, pressing herself against the wall until they are gone.

She reaches a small stone cottage on the corner of Marygate. Wooden shutters are closed over the windows, but a thin thread of smoke is rising from the chimney. Harriet taps lightly on the door, edgy with anticipation. She glances over her shoulder. The street is empty, save for a fox that scuttles down a dark alleyway and disappears.

The door creaks open to reveal a dark-haired young woman. She is unfamiliar—and on this island that is something of a novelty. Harriet has not seen her at church—a Catholic, perhaps, and in that case, almost certainly a Jacobite. Michael's lover? Or just someone willing to help further the Jacobite cause? She is dressed in a dark woollen dress and shawl, as though she is trying to blend into the night, her hair scraped back in a severe bun. The single candle in her hand casts shadows over her cheeks and gives her a faintly hunted expression.

"Did Michael send for you?" she asks brusquely. Her Northumbrian accent is thick and harsh, and Harriet has to concentrate hard to catch her meaning. She nods.

The woman gestures for Harriet to follow her into the cottage. She leads her through a narrow passage, closed doors on either side and the salty stench of tallow thick in the air. She shoulders open the door to the kitchen. It is small and cramped, with a single table in the centre cluttered with stacked wooden bowls and a half-eaten loaf of bread. Firelight glows in the range, the air thick with the smell of old boiled meat.

Michael Mitchell is sitting at a chair with his long legs stretched out and his hat sitting on the table in front of him. He is wearing the same dark greatcoat he had appeared in at Julia's shop. Harriet is surprised to see him alone. She had half expected to be walking into a Jacobite meeting.

"You came," says Michael.

"You sound surprised."

"A little."

Harriet stands with her back pressed to the cold stone wall. "Are you not worried I've brought the redcoats with me? Or that I'm going to tell every soul I meet where you're hiding?"

"And are you not worried I might have some fellow Jacobites tucked away in the corners ready to come after your family?"

"I suppose I ought to be, yes." Michael's words about her being disloyal to her family echo in Harriet's head. There's a truth to them, no doubt. Is that why she has come here tonight? To create trouble for the family she has begun to feel so detached from? The answer is an uncomfortable one, and she pushes the thought away quickly.

The dark-haired woman steps into the kitchen and places the candle on the sideboard. She looks at Harriet with slightly narrowed eyes.

Michael drums his fingers against the table top. "I know you're not a spy. I told you, I've had time to think about it. If you were, you would not have said a word about where the Jacobites were gathering. I've heard others speaking about Lesbury Common since. The rebels are waiting there for directions from France or Scotland. I think it's like you said; you just overheard something." He shifts forward in his chair to eye her. "And I think you just like to cause trouble. Stir things up."

"Is that why you wished to speak to me?"

Michael exchanges glances with the dark-haired woman. "I need to get to Lesbury," he tells Harriet. "To re-join the rebels."

"I thought you were waiting for your older brother."

Something passes across Michael's eyes. "Well. As much as I hate to say it, the prospect of Hugh returning seems less and less likely with each day. And I'm a wanted man now. I know it's dangerous for me to be strolling around the place, especially now the redcoats are so active in these parts."

Harriet snorts. "That did not seem to bother you much before."

Michael ignores her comment. "I need your help to get to Lesbury."

"My help?" She raises her eyebrows.

"Aye. It's dangerous for me to make the journey on my own. I can't take the chance that I might be recognised. But if were to make the journey with you, I'd be under less scrutiny."

Harriet frowns. "Why?"

"You'll pose as my wife," says Michael matter-of-factly. "The redcoats will be on the lookout for men on their way to join the rebel army. But they'll never suspect that a man travelling with his wife is headed for Lesbury Common. You'll be the perfect cover for me."

Harriet doesn't speak at once. She had not expected this. On the other side of the room, the other woman stands with her back to the door, studying Harriet with a look of open distrust.

Harriet sits at the table. Michael's request is laughable. But she cannot deny she is curious. "And how exactly do you propose I return to Lindisfarne once I've deposited you into the hands of the rebels?"

"Anne will accompany us," Michael says, nodding to the other woman. "She can pose as your lady's maid. And she will be able to drive the wagon back to Lindisfarne."

Harriet's eyes meet Anne's for a second, then she turns back to Michael. "If that is the case, why do you need me? Why not just take her?"

"It's a long journey back, and you'll be travelling late at night. Safer for there to be two of you." His lips quirk. "I'm not a complete bastard, regardless of what you might have heard about me. I don't want either of you to get in trouble."

"And you do not think two women travelling alone will raise suspicions?"

"Not if we have our stories prepared," Anne speaks up. Harriet turns to her in interest. "Why do you think so many women are working for the Jacobite cause? Because we don't arouse as much suspicion. If the redcoats stop us, we'll tell them your husband has died and you're on the way home to your family."

Harriet smiles crookedly. "It sounds as though you have done this before." When Anne doesn't respond, she leans back in her chair and looks at Michael. She ought to have shut this down already. Ought to have laughed in Michael Mitchell's face and marched right out of the house.

But she finds herself saying, "Why should I do this for you? I hardly know you. And all I do know of you is that you're a violent man and a liar."

The smile doesn't leave Michael's lips. "Harsh. But probably fair." He reaches into his pocket and produces a coin pouch. Sets it on the table in front of him. "I can pay you."

Harriet straightens. "Well. Why did you not tell me that before?"

"I suppose I wanted to see if you would do it out of the kindness of your heart."

Harriet snorts. "I'm not an idiot. And I'm afraid there's little kindness in my heart."

"One guinea and ten," he says.

Her heart skips. One guinea and ten. Enough, she imagines, to get her to Paris. But she senses Michael's desperation.

"Two guineas," she says.

"One and fifteen." And at once, Harriet's mind is racing. Thoughts of her paintings on the Baillieus' walls, thoughts of being in Paris with Isabelle—thoughts of being somewhere other than this cursed island. There is no way she will make the journey to Lesbury and back without Edwin noticing, of course. But what is the worst he could do to her? Yes, he could strike her, cause physical pain, but such a thing would only be temporary. He could declare he was washing his hands of her and leave her to her own devices—and what a blissful outcome that would be. Really, she thinks, the worst he could do would be to take her upstairs and put another child inside her. She wonders if he is more or less likely to do so if he is angry with her. Even that would almost be worth it if she has the means to make Paris a reality.

Thoughts of Thomas tug at the back of her mind. He will be without his mother for a day or more. Jenny will care for him; feed him—milk and flour from the pap boat, like Harriet has pushed for in the past. Best she begin to sever his reliance on her. After all, she cannot take him with her to Paris.

She lets Michael see none of her racing thoughts. Lets him see nothing but a cool façade of indifference. "I will think about it," she says.

Irritation flickers across Michael's eyes. "Think quickly," he snaps. "The army won't stay there forever. When you've made up your mind, leave word with Anne."

CHAPTER FIFTEEN

"If I did not know better," says Julia, picking her way across the mudflats towards Nathan, "I would say you had come here looking for me."

Nathan plants his boots in the damp sand at the top of Saint Cuthbert's Island. "I hardly think so. My daughter likes this part of Lindisfarne the best. Nothing more than that." He knows there's a hollowness to his words. Because when Theodora had asked to be taken out to the islet off the coast of the village, Nathan's first thoughts had been of Julia. He has seen her and her son out here on many occasions. Knew there was more than a small chance they might run into one another. He had found himself agreeing to Thea's request anyway.

He trudges down the sandy embankment towards Julia. Slate-coloured clouds weigh on the horizon, and the cold air smells of rain. He can feel his cheeks reddening in the wind. Can taste the sea on his lips.

Julia gives him a half smile. "It does not suit you, you know. This rudeness. It sounds very forced."

Nathan doesn't speak at once. Because the truth is, it feels forced as well. He hates confrontation, hates rudeness. Is uncomfortable with anything other than easy cordiality. But given the way Julia has deceived him in the past, he knows he needs to keep his guard up. It is too dangerous not to. Both in regard to Holland's warning—and in regard to his own traitorous heart.

"Well," he says, avoiding her comment, "I do suspect Theodora wished to come down here in the hope she might see Bobby." The two children have already scrambled onto the islet and are pointing and laughing at the diving seals.

"Aye," says Julia. "They do seem rather fond of one another." Nathan realises he is standing close to her; close enough to count the pale explosion of freckles on her cheeks. He is strangely comfortable at her nearness, he realises. That fact in itself makes him uneasy.

Theodora bounds over the rocks on the edge of the island. "Stay out of the water, Thea," Nathan calls. "It's far too cold for wet feet." His daughter ignores him, scrambling up the outcrop on hands and knees, giving them a fine view of her underskirts and stockings. Nathan rubs his eyes.

"I hope you took the telescope in out of the rain," says Julia. "It's quite a high-quality piece. At least, the fellow who sold it to me assured me it was. I hope he wasn't trying to swindle me."

"It is a high-quality piece," Nathan agrees stiffly. "I shall return it to your shop when I have a free moment."

Julia smiles to herself. "You do that." She bends down to pick up a seashell, running her gloved finger over its pearly surface. She tucks it into the pocket of her cloak. "How is Harriet?" she asks. "I've not seen her in more than a week. I'm a little concerned about her."

Nathan hesitates. Some selfish part of him is pleased Harriet has not been spending her time with Julia. Another part knows it would do his sister good to see her friend. Tentatively, he asks, "Has she told you…"

Julia catches the hood of her cloak before the wind whips it off her head. "She's not told me anything. I only gathered something was amiss after you sent me to fetch Eva."

Nathan nods stiltedly. "Well. I am sure Harriet will speak with you when she is ready."

Julia's gaze drifts past him to a figure making his way down the hill towards them. Nathan's stomach dives at the sight of Joseph Holland. He knows it will do neither of them any good if Holland sees him and Julia together. He is about to make his excuses when Julia says, "I'd best go." Her jaw tightens, her eyes hardening at the sight of Holland. "Bobby!" she calls. "Come on, now. Quickly." When her son doesn't turn, she gathers her skirts in her fist and strides across the mudflats towards him, barely reacting when a wave jolts off the edge of the island and washes over her shoes. Nathan stares after her, baffled by her unease. Holland has his eyes on Julia, yes, but there is no way she ought to know that.

Unless she has somehow caught wind of Holland's position. Unless the men spying for the government are not as well hidden as they believe.

Nathan's heart begins to bang against his ribs. What would such a thing mean for the safety of his family? If Jacobite sympathisers like Julia have somehow learnt of Holland's role, there is every chance they might also have learnt that the government spies are using Highfield House.

If Julia knew such a thing, surely she would not have spoken to him so genially today. Surely she would not have helped him by sailing out to Longstone. Surely she would not have given him the telescope.

Unless she was playing him like she has done in the past.

Nathan rubs his eyes, feeling the beginnings of a headache. If he is honest with himself, he had been pleased to find Julia on the beach today. But he knows that was foolish. Knows he must be stronger than that. He will not, he tells himself firmly, allow her to mislead him a second time.

"I thought it was your intention to keep Miss Mitchell away from your family," says Holland, his footsteps crunching across dried seaweed as he makes his way towards Nathan.

Nathan folds his arms. "It's a small island. Sometimes running into her cannot be helped."

Holland hums noncommittally. For a moment, Nathan considers telling him of his suspicions that the government spies may not be as hidden as they believe. The moment the thought arrives, he dismisses it. Untrustworthy though she may be, he cannot put Julia and her son in danger like that. Besides, Holland and the other spies have been careful. Discreet. And Nathan is certain his family has been too. If anyone has come to learn what the house is being used for, he cannot make sense of how.

"Is that why you're here?" he asks Holland. "To warn me away from her? Because I can assure you, there's no need."

Holland chuckles humourlessly. "Are you certain about that?"

Nathan shoots him a glare. "Perfectly."

"I saw you while I was up on the Heugh," says Holland, nodding towards the hill behind the ruins of the monastery. He stops speaking for a moment as Julia charges past, dragging Bobby along behind her. "Miss Mitchell," he says with a nod. She gives him a strained smile of greeting and hurries away, ignoring Nathan. When she is gone, Holland says, "We need the house for another meeting. Tomorrow evening."

"As you wish." Nathan knows there is no point in arguing.

Holland gives him a nod of thanks. "I appreciate it, Blake," he says, clapping Nathan on the shoulder, as if he had even a hint of a say in the matter.

Eva finds Nathan striding back up the hill from Saint Cuthbert's Island. Theodora is just ahead of him, pink-cheeked and windblown, with her woollen bonnet pulled almost to her eyebrows. The hems of her blue checked skirts are sodden and tangled around her legs. At the sight of her aunt, she bounds forward and throws her arms around Eva's waist.

Nathan doesn't look particularly pleased to see her. "Planned to accost me did you?" he asks.

Eva ignores his sharpness. "I went to the house. Edwin told me you had taken Thea out here."

"I was looking for selkies," Theodora puts in. "Magic seals."

Nathan raises his eyebrows. "Where on earth did you hear about selkies? Did Bobby tell you?"

"No," she says airily. "Mrs Brodie did. After Miss Jenny took me and Thomas to see the seals one day. And then I had cocoa."

"I see."

Eva eyes her brother. His hands are dug deep into the pockets of his greatcoat, a faint frown creasing the bridge of his nose. "Are you all right?" she asks. "You seem bothered."

"I'm fine." He doesn't look at her.

"Are you sure?"

"What do you want, Eva?" he says tautly.

She reaches for her niece's hand. "I thought perhaps I might resume Thea's lessons?"

"Yes!" Theodora sings, before Nathan can speak. "But no arithmetic.

Just reading and writing."

Nathan manages a half-smile. "It seems your niece has spoken." He gives Theodora a pointed look. "But she will do arithmetic too. And Latin."

Theodora screws up her nose.

"You shall have to come to the house," Nathan tells Eva, watching his feet. "I'll not be taking her all the way out to you."

Eva gives a short laugh. "I figured. I'm learning to sail," she tells him. "I shall be able to come on my own before too long. At least as soon as I can come about without ending up right back where I started."

"I see," says Nathan, her meagre attempt at humour either ignored or unregistered.

"Bobby hates arithmetic too," Theodora says suddenly. "At school, he has to do the mul-ta-pa-cation tables." She speaks the word out carefully. "But they also do reading and writing. He said I should come too, but Papa won't let me."

"Is that so?" Eva looks sideways at her brother. "I wonder why that is."

Nathan ignores her.

"I'm writing a story," Theodora announces. "About the fisherman's wife who asked the selkie to take her to the moon. Mrs Brodie told me all about her. I'm putting her in my own story. But I'm giving her a better ending. I'll read it to you in our next lesson." She pauses for breath. "Can we have it tomorrow?"

"Of course." Eva releases her hand and Theodora runs ahead into the open grassland behind the village.

Nathan watches after her. "I'd forgotten those tales," he says. "About the selkies. I suppose you were too young to remember folk tales like that." He digs his hands into his pockets. "Perhaps I ought to have a word with Mrs Brodie. Ask her not to speak to Thea about such things. I know there's talk of the… old ways up here. Do you think I ought to be concerned about her getting carried away with such ideas? Folk tales and superstitions and the like drifting down from Scotland. I'd hate for her to get lost in them."

Eva laughs, buoyed by his attempt at conversation. "You've a very imaginative daughter, Nathan. As you well know. Only you could make such a thing a cause for concern. Just because she is writing stories and listening to folk tales does not mean she is about to lose herself in the old ways."

"Mm." He does not sound convinced.

"Why not send her to the dame school?" Eva asks. "I'm sure such a thing would be good for her. Better than sitting around in that creaking old mansion all day. Need I remind you that you did not want Thea in the house at all."

"Believe me, I do not need to be reminded," Nathan snaps. "And I'd say you lost any input you might have had in Thea's upbringing when you absconded across the sea."

"Absconded across the sea?" Eva shakes her head. "You're impossible. And offensive."

"I'm sorry," he says, not sounding sorry in the slightest.

"How long are you planning on holding this grudge for?" asks Eva. "Because the thing is done. Finn and I are married. And nothing is going to change that. I hoped marrying for love would not cost me a brother."

Nathan looks at her witheringly. "That's a fine attempt at guilting me, Eva. I thought you above such things." He walks with his eyes down for several paces. Finally, he says, "I can't send Thea to the dame school. Not while there are so many people here who do not trust our family. I hate the thought of leaving my daughter with people I'm not sure would have her best interests at heart."

Eva nods. She understands, of course. How could she not? But surely Nathan is holding on too tightly. Seeing danger where there is none. She dares to say, "I suspected it was because you did not want Thea around Julia Mitchell's son."

"Well. That too."

Eva sees something flicker across his eyes at the mention of Julia. The sight of it tugs at her chest. She knows how rare it is for Nathan to be drawn to someone the way he was to Julia. She regrets that he had been deceived by her as he had.

"I think you're right to stay away from Miss Mitchell," she tells him. "But I don't think that's a good enough reason to keep Thea away from school…" The last words of the sentence are strangled, but she does her best not to let Nathan see her sudden unease. She tries to hide the way her eyes pull towards the man striding up the hill from the anchorage.

He is impossible not to notice. Striking and sculpted Henry Ward, who walks in giant strides and spills confidence, has the kind of charisma that draws eyes and stops conversations. At the sight of him, any doubts Eva had had about Harriet's parentage fall away. Because there in Henry Ward is her sister's beauty. It was not found in plain and mousy Abigail, or rugged and red-cheeked Samuel Blake.

Eva lowers her eyes and pulls up the hood of her cloak, praying Ward doesn't see her.

Once, Henry Ward had shown her kindness. When he had learnt she was Abigail Blake's daughter, he had taken her to his dinner table and lavished her with care and attention. But she is sure all of that kindness was erased when she helped Finn escape his ship.

What is Ward doing here on Holy Island? Panic rushes through her at the thought of her husband, waiting for her at the Lindisfarne anchorage. She knows Finn will be aware—knows he is always on the lookout for Ward. But all it would take would be a stray pistol shot. A moment of diverted attention for Ward to get what he has been seeking.

No. There has to be more to it. If Ward merely wanted Finn dead, he has had ample opportunity to see the thing done. But this knowledge goes far from reassuring her. Because the sight of Ward, who has given almost all his looks to his daughter, reminds Eva that he is inexorably linked to her own family. In ways she is only just beginning to untangle. Does he know about Harriet? Is that what this is about?

"Eva? What is it?" Nathan follows her gaze. He glances at Ward, but looks away without comment. Nathan has heard of Henry Ward, of course. Eva had told her brother all about him after she had returned from his ship several weeks ago. But Nathan has not seen Ward for twenty years—if, indeed, ever. Surely he has no idea who the man in front of them is.

But now she sees Harriet in Henry Ward, it seems impossible that her brother cannot. Still, she reminds herself, to Nathan, the man in the tricorn hat striding up the street with two of his crewmen is a stranger, barely worth a passing glance. And it is best that it stays that way. Eva does not want her family drawn into this sorry business she and Finn have with Ward. At least no more than they are already.

"I'd best get back to the anchorage," she says, forcing herself to keep her voice level. "I do not wish to keep Finn waiting." She is suddenly desperate to get back to Longstone as quickly as possible. She flashes Nathan a strained smile. "I shall see Thea for her lesson tomorrow at noon."

Nathan watches Eva disappear towards the anchorage, then he strides back towards the house at the same brisk pace, calling Theodora to keep up with him. He desperately hopes his sister had not registered the look of horror on his face.

He dares a glance over his shoulder. Watches the man in the cocked hat disappear into the tavern, flanked by two others. The door thumps shut behind them.

Nathan knows he ought not be surprised to see him. But every time he glimpses Henry Ward's face, he cannot help but be filled with dread.

CHAPTER SIXTEEN

"Why are we walking so fast, Papa?" Theodora whines. "Slow down."

Nathan reaches out to grab her hand. The physical contact sends an unpleasant jolt through him, but it has the intended effect of making her skip to keep up with him. Her narrow fingers curl tightly around his gloved hand.

He cannot bear for Ward to see him. Worse, he cannot bear for Ward to see Theodora; to see that which Nathan holds most dear. That which would fell him the hardest if it was taken from him.

He touches a hand to his forehead. Even through the thick leather of his gloves, his skin feels hot and cold at once; dread mixed with the icy wind. Dead and alive. The swirling in his belly is telling him to let go of Thea's hand, but he is physically unable to. It feels as though he must keep hold of her forever, forever, forever, because how easily Henry Ward might take her if he untethered himself from her. At the sight of Ward walking through the village, the threats he has made feel all too real.

Beyond the town, the land opens out to gold-tinged grassland. In the fading daylight, Nathan feels intensely vulnerable. Insignificant in the expanse of this openness; and beside him, tiny Thea, the height of fragility. His heart is thumping hard, goaded on by his daughter's tight grip on his hand. There's a smile on her lips—he knows she is enjoying the rare contact. Knows she has no thought of the chaos roiling inside him.

He feels watched. He whips his head around, trying to catch sight of the eyes he can sense boring into him. Nothing, of course. Just his imagination charging. As it so often is, this part of the island is almost impossibly empty.

He knows he shouldn't be carrying this alone. Eva has had her own run-in with Henry Ward, and so, apparently, has her husband. He ought to tell them of his own dealings with the man. The demands Ward has made. But things have gone too far for that. He is too deep into the charade to dig himself out of it now. He shakes his head wryly to himself. He had cursed Julia for her lies and deceit. Is he really any better?

They step through the front door of the house, and Nathan lets himself breathe. He releases Theodora's hand and locks the front door. And before he can really understand what he is doing, he is marching up to his study and pulling that damn box out from under his desk. Setting the telescope up at his study window.

In the early-evening light, the first stars are beginning to glitter, and he angles the telescope to catch their glow. He lowers his eye to the lens and pulls in a long breath. A little of the tension in his muscles evaporates.

There is something oddly calming about peering through the glass into the oceanic depths of space. Somehow, the sight of the stars that the telescope pulls from the blackness dulls the panic, fades out the image of Theodora in Ward's grasp. Against the enormity of the night sky, and cradled behind locked doors, Nathan feels blissfully insignificant. And so does Henry Ward.

"What's that, Papa?" Theodora is standing in the doorway, chewing the end of her plait. He had not heard her approach.

"Come and look," he tells her.

She hurries towards him. He angles the barrel towards the waning moon, its peaks and valleys stark against the darkening sky. He guides Theodora to stand in front of him and peer through the eyepiece. A faint murmur escapes her.

"Oh," she says. "The moon." When she looks back at him, her eyes are wide and her lips parted in a look of entrancement.

Nathan smiles to himself. He had had the same reaction when his father had first set the telescope up for him, and he had peeked out into the night through this very same window.

"Can you see all the peaks and depressions on the moon?" he asks his daughter. "As if someone has scooped out spoonfuls of it?"

Theodora nods, her eye still to the glass.

"Some people think some rocks crashed into it," he tells her. "And that's how all the holes got there."

She looks over her shoulder at him. "Maybe the fisherman's wife did it after the selkie sent her to live there."

He chuckles. "My nurse used to tell me stories about the selkies when I was a boy," he says. It's a memory that had been frayed and distant until he had heard Theodora speak of the old folk tales that afternoon. A memory of windblown hair and muddy boots, and legs aching from running the dunes. Of being an island child who believed in the shape-shifting selkies and spoke with the rounded vowels borrowed from the Scots. A part of himself he had forgotten. Certainly, his mother had never sought to remind him of it. Once they had left Holy Island, she had barely spoken of the place. Running the dunes with folk tales in his head had been replaced by arithmetic tutors and cricket matches. Later, by the rigidity of a business degree at Cambridge. Coffee house debates about unemployment figures and Britain's involvement in Continental wars. A merchant enterprise; a wife, a daughter. And then grief and failure that had stripped the last of the magic from the world.

But, "I remember hearing about the selkies taking off their seal suits and turning into real people," he tells Theodora. "Although I never heard of them living on the moon."

Theodora giggles as she looks up from the telescope. "The selkies don't live on the moon. Only the fisherman's wife who asked the selkie for a wish. Mrs Brodie told me about her. Her house wasn't big enough and she wanted a castle on the moon. Mrs Brodie said she got lonely there after a while and wanted to come home. But in my story, she likes it, and she decides to live there forever. Look." She nudges him gently towards the telescope, pulling her hand away from his shoulder quickly. "That mountain on the side looks just like a castle where she might live."

Nathan smiles faintly. "You know these are just stories, don't you? The selkies are not real."

Theodora laughs. "Of course I do. Don't be silly, Papa." She presses her eye back to the lens. And though his problems have rarely felt more weighted, Nathan feels an immense pull of gratitude for Julia's telescope, and the space it has given him to breathe.

CHAPTER SEVENTEEN

Finn scrawls the tide times in his logbook, his pencil scratching across the page. Eva is pacing the living space, her stockinged feet sighing against the floorboards.

"Do you think Ward knows about Harriet?" she asks. "Do you think that's why he came to Northumberland in the first place? Do you think that's why I saw him on Holy Island today?"

Finn leans back in his chair, following her with his eyes. Her fingers are intertwined in her worn yellow shawl, dark hair hanging loose down her back as she marches from the sideboard to the doorway and back again. She is making it hard for him to concentrate.

Finn puts down his pencil. He wraps his hands around his teacup, listening to the wind rattle the open shutters. A blaze of firelight is pouring through the window and casting long shadows across the cottage. He can hear faint snoring coming from the Mitchells behind the closed door of the bedroom. The spring watch open on the table beside him tells him it's a couple of hours from dawn.

Though he is doing his best to stay calm, he can't deny he is on edge. Longstone is feeling far from the place of isolation it has done for the past five years. But he is fairly certain it is not Henry Ward's daughter that has brought him back to Lindisfarne. "If he knows about her, and wants to meet her, why would he wait twenty years to do so?" He shakes his head.

"I don't think this is about Harriet. But I do think it's about your family. It's too much of a coincidence that he would appear now, at the same time you all returned."

Eva nods slowly, her eyes glassy as she stares into the grate. A log breaks open, sending sparks flying up the chimney. "You're right." A frown creases the bridge of her nose. "He has been in Northumberland for more than a month. If he wanted to see Harriet, surely he would have done so already." She sits opposite him and begins bouncing her knees up and down. Finn presses a hand to her thigh and she stops jolting. Picks up her teacup. He wishes he could take the rest of her anxiety away as easily.

"And you've not told her who her father is?" he asks.

Eva puts her cup down without taking a sip. "How can I?" She is suddenly defensive. "What if she seeks him out and he tells her everything?" She shakes her head in frustration. "You of all people ought to understand why I cannot say anything!"

Finn nods. It's a conversation he does not want to get into again. Of course he understands.

He wants to go to her, hold her, promise her everything be all right. Promise her that Ward will not hurt them. But Eva is far too involved in this, far too aware, far too intelligent, to accept his empty assurances. He hates that he cannot protect her. And while having her on Longstone with him is every dream he never knew he had, he hates that he has brought her here to live a life so full of worry.

He stares out the window, past the glow of the firebasket to the inky plain of the sea. Lights out there, but they are far too low in the water to be Ward's ship. Lindisfarne fishermen, no doubt, out for the herrings that swarm at night, threading between the rocky outcrops of the Farnes in the glow of the firebasket.

He scrawls in the log: *fishermen sighted.*

He had started keeping the logbook when he had returned to Longstone five years ago after almost fifteen years of living a rootless, transitory life. Back then, in the wake of his father's death, the loneliness of the island had weighed on him, and the log had been a way to fill the empty hours of firelit night. A way of reminding himself that the rest of the world was still out there. Now, it has become a daily habit to record the high and low tides, the weather, the ships that pass the island. He is also well aware that by doing so, he is tracking the days in which Henry Ward has not come for him. Recording yet another day he has survived.

A part of him wants to leave this place. Climb into the skiff with Eva and sail somewhere Ward will never find them. He has made the Longstone light his responsibility, but he does not want it to cost him his life. Nor does he want to condemn himself to a life of running, of constantly looking over his shoulder. Of waiting for Henry Ward to spill his most damaging of secrets.

Finn knows Ward wants to punish him for Oliver's death. But what is he waiting for? Is his marriage to Eva somehow protecting him? Perhaps Ward is unwilling to send his crewmen to Longstone and put Abigail's daughter in the line of fire. But Ward has had plenty of opportunity to come after Finn alone. Times when he has been on the mainland; times when Eva has been away on Lindisfarne.

Perhaps he is simply not as important to Ward as he might have imagined.

Either way, he has had enough of waiting. He thinks of Eva standing at the window on their wedding night; thinks of the fear in her eyes when she had looked out over the water in search of Ward's ship. He does not want this to be his life. And more than anything, he does not want it to be Eva's.

At the first hint of dawn, Eva throws the Mitchells out of the bedroom and climbs into bed. She falls asleep quickly. Finn's eyes are heavy with sleeplessness, but he knows if he is to catch hold of Henry Ward—and if he is to do so without his wife knowing—he needs to leave now. Eva will be awake again in a few hours, ready to go to Holy Island for her niece's lessons. With luck he can make it there and back without her having any inkling of it.

"You going somewhere?" asks Angus, as Finn reappears in the living area, tugging on his coat.

"Nowhere of any importance," he says. And in case it didn't sound suspicious enough, he adds, "Not a word to Eva."

Navy blue sea fringes Holy Island in the early morning, the pale stripe of dawn glowing on the horizon. Cold wind skims the water, promising an early winter. Finn shivers, turning up the collar of his greatcoat and flexing his frozen fingers. He sails past the village, out towards Emmanuel Head, where the *Eagle* is moored. He looks up at the barque. He can see a man on anchor watch, but the dark portholes suggest only a skeleton crew is aboard. He knows there is a good chance Ward and his crew are still in the village tavern.

Finn has vivid memories of Ward's privateering crew spending long nights in sordid drinking holes. Whenever the captain had allowed it, they would disappear into the taverns dotted along the coast of east England and the Spanish Netherlands. As a child, he had stayed aboard the ship with a cleaning rag in hand and list of hideous chores to complete. He can still conjure up the smell of beeswax polish, the stench of the congealing stew in the galley; the scrapes and slops as he emptied the vats into the sea.

He takes the skiff back to the village and secures it to the jetty. In the early morning, the first of the fishermen are bustling around the huts, arms loaded with bundled nets. Finn feels their eyes on him, but he keeps walking with his head down, making it clear he is in no mood for questions.

His footsteps echo across the cobbles as he approaches the tavern. Drunken laughter bounces between stone walls. Two men stumble past him, crooked with drink; another sits slumped against the outside wall. Finn pushes open the door. He is greeted with a fog of stale smoke, air thick with liquor and sweat. Men laugh and chatter loudly.

Finn hopes Ward is here among his crewmen. Far safer to confront him in the village than in the privacy of his ship.

The moment he steps inside, he catches sight of Ward standing at the back of the tavern. He seems locked in a heated conversation with a greying, narrow-faced man. The man has a faint familiarity to him, and Finn guesses him a long-time member of Ward's crew.

Ward turns towards Finn, as though sensing his arrival. Their eyes meet. Ward makes his way towards him, picking his black tricorn hat up from the large table in the centre of the tavern as he passes. He nods towards a smaller unused table at the back of the room.

"I thought you and your crew would be more discreet than this," Finn says, following. "Now that you've turned to piracy."

"And I thought you would be wiser than to seek me out." Ward is dressed in a dark waistcoat with silver buttons, his ornate white shirtsleeves buttoned neatly at his wrists. The faint red webs in the corners of his eyes hint at a long night, though his clothes are unstained and his greying hair is tied back in a neat queue. He pulls out a rickety chair and stiffly lowers himself onto it.

Finn slides onto the chair opposite. "I figured you're unlikely to shoot me with so many witnesses."

Ward's eyes dart momentarily to his crewman at the back of the tavern, then he looks back at Finn. "From what I hear, I don't imagine there would be all that many people on this island too distraught over your death. You've a reputation for being somewhat light-fingered. It seems folks are not all that willing to have their hard-earned coal used to keep the Longstone firebasket burning."

Finn smiles wryly. "I'm sure they're not." In truth, he knows Henry Ward is unlikely to shoot him at all; at least, not here in a cold-blooded murder. If he is to kill him, it will be done according to the laws of his ship's articles: a hanging from his yardarm, or a keel-hauling in the lightless water beneath the ship. "What of you?" he asks. "Are you not worried about being caught? You know they love to see pirates hanging over the Thames these days."

Ward sits upright in his chair, his spine rigid against the backrest. He folds his hands neatly on the table in front of him. "Well. Some risks are worth taking. In any case, we sailed over from San Salvador without engagement. So it's safe to say the authorities are not on our tail."

"What risks?" Finn pushes. "Why leave the Caribbean? Why come to Northumberland, of all places?"

"Because I have matters to attend to here."

"And your crew is happy to sit about in the bay for weeks on end? Are they not craving action?"

Ward smiles thinly. "Hence the long night in the tavern."

Finn leans back in his chair, considering. Back when he was Ward's cabin boy, he'd had a strong rapport with his captain. There had been trust between them; openness. Ward had filled the gap left by the father Finn had never seen eye to eye with. The father he had fled Longstone to get away from.

Ward had taught Finn to make a three-masted barque bend to his commands. To fire a pistol with striking accuracy. To stand on deck with a quadrant to his eye and trace a path through the sea by starlight. And he had made it clear that Finn could always come to him with his questions. His fears. That grand, polished great cabin had never been inaccessible, even if it did manage to instil in him a sense of awe. Somehow, under Ward's guidance, Finn had rarely felt afraid. Even with French gunfire roaring around his ears, he had felt steadied by Henry Ward's presence. If they were to die, Ward had always said, they would do so for their country. And what greater honour was there than that?

Finn had believed those words as a child. Ward had led him to foolishly trust in his own invincibility. But now, he sees the hollowness of that refrain his captain had spouted. He has been far too close to death by Henry Ward's hand to believe that dying will come without fear.

While he knows, of course, that there is no chance of rebuilding the trust he and Ward had once shared, he wonders if he can at least get his former captain to open up a little. Speak in something more than riddles.

"Why piracy?" Finn asks. "You were always so adamant that we only attack enemy ships. No conflict without a letter of marque, was that not what you always said?"

"The war with France is over," Ward says evenly. "There's no role for privateers. It leaves men like me with few options, wouldn't you say?"

"Find yourself a nice little cottage to retire in and leave us all alone."

Ward gives a short laugh that disappears quickly. "I'm glad you're here, Finn," he says suddenly. "There's something I would like to speak to you about."

Finn raises his eyebrows. "If that's the case, why did you not send your thugs to collect me like last time?"

Ward ignores the barbed question. He waves a hand towards the bar. Moments later, two cannikins of whisky appear on the table. He nudges one towards Finn. "Here. I suppose you're to be congratulated on your marriage. You and your new wife are the source of much gossip here on Lindisfarne."

"I'm sure." Finn turns the cup around in his hand, without drinking. "I didn't imagine my marriage to Eva would be something you wished to celebrate.”

Ward brings his cannikin to his lips. “Well. Had things not happened the way they did between you and Oliver, it would have brought me much joy to see you marrying Eva Blake. But if Abigail knew Eva had married the man who killed her brother, it would destroy her.”

Finn bristles. He knows Ward is right, and the truth of it is an ache. “Eva’s mother is dead,” he says tautly. “What she would think is of no consequence.” But he can’t make himself believe his own words. He knows Oliver’s death has been at the forefront of Eva’s mind since she learnt who Harriet’s father is. He knows she is afraid of what Henry Ward could tell her family. But he also knows there is more to it than that. He can see it in her eyes sometimes. He can tell she thinks of her mother, of Oliver. Thinks of the betrayal she has committed by marrying him.

He cannot let Ward see his doubt. Ward had always taught him to find a man’s weakness. Finn knows it is no secret that Eva is his. But what of Ward? Had Abigail Blake been his weakness? Had he loved her? Had she loved him?

He can feel Ward studying him. “Does Eva know you’re here?” he asks.

“Of course not. She’d skin me alive for being so foolish.”

“She’s a wise lass.” Ward tosses back the rest of his whisky. “Why are you here, Finn? Is it to try and convince me to pardon you, now you’ve tied yourself to Abigail’s daughter?”

“No.” Finn looks at him squarely. He’s had enough of dancing around the issue. “I want to know why you’re here on Lindisfarne. I know it’s no coincidence you appeared at the same time as Eva’s family. And what do you want with me that makes you so pleased to see me?” He does not dare speak of Harriet. He knows there is a good chance Ward is unaware of her existence. And he is not about to plant the idea in his head.

“My business on Lindisfarne is none of your concern.”

“Of course it’s my concern,” Finn hisses. “Eva is my wife. And you clearly want something from her family.”

Ward leans back in his chair, rubbing his shorn chin. His refusal to give a straight answer is all the confirmation Finn needs.

“Where d’you find all these men?” he asks, inclining his head towards the large table in the middle of the tavern. Despite the pink dawn filtering through the windows, there are at least twenty or thirty men still lolling around the tavern with tankards in hand. No doubt most of them belong to Ward's crew. Finn wonders how many more men are crammed between decks on the *Eagle*.

"I've spent some time in Nassau," Ward says. "New Providence."

Finn snorts. "Henry Ward in the Republic of Pirates. Never thought I'd see the day."

"I imagine you'd be quite intrigued by the place," says Ward with a thin smile. "Most of the men there were once privateers, like ourselves. Turned to piracy because peacetime has left them with little choice. The men have drawn up their own articles of agreement to live by. Crews vote on who is to lead their ships. They treat one another with much more civility than most of the sorry souls here in enlightened England. A rather fascinating social experiment, you might say."

"A social experiment? For privateers who are unwilling to accept that their privateering days are over?"

Ward chuckles. "Something like that. In any case, Nassau is the easiest place to fill a ship. At least if you're a captain with a notable reputation." There's a forced bravado to Ward's words, Finn realises. A hint of uncertainty he has never heard from him before. It catches him by surprise.

"And did these men know when they signed with you that there would be no action to be had?" he asks. "Outside the tavern, at least?"

The corner of Ward's lips tilt up, but it's a hollow smile. "They jumped at the chance, lad. I can offer them something that no one else can."

"And what is that?"

"Immunity. From the British government at least."

"Immunity?" Finn repeats, incredulous. "How?"

"That is for my crew alone to know." He leans forward. "Although I am willing to extend that invitation to you."

Finn lets out a short laugh. "Are you just? A few weeks ago, you were determined to see me dead. Now you're offering me a place in your crew?"

"Call it a truce. I am willing to overlook the punishment due to you for Oliver's death, in exchange—"

"—for me leaving Eva behind," Finn finishes, the pieces falling into place. Something tightens in his stomach. He supposes he can't be surprised at this. But that does nothing to dull the sting of the blow.

Ward's arctic-blue eyes spear Finn's. "It's what Abigail would have wanted. Nothing will bring her son back, but at least she would be spared the knowledge of her daughter spending her life with Oliver's killer."

Finn's fingers tighten around his cup. "I've done nothing but treat her well, Ward. I'd never dream of doing otherwise."

"That's hardly the issue. As you well know."

Finn grits his teeth until pain shoots through his jaw. "You truly think I will agree to this?"

"I would at least think you would have the brains to consider it. A better offer, surely, than sleeping with one eye open, wondering when I might see fit to deliver the punishment you have so far escaped." Ward gives him a knowing smile. "Surely that is not the life you wish for for your wife."

Henry Ward's words are tinged with bluster, yes, but that does nothing to take away their impact. Because for not the first time in his life, Finn feels as though his captain has the ability to look inside him and read his every thought.

Sunlight is pouring over the horizon by the time he returns to Longstone. His body is aching with exhaustion, and though his thoughts are rattling, he is craving sleep. He leaves his damp, sea-scented greatcoat in the living quarters and slips back into the bedroom. Is relieved to see Eva breathing deeply with sleep.

As he slips under the blanket, she opens her eyes. "You're just coming to bed now?"

"Aye. I wasn't tired yet."

She sits up on her elbow, reaching out a hand for him. Her hair is tangled around her face, her thin nightshift sliding off one shoulder. "You're cold. Have you been out?"

"Just to empty the basket." The lie stings, and he curses himself for it. But it's for the best, he tells himself. Eva would tear him apart for going to see Ward, but it is more than that. Of all things, he does not want her to know of the offer his former captain has made him. It will anger her, cause her to act rashly. But perhaps, worst of all, it will cause her to question whether Ward is right to be asking for this. Whether her marriage to him is a betrayal to her family she ought never have agreed to.

For a horrifying moment, she is silent, as though turning his answer over in her mind. "Get some sleep," she says finally, sliding back beneath the blanket and pulling it to her neck. "I told Nathan I'd be there for Thea's lesson at noon."

CHAPTER EIGHTEEN

Eva senses movement in the corner of her eye. She stops walking. She whirls around, catching nothing but the blurred figure of a roe deer darting into the dunes behind Highfield House. She quickens her stride toward the manor.

As she walks, gripping tight fistfuls of her skirts, she cannot shake the feeling she is being watched. Deep billowed clouds are low on the horizon, sucking the light from the day and adding to her unease. Wind sighs through the grass, a barely audible whisper.

Eva pushes back the hood of her cloak to open up her vision. "Henry Ward," she hears herself say, "if you're there, show yourself."

Silence, of course. Wind sighs through the grass, meeting the constant lash of the sea. She feels like a fool. Henry Ward is not the kind of man to crouch in wait in the undergrowth. He is a man who will show himself at the very moment he chooses to. She puts her head down and hurries towards the house.

"Eva. Good." Edwin staggers out the shed at the back of the property, arms overloaded with timber. "Nathan told me you were coming today."

Eva raises her eyebrows. She is not sure her brother-in-law has ever been pleased to see her before. Although she can't deny that, after the troubling walk across the island, there is a part of her that is glad to see him too. "Is something the matter?" she asks.

"I need you to speak with Harriet," Edwin says, resting the wood against the wall of the house beside withered brown threads of ivy. "She has this outlandish idea about travelling to Paris to show her paintings."

"Why is that an outlandish idea? She is very talented. So her tutor used to say, anyway."

Edwin sighs. "I'm sure. But you know what she's like. Given the chance, this will take over her life. It's not healthy for a person to be so single-minded. And these artistic types she associates with, they're not good for her. They fill her mind with all sorts of fanciful ideas." He shakes his head, as though catching himself about to run away with his thoughts. "I need you to talk her out of it."

"You're the one who does not wish her to do it. Why do you not talk her out of it?" She pulls her cloak tight around her body. "I think it would be a good thing for her. And I think her work deserves a little recognition."

Edwin sighs wearily, as though expecting such a response. "This is not the time for her to be doing such things," he says. "This business with her father… it has upset her. I can tell. Not that she would ever admit such a thing to me." He sounds faintly regretful.

Eva wonders distantly what he would think if knew his wife was the daughter of a man like Henry Ward. She knows how much Edwin Whitley prides himself on his good name.

He digs the key to the front door from his pocket and opens it, gesturing for Eva to enter. "She listens to you," he says. "At least, she listens to you more than she listens to me. Perhaps you might consider speaking with her? Please? I would appreciate it."

Eva gives him a small nod—a gesture signifying the conversation is over, rather than any agreement to his request. He murmurs his thanks, then gathers up the timber and clatters into the house behind her.

Theodora thunders down the stairs and rushes at Eva, grabbing her hand and tugging her into the parlour. Harriet is inside, perched on the edge of the settle. At the sight of her, Eva's stomach knots.

"Sit down," Theodora orders. "I'm going to perform a reading of my story."

Eva sits obediently beside her sister.

Finn is right. She ought to tell Harriet about her father. Right now. Of course she should. But with the knowledge of who Ward is, and the terrible truths he could reveal, her precious new life has begun to feel fragile. Eva is all too aware of how easily it could be taken away. She is certain that if the truth of Oliver's death came out, she would be forced to choose between her husband and her family. Nonetheless, she knows keeping this knowledge from Harriet is the height of selfishness—or is it?

Because despite Harriet's self-assured façade, Eva is aware of how breakable her sister really is. She has not forgotten the sight of Harriet's ruined painting. Has not forgotten the sight of her sister slumped in the armchair with a whisky glass at her fingertips to take away reality. What would the knowledge of Henry Ward do to her? Would it be any worse than the uncertainty? The question goes someway to easing Eva's guilt, though she is well aware she is making excuses.

"Wait here," Thea orders. "I have to fetch my notes." She rushes out of the room.

"Well," says Eva, giving Harriet a smile she doesn't feel, "it seems she'll do anything to get out of arithmetic these days."

"I told her she has ten minutes," says Harriet, tapping her heels edgily. "I've a lot of work to do."

"Oh," says Eva, too brightly, "you've started a new piece then?"

Harriet looks out the window. "Not yet."

"I see." Eva folds her hands in her lap. Unfolds them again, then toys with the embroidery on the edge of her bodice.

"What?" Harriet demands.

"What?" Eva echoes.

"You keep looking at me. Do you have something to say?"

"No."

"Then stop it. You're driving me mad."

Eva had not realised how many sideways glances she had been giving her sister. But sitting here with Harriet, all she can see in her is Henry Ward. "Thea," she calls desperately. "Are you ready?"

"Almost. I just have to put my costume on. And fetch Papa."

"Papa is working," Eva calls back. "You'll have to read it to him another time. Quickly now." She starts to gnaw on a fingernail, a habit she had left behind in childhood.

"You're acting strangely," says Harriet accusingly.

"No I'm not."

Harriet snorts.

"Edwin told me about your plan to go to Paris," Eva blurts. She had not intended to go near such a thing. But it is better than the silence.

Harriet smiles wryly. "Let me guess. He sent you to do his bidding. Talk me out of it."

Eva doesn't answer at once. "He is just worried about you," she says finally. "He does not think now is the best time for you to be thinking of such things."

Harriet hums. "So he is not going to give me the money I need then. She twines a loose strand of hair around her finger. "I have to say, I expected such a thing from him. But not you."

"I'm not going to try and talk you out of it," Eva hisses, taken aback by Harriet's aggressiveness. "If you must know, I told him I thought it would be good for you. I just thought you ought to know what he asked of me."

"Is that so?" Harriet's words sound full of doubt, full of accusation.

"What is the matter with you?" Eva demands. She regrets the comment the moment it is out, but her sister is utterly infuriating. She did not mean to get into this argument, but somehow this feels safer. It's old, well-worn ground, if more bitter than usual.

Theodora struts into the room. She has a worn grey blanket wrapped around her shoulders and crown of sea thrift on her head, a wad of crumpled papers in her fist. Eva has never been more relieved to see her.

"Well, this is an interesting costume, Thea," says Eva.

Harriet wants to smack that forced brightness right out of her. She's surprised by her sudden fury at her sister. Or perhaps she's not. Because really, honestly, she has been angry at Eva for weeks. Furious at her for flying out of their lives and leaving Harriet to face her starched and stilted marriage alone.

This was not how it was supposed to be. This life as Edwin's wife, it was supposed to be tolerable because she had Eva beside her. Nathan and Edwin and Matthew would gallivant around the coffee houses, and she and Eva would hide themselves away to gossip about their beastly, uptight husbands, and everything would be all right.

"I'm a selkie," says Theodora. "Half a seal and half a girl."

Eva gives her a stiff smile, painfully obvious in not looking Harriet's way. "Very good. Read us the story then."

Eva is impossibly twitchy today. Harriet does not like it. It makes her feel there is something her sister is hiding.

Theodora looks down at the papers in her hand, the blanket sliding from her shoulders and pooling at her feet. She picks it up awkwardly with one hand and drapes it back over her shoulder. "Once upon a time," she begins, "there was an old man and his wife who lived by the sea. The man was a fisherman, and one day he rescued a seal who was trapped in his net. But it was not just a seal. It was a magical selkie who turned into a lady when she climbed out of the water."

Harriet sighs, louder than she had intended, and receives a brisk kick in the foot from Eva. She grits her teeth.

Being around her sister, Harriet realises, it makes her feel abandoned. Betrayed. And beneath it all is that which Harriet has been doing her best not to acknowledge: that thick, searing pull of jealousy.

Because impossibly, unfathomably, Harriet wishes she were Eva.

She cannot believe she feels this way. As soon as she was old enough to do more than trail after her like a blindly doting little sister, Harriet had seen Eva as dour and dull. A rigid follower of the rules, dreamless and hemmed-in by expectation. The fact that her colourless sister might be living this impossible sea-drenched life is too much to take in. Especially when Harriet knows that Eva also has the kind of love that Harriet will never have. Can never have.

Eva has told her none of this, of course. But she doesn't need to. Harriet can see it in her eyes. Can see it in the way she and Finn exchange those wordless, doting glances when they think no one is watching. It makes something burn in Harriet's chest; a thorny mix of jealousy and grief.

At least, she thinks, she is still capable of feeling something.

"And on the moon," says Theodora, "the fisherman's wife found mountains that looked like a castle. And holes that were made when a rock crashed into it."

Suddenly the thought comes to her, fervent and fierce. Harriet covers her mouth to silence her gasp. The images fly at her: the rise of the dented moon, with its peaks and valleys. Its depressions and shadows. This, she thinks, will be her unique way of putting the natural world to the canvas. She will build on the work of Maria Eimmart, whose depictions of the planets she had once seen in her brother's study. She will paint the moon, the stars, the planets. Track the changing hues of the night sky.

The moment Theodora's story is finished, Harriet races to her workroom. She throws open her notebook and begins scrawling furiously.

The piece takes shape at once: the globe of the full moon, silver-gold on the horizon, shedding its light on the water as it rises. Night, she thinks—that is far more her style than the sun-streaked vista she had attempted last time. As her pencil moves without pause, a weight is lifted from her shoulders—that irrational fear that she might never find inspiration again. The fear that these interminable months on Lindisfarne might have drained the creativity out of her. She thinks of the other pieces that will follow this one: a collection of starlit landscapes. Eclipses. Comets. Fresh and new and daring. Enough to provoke discussion at the salons of Lord and Lady Baillieu—especially if they are signed with the name of a woman.

So Edwin will not give her the money she needs. It is no surprise, of course. Nor is it a surprise that she has found out this way: through her sister rather than direct from her husband's mouth. But it is no matter. She does not need him. She just needs to find the courage to take that journey to Lesbury with Michael Mitchell—and then she can go about bringing her dream to life.

"I'm concerned," Nathan says, voice low, "that people may be aware of Joseph Holland's involvement with the government." He and Edwin are clustered together at the top of the dining table, beneath a fug of pipe smoke. He can hear faint murmurs coming from the spies' meeting in the parlour. Before the meeting had begun, Nathan had gone from room to room, closing all the curtains in the house. Then he had decided that that made things look far too suspicious and had gone around opening them again.

Edwin blows a line of smoke up towards the beamed ceiling. "What makes you say that?"

"Just a suspicion." Nathan takes a long draw on the pipe, willing it to take away a little of his unease. "If the Jacobites on the island know Holland is a spy, there's nothing to say they don't know what the house is being used for. And there is no saying what they would do to our family."

"If the Jacobites on the island knew Holland was a spy, he'd be dead," Edwin says matter-of-factly. "He'd probably be taken out to sea and thrown overboard. They'd make it look like a fishing accident."

Nathan winces at Edwin's bluntness. He is not sure he agrees. Surely the fact that Holland is alive does not necessarily mean the Jacobites are ignorant to what he is doing. Deceit might come easy to people like Julia Mitchell, but he suspects that murder does not.

Edwin leans back in his chair. "You ought to have discussed it with me before you agreed to let the spies use the house in the first place."

Nathan brings his pipe to his lips. This is far from the first time Edwin has raised the issue. He does not regret his decision. Letting the spies use the house had saved Eva from suspicion at best—and death by hanging at worst. It had been a decision he had not had to think on.

The thud of the door knocker echoes through the house, making him jump. He leaps to his feet, racing towards the door before Mrs Brodie can get there. He had not expected anyone else for Holland's meeting—but he had also been deliberate in not asking too many questions.

Julia stands on the doorstep, clutching her son's hand. Nathan's heart begins to thunder.

"What are you doing here?" he blurts.

Julia looks surprised at his outburst. She falters. "I was worried about Harriet. I thought to see how she was faring." She glances down at her son. "And if you don't mind, Bobby was eager to see Theodora."

Bobby digs a large cockle shell out of his pocket. "I found this near the anchorage this morning," he says with a gap-toothed smile. "I want to show her."

Nathan realises he is standing with his arms stretched out across the doorframe, as though to prevent them from entering the house. And in the somewhat desperate hope of preventing Joseph Holland from hearing Julia's voice.

"I'm sorry," he says hurriedly. "Harriet and Theodora are sleeping." The lie feels clumsy. Transparent. "I shall be sure to tell them you came by."

Before Julia can manage a word, the door is locked. Nathan leans his back against it, closing his eyes to gather himself. He can hear the dull murmur of voices coming unbroken from the parlour. Nothing to suggest the men inside had caught on to Julia's appearance.

He goes back to the dining room and collects his pipe from the ash tray.

"Who was that?" Edwin asks, voice low.

"Julia Mitchell. Here to see Harriet. I told her now was not a good time."

"Interesting." Edwin blows out a thin line of smoke.

"What is that supposed to mean?"

He leans back in his chair. "I think you know what that means, Nate. Don't you think it rather a coincidence that Miss Mitchell happened to arrive right when Holland and his cohort are meeting?"

"With her son," Nathan hisses, inexplicably defensive. "I hardly think she would drag her child along if she were…" *A spy.* He can't bring himself to finish the sentence, in case it solidifies his own doubts about Julia, and her ill-timed appearance. What would she even be hoping to achieve by doing such a thing? She could hardly stand with her ear to the parlour door and listen.

Then again, one step inside the house would tell her something secretive was taking place here. And perhaps that is all she wished to know.

Nathan shakes the thought away.

"Be careful around her, Nate," says Edwin. "We know her brothers are active Jacobites. It's no stretch to think that she might be as well. If she were to find out what is happening at the house, she might—"

"She'll not find out what's happening at the house," Nathan says brusquely. He rubs the back of his neck, keen to change the subject. "Where is Harriet? I hope she did not hear me sending Julia away."

"In her workroom," Edwin tells him. "She's been in there since before

Eva left. It seems she's working on something new."

"I trust she has no thought of what is happening in the parlour?"

"Of course not," says Edwin. "And even if she did, I doubt she would have much of an opinion on the matter."

Harriet is not in her workroom. When Nathan returns to his study, he finds her lounged in the high-backed chair behind his desk. Her long blonde hair cascades freely over her shoulders, and she has a dark smudge across one cheek.

"May I use your telescope?" she asks.

Nathan blinks. "The telescope?" He did not even know Harriet was aware of the thing's existence.

"It's for my new painting," she explains. "Thea's story inspired me." She slides forward in the chair. "I want to paint the moon in detail, like Maria Eimmart did."

Nathan smiles faintly. It has been a long time since he has heard his sister speak with such aliveness in her voice. "Of course." He reaches beneath the desk for the box containing the telescope and sets it up at the window. "It's cloudy tonight," he says. "But clear enough to see the moon, I think." He peers through the eyepiece, angling the telescope until it catches the thin white crescent. "Ah. Yes. Quickly." He steps away and nods to Harriet to catch a glimpse of her subject before it disappears behind the clouds. "Do you see it?"

"Yes." A smile appears on her lips. She looks up and snatches her notebook and pencil from the desk. She begins to draw quickly, looking alternatively between the telescope lens and the book. Nathan watches in fascination as the familiar contours of the moon appear on the page. "It's waning tonight," he tells her. "So there is not a great deal to see. But hopefully enough to get you started. Will it show you what you need?"

"Yes. Certainly. In any case, I don't wish my piece to be a scientific representation, but an artistic one. There's no need to capture every specific detail. I just hoped looking at the real thing might give me some more inspiration."

"And has it?"

"Very much."

Nathan smiles crookedly. It is only when Harriet speaks of her art that he feels he gets a glimpse of who she truly is. The only time the façade she hides behind comes down. He is also somewhat relieved that she does not appear to have heard Julia coming to the house. Or at least, if she has, she has not bothered to raise the issue. "I shall leave you to your work," he says, taking paper and an ink pot from the drawer. "Take as much time as you need."

Harriet nods her thanks. Before he reaches the door, she says, "Nathan?"

He turns to look back at her.

Harriet leans back in the desk chair, her fingers tightening around her pencil. "I've been invited to Paris," she says. "To show my work. A nobleman and his wife are interested in sponsoring me."

Nathan's face breaks into a smile. "Harriet, that's wonderful. I'm so pleased for you." He is not surprised. As little as he knows about art, he can tell his sister is immensely talented.

She does not return his smile. "Edwin does not wish me to go," she says. "He tried to have Eva talk me out of it today. He believes my place is by his side. As Thomas's mother."

Nathan hesitates. "Well. That is hardly an unreasonable position."

Harriet gives him pleading eyes. "Will you speak with him? Try to change his mind? Please?"

Nathan sighs. He can practically see the weight that has descended on Harriet's shoulders. The passion and lightness she had spoken with moments earlier has all but disappeared. But, "He is your husband, Harriet. The decision is his. It is not my place to interfere."

Harriet opens her mouth to speak, then decides against it. She nods shortly and slides around on the chair. Put her eye back against the glass and retreats into silence.

She stays in Nathan's study until the spies have finished their meeting. No eavesdropping tonight; she cannot risk Edwin catching her and sending her up to the bedroom like a child. Besides, the pieces of knowledge she has gathered have already come in use. She has Michael Mitchell's attention, and soon she will have his money too.

If she wants to see Paris, making the journey to Lesbury Common is her only option. Edwin and Nathan have both made that clear.

She waits until they are both in bed. Puts her notebook of lunar images on the table in her workroom. And she slips out the front door.

Overhead is the dinted shard of the moon she had been peering at so closely, now nothing more than a glow behind the clouds. It's a ghostly, faraway kind of light; one that makes her think of otherworlds, and a magic she no longer believes in. It guides her way into the village.

The town is still. The sea is rhythmic against the shoreline, and in the eerie stillness its sigh seems to echo and bounce between stone walls. The stench of drying seaweed hangs on the air.

Harriet hurries through the streets with her head lowered and her lamp held out in front of her. She knocks on the door of the house at the corner of Marygate.

Anne answers without speaking. She gives a nod that is so conspiratorial that Harriet would have laughed had she not been about to leap into something so reckless.

"You can get word to Michael?" she asks, voice low.

"Aye." Anne's eyes glow within the shadows hanging over the doorstep. There's a seriousness about her, and a heaviness Harriet recognises in herself. For not the first time, she is pricked by curiosity. What drew Anne into helping Michael Mitchell? Harriet has never seen any particular affection between them; around Michael, Anne seems just as grave and unyielding as ever. Or perhaps this is just a cover she presents to hide her true nature from outside eyes. Harriet knows all too well about that. Likely though, and this brings her no small amount of satisfaction, Anne's actions have little to do with a man—or rather, little to do with any man but James the Old Pretender. As Michael had told her, there are more than a few women who are willing to risk their own safety to advance the Jacobite cause.

Her mind leaps to Julia. She can never find out that Harriet is to help Michael re-join the rebels. Once the army mustering at Lesbury engages, there is every chance Michael will die in battle. Surely, in Julia's eyes, for Harriet to help him do so would be a far greater betrayal than her hiding her brothers in the attic of Highfield House.

But right now, she has no room for Julia's concerns, or what will happen to Michael once the Jacobite army begins to march. Right now, all she has room for are those coins in his pouch—money that will be hers once she completes this task. It will lead her towards the life she craves with every inch of her being.

"Tell him I will do it," she says. "For the sum agreed."

"Your timing is good," Anne says brusquely. "He plans to leave tomorrow evening. Told me he can't wait any longer for you to make up your mind."

Harriet nods. As she turns to leave, Anne says:

"You are one of the Blakes, aren't you?"

Harriet smiles wryly. No, she wants to say. She is not. She never was. But that is a conversation she is not willing to go into with this near stranger. Instead, she nods.

"Interesting," says Anne. "That you're doing this."

"My family are not spies," Harriet says. "If that is what you're suggesting."

"I did not say they were. But I imagine it unlikely that a family from London might have Jacobite leanings. So I can only imagine you are doing this for other reasons." She tilts her head, as though trying to see behind Harriet's eyes. "Is it as Michael says? That you have no loyalty to your family?"

Harriet bristles at the accusation, though she knows there is more than a small grain of truth to it. She does not wish to see her family in danger, of course, but perhaps there is a part of her that wishes to defy them. Defy Edwin for his refusal to support her trip to Paris, and Nathan for refusing to speak to her husband on her behalf. Defy Eva for flitting off to Longstone and abandoning her.

"My reasons are none of your business," she says tightly.

Anne opens her mouth, as though debating whether to press the issue. After a moment, she nods. "Be here tomorrow evening," she says. "Just after sunset."

CHAPTER NINETEEN

The sunsets are coming earlier now, as the year draws closer to winter. The sun careens towards the horizon, bathing the island in the cobalt blue of evening. Harriet has told Edwin she will not be at dinner tonight, but that she will take her meal alone in her workroom. He had not argued, just as she expected. He has been reluctant to raise his voice with her since this news of her father. At least, she supposes, it has been good for something.

Her new piece is coming alive. The first layers of paint are on the canvas, colours carefully blended to depict the unending depth of the night sky. She is not sure if the thought of the journey to Lesbury is fuelling her inspiration, or if her inspiration is fuelling her desire to complete the journey. Her desire to see Michael's coins in her hand, and her paintings hung on the Baillieus' walls.

She knows she will not make it all the way to Lesbury and back without her family noting her disappearance. But she hopes she will be far enough from Lindisfarne by the time they notice her missing that they will have no way of finding her. No doubt when she returns, Edwin will have rediscovered his will to raise his voice with her, but the money Michael is paying her will soften the blow of that. It is hard to care how Edwin will retaliate when she has the means to bring her dreams to life.

She has stowed her travelling cloak and bonnet behind the chair in her workroom, along with the lamp she will need to light her way into the village. Has forced down a few mouthfuls of the soup Mrs Brodie had brought her. But after she has wiped her pallet and set the brushes aside to dry, she does not go to the window to make her escape. Instead, almost without conscious thought, she finds her way to the nursery. And she sits with Thomas in her arms, drawn here, to him, by the pull of guilt she had hoped would not show itself. His eyes, round and blue, are piercing hers, and she is finding it impossible to look away. What is he seeing, she wonders? Does he recognise his mother, or does he see a stranger? She cannot deny he sometimes feels that way to her. An unknown entity she had never longed for, the way she knows she is supposed to. She knows well there is something wrong with her; this woman who never craved a child, or the touch of her husband's body.

She traces a finger along Thomas's smooth cheek; a gesture she has done so many times in the past, in an attempt to know her son—to recognise a little of herself in him. Perhaps it's best that she finds none—after all, why would she ever wish any of her brittle self-loathing on her child?

She pulls her eyes from his and settles him into the crib, then makes her way down into her workroom before she changes her mind.

She ties her bonnet and takes the lamp from the shelf. She keeps a candle burning on the mantel in her workroom so it might cast a little light beneath the closed door and buy her time before anyone notices her missing. She wrestles open the window. The creaking front entrance of the house is an impossibility, of course, as is creeping to the back door while Mrs Brodie is at work in the kitchen. Sea-scented air gusts inside and flutters the flame of the candle. Harriet leans out the window and lowers the lamp to the earth, then lifts her skirts to her knees and clambers over the sill. She slides, somewhat ungracefully, the short distance to the ground.

Though the sun has just disappeared, there is already an inkiness to the dusk, a silver-dark light that feels almost otherworldly. The first stars are dusted across a clear sky, beside the thin crescent moon. The roe deer are active as she makes her way through the dunes, skitting between the shadows and rustling the grass. Each soft thud of their hooves makes her heart thump a little louder. She follows the rusty glow of her lantern into the village. She feels an odd sense of detachment. A sense of being utterly outside herself. Completely removed from the life she knows. And that, she thinks, is a blissful thing. She has had quite enough of being inside her own head.

"Good evening, Mrs Whitley." Harriet whirls around. It's the pastor, of all people, his voice distrusting—or at least made that way by her own racing heart. He looks past her into the empty street, then back to meet her eyes. "What are you doing out alone at night?"

"Visiting a friend," she says, sharper than she intended. Will he go to Highfield House and tell Edwin he has seen her? Unlikely, she supposes; he has no lamp, and will not set off on the trek to Emmanuel Head without one. In any case, by the time he makes the journey up to the house, she and Michael will be on their way.

The pastor—young, but with dark, scrutinising eyes beyond his years—looks her up and down, but doesn't prod. "Mind yourself," he says finally. "And have a safe journey home."

Harriet cannot get to Anne's door quick enough. She and Michael are already in the lane beside her house. Michael is tethering a horse to a small covered wagon, while Anne stows a basket of food beneath the bench seats. Michael is dressed in a dark greatcoat and breeches; Anne in simple grey skirts befitting a maid, her dark hair tucked up beneath a white mobcap. They turn in unison towards the glow of Harriet's lantern. A satisfied smile appears on Michael's face. Anne gives her a brusque, wordless nod.

"I want the money now," Harriet murmurs. She feels on edge after her run-in with the priest. Having the coins in her pocket will go some way to steadying her, reminding her of why she is doing this.

Michael raises his eyebrows, the corner of his lips turning up into a half-smile. "I didn't realise you were so distrusting."

"You were hiding in our roof. I think it fair to say you're a man who cannot be trusted."

"Very well." He digs into his pocket and produces a pouch of coins. Hands it to Harriet. "Keep it hidden while we travel. In case we run into trouble."

Her mouth feels suddenly dry. "Is that what you expect to happen? We will run into trouble?"

"I hope not," says Michael, too lightly. "That's why I have you." He finishes securing the harness and pats the horse on its broad neck. He offers Harriet a hand to climb into the wagon, Anne scrambling up behind her without waiting for assistance. Michael swings himself into the box seat and takes up the reins. And the carriage begins to move out of the village before Harriet has a chance to regret her decision.

CHAPTER TWENTY

Nathan is infuriated with himself over how much he loves the telescope. Of course he loves it. It's just like the one he had begged his father for back when he was a boy.

"You keep this away from Oliver, now," his father had said to him, the day he had handed Nathan the box. Had even let him hide it in the study until it was time to set it up at the window. Exploring the sky with his father—and without his coldblooded brother—are some of Nathan's most cherished childhood memories.

So yes, he wants to use the telescope. And yes, he wants to share it with his own child; give her similarly precious memories; show her places that hide beyond human comprehension. The fact that the telescope came from Julia is a fact he will just have to do his best to ignore.

After dinner, he and Theodora head out into the night. Thea is bundled into her cloak and woollen bonnet, and she holds the telescope close to her chest, carrying it like the most precious of bundles. Nathan walks with the stand in one hand and a lamp in the other.

It's a still night; clear and cold. The sea is sighing loud against the shoreline; seems to fill all the empty spaces. Overhead, the stars are a blaze. Nathan cannot wait to lift the telescope to them and pull more pinpoints of light from the darkness. This morning, in a burst of childlike excitement, he had written to the circulating library at Cambridge and ordered copies of the Kepler star maps he remembers poring over with his father. He cannot wait to show them to Theodora; to teach her to track those glittering trails of light across the night sky.

Once they are far enough from the house that the lamps behind the windows will not dim the brilliance of the sky, Nathan blows out the lantern and lets the oceanic wash of the stars intensify. In the darkness, Theodora takes a step closer to him, stopping, instinctively, an inch from making contact. Nathan takes the telescope from her hand and settles it into the stand. He peers into it, adjusting the eyepiece to track past the pointer stars and find the blaze of Polaris.

He steps aside, and Theodora hurries to the telescope. "Do you see the bright star in the middle?" She nods. "That's the North Star. It's how ships find their way across the sea."

She looks over at her shoulder at him, slightly doubtful. "How?"

"Well… It does not move across the sky like the other stars do. And it always points to the north, you see."

"What about these stars? And these ones?"

Nathan answers her questions and guides the telescope through the darkness, pointing out the dragons and bears and winged horses the constellations paint across the sky. And then he lowers the telescope for a moment, catching the glitter of a light on the sea. Henry Ward's ship, he thinks dully. He hates that that ship, that man, is always at the forefront his mind. But how can it be any other way?

He tilts the telescope until it catches the tinderbox blaze of the Longstone light. The life Eva has made out there is something of a mystery to him, and the darkness on every side of the beacon goes little way to answering his questions.

It is past nine when they return to Highfield House. Thomas is wailing steadily from upstairs, and Nathan feels his serenity dissipate. He unties the cloak from his daughter's shoulders, the telescope and stand tucked under one arm. "Up to bed, Thea. It's getting late."

"A story?" she begs.

"A short one. I shall be up in a moment."

She gambols upstairs just as Edwin strides out from the parlour. "She's gone again, Nathan," he says, scrubbing a hand over his eyes. "The window was open in her workroom. I think she used it to leave the house." He rakes a hand through his dark hair, which hangs uncharacteristically loose on his shoulders. "I've waited here long enough, hoping she'll show herself. I need to go out and find her."

The last of Nathan's calmness evaporates. He tries to keep his own anxiety under control. The memory of Eva's disappearance is far too fresh in his mind. It had been barely two months ago that she had been forced into Donald Macauley's boat and had spent the night on Longstone.

But this, Nathan feels certain, is not the same thing. He has little doubt that Harriet's disappearance is her own doing. An act of rebellion. Anger, perhaps, that she has not been permitted her trip to Paris. Perhaps he ought to have made more of an effort to convince Edwin on her behalf.

The fact that she has left of her own accord does not ease the worry in his chest. Especially with Henry Ward's ship glowing in the bay.

"I'll come with you," he tells Edwin. He sets the telescope down carefully in the corner of the parlour, regretting that Theodora will have to go without her tales of magic and moonlight tonight.

The blackness feels thick as they head into the village. As he had made his way across the dunes with Thea and the telescope, the starlit night had felt like a thrill. Full of magic. Now, the dark feels vaguely threatening. A reminder of how much his family has stacked against them.

As much as he does not want to admit it, he knows the first place they need to go is Julia's shop.

"I'll ask at the tavern in case anyone passed her in the street," says Edwin. "You check if she's with Miss Mitchell." Nathan nods, fighting off a pull of unease. Julia will likely have questions for him, after the way he had thrown her and Bobby off his doorstep yesterday. Questions he has no thought of how to answer. The thought has his heart racing, but it is with something that is not entirely dread.

He peers through the front window into the shop. It is dark, lit only by the glowing remains of the fire. He can see the bulbous shadow of the cat curled up on the tiles by the hearth. Can see a stack of books, and what appears to be clothing, piled up upon the counter. Two chairs are crammed between the shelves beside what looks, inexplicably, to be part of an old wrought iron bed head.

Nathan goes into the alley beside the building and knocks on the side door. Silence at first, then he hears the stairs creak. Julia pulls open the door. Her lips part at the sight of him.

"Mr Blake."

"Is Harriet here?" he asks.

"No." She tugs her shawl around her shoulders. "I've not seen her in days." Concern creases her brow. "She's missing?"

Nathan nods. "Perhaps it's too soon to worry. But… well, as you know, she has not been quite herself of late."

"Is there someone else on the island she might be visiting?" Julia asks.

He sighs. "As far as I know, you're the only person she spends her time with."

"Perhaps she's with her sister. She could have paid one of the fishermen to take her out there."

Regretfully, Nathan is well aware of this possibility. He is also well aware that he ought to have sent Edwin to the curiosity shop. Because at the thought of making a journey out to Longstone, that thumping in his chest veers a little closer to dread.

"I'm sure it's too dark to sail out there tonight," he says, a little more hopefully than he knows he ought to.

Julia strides back into the shop, making Nathan follow almost instinctively. She takes her bonnet and cloak from the counter. "I'd like to know if she is out there or not. If she is, at least we can stop worrying." She tosses her cloak over her shoulders and heads for the staircase. "I'll have to go by my friend Alice's house. Leave Bobby there. I don't fancy taking him with me at such an hour. It's not the safest of journeys in the dark."

Nathan's throat is suddenly dry.

Julia looks back over her shoulder at him. "Are you coming?"

And what can he do but say, "Of course"?

CHAPTER TWENTY-ONE

He tries to tell himself this flimsy fishing boat is seaworthy. That there is nothing beneath the water for them to strike. That this rolling, ink-dark sea does not have the power to swallow him.

But Nathan does not believe a single word he tells himself. Outside the Lindisfarne anchorage, the sea melts into the sky and his body cannot settle into the up-and-down rhythm of the boat on the swell. He can see the faint rose of light from the mainland, and out ahead, the shipping beacon on Longstone.

He pulls in a breath, fingers wrapped tightly around the edge of his seat. Despite the cold night, his shirt is damp with sweat beneath his greatcoat. How far to Longstone? Five miles? Ten? Twenty? With the dark distorting his surroundings, it seems impossible to tell.

"Are you all right?" Julia asks from behind him.

Nathan looks over his shoulder at her. Tries for a smile he knows looks more like a grimace. "I'm not fond of the sea."

"You are living in the wrong place then, aren't you."

"I'm becoming more and more certain of that each day."

Her eyes soften in the lamplight. "It's not far. A mile more perhaps."

He nods stiffly.

"Keep your eyes on the firebasket," she says. "It may help the seasickness."

He glues his gaze to the blaze out ahead of them. And it goes someway to calming the clamouring in his belly. Unbidden, he feels a pull of gratitude towards Julia.

She has not spoken a word about his refusing her entry into the house yesterday. Perhaps she has just let the matter slide out of concern for Harriet. Or perhaps she too is afraid of what questions may arise if she goes near the issue. Nathan pushes the thoughts away. He has far too much on his mind right now to even entertain the idea of Julia spying for the Jacobites. Besides, she has done him a great favour by sailing out here to help his family. He owes her more than suspicion.

He watches her lean on the tiller. "Are you certain you know what you're doing?"

"Do you wish to take over?" she asks pointedly.

He swallows. "No. I'm sorry. I just… Have you sailed out here in the dark before?"

"Yes. Well, close to dark. Not like this," she admits. "But I can manage it. The Knavestone reef is to the north-east of Longstone. We'll come in from the south."

"The reef?" he repeats sickly.

A faint smile appears on her lips. "We shall give it a wide berth, I promise. And we can thank your sister and her husband for guiding our way."

Nathan says nothing. If it weren't for his sister and her husband, he wouldn't be needing to make this infernal journey in the first place. "When did you learn to sail?" he asks.

Julia tucks a coil of red hair beneath her cap. "When I was a child. My older brother Hugh taught me. Of course, I thought I knew everything back then. Told him I did not need instruction." She smiles to herself. "Hugh threw me into the boat and told me to sail it without him. That sorted me out nice and quick."

Nathan gives her a faint smile that disappears quickly. "You must miss him terribly."

Julia looks up at the taut sail, as though to hide the sudden emotion in her eyes. For several moments, she doesn't speak. Perhaps debating whether to discuss her missing brother with him—or whether he will use it as another opportunity to condemn her family. "It's the uncertainly that is the worst thing," she says finally. "Not knowing if he is alive or dead. Not knowing if I will ever see him again." She lowers her eyes. "When I found myself with child, my father threw me out of his house. Hugh and his wife took me in. Kept a roof over me and Bobby's heads til I could stand on my own. I owe him a lot." She sighs. "He became obsessed with the Jacobite cause after his wife and son died. A way of giving meaning to his life, I suppose. After all he lost." Her jaw tightens. "In any case, I'm sure you have little interest in Hugh's whereabouts. My brothers have caused enough trouble for your family."

Nathan looks her in the eye. "That does not mean I wish them any ill will."

Julia doesn't answer. She turns away suddenly, as though unable to hold his gaze.

After a long silence, she brings the boat up to a small jetty protruding from the island. Firelight spills over the rocks, turning the surfaces of the pools bright gold. A lamp glows through the window of the small stone cottage, but beyond the reach of the firebasket, the rest of the island seeps into darkness.

Nathan did not know what he was expecting his sister's new life to look like. He only knows it was not this. He is simultaneously appalled and awed at its remoteness; its eerie, shadowed beauty. At the responsibility Eva and Finn have made their own.

He feels an uncomfortable pull in his stomach—a tug of protectiveness towards his younger sister. He is not sure if it's a fear of Eva being out here, so vulnerable to the ocean in this tiny, towering house, or worry that she might have latched herself to this life—and the man that comes with it—thoughtlessly, too quickly, too blinded by love to turn an eye to the future.

But when Eva emerges from the cottage, expertly navigating the pools and rocky crevices, there's a look about her that says she belongs here, has always belonged here. And perhaps a part of her has always known that, even as a young child when she had slept in a bedroom with the Longstone light straining through the window.

"Nathan?" she says. "What are you doing here?"

He climbs shakily from the boat, gripping tightly to the posts of the jetty. The feel of solid rock beneath his feet is somewhat steadying, though the island feels as though it could succumb to the sea at any minute. "Good Lord, Eva," he says, "this is—" She raises her eyebrows, and it has the effect of silencing him. He swallows. "Is Harriet here?"

"Harriet? No, of course not."

Nathan feels something sink inside him. Eva glances at Finn, who has followed her out of the cottage.

"Come inside," he says. "Warm yourselves."

Nathan teeters across the dark rocks and follows Eva and Finn up the steps to their cottage, Julia close behind. Finn shoves open the door and it squeals against the floorboards. Warm air billows out into the night. Nathan is grateful for the fire blazing in the grate. Even more grateful for the bottle of whisky he spies on the sideboard. One of Julia's brothers is sitting at the table, surrounded by three empty soup bowls. He stands as they enter.

"What in hell are you doing sailing here so late at night, Jul?" he demands. "It's far too dangerous a crossing."

"Calm yourself, Angus," she says, holding her hands up to the fire to warm them. "We're here in one piece." She rubs her palms together. "Where's Michael?"

"Thought to ask you that," Finn shoots. He leans up against the door and folds his arms across his chest. "If your brother wants to use this place to hide then I suggest he damn well stays hidden."

Julia straightens suddenly. "Michael has left again?"

"Aye," says Angus. "He says he's off to another…" He eyes Nathan warily. "Well."

"Another meeting?" Julia finishes tautly. "You can trust him, Angus. If you couldn't, do you really think your neck would still be unbroken?"

She looks sideways at Nathan, and for a moment, he tries to see behind her eyes. Does she truly trust him, she wonders? Or is this all part of some game she is playing?

Eva follows Nathan's longing glance to the whisky bottle. She goes to the sideboard and clatters through it for the cups. Fear for her sister is coiled tightly at the base of her stomach. She knows Harriet has been on edge lately. Knows she is likely to behave rashly. And she also knows the villagers do not trust her family. Whether this disappearance is Harriet's own doing or not, Eva fears she is in danger.

She fills four cups—all they have in the house—and hands the cannikins around. Nathan nods his thanks. Drinks hurriedly.

"When did you last see Harriet?" Eva asks him.

"Sometime before dinner tonight," he tells her. "She said she was going to work on her painting. No one heard her leave. She must have gone out through the window."

Eva takes a sip from the fourth cup, then hands it to Finn. "I'll come back to Lindisfarne with you," she tells Nathan. "I'll help you look for her. I cannot just stay here and wait for news."

Finn empties the cup in one gulp and sets it on the table. "Wait for the slack tide," he tells Julia. "A quarter of an hour. It will make your journey back a little safer."

She nods. Crouches back beside the fire to warm her hands.

Eva goes to the bedroom to gather her things. She is not sure what is rattling her more: anxiety over Harriet's disappearance, or the prospect of the treacherous journey back to Holy Island in the dark. Finn follows her into the bedroom. Closes the door behind him. "I'm coming too. I'll take you over."

She pauses, her duffel bag in one hand and her spare shift in the other. "No," she says. "Not to the house. I couldn't ask that of you."

"You're not asking it. I'm suggesting it. I want to help you find your sister."

She hesitates. "I do not know how long I'll be there. It could be days."

"It's no matter. Angus can keep the light. And Michael, if he ever bothers to show himself."

"What about…"

He steps closer and cups her elbow in his broad palm. Eva smells woodsmoke and ocean on his skin. "Do you not want me there?"

She lets out her breath. "Of course I do. But…" She does not want memories of Oliver's death to return to the front of his mind. And perhaps there is also a fear of what her family might see if Finn was to step back into Highfield House. Perhaps this secret they are carrying might become a little harder to keep.

He presses his rough palms to her cheeks. "I'm coming with you, Evie." He lets his hands fall and reaches for his greatcoat slung over the foot of the bed. Eva tries to catch his eye, but he is looking away, wearing a closed-off expression. And perhaps closed off is exactly what he needs to be to set foot in Highfield House again. She feels a swell of love for him, coupled with a pull of unease. "Finish packing your things," he says stiffly. "We need to catch the tide."

With the slack tide, the water is black ink, rippled orange by the firebasket. Finn glances over his shoulder at Julia's fishing boat edging away from his jetty. Once she is clear of the island, he tugs on the sheet to open the mainsail, catching the breeze. He navigates slowly around the rim of the Farnes, letting Julia follow close behind. To his right, he sees white water glowing as it breaks on the Knavestone rocks. For all the years he has lived on Longstone, he can count on one hand the number of times he has made this journey in the dark.

Eva's eyes are wide in the glow of the lamp she is clutching. "You don't think she's with Ward, do you? What if she found out about him somehow?"

Finn fears such an outcome as much as Eva does. He can't bear the thought of her family finding out the truth about the night Oliver died. If that happened, he'd have little choice but to accept Ward's offer to join his crew and disappear from their lives. It's a prospect he can't bear to follow far.

He glances over his shoulder at the firebasket. It's a strange feeling to see it from the sea like this. Unmooring, like he is heading to places he was not meant for.

Places like Highfield House.

The house is visible from far out on the water, lamps in windows glowing like moons. He has seen this house from the sea on countless occasions. How many times had he stood on the deck of the *Eagle* while Ward was inside the manor, spending his nights with Abigail Blake? It had looked just as it does now.

Though they are memories he rarely revisits voluntarily, he finds himself combing through his recollections of Ward's visits to Abigail. Whenever they had returned to England after privateering in the German Ocean, she had offered the *Eagle's* officers comfortable quarters for the night. Had the visits taken place across months or years? Had Ward and Abigail known each other before her husband had died? How long had they shared each other's bed? Finn has no thought of it. He himself had only set foot in the house on one occasion—the night that has stayed with him ever since.

It's a fresh kind of stupidity, perhaps, to be willingly stepping back into the place. But as he watches the hazy shape of Highfield House sharpen, Finn knows he has no choice. Eva must be here, therefore so must he. Not for a second had he questioned that.

That doesn't change the hollow, falling sensation in his stomach as he eases the skiff towards the beach.

Eva glances sideways at him, her fingers clenched tightly around the handle of the lantern. "You can change your mind, Finn. I'll not—"

"I'm not going to change my mind." The words come out sharper than he intended, and Eva falls silent. He flashes her an apologetic look and covers her hand with his, but doesn't trust himself to speak.

The past cannot hurt him, of course. Oliver Blake's ghost is not going to rise from the woodwork and end him. But the truth that he is hiding; that can hurt him. Worse, it can hurt Eva. And it has the power to tear them apart.

CHAPTER TWENTY-TWO

Harriet is not sure she has ever seen darkness quite as thick as this. There is barely a thread of a moon, and the stars have disappeared behind a solid bank of cloud. Cold wind gusts through the open front of the wagon, fragrant with the smell of damp earth. All that lights the road is the flimsy lamp in front of the box seat. Still, the horse trots onwards, the rhythmic rattle of hooves lulling Harriet into something trancelike and quiet. And perhaps this is the best state to be in; a state which does not allow her to think too closely about all she is doing. About her family, who will no doubt be looking for her by now. About the son she has left behind. About what might lie in that impenetrable darkness.

There's an uncomfortable tightness in her chest. A shallowness to her breath. Fear, she realises. She tries to swallow it down. Fear is one of those gruelling emotions she does her best not to feel. And more often than not, she succeeds. Is able to detach herself from her reality enough to let the fear pass her by. But it is here now, simmering at the back of her mind like a contagion.

From the dark innards of the wagon, Harriet can just see through to the box seat. She can see Michael in profile, his features underscored by lamplight. His square jaw is set firm, eyes fixed ahead in intense focus. What is he thinking? Is he imagining the moment he will re-join the Jacobite rebels; or that moment when he has sword and pistol in hand,

and it is a toss of a coin whether he will live to see the next sunrise? Or is he merely focused on the next moment ahead; the next yard of dark road; the next tug of the reins? Is he, too, afraid? Or is his passion for his cause too consuming for that?

Harriet had assumed her own passion for her cause was too. But the fear is here, thick and cloying, turning her stomach and making her fingers clench hard in her lap. Now identified, it will not lie down.

She slips a hand beneath her cloak, feeling the bulge of the coin pouch inside her stays. Coins that will make all this—and whatever fury she returns home to—worth it.

She can feel Anne's eyes on her. Dark brows, full of expression. "So what is it then?" she asks. Her voice cutting through the silence make Harriet jump. They have barely exchanged a word since they left Holy Island several hours ago. "Why are you here?"

"Pardon?" Harriet heard her perfectly; just needs a moment to craft an answer. Decide how much to share.

"Your reason for being here," says Anne, toying with the hem of her apron. "What is it?"

Harriet peeks through the front of the wagon at the barely lit road ahead. "He is paying me well," she says simply. "And I have a great need for the money."

Anne gives a short laugh. It's a judgmental sound that adds to the faint nausea in Harriet's stomach. "What need does a lady like you have for money? Your family is the wealthiest on the island."

Harriet would laugh if it weren't for the sense of dread she feels creeping up on her. If the villagers were to see the broken window panes of Highfield House, or the holes in Nathan's boots, she feels certain they would change their assessment of the situation. But she says, "That money belongs to my brother. My husband. It is not for my own purposes."

"Your own purposes. And what might those be?" Anne sounds disparaging, and Harriet desperately wishes for their old silence.

"It's of no matter," she says.

She hears another laugh come from the darkness. She can just imagine what Anne is thinking: that this polished young lady from the house on the head needs the money for silk gowns and fancy scents, and jewels to hang from her throat. When she compares her plans for Paris with the way Michael is about to risk his life, they feel barely less trivial than a new wardrobe.

She finds herself thinking of Isabelle. What will she think when Harriet tells her of this journey she has undertaken to make Paris a reality? Pride, perhaps? Admiration? Or will she scold her for leaving her son behind; leaving her husband and siblings to worry? Isabelle is far more caring than she is, Harriet knows. Far less selfish. It is part of what had drawn her to her in the first place—that glimpse of something she knows is all too lacking in herself.

Inexplicably, she feels tears prick her eyes. She blinks them away quickly.

"What of you?" she asks Anne. It feels like the silence is over, at least for now, and if they are to speak, Harriet would rather steer the conversation away from herself.

Anne lowers her voice. "I wish to play my part. And they'll not accept a woman in their army. We're consigned to running messages. Raising the next generation of men who will fight for the Stuarts."

"Would you fight for them? If you could?"

"Of course I would," Anne says, with a touch too much conviction. Enough to let Harriet see the hint of doubt beneath. Anne is quiet for a few moments, as though she too has caught a glimpse of her own uncertainty. "I think of it sometimes," she says. "Pulling on a pair of breeches and tucking my hair up under a cap. Wouldn't be the first woman to do so. But I couldn't do that to my husband. He needs me."

Anne is aware her reasons sound like an excuse, Harriet can tell from her tone of voice. And it brings her a hint of satisfaction. Still, Anne obviously has more than a hint of passion for the Jacobite cause. She wouldn't be here if she didn't. What would it feel like, Harriet wonders, to fight for something so selfless? If she is ever to place her survival upon the toss of a coin, it will be for her own purposes, not that of some distant would-be king.

"What does your husband think of you doing all this with Michael?" she asks.

Anne snorts. "I'd tell you if I thought he had any knowledge of it. Poor fool can't hold his liquor. Just have to feed him a glass or two and he'll sleep through til morning. He'll have no inkling I'm even gone."

Harriet squeezes her hands together even tighter, forcing down a swell of panic. She will have no such luxury; of that she is certain.

"And you?" asks Anne.

"My husband will know I am gone," she says. "And I shall pay for it when I return. But this is something I have to do."

Finn draws his sloop up beside Julia's fishing boat, allowing Nathan to stumble from one vessel into the other. He curses as he lands heavily in the skiff beside his sister.

"All right, Nathan?" Eva asks, the faintest hint of a smile on her lips.

"Fine." He looks over his shoulder at Julia and gives her a brisk nod. "Thank you," he says stiffly. "For taking me out there."

An unreadable look passes over Julia's lamplit face. Then she nods and tugs on the mainsail sheet. "I shall let you know if I hear anything."

Eva looks questioningly at her brother as Finn rows the skiff towards the shore. "That was rude. You might have asked her to the house."

Nathan watches Julia's boat round the point and head back towards the village. "She has Jacobite sympathies," he says. "It's too dangerous her being at the house when Holland and the other messengers could turn up at any time. Besides, when did you become her biggest supporter?"

"I just think—" Eva jolts forward as the boat crunches hard against the pebbles on the sea floor. She grabs at the gunwale to keep from falling. "What are you doing, Finn? Are you all right?"

"Sorry." He is distracted. On edge. He can feel it behind him; Highfield House. Can see it in his mind's eye: cobbled brick and stone walls, crooked chimneys, the weather-worn red tiles of the roof. Perpetual darkness behind the rows of gabled windows.

He feels the boat tilt as Nathan steps out into the shallow water. Still, he doesn't turn.

"All right?" Eva asks again, voice low.

Finn nods. Stands and leaps out of the boat in one swift movement, to prevent himself from changing his mind. He holds out his hand for Eva. She takes it, then watches him closely as he drags the skiff up onto the beach. She hangs back, letting Nathan go on to the house ahead of them.

In the moonless night, the house is a beast, candles glowing in windows and the front door thrown open, letting a blaze of light out onto the dunes. Finn forces himself to walk. To breathe evenly. To step through the front door.

Here is the foyer, hung with paintings of weatherworn lands and men in wide Elizabethan collars. There is that wide staircase Abigail Blake had looked down on him from, before leading him upstairs to her son's bedroom. The air feels thick and close, fragrant with candle wax and freshly cut wood. The faint hint of pipe smoke and the lingering mustiness of neglect. He feels it tighten his chest. Hears the blood rushing in his ears. His hand tenses around Eva's.

She glances at him. "We do not have to…"

He shakes his head faintly, silencing her. He can feel the unease pouring off her; fear over her sister, and anxiety over his being here. He had not come with her so she might feel anxious. He knows that right now, his presence is having the opposite effect to what he had intended. He presses a hand between her shoulder blades, nudging her forward. Nods. It's all right.

He follows her into a sitting room, where an enormous fire is roaring in the grate. After the icy journey across from Longstone, the room feels hot and airless. He feels the back of his neck prickle with something that is either heat or dread. Finn finds his gaze travelling around the room; to its worn embroidered armchairs and polished tea tables. A large bookshelf stands against one wall, the gold-embossed spines of the volumes tatty and faded.

He wonders if this is the room where Abigail had entertained Henry Ward and his crew. He pictures Ward reclined on the settle with his long legs stretched out in front of him, pictures his crewmen in front of the fire with glasses in their hands. And what about Abigail herself? Had she welcomed them? Drunk with them? Had she sought time alone with Ward? Or had that been all his doing?

Tonight, Harriet's husband is the only man in front of the fire. His greatcoat and hat have been tossed carelessly over the arm of the settle, his shirt half-untucked and his hair windswept and tangled. He looks a different person to the wigged and polished gentleman Finn had met at his wedding.

"The pastor saw her in the village," Edwin tells Nathan. "She told him she was going to see a friend. I assume it was a lie." He looks past Nathan to Finn and Eva. "I see you brought the cavalry." Finn feels Edwin looking him up and down, assessing him. Eva takes a step closer to him, perhaps unconsciously. Perhaps a defensive, protective move. But after a moment of consideration, Edwin says, "It was good of you both to come."

A housekeeper bustles into the room with a tray and places a large porcelain teapot on the table, along with a plate of colourless biscuits. Nathan nods his thanks and she disappears silently from the parlour.

This housekeeper, this tea tray, this cavernous, embroidered parlour—it's a reminder of the status of the family Finn has married into. A reminder—as if he needs one—of how much he does not belong here. He knows the Blakes' money is running out; Eva has told him everything. But it does not feel that way. Sometimes it is easy to forget the old wealth his wife comes from when her hair is windblown and her hands are streaked with coal dust.

Eva goes silently to the table and fills the teacups. The faint mewling of a baby floats down from the top storey.

"We ought to be out there looking for her." Edwin begins to pace. "Not sitting here drinking tea."

"You know there's little more we can do in the dark," says Nathan, taking a bottle of brandy from the cabinet and sloshing an ocean of the stuff into his cup. "We'll go out looking again at first light." He nods vaguely towards the plate of biscuits. "Please. Eat."

"No, thank you." Finn's voice comes out strained. He doesn't want to be here, making these forced, unfamiliar pleasantries. Despite the vastness of the room, the air feels too thick, too heavy, making something close in his chest like a fist. It is taking everything in him not to tear out of this house and never return.

Eva glances at him. "I'm going to try and sleep," she murmurs. "Will you join me?"

Finn nods wordlessly. They make their goodnights then, alone in the dark hallway, Eva takes his hand. Her grip is tight; for her own sake or his, he can't quite determine. She takes a step onto the staircase.

Finn's free hand shoots out, grabbing hold of the banister. Because at once he is a child again, following Abigail Blake up these stairs, the smooth, time-worn wood of the rail beneath his palm. He hears his breathing quicken.

Eva stops walking. "Let's go back downstairs. We can—"

"No," Finn says quickly. "It's all right. Really." He starts climbing again, before she can question him. Before he can change his mind.

There are reminders. Will always be reminders. Reminders he has learnt to deal with. The faint scar on his forearm from Oliver Blake's knife. The dark shape of Holy Island, visible through the cottage window. And yes, the sky blue eyes of the woman he loves—the same eyes as her elder brother; the same eyes that had stared lifeless at him from the floor of the bedroom with the priest hole within the wall. This house is just one more reminder. It does not need to consume him.

Eva pushes open the door to what he assumes is her old bedroom. It's sparse and cold, the grate empty and the wash basin dry, as though no one has entered since she had come to live in his cottage. A chipped chest of drawers is pushed up into one corner, a worn gold-rimmed mirror sitting above the mantel. Like the rest of the rooms in the house, the walls are lined with dark wood panelling, but through the open curtains, Finn can see the faint bloom of the Longstone light.

In spite of himself, he smiles. "You can see the firebasket from here?"

Eva comes towards him. Slides her arms around his waist and looks up at him, her chin against his chest. "I may have spent a little time pining at that window." She holds him tightly, as though trying to shield him— from what? The past? The house itself? He lets himself sink into her. She stands on her tiptoes to kiss his lips. "Thank you for coming. I'm glad you're here."

At a knock on the door, she releases her grip on him, and goes to collect a jug of water from the housekeeper. She murmurs her thanks and closes the door quietly behind her, setting the jug on the washstand.

Finn sits on the edge of the bed. It groans loudly beneath his weight. "I came back here once, you know. After Oliver... I came back to see your mother."

"You did?" Eva perches beside him, kicking off her shoes and curling her legs beneath her.

"Aye. A couple of months after it happened." The beams above their heads creak softly as the house settles around them. "I'd found work on a farm in Berwick by then, but I knew I had to come back. I wanted to tell your ma what happened. How he died." He lowers his eyes. "Tell her I was sorry." They come out sounding husky, these words he has never spoken before. His visit to the house, his failed attempt at an apology, in a desperate attempt to ease his guilt—these are things he had almost forgotten. Being back inside the place has drawn the memory out into the light.

Eva covers his hand with his. "What happened?"

"When I got to the house, it was dark. But I looked through the window of the parlour, and I could see the coals in the grate were still hot. I knocked, but there was no answer."

Eva lets out her breath. "I wonder if it was the night we fled. Mother left everything behind that night. No doubt she left the fires in the grate burning too."

"Ward's ship was in the bay that night," Finn tells her, watching Eva trace her finger over his thumbnail. "I could see it—in the same place it is now. After I looked through the parlour window, I saw someone from his crew coming towards the house."

Eva frowns. "Was it Ward?"

"I don't know. Probably. It was too dark for me to see properly. I didn't want him to catch me, so I ran. Didn't come back to Lindisfarne for years."

Eva shifts on the bed, leaning her forehead against his. "I'm sorry you never got to tell my mother what you needed to."

Finn tucks a loose strand of hair behind her ear. "It's probably for the best," he says. "I can't imagine she would have let me just walk away unpunished, do you?"

Eva sighs. "Honestly, I don't know what she would have done. I have no sense of who she was anymore. I like to think she would have understood it was a mistake. But I know that may well be wishful thinking." She sighs. Unpins her hair and begins to unlace her shortjacket. "The bed is a little small, I'm afraid," she says, veering abruptly away from the subject of her mother. "We shall have to make do."

Finn leans over and kisses her neck, the feel of her soft skin going some way towards steading him. If he is to spend a night inside this house, he is glad he will have Eva's warm body curled up beside his own.

CHAPTER TWENTY-THREE

Here is Lesbury Common. Dark and still, barely touched by the streetlamps of the village. Not a soul in sight. No hint of a gathering army.

Michael stops the wagon and leaps out of the box seat, the thud of his boots loud in the late-night stillness.

Inside the wagon, Harriet can hear herself breathe. Her fingers curl around the edge of the bench seat. Will he blame her? Insist the information she provided was wrong? Will he demand she return the money?

She cannot let that happen.

Tentatively, she climbs from the wagon, shoes landing on the soft grass of the common. Her legs feel weak, unsteady with the fear that has been growing with each dark mile they have covered. "I know what I heard," she tells him, with as much firmness as she can gather. "This is where the army was mustering."

Michael barely acknowledges her. He just stands with his arms folded across his chest, looking out across the dark plain of the common. His jaw is set tightly and she can see the faint tick of the muscles within. The wagon creaks. Anne climbs out and stands behind Harriet.

"We're too late," she murmurs uselessly.

The glow of a lamp appears on the edge of the common, and Michael whirls around towards it, catching sight of a young man picking his way back towards the village.

"You," he calls.

The man stops walking, lifting the lamp to help him see into the darkness.

"Where'd they go?" Michael demands. "The rebel army?"

"They left days ago," the man calls, keeping his distance. "They heard the redcoats was coming. Four whole regiments turned up here day before yesterday." He chuckles dully. "Shame they didn't catch the bastards, if you ask me."

Michael bristles. "Where'd they go?" he repeats. "The rebels?"

"They were off to Alnwick last I heard," he says. "Proclaiming James as king. That were days ago, mind. I daresay they'll not be staying in one place too long. Not with dragoons on their tail."

Michael begins to pace across the grass, boots sighing rhythmically. Harriet's hand goes instinctively to the coin pouch inside her stays. The man with the lamp disappears into the village, making the dark thicken.

Michael marches back up to the wagon and swings himself into the box seat. "Get in," he says. "We're going on to Alnwick. We can be there in less than an hour."

"Did you not hear the man?" Anne hisses. "They've four regiments on their tail. Do you really think the rebels are going to be sitting around in Alnwick waiting to be caught?"

Michael's eyes flash in the lamplight. "Get in," he says again, more firmly this time. "I've not come all this way to turn around and give up."

At the firmness in his voice, Harriet finds herself obeying. She climbs into the wagon without a word. And that woman that does not take orders, she thinks distantly, how painfully far away she is. Because she might have defied her husband by taking this foolish journey into the night, but here she is nodding along to the next man, following his instructions without complaint. Allowing him to tug on those reins and lead her towards four regiments of redcoats. She swallows down a wave of nausea.

Anne doesn't move. She glares up at Michael in the box seat. "You're a fool," she says.

"So be it," he hisses. "Just get in the wagon and do your part, like you told me you were so damn desperate to do."

Anne hesitates for a moment. Harriet clenches her hands around fistfuls of her cloak as she watches, willing her to climb into the wagon. Out here in the openness of the common, she feels intensely exposed. Feels her fear creep towards terror.

Finally, Anne turns and climbs into the wagon, a closed-off expression on her face.

The lights of Lesbury disappear, leaving long, dark ribbons of road out ahead of them. Harriet closes her eyes. This was supposed to be over by now. Michael was supposed to be gone, and she and Anne were supposed to be on their way home to Holy Island. She is suddenly, painfully aware that she is travelling with a man the British army wants to see on the scaffold. A man whose passion for his cause is preventing him from acting wisely.

Just like herself, she thinks.

Michael stops the wagon. At once, it is too still. Too silent. Lamplight pools in front of them. On either side of the road, the fields are impossibly dark.

Anne leans forward. "What is it? Why have we stopped?"

And it is not too still at all, Harriet realises. Or too silent. Or too dark. Because there are lamps moving through the darkness now, growing brighter. Horse hooves rattling the earth.

Perhaps they are just travellers. Or more Jacobites stealing towards Alnwick in an attempt to catch up with the rebel army. These, she knows, are likely possibilities.

But: *troops active.* And Harriet knows there is every chance this is the redcoats moving towards them, ready to intercept any rebels that might cross their path. Four regiments, she thinks sickly. *Shame they didn't catch the bastards if you ask me…*

She draws in a breath. Even if this is the redcoats, on the trail of the Jacobite army, it's of no matter. Is that not what she is here for? This is why her bodice is heavy with coins. They have rehearsed their story, taken their roles. The man in the box seat is a simple merchant, travelling to Lesbury to meet a client. And she is his wife. She tries to untangle her thoughts; prepare herself to adopt her role.

But before she can make sense of what is happening, Michael blows out the lamp, and the wagon is drowned in blackness.

It's a grave error. Harriet knows it at once. She and Anne are here to support Michael's cover story. The merchant, the wife, the lady's maid. But in his impulse, in his blowing out the light, he has marked them as rebels. Jacobites.

"What in hell are you doing?" Anne hisses. "Light the lamp." She lurches forward, but Michael puts a sudden hand out into the wagon, forcing her back. Though she can see little more than his outline, Harriet can tell he is shaking. As though he knows he has made a crucial mistake. As though the bravado he has been putting on the whole time he has known her has been nothing but a cover for a deep fear of capture. Of death.

"Light the lamp," Anne says again, but her words fade out as she speaks them. Because the sound of hooves is coming closer.

The thunder of horses stops and a globe of light shines into the wagon, illuminating a bearded face. A scarlet uniform trimmed with gold braiding. The soldier lifts his lamp, shining it into Michael's eyes. "Well now," he says. "What do we have here?"

Does he recognise Michael Mitchell as the man who shot a dragoon at the protest in York? Harriet cannot tell. Michael says nothing, just stares the soldier down, though the trembling of his entire body betrays him. Betrays all of them, Harriet realises sickly. Sweat rolls down the side of his face.

"I'm on my way to Alnwick with my wife," he says. But there is no substance to his words.

The soldier pans the light past him, spearing it into Harriet's eyes. Her heart is thundering, her skin damp beneath her shift. Perhaps she ought to tell them her name. Tell them her family's house is being used by government spies, and that of course she is no Jacobite. But she knows her actions speak louder than these hollow words.

Somehow, she knows before he pulls the trigger that Michael is going to shoot. And she is leaping from the wagon seconds before the sound breaks the cold night air. She lands heavily, pain shooting through her shins as she stumbles forward, her palms planting hard against earth. And this blind instinct, it gives her the few yards' head start she needs to tear away from the soldiers and across the unseen veneer of the land. The ground seems to tilt beneath her as fear floods her body. Harriet hears

Anne cry out as the dragoons seize her. And she hears a volley of gunfire.

Harriet runs, with no thought of where she is going, or where the soldiers might be. Lamplight illuminates the sorry sight of the wagon, but beyond it is inky blackness. She stumbles over uneven ground and ploughs through tangled greenery. She does not see the low-hanging tree branch until she is an inch away from it. She ducks and stumbles, feels the branch tear at her hair, scrape along her cheek. And when she lands, heavy and breathless on the cold, damp earth, it is no small part of her that is surprised she is still alive.

CHAPTER TWENTY-FOUR

Finn lies staring at the rugged ceiling as dawn lights Eva's childhood bedroom. He shifts in the narrow bed, careful not to wake her. She is curled up on her side, her back pressed against him. He can feel her warmth through her thin nightshift, her hair tickling his bare shoulder. He has slept little, but it had felt much more reassuring to lie in bed beside his wife than to roam the house in the lightless hours of early morning, wondering at the depths of the shadows. There was something reassuring, too, about the firebasket glittering through the gap in the curtains, a reminder that he is doing all he can to make amends for Oliver's death.

In the pink dawn, the beacon is extinguished now, but Angus had kept it burning steadily throughout the night. He wonders if Michael had bothered returning to Longstone last night. When he returns, Finn will let the man know he has had enough. If Michael is willing to risk their safety by gallivanting around Lindisfarne and the mainland every two minutes, then the offer of shelter is retracted. He has enough to worry about without the threat of redcoats on his doorstep.

Eva stirs and rolls over to face him, letting her fingers run absentmindedly over his bare chest. "Are you all right?" she murmurs. Finn allows himself a smile. It must be the tenth time she has asked him that question since they set foot inside the house.

"I'm all right." And he means it. Because beyond the unease is a strangely steadying reminder that this house had let him live. This house, with its priest hole beside the fireplace and the passage within the walls, it had given him a reprieve. A chance to escape, and to try to atone for his mistakes. Somehow, that gives him the courage to believe that nothing will collapse today.

"Have you slept?" Eva asks, rubbing her eyes.

"A little." He gives her a smile he hopes looks genuine. "You know I sleep better in the daylight."

"I've not slept much either. I'm so worried about Harriet." She slides out of bed, reaching for the underskirts she had left on the floor. "Can we take the skiff out this morning? Follow the shoreline? In case there's any sign of her?"

"Aye. Of course." Finn follows her out of bed and pulls back the curtain. The tide is high, knocking roughly against the embankment. If they leave now, they will be able to circle the entire island. But if Harriet has left any hints of her whereabouts on the beaches, they will be hidden beneath the surface.

They are on the water before the sun is more than a glow on the horizon. A thin layer of mist lies over the sea, the water soupy and grey. Finn eases the skiff along the east coast of the island, past the castle and through the anchorage. Neither of them speak, unwilling to disrupt the thick silence that hangs over the sea.

As they are making their way across the ribbon of water between Lindisfarne and the mainland, Eva gets suddenly to her feet. "Over there." She points. "What is it?"

Finn squints into the rising sun, following her outstretched finger. He sees a small unidentifiable shape hanging on the tangle of greenery by the edge of Holy Island. Something woollen, perhaps. He cannot make it out.

"Clothing?" asks Eva. Finn pulls on the oars, guiding the skiff into the shallow water. Eva remains standing, hunched over and gripping the gunwale. When the water is shallow enough, she gathers her skirts in her fist and leaps out towards the edge of the island, sending a flock of gulls shooting upwards.

Finn jumps out after her and pushes the skiff up into the reeds at the water's edge. Eva grabs the piece of clothing from the bush and holds it up. It looks to be a woman's shawl, but the wool is frayed and worn to the colour of mud, with only the barest hints of its former blue still visible.

It has clearly been out here for far longer than the day Harriet has been missing.

Eva drops it back onto the bush. "It's not hers. That's a good thing, I'm sure." Her voice is thin.

Finn presses a hand to the small of her back to guide her back to the skiff. And he stops at the sight of a longboat approaching. Henry Ward is watching them as his boat nears theirs, two of his crewmen manning the oars.

Finn feels Eva's muscles tense beneath his palm. "He followed us," she murmurs.

He nods. He knows there is no way Ward has come upon them by chance. No doubt he had seen them set out from Emmanuel Head this morning.

Eva tugs Finn towards the boat. "Come on. Quickly." She thrashes through the reeds and scrambles ungracefully over the gunwale.

"There's no need to run, Eva." Ward's voice carries across the sea. "I just wish to speak with your husband."

Finn shoves the boat into the water and leaps inside. He settles the oars into the oarlocks, but does not row. The skiff drifts out towards Ward's longboat. He knows there is little point trying to avoid the confrontation. After all, Henry Ward knows exactly where to find them.

"I wondered if you have had time to consider my proposal," says Ward, when they are close enough for him to speak without raising his voice. Any last doubts Finn had had about Ward following them evaporate. He knows every piece of this is deliberate; knows Ward is speaking of his invitation to join his crew in front of Eva to put him in a difficult situation.

"I've given you my answer," Finn says tautly. "That is not going to change." He takes up the oars and pulls hard.

"Your answer to what?" Eva demands. "What is he talking about?"

"Stop, Finn," Ward orders, that forced bravado tainting his words again. "I'm speaking to you." Smoothly, he produces a pistol from within his greatcoat. He holds it in Finn's direction in a vaguely threatening manner.

Finn lets out a humourless laugh. "Really?" He lifts the oars from the water anyway. Hears Eva's sharp intake of breath.

"Your answer to what?" she repeats, voice low.

Finn presses a hand to her knee; squeezes gently. He will pay for his secrecy later, he has no doubt. But right now, he needs her to stay quiet. He looks squarely at his former captain. "My answer is no, Ward. So if you are going to kill me, just do it. This has gone on long enough."

"Are you mad?!" Eva lurches in front of him, making the boat tilt on the swell. She stretches out her arms in an attempt to make herself as wide as possible, blocking him from the path of Ward's bullet. Ward chuckles lightly.

Finn eases her aside, doing his best to ignore the fierce glare she gives him. "It's all right," he murmurs. "Trust me." He looks back at Ward. "You can't do it, can you. Not to my face. Not when there are no crewmen willing to keel-haul me so you can keep your hands clean."

"You sound very sure of yourself," says Ward.

"That's because I know you too well. Get out of our lives, Ward. Take your crew and use that precious immunity." Somewhere at the back of his mind, Finn knows this boldness is misplaced. Knows Henry Ward has an entire crew at his disposal who will have no issue with effecting the killing that Ward is unable to execute. But he is also certain that Ward will not shoot him here, in cold blood, in front of his wife. Not the boy he had spent so many hours with in the great cabin of the *Eagle*, teaching to read nautical charts and navigate by starlight. Ward has always valued loyalty, and Finn knows he will not stoop to such a callous execution. In a strange sort of way, Henry Ward has far more decency than that.

Finn pulls on the oars to ease the skiff back around the point, then unfurls the mainsail, letting it catch the cold wind. Eva stares over her shoulder, eyes fixed to Ward's longboat. Best that way, Finn thinks. Because he is fairly certain that when she looks back at him, the anger in her eyes is going to turn him to stone.

Finally, she whirls around. And her fierce look does not leave Finn disappointed. "Your answer to what?" she hisses. "What in hell was he talking about?"

He tells her in pieces. His visit to the Lindisfarne tavern. Ward's desire to have him back in his crew. His outlandish claim of offering immunity to those who sign his pirates' articles. He says nothing of Ward's reason for wanting Finn back on his ship: to keep him away from her.

He says nothing, because there is a part of him that knows Ward is right to demand such things. Knows he had no right making Eva Blake his wife. Most of all, he says nothing, because if he speaks it out loud, it will remind him that this offer—a life for Eva without the fear of Ward in it—is exactly what is best for her.

Finn knows he's a coward. Selfish. But finding Eva had been so unlikely, so miraculous, that he does not have the strength to take what Ward is offering. How can he give her up?

Eva sits with her hands tightly clasped in her lap, spearing him with a fierce glare. "You did not think to tell me this earlier?" She flies at him suddenly, throwing her fists into his arms and chest. The boat rocks on the swell. "How could you be so foolish as to go to him in the tavern? And to goad him into shooting you? Do you truly think you know him so well? What if he's a changed man? What if I had sat there and watched him kill you?" Her voice rattles with emotion.

He takes her wrists, eases her away from him. "It's all right," he says again, running his thumbs over the backs of her hands.

She pulls away. "It is not all right," she hisses. "You are damn lucky you are still alive." She stares out across the water, avoiding his gaze. Her eyes overflow suddenly and she swipes away her tears with her palm. "It is not just you anymore," she says. "You're not alone out on that rock any longer. You do not have to keep everything to yourself." She swallows down her tears and looks at him squarely. "Henry Ward is my sister's father," she says, levelling her voice. "I am as much a part of this as you are. You ought to have told me you were going to see him. And you ought to have told me what he was offering you."

"You would have stopped me from going to see him."

"Of course I would have!" she cries.

"I'm sorry." Eva looks at him expectantly, clearly wanting more. "You are right," Finn says after a moment. "Ward *is* a changed man. His confidence, it seems forced somehow. Unnatural. As though something is troubling him. Maybe it's because he's had no choice but to turn to piracy, like he never wanted to do. Or maybe there's something more."

Eva doesn't respond at once. She stares out over the water as a gull swoops and ripples the surface. Her eyes are glassy. "Promise me," she says, "you will tell me if he comes to you again." She narrows her eyes.

"Or if you go to him."

Finn says nothing. It is a promise he cannot make. Because while Henry Ward might be Eva's problem too, he longs for that not to be the case. He thinks of her standing at the window on their wedding night, looking out into the dark in fear of seeing Ward's ship. The voice in the back of his mind gnaws at him, reminds him he has a way to get Ward out of Eva's life forever. He wills it to be silent.

CHAPTER TWENTY-FIVE

Harriet cannot make sense of how long she has been hiding in the undergrowth for. All she knows is it's eerily silent, with morning light bringing shape to the blackness that had surrounded her for what seemed an eternity. She is on the edge of a wide, flat plain, fringed with tangled gorse and low, gnarled trees. Her body is aching from a night spent huddled on the ground, and she is shivering violently. A part of her is afraid to move, her fear pulsing inside her. But stay here, and she knows it will not be long before the cold seizes her.

As she shifts slightly, trying to return feeling to her numb toes, she hears the dull shudder of the coin pouch tucked inside her bodice. The sound of it drives her to move. She crawls forward, entangling herself in mud-caked skirts. Twigs crack beneath her weight as she wriggles out from beneath the low branches. Gets shakily to her feet.

It ought to be the thought of her son driving her to self-preservation, she knows. She ought to want to live for him and him alone. But somehow, Thomas has become a symbol of the false life she is living. A life of hiding and pretending. A symbol of her loveless marriage.

Poor Thomas, she thinks. It is not his fault he was born to a woman incapable of doting on her child. Of loving him as much as she should.

The land is dizzyingly green beneath the curtain of mist. She squints into the haze, trying to catch the shape of a farmhouse or shed. She cannot be far from Lesbury. But she can see nothing around her but trees bent crooked in the wind. She cannot even tell where the road is. She stands motionless, arms wrapped around herself.

Somewhere distant, hooves echo. Harriet's heart jolts, then she realises it is just a passing wagon. In the distance, she sees its hazy shape move through the cloud. She begins to stumble towards it. She will find the road. And for better or for worse, it will lead her back to Lindisfarne.

She is following the trail before she can make sense of it; not the road, but something far worse. Dark, rusty beads, splattered against the earth. One step, then another, she follows them, not daring to look up.

And at the end of her tunnel vision, she sees it: the motionless hand, attached to the motionless arm, the motionless body. Michael Mitchell's coppery hair is plastered to his head, his beard matted with dirt. Blood has pooled beneath the bullet wound in his neck, congealing beneath a whirring black raft of insects. He lies face down beside the road, and Harriet is glad she cannot see his eyes. The horse and wagon are no longer beside him. Had the soldiers taken them and left Michael to rot?

She stands over him for several minutes, oddly transfixed by the fly crawling up his bloodstained neck. It feels wrong to leave him here. But what choice does she have?

She begins to walk, pain shooting through her legs with each step as feeling returns to her frozen feet.

None of this feels real. Not Michael's lifeless body, or this profound emptiness, or the unnameable green vastness around her. This is not the shape of her life. Her life is neat edges: a respectable husband and son. She is *wife* and *mother* and none of this. But she knows this is a lie. Knows there are parts of her that exist far beyond those neat edges.

Because as she walks, her thoughts are pulled back into smoke-hazy rooms with her artists' circle. To lazy afternoons in Isabelle's parlour, with shoes and stockings on the floor. To glasses being filled as though the rest of the world had ceased to exist. To a wine-tainted kiss they can never speak of.

An ocean of grief surges at her. Hot and torrential and fierce. Harriet hears herself cry out in a desperate sob. Feels tears fill her eyes and spill without warning.

Beautiful, talented Isabelle. How can one person can bring her so much joy and yet so much regret? How can she be so happy in her presence, and yet simultaneously filled with such deep self-loathing and shame?

Tears pour down her cheeks, dripping unhindered from her chin. Tears she has been holding inside for longer than she can remember. Tears she learnt to push aside the moment she realised there were parts of herself that could never be spoken of. Never be brought to the light.

Because only someone with the heart of a sinner would feel such things for another woman.

She keeps following the road. Back towards her husband, her son, towards the life she has been taught she should be living.

They are sirens, they say, the women whose wicked hearts draw them in this direction. Cursed, unnatural creatures. Witches. And isn't that how she has always felt? An unnatural being?

The broken, ill-fitting piece.

It is late morning when Eva and Finn return to the house. The sun has broken through the cloud bank in neat gold strokes, turning the water turquoise at its edges. Eva's heart is still fast after their run-in with Ward. At the knowledge that Finn had gone to him alone, and at the offer Ward had made him.

In a strange sort of way, there is something faintly settling about Ward's invitation for Finn to re-join his crew. The offer—and Ward's reluctance to pull the trigger today—suggests he is not so adamant on seeing Finn dead as she had believed. It also suggests that Ward is somewhat delusional—surely he did not imagine Finn might accept such an offer? She might have known Finn for a fraction of the time Ward has, but Eva knows with a deep certainty that no offer of pirating wealth would ever tempt her husband from her side.

Not that that knowledge does anything to lessen her anger towards him right now.

Theodora is rolling her hoop outside the house when they approach, Jenny watching from the doorway with Thomas in her arms. There's a flatness to Thea today that suggests that, while she may not know exactly what is going on, she is aware that something is amiss. Eva wonders what Nathan has told her to explain Harriet's absence.

She catches the hoop as it escapes Theodora's control and trundles over the ground towards her. She hands it back to her niece. "You're getting better," she says, forcing a smile.

"Not really," Theodora says irritably. "The ground is too bumpy here." Hunching, she attempts to twirl the hoop, but it catches on a knot of grass and falls flat. She huffs. "See?"

Eva puts a hand to her shoulder, guiding her back towards the house. "How is your story coming along?"

"Good." She looks past Eva to Finn. "The selkie made a castle on the moon for the farmer's wife to live in," she explains.

"Obviously," says Finn.

Eva smiles.

"My ma used to believe in selkies," Finn tells Theodora. Her eyes light. "She used to say that if she ever found one, she'd wish for a pot of gold and sunny skies every day."

"Mhm." Theodora nods thoughtfully. "That would be a nice wish."

Finn follows Eva up the front path towards the house, then stops walking and catches her wrist. "How angry are you?" he asks, voice low.

Eva snorts. "Do you really need to ask that?"

"Just trying to be optimistic." He squeezes her wrist gently. "You know this is what Ward wanted, aye? To unsettle us, by making sure you knew what he asked of me."

Eva narrows her eyes. "He succeeded."

Finn drops her wrist and glances up at the house. "Go on without me. I'll be in in a minute." In spite of her anger, Eva's heart lurches. She can hear the strain in his words. Can see the weariness in his eyes. Though he has not said it—would never say it—she knows he is finding it difficult to be in the house. She is finding it difficult too. Having him here reminds Eva of what she has known from the beginning: that now she has married Finn, she is condemned to keeping secrets from her family. It's a burden she had accepted when she had agreed to become Finn's wife. A burden she is willing to carry if it means spending her life with the man she loves. But it is a burden that feels twice as weighted when they are inside Highfield House.

She gives him a nod of understanding. He sinks onto the grass of the dunes, his gaze cast out to sea. A deliberate attempt, she can tell, to keep the house out of his eyeline.

Theodora tosses her hoop into the air then plants herself on the grass next to Finn. "Papa says the selkies are make believe, but Mrs Brodie doesn't think so. What do you think? Have you ever seen one?"

Eva allows herself a faint smile and makes her way inside. She had managed little more than a tiny triangle of toast this morning, and her stomach is groaning with hunger, in spite of her fear for Harriet. The smell of onion soup is drifting out from the kitchen, making her mouth water.

The house is quiet. Dust motes dance in the stream of light pouring through the narrow window above the door. It feels oddly empty without the constant barrage of hammering. No doubt Nathan and Edwin are still out looking for Harriet on the mainland. But as she makes her way towards the kitchen, Eva sees the door to the parlour open. She catches sight of her brother in an armchair, reading through a ledger with a quill in hand. A half-eaten bowl of soup sits on the tea table beside him.

She debates whether to enter. Ask if he has any news. She decides against it. Surely if he had heard word of Harriet, he would have sought her out himself to tell her. And she is far too tired to deal with any more of Nathan's saltiness.

"Is that you, Eva?" he calls, before she can leave.

She steels herself, then steps inside. "You're working?" she asks.

"Trying. I hope to have something of a business to return to once we leave this place."

The words strike her unexpectedly. Of course, she has always known her family never planned to stay here forever. But Nathan's words remind her that soon they will be so far away. She pushes the thought aside. Thinking of that future feels too difficult with Harriet missing.

"No word?" she asks.

Nathan shakes his head. "No one in Bamburgh or Beal has seen her. Edwin has gone back to the village in case anyone has heard anything since we were last there."

"Finn and I circled the island," Eva tells him. "There was no sign of her."

Nathan nods towards the armchair opposite him. "Sit down, Eva. You look exhausted."

She sits. She is exhausted, yes, but that exhaustion has come from tiptoeing around her brother, and her own secrets, for the past day. Nathan sets the ledger down beside the soup bowl.

"Where is your husband?" he asks.

"Outside. Having a pressing conversation with Thea about the potential existence of selkies." She pauses. "That is all right, isn't it?"

He chuckles. "Of course."

She dares to meet his eyes. "How are you?" she asks finally.

Nathan pinches the bridge of his nose. "That is a complicated question."

"I know."

He sighs. "I regret bringing us here. I ought to have found another way…" He fades out, but catches the faint smile on Eva's lips.

"I'm rather glad you did," she says. "Or rather, I'm glad I had no choice but to follow you up here." The moment the words are out, she regrets them, fearing they will remind Nathan of her mutilated betrothal to Matthew Walton.

To her surprise, he smiles. There's a sudden warmth in his eyes, and it makes Eva realise how much she has missed her brother's company. "You seem happy," he says after a moment.

"I am happy. Very much so." She falters. "Well. At least, I would be if it weren't for Harriet…" She decides not to mention her irritation at her husband.

Nathan toys with the cover of his ledger. "I'm glad you're happy."

"Really?"

"Yes, really. Do you truly doubt that?"

Eva hesitates for a moment. "No," she decides. "I don't."

Nathan takes a piece of bread from the plate beside the soup, but then changes his mind and puts it back on the plate without eating. "It was good of you and Finn to come," he tells her. "I suspect it was the last thing you wished to do."

Eva's heart jolts, fearful her brother has picked up on Finn's unease at being in the house. But then she realises Nathan is referring to their own strained relations. "I'm as worried for Harriet as you are," she tells him. "I could hardly stay on Longstone and just hope for the best."

Nathan looks out the window for long moments, rubbing at his jaw. "I know she has been unhappy. Even before this business with her father. Do you think it because I pushed her to marry Edwin?"

It is times like this, when Eva can see the guilt hanging on Nathan's shoulders most heavily, that she wishes he was not so averse to human contact. The touch of a hand, an embrace—she finds it hard to comprehend how these things might bring him such unease. She hates this isolation her brother has imposed on himself. Cannot imagine the loneliness that might come with it. "I don't know," she admits. "She rarely speaks to me these days. And perhaps I don't try as hard as I ought to. But none of this is your fault." She leans forward in her chair, trying to catch her brother's eye. "You have to know that."

He gives her a thin smile. But she can tell he is far from convinced.

When Theodora is herded inside by the nurse, Finn gets to his feet and follows her into the house. He knows he cannot stay outside forever.

The moment he steps through the door, the gloom of the house swallows the daylight.

His heart is hammering. He feels too unsettled to eat, too restless to sleep. He is unsure if it's the house, or concern over Ward and his cursed offer—and Eva's fresh knowledge of the situation. Either way, he needs something to occupy his thoughts.

He can hear voices coming from the parlour; Eva and Nathan. Cannot make out their words. He goes upstairs and tosses his coat across Eva's bed. A door is ajar on the other side of the hall. He steps back out into the passage and peeks inside.

The room looks like an earthquake has hit. The fireplace lies in pieces, and he can barely see the floor between the strewn bricks and fallen wood panels. A hammer and pry bar lie discarded in the corner, as though whatever attempt at restoration was being made here has been forgotten about in the stress of Harriet's disappearance. Finn steps out of the room, pulling the door closed behind him.

In a daze, he continues down the hallway to the door at the end of the passage. And he is standing outside the room in which he had killed Oliver

Blake. When he had followed Eva upstairs last night; when he had glanced down this hallway at the rows of closed doors, he had been unsure of which room it was. But now it feels as though his body has led him here instinctively. As though a part of him has never forgotten.

The second storey of the house feels oddly quiet. Too empty. Hollow, somehow, with few threads of light making it into the hallway through the rows of closed doors. Finn feels the need to turn that handle and step inside. It's a strange urge; frightening. But somehow, he feels it will be easier this way, if he just confronts the reality of what lies behind that door. Like facing a predator instead of living on the run.

He steps into the room.

Oliver's bedroom does not look like he remembers. Not really. The bed is gone, leaving an empty, uninhabited space, and there has clearly been restoration work done. But he can tell the structure of the room has not been altered. The fireplace; he remembers that. Remembers searching the wooden panels around it for the priest hole behind. But the windows seem much larger, the panelling lighter, the thick beams across the ceiling not so close to the top of his head. As though his memories have distorted over time. As though he has spent so long with his thoughts in this place that the room had shrunk in on itself inside his mind, until all it consisted of was that yard of bloodstained floor where Oliver's body had fallen.

He stands there for a long time. Can't comprehend why. Perhaps there is a sense of confronting the past, somehow. Of meeting his memories head-on, rather than letting them steep in the back of his mind. He feels rooted in place, feels old fear and desperation and guilt pushing to the front of his thoughts. He hears the footsteps distantly, but does not fully register them.

"Theodora, is that you?" Nathan appears in the doorway. Finn whirls around, jolted from his thoughts. "Oh. Forgive me. I usually keep this door locked. I forgot to close it up in all the chaos. Thea is always trying to get in here." Nathan Blake is uneasy in this room, Finn can tell. Even after all this time. Not that he blames him. Not one bit.

"Why do you lock the room?" Finn finds himself asking.

There's a moment of silence so brief he is not sure if he is imagining it.

"There's a double-barrel priest hole beside the fireplace," says Nathan.

"It leads to a passage within the walls. Edwin blocked the outside entrance up after we discovered the Mitchells had been using it to get into the attic. It's not a place for children to be playing."

Finn nods. He wonders distantly what the right reaction to this is. He ought to feign some surprise, surely. Something that might suggest he is hearing of this for the first time. But it feels suddenly as though Nathan is watching him too closely, and he cannot bring himself to do anything more than nod.

Nathan holds out a ring of keys. "Look as you wish. But lock the door when you're done."

"I've no need to look any further," Finn says quickly. He follows Nathan out of the room. "The fireplace," he says. "In the other room. I can help you restore it. I rebuilt the fireplace on Longstone last year."

Something flickers across Nathan's eyes. Surprise at the offer, but something else that Finn can't read.

"Thank you," he says after a moment. "But there's no need, really."

"Truly? It looks like there's a great deal of need. And I'd rather keep busy than sitting around waiting for news."

Nathan looks away for a moment, caught in hesitation. "Very well," he says finally, though his words are anything but decisive. "Do as you wish. You'll find the mortar in the shed behind the house."

CHAPTER TWENTY-SIX

Harriet's legs and feet are aching, her head spinning with thirst. She has been walking for most of the day.

The sun is low in the sky now, much of the daylight sucked away, and the inky pall of dusk beginning to settle over the land. There's a deep ache inside her; an ache of grief, of self-loathing. Pure and utter exhaustion at this letting out of emotions she has held tightly to her chest for so many years. And yet her tears feel anything but cathartic. They have torn something open, something gaping and unfixable.

She curses this emptiness, this vast open land with its absence of life. Because it has given her the space to admit that which she cannot bear to acknowledge.

She walks slowly, crookedly. She has been following the road, keeping the ocean on her right. Has long given up attempting to stay hidden.

No redcoats have found her. But no one else has either. No rides have been offered. It is a bleak and lonely part of the country up here, especially now, with the early-autumn dusk closing in and the threat of conflict around every corner.

Now, here is Beal; beyond it, Lindisfarne. The middle of the sandy path onto the island is covered in a ribbon of sea, though the edges are still dry. How deep is the water? Harriet has no thought of it. No thought of whether the tide is rising or falling. Somehow, it had not even crossed her mind to think of such a thing as she had followed the ocean back to Lindisfarne. What a fool she is. A naïve child. How had she ever imagined she might live out from beneath the protection of her husband's shadow?

Wearily, she stands on the tiny jetty at Beal and looks out across the water. A small row boat is beached in the mud, like a forgotten children's toy. Clouds are beginning to roll in, bathing Holy Island in blue mist that seems to rise from the water. At once the island feels so close, and so far away.

Harriet sits on the edge of the jetty and pulls off her mud-caked shoes and stockings. She gathers them up in one hand, lifting her skirts above her ankles with the other. The path is cold beneath her bare feet, and sharp twigs protruding from the mud bite at her skin. She walks, attempting deliberateness, letting seawater cover her toes, her ankles, her calves. The chill of it stings, but she keeps walking. Now she has begun, she cannot stand to turn back.

How many times has she stood on the edge of Holy Island, wishing to make her escape? And now here she is, so desperate to return that she is willing to wade through the sea? The thought is so ludicrous she laughs. It's a desperate, hysterical sound; one that quickly turns into a sob of fear. Because water is gathering around her skirts now, pulling her one way, and the other, trying to yank her feet out from beneath her. The water is rushing in from the ocean, she realises sickly. The tide is rising. To trap her on Lindisfarne, or keep her out?

The water surges and her feet fly out from beneath her. She drops her shoes, unable to catch them before the tide tugs them away. She feels herself grapple with the sea floor, trying to right herself as the water rushes over her head. She kicks hard, her legs tangling in her skirts. Saltwater floods down her throat. She tries to keep her eyes open; tries to focus on those last pale threads of daylight glimmering through the surface of the water. But her eyes close instinctively, and when she next opens them, she has no thought of which way is up and which is down.

And this is right, is it not? She is the wicked siren, with her heart and her body aching after another woman. Is this not what she deserves? To drown in the sea where women of her kind come from.

She will die—the thought comes to her, violent and terrifying. But she finds herself kicking again, seeking the sea floor with her feet. She breaks through the surface, gasping and coughing. She is no closer to Lindisfarne. But she is alive. A strange thing. She had not imagined her will to live was so strong.

She drops onto her knees in the shallow water. And her hand goes instinctively to the bulge inside her bodice—to Michael Mitchell's coin pouch. To her chance at an unhemmed-in life. But that life, she realises now, it will not be unconstrained. Not really. She had tried to tell herself that being in Paris with Isabelle would bring her the greatest joy, but really, how can it do anything but cause her pain? It will only remind her of her own sin, and the things she will never have. Even if her work is to hang on gallery walls, she will still be forced to keep these darkest parts of herself hidden away.

Besides, how will she ever find the courage to step out on her own like that? She had told herself she was strong enough, but her façade of bravery had crumbled with the first hint of pressure.

"You there!" Footsteps slosh through the mud towards her, and then a man is pulling her from the shallow water, helping her stand. "What in hell are you doing out here?"

The man is wearing a long, dark greatcoat, his white beard thick and uneven. Harriet recognises him as one of the fishermen from Holy Island. Tom Cordwell. He looks her up and down, surprise in his eyes. There's recognition there too, of course—everyone from Lindisfarne knows who her family is.

"What happened to you?" he asks.

Harriet doesn't speak. Can't speak. Cordwell hauls her back towards the jetty and into the row boat, which has begun to float again on the shallow water.

He climbs in and tosses her a ream of filthy hessian from the bottom of the boat. "Warm yourself," he grunts.

Harriet wraps herself in the hessian. It is coarse and stiff, and reeks of old herrings, but it eases the violent trembling in her body.

"Water," she coughs.

Cordwell pulls on the oars without taking his eyes off the pitiful shape of her, huddled in the bottom of his rowboat. He reaches for a waterskin beside him and tosses it in her direction. Harriet gathers it from the damp floor of the boat. Fumbles with the cork and takes a long sip.

"You ought to be careful," Cordwell grunts. "Them bastards working for Cotesworth are not to be trusted." His voice is dark with threat. "Were they the ones who sent you out here? Typical, wouldn't you say?" he continues, before she can manage a word. "Sending young lasses out to do their bidding instead putting themselves in danger. Were they the ones who told you to cross back onto the island? Or was that your own wise idea?"

Harriet lets out her breath. Of course he suspects she has been working with the government spies. "No." She finds her voice. "You have it wrong. All of you." Because perhaps she has a chance here. A chance to show the villagers her family is not intertwined in the government cause. A chance, perhaps to undo a small piece of the damage this ill-fated journey has caused. "I was helping one of the rebels get to Lesbury. To re-join the Jacobite army." Even to her own ears, her words sound foolish. Like a lie. And she knows at once that this man is not going to believe her.

He snorts a laugh. "Is that so?"

"Yes. That is so." Her voice comes out sounding tiny. Weak.

Cordwell snorts. "The army moved on from Lesbury days ago, lass. You'll have to try better than that."

Harriet shoves the cork back into the mouth of waterskin. Says nothing.

"What does your husband think about this?" There is humour in Cordwell's voice now. "He know you're out here? Or are you another one of them foolish lasses gone out on their own thinking they could change the world?"

Harriet closes her eyes. "I am not trying to change the world," she mutters.

"Not sure I believe you," says Cordwell. "You see, we've heard things about your family. About all them workmen that come to your house. In and out the door, far too quick to get anything done."

Harriet's heart quickens. She opens her eyes. Tries not to react to the knowledge that the Jacobites have been watching her house. Watching her family. Watching her. She cannot be surprised at the conclusions they have drawn.

Perhaps this is the piece of knowledge that will finally get her husband to leave Lindisfarne. Get them off this cursed island. Muted hope flickers inside her for a moment, but its spark is extinguished quickly. The thought of her husband only serves to remind her of the reprimanding she is about to face.

"So you see, lass," says Cordwell, "I'm not so inclined to believe you when you tell me you're helping Jacobites get to Lesbury."

The shore is close. In mere moments, Harriet will climb from this boat and begin the long walk back to Highfield House with her clothes trailing water and her feet bare. Her soul torn open and the image of Michael Mitchell's lifeless body burning behind her eyelids.

Her family can know nothing about Cordwell's rescuing her, or the suspicions she has just confirmed. If they were to find out about the danger she has put them in, they would never forgive her. And if this journey has taught her anything, it is that she does not have the strength to face the world alone.

Rebuilding the fireplace is a simple enough task. Most of the bricks are in fine enough order to be reused, and the stone of the chimney is still entirely intact. But the chaos surrounding him has Finn on edge. It's the good condition of the bricks that tells him the fireplace has been pulled apart, rather than having fallen of its own accord. The wood panelling, too, has clearly been torn from the walls. The panelling is old, and in need of replacement. But why tear it down while the fireplace is still in pieces? Why not complete one job at a time? There is no order to this. No plan.

The room does not look like it is being restored. It looks as though it has been torn apart, as though part of a destruction mission. Or a desperate search for something. Finn presses the last brick into the row he is working on, then takes the lamp from the mantel and steps out into the passage. He hears Nathan talking to his daughter downstairs.

Finn rattles the door to Oliver's room. Locked, as he had expected. Then he nudges open the door of the room beside it. A large wooden desk is pushed up against one wall, a spying glass set up on a stand at the window. He guesses this to be Nathan's study.

The fireplace catches his eye. Like the hearth in the room he has been working on, the bricks seem to have been torn down almost haphazardly. Several of the wood panels appear loose, propped up against the wall. Had they fallen? Or have they been torn down?

Finn steps out of the room before he is caught, the floorboards creaking beneath his feet. He nudges open the door of Eva's bedroom. The floorboards creak loudly as he paces across the room. He feels them shift beneath his weight, as though they have been prised up and hastily hammered back down, in a haphazard, unplanned way.

It's an old house, he tells himself. Bound to squeak, to groan. But he finds himself returning to the room in which he is rebuilding the fireplace. Staring at the panels torn from the walls, the half-built hearth. Is Nathan tearing the room apart to start again? It's possible, of course. But it feels like much more than that. This room, it feels like desperation. Like a frantic search has taken place. Like fear.

Finn scrubs a hand across his eyes.

He's imagining things, surely. The house has worked its way inside his head, and he is seeing drama where there is none to be found. Nathan Blake is no trained craftsman, he tells himself. The restoration has been haphazard because he has come here with no plan. Likely, Nathan was overwhelmed by the size of the task he had taken on. Any sane man would be. There is nothing more to it than that.

But the thought gnaws at him. Reminds him that this is a house full of things that hide. And as he returns to the fallen bricks of the fireplace, the thought circles through Finn's mind without pause, telling him this is not about a restoration at all.

CHAPTER TWENTY-SEVEN

Nathan pokes his head into the dining room. Theodora is sitting at one end of the table with Jenny. Thomas lolls in the nurse's arms, mercifully quiet. Nathan watches his daughter bring a spoonful of stew to her mouth. He has been trying his best not to let her see that anything is wrong. Suspects he is doing a rather terrible job of it.

"All right, Thea?" he asks.

She nods. Dips her spoon into the bowl for another mouthful.

Nathan flashes her a smile that he knows doesn't reach his eyes, then pulls the door closed. Eating with his daughter would have been wise, he supposes, but he cannot stomach the thought of food right now. Perhaps he will force something down later with Eva and her husband, at whatever ungodly hour those creatures of the night eat their supper.

He makes his way towards the parlour, and the dreary account book he had left in there. He knows he ought to have accompanied Edwin back into the village on another search for Harriet. But really, such a thing has begun to feel futile. Harriet is not in the village; of that he is certain. And wherever she has run away to, she has done her best to make sure she is not found. Besides, now Finn has set to work on the fireplace, Nathan feels a strange need to be here. To ensure he is on hand to cut off any questions that may arise.

When he steps into the parlour, he finds Julia waiting. He freezes in the doorway.

"Eva let me in." She rises from the armchair as he steps tentatively into the room.

"I did not hear the door."

"She must have seen me coming. She opened the door before I could knock." Somewhere distantly, Nathan tells himself to remind Eva of Holland's warning about having Julia in the house. But a part of him is glad she is here.

When he doesn't speak, she says, "No word on Harriet?"

"No. I'm afraid not."

"I asked around the village again this afternoon. No one has seen her."

"Thank you. I appreciate your help." Nathan tugs edgily at the hem of his waistcoat.

A faint smile flickers on the edge of her lips. "Do you?"

"Yes," he says. And somehow, he means it. He sinks onto the settle.

Julia crosses the room and sits beside him. He is too tired to protest. Too tired to pretend he does not want her here. Too tired to maintain this veneer of anger he feels he ought to put up in her presence.

She is close. Close enough for him to see the gold flecks in her eyes, the loose threads on the hem of her bodice. Close enough to smell the intricate weave of scents on her skin: ash soap and sea and something faintly floral. Her nearness makes his heart quicken. But somehow, this quickening of his heart, it is only partially in fear. Beneath the discomfort is something far warmer. Something far more alluring.

He knows that if Joseph Holland or any of the other spies were to see her at the house, they would both be in danger. But something about her makes him forget himself. And he says, "I'm afraid for Harriet. I ought to have done more to stop this from happening."

"I feel the same," Julia agrees. "I ought to have sought her out more often. Asked how she was faring."

Nathan smiles wryly. "I am sure I did not make it easy for you to come here to see her."

"Well. I know I cannot expect a welcome after all I did to your family."

Nathan doesn't respond. For several moments, they sit in a stilted silence, filled by the dull crackle of the fire in the grate.

"The other day on the beach," Nathan begins carefully, "you rushed away when you saw Joseph Holland. Why?"

Julia looks at him intently for a moment, as though trying to determine the meaning behind his question. Perhaps trying to determine how much to share. "I am not sure I trust him," she says finally. "There are rumours about him."

"What kind of rumours?"

Julia smiles crookedly. "I am no fool, Mr Blake. And neither are you. I am sure you know what rumours I am referring to."

Nathan nods faintly. He knows there is little point in pretending. If he wants Julia to be open with him, he needs to do the same for her. "They say Joseph Holland is spying for the government," he says.

"Indeed."

Nathan stares into the fire, letting his eyes grow glassy. It seems his fears about Holland's role being uncovered are not unwarranted. Does Julia have any inkling of what Highfield House is being used for? Would she tell him if she did? Would she even care?

He rubs his eyes. He cannot find space in his mind for these concerns right now. Right now, he does not want to doubt Julia, or sift through everything she says in a desperate search for the truth.

Right now, he just wants to be in her company.

"I hope you are not involving yourself in the Rising," he says gently. "I would hate to see you in danger at the hands of Holland and his kind." And his fear for her safety is real; goes far beyond his wariness over what she might be entangled in.

"It makes little difference if I am involved in the cause or not," says Julia. "My family are known Jacobites. I am aware Holland is keeping a close eye on me. And I'm sure there are others who are doing the same. I just have no thought of who they are."

"Be careful," he says. "Please."

Julia's eyes soften as they meet his. "I will. Nathan, I…" Before he can make sense of what she is doing, she reaches out and puts a hand to his wrist. Panic courses through him at the unexpected contact. He flinches violently, tossing her hand away.

She leaps to her feet and backs away. "I'm sorry," she splutters. "I'm sorry."

Regret seizes him. "Forgive me," he says hurriedly. "You took me by surprise, is all." The half-truth stings, but it is easier than honesty. He has no thought of how he would even begin to explain his fear to another person. What sane man is so adverse to another's touch? What would Julia think of him if she knew?

Nathan hears the click of the front door and hurries out of the parlour. He had not expected Edwin back so soon, and wonders if he has news. Harriet is standing in the entrance hall, her husband's hand wrapped tightly around her upper arm, as though to prevent her from escaping again. She is barefoot and shivering, wrapped in Edwin's greatcoat, her hair wet and tangled down her back. A long, thin cut scars one cheek. Nathan is not sure if he is relieved at the sight of her or horrified by the state she is in.

"Where have you been, Harriet?" he demands. "What on earth has happened?"

At the sound of the door, Eva hurries down the stairs, Finn at her shoulder. Harriet's gaze shifts between them. "I…"

"The truth," Edwin hisses, shaking her arm forcefully. "Tell them everything you told me." His gaze snaps to Mrs Brodie as she hurries in from the kitchen. "Prepare hot water for a bath."

"Yes sir." The housekeeper disappears back down the passage.

Harriet's eyes linger on Julia, who is hovering behind Nathan, careful to keep her distance. "Your brother. Michael." Her voice is cold and expressionless. "He wanted to re-join the rebels. At Lesbury Common… I said I would help him…"

"You were with Michael?" Julia's eyes widen. "He left? He's re-joined the army?"

Harriet looks down. "We were caught by dragoons. He… Michael was killed."

Julia makes a sound from her throat, presses a hand to her mouth.

Nathan feels something twist in his belly. But he has no thought of whether it is empathy for Julia, or the knowledge that once again her family has put his in danger. This news is a reminder of what he has allowed himself to forget all too easily: that the Mitchells cannot be trusted. And this, he thinks, this is why he cannot allow himself to get close to Julia. This is just another in a long line of reasons why he cannot allow these feelings he has for her to turn into anything at all.

"What happened?" Julia coughs. "Where is he?"

"I hardly think that's of consequence right now," Edwin snaps, a firm hand on Harriet's arm guiding her towards the staircase.

Julia grabs Harriet's wrist before Edwin can whisk her away. "What happened, Harriet?" she asks, her voice rattling. "Please tell me. How did he die? Are you hurt? What did—"

"Leave," Edwin tells her firmly. He pushes past Eva and Finn as he marches Harriet up the staircase.

Julia looks questioningly at Nathan. He swallows. "Edwin is right," he says after a moment. "It's best that you leave. I'm sorry."

Her eyes flash. And she charges out of the house, as though her hatred for his family is suddenly far more intense than his loathing of hers.

CHAPTER TWENTY-EIGHT

Edwin banks up the fire in the bedroom and guides Harriet towards it, his grip on her arm unyielding. Mrs Brodie elbows open the door and carries in a pot of boiling water. She tips it carefully into the tin bathtub she has set up in the corner of the room. She tops it up with cold water from the washbin. "I've some more water on the range now, Mr Whitley. Shouldn't be too long."

Edwin nods brusquely.

Once the door has clicked closed behind her, he pulls his coat from Harriet's shoulders and tosses it on the bed. "Get in the bath." His voice is low.

Harriet shivers. "I wish to see Thomas." She keeps her eyes down, unable to look at him.

"He's with Jenny." Edwin folds his arms. "Get in the bath," he says again.

"I wish to hold him. I missed him." It's true, she realises. She wants her son. Needs him. At least, she needs the comfort of his warm body pressed against her own. Her infant child feels like the only person in the world not yet capable of judging her.

Edwin snorts. "Curious that you only feel such things now."

She does not press the issue. She knows he is right. Wordlessly, she reaches down to open her shortjacket, but her cold, stiff fingers fumble with the laces. Edwin pushes her hand aside and steps close to her, working at the lacing down her chest.

"I can do it myself," Harriet coughs, suddenly remembering the coin pouch inside her bodice. She turns away, fumbling with the last of the eyelets. She pushes her shortjacket and dress from her shoulders, hiding the pouch in the pile of her clothing as she lowers it to the floor. She unlaces her stays and wrestles off her shift, the damp fabric clinging to her skin. Instinctively, she wraps her arms around herself, hiding her naked body from her husband. But when she glances Edwin's way, his eyes are fixed to the floor.

She steps into the bathtub and draws her knees to her chest, shivering in the thin puddle of water. Edwin takes the jug from the washbin and comes to kneel beside her. He scoops up the bathwater and pours it over her bare back. The feel of it is faintly soothing, but her husband's wordlessness chills her. He pours another jug of water over her shoulders, lifting her damp hair from her neck. For a moment, he leans close, his lips at her ear. But then he seems to decide against speaking. He puts the jug down and gets to his feet, moving across the room to stand by the window.

When a knock comes, he opens the door and takes the fresh pan of hot water from Mrs Brodie. He pours it into the bathtub, then lets it clatter to the floor. The sound echoes, making the muscles in Harriet's neck tighten. Hot water swells around her legs, but she can find no comfort in it. Everything feels so colourless and cold. Michael, dead. Anne in the hands of the redcoats. The Jacobites in the village spying on the house, their suspicions heightened by her own foolish behaviour.

"That's enough," Edwin says after a few more minutes. "Get out."

Harriet stands slowly and climbs out of the bathtub, refusing his hand. She trails water across the floorboards as she reaches hurriedly for her robe. She slides it on over her wet shoulders, barely bothering to dry herself. The need to cover herself feels far more pressing.

For long moments, Edwin stares at her, as though trying to see behind her eyes. "Why?" he says finally. "Is this whole sorry escapade because I did not agree to you travelling to Paris?"

Harriet says nothing.

"This family is under enough suspicion," he hisses. "Did you stop for a moment to think how your actions might affect me? Your brother and sister? Your son?" He shakes his head. "Lord only knows who saw you creeping across the island barefoot and soaking wet. I hardly dare imagine how suspicious the villagers will be if they hear about it."

"No one saw—"

"Quiet!" Edwin's palm flies to her cheek, silencing her lie. She reels backwards with the shock of it. Tears well behind her eyes at the sudden sting, but she refuses to let them fall. She stares him down with hard eyes.

At the sight of her unshed tears, Edwin's lips part. Harriet knows he has never seen anything close to such emotion from her.

But there is no reaction from him. No vague sense of regret, or even satisfaction, at his raising his hand to his wife. He is as emotionless and wooden as he always is.

She has made the right decision, she thinks, in not telling him all that Tom Cordwell had said to her. If this is what happens when she opens her mouth, she will keep to herself the fact that somehow, Cordwell already knew what the house was being used for. His finding her in the water this evening may have confirmed the suspicions the Jacobites have about this family, but it was not what had sparked them. Clearly, there are people in the village who have been watching Highfield House since long before she involved herself in Michael Mitchell's plans.

Harriet turns and walks towards the door.

"Where do you think you're going?" Edwin demands, suddenly sparking to life.

"I'm going to my workroom." Harriet doesn't look at him. The need to escape the bedchamber is suddenly overwhelming. A physical ache.

"No. I'll not have you leave my sight. And you are not to go anywhere near that workroom." Edwin paces across the room, blocking her path to the door. "I gave you your liberties, Harriet. I allowed you to keep painting. Allowed you meet with your artist friends. And this is how you repay me?"

Harriet closes her eyes, forcing her tears away. This is to be expected, she supposes. But Edwin will sleep. He will work. He cannot keep watch over her every hour of every day. And she will sneak back into her workroom then. Bring those moonlit scenes to life.

But he watches her, and for a horrible, fleeting second, it is as though he can read her thoughts. Perhaps it is not surprising. What other thoughts would she have other than ones of rebellion, railing against this harshest of punishments?

Edwin throws open the door and strides down the stairs.

"Where are you going?" Harriet dares to ask.

He does not respond. She races down the staircase after him, her robe clinging to her damp legs.

Edwin charges into her workroom, the door thumping loudly against the wall. He grabs at the cloth she has wrapped her brushes in and they clatter to the floor. He reaches down to gather them. With his spare hand, he snatches her half-finished painting from the easel. Harriet makes a desperate grab at her canvas, but Edwin charges past her into the passage.

"Where are you going?" she cries. "Edwin. Please. *Please.*"

She chases him into the parlour, where a fire is roaring in the grate. He flings her brushes into the flames. Harriet flies at him, trying to grab the painting, but he shoves her back.

The canvas is large. Too large to be swallowed by the fireplace in one mouthful. But Harriet watches in horror as Edwin feeds the painting into the fire, and lets the flames burn away the moon. Her stomach dives, but she has gone far beyond tears now. Hatred burns inside her. And for a fleeting, foolish second, she wishes she was back on the road to Alnwick, hiding in the undergrowth, with nothing and no one around. For right now, the thought of sleeping, waking, breathing, next to this man feels like a trial she would rather not survive.

Edwin stares glassy-eyed into the flames. "I thought to allow you to take the trip," he says distantly. "Before you ran away. I decided it might do you some good. I thought once the restoration was done, you and I could go to Paris together and you could meet with these sponsors." His words strike her. He is lying, surely. After all, he had sent Eva to try and talk her out of meeting with the Baillieus. "Your brother and sister," he continues, "they both convinced me this was a fine opportunity for you. I did not want you to miss out on such a chance on account of me."

Harriet swallows hard. She cannot look at her husband in case she sees something in his eyes that tells her he is speaking the truth.

Edwin watches the corner of the frame splinter into the fire. The canvas curls like a slow-moving wave. He looks back at her with a faintly bewildered look. "What was I to have done, Harriet? Tell me."

She doesn't reply. Just stares into the fireplace until the last of her painting is gone.

Nathan closes the door of the study and leans his back against it. He closes his eyes, a sick feeling in the pit of his stomach. He is not sure if it comes from the thought of whatever punishment Edwin is inflicting on his wayward wife, or the look in Julia's eyes when she had run from Highfield House. He can feel the ghost of her touch on his arm, as though her fingers are still pressed to his skin.

He goes to the desk chair and opens his account book. He stares down at it blankly, numbers swimming in front of his eyes. His unease ought to have settled now Harriet has returned. But the sight of his sister appearing at the house in such a state had done little to calm his anxiousness. Of all the things he had imagined her doing, running off to assist the Jacobite cause had not been one of them. He cannot imagine what could have driven her to do such a thing. Was it merely an act of rebellion? Or has Harriet become even more of a stranger to them than he had imagined?

There is a knock at the door of the study. "Come in." He looks up, surprised to see Finn. He wears rolled-up shirtsleeves, with the grime of the broken fireplace clinging to the linen. Light-brown hair is coming loose from his queue, his shirt open at the neck.

"I'm sorry you had to witness all that business with Harriet," says Nathan, before Finn can speak. "I'm sure you and Eva are in quite some hurry to get home. Are you finished with the fireplace?"

For a second, Finn does not reply. He hesitates for a moment, and his eyes shift, as though seeming to change his mind about whatever it is he has come here to say. Then he closes the door behind him. Folds his arms across his chest.

"Nathan," he says, "what are you really doing in this house?"

CHAPTER TWENTY-NINE

"What do you mean? Edwin and I are restoring it." Nathan forces a laugh. "As you can see, I'm not much of a handyman."

"This is not about a restoration." His guess is not wrong; Finn can tell by the look in Nathan's eyes. It's a look of defeat; fear, perhaps. It is mere seconds before his shoulders slump forward. He rubs his eyes and plants his elbows against the pages of the ledger opened in front of him.

"I'm searching for something. A document. Apparently my mother hid it somewhere in the house. And now its owner wants it back."

Finn leans his back against the door. Keeps his voice low. "Its owner. And who is that?"

"Henry Ward."

Finn nods slightly. He had expected the name before Nathan had spoken it. It feels like a piece falling into place. He takes a chair from the corner of the room and plants it in front of Nathan's desk. Sits. "What's the document?" he asks.

Nathan sighs. "A letter, I'm told. Kept safe in a brass box. Revealing the Jacobite leanings of someone high up in the Whig government."

"A dissenter," says Finn. "That's not so uncommon, surely."

"Ward says this letter has blackmailing power—particularly now the Whigs are in such a position of strength. Far more so than they were twenty years ago when Ward would first have received the letter." Nathan drums his fingers edgily against the arm of his desk chair. "I don't know who the letter speaks of. Or how Ward got it. But he seems certain that the government would go to great lengths to keep this a secret."

Finn nods slowly. So this is how Ward plans to offer his crew immunity: by blackmailing the authorities and threatening to reveal this damaging information.

None of this is a surprise to him—he knows how shrewd and calculating Henry Ward is. But fearing Ward had his eye on the Blakes was one thing. Knowing it for certain makes him distinctly afraid.

"Apparently he gave the letter to my mother to keep safe," says Nathan. "And now he wants it back." He rubs his eyes. "I do not know if Ward truly ever owned such a letter, or if these are just fanciful stories."

"There's every chance he's telling the truth," Finn says. "Ward was a respected privateer. He was active in the war at the end of last century, so someone may well have shared information with him about the French and their Jacobite allies."

"You sailed with him."

"Aye. For a short time." Finn hopes he does not ask any more questions. Nathan's assumption, surely, is that he sailed with Ward as a young man—not as the boy he was when he had fought with and killed Oliver Blake. "Ward's a dangerous man," he says. "But he's not one to lie."

"I see."

Finn can tell this was not news he wished to hear. For long moments, Nathan turns to look through the undrawn curtains. The night is black and starlit, the sea invisible behind the glass.

"Ward was adamant that I return to Lindisfarne and recover this letter," says Nathan. "He's made threats. Against me. And my daughter."

Little wonder Nathan Blake looks so haunted. Finn thinks of the way Ward had spoken so brassily about offering his crew immunity; spoken as though he already had the letter in his hand. No doubt he has made promises to his crew; promises he will struggle to keep if the letter is not found. Finn knows how much such a thing will gall a man who prides himself on honour as Ward does. But are these empty threats he has made against Nathan and Theodora? Finn can't be sure. Would Ward's affection for Abigail prevent him from harming her son and granddaughter? Or has that been overridden by his need for this letter? His need to keep his word to his crew, and prove himself a man of honour?

"Who knows about this?" Finn asks. "Who knows the real reason you're here?"

"Edwin knows I'm here looking for the box containing the letter," says Nathan. "But I've told him nothing about Ward. I told him the box contains my mother's jewellery. He doesn't appreciate the seriousness of the situation. He thinks I ought to put an end to the search and concentrate on restoring the house. Eva and Harriet know nothing about it. And I would appreciate it if you did not tell them."

Finn bristles. "You're asking me to keep this a secret from my wife?"

Nathan looks at him squarely. "I'm not asking you. I'm telling you."

The sharp look in Nathan's eye catches Finn off guard. It's a look of hardness he has not seen from Eva's brother before. And for a horrifying second, Finn is afraid he has been recognised. It's an irrational thought, of course—the night of Oliver's death, he and Nathan had been boys. This is just the house playing tricks.

"Eva could handle the truth," Finn says.

Nathan passes a quill between his fingers. "Perhaps. But not Harriet. Certainly not after…all this." He waves a hand in the vague direction of Harriet and Edwin's bedchamber.

Nathan reaches down and pulls open the cabinet beneath his desk. He produces a bottle of brandy and two glasses. The bottle is ornate, old-looking, and Finn wonders if it has been here since Abigail had lived in the house. Perhaps a bottle Henry Ward had brought her. Nathan fills the cups and hands one to Finn.

He gulps it down. It's rich and fragrant, smooth on his tongue. Far better than the moonshine he usually tosses back on Longstone.

Nathan leans back in his chair as he drinks. And that look in his eyes, it is not a threat, or recognition, Finn realises. It is complete and utter exhaustion. Finn knows all too well what it's like to be pursued by Henry Ward. Knows the stress of trying to protect those he loves.

The stress of trying to keep a secret.

It's almost a relief to share this after so many harrowing months. And while Finn Murray is not the man he had imagined unloading all this on, Nathan can't deny that speaking of it makes the weight upon his shoulders a scrap more manageable.

"It was not supposed to be like this, with the whole family here," he says. "I thought it would just be Edwin and me. I thought we'd come up here and I'd find the damn letter, and that would be the end of it. Then I could sell the house and be done with it. I did not expect Edwin to bring Harriet and Thomas with him. And I certainly did not expect Eva and my daughter…" He scrubs a hand over his eyes. "I told my sisters I was coming up here to restore and sell the house. Once they were here, I had to carry on with the charade."

Nathan knows he ought to have told them the truth. But how could he have admitted to the trouble he was in? He is supposed to be the head of this family—and all he has done is drive them into financial ruin. Secure Harriet into an unhappy marriage and turn Eva wild. He feels like an utter failure.

The first letter from Ward had arrived at Nathan's office several months ago. Ward had introduced himself as an acquaintance of Nathan's mother. Had expressed his sadness at Abigail's passing. Nathan had vaguely recognised Henry Ward's name. A distant figure from a forgotten childhood on Holy Island. He wondered how Ward had come to hear of his mother's death, but did not dwell on it. No doubt she and Ward had shared acquaintances who had passed on the news.

Ward had explained, in polite and reasonable terms, of the valuable letter he had given Abigail for safekeeping more than twenty years earlier, sealed in a brass box to protect it.

And then: *Some months before your mother's death, I managed to contact her through my London solicitors, after searching for her for many years. She assured me the letter was securely deposited in the safe I had opened under my name at the Bank of England.*

I returned to London last week after several years abroad. Imagine my surprise when I discovered the letter was not in the safe.

The tone of Ward's letter had grown increasingly threatening. *I struggle to believe Abigail would have lied to me on such an issue. Therefore, Mr Blake, I must ask you if you know of the whereabouts of this most valuable of my possessions.*

Nathan scrawled back a short reply. He knew of no such letter, and had certainly not taken it from a safe at the Bank of England. Ward's correspondence was bewildering. Nathan had never known his mother to own anything valuable enough to be stored in a bank safe—and surely something as insubstantial as a letter could not have the immense value Henry Ward attributed to it. He wondered at the truth of the issue. Surely there had to be more in this locked box than a mere piece of paper. Jewels, perhaps. The pirating treasures he had imagined Henry Ward collecting back when he was a child. In any case, he told Ward, everything his mother had owned in those years she had left behind at Highfield House the night they had made their hurried escape. Of this, he was certain. The night they had fled, Abigail had taken nothing but the clothes on her back. Her hands had been far too full of her screaming children to have taken Ward's precious box with her, no matter how valuable it might have been.

The next letter came quickly, Ward's accusation thinly veiled. *Once again, I am certain Abigail would have had no cause to lie to me. If, however, the letter remains at Highfield House, as you so adamantly believe, I humbly request you return to Lindisfarne at your earliest convenience and retrieve it…*

It was a request Nathan had no time for. He was struggling to rebuild his business, struggling with a daughter plagued by nightmares. Traipsing up to Lindisfarne at the whim of this man from his mother's past was not something he was willing to entertain.

But when Ward turned up on the doorstep of his Islington townhouse, Nathan knew he did not have the luxury of ignorance. He had recently sold the family home, and knew it was no easy thing for a stranger to hunt down the address of his rented house on the outskirts of the city. No doubt Henry Ward had put the same effort into finding him that he had put into hunting down Abigail in those months before her death.

"I need that letter," said Ward. "Urgently. It is non-negotiable"—his words highlighted by the pistol tied to his belt, deliberately positioned, Nathan felt sure, to provide him with nothing more than a glimpse of the threat at hand.

"I do not have this letter," he hissed. "If Mother had deposited it in a safe in your name, how would I even have got to it?"

Something passed across Ward's eyes. "The safe was in your name too, as her eldest surviving son. As I suspect you well know."

Nathan blinked. "What?"

Ward hesitated. "Abigail wanted security for you and your sister. She could not bear the thought of you returning to the same financial trouble she was in after your father died. Of course, I respected her wishes. She and I…" He cleared his throat. "Well. Suffice to say the future I had planned with her did not come to fruition."

Nathan frowned. He had had no idea his mother had ever planned a future with a man other than his father, or that she had ever suffered financially. The knowledge was unsettling. After they had left Lindisfarne, Abigail had never shown the slightest interest in taking another husband. Nathan had assumed their finances secure enough for her not to need to. What else had he been wrong about?

"Why would I even think to steal a letter, of all things?" he demanded, rattled at Ward's upturning of his version of the past.

"You seem an intelligent man, Mr Blake. I am sure you can see the value in such a piece of correspondence. If the nation was to find out a covert Jacobite had made it into the upper echelons of the Whig party, their support would weaken considerably. I imagine they would be willing to pay a substantial fee to make sure the knowledge of such a betrayal was not made public."

The back of Nathan's neck prickled. "I am not the kind for extortion."

"I suspect that's the truth," said Ward. "But I also know your business has suffered something of a setback. And an intelligent man like you would know he could fetch a hefty price for a letter of such value. Enough to cover the losses you have incurred of late."

Nathan pressed his shoulders back, trying not to let Ward see his unease. He felt like a child under the thrall of an angry guardian; far from the head of a respectable family he was supposed to be. "If you truly believe I've sold the letter, why are you here demanding I give it back to you?"

Ward smiled thinly. "Because I am hoping you will have the sense to buy it back from whoever you sold it to. And return it to me."

Nathan closed her eyes. "I told you, I know nothing of this letter. If it is not in your safe, it must still be in Highfield House. Or else Mother rid herself of it."

"She would not have done that," Ward said firmly, as if that was the end of the matter. "I'm certain of it. But if you truly believe the letter to still be in the house, then you will go up to Lindisfarne and find it for me." Ward produced a key from his pocket and held it up for Nathan to see. "A small brass box. The lock fits this key. The last I saw of it, Abigail was keeping it in a drawer in her nightstand." He slid the key back into his pocket.

"I'm sorry, Mr Ward," said Nathan, trying hard not to think of how in hell this man knew anything of his mother's nightstand. "But I am afraid this is not my problem."

Ward was silent for a moment. "You have a young daughter, I believe?" The words were spoken warmly enough, but Nathan could see through to the threat beneath. He had been painfully deliberate in keeping Theodora out of sight. And yet somehow, Ward had known of her anyway, just as he had known of the collapse of the business. And just as he had known where to find them.

Nathan felt hot and sick with dread. He wanted to tell Henry Ward he was not the kind of man he could coerce with hollow threats. But he knew that was a lie. He could see the distrust in Ward's eyes. Could tell the man did not believe him when he promised he knew nothing of this precious letter in a box.

Nathan was wracked with fear over what Ward could do to his daughter, to his sisters, to him. And so, with no other choice, he promised he would return to Lindisfarne for the first time in twenty years. Find the box his mother had left behind in her hurry to escape the island.

He told his family he was going north to meet with a new manufacturer. Told them he would be home in a matter of weeks. Surely this damn box would be tucked away in a drawer or cupboard, forgotten about by their mother when she had torn out into the night.

Once on the island, Nathan had done his best to hurry out to the house without any of the villagers seeing him. He had known, even then, before they had branded his family as spies, that his being there would raise questions. And they were questions he had no thought of how to answer.

It was dusk when the hulk of Highfield House loomed between the dunes, a deep shadow, a shape from half-remembered dreams. The sight of it drew him back into all the worst pieces of the past: to burying his father, to being trapped in the priest hole, to his brother's lifeless eyes staring up at the beams of the ceiling. His mother tugging at his hand as they ran across the Pilgrims' Way towards the mainland, water licking at his ankles, knees, thighs.

He had wondered then, as he had trudged grimly towards the house, what bearing Henry Ward had had on his mother's leaving. What had his mother gotten herself involved in all those years ago? Why would she have promised to keep this letter safe for a man like Ward? What was between them? Ward had spoken of them planning a future together—if this was the case, why had Abigail fled Holy Island so impulsively?

As a boy, Nathan had known of the man from the sea who would come to the house. He had met Henry Ward once or twice, but most of his memories of him were hazy, formed by overhearing conversations on the edge of sleep. Now, with Highfield House looming ahead of him, those nights spent listening to Ward's deep laughter felt far more present. Felt like they belonged to something other than the distant past.

Nathan had always assumed their leaving Lindisfarne had come from his mother's grief. Her need to escape the house where her husband and son had died in quick succession. But now he began to wonder if there was more to the story. Was Henry Ward somehow tied into their reason for escape?

He slid the rusty house key from his pocket, dimly aware that he had spent most of the journey, and certainly the entire walk up from the village, with his fingers tight around its cold metal. He would get inside, find the damn box, and suffer through one night in this lonely old place. When he returned to London, he would give the letter to Ward and get him out of their lives. And then start the process of getting the house out of their lives too.

Nathan wondered why he had been so reluctant to sell the place. Until last year, when his business had collapsed, he had not needed the money, and he had always been certain the house was in a state. Selling it had all felt too hard. But at the back of his mind, he could not help but wonder if there was more to it. If it was some misplaced loyalty to his brother that kept him holding on to the place where Oliver had lost his life.

Nathan shook the thought away. Oliver had been a callous bully, and his body had long turned to dust. He deserved no loyalty.

Inexplicably, his heart quickened as he followed the faint path through the long grass leading up to the house. Strange that a track might still be worn into the earth, given two decades had passed since anyone had lived here. He supposed the house was something of a curiosity to the people of Holy Island, lonely and windblown out on Emmanuel Head. No doubt it had had its share of curious eyes pressed to the grimy windows.

Nathan slid the key into the lock, half surprised when the front door opened with little more protest than a loud groan. Ahead of him, the house was dark and cavernous, the air stale and thick as water. As he stepped across the flagstones in the entrance hall, he heard the faint scrabble of unseen mice. In the last light of dusk, he could feel the painted eyes of an ancestor boring into him, the sight of the familiar portrait making the years unwind. Another painting lay on the floor at his feet, its frame in pieces and its hook fallen from the crumbling mortar of the wall.

Nathan pulled a tinderbox and candle from his bag and lit the wick with mildly trembling hands.

It was too dark to search the house properly. Long shadows lay over everything, and the dark was seeping in like liquid. But he felt restless, impatient. He did not want to look too closely at the house they had left behind. He wanted to find that box by lamplight and be saved from having to delve too deep.

With the lamp in one hand, he went first to his mother's old bedchamber and opened the drawer of the nightstand. In spite of his need to find the letter, he was mildly relieved to find Henry Ward had not been correct about her having stored it there. He made his way through the house, opening the cupboards and drawers, and peering under the beds, every glimpse a piece of his old life. Old clothes still hung in the wardrobes; his own boyish trimmed coats and Eva's tiny smock dresses. The sugar loaf hat his mother had worn to church. Plates and bowls with chips in the same places, books that were familiar before he was even old enough to read them. So many years had turned over while this house had lain entombed in the past. In the morning, he would pack up all these old clothes and memories and take them to the church for the charity collection. Start the process of setting time moving again in Highfield House. Because what good was it doing to keep the past locked up in here, poisonous and unbreathable? But among all those old clothes, those old memories, he found no box. No letter.

Finally, exhausted, his instinct drew him back down the passage to his old childhood bedroom. He lay beneath the blankets and their decades-long veneer of dust, his mind refusing to still. He thought of the night Oliver had died. The memory was vivid and bitter, though he had no thought of how much time had distorted it. He remembered the laughter of the men in the parlour floating up the staircase. Somehow, he knew one of the men was Henry Ward; the boy who had fought with Oliver, a member of his crew. Whether a long-buried childhood memory, or a piecing together of this puzzle he had now become entangled in, Nathan was not sure.

The next morning, with bronze light pouring through the windows, he searched and searched. Every cupboard, every drawer, every shelf. If this letter truly was as valuable as Ward claimed, there was every chance his mother had hidden it somewhere more secretive. Beneath a floorboard. Behind a wall panel. Inside an unused chimney, perhaps. And in a place as sprawling as Highfield House, the list of places to hide—or be hidden—was near endless. Impossible to search alone, and with his bare hands.

He went back to London. *A box*, he told Edwin, *containing some of my mother's jewellery. I need to sell it to rebuild the business.* Somewhere in the back of his mind, Nathan knew lying to his brother-in-law was not the wisest course of action. But he knew Edwin considered him weak. Knew that if he told him about Ward, Edwin would insist they fight. Whether in the courtroom, or with pistols on Tothill Fields, Nathan had no thought. And it didn't matter. He had seen the pistol in Ward's belt. *You have a young daughter, I believe?* No. There would be no fighting. With Edwin's carpentry expertise, they would tear the house apart as quickly as possible. Find the box containing the letter. Get Henry Ward out of their lives.

Edwin had jumped at the chance. "About time you did something with that old place, Nate. You'll thank yourself when you sell it." He chuckled. "It will do far more for your business than a measly old box of jewellery."

Nathan tried to hold him back, tell him he had no desire to restore the house, or sell it, or do anything other than burn it to the ground. But Edwin was already running with the idea. Besides, Nathan knew Edwin was right: if he was to have any chance of rebuilding his business, he needed the money that would come from the sale of the house. He would let Edwin do as he wished to the place, as long as he also did all he could to find the letter. Soon Henry Ward would be nothing but a memory and Nathan could begin to rebuild his life.

By this point, his finances were dire, and continuing to rent the house in London while he was unable to work was not an option. But nor was taking his daughter with him to Holy Island with a man like Henry Ward breathing down his neck.

Nathan had not expected Edwin to rent out his home and cart his entire family up to Northumberland.

"Lindisfarne is no place for Harriet," he had tried to argue. "You know how much she loves the city. Why not let her stay in London with Eva and Theodora? Matthew Walton has offered them his empty townhouse."

"Getting away from London will be good for her. She's far too absorbed in that dreadful clique of painters. She could use some time away from the city. Might remind her she's also a wife and mother."

With Harriet present, Nathan had had no choice but to play up the lie that he was in the house to restore it. His cover story had become a reluctant truth.

With a bowed head, he tells Finn everything. His new brother-in-law knows Henry Ward, of course. Knows what he is capable of. And Nathan is sure that, unlike Edwin, Finn appreciates the gravity of the situation. Finn nods along slowly to the story, bringing his glass to his lips with almost rhythmic regularity. He is quiet for several moments after Nathan finishes speaking. Turns his glass around in his hand.

"I saw Ward's ship passing Longstone not long after Eva first came to stay with me," he says finally. "Was that when he first returned to Northumberland?"

"I believe so," says Nathan. "I told him I would need longer than I initially thought to find the letter. He turned up at the house a few weeks after we arrived, hounding me to produce it. I asked him not to come here again. I told him I would leave word at the village tavern the moment I found the letter."

Finn taps his fingers against the side of his glass, his brow creased in thought. "And he agreed to that?"

"He did. But his ship has been moored in front of the house for the past few weeks. A means of threatening me, I presume."

Finn nods slowly. Nathan appreciates his calmness. It goes some way to settling the deep panic that had taken root inside him when Ward had first appeared at his door. When he had first decided to keep this a secret.

"Your family has never been suspicious?" Finn asks.

"Eva has been out on Longstone with you, and Harriet is far too absorbed in her own world to take note of what's going on around her. I told Edwin that Henry Ward was just a potential buyer interested in seeing the house." He leans back in his chair and rubs his eyes. "As you can see, I've torn the place apart. There is no letter. I'm sure Ward knows that by now. I think he is just doing all this to punish me for that."

"Are you sure your mother didn't take it with her when she left the house?" asks Finn.

"I'm certain. I remember that night like it was yesterday. Mother had nothing with her."

"She could have carried the letter in her pocket. Or inside her stays."

"Ward gave it to her in a locked brass box," says Nathan. "I suppose it's possible that she might have smashed the box open and taken the letter with her in her pocket. But I suspect she got rid of it before we left. Perhaps she did not want something so inflammatory in her possession." He sips his brandy. "I told all this to Ward. He did not seem to want to hear it."

Finn smiles wryly. "I can imagine. He's lured a shipful of men into his pirating crew with the promise of the immunity that letter will give them."

Nathan curses under his breath. Having Henry Ward in his shadow is bad enough; he had not stopped to consider he might have an entire crew at his disposal.

Finn looks out the window, scratching his bristled chin. "Ward said nothing of this to Eva when he met her aboard his ship."

"I told him I wished to keep it from the rest of the family," says Nathan. "It seems he has respected my wishes."

Finn nods, clearly unsurprised. "He has a strange sense of honour. Some decency about him. But he'll not hesitate to punish people he thinks have deceived him."

Nathan stares into the bronze halo at the bottom of his glass. "I've not deceived him. But perhaps my mother did."

"Aye. And I suspect that's the last thing Ward wishes to hear."

"Yes," says Nathan. He opens his mouth to speak, then wavers. "Harriet…" he begins. "I suspect she is…" He catches Finn's faint nod. "You knew."

"Eva came to suspect it, aye."

Nathan shifts uncomfortably in his chair. A part of him had been hoping Finn would argue; tell him he is mistaken about Ward being Harriet's father. Not that Nathan had really had any doubts. The resemblance between father and daughter is far too strong to be a coincidence. The knowledge is uncomfortable, but Nathan knows trying to ignore it will do him no good.

He has little doubt now that Henry Ward had had something to do with why they had left Holy Island. Had Abigail been shamed by the villagers for her relations with him? Or had she fled to prevent him from finding out about his child? Perhaps both.

"I've not told Harriet," Nathan says. "I do not want her to know anything about the man. How can it do her any good to know she's that scoundrel's daughter?"

Finn nods. "Let me tell all this to Eva," he says. "She can help. You know she can."

Nathan sighs. "I did not want her involved in this. She was not even supposed to be here. She was supposed to be—"

"In London marrying that toff Walton," Finn finishes tautly. "Aye, I know. But things have not worked out the way you planned. And it sounds as though you could use a little help."

Nathan draws in a long breath. Involving his sister in this was the last thing he had ever wanted to do. But he knows it is too late for that. Eva has already entangled herself with Henry Ward. Besides, perhaps it would do him good to have her input. Eva is intelligent, level-headed. Perhaps she really can be of some assistance.

"All right," he says finally, tossing back the last of his brandy in an attempt to steel himself. "But let me be the one to tell her." He needs the chance to explain. A chance to apologise for his failures. "If she must hear it, I would like her to hear it from me."

Harriet stands motionless outside Nathan's study.

Listen. Observe. Gather the pieces.

Listen. Observe. Gather the pieces.

The raw anger she had felt after watching her painting burn has been sloughed away by her brother's words: *How can it do her any good to know she's that scoundrel's daughter?*

Harriet closes her eyes, pressing her back against the wall to keep her balance. Once again, she has just fragments of the story. But those fragments are enough.

How many people have sought to keep this a secret from her? How many people know the truth of who her father is? Nathan and Finn. Eva too?

She has no idea who this Henry Ward is. The scoundrel. Faceless— but she has a name. Precious pieces of the story.

The floor creaks in Nathan's study and Harriet darts across the hallway into her bedroom. The tin bath still sits in front of the dying fire, the pile of her wet clothes beside it. Michael's coin pouch she has tucked beneath her mattress.

She goes to the desk in the corner of the room and pulls paper and an ink pot from the top drawer. Dips her quill into the ink and begins to write words that at once mean nothing and everything to her:

Come at once to Highfield House. Letter has been found.

What this letter is, she has no thought of. She has caught just pieces of Nathan and Finn's conversation. But those pieces are of infinite value.

She signs the letter with her brother's name. Throws a dress on over her nightshift and hunts around the room for her cloak.

CHAPTER THIRTY

Eva knocks on the side door of the curiosity shop. It's late—far too late to be traipsing alone across the island. But Finn has finally dropped into an exhausted sleep, and Eva knows Nathan's stubbornness would never allow him to visit Julia. In spite of all Julia has done, Eva is more than a little ashamed at the way her family sent her on her way after hearing of her brother's death. When had they become so heartless?

For a long time, there is silence. Eva steps around the corner to peer through the dark windows, the globe of light from her lantern reflected back at her. She squints. Is that movement in the darkness of the shop? Or is it just her imagination? She darts a glance over her shoulder, wary of eyes upon her.

Just as she is about to begin the unnerving walk back to the house, she hears the door creak open. Julia's eyes are red rimmed and swollen, a tatty green shawl draped around her shoulders. Her curls hang messily around her face. At the sight of Eva, she wraps her arms about herself tightly, an almost protective gesture.

"Have you come here to criticise me?" she snaps. "Blame my family for the trouble Harriet got into?"

Eva absorbs her sharpness. "I've come to see if you are all right."

Julia lets out a breath, shaking her head incredulously.

"I'm sorry," says Eva. "I'm sure that's a foolish question." Julia stays planted in the doorway, making it clear an invitation to enter will not be forthcoming. Eva shifts the lamp to her other hand. "I am sorry about your brother. And I'm sorry for the way Edwin and Nathan treated you this evening."

Julia snorts. "I thought you despised me as much as they do."

"Nathan does not despise you," says Eva. "Believe me."

Julia lowers her eyes. A ginger cat appears from behind her and she bends down to scoop it into her arms. She smooths the cat's fur for a moment, lost in her own thoughts. "In the morning, I need to go to Longstone and tell Angus what happened to Michael," she says distantly. "I'd appreciate it if you didn't say anything to him. I would like to be the one to tell him."

Eva nods. "Of course. And I'm sorry. I ought to have told you how often Michael was leaving the island."

Julia shakes her head, her eyes softening a little. "It was not your fault, Eva. It was not your job to keep watch over him."

"Angus will go to London?"

"I suspect so. It's clear by now that Hugh is not coming back." Julia speaks in a thin, guarded voice that Eva suspects is only just keeping her grief at bay. She can only imagine how Julia must feel: one brother dead, one missing, one about to flee into the city.

"I'm sorry," she says again. Her sympathy feels hollow, empty. "If there is anything you need…" She trails off, Julia's closed expression letting her know she is the last person she will come to with her needs. "I'll leave you be," Eva says finally. "But you know where to find us."

Julia nods.

As she is about to close the door, Eva turns back suddenly. "Julia," she says hesitantly. "Do not give up on Nathan."

Julia raises her eyebrows, clearly caught off guard. "I would have thought I was the last person you wanted around your brother."

Eva hesitates. "Well. The way he is around you… it's a rare thing. What I think has little to do with it."

Julia frowns. But she nods slightly. Doesn't speak. Just closes the door, making it clear the conversation is over.

Harriet presses herself against the stone wall of the apothecary, holding her breath as her sister passes on her way back to the house. When she is sure Eva has not seen her, she hurries towards the tavern.

Lamplight spills out onto the cobbles, along with the soft murmur of voices, punctuated by a loud laugh. Harriet pulls up the hood of her cloak and steps inside. Her heart is quick, but somehow, this piece of knowledge about her father, and his unexpected nearness, has allowed her to find some hidden reserve of courage.

The place is sparsely lit, with the hearth smouldering orange. A few men cluster in corners, chatting in low voices beneath curls of pipe smoke, but Harriet is relieved to find the tavern largely empty. Surely if she is seen in such a place, it will raise far more questions than her rescue at the hands of Tom Cordwell. She approaches the bar with her head down. Hands the folded page to the barkeep. "A message," she says. "For Mr Ward."

She holds her breath, hoping the man will not ask for more information. A look in his eyes tells her he recognises her, but he does little more than nod. Perhaps the mention of this Mr Ward's name has encouraged him into silence.

Perhaps he has learnt well enough not to ask questions.

Nathan takes the telescope outside. He needs to escape the house and the poisonous air the last few hours have filled the place with. Needs the calmness of the night sky to ease the shame of his unearthed secrets, the stress of his predicament. The memory of the anger in Julia's eyes as she had charged away from the house.

He finds a flat patch of earth behind the manor, away from the lights of the mainland. He sets the telescope up on its stand, angling it towards the sky. Mars is at its brightest from now until Christmas, and he hopes to examine it through the glass. Let the enormity of the universe, the mystique of distant planets, quieten his racing thoughts.

Footsteps in the dark make him turn. On edge, he whirls around. Somehow, he is not surprised to see Julia emerging from the dunes.

"You," she hisses, jabbing a finger in his direction. Her curls are untamed, whipping around her face like bracken blown wild in a storm.

In the glow of her lantern and the sparse light spilling from the house, he sees the clutter of emotions on her face. "You act so damn self-righteous. But you're no better than I am. In fact," she snaps, "you're worse. I might have deceived you to save Angus and Michael's lives, but at least I have some damn compassion in me. My brother has just been murdered, and all you can do is let Harriet's husband order me from the house?" Her eyes are wide and tearful. "Do you not think I have a right to know how my own brother died?" Her voice wavers. "I have no thought of what has even happened to his body. I cannot even bury him. Give him a proper farewell."

For several moments, Nathan doesn't speak. Everything she has said is right, and he can think of nothing to say but a meagre, watery apology. He can imagine how little good that will do. Julia lets out a frustrated breath and turns on her heel. And all Nathan can think about is how much he does not want her to leave.

Impulsively, his hand shoots out and snatches hers. The gesture surprises himself as much as it does her—that searing jolt up his arm, hot and cold at once, a flood of goosebumps over his skin. And the feel of her, it is not unpleasant, he realises. It is not unpleasant at all. But it is almost painfully overwhelming, and he lets his hand fall.

"Please don't go," he hears himself say.

For a moment, Julia is frozen, lips parted, eyes wide. Nathan takes a step towards her. "I am sorry about your brother," he says. "I truly am. And I am sorry for letting Edwin send you away like that." Shame churns inside him.

She swallows. Nods.

Nathan's heart is thundering with the remnants of the contact, and with the knowledge that he has only just allowed himself to admit to: that he wants to be around her. That he wants her close to him.

Julia scrubs away a stray tear, wind off the sea blowing hair across her eyes. "I'm glad you are using the telescope," she says finally. Her lips tilt upwards slightly. "I thought you planned to return it."

Nathan gives her a sheepish smile. "Well. It's a fine piece. It would be a shame to let it go to waste." He bends, training the barrel across the sky until he captures the faint red eye of Mars. "Here." He nudges her towards the telescope. "Look."

Julia bends. Looks through the eyepiece for a moment. He can see her back and shoulders rising and falling with slightly quickened breath.

"Mars is at its brightest for the next two months," Nathan tells her. "If you look carefully, you can just make out the dark spots on its surface. Huygens spoke of them when he first depicted the planet last century."

"You know a lot about this," says Julia.

"A little. My father taught me when I was a lad."

She stands and turns back to Nathan. There is a ghost of smile on her lips at his use of the Northumbrian vernacular. It disappears so quickly he is not sure if he imagined it. "I'm sure it was Michael's fault that Harriet got involved in his business," she says. "But I just want you to know that I knew nothing of it." She looks down. "For whatever that's worth."

Nathan nods shortly. He believes her, he realises. "Well. For whatever it's worth, I do not imagine Harriet would have taken much convincing." He clears his throat. "Mars will get brighter as it gets closer to dawn," he says. "I am sure it's of no interest to you. But… I do find looking at the sky makes one's problems a little easier to carry. If you would like to stay…" He shakes his head. "I'm sorry. It was a foolish suggestion. I'm sure you've too much on your mind to—"

"I'd like that a lot," Julia cuts in. Her smile is pale, but this time he knows he is not imagining it. "Thank you."

She cannot be here—at the back of his mind, Nathan knows that. Knows it is only a matter of time before Holland and the other government spies are back at Highfield House. And he has no thought of how deeply Julia is entrenched in the Jacobite cause. Her reaction the day she had seen Holland on the Heugh suggests she has much to hide.

Nathan pushes those thoughts away. He will revisit them again when the sun rises and the stars disappear into the daylight. Because surely, surely, he and Julia will not be spotted together now, so late at night. Surely, just for these few hours, they are safe in this moonless darkness, with their eyes turned to the sky.

CHAPTER THIRTY-ONE

Nathan is surprised when pale dawn begins to push against the bottom of the sky. He had not intended to stay out here all night, but the stars are disappearing into the light now, after moving in their wide arcs towards the horizon.

He and Julia sit side by side on the dunes. So close that from time to time, her shoulder brushes his. He finds himself welcoming the soft jolt it sends through him. Finds himself almost craving it.

Julia lifts the telescope from her lap and brings it to her eye, looking out over the lightening water towards the firebasket her youngest brother is keeping alive. Throughout the night, their discussion had shifted from the stars and planets to the safe ground of their children, to finally touching on their own parallel childhoods on Holy Island. Julia had wanted to speak of her lost brother, Nathan had realised, her stories peppered with brash and headstrong Michael, who could swim across to the mainland and liked to play in the rain. From time to time, she would bring the telescope to her eye to pull in some more of the universe, and its power to make trouble seem distant.

"I ought to get back," she says finally. "I need to collect Bobby from Alice's. The poor lad'll think I've forgotten him."

Nathan can't take his eyes from her. With each minute, the sky grows lighter, and her profile becomes sharper, clearer. He can see the freckles on her cheeks and nose, the stray piece of grass caught in one of her curls.

He gets to his feet, offering her his hand. She takes it as she climbs to her feet, then releases her grip quickly. He has not said a word to her about his difficulty with physical contact. But he can sense she is aware of it, at least on some level.

She hands him the telescope. "Thank you, Nathan. For all of this." Her eyes meet his and he feels a warmth in his chest.

He nods. "Of course. I hope it helped a little."

Julia smiles faintly. "More than you could know." Her look is pointed and meaningful. And where do they go from here, Nathan wonders? The safest thing, he knows all too well, is to turn his back. Put as much distance between himself and Julia as he can. But right now, that does not feel possible.

"Shall I see you back to the village?" he asks.

"No. It's all right." She takes a step closer, and Nathan can feel her breath against his chin, mingling with the cool breeze of morning. A shiver goes through him. "But will you call on me?" She sounds tentative, more uncertain than he has ever heard her before.

He swallows hard. "I will, yes."

Julia flashes him a short smile. Then she turns towards the path that leads back to the village.

At the sound of footsteps, she stops, frozen on top of the shallow dune. There are men coming towards them, Nathan realises sickly, their figures emerging from the early-morning dimness. Men charging towards the house with hunting muskets in their hands.

Nathan recognises Tom Cordwell. Martin Macauley. Two other men from the fishing fleet. All four of them known Jacobites. His heart begins to thunder.

Julia whirls around to face him, panic in her eyes, but something else beneath. Something questioning. "Why are they here?" she demands. "What do they want?"

Nathan shakes his head. "I don't know." It's only a half-truth, of course. But how can he manage otherwise, with four armed men charging towards his house and this look of bewilderment in Julia's eyes?

She rushes down the side of the dune and blocks the men's path. "What do you want with them?"

"Get out the way, Miss Mitchell," Cordwell snorts.

Julia grabs Martin Macauley's arm as he charges past. "What do you want with them?" she repeats.

"What do you think we want?" he says tautly. "Bloody spies, aren't they. Keeping government intelligence at their house. Spies coming and going at all hours. And Tom caught one of them out running messages for Cotesworth."

Nathan's stomach dives. "No. You're wrong. You're—"

Macauley swings the butt of his musket, pounding Nathan in the stomach. He hunches over, gasping for breath, the telescope falling from his hand and thudding dully to the grass. A cry of shock from Julia, but when he looks up, there is no hint of sympathy in her eyes.

"Government intelligence?" she repeats. "Is this true?"

"I..." His moment of hesitation is enough. Because that look of betrayal he sees, Nathan knows it well. He had given her that very same look when he had found her brothers hiding in his attic.

"I trusted you," she hisses. "Even after everything people said about you. I told them they were wrong."

Nathan reaches for her, but she pulls away. "Julia," he manages. "Please. I..."

She shakes her head. Backs away. And she is charging down the path away from the house, without a single look in his direction.

Harriet hears them come to the door. Hears them thunder inside, searching, breaking. Edwin flies out of bed, snatching his pistol from the nightstand and rushing downstairs. Harriet hears more footsteps on the stairs; guesses they belong to Eva and Finn.

She slides out of bed and steps out into the hallway. At the bottom of the stairs, she sees Tom Cordwell, and three—four?—other men with muskets in their hands, shoving their way past Finn in an attempt to get to the parlour. Harriet knows what they want. Last night, as Cordwell had scooped her from the rising water, she had confirmed his suspicions that there are government missives hiding in Highfield House. No doubt they have come here to find them.

It is her doing that has brought these men here, Harriet thinks distantly. She knows she ought to feel shame. Regret. But she cannot quite make herself do so. Because her family had kept the truth of her father from her. And for that, it feels as though they need to be punished. If that punishment comes at the hands of the Jacobites, so be it.

She goes back to the bedroom and dresses slowly, lacing herself back into the bodice and skirts she had only stepped out of a few hours earlier. She feels oddly calm. Oddly detached. Downstairs, she hears the crash of breaking glass, shouts of men.

"You will find nothing," she hears Nathan say. And, "You are mistaken."

"Get out of our house this instant," Edwin demands, his hollow threat punctuated by the dull thud of what she assumes are books being torn from the shelf. There is something oddly enjoyable about this cursed house being ravaged like this, as though the men are only hastening the ruin it has already started to descend into. She wonders if they will find what they are looking for. Nathan can claim they are mistaken all he wants, but Harriet knows that, more often than not these days, there really are government missives tucked away in this house somewhere.

She pulls on her shoes. As she steps out into the passage, she sees the men charging up the staircase, muskets held out into front of them. Her calmness evaporates, and her heart jumps into her throat.

She thinks suddenly of her son. Is afraid for him—a belated reaction, but at least it has come at all. She flies towards the nursery, waiting to be hit, the thunder of the men's footsteps on the staircase rattling around inside her.

Before she can reach the nursery door, a shot breaks through the chaos. The bullet careens into the stone wall of the stairwell, inches above Cordwell's head. Stone sprays out across the steps.

"Stop." It's a voice Harriet doesn't recognise. A voice with far more gravity than Nathan or Edwin's. Cordwell and the other men halt their charge up the staircase and turn back to face him.

Harriet looks past them to the man who had pulled the trigger. He is a stranger. And yet, she feels instinctively that he is anything but. Because somewhere deep inside herself, she knows this is the man she had summoned with the message she had left at the tavern.

She knows this man is her father.

She wraps longs fingers around the banister, feeling strangely unsteady.

The four men hold their muskets out in front of them. Undaunted, her father meets their weapons with his own single pistol. Despite the early hour, he is dressed in a neat maroon justacorps with a row of brass buttons, a fine lace cravat tied at his throat. "Get out," he says. And there is something in his voice that makes the men obey him. Something cold, even, authoritative. Perhaps, with his firing into the wall above Cordwell's head, he has proven himself the only man willing to pull the trigger.

Footsteps thump down the staircase, and in moments, Cordwell and the other men are gone, leaving a weighted silence in their place. One of the paintings in the entrance hall has fallen, another hangs crookedly. Someone shifts their feet, and Harriet hears the crunch of broken glass. In the open doorway of the parlour, she can see books strewn across the floor.

Nathan stands opposite her father at the bottom of the stairs. The look of fear on his face is blatant. Finn has a tight grip on Eva's wrist, and she takes a step backwards, putting as much space between herself and this man as possible. This Henry Ward, he feels like an impossibly imposing presence.

Harriet watches from halfway down the stairs. No one looks at her, acknowledges her. They are all far too entranced by her father. This man is not a stranger to any of them, she realises. Not Nathan, or Eva, or Finn. They all know him, and they all fear him. And not one of them had seen fit to tell her who he was.

Ward looks at Nathan. "Where is the letter?" His words are sharp and measured. Impatient, but not angry. "Give it to me."

"You know I've not found it, Ward," says Nathan. "And I have asked you before to please stay away from this house." There's a thinness to his words, belying his pathetic attempt at forcefulness.

Eva's eyes dart between Finn and her brother, then back to Ward. "What are you talking about?" she demands. "What letter?"

"A very valuable letter your mother took care of for me," Ward tells her, "that your brother seems unwilling to part with."

"There is no letter, Ward," Nathan hisses. "I've torn the whole damn house apart."

"This is why you came to Holy Island?" Eva demands. "At Henry Ward's bidding?"

Harriet lets out her breath. This man is not only known to her brother; he had been the reason they had come to Lindisfarne in the first place. Little wonder Nathan's restoration has been so chaotic—it is all an utter lie.

Before Nathan can manage a word, Ward says, "Is this why you sent for me? To tell me this same sorry story all over again?"

"Sent for you?" Nathan repeats. "I did not send for you."

Ward shoves a crumpled note into his hand. Nathan unfolds it and reads. His face turns blank, pale, and it brings Harriet more than a little satisfaction. Almost absentmindedly, he passes the page to Eva.
As she registers her sister's handwriting, Eva's gaze drifts upward, finding Harriet on the staircase. The horror in her eyes is blatant, but there is confusion there too.

Ward lurches forward suddenly, shoving Nathan back against the wall. "I have had enough of these games, Blake. Just give me what I came for."

"I have nothing to give you," Nathan hisses. "If I did, do you truly think I would have let this go on so long?" Nathan lets out a feverish laugh. "The damn letter does not exist. It is not here. I think it's time you accept that." His voice wavers with forced bravado. "Whatever my mother did with it, she did not keep it safe like she told you she did. Whatever was between the two of you was not what you think it was."

Harriet watches something almost imperceptible pass across her father's eyes. "You know nothing of what was between your mother and me, Mr Blake." She can hear the strain in his voice. Harriet's hand tightens around the banister. She feels oddly invisible, excluded from this conversation between people who, she sees now, are already entangled in each other's lives. And yet somehow, she is at the centre of all this. No longer the ill-fitting piece, but rather, the connecting one.

Ward takes a step closer to Nathan, but Finn steps in front of him, holding a palm flat to his chest, pushing him away. "The letter is not in the house, Ward. Threatening them is not going to change that. Just take your crew back to Nassau and get the hell away from here."

A wry smile appears on Ward's face at Finn's outburst, but it disappears quickly when Edwin whips his pistol out from inside his coat.

It's an almost theatrical gesture, and Harriet has to bite her lip to keep a burst of hysterical laughter from escaping.

"He's right," says Edwin, almost managing to sound threatening. "Get out of our house."

Ward looks at the pistol, then back at Edwin. "I rid your home of those thugs, and this is how you seek to repay me?" Edwin falters. "I was sent for," Ward hisses. "I only came here because I believed the letter had been found." He turns to look at Nathan. "What else was I to think when the note was signed with your name?"

"Nathan didn't send for you," Harriet says suddenly. "I did."

At the sound of her voice, her father turns, noticing her for the first time. He frowns in confusion, pins her with his gaze. It's an intense look, one full of questions. She finds herself returning it.

"Please, Harriet," she hears Eva murmur. "Don't."

Harriet ignores her. She makes her way down the staircase, gripping tightly to the banister.

"Who are you?" Ward asks. "Why did you send for me?"

Harriet swallows. "I need to speak with you."

An odd look comes over Ward's face. Harriet can tell that, somehow, he senses the gravity of this situation. Does he see himself in her, as she does in him? He glances briefly at Nathan, then at Finn. And then he turns back to Harriet and nods without speaking. Makes his way out the open front door.

"Please, Harriet," Eva says desperately. "Please don't go with him." The look on her face is one of blatant dread.

"Why?" Harriet hisses. "What are you so afraid of?"

Eva's lips part. "I..." She falls silent. Take a step closer to her husband. He murmurs something to her that Harriet cannot make out.

She shakes her head. "You knew," she hisses, "didn't you? You knew and you did not think to tell me." She glares at Nathan. "You all knew."

Her brother says nothing.

"Harriet." Edwin takes a step towards her. "Don't." He wraps a hand around her upper arm, but there's a forced gentleness to it, as though he does not want the rest of the family to see the harshness with which he had treated her last night. She pulls easily from his grip.

"Do you not think I have the right to speak to my own father?"

She does not wait for a response. Just turns and walks out the door. And despite the looks of horror and despair that Henry Ward has the power to elicit from her family, not one of them attempts to stop her.

CHAPTER THIRTY-TWO

Henry Ward stands on the edge of the embankment with his back to the
sea, passing his tricorn hat between his hands. Wind ruffles his powdered
hair, lifting a single stray strand from his cheek. For a long time, he looks
at Harriet without speaking.

She stares back at him. A part of her had not truly believed it until
now. But when she looks at Henry Ward, she sees her own straw-coloured
curls, her own hooded blue eyes. That darkness at her edges. And she
feels a greater sense of belonging than she ever has with her husband, or
with her half-brother and -sister.

She glances back towards the house. No one has come after her. Still,
she can practically feel the eyes at the windows. She has no doubt every
one of her family is watching her.

Beneath Ward's open justacorps, she can see the glimpse of the pistol
tucked back into his belt. It feels right that she might be the daughter of
a man with a pistol in his belt. A curious thing though, that he had not
sought to reload it after firing at Cordwell and the other men. Not even
as he had looked down the barrel of Edwin's weapon.

He knows who she is, Harriet can feel that instinctively. But she also
senses that he does not wish to put his suspicions—his knowledge—into
words. In case he is wrong. Or perhaps, in case he is right.

"You are Abigail's daughter," he says finally.

Is he asking or stating a fact? Harriet cannot tell. But she says, "Yes."

"Why did you send for me?" His voice is husky, uneasy, devoid of the commanding tone he had spoken with inside the house.

She swallows, her mouth suddenly dry. Away from her family, she feels suddenly vulnerable. Raw and exposed. "I suspect you know the answer to that."

Ward nods, so faint it is almost imperceptible. He looks wide-eyed and haunted. And what is it that has rattled him so, Harriet wonders? Is it the knowledge of her, or the knowledge that her mother had hidden her away; perhaps fled Holy Island so the two of them might never meet?

"What's your name?" asks her father.

"Harriet. Harriet Whitley."

"Harriet." He speaks her name slowly, tentatively, as though testing himself. He stays planted in the shingle at the top of the beach, barely noticing when the fringe of a wave reaches his boots.

"Did you know about me?" she asks. Her heart quickens in anticipation of his answer.

"No."

"Then she betrayed you as well as me."

"Yes." She hears regret in his voice. "I suppose she did."

"The letter that you and Nathan were speaking of," she says. "What is it all about? What do you want with my family? You have made threats against them?"

Ward rubs his eyes. There is a heaviness to him, Harriet realises. An almost visible weight on his shoulders, as though he is carrying a perpetual strain. A burden he cannot lift. "I know the way it looks," he says. "But these threats. They do not come from me."

She eyes him. "Who do they come from?"

He exhales slowly. "A man I ought never have allowed to remain in my life."

Harriet lets out a short, humourless laugh. "So it is going to be like this, is it? We are to speak in riddles?"

A look of curiosity passes across Ward's eyes, as though he is taken aback by her boldness. He tilts his head, taking her in, contemplating. "You are my daughter," he says, as though finding the courage to speak the words.

Harriet nods, his own frankness stealing her own.

Ward begins to walk along the top of the beach. Wind flutters his open justacorps, making him appear broader, and even more imposing than before. Harriet's eyes are drawn to the sailing vessel sitting at anchor in the sea beyond Emmanuel Head. His ship, she realises now. All these weeks, her father's ship has been visible from the window of her workroom. She finds herself walking beside him.

"Your mother used to have a saying," Ward says, watching his boots as he walks, "that come midnight, all truths would be revealed. She believed we could not hide things forever. That sooner or later, we all grow tired of keeping secrets." He glances sideways at her. "I suspect she thought you were the exception. No doubt she thought she had succeeded in keeping you hidden away." He nods at the longboat beached on the embankment. "I would like to speak with you further," he says carefully. "If you will permit me?"

Harriet glances at her father, then back at the house. Climbing into his longboat, she feels instinctively, will untether her from her family even further. But such a thing no longer feels so frightening. Because just like her mother, her siblings have shown themselves adept at hiding things. And she has had quite enough of being shielded from the truth.

She accepts her father's hand. Allows him to help her over the gunwale. And she feels herself become weightless as the boat rises. Pulls her out to sea.

Book Three:

Midnight Rising

NORTHUMBERLAND, ENGLAND

OCTOBER 1715

CHAPTER ONE

Silence feels safest. The easy way out. Because Julia Mitchell knows all too well that this could be the last time she ever sees her youngest brother.

The sea between Longstone and the mainland is thrashing against the hull of the dory, churned and restless. Pale sunlight ripples over the water, peaking grey and silver. It's a soupy, wintery half light that makes the morning feel closer to dusk. Julia has her hood pulled up over her head, a shawl bundled around her neck. Keeping out the cold, yes, but also preventing her brother from seeing too much of her grief.

Julia looks over at him, but neither of them speak. What is there to say?

Gentle, soft-spoken Angus has been pegged as a dangerous Jacobite, and has little choice but to hide away in London—out of sight of the British army, but also out of reach of his family. Julia knows that if he was to write to her once he reaches the capital, it would put her and her son in danger.

And so: silence. Speaking will take her far too close to tears.

Angus is deliberate in not looking her way, his green eyes fixed to some distant, intangible point on the mainland. Best this way, Julia thinks. Less painful, somehow.

Her body aches with exhaustion. She had not slept a minute last night, upturned by the news of her brother Michael's death at the hands of the redcoats; and then calmed by hours spent with Nathan Blake on the darkened dunes of Emmanuel Head. The two of them had spent the entire night peering through the telescope she had given him, sharing pieces of their lives while the sky glittered overhead.

But those hours, starlit and fragile, they're marked by betrayal now. Because as she had gone to leave Highfield House, the place had been stormed by village Jacobites, with accusations against the Blakes on their lips. Accusations Julia has spent the last three months trying to ignore.

Government spies.

"Keeping government intelligence at their house," Martin Macauley had told her, as he charged towards Highfield House with a musket in his hand. "Spies coming and going at all hours."

How could she have been so blind?

Ever since their arrival on Holy Island almost four months ago, the Blakes have been under suspicion of spying for the government against the Jacobites. Julia had denied and doubted, convinced herself that everyone was wrong. She needed her friendship with Harriet. And perhaps, even more so, she needed whatever this fragile thing was that was simmering between her and Nathan. Had refused to see what was right in front of her eyes.

She feels like the biggest of fools.

The mainland is coming up on them far too quickly, a sorry cluster of sand-coloured buildings shepherded behind thick town walls. The sea drains of colour in their shadow.

Julia has taken Angus up to Berwick in her brothers' fishing boat. It's a longer journey than the quick crossing to Bamburgh, but from here it will be easier to find transport down to London. And then? She cannot think of it.

Angus has already stayed here in Northumberland far too long. The anonymous chaos of London is the only place he will be safe. But Michael's death, so raw in the harsh light of morning, is weighing almost impossibly heavy on her shoulders. Julia does not know if she has the strength to let another of her brothers go.

Angus hands in the sail, allowing Julia to ease the boat towards the jetty. She reaches for his gloved fingers.

"You'll manage on your own?"

Angus smiles, but it doesn't reach his eyes. "Course I'll manage."

Julia's chest aches. Her youngest brother is barely past twenty, and she can't push aside that fierce swell of protectiveness she has always felt towards him.

"There's a part of me that's glad to leave," Angus admits. "With luck I can put this mess behind me and start again."

Julia nods. She knows Angus had never truly wanted to fight for the Jacobite cause. Knows he had been coerced into joining the rebel army by Michael's blind enthusiasm, and the ox plough that is their eldest brother Hugh. Julia has little doubt that, the day her brothers had fired at redcoats at the protest in York, gentle Angus had not been the one to pull the trigger.

"You'll start again, aye," she says, trying for a smile. He deserves it, after all he's been through: three lightless months in the attic of Highfield House, and weeks marooned out on Longstone with a constant eye on the horizon. "And once all this is passed, you'll find me and Bobby again. Hugh as well, perhaps." She cannot keep the waver from her voice. She reaches for the mooring post, forcing down tears.

Angus puts a hand to her shoulder. "Stay here, Jul. There's no need to come into town. Let's not make this harder than it already is."

He's right, of course, but teetering in the boat, they can manage no more than a brief, unbalanced embrace that is over far too quickly. For the best, Julia tells herself. Any longer and her tears will spill. She kisses his bristly cheek. Lowers her eyes.

She feels the boat tilt as Angus steps out onto the ladder of the jetty, but she does not watch him leave. Does not turn as his footsteps echo against the cold morning sky.

He knows where to find her, Julia reminds herself. One day, Angus will return to Holy Island, and they will climb the dunes with wind in their hair, like they did as children.

No. That memory is far too difficult now Michael is gone.

But she clings to that hope of seeing her brother again, as she guides the fishing boat back down the coast to Holy Island. She clings to it as she makes her way through the narrow streets of Lindisfarne, the maze of stone silver-grey in the weak late-morning light. The sun struggles to reach into the corners of the village, and the shadows sharpen the dull sense of dread beginning to roil in Julia's stomach.

She unlocks the door of her curiosity shop, the fresh holes in her life highlighted by its quietness. Dust floats undisturbed through a shaft of pale sunlight that pools on the floor beside the first row of shelves. Light picks out the gold rim on an old tobacco box.

Julia finds herself standing in the circle of sunlight, willing it to take away a little of her grief. How many hours until her son is due home from the dame school? She is craving his company, craving his boundless energy that is so far undented by the friction of the Jacobite Rising. She has not yet told him about his uncle's death. And she has no idea how to do so. Bobby had adored Michael. Learning of his loss will break him.

Her cat, Minerva, slinks out from between the shelves and rubs up against Julia's skirts. Julia bends, runs a hand across Minerva's back, trying to enjoy the feel of the silky coat beneath her touch.

Once, this was her favourite time of day; when the doors had just been unlocked and she had time to herself to explore the wilds of her shop. To walk the cluttered aisles and admire the pieces of other lives that had ended up on her shelves. A moment to take a breath and celebrate the fact that she was here for another day. Celebrate the fact that somehow, she had made it this far, had built this unlikely life from nothing.

Today, though, with grief over Michael and Angus pouring into her heart, it feels as though it will only be seconds before everything collapses beneath her.

She turns towards the cellar. The door at the bottom of the stairs is swinging open. Unease pulls at her as she hurries down the staircase. The cellar is empty, the blankets on the bed tossed aside. An unlit lantern sits on the floor by the doorway, still giving off a faint stench of tallow. There is a stale warmth to the space that suggests her unwanted guest has only just left.

Julia curses under her breath as she closes the door of the cellar. She pulls a key from her pocket and slides it into the lock to hide the room from prying eyes. And she imagines that day when everything will topple. Feels it creep a little closer.

CHAPTER TWO

His mother had been right to leave Highfield House. Nathan feels that deeply, instinctively. Whatever her hazy, indiscernible reasons for leaving, she had been right to do so. This house; somehow, it has the potential to suck any goodness from the world. Poison the water and pollute the sky.

Twenty years ago, Abigail Blake had fled the family home. Fled Holy Island. Nathan wishes he had that option. Disappear and never look back.

Then again, perhaps it's not the house's fault. Perhaps he only has his own foolishness to blame for his situation. Because he can hardly claim he has any good sense in him when he is standing here outside Julia's door in a desperate hope of making amends. How can he blame anything other than his own stupidity when he has come here by choice? No, perhaps not by choice. Because the need to explain himself to Julia after all she saw this morning feels as crucial as taking a breath.

Spies and muskets and dangerous accusations.

Step through that door, and he knows he can expect a raft of angry Jacobites at worst. A red-hot poker in the eye at best.

He does it anyway.

The bell above the door bellows as he enters. With the high tide, the curiosity shop is empty of customers, and Nathan is not sure if being alone in Julia's presence makes him relieved or terrified. She whirls around from where she stands at one of the shelves, a dusting rag in one hand and a gaudy brass trinket box in the other. A look of unbridled rage makes her green eyes blaze.

"Get out," she says.

"Please let me explain."

"I've no need for an explanation. I've already been foolish enough."

No, he will not let things unravel like this. This balancing game with Julia Mitchell, it is infuriating, it is confounding, but it also undeniably precious. He prays it is not lost forever.

Nathan dares to take a step towards her. "I've not been entirely honest with you," he admits. "But I'm no spy. I swear it. And I wish to tell you everything." The words make something close in his chest, because he knows how dangerous they are. Dangerous, but utterly necessary. If he is to have any chance at resurrecting his fledgling relations with Julia, there can be no more secrets between them. No more lies.

She eyes him. Her red hair is chaos, loose curls escaping from the knot at the back of her neck and clouding around her face. Her cheeks are flushed with anger, eyes shadowed with sleeplessness and heavy with grief. At the sight of her, his heart is pounding. He can feel the resentment radiating off her body.

She slams the trinket box back on the shelf and strides towards the door. Turns the key, locking them in. Then she looks at Nathan with fierce eyes. "Start talking then."

Start talking. Start talking. Really, he has no idea where to begin.

Maybe it's a blessing that his house has been revealed as a meeting place for government spies. Because now the informants will use the house no longer, and he will be freed from the knot of the Jacobite Rising he has found himself tangled in.

But even as the thought comes to him, Nathan knows he's being naïve. Of course it will not be that simple. Because as much as he does not want to admit it, he fears Julia is also deeply entangled in the Rising. And if this attempt at explanation capitulates; if she continues to believe his family are government informants, it could put them in even more danger. This conversation is not just about him and Julia, he realises. It's about putting an end to these foolish rumours of his family spying for the king.

"I'm no spy," he says again, deciding this is as fine a place to begin as any. "No one in my family is. The men that attacked Highfield House this morning were mistaken."

Julia stands with her arms pinned across her chest, her back pressed up against the door of the shop. "Martin Macauley said they were watching your house. He said there have been messengers coming and going. And that they saw one of you delivering government intelligence from William Cotesworth."

"They saw Harriet returning from Lesbury Common," Nathan tells her. "After she helped Michael try to return to the Jacobite army. And they drew their own conclusions." He sees a faint wince from Julia. Regrets having to go near her brother's death.

"And the messengers coming to your house?" Her voice has lost a little of its sharpness.

Nathan swallows. "That part is true."

Julia exhales and reaches for the door handle.

"Wait. Please." He knows what he is about to say could be an enormous mistake. But it's a mistake he needs to make. If Julia is to trust him, he needs to trust her too.

He closes his eyes for a moment; that dizzying point of no return. A dive off a cliff.

"My family are not spies," he says, "but Cotesworth's informants were using Highfield House. I had no choice but to agree to it. For reasons…" He hesitates. "For reasons that are best not to go into."

"No. You cannot tell me your house is being used by government spies, and then refuse to tell me why. At least, you cannot do that if you expect me to believe a word you say."

Nathan nods resignedly. He had expected this much. "The day Donald Macauley disappeared, he forced my sister into his boat and took her out to sea." His chest tightens with the knowledge of what he is to reveal. And what it could mean for Eva if this knowledge falls into the wrong hands. "He accused her of being a spy, and tried to kill her. She defended herself and knocked Macauley unconscious. He fell into the water and drowned." He watches Julia for a reaction, but her face remains almost eerily empty. A slight parting of her lips is the only thing that lets Nathan know she has heard what he said.

"One of the government spies told me he had a way to clear Eva's name. A way to ensure the villagers did not come after her over Macauley's disappearance. In exchange, they asked to use the house as a rendezvous point for the exchange of government messages. I had no choice but agree to it. For my sister's sake."

Julia is silent for a long time. Nathan can practically see her turning this information over in her head, picking at its seams. She toys with the edge of her dusting cloth. Finally, she looks up at him. "Are you telling the truth?"

"Do you truly think I would tell you such a thing if it were a lie? Do you think I would do that to Eva?"

"No," Julia says finally. "I don't suppose you would."

He cannot read her, Nathan realises. The closeness he had felt towards her out on the dunes last night has been washed away by Cordwell and Macauley's accusations. He has no thought of whether she believes him; whether she is angry at him for keeping the knowledge of Donald Macauley's death a secret. No thought of whether, the minute he steps from the shop, she will take this information straight to Donald's son.

Julia stares out the window, her eyes glazed over in thought. Wind pushes against the pane, making the old wooden frame creak. "How did Cordwell and Martin Macauley know what the house was being used for?" she asks. "Why did they attack you?"

"My family has been being watched," Nathan admits. "For some weeks. We've been under suspicion since we arrived here on Lindisfarne. Cordwell and Macauley must have seen the messengers coming to the house. Drawn their own conclusions."

"Did they hurt any of you?"

"No."

Julia sets the rag down on the counter. "I'm sorry I didn't stay to make sure you were unharmed."

"I can hardly blame you for running away as you did," Nathan says with a faint smile. "I'm aware I've been more than a little hypocritical. Given all the trouble I gave you for keeping secrets from me."

"Well." Julia swallows. "I suppose I can understand why you did."

Nathan looks at her for a long second, their eyes meeting. His heart is quick, and he cannot tell if it's his fear of human contact that is causing it, or the heat rising from Julia's body, or everything he has just revealed. Perhaps all three. "You will… keep all this to yourself?"

"Of course."

Nathan dares a small smile. Feels his chest swell when she returns it. "I'd best get back," he manages. "I'm needed at the house."

He decides not to say anything to Julia about the way Harriet had disappeared onto Henry Ward's ship this morning, wild with rage at her family for keeping the truth of who her father was from her. Nathan and Edwin had spent most of this morning pacing in front of the windows, waiting for her to return from Ward's clutches. And she would return, they had told each other, over and over, a feverish chant. Of course she would. As much as Harriet likes to leave most of her mothering duties in the hands of her son's nurse, Nathan knows she would never abandon Thomas completely.

Edwin had been adamant that they go after his wife. Somehow, Nathan had managed to convince him that blundering out to the ship on a misguided rescue mission was not the wisest course of action. Besides, for all Henry Ward's darkness, he is still Harriet's father. And she deserves a chance to know him. Perhaps if they had given her that from the beginning, she would not have run off with him like this.

Eventually, the need to see Julia had overridden Nathan's desire to hover at the window and wait for his sister to show herself, and he had left Edwin to his own devices.

Julia walks him to the door and turns the key. When she looks back to face him, she is close, and he can make out the mist of pale freckles across her cheeks.

"If you…" He lets his words trail off. Doesn't know where they are going. His gaze drifts instinctively to her parted lips and he looks away hurriedly.

There is a hint of warmth in Julia's eyes. "Thank you for telling me all this."

"Everything I've told you is the truth," says Nathan. "You know that, don't you?"

"Yes," says Julia, her fingers curling around the doorframe. "I do."

And that, Nathan thinks, is something well worth celebrating.

CHAPTER THREE

Eva stands at the window of her childhood bedroom, her forehead pressed to the glass. It's late afternoon and the sun is pale; feels as though it barely rose before plummeting back towards the horizon. Beyond the window, the sea is the same ash grey as the sky, the water punctuated by the dark shape of Henry Ward's ship.

Unease is coiled tightly in the bottom of Eva's stomach. She hates the thought of Harriet being out there alone with Ward. Hates the thought of all he could tell her.

Nathan appears around the corner of the house, striding over the dunes from the direction of the village. Eva had had no idea he'd even left. She hears the click of the front door. Hears his footsteps thump steadily into the house.

From the ship out beyond the embankment: nothing. Henry Ward's barque is as still and silent as it has been since dawn, when Harriet had followed her father out there.

Eva knows she ought to have told her sister she was the daughter of Henry Ward the moment she had learnt of it. Knows she should not have left it to Harriet to find out by overhearing Nathan's words.

But telling the truth had felt like far too much of a risk. One word from Ward and Harriet would know Finn had caused their brother Oliver's death. Eva had hoped it was a secret that would never find its way out. Now, with her sister aboard Ward's ship, such a thing feels like the greatest naivety. She cannot bear to think about what knowledge Harriet might bring back to the house with her. Everything feels dizzyingly close to collapse.

She yanks the curtains closed. The sight of that motionless ship, silhouetted with distance, has her on the edge of madness.

"Perhaps we ought to just tell them," Finn says from behind her, his voice low. He's sitting on the floor by the hearth, brown eyes glassy as he stares into the grate. The firelight casts shadows over his bristly cheeks. "If they hear the truth from me…" He fades out, unable to finish the sentence. Because surely he knows this truth will be just as brutal whether it comes from Henry Ward's mouth or his own. He scrubs a hand across his eyes.

Eva reaches down and runs soft fingers through his hair, wishing she could take away his unease. He has been quiet all day, clearly tossing these thoughts around his head as he worked away at rebuilding the fireplace in her mother's old dressing room.

Eva is craving the emptiness of Longstone. She longs to disappear and leave her sister to her own devices. But she can't push aside the worry. Worry over Harriet's safety, or her own secrets, she cannot quite determine. She only knows she cannot leave until her sister has returned.

"We cannot tell anyone," she says stiffly. "My family cannot find out…"

Finn reaches for her hand and tugs her down to sit beside him. "You know there's every chance Harriet already has."

Eva picks at her thumbnail. Up close to the fire, she feels hot and unsteady. She tugs edgily at her shortjacket. "Harriet is the daughter Ward never knew he had. Surely the first thing they discuss will not be you and Oliver. Why would it be?" But she can hear the desperation in her words. Because the fact that Finn killed Oliver may not be the first thing that Ward tells his daughter. But there is every chance it may be the second, the third, the fourth. Eva knows she is kidding herself if she imagines Ward will keep this a secret. Ever since he had returned to Northumberland, he has been determined to make Finn pay for Oliver's death. What better way to do so than this?

"Let's go back to Longstone," she says suddenly. "Right now."

Finn raises his eyebrows. "I thought you wanted to make sure Harriet got home safely."

"I know. I did. But I cannot just sit here and wait any longer." With each minute, each hour that passes, she is coming to see the danger of staying. Because it's another minute, another hour, in which Henry Ward could tell Harriet the truth. Another minute, hour, in which everything could fall. "Besides," she says desperately, "Angus may have left the island by now. And it will be dark in a few hours. We need to go back to keep the light."

Before Finn can reply, the front door creaks open. There's a muffled flurry of footsteps. Voices.

Eva's stomach rolls. This is it, she thinks. This is the moment she has been dreading since she learnt the truth of how her eldest brother died. Since she stood at the altar with Finn and committed to honour, obey and keep secrets from her family.

She gets to her feet, sucking in her breath and pushing open the door. She reaches for Finn's hand as she steps out into the passage; a gesture of solidarity. Voices float up the staircase. The smell of overcooked lamb stew turns the air—food their housekeeper had prepared earlier in the day, and that has gone untouched. None of them have been in the mood for eating.

"Are you unharmed?" Eva hears Nathan ask.

"Did you imagine I wouldn't be?" Harriet's voice is oddly level. Expressionless.

Nathan replies only with silence.

Eva looks down the staircase at her sister. Harriet is standing in the entrance hall with Edwin and Nathan, though both men are hovering an uncomfortable distance away from her.

Harriet's cheeks are pink with cold, her chin lifted, shoulders pressed back. She is without a cloak or bonnet, and wearing just a light woollen day dress, her blonde hair in a long plait down her back. There's a new hardness about her, Eva realises. A look in her eyes that goes beyond her typical emotionlessness.

At the sound of Eva and Finn's footsteps on the stairs, Harriet looks up. Her eyes meet her sister's, but Eva cannot read them. Harriet says nothing.

She knows. She must know. This wordlessness, it is all part of some twisted game she is playing. Punishment for keeping the truth of her father a secret. Eva's fingers tighten around the banister. She forces herself to keep walking.

Nathan clears his throat. Rubs a hand across the back of his neck as he calls for the housekeeper. "Mrs Brodie, that stew you prepared earlier. Perhaps you might serve it up for dinner?"

This family, Nathan knows, is at risk of fracturing. There have been far too many secrets between them, and he knows he is mostly to blame. This entire venture to Lindisfarne had been built on his own lies. A restoration of the house, he had told his family. In truth, he had been coerced up here by Henry Ward, on a search for the valuable letter his mother had apparently been keeping safe at Ward's request. The valuable letter that Ward now wants back.

Henry Ward has not found his precious letter. But he has found his daughter. And this is arguably more problematic.

Nathan sees clearly now that, just as it was with Julia, the time for keeping secrets from his family is over. He has already done enough damage. He will put an end to all this falsity now, before things are broken beyond repair.

So. They will sit down to a meal like civilised human beings. They will be open and honest with each other. And no one will flee, or lie, or go gallivanting onto a pirate ship.

At least he hopes that will be the case.

"Finn and I need to leave," Eva blurts. "We need to get back before dark. Angus may have left and we need to light the firebasket…"

Two hours, probably three, until nightfall. Nathan knows she is making excuses. He doesn't blame her. "This is very important, Eva," he says, doing his best to conjure up some kind of firmness. "I'd appreciate it if you could stay."

"We can't. I'm sorry." Eva lurches towards the front door, but Finn grabs her hand, tugging her back. For several moments, Eva doesn't speak, eyes meeting her husband's in a moment of unspoken dialogue. Finally, she gives a nod of reluctant agreement. Accepts her fate and creeps towards the dining room like a prisoner approaching the gallows.

Nathan watches after her for a moment. He meets Finn's eyes. Gives him a faint nod of thanks.

They make their way into the dining room, barely speaking, as though driven to silence by the weight of their combined secrets. Mrs Brodie is shuffling her way down the long wooden dining table, lighting candles to brighten the late-afternoon gloom. A fire crackles steadily in the grate, making shadows dance across the dark wood wainscoting of the walls.

Rapid footsteps patter down the hallway and Theodora explodes into the dining room, blonde plaits flying. The children's nurse hurries inside in her wake.

"I'm sorry, Mr Blake," Jenny says, half breathless. "She darted out when I weren't looking."

Nathan gives the nurse a knowing look. "Back to the parlour, Theodora," he tells his daughter. "Mrs Brodie will bring you your stew in there."

Her face wrinkles. "No! I want to eat in here with everyone else!"

He is not in the mood. "Back to the parlour," he says sharply. "No arguments."

Theodora huffs loudly. She drags her feet and looks wistfully over her shoulder as Jenny hauls her out of the dining room, mumbling fresh apologies.

Nathan takes a seat at the head of the table as the housekeeper sets a bowl of congealing stew in front of him. His throat closes in protest.

This high-backed chair in front of the fireplace, it's where he remembers his father sitting. He has never sat here before; the dining table is so vast, there has never been any need to fill this chair. And if he's honest with himself, he has never truly felt worthy. But today, he feels a need to take this seat at the head of the table. He knows he needs to conjure up a little authority. Perhaps sitting in this chair will allow him to absorb a little of his father's influence. Allow him to act like the patriarch of this family he is supposed to be.

Silence hangs over the dinner table. Edwin and Harriet sit on one side of him; Eva and Finn on the other. Nathan has not missed the extra inches Harriet has put between herself and her husband. She has made herself into an island. Disconnected and inaccessible. On the opposite side of the table, Eva and Finn sit shoulder to shoulder, unnaturally close, as though bolstering each other against wherever this discussion is going to take them.

Nathan lifts the bottle of claret from the table and fills the glasses, trying to order his thoughts. He murmurs a hurried grace, then turns to look at Harriet. She picks up her napkin and spreads it carefully over her lap. She lifts her chin, glances around the table with a look of defiance. She knows, of course, that they are all impatient to hear what happened on that ship. Nathan can tell how much she is enjoying it.

He forces down a mouthful of stew. Chases it with a hurried gulp of wine. "Well?" he says. "What did Ward have to say to you?"

Harriet lifts her wine glass and takes a miniscule sip, before setting it carefully back beside her bowl. "Do you not think you ought to be the one answering the questions, Nathan? It seems you have been keeping plenty of things to yourself." Her eyes dart around the table. "You all have. Did not one of you think I might wish to know who my father was? Why did you all think it such a good idea to keep it to yourselves?"

"Harriet, that is enough," Edwin says stiffly. Her eyes flash at him, but she does not respond. Edwin turns to Nathan. "She's right, though, Nate. I think it's time you told us everything."

Nathan nods slowly. At least when he lies down to sleep tonight, he will do so with no secrets on his shoulders. "Ward came to me several months ago," he begins. "He had his lawyers track me down in London. He told me he needed a valuable letter he had given to our mother for safekeeping. Apparently the letter speaks of the Jacobite leanings of someone high up in the Whig party. Prime blackmail material." He feels Edwin's eyes boring into him. "Ward tracked Mother down before her death and wrote to her, asking about the letter's whereabouts. Mother told him it was in a safe at the Bank of England. That turned out not to be true."

He turns his wine glass around by the stem. His family are silent on either side of him, Edwin nodding at him to continue. It's a strange feeling. Nathan cannot remember the last time he commanded such authority from them. "Ward accused me of taking the letter. He believed I sold it for my own purposes. I told him he was mistaken. I was certain Mother had not taken the letter with her when she ran from the house, so

Ward was convinced it must still be here. He ordered me to come up to Lindisfarne and find it. When I refused, he made threats against me." His voice drops involuntarily. "And against Theodora."

Edwin sighs. Shakes his head. "You ought to have told us the truth from the beginning. Why lie to us with this nonsense about the restoration?" But the brazenness with which he usually speaks is gone. Nathan senses he too is unnerved by this new hardness of Harriet's.

New? Perhaps it has always been there. Perhaps he has just never looked hard enough. Perhaps the day she has spent in her father's company has given her the courage to bring it to the surface.

Nathan turns to Edwin. "I did not tell you the truth because you would have insisted we fight Ward," he admits. "I know you. And that was a risk I couldn't take. Fighting him is far too dangerous."

"You have it wrong," Harriet says suddenly. "Henry Ward does not wish to hurt you."

"You may wish that to be the case, Harriet," Nathan tells her. "But your father tracked me down in London. He found the house we were renting and came there to threaten me. He forced me to upend my life and come up here to tear the house apart. He made it perfectly clear what the consequences would be if I did not find that letter."

"You've not found it," she reminds him. "And what has he done to harm you? Nothing."

His thoughts collide. It's the truth, he realises. For all his bluster, all his threats, Henry Ward has not harmed a hair on their heads. More than that, if Nathan is not mistaken, Ward had even sought to protect them against the Jacobites who had stormed the house yesterday.

He looks squarely at Harriet. He needs more from her. Needs her to be open; to tell him what had happened on the ship. Needs her to stop playing these infuriating games. "Did Ward say something to you about the letter?" he asks, trying to see behind her eyes. "Is there something you know that you are not telling us? Or is all this talk about him not being dangerous just wishful thinking?"

"Wishful thinking," she snorts. "You really do think me an empty-headed fool." She tears at a piece of bread with long fingers. "The threats do not come from him, Nathan. He is acting on another's bidding."

Finn looks up suddenly. "Whose bidding?"

Harriet glances at him, as though surprised at his question. Nathan is surprised too—he has barely heard a word from him all day. "It doesn't matter who," she says. "You just need to know my father is not a danger."

Nathan rubs his eyes in frustration. "Harriet. If you have that information, you must tell us. Do you not appreciate the seriousness of the situation? Do you not appreciate the trouble this family is in?"

Harriet's laugh is thin, icy. "You are berating me for not telling you important things, Nathan? A little hypocritical wouldn't you say?" Her eyes move around the table before landing back on him. "You need to find that letter," she says. "But you do not need to fear Henry Ward. He does not want to hurt us." She looks down, her voice softening a little. "He loved our mother."

Nathan has no idea if this is true. Though his mother's reasons for escaping Holy Island are hazy, he has little doubt Henry Ward is tied up in them. If Ward had truly loved Abigail Blake, he doubts that love was reciprocated.

Harriet's eyes narrow at Nathan's lack of response. "*You* know he does not want to hurt us, Eva," she says pointedly. "You have been aboard his ship. He told me as much. And did he not treat you with kindness?"

Eva's hand tenses around the handle of her spoon. She has not touched her food. "He tried to kill Finn," she hisses. "We almost drowned trying to escape."

"Well." Harriet brings her wine glass to her lips, then peers across the rim, eyes shifting between Eva and Finn. "Perhaps you did something to deserve it."

CHAPTER FOUR

Eva leans back against the gunwale of the skiff and lifts her face to the sky. The last glow of dusk is turning the sea purple, a fine sheen of rain glittering in the lamplight.

They had been stuck at that cursed dinner table for far longer than she had hoped, and the sun is no more than faint patch of light above the horizon. She prays no ships have come out here tonight to find the ink-dark rocks of the Farne Islands. Prays no one has got themselves in trouble on account of her family's dramas. There are no lights on the sea beyond their own, and she is not sure if that reassures her of its emptiness, or suggests that those ships' lights have dipped beneath the surface.

She curls her fingers around the handle of the lamp, letting her body meet the rhythm of the skiff as it moves on the sea. Even now they have left Highfield House, even now they have made it through dinner without their secrets being spilled, she cannot let go of the unease. The muscles in her back and shoulders feel like iron, and a headache is pressing behind her eyes.

Finn leans back against the gunwale, his gaze drawn towards the inky shape of their cottage, just visible in the disappearing light. "I don't think Ward told her about Oliver," he says finally. "Harriet's clearly furious at everyone. If she knew about Oliver, she'd have spoken of it, don't you think?"

In spite of all they are carrying, Eva can see the difference in Finn now they have left Highfield House. The rigidity with which he had carried himself in the house seems to have drained from his body, and the tension is gone from his voice. She hates that she had put him through such a thing.

She wants to believe Finn is right about Harriet. But she cannot quite bring herself to do so. She lifts her face to the sky, letting the rain dampen her cheeks. "You do not know her like I do. She likes to play games. It is just like her to have this knowledge but keep it close to her chest. Not let it out until she feels it will do the most harm."

Finn leans on the tiller, guiding the boat around the foam-tipped fringes of the archipelago. "D'you think she's right about Ward not wanting to hurt your family? About there being someone else behind these threats over the letter?"

"No," Eva says bitterly. "Do you?"

Finn tilts his head, considering. "Maybe. I know Ward really did care a lot about your ma. It makes sense that he'd not want to hurt your family."

"He threatened Nathan and Theodora."

"Empty threats. He's never hurt either of them. And honestly, I'm not sure he ever would."

Eva uses her free hand to pull her cloak closed. She does not want to consider that there might be someone else, someone unknown, with an eye on her family. At least Henry Ward is something of a known quantity. "How can you even think that way after all he has done? Have you forgotten he almost killed you?"

Finn squeezes her shoulder to calm her. "Of course not. But you said I don't know Harriet like you do. Well, you don't know Ward like I do. And he has a sense of honour. A twisted one, maybe, but a sense of honour nonetheless. I've never known him to lie."

Eva lets out a long breath. "I wish I had your faith in him."

"Besides," Finn says, "there's something different about Ward lately. His confidence, it seems forced. Makes sense if he truly is being forced into this by someone else."

Eva nods faintly. Even if Finn is right, she knows she will never bring herself to trust Henry Ward.

She lifts the lamp, trying to catch the outline of their cottage, and the skeletal shape of the firebasket, half lost against the night. It's a strange thing to see Longstone dark like this. Even on the wettest, wildest nights, when there is no chance of keeping the beacon lit, there is always a fire glowing inside, or at least a lamp on the table. The darkness is unsteadying. A reminder, perhaps, of what their home would look like if they let it be reclaimed by sea.

Eva gathers her skirts in her fist and climbs towards the bow of the skiff, holding up the lamp to guide Finn's way into the moorings. She climbs from the boat, the high tide pushing though the slats of the jetty with each swell of the sea. Finn steps out behind her.

The sea is restless and loud tonight, swallowing much of the island and teasing the stairs at the front of the cottage. Eva carries the lamp around the fringe of the water, guiding Finn's way towards the coal shed. He loads up a bucket with kindling and coal, then carries it back to the firebasket. The chain groans as he lowers the brazier to the rocky ground. He shovels in the fuel and uses the lamp to spark it to life. Firelight spills across the island, thinning out the darkness.

Eva stares up at the flames, which are roaring against the rain shower. Feels a little of her restlessness drain away. She knows keeping the light has always been a way for Finn to try to atone for Oliver's death, so close to the forefront of their minds after two days at Highfield House. Eva cannot help but feel the same need for redemption. Because she can tell herself as often as she likes that Donald Macauley's death was an accident, but that does not change the fact that she has killed a man. The sight of the blazing beacon, of the responsibility she has chosen to shoulder, to protect the lives of strangers, takes away a scrap of the guilt and regret.

The moment she steps through the door of the cottage, Eva feels tension drain from her shoulders. She is glad to be home. Glad for the familiar smell of woodsmoke and candlewax. For the sight of their wobbly kitchen chairs, the smoke-stained bricks of the hearth, their tin teacups that seem to have found permanent lodgings in the middle of the table. Glad for the creaks of the windows and the faint crackle and groan of the beacon. The soothing lash of the sea. A strange thing, Eva thinks, that this cottage has come to feel like home so quickly, while Highfield House, the very place in which she was born, has always felt like a piece of someone else's life.

The sleeping pallets belonging to Angus and Michael Mitchell are gone, the crates they had sat on around the table no doubt taken back to the coal shed. There's a deep stillness to the place that has not existed for weeks.

Eva sets the lamp on the mantel. "Poor Angus," she murmurs. She cannot imagine how difficult it must have been to have packed up his dead brother's belongings with the long, dangerous journey to London laid out in front of him.

It is a strange feeling to have the cottage to themselves again. It takes Eva back to her first days on Longstone; days when she and Finn were little more than strangers. Hiding secrets from each other, instead of from the rest of the world.

As much as she feels for Angus, she is grateful for the space, the privacy. This precious time alone with her new husband.

Finn comes towards her. He cups her cheek with his rough palm. "My wife," he says. And it makes her smile. This is the first time they have had the cottage to themselves since they married, and right now, there is nowhere she would rather be.

He pulls her into a deep kiss. Eva feels herself sink against him. Feels his broad arms circle her body. She closes her eyes, drinking in every piece of him. The coarseness of his beard against her cheeks, the scent of woodsmoke infused in his shirtsleeves, the warmth of his palms against her skin. She feels herself being lifted onto the table. Feels rough hands sliding beneath her skirts. Hears herself sigh against his mouth.

And this is her choice, Eva thinks distantly, as Finn's lips work their way down her neck. If their secrets spill and everything falls, and she must make the choice between her husband and her family, this is her choice. It is right here that she will stay, with the sea on her doorstep, restless beneath the firelight.

Nathan can see little through the telescope tonight. A faint glint of starlight there; a glimpse of the moon between the cloudbank. Still, the very act of turning his gaze away from the earth has the effect of slowing his heart. Of taking him away from his problems for a time. Of making Ward, and the letter, and that godawful dinner he had insisted on tonight, feel a little more distant.

He yawns. The house is dark and quiet around him. No sound but the groans of beams contracting with the cold; the occasional scrabble of an unseen mouse. No light but the single candle flickering on the far end of his desk. The darkness around him pulls more light from the stars.

A fresh plume of cloud blows across the moon and Nathan stands up from the telescope. He takes the candle and makes his way into his darkened bedchamber. He can make out the shape of Theodora, lying on her side in the truckle bed in the corner of the room.

He sets the candle on the side table and crouches beside the bed. His daughter rolls over to face him. He puts a hand to her shoulder. "I'm sorry, my love. I didn't mean to wake you."

"I wasn't asleep," she announces. "I was lying here thinking about the new story I'm going to write."

"Oh yes? And what is that?"

Her eyes are wide and ridiculously sleepless, though it's well past eleven. "It's about a bold adventurer," she tells him. "Who sails to faraway lands in his magic ship."

"Faraway lands? That does sound like a great adventure." He tries not to think about the fact that she has likely been inspired by the ship moored outside the window. When he was a child, he had seen Henry Ward as a bold adventurer too.

He keeps his hand to Theodora's shoulder. Despite the flicker of unease the physical contact brings him, there is something reassuring about the feel of her. She is here with him, she is safe. For everything that has unravelled, the threads have not yet slipped through his fingers entirely.

He removes his hand, but stays sitting on the floor beside her bed, watching as her breathing slowly morphs into the deep inhalations of sleep. Nathan leans back against the wall and lets his own heavy eyes drop closed.

Though his much-insisted-upon family dinner was as painful as that poker in the eye, he is relieved to have relinquished himself of his sizeable pot of lies. Even more relieved at not having to maintain this charade of restoring the house. Tomorrow, he will not have to hammer floorboards or rebuild fireplaces, or do any of the other godawful tasks Edwin dishes out to him. For all he cares, the place can sit in ruin until the end of its days. As for Ward's precious letter, well, it is not in the house. That much is clear.

Nathan tosses Harriet's words around his head. He knows better than to take what she says as the gospel truth, especially now, when she feels so angry and betrayed. But he cannot deny that some of her claims had struck a chord within him.

Ward has made threats, yes, but he has never acted upon them. Never done anything to harm their family. Even when he had come to the house and stared down the barrel of Edwin's pistol, Ward had not fired in retaliation.

So perhaps Harriet is right. Perhaps Ward will not hurt them, Abigail's children. Perhaps he really had cared for their mother too much to do so. Perhaps there really is someone else behind these threats. Someone who is forcing Ward to do their bidding.

The prospect does not quite sit right. From what Nathan knows of Henry Ward, he is far too imposing a man to bend to another's will. But perhaps that is exactly why he had sought to carry on this pretence of being the one behind the threats. Surely it cannot be easy for a man who has been a leader all his life to capitulate to the demands of another.

But in a way, Nathan knows it does not matter. Whoever it is that wants the letter, he cannot produce it.

He looks over at Theodora, her chest rising and falling, a hand splayed out beside her cheek. The urge to run is building up inside him. He imagines he feels the way his mother once felt: that searing need to leave Holy Island—to escape Henry Ward. Because it was Ward his mother was escaping, surely. Escaping so he might never know about his daughter. Nathan can only imagine how horrified Abigail would have been if she knew Harriet had spent the day on her father's ship.

He is certain things had not been simple for his mother, but he is aware they are even more complicated for him. Because he can take Theodora and run, but they will surely be followed—by Henry Ward, or by whichever other nameless, faceless bastards are so desperate for this letter. And even if he did run, how much of his family would he leave behind? Eva has made her life on Longstone, an easy target for Ward and his men if they ever sought to come after her. And Harriet? As much as she has rallied to return to London, Nathan knows she will not take it well if he and Edwin drag her away from the father she has only just come to know.

Nathan knows his relationship with his youngest sister is beginning to fray. Since he had learnt that Samuel Blake was not Harriet's father, he has done his best to make her feel as much a part of the family as ever. But he can sense Harriet sliding apart from them—largely thanks to all they have kept from her.

No, Nathan thinks sickly. He cannot run. He cannot do that to his sisters. Nor can he condemn himself and Thea to a life of always looking over their shoulders, wondering who might be on their tail.

And then, of course, there is the other reason that is making him so hesitant to flee. No, he is not going to think about Julia. Not now. At least, he is going to do his best not to.

He cannot run. But somehow, he needs to get the truth out of his sister. Whatever passed between Harriet and Ward on that ship, he needs to know.

CHAPTER FIVE

Harriet can't quite make sense of why she continues to use her workroom. Since Edwin had condemned her brushes and canvas to the fire after her ill-fated venture to Lesbury with Michael Mitchell, the place has been painfully empty. The table is bare without her brushes and water tray, the armchair made more tattered and wretched by her own misery. Her empty easel stands by the window, holding nothing, mocking her.

But even without her paintings, this is still her space—at least, she wants it to be. The place where it feels most possible to let the real world disappear for a time. Because the real world has become almost impossible to carry.

Now Edwin has forbidden her from painting, now her notebooks have followed her canvases into the fire, she has no idea where to put this chaos of emotions that is thrashing around inside her. How does she navigate the knowledge of her father the pirate? Of his crewmen who have her family in their sights? How does she temper her anger at her siblings for all they had kept from her? Or the aching knowledge that Edwin will likely forbid her from ever seeing Isabelle or any of the others in her artists' circle again? She feels constantly airless, weighed down from above.

A knock at the door, and the muscles in her shoulders tighten instinctively. It's not Edwin, at least. These days, he does not even bother knocking.

"Come in," she murmurs, not bothering to move from the armchair.

When Nathan steps inside, he's wearing a fragile look; a look of uncertainty and faint hope. If he's still angry at her for escaping onto Ward's ship, his expression does not give it away. Harriet is grateful.

"How are you?" he asks.

"Is that really why you're here? To see how I'm faring?"

He knots his hands awkwardly. "In part, yes."

"And the other part?" She knows why he is here, of course. Knows he has come for information about her father and this damn letter. About who might be hiding behind it.

Nathan sighs. He hesitates, as though debating whether to keep pounding away at this pretence of caring. "I need you to speak openly," he says. "About what happened between you and your father on his ship yesterday. I need you to tell me exactly what he told you about the letter, and who it is that is really threatening us."

Harriet examines a fingernail. "And why should I do that?"

"For the good of this family," Nathan says tautly. "I assume that still matters to you."

For the good of this family. That's a hypocritical turd if ever she heard one. *The good of this family* hadn't seemed to matter much when Nathan was spouting lies and swinging hammers to keep up the façade of his mock restoration.

She watches his expression falter, as though he too can see the hypocrisy in what he is asking. He rubs the back of his neck. Continues to hover in the doorway. "Please, Harriet. I know we have all done wrong by you, and I'm truly sorry. But I'm afraid." His voice thickens. "I'm afraid for Thea, and for Thomas, and for you and Eva. I have no idea how I'm to keep everyone safe, because I have no thought of who or what we are really up against."

Harriet picks at a thread on the armchair, not speaking. In spite of herself, she feels a tug of pity towards him. Nathan has always had a propensity for shouldering all the world's problems; for blaming himself for every speck of dirt in the family's treasury. Besides, this is the first genuine apology she has received from anyone about keeping her father from her.

Nathan takes a step further into the room and leans up against the empty table. "What happened between you and Ward when you went aboard his ship?" he asks again.

Harriet looks out the window of the workroom. The ship is still out there, watching the house, as it has been for weeks. "I told you what happened last night."

"No you didn't. You only told us pieces. That pieces that would leave us with the most questions."

Harriet shifts uncomfortably. She had not realised she was so transparent.

In truth, a part of her had feared him, her father, the man who had appeared at their house with a pistol in his pocket. Some part of her was afraid to trap herself by stepping aboard his ship. After all, whether she had his blood running through her or not, Henry Ward was still a stranger.

But there was a part of her that needed to know him. Desperately. She has always felt as though she were on the fringe of her family, the ill-fitting piece. A creative fantasist against her level-headed siblings; sharp-tongued against their compulsive geniality. Ice-blonde against their mousy darkness.

Perhaps, she thought, Henry Ward might help her find some sense of a place in the world. Might anchor her somehow. Give her the sense that she was doing more than being dragged through a life she had no say in crafting. Besides, she had spent the first nineteen years of her life certain she would never know her father. How could she not take this chance she had so unexpectedly been gifted?

In any case, when she had stepped out of Highfield House yesterday morning, her anger at her siblings had been almost blinding, and she felt like she had nowhere else to go. And so, when Ward had invited her aboard his ship, she had accepted without question.

She had felt the eyes on her from the moment her feet touched the polished deck of the ship. The men at the davits murmured; others looked up from their polishing, their carving, their card games. The eyes of Ward's crew told her she was not welcome. A bad omen. She knew the stories: a woman onboard sends a ship to the bottom of the sea. But her father's glare had told the men not to ask questions.

He led her down into the cramped and shadowed depths of the ship, along a narrow corridor that creaked with the shifting of the sea. Into a large cabin unlocked with a key he pulled from his pocket. A table stretched out beneath an ornate black lantern, and embroidered curtains were pulled back to reveal the narrow bed against one wall. The windows at the back of the cabin had been boarded up, and shards of morning sunlight strained through the gaps in the wood, painting a cross-stitch of shadows on the floor. The ship smelled old and sour; sweat and bodies and men who had given up caring. The stench turned Harriet's stomach. Her father made no mention of it, and she wondered if he had ceased to notice.

Ward took the lamp from its hook above the table and lit it with a flick of his tinderbox. The shadows that fell across the cabin seemed to only heighten the gloom.

With a wordless nod, Ward gestured for Harriet to sit. She gathered her skirts and slid awkwardly onto the bench at the table. Her eyes drifted upwards, to where footsteps thumped above their heads.

She folded her hands in her lap, feeling wildly out of place. Her father took the pistol from the pocket within his crimson justacorps and set it on the desk. Slid off his coat and hung it on the back of the chair. He yanked the cork from a half-drunk wine bottle and filled two glasses, setting one in front of Harriet. She glanced at it in disinterest, wishing instead for tea, but unable to find her voice.

Ward took a long gulp of wine, then slid onto the bench opposite her. He looked at her for a long second. A strange thing, Harriet thought, to see herself in the face of this stranger; in his hooded blue eyes, the coils of hair tied at a long and slender neck. Felt as though she had caught hold of a thread that could cause her to unravel.

"How old are you?" he asked finally.

Harriet cleared her throat. "I shall be twenty in June." Her voice came out far softer than she intended. She could practically see his mind whirring, calculating. But surely he knew there was no need for uncertainty. She looked every inch her father, and in a way, she was grateful. It took away the doubt.

Ward stared into his clasped hands. "Abigail never told me," he murmured. "If I had known, I would have..." He trailed off, as though unsure exactly what he would have done. He turned his glass around by the stem, unable to meet her eyes.

"She did not want you to know," Harriet said bluntly. "She did not want me to know either. I grew up believing Samuel was my father until

I found his gravestone."

He nodded slowly. Harriet could tell the words pained him, but which part? The fact that Abigail had kept his child from him? Or the fact that he had missed so many years of her life? Perhaps both.

Or perhaps she was just fooling herself. Perhaps she was nothing to her father, this man who crossed oceans in trails of cannon fire. Perhaps she was just one in a long line of achievements he had left in his wake.

She desperately wanted to be something to him. Desperately wanted him to care about her. She wanted to fit into this foreign life, this hatched-light cabin. Because she did not feel as though she fitted into her own life.

She was here on his ship, at least. That had to count to for something. It suggested that, if nothing else, she was a source of curiosity for him.

Harriet knew there were questions she ought to ask. Such as why he had threatened her brother, and what this mysterious letter was all about. But she did not want to bring the rest of her family into this. Right now, she felt painfully disconnected from them. Right now, she wanted this time alone with her father. Were they not owed that, after all the lies they had been put through?

"Tell me about yourself," Ward said. It was a question no one had ever asked her before. A question she had no thought of how to respond to— and one with answers that were not altogether comfortable.

"I want to know about you first," she said. "What manner of ship is this?"

His eyes shifted. "I am afraid I cannot give you the answers that would please you."

"How do you know what answers would please me?"

A faint smile flickered on his lips.

Harriet lifted her glass and took a shallow sip. "A pirate vessel, then," she said easily.

"Much to my shame, yes. The *Eagle* was a successful privateer for many years. But since the war with France ended, there has been no place for privateers. And too many men in my crew support the Stuarts for me to consider offering the king my services against the Jacobites."

It was amusing, almost, the way his eyes lowered in shame. Did he really care so much what she thought of him? But there was something thrilling about this, having a pirate's blood in her. She felt oddly emboldened by the knowledge. It gave her courage, somehow—however misguided and foolish that courage might be.

He told her stories then, of the battles he had waged against the French enemy in the dying years of last century; a time, she saw now, which had been interspersed with visits to Highfield House. And then the stories shifted. Goaded on, perhaps, by the deep interest he saw in Harriet's eyes. Peacetime, and a fleeing to the Caribbean; long hot months spent in the Republic of Pirates. He told her of the men he had gathered on his ship under the black flag. Of his first unlawful attacks against East Indian trade ships in the clear waters outside Nassau.

"The *Albion*," he said, shaking his head. "I'll always remember that name. Full of cotton and silk. We plundered her dry." The candlelight caught the brass buttons on his waistcoat. Made them glitter. "It is not something I'm proud of."

The stories felt faraway. Difficult to grasp, those sun-drenched Caribbean islands, running with stolen gold. Hard to acknowledge as real. After all, Henry Ward's life was so far removed from what Harriet knew to be reality. But there was a sincerity in his eyes that told her the stories were true.

"Where did you meet my mother?" she asked.

"I met her on Holy Island not long after her husband died. She was… not herself then, I suppose you could say."

Harriet frowned. "What do you mean?"

"Well. She was grieving. Concerned about her security. And your brothers and sister's future. She made some rash decisions."

"What decisions? You?" Harriet felt her chest squeeze. She had never imagined herself the consequence of a rash decision.

"I suppose so, yes," said Ward, his eyes drawing downward.

"That is not what you meant, is it," Harriet pressed. "What other rash decisions did she make?"

He shook his head. "It was a long time ago. There's no need to revisit them. I know your mother would not wish us to speak of her mistakes."

Harriet snorted. "My mother would not wish for us to be speaking at all." Her fingers tightened around the stem of her glass in frustration. "'Come midnight, all truths will be revealed.' That's what Mother used to say, was it not? That's what you told me."

Ward nodded faintly.

"And do you not think that time has come? Do you not think we have gone past the point of keeping her secrets?"

Ward didn't answer immediately. He rubbed his smooth jaw. "I know you are angry with Abigail for all she kept from you," he said. "And I confess, I am too. But your mother was a good woman. I do not want you to lose sight of that."

"And what if I already have?"

His eyebrows rose at her brusqueness. "Well. Then that would make me most regretful."

"Did you love her?" Harriet asked boldly.

He lowered his eyes. "I did, yes."

"And did she love you?"

Ward didn't speak immediately. "I believed so, once," he said finally. "But perhaps I was mistaken."

"She fled Holy Island so you'd not know about me."

It was a question more than a statement; a need to piece together these hazy fragments of the past. Ward sighed as he refilled his glass. "It would seem that way." Harriet heard grief in his voice.

"This letter," she began, "you told me it is not you who wants it so desperately. You told me there is another man who is forcing you to do his bidding. Who? Someone else from your crew, I assume?"

The look in Ward's eyes told her she was not mistaken. But he said, "I do not want you involved in this. At least no further than you are already."

Harriet laughed incredulously. "Really? That is all you are going to tell me?"

"Is that why you came here?" he asked. "Because you hoped I would tell you what you wanted to know about the letter?"

"No. I came because I wanted to know who you are. I needed to know."

Ward brought his glass to his lips, studying her closely. "Tell me about yourself now," he said. "I want to know who *you* are."

And where to begin? Surely with *wife* and *mother*, because was there anything beyond that? Surely she ought to tell her father about his grandchild, and his cavalier of a son-in-law who had waved a pistol beneath his eyes. But the words that came out: "I am an artist. A painter.

I have been invited to go to Paris to present my work."

Ward lowered his glance. He gave her a faint smile. "Harriet." Said her name carefully, experimentally. "Will you stay a while? Or do you need to get back to your family?"

"I do not need to get back to my family."

She had stayed. Over bread and cheese, and wine that tasted as though it had come from somewhere far away, he had told her more about his travels, his seafaring father, his invitation to the court of William and Mary. Harriet had told him about her childhood in London; about the townhouse in Chelsea where she had been born, and the neat childhood of governesses and painting tutors her mother had built for her. And then dutifully, she had told him about her husband, her son.

As they spoke, she had the distinct sense that Ward was not allowing her beneath the surface. They were polished stories he told her, empty of emotion, cut and curated for an audience. Perhaps she was not letting him in either—but only because beneath the surface was a far too painful place to go. Perhaps her father felt the same.

But now, as she sits with Nathan in this sorry shell that was once her workroom, Harriet wants to give the impression to her brother that Ward had let her into his secrets. In truth, she has no pieces of useful knowledge to dangle in front of Nathan. If she is honest with herself, she had left her first meeting with her father disappointed by their shallow conversations. By the secrets and truths he refused to share. In so many ways, Henry Ward still feels like a stranger. Not, she supposes, that she could really have expected anything else. Impossible, surely, to overcome almost twenty missed years in a single morning.

"Will I see you again?" she had asked Ward as he had deposited her back on the embankment in front of Highfield House yesterday afternoon.

"Is that what you wish?"

"Yes." The answer made her feel vulnerable. Exposed. She was relieved when he said:

"Then it shall be so."

That vague response had given her hope that maybe one day he would be more than a stranger. That one day, he might let her beneath the surface.

She looks at Nathan. "There is someone else behind the letter. He told me that much. Someone from his crew, I assume. But I do not know who it is," she admits. "Ward said he did not wish for me to be involved."

Nathan glances out the window for a moment before turning to look back at her. "Is that the truth?"

Harriet bristles. "Yes."

"I see." If he is attempting to hide his disappointment, he is doing a rather terrible job of it. He twists a button on his waistcoat, his brow furrowed in thought. "Do you trust him?" he asks her finally.

"Yes," says Harriet. "I do." She prays she is right to do so. For her own sake more than anyone's.

CHAPTER SIX

He must be a fool to be inviting Ward back into the house. But that is exactly what Nathan finds himself doing.

He scrawls the note quickly, before he can change his mind. He needs answers. Clarity. Needs to know where these threats to his family are truly coming from. And he needs to hear this information from Henry Ward himself.

He makes his way to the tavern, where he has been instructed to leave Ward's messages. He has been forthright—at least as forthright as he can manage; has specified Ward is to come to Highfield House at one tomorrow afternoon. This way, he can ensure Thea and Thomas are out of the house in Jenny's care, plus it will give him time to determine exactly what it is he wishes to say—or time to stew madly over the conversation, in any case.

On his way back to the manor, he collects the mail from the post house. The correspondence he was waiting for has arrived: responses from two potential new watch manufacturers from London. The prospect of rebuilding his failed business is one he is not looking forward to. But at least it gives him a glimpse of a future in which he is free of Holy Island and Henry Ward's grasp.

He has no idea if that future is completely fictitious.

Among the dreary financial outlines of business proposals is something which brings him endlessly more joy: copies of the Kepler star charts he had requested from the circulating library at Cambridge. Nathan remembers these same maps spread out over the desk in the office at Highfield House, back when it belonged to his father. Remembers the two of them huddling at the telescope, translating the ocean of stars to the neat black and white lines of Kepler's charts. Perhaps tonight the sky will clear and he will be able to do so again. A few hours' reprieve from thinking about Ward and the cursed letter.

Nathan hurries out of the post house with the charts tucked under his arm. He glances upwards at the thick bank of clouds. Looking at the stars tonight feels like wishful thinking.

He does his best not to make eye contact with anyone as he strides through the narrow streets. Word must have spread by now about Tom Cordwell and his cohort descending on Highfield House. Nathan wonders what stories are being told. Had Cordwell told the villagers the truth—that he had found nothing in the house? Has it gone someway to easing their suspicion about the Blakes? Or had the appearance of Henry Ward and his wayward pistol added fuel to the fire of the villagers' distrust?

Nathan has barely made it past the churchyard before he hears footsteps thudding behind him. He whirls around to find Joseph Holland closing the distance between them. Holland is dressed in a long dark greatcoat, a woollen cap pulled down low on his head. His bristly cheeks are red with cold. "We need to speak," he says gruffly.

Joseph Holland is the government spy who had initiated the use of the house, and Nathan is surprised he had not come asking questions the moment he heard about the attack. No doubt he felt that would raise too many questions, especially if the manor is still being watched. How Holland managed to catch him at the very moment he was striding through the village is a question Nathan does not want to know the answer to.

Holland's eyes dart. It's that same wary, hunted look that Nathan had seen in Julia's eyes when he had gone to her shop yesterday. The same look he has seen from so many of the villagers since the Jacobite Rising began. A look of suspicion and distrust, and faintly, of fear. Sensations he knows all too well.

"I'm going on ahead to my cottage," Holland murmurs. "Wait five minutes and then follow me." He is off before Nathan can reply.

Nathan turns in the opposite direction and circles the village before approaching Holland's small wooden cottage at the end of Prior Lane. He checks his pocket watch. Five minutes, as instructed.

Holland opens the door before Nathan knocks. Nods for him to enter. Holland's dog, a scruffy black and white thing with legs far too long for its body, gambols across the room and sniffs Nathan's shoes before winding around the table and settling down on the stones of the hearth.

Despite the pallid daylight, the single room of the house is dark, with shutters closed tightly across the windows and a lamp sputtering in the middle of the table. The place smells of damp and dog.

Nathan sits at a lopsided chair at the table, placing his mail down beside the lamp. The place is freezing, and he makes no effort to remove his greatcoat.

Holland paces, making the floorboards creak. "I heard what happened up at the house. Is your family unharmed?"

"We're all right. Thank you."

Holland takes off his cap and twists it between his hands. "Obviously we can't use the house anymore."

Nathan nods. Doesn't speak, for fear his relief will be too evident.

"Any idea what happened? Any thoughts on how the Jacobites came to know what the house was being used for?" Is there a hint of accusation in Holland's words, Nathan wonders? Or is he just imagining things?

He knows, of course, that Tom Cordwell catching Harriet returning from Lesbury had heightened the suspicions the villagers had had about the family. But there has to be more to it. If his sister is to be believed, Cordwell knew the house was being used for an exchange of messages long before Harriet's ill-advised journey with Michael Mitchell. And though Nathan knows Harriet is not always to be trusted, he is fairly certain Edwin's interrogation the night she had returned from Lesbury had succeeded in getting the truth out of her.

"We've been being watched for the past few weeks," he tells Holland. "Several of us have sensed it."

"Villagers just sitting outside Highfield House and watching for days on end in hope of seeing something untoward?" Holland shakes his head.

"I don't believe that. There has to be more to it. Someone working for the Jacobites must have seen something specific."

Nathan grits his teeth. "You think it was Julia Mitchell."

"Hardly the most outlandish of suggestions. We know her family are active Jacobites. And if I'm not mistaken, she had the good fortune of turning up at the house at the very moment we were meeting."

Nathan curses inwardly. Last week, Julia had appeared on the doorstep while the government spies were gathering beneath his roof. An innocent coincidence, Nathan had told himself, however naively. Julia had claimed she was calling after Harriet, and Nathan had believed—or at least, desperately hoped—that Holland and the other spies had not been aware of her being at the house. He had done his best to get her off the property as quickly as possible, without anyone catching on to her presence. This, he thinks dully, is exactly where he feared such a thing would lead: to baseless accusations hurled in Julia's direction.

"Miss Mitchell had nothing to do with it."

Holland's eyebrows rise—and Nathan's outburst manages to surprise himself just as much. For weeks, he has been as suspicious of Julia as anyone.

But two nights ago, as they had huddled by the telescope together, he had felt something shift. Not just because he had finally managed to break through his fear and make physical contact with her. That night, with no one else around, and any pretence eroded by grief over her lost brother, he had felt a genuineness to her. He had seen a new side to her as she had spoken of her son, her cat, her tomboyish childhood on Holy Island, spent running the dunes and beaches with her skirts tied at her knees. He had glimpsed a softness, a vulnerability he got the sense she rarely allows herself to reveal.

"Careful, Blake," says Holland. "Now is not the time to let a woman cloud your judgement."

Nathan bristles. He feels a swell of anger at Holland, and at himself for being so transparent. For letting his feelings slip without. But beyond it all is that low, rumbling undercurrent of fear for Julia about where Holland's suspicions will lead.

He needs to warn her.

CHAPTER SEVEN

The curiosity shop is empty, the front door locked. Nathan pounds on the side door. Calls Julia's name. Nothing.

He tries the church and shops of Marygate before catching sight of her at the anchorage. She is marching down the jetty in her dark green cloak, a basket of food slung over her arm. He guesses she has just returned from the mainland.

"You look worried," she says. "Has something happened?"

Nathan is fairly certain he has looked worried the entire time Julia has known him. And probably several years before that. He opens his mouth to speak, then stops, glancing edgily over his shoulder. Since the raid on the house, he feels eyes on him everywhere.

Julia hurries towards one of the fishermen's huts dotted along the beach, gesturing for Nathan to follow. "In here." She shoulders open the door and he follows her inside.

It's a bent and tiny place, hung with the smell of herrings and ocean, and creaking loudly with each gust of wind. A small table sits in one corner, cluttered with hooks and tangled twine, and hunks of what appears to be beeswax. Salt-encrusted nets hang from nails along the walls.

Julia puts her basket down on the sandy floorboards and looks up at him expectantly. Nathan stands with his back pressed up against the door. Feels it teeter against his weight. He is acutely aware of the distance between himself and Julia; two feet, perhaps. It's both far too much, and nowhere near enough. His pulse thunders in his ears.

"Joseph Holland," he begins, and that is enough for a look of unease to darken Julia's eyes. He knows she has been wary of him. Knows she has suspected him of spying for the government for some time. "You need to be careful. Keep your distance from him."

"Why? What's happened?" She looks at him squarely. "They are not just rumours, are they. This talk of Holland spying for the government."

"No," Nathan admits. "They're not." The words feel weighted, dangerous. Since setting foot back on Lindisfarne, he has been doing his best to stay out of the Rising. But with every passing minute, he seems to find himself more deeply entangled in it. And he is acutely aware he could be seen to be playing both sides. "Holland was the one who coerced me into letting the government spies use the house in the first place," he says. "And now he's desperate to find out how the Jacobites knew what the house was being used for."

Julia nods slowly. "He thinks I'm the one who told them."

"You came to the house once while the spies were meeting," Nathan admits. "I suspect Holland heard your voice. He knows your brothers are active Jacobites. He suspects you're working for them too."

Julia draws in a breath, as though turning this information over in her mind. "Who else?" she asks. "Who else on the island was coming to these meetings at Highfield House? Who else do I need to be wary of?"

"I didn't recognise the others," Nathan tells her. "They weren't from the island, as far as I could tell. Men Cotesworth recruited from around Northumberland to find the Jacobite nobles. They were using Highfield House because they believed Lindisfarne a key post for the rebel cause."

"I see."

Nathan finds himself taking a step towards her. "You need to watch yourself," he says. "Keep a close eye on Bobby."

There's more he wants to suggest, of course. Outlandish suggestions where he can all but ensure her and her son's safety: close the shop, keep Bobby away from school. And most treacherous—*stay with us*. But of course, he can hardly claim that Highfield House is any kind of safe haven. Not with Ward's ship in the bay and a bullet from his pistol lodged in the stairwell. Besides, it was her being at the house that had landed Julia in this trouble in the first place.

"This was risky," she says. "You telling me this. If Holland were to find out about it, you would be in as much danger as I am."

Nathan allows himself a small smile. Of this, he is well aware. "I could hardly say nothing, could I."

"Many would say that's exactly what you ought to have done." Julia looks up at him for a long, wordless moment, as though debating whether to speak further. The hut creaks loudly above their heads. "Nathan," she says finally, "I am so confused. You have put yourself in danger by telling me all of this. Why would you do that for me?"

He feels his fingers tighten around the star maps in his hand. Hears the steady thud of his pulse become a roar.

Julia continues before he can speak, her voice thin, uncertain. "Sometimes I feel as though… as though you care for me. And other times, it's as though you cannot wait to put distance between us." The intensity of her eyes brings heat to the back of his neck. "I know we've made it difficult to trust one another. But it is not just that, is it. I know it's not." She draws in a breath. "Is it because of my reputation? My past? Does it offend you that I have a child outside of wedlock? I know I couldn't blame you. I—"

"No," Nathan blurts. "It is not that, Julia. It is not that at all." He is not ready for this conversation. His fear of human contact is something he rarely discusses. He has little idea how to even put it into words. But how can he do otherwise when Julia is carrying his imperfections on her own shoulders? Besides, if whatever is between them is to have a chance of turning into anything real, this is something she needs to know.

Her being an unmarried mother had barely even registered with him. When he is in her company, his mind is far too full of determining whether or not she might be spying for the Jacobites, and whether or not he is going to self-combust in her presence, that there is barely room for such things.

And that in itself is somewhat unexpected. The starched and upright man he was in London would never have gone near a woman with such a past. Then again, the man he was in London had never considered going near a woman at all. Somehow, against all odds, his wife, Sarah, had just happened. And then, just as abruptly, she had been taken away.

He looks into Julia's gold-flecked eyes. Reads confusion there; uncertainty. And he knows he needs to be open with her. Here, now. After all the dangerous things he has shared with her these past two days, he needs to share this one more thing. And it is this that most has his heart racing.

"It's not…" He stumbles. Tries again. "It is not that I don't want you around me." His mouth feels dry, his skin hot. It has been so long since he has spoken openly of this. Not since Sarah. Aware he is crushing the star maps between his fingers, he sets his pile of correspondence on the table.

He swallows, choosing his words carefully. He knows that if he misspeaks, he could offend her irrevocably. "I find it difficult to be close to anyone," he says. "Physically… I…" His eyes are down, but on the edge of his vision, he sees Julia nod at him to continue. "When I feel the touch of another person, it's often too much to bear." He knows how foolish it sounds. "I don't know how else to describe it. It's a fear, of sorts, I suppose. One I cannot really make sense of." He scrubs a hand across his eyes. "I'm sorry. I can only imagine what you must think of me. What a madman you must think I am."

Julia frowns. "I don't think that at all." She swallows visibly. "Have you always had such a fear?"

"Since I was a child. I do not know for certain what caused it. Although I suspect my older brother may have had a little to do with it."

Julia nods. Nathan knows she remembers Oliver. She has told him as much; besides, he's sure everyone on Holy Island remembers him. A difficult child to forget. But Julia doesn't speak of his long-gone brother. Instead, she says, "Theodora. Is she…"

"She is my blood daughter, yes," Nathan says, answering her unspoken question. "I never imagined I would have a child. But when I met her mother… it was easy, somehow. Or, easier at least. I did not feel this fear quite so intensely." He looks down. Knots his hands together and squeezes. "Since Sarah died, I've never felt the desire to be near another woman—" Julia shifts and Nathan finds himself reaching for her. Finds his fingers closing around her wrist. He feels a bolt of hot energy shoot through him. Doesn't let go. "Except perhaps with you." The words feel dangerous. As though they could lead him to a path he cannot follow.

For long moments, Julia doesn't speak. Nathan's heart is pumping so hard he is afraid she will hear it. He fears he has said too much. Against her freckled skin, his fingers are blazing.

Julia's lips curl into a faint smile. She holds his gaze for a long, wordless moment, and Nathan is overcome by the sudden urge to pull her close, to feel her body against his own. But that urge is coupled with a sudden wave of overwhelm, and he holds himself back.

"Thank you for telling me," she says. "I'm sure it cannot have been easy."

His thumb traces a faint line across her bare forearm, testing himself. He can feel the smooth plane of her skin, the outline of bone, the fine hairs that dance against his fingertip. He hears loud breath against the background sigh of the sea. Cannot tell if that breath belongs to him or her.

"Where do we go from here?" Julia asks.

Nathan stands motionless, gathering his courage. He takes a step closer. Puts a hand to her shoulder, feels the curve of her, the heat of her body beneath the coarse wool of her bodice. Julia is still. He slides his hand down her arm, over her elbow, over the rough stitching on the sleeve of her shortjacket. His hand is pulsing with energy, blood rushing in his ears. And then, like a dam breaking, it is too much. At least, it is enough. He pulls away.

Julia looks him in the eye. "All right?" There is no judgement there, and he feels a deep gratitude.

He nods. Perhaps he is even a little more than all right. "I don't know where we go from here," he admits.

She smiles. "We shall work it out."

And suddenly there are voices; low murmurs coming towards them.

"I ought to go." Julia snatches her basket and throws open the door. She flies out of the hut without another word, marching, head down, back in the direction of her shop.

Julia stops on the corner of Marygate and watches Nathan slip from the fisherman's hut. With the collar of his greatcoat turned up and rolled papers tucked under his arm, he strides off the beach into the village.

A deep current of guilt runs through her, making her chest ache. After all he has just shared with her, after the danger he has put himself in by confirming her suspicions about Joseph Holland, is secret-keeping the best she can manage? She wishes so desperately that things were different.

She knows her eldest brother is nearby. It was his voice that had made her charge from the hut and put an end to her and Nathan's conversation. She prays Nathan made it off the beach before Hugh has any inkling of who she has been spending her time with.

She hurries back towards the shop, glimpsing the scarlet coats of two militiamen at the other end of the street. Doesn't stop to pick up the apples that escape out the top of her basket and roll into the gutter.

She will not wait for her brother to catch her. Right now, she wants nothing to do with him. And in any case, they cannot be seen in one another's company. Not by anyone. Nathan's warning about Joseph Holland has reminded her that even in a village so skewed with Jacobite support, there are plenty of people who wish the cause to fail. She knows there is every chance that word of Hugh's run-in with the authorities has spread back to Holy Island. Knows there are plenty of people here who would turn him over to the militia if they were to see him. And turn Julia in alongside him for providing shelter to a Jacobite criminal.

She unlocks the front door of the shop, dumping her basket on the floor behind the counter. She will take the food upstairs later. She knows Hugh will not be far behind her, and in the vain hope that he had not seen her at the anchorage, she wants to make it look as though she has been here at work all morning. She unlocks the chest where she keeps her pocket book. Dumps the coins on the counter and begins to count them.

When the bell above the door chimes, Julia doesn't look up. She knows it's Hugh. She has lost track of how many times she has begged him to at least use the side door off the alley when he returns to the shop. Using the front door, where anybody could see him, seems like an act of defiance. Like he is challenging the villagers to turn him in. Michael had been exactly the same. And look where that had led him.

Just after the siege at Lindisfarne Castle three weeks ago, Julia had been awoken in the night by a thumping on the front door of the shop. At first, she had been elated to find herself standing face to face with her eldest brother. After they had fled the conflict in York, in which they became wanted men, Angus and Michael had been separated from Hugh, and Julia had not heard word from him in months. She had begun to believe he was lost to them forever. Finding him on her doorstep had been an astonishing joy. She threw her arms around him, squeezing tightly.

"Where have you been?" she cried, tugging him into the dark shop. "Michael and Angus are waiting for you. They're out on Longstone. They don't want to leave for London without you."

"I'm not going to London. I'm needed here." There was a hardness in Hugh's voice that made Julia wary. Not a hint of warmth in his green eyes.

"Needed how?" she dared to ask.

"You don't need to know." He strode towards the staircase, but Julia darted in front of him, preventing him from going upstairs to her living quarters.

"I do need to know. Tell me, Hugh. Please."

He glanced back at the front door to ensure it was locked. Sighed. "The seizure of Lindisfarne Castle should have been successful," he told her. "Bamburgh and Lindisfarne are Jacobite towns. We've an entire army mustering at Lesbury. But word of the attack on the castle never reached them."

"And what do you plan to do about that from my shop?"

Hugh pulled off his dark wool cap and his thick red hair sprang free. "The Jacobites are using hollow trees and bushes between here and Bamburgh as communication posts. Our messages are being intercepted. We need to know who the government supporters are on Lindisfarne. And who might be intercepting the messages." He clenched his fist around his cap. "It's risky trying to get back to the army. But I can do my part here. Find out who's working for Geordie out on Holy Island."

"You can't stay here," said Julia. "I'm sorry. There are militia in the streets now. They came up from the south last week. If they find you here, we'll both be arrested. I'll not put my child in danger like that."

"Would you rather I return to my own cottage?"

"Of course not. Don't be foolish. If anyone saw movement in your house, they'd be suspicious."

"Then I'm staying here." That unyielding look in his eyes, Julia knew it well. But it had intensified in the months he had been away. Grown harder, colder. Almost made her fear him. He nodded towards the cellar. "I'll sleep down there, if you're so worried about having me in your home. No one will know I'm here."

Once, Hugh had been warm and caring. He had taken her in without question when their father had thrown her into the street after she found herself with child at seventeen, Bobby's father a distant, liquor-hazed memory. It was Hugh who had lent her the money she needed to open the shop; had rented the property for her in his name. But since the death of his wife and child two years ago, he had become fixated on the Jacobite cause. Nothing and no one else seemed to matter.

He had refused to let Julia tell anyone of his being there, not even their other brothers. Michael had died believing Hugh lost to the cause, and when Julia had sent Angus off to London alone, it had been with lies on her tongue and regret surging in her chest.

This was a cause greater than their own personal trials, Hugh had said. If the Stuarts were to be restored to the throne, as God wished, each man, woman and child had to do their part.

Julia wishes she had the courage to stand up to him. Wishes she had the strength to throw him out of her home. After all, she had been so adamant that her brothers stay away from her shop that she had hidden them in the empty shell of Highfield House. But each time she considers forcing Hugh out, the voice in the back of her head reminds her of everything he has done for her. And she cannot quite find the words.

Has she managed to keep Hugh's presence a secret? Julia cannot be certain of it. Harriet and Michael had both been at the shop while Hugh was hiding in the cellar—Nathan and Eva too. And then there are the blatant lies she had told Nathan about not knowing her brother's whereabouts. Julia had almost convinced herself he could see the untruths behind her eyes.

Today, Hugh is dressed in a long dark greatcoat, his hair tucked up beneath a knitted cap. His square jaw is clean shaven, free of his tell-tale red beard. He's far better at this game than Michael was, Julia thinks dully. With the hat pulled low on his forehead, hiding his fiery hair, she would have easily strolled past Hugh in the street without paying him a second glance. At least if it weren't for the racing pulse and deep dread his presence seems to instinctively stir up within her. She can tell by the look in his eyes that he had seen her with Nathan.

Hugh strides up to her and plants his hands on the counter. Julia can smell the sea on him; guesses he has been on the mainland, exchanging words with the Bamburgh Jacobites that have not left to join the rebel army. She has not seen him since yesterday morning.

"The Northumbrian Jacobites met up with the Highlanders in Kelso," he announces. "We're nearly two thousand strong now." She sees a fire behind his eyes. "Almost enough to outnumber the government troops."

Julia purses her lips. Unless the rebel army is about to storm Lindisfarne, she has little desire to know where they are. "Angus has left," she says. "Gone to London. Alone. I took him over to Berwick yesterday."

Hugh nods. "Good. It's what's best for him. You didn't tell him I was here, did you?"

"No," she says bitterly. "I wouldn't dare."

He nods. "It's for the best, Julia. The less people who know where I am, the better."

"Even your own brother?"

Hugh opens his mouth to respond, then seems to change his mind. He begins to walk down the steps towards the cellar. Looks back over his shoulder at her, a wordless instruction for her to follow. And in spite of every last scrap of self-respect, Julia finds herself following.

Hugh takes the tinderbox from the chair in the corner and lights the lamp, then shuts the door behind them. The room feels suddenly thick and airless, as though the stone walls are closing in.

"You know Nathan Blake," Hugh says.

Julia had been more than a little grateful that Hugh had not been at the shop when Nathan had appeared yesterday afternoon, begging for the chance to explain himself. This time, she knows she has had no such luxury.

Surely Hugh knows of the rumours pegging the Blakes as government spies. She cannot bear to think on who he might have shared these rumours with. He has no proof, she reminds herself. There is no proof. Because Nathan is not a spy.

She stands with her back pressed to the wall of the cellar. "Yes," she says tautly. "I do know Mr Blake."

"And what did you have to speak about that was so important you saw fit to hide away in a fisherman's hut?"

Julia feels her cheeks blaze. "That is none of your business."

Her mind is still churning from everything Nathan had told her, and she wishes she had a little time to take it all in. Joseph Holland, yes, but that is no surprise. Rumours of Holland's involvement in the government cause have been swirling for months. It is Nathan's other revelation that has most unbalanced her.

Since Bobby had arrived; since the village—and her own father—had labelled her a harlot, Julia has done her best to live up to the reputation. If she is to be perceived that way, why not embrace it? A subconscious thing at first, then a deliberate choice. An act of defiance. An attempt at not caring what people say about her. More than once, when she had opened her cellar to lodgers in the days before the Rising, she had ended up sharing their bed. Empty dalliances, chased away with Queen Anne's Lace, to prevent a brother or sister for Bobby.

And how is it that, after all the trysts and meaningless entanglements she has found herself in; after all the men she has curled up beneath the sheets with, that single touch of Nathan's hand against her shoulder had set her so alight? She is not sure any man has ever elicited that reaction from her. Bobby's father, perhaps, but he was just a fleeting mistake who had disappeared before he'd even swallowed the last of the whiskey.

She supposes it makes sense, in some strange way. Because Nathan Blake is the opposite of those brash and bawdy men who used to find their way to her cellar. He's a man ill at ease with himself. Self-doubting and uncertain. She had sensed that from the moment he had first walked into her shop to buy a doll for his daughter. A man who seems entirely unaware of his own strength, his own grace. Unaware, she imagines, of how hard her heart beats in his presence.

How can he be anything but strong, given all he is facing? Nathan may not be able to see his own quiet strength, but it was what had drawn Julia to him in the first place. And that need to make him see it himself, well, that is almost overwhelming.

When I feel the touch of another person, it's often too much to bear. Though she could tell the words had not come easy to him—no doubt it is a thing he rarely speaks of—Julia had been almost reassured to hear of his fear. Because while this is an intricacy she had never imagined she would have to navigate, she is relieved to know Nathan is not disgusted by her being an unwed mother, as she had feared.

The hard look in Hugh's eyes sloughs away her thoughts of Nathan.

"It is my business," her brother says, his voice low and slow, "because the Blakes are believed to be working for the government. And you are either sharing Jacobite secrets with him, or you are sharing his bed. Or both."

Julia snorts. "That's quite some conclusion to jump to." When Hugh doesn't respond, she says, "The Blakes are not working for the government. Of that I can assure you. And what is between Nathan and me has nothing to do with you." She meets her brother's eyes challengingly. "If you must know, he was putting himself in danger to ensure my safety."

Hugh's expression suggests he does not believe her. "I would hate to think you were betraying our family, Julia."

"When did the Jacobite cause become our family's cause?"

"When it caused Da to lose his spirit in the battle at Dunkeld. And when Michael lost his life."

"Michael was a fool," Julia hisses. "You know that as well as I do." But Hugh is right, she thinks distantly. This has always been her family's cause. Her father had watched men burnt alive in the houses of Dunkeld, and the weight of it has hung over him ever since. Now Michael is lost to them forever; Angus forced from his family and home. This conflict, bubbling beneath the surface since Julia was in the cradle, has shaped their entire lives.

"Michael was doing what he thought was right," Hugh shoots back. "Instead of hiding away like a coward. Or worse—helping the other side."

"I am not on any side," Julia snaps. "All I want is to keep my son safe."

"Is that what you and Nathan Blake were doing then? Keeping Bobby safe?"

Finding a sudden burst of rebellion, she throws open the cellar door. Hugh catches her wrist before she can charge away.

"Julia." His voice softens slightly. "I'm sorry. I didn't mean to put you on edge."

"How exactly did you imagine I would feel?" she hisses. "I'm being interrogated."

"I'm sorry," he says again. "You know I'm only doing this because I care about you."

She snorts. "No, you're doing this because you've become so passionate about the Jacobite cause you've lost sight of everything else around you."

He seems to consider her words for a moment. "I am passionate about the cause," he agrees. "But I do care about you. You know I do."

Julia is silent. She had known that once, yes. But lately? She's seen little sign that Hugh cares a scrap about her or Bobby. Even the news of Michael's death, told to him with tears running down her face, had elicited little more than a regretful nod. A few steely words muttered about sacrifice and troop numbers, as though Michael were some nameless soldier instead of their own younger brother. Julia has begun to wonder if the empathetic part of Hugh has been scoured away.

He releases his grip on her wrist. "I don't want you to get hurt," he says. "I know how difficult life has been for you. But there cannot be anything between you and Nathan Blake."

Julia glares at him. "It is not your place to decide that."

"It's too dangerous. You can't be associating with government spies."

Julia clenches her hands into fists. Clearly her words about Nathan's innocence have not even registered. "Highfield House was attacked at dawn yesterday," she says tightly. "Did you have anything to do with that?"

"No. It was Tom Cordwell and some others."

Julia grits her teeth. Hugh's knowledge of the situation does little to support his claim of innocence. "Nathan says he's been being watched," she snaps. "He says Cordwell and the others came to the house because they saw the government messengers using it. Was that your doing? Have you been watching Nathan and his family?"

Hugh's silence is all the answer she needs. She knows this is the worst kind of betrayal to Nathan; to be hiding Hugh here after what he has just confessed to. Far worse than anything else she has done to the Blakes. "The government spies think I'm the one who told the Jacobites what

Highfield House was being used for," she says pointedly.

Something sparks behind Hugh's eyes. Julia expects some outburst about her safety, but he says, "Who?" Something close to excitement in his voice. "Who's working for the government on Holy Island? If you're so adamant it's not Nathan Blake, tell me who it is."

She snorts. "You were watching the house. Don't you already know that?"

"I saw men coming and going, aye," he says. "But I didn't recognise any of them. They were all dressed as laborers. And did a fine job of keeping their faces hidden. Tell me who they are."

"I've no idea." She cannot speak Joseph Holland's name. It would put Nathan in far too much danger.

Hugh gives a thin laugh. "What happened to you, Julia? You used to be a far better liar."

CHAPTER EIGHT

There has been a debate, Harriet is aware, over whether or not she ought to be told her father is coming to the house this afternoon. It has been going on for much of the morning; she has caught snatches of it through closed doors and around corners. Nathan, clearly still feeling guilty over his secret-keeping, thinks she ought to know; ought to be given the chance to let Henry Ward into her life. Edwin, unsurprisingly, is all for shunting her up to her bedchamber so she might never lay eyes on her troublesome father again.

Well. She listens, and she learns, and she slips out of the house before Edwin and Nathan can make up their minds what to do with her, and when Henry Ward's longboat sighs up against the embankment, she is ready and waiting.

It had crossed her mind, fleetingly, to pretend to be engaged in some other activity: an afternoon stroll perhaps, or removing the dead ivy scrawled across the walls of the house. Something that will make her look less desperate for her father's company.

She decides against it. Her fledgling connection to Henry Ward has already been tainted enough by lies and deceit. She will not poison it further with foolish games.

Showing her father how much she wishes to be a part of his life makes her feel impossibly vulnerable. It is not often that she willingly lets anyone see her weakness. But she knows how easily Henry Ward could weigh anchor and sail out of her life. She could not bear for that to happen.

Ward approaches the house with a deliberate stride, but halts in his step when he sees her. There's something faintly reassuring about that falter. A sign, perhaps, that she matters to him; makes a dent on the vast tableau of his life.

He takes off his cocked hat and passes it between his hands. "Good afternoon, Harriet." His address is stilted; uncertain, somehow, and too formal. The effect of two decades of distance. "Were you out here waiting for me? Surely there's no need for such a thing."

"My husband does not wish me to see you," she admits.

Ward nods, unsurprised. "I'm sure I cannot blame him for that."

Their eyes meet for a silent, stilted moment. "I told Nathan he could trust you," Harriet says finally.

"I'm glad you feel that way."

She hesitates. She thinks to invite him inside with her; show him pieces of her life. Her son, perhaps. What she really wants is to show him her paintings, but thanks to Edwin, those are nothing but ash now. She wants to impress Henry Ward, she realises. Wants to make her newfound father proud of her. How petty, she thinks, chasing the thought away bitterly. Has she not grown up from the child who used to wave her sketches under the nose of her mother, craving validation?

Besides, she is all too aware that Henry Ward has not come here for her. He has come at Nathan's bidding, come to tell the full story. Come to share those midnight truths. To admit, perhaps, that he is not the all-powerful man he once was, and that there are other men at the tiller of his ship. Yes, she has caught pieces of the story, no matter how much Nathan and Edwin have tried to keep her blind and deaf to it.

And so this will have to be enough for now; the fact he is glad to have her trust. Harriet gestures towards the front door and slides a key from her pocket. "My brother is inside waiting for you."

It's Harriet who has let him in, Eva knows. She is making no secret of it, standing at her father's shoulder in the entrance hall with a brittle look on her face. A look that says she has chosen her side.

Eva tries to glimpse behind Ward's eyes. Tries to catch any hint as to whether or not he has spilled the story of Finn and Oliver. She sees only his lifted chin, his hard eyes—a rigid façade of confidence. She cannot bring herself to look at Harriet.

Eva desperately does not want to be here. Desperately does not want Finn here. It feels as though they had escaped just long enough to draw breath before being pulled back below the surface. But when she had come to the house for Thea's lessons yesterday, Nathan had told her of his plans to speak with Ward. And what other choice does she have but to be here? If Ward is to speak of the past, she needs to hear what he has to say.

His eyes move over them, all gathered in the entrance hall like expectant children. Nathan and Edwin, her and Finn. He seems to look down on them, despite being no taller than Nathan and Edwin, and inches shorter than Finn. He greets them only with a wordless nod.

Nathan swallows visibly. "Thank you for coming." He clears his throat and gestures towards the parlour. "Please. This way."

Ward begins striding down the passage before Nathan even finishes speaking. Harriet trails after him, but Edwin steps in front of her, blocking her way before she can enter the parlour. "Upstairs," he murmurs.

The look in Harriet's eyes is so fierce it makes Eva's chest tighten. Harriet looks to her father, as though hoping he might intervene, might allow her to stay. Ward glances over his shoulder at her, but says nothing. Just steps inside the parlour with Nathan. Harriet whirls around and disappears down the passage.

Edwin looks expectantly at Finn. "I'm sure Harriet would welcome her sister's company," he says pointedly.

Finn looks at Edwin, then at Eva. He puts a hand to the small of her back, guiding her into the parlour beside him.

"Thank you," she murmurs.

"If I have to sit through this, I'm not letting you escape it." His half-smile doesn't quite reach his eyes.

Ward takes the armchair in the corner of the parlour without waiting for an invitation. He looks as though he belongs there, Eva thinks sickly. Looks as though those faded blue cushions have been worn smooth with his own weight. Nathan and Edwin sit opposite him on the settle, leaving Eva and Finn to hover in front of the mantel.

The fire is blazing. Sweat prickles Eva's skin, dampening her shift at her lower back. She shifts her weight edgily, alight with nerves. The fluttering of her heart, her stomach, is almost unbearable. Firelight glows off the dark wood panels of the walls, making the room feel close and cloying, despite the pale sunlight struggling through the windows.

"I was glad to receive your message," Ward says to Nathan. "I'd hoped for the chance to speak with you."

Eva hears a murmur escape her. The men turn to her.

"Do you have something to say?" Ward asks tightly.

Her body turns hot, then cold under his hard blue eyes. "Just that you are hardly one to wait for an invitation."

A few months ago, she would never have spoken out like this. Would have kept quiet in an attempt to veer away from conflict. But conflict has become such a part of her life of late that she is no longer so afraid of it. Still, she knows the only place her outbursts can lead here is to her and Finn's secrets being spilled. Perhaps she ought to have been sent upstairs with Harriet.

Ward seems unfazed by her blundering. "I promised your brother I would not come to the house uninvited," he says firmly. "And I am a man who keeps his word. As I'm sure your husband will tell you."

Eva swallows. Feels herself take an involuntary step towards Finn. He shifts his hand slightly to graze his knuckles over hers. She can sense the tension in his body.

"Well," Edwin shoots an irritated glance at Eva, before turning back to Ward, "now that you're here, I think we would all appreciate you giving us a full explanation of the situation we're facing."

Nathan shifts awkwardly on the settle. He is well dressed today, Eva notices, in a deep blue waistcoat embroidered with gold thread. Brown hair powdered and tied with a matching ribbon. To give him confidence, perhaps. It does not appear to be working.

"You've not told us the truth about this letter," he tells Ward. "I need to know who is behind it. And why."

Ward leans back in his chair, curling his weather-worn hands around the arms. "Those are quite forward requests, Mr Blake. Rather hypocritical of you to demand such openness from me when you yourself have kept so many secrets. Did you not imagine I might care to know I had a daughter?"

Nathan bristles. "Can you blame me for not telling you about Harriet after the threats you made towards me and my child?"

"I suppose not." Ward's eyes shift to Eva and Finn. "Although I cannot help but wonder if your silence might have come from more selfish reasons."

"You've been threatening our family," Eva snaps, the words tumbling out before she can rein them in. "Can you really be surprised that we kept such a thing from you?"

"Indeed I can't." Ward's eyes pierce her. "Mrs Murray."

She falls silent, cursing herself for her outburst. The drumbeat against her ribs is dizzying. Ward's threat, unspoken, presses down on her, making the air unbreathable. Finn meets her eyes in silence.

Ward looks their way for a long second, before turning back to Nathan. "I will tell you what you wish to know, Mr Blake," he says. "But perhaps once I do, you will understand why I kept the truth from you for so many months."

Eva feels Nathan glance at her. Unease in his eyes. He nods for Ward to continue. Eva hears the faint creak of the floorboards in the passage outside the parlour. She knows Harriet is listening.

"When I met your mother a little over twenty years ago, she had got herself in trouble," says Ward. "The first Jacobite Rising had failed some years earlier, and the cause was struggling to find its feet. After your father died, Abigail involved herself in the cause, raising money, as it were."

Nathan's hands tighten around his knees. "Mother was not a Jacobite."

"No," says Ward. "But she was in desperate need of money after your father's death. Samuel had little wealth to leave her. Her settlement was terribly small, and she had no rights to sell the house. She aligned herself with the Jacobites on this island, under the guise of friendship. The Jacobite cause was languishing after Dundee's failed rebellion. Their morale was low and they desperately needed funds. Abigail volunteered to visit the noble Jacobite families around Northumberland, raising money for the cause. She kept a large percentage of that money for herself."

"No." The word falls out of Eva's mouth on its own accord. "You're lying. She would not have done something like that. She was a good person."

Ward's eyes soften slightly, and his expression of sympathy hits her hard. "She was a good person in many ways, yes," he says. "But not all. I'm sorry, Eva. It brings me no joy to tell you this." She hates the sincerity in his voice. Hates that that sheen of bravado has come down, to reveal an authenticity beneath. Because it makes it so hard to doubt him. So hard to brand him a liar. And beneath it all is that thorn Eva has been doing her best to ignore: that she has been questioning exactly who her mother was since she learnt Harriet was Henry Ward's daughter.

Eva looks at Nathan, willing him to protest. Willing him to drop some piece of information from their childhood that will prove Henry Ward is wrong about this. But the look in Nathan's eyes, it's almost as unsettling as Ward's sympathy. Almost as though these words have triggered some forgotten memory within him. Does he remember their mother making fundraising trips around the county? Does he remember her spending time with the Jacobites on Lindisfarne?

"The letter I have been so eager to get my hands on was written to me by a Scottish nobleman I sailed with in my youth," Ward tells them. "I knew the value of the letter immediately, especially given it contained the signature and seal of a prominent member of the aristocracy. I knew how much damage it could do if it fell into the wrong hands. And how much the Whig party would pay to ensure that did not happen.

"Your mother found it among my belongings one day. Offered to hide it in the house. She argued that it would be much safer locked away here, than travelling around Europe aboard my ship. I regret that I agreed."

He turns to look out the window, his eyes growing glassy. "I assumed Abigail took the letter with her when she left the island, given its value. And when I contacted her before her death, she told me she had put it in our safe at the Bank of England. That turned out to be a lie."

Nathan shifts forward on the settle. "Why did she lie to you? What did you do to her?"

Ward's eyes flicker at the accusation. He does not speak at once. "I suppose something made her change her mind about what was between us," he says finally. "But I know no more than you do. I've not seen her since the night your brother died."

Eva's heart thunders at the mention of her brother. She stares at her feet, unable to meet Ward's eyes. But Ward's thoughts are not with Finn and Oliver, she realises—at least not at this moment. They are with Abigail, and whatever had been between the two of them.

"Given you have been unable to find the letter," Ward tells Nathan, "I can only assume she sold it and used the money to fund her new life in London. And that she was too afraid to tell me the truth when I asked after the letter before she died."

Eva's stomach rolls. Her childhood in London had not been filled with wealth, but nor had it been penniless. She and her siblings had grown up in her late father's townhouse in Chelsea; had never been cold or hungry, had never walked the streets with holes in their boots. The three of them had been well educated: herself and Harriet with sought-after governesses, Nathan at Tenison's, and then at Cambridge. Eva had always assumed such a life had been possible because of the settlement her father had left Abigail after his death. But is it possible that life had been paid for with the funds from a stolen Jacobite letter?

"Why do you want the letter so badly now?" Finn says suddenly. "Why come for it after twenty years? Is because you want to offer your crew immunity like you told me?"

Ward rubs a hand over his shorn chin. Eva catches a hint of shame in his eyes. "My crew is largely English," he says. "And like all Englishmen in this day and age, they are divided."

"You have Jacobites in your crew," says Nathan.

"Indeed. One particularly fervent supporter of the Stuarts is my quartermaster, John Graveney. He has been a part of my crew for more than two decades." He looks at Finn. "Perhaps you might remember him."

Finn says nothing.

"Mr Graveney is—or rather, was—a loyal member of my crew. When we were in Nassau several years ago, he came across correspondence that Abigail had written to me while she was living at Highfield House. In it, she speaks of the theft she committed against the Jacobites she pretended to be working for."

His words catch Eva by surprise. "You kept her letters," she murmurs.

"They were precious to me," Ward admits. "But I can see now that it was foolish to do so. When my quartermaster discovered the damage

Abigail had inflicted on the Jacobite cause, he became determined that she be punished for her crimes. See the money she stole returned, and justice done. Of course, such a thing is no longer possible. At least from Abigail herself."

"He wants the money our mother stole," Nathan says dully.

Ward nods. "Indeed."

Nathan gets to his feet and strides to the window. He stares through the glass for long moments, his hands folded behind his back and his shoulders rounded. Eva can practically see the weight of the situation pressing down on him.

"You're Graveney's captain, Ward," Finn snaps. "Do you not have control over what he does?"

"I have control over him as a member of my crew, yes," says Ward. "But not as a man." He looks at Finn pointedly. "You ought to understand that better than anybody."

Eva sees the clench of Finn's jaw. Sees the rapid rise and fall of his chest. After a moment of silence, he asks, "How did Graveney learn of the letter?"

"I told him of it," Ward admits. "I hoped it would appease him. I truly believe it has the power to offer my crew immunity. The Whigs have far more influence than they did twenty years ago, when the letter was first written. And the man it speaks of is still holding office."

"So, what?" Edwin demands. "You plan to blackmail the authorities with the information in the letter in the event of your pirate crew being captured?"

"Indeed." More poorly hidden shame in Ward's voice. "Without the threat of capture in British waters, my crew could make great wealth. Wealth that Mr Graveney could funnel back into the Jacobite cause, if he chose to do so." He lowers his eyes. "I hoped such a promise would be enough to keep him away from your family. But without the letter, I cannot say what he will do."

"Why not tell us all this from the beginning?" Nathan asks. "Why let me believe you were going to kill me? Come after my child?"

Ward sighs. "It brought me no pleasure, Mr Blake. But whatever you might believe, I loved your mother. And I know she never wished you to find out what she had involved herself in. It was something she was not proud of."

"Why tell us the truth now?"

"Is that not obvious?" Ward says tautly. "I have just learnt I have a daughter. I do not wish her to see me as a monster I am not." His voice hardens. "And given all Abigail kept hidden from me, I am less inclined to keep her secrets. Especially when doing so reflects so poorly on me."

Nathan leans back against the window. "The letter is not in the house," he says finally. "Whether it's you or your quartermaster that wants the damn thing, it doesn't change that."

Ward nods. "Mr Graveney knows you have been unable to find the letter."

"And?"

"And he wishes repayment in another way. He wants the money your mother stole to be returned to the Jacobite cause."

"There is no money," Nathan says thinly.

"That's an argument you can attempt to make, Mr Blake," says Ward. "But I'm afraid Graveney is unlikely to believe it when you are sitting in the biggest house on Holy Island."

CHAPTER NINE

Finn follows Ward out of the house, letting the door thud shut behind him. A fine, misty rain has begun to billow in across the sea. "How many?" he asks. "How many men will side with Graveney to force this money from Eva's family?" Their boots sigh over the soft earth of the dunes.

Ward presses his lips together. "Enough."

"You can't let him take the house," Finn hisses. "It's all they have."

"Do you really think any of this is my choice? Do you really think I'd choose to be here, floating around this cursed house for weeks if I had an alternative? Don't you think I hate this place as much as you do?"

His outburst catches Finn off guard. "You don't want to be here?"

Ward turns away. Lowers his voice. "Of course I don't. There's nothing here for me but bad memories. But Graveney and the other Jacobites… they're determined that the Blakes pay for what their mother did. They want the letter. Or payment, in its place."

"Fight them," Finn snaps. "When have you ever let your crew do something against your will? Surely you can't support Graveney taking the house."

"Of course I don't."

"Then put a stop to it!" Finn hisses.

Ward looks down. "I'm afraid it's not that simple."

And Finn sees it clearly now; sees that Ward's captaincy is not as secure as it had once been. He has a ship full of angry Jacobites seeking justice for Abigail Blake's twenty-year-old crimes, and he's made promises of immunity that he cannot deliver on.

Finn looks out to the ship lying at anchor beyond the house. It's barely visible behind the fresh curtain of mist. "You fear Graveney will mutiny, don't you. And you think if you leave Lindisfarne without the letter it'll turn your crew against you."

Ward doesn't answer. He doesn't need to.

For the first time in his life, Finn sees through Ward's brassy façade to the flawed and frightened man that lies beneath. There is something unsteadying about Ward's weakness being on such glaring display, especially with the fate of Eva's family depending on him.

"So your captaincy is more important to you than the family of the woman you loved," Finn says bitterly. "Is that the kind of man you are now?"

He sees something flicker behind Ward's eyes. Anger. He knows he has gone too far.

"I could sail away from this house right now without the letter or the money," Ward says tautly. "But how long do you think it would be before Graveney and his supporters wrestled the captaincy from me? And the first thing they would do would be to come right back here to Holy Island and force the house from Nathan in exchange for the money his mother stole." His eyes bore into Finn's. "I'm trying to keep Abigail's family safe. That is all I've ever wanted to do."

Finn says nothing. Ward is right, he realises. He hates that he is right.

"Do you really think this is acceptable, Finn?" Ward asks suddenly. "For you to be sitting at their table? Giving your input into these matters? Do you really think you ought to be a part of this family?"

Finn swallows. "Eva and I are married," he says. "It's time you accepted that."

Ward laughs thinly. "Don't tell me what I ought to accept, lad. You know me better than that."

Finn's stomach knots. "Abigail deceived you. She left this island so you'd never know about Harriet." He knows Ward does not need the reminder. "And you're still pressuring me to leave Eva as you think her mother would have wanted?"

"Yes. Because it's the right thing to do. You do not belong in this family, Finn. Surely you can see that." Ward looks at him pointedly. "My offer still stands. Join my crew, and I will let the punishment due to you over Oliver's death slide."

"I am not going to join your crew, Ward. I've no intention of leaving my wife. So if you mean to kill me, just do it." He folds his arms. "What exactly are you waiting for?"

Ward chuckles dully at Finn's clumsy boldness. "I'm waiting for you to see sense and take up my offer. It would bring me no pleasure to kill you, Finn. You know that."

"Because you want my support against Graveney?"

Ward ignores his barbed comment. Raindrops glitter on the shoulders of his justacorps. "You can't go your life without being held accountable for what you did. Sooner or later, the truth is going to come out."

The muscles in Finn's neck tighten. One word from Ward to his daughter and the truth about Oliver's death will spill. If he has not told Harriet already.

As if reading Finn's thoughts, Ward says, "Fetch my daughter for me. I wish to say goodbye to her before I leave."

"Can you sail this boat to the North Pole?" asks Theodora. She is clambering over the benches of the skiff, which is beached high up on the embankment. Ward's longboat lies barely thirty feet away. The rain has eased to a fine drizzle, making the grass of the dunes glitter.

"You'd have to find it first," says Finn. "And you might get a little cold."

Theodora's shoes skid over the wet palings of the boat. His hand darts out and grabs her arm to keep her upright.

"Careful, Thea," Eva says edgily. She glances back to where Harriet is talking to her father just outside the house.

Theodora ignores her. "What about the South Pole? I think the adventurers in my story would like to go there. I bet there's sea monsters."

Eva gnaws at her thumbnail, trying to gauge Harriet's expression. Her face is too hard to read from side on. Ward presses Harriet's hand between both of his for a moment, before turning from the house and striding towards his longboat.

Theodora follows him with her gaze. Eva steps protectively in front of her, trying to block her view.

"Who is that?" Thea asks, peeking out from behind her. When she gets no response, she pulls at Eva's skirts. "Auntie Eva? Who is he?"

"He's no one," Eva says tautly.

Despite all he had told them about not being the one behind the threats over the letter, trusting Henry Ward is not something that comes easily. Harriet glances their way, then disappears inside.

"Wait for me," Eva tells Finn suddenly. "I'm going to speak to her. I want to find out what she and Ward were talking about."

She grabs Theodora's hand and tugs her back into the house behind her. Sends her niece upstairs, before making her way tentatively down to the workroom, where she feels certain Harriet will be hiding.

She knocks, but steps inside without waiting for an invitation. With the fire almost out and the lamp unlit, the room is a misery of shadow.

Harriet doesn't look surprised to see her. "Come for more information, have you?" She wipes away the condensation on the window and watches as Ward's longboat glides back towards his ship. Her damp hair is frizzing slightly around her face, escaping the confines of the long plait down her back.

"Of course not." Eva knots her hands. "Well. Perhaps a little." She shakes her head, hating how on edge she is around her sister these days. "I just wish to speak with you." And yes, she had come here so she might manage a glimpse beneath Harriet's prickly shell, to determine whether Ward has told her about Finn and Oliver. But as she stands opposite her, Eva realises this is about more than that. It is about rebuilding their fragile relations before they are frayed completely. If Harriet knows how Oliver died, such a thing will be impossible. But if not, perhaps she has a chance to keep her sister in her life. Eva suddenly realises how much she longs for that to be the case.

"Speak with me about what?" Harriet asks tautly. She doesn't turn away from the window.

Eva toys with the splintering edge of the table. "I wondered if you might like to come back to Longstone with me," she says hopefully. "I know I spoke about showing it to you one day. The rain has almost stopped and the sea is quite calm."

"No thank you."

"Very well. Then perhaps we could have tea?"

Harriet turns to look at her. "Why?"

"What do you mean, why?" Eva takes a step forward, closing the space between them. "I'm sorry," she says, "for not telling you about Ward. It was wrong of me."

Harriet eyes her closely, making Eva's heart quicken. She has always struggled to read her sister, but now such a thing is near impossible. She hates this roiling in her stomach when she is around Harriet. Hates that she cannot trust her. Ward's daughter or not, it does not change the fact that Harriet is Eva's only sister. And she cares about her far too much to let their relationship be destroyed by this.

Perhaps it is too late. Perhaps Harriet knows about Finn and Oliver, and their sisterhood is already in pieces. But until Eva knows that for certain, she is not going to stop trying.

"Come on," she says, in the firm voice she used on her flighty younger sister back when they were children. "It is not doing you any good being down here. Let's go to the parlour. I'll have Mrs Brodie bring us some tea."

Harriet stiffens. "Your husband is waiting for you."

"He'll not mind waiting a little longer." Eva knows he'll be particularly willing to wait if she can determine just how much her sister knows.

Harriet sighs heavily and follows Eva down the passage towards the parlour. Eva rings the handbell on the side table; asks Mrs Brodie for a pot of tea. For long moments, they sit silently beside each other on the settle, Harriet perched on the edge, her back rigid and her eyes unreadable. Eva knots her fingers. This suddenly feels like a terrible idea.

"Why did you not tell me?" Harriet asks abruptly.

It feels like a test. "Because I believe Henry Ward is a dangerous man," Eva admits. "He dragged Finn aboard his ship a few months ago. Tried to kill him for something he did back when he was a child." She is sailing far too close to the wind, she knows. But if she is to have any hope of resurrecting things with Harriet, she needs to give her something other than empty lies.

"What did he do?"

"He fought with someone," says Eva, trying to keep her voice level.

"He was just defending himself. He did not deserve to be punished for it."

Harriet snorts. "You would say that, wouldn't you."

Mrs Brodie shoulders open the door, a tea tray in her hands. Eva murmurs her thanks as the housekeeper sets the pot on the tea table and fills two cups.

Eva picks up her teacup, letting the warmth seep into her fingers. Once the door has closed behind Mrs Brodie, she says, "I do not want this business to destroy what is between us, Harriet. You are my sister and I want you in my life."

Harriet takes her cup from the table, but doesn't drink. "Why does it matter?" she asks. "In a few months, I will be back in London and you will be up here, more than a week's journey away. We are hardly going to be at each other's supper table every Sunday." She lets out a faint, private laugh. "Assuming you have a supper table, that is."

Eva sets down her teacup. Tries to swallow the hurt and anger. "So that is all I mean to you then? I'll be forgotten once you return to London?"

Harriet sighs, with a faint hint of regret. "I did not mean it like that. I just meant… Well. Once I leave, are you and I ever going to see each other again?" Her words feel too dramatic, too weighted.

"I certainly hope so," Eva says. "Is that not what you want too?"

Harriet gives a snort of humourless laughter. "I can promise you, Evie, once I get out of this place, I shall not be returning."

"Very well. But I can come and see you in London from time to time." She swallows. "If you wish it."

Harriet seems to consider her question. Then she nods faintly. It's a meagre, hollow promise, Eva knows, but one that clearly shows she does not know the truth of how Oliver died.

It feels like an enormous victory.

CHAPTER TEN

"I assume you're going to the authorities with this," says Edwin, following Nathan out of the house. "It'll be easy enough with the militia in the village."

Nathan curses under his breath. He had hoped to slip out without Edwin noticing. Had hoped for an uninterrupted hour to drift around the island and let the chaotic thoughts in his head fall into some kind of order.

He has no idea what he is supposed to think of Ward's claims. He does not want to believe his mother was a thief. But he cannot deny that Ward's story had pricked at some hidden thread of memory. At some unnameable unease that always comes when he thinks of his childhood. His mother's vague, insubstantial answers to his questions, perhaps. Her long absences from the house.

In a way, he is glad she is not here to see what her choices have led to. But he cannot go to the authorities.

"Ward and Graveney have not done a thing to us." Nathan tucks his hands into his pockets and strides with his head down. "The authorities are not going to go after them based on threats that may amount to nothing."

Edwin raises his eyebrows. "Is that what you believe? That this will come to nothing?"

"Of course not. But you know that's how the militia will see it."

"These men are pirates, Nathan," Edwin says. "You're telling me you don't think the authorities will be interested?"

Nathan doesn't reply. He never ceases to be amazed by his brother-in-law's ability to make him feel so small and foolish. Edwin quickens his pace to keep up with him. Gulls swoop above their path as they trudge towards the village.

"Ward's men are watching us," Nathan says finally. "Their ship is right outside our house. Who knows what they'll do if they see us going to the militia? I can't take that risk."

Edwin walks in silence for several paces. Nathan expects a retaliation; a recitation of all the reasons why this is the wrong thing to do. But Edwin says:

"Very well. You may be right."

Nathan gives a humourless laugh. "I'm surprised to hear you say that." He folds his arms across his chest, bracing himself for what's to come. He knows Edwin's solutions will revolve around pistols and counter-threats. And while Nathan can see that this is likely the way forward, he aches for a peaceful resolution.

Edwin says, "We need this Henry Ward removed from our lives."

"By killing him, you mean?"

"Well, he's hardly going to go on his own accord, is he. He's made that perfectly clear." Edwin digs his hands into the pockets of his coat, his shoes sighing through the mud on the edge of the village. "I know you don't have it in you to kill a man, Nate. But for the safety of this family, I can assure you I do."

Nathan is a little taken aback by the blasé tone to Edwin's voice. He suspects it's little more than bravado. He has known Edwin for almost a decade, and has never known him to so much as swing a punch at another man. Then again, he has brandished a pistol at Henry Ward before. Not that he had the courage to pull the trigger. "Does it not faze you that he is your wife's father?"

"No," Edwin says matter-of-factly. "Quite honestly, we'd all be better off without him in our lives. Harriet especially."

"Killing Ward is not going to solve the problem," Nathan says irritably. "You heard what he said; he's not the one behind these threats. And even if he is lying about that, he has a whole crew behind him. Or at least part of one. We can't fight all those men."

Edwin makes a noise in his throat. He doesn't respond with suggestions of duels and pistol fire, and Nathan feels faintly relieved.

"Then we leave," Edwin says finally. "We pack our things and we leave Lindisfarne as quickly as we can."

"They'll be watching the house. They'll expect us to run."

"Then we leave in the night."

Leave in the night. Just as his mother did. How many times in his life is he to be forced from Highfield House on account of Henry Ward?

"What of Eva and Finn?" Nathan says. "This is their home now. Are we just to leave them to the devices of Ward and his crew?"

Edwin keeps his eyes down. "Eva and Finn can make their own choices."

Nathan is aware, suddenly, of two men walking behind them along the row of stone fences on the outskirts of the village. He feels a tug of unease as he realises the men are gaining on them. Deliberately so.

They're unremarkable men, both grey and leathery, in colourless sailor's slops and cavalier boots. They fall into line beside Nathan and Edwin, forcing Nathan into the muddy grass on the edge of the path.

"Can I help you?" Edwin says brusquely.

He doesn't need an explanation, Nathan realises. He knows instinctively who these men are. "Mr Graveney," he says dully.

"You're him then are you?" says Edwin. "The man seeking to make his fortune off our family?"

"Rather, the man seeking to reclaim what was stolen from the Jacobites." Graveney is the older of the two men; taller than his crewmate, with a narrow face and eyes pitted in the hollows of his cheeks. A patchy grey beard hangs in threads down to the top of his chest.

Nathan feels something sink inside him. The dull knowledge that this man is not a figment of Ward's imagination. Not a fictitious vessel to make him look better in his daughter's eyes. He wonders why Graveney has chosen to show himself now. Perhaps he's grown tired of waiting for Henry Ward to produce the letter. Decided to take matters into his own hands.

John Graveney has a self-righteous look about him. That proud glow in his eyes that Nathan has seen in the faces of other Jacobites when they spout words like *true king* and *by the grace of God.* The glare Graveney gives him is one of a victim towards a criminal. Nathan can't help but shoulder a little of his mother's guilt.

"I don't have the letter," he says, expressionless.

"So I hear." Graveney's voice is gravelly. "But a family as wealthy as yours no doubt has other ways to repay your mother's debts."

Nathan says nothing. There's little point, of course, telling this man how empty his family's coffers are. Because the fact remains, he is the freehold owner of Highfield House, and the pocket of land that surrounds it. No doubt Graveney is aware of this. No doubt it's the house he's seeking. After all, these men seem to have little difficulty in finding out all they wish to know about his family.

Graveney digs his hands into the pockets of his greatcoat, as casual as if they were discussing the weather. "You have until the end of the week," he says. "Saturday. The letter or the house."

Nathan glances at Edwin. He's silent, staring at the two men, a muscle ticking in his jaw. Nathan grits his teeth, hating his own rote nod of acceptance.

Graveney and his crewmate turn down the path and disappear. Edwin watches after them. "We need to leave," he says finally. "Tonight. I'm going home to pack our things."

Nathan feels the pit in his stomach widen. Edwin is right, of course. Leaving is the only way forward. The only way to ensure his child's safety. His own safety. And as much as he hates the thought of leaving Eva out on Longstone in Ward's purview, Edwin is right: she and Finn can make their own choices.

But, "Saturday," he says desperately. "We have six days."

"Six days to do what?" Edwin hisses. "You've been looking for this letter for months. You know it's not in the house. Your mother probably sold the damn thing years ago. "

"I know. I just…" He trails off. He cannot bring himself to speak of that sickening parallel of being forced from the house once again. For weeks, the urge to run has been building up inside him. But now it's becoming a reality. And he is beginning to realise that running is not what he wants to do at all.

He knows it's foolish to stay, but he cannot bear the thought of history repeating. Nor can he bear the thought of walking away from this fragile thing he and Julia have begun to build. "Just give me these six days." He looks at Edwin pointedly. "If Graveney can give me that time, surely you can too."

Edwin lets out a breath. "What in hell happened to you? A few months ago, you were desperate that none of us were even in the house with you. And now you're refusing to leave?"

Nathan doesn't reply, making Edwin scrub a hand across his eyes in frustration.

"Six days," Edwin says tautly. "And then we're leaving. All of us."

"As you wish." Nathan turns suddenly and begins to stride away.

"Where are you going?" Edwin demands.

And Nathan does not feel the need to answer.

The sight of her husband makes Harriet's heart jolt. What is he doing here in the village? She thought he and Nathan were locked away in the office at Highfield House, piecing together their plans to rid the world of her father. She darts down the nearest alley, catapulting through a puddle and soaking her stockings to the shins.

It's no use. Edwin has seen her.

His footsteps echo on the cobbles as he rounds the corner to face her. "What are you doing here?" he demands.

"A walk." The lie is so clumsy she would almost have laughed if he had believed it. He rubs his eyes. Looks around them at the narrow lane leading towards the anchorage and tavern. A hunched old man drowning in a long black cloak watches them from a corner as he brings a pipe to his lips. Edwin puts a hand to Harriet's shoulder, ushering her away.

"That is not the kind of street you ought to be seen on," he says. Harriet watches the realisation dawn on him. "Were you going to the tavern? To get word to your father?"

"No."

He sighs. Holds out a hand. "May I see the message?"

What would he do if she refused, Harriet wonders distantly? He would cart her back to the house no doubt, probably put her behind locked doors. Any chance of getting word to her father, of telling him how much she longs to speak to him, would be gone. Probably forever.

Reluctantly, she pulls the note from her pocket and presses it into Edwin's palm. He unfolds it. Reads slowly. Harriet turns away, huddling into her cloak. She feels as though she is burning under his scrutiny. It's not the fact that he has caught her that makes her feel so unbalanced; it's the fact that he might sense the vulnerability she knows is all too evident in her words to Henry Ward.

I would very much like to spend more time with you…

Know you a little better…

Very important to me…

Edwin crumples the page in his fist. "Things have changed, Harriet. We cannot stay here any longer. We shall be leaving for London by Friday at the latest."

Harriet feels suddenly breathless. A return to London. She cannot make sense of why the idea leaves her feeling so hollow. Is this not what she has longed for? "Why?" she finds herself asking.

A look of hesitation passes across Edwin's eyes, as though he is debating how much to share with her. "Because it's not safe here," he says. "There are men in your father's crew who are threatening our family."

Harriet's thoughts begin to race. She knows there is little point arguing about the intentions of Ward's crew. Knows she has little chance of convincing Edwin to stay. Besides, is that even what she wants? All she knows is that the need to speak with her father has just become even greater.

"If we are to leave, will you not give me this last opportunity to get to know my father?" Edwin opens his mouth to speak, but Harriet presses on before he can get a word out. "Once we leave Holy Island, he will be out of our lives. Can you not just give me this one chance? Please?" She hates imploring him like this. But she is desperate. She needs to be a part of Henry Ward's life. Needs that sense of belonging. Needs to matter to him. He is a man with his own ship, she thinks distantly. Surely he has the means to travel to London to spend time with his daughter when he wishes to. Surely her leaving Lindisfarne does not have to mean cutting her father out of her life.

Edwin looks down at the wet cobbles, deep in thought. Finally, he says,

"One meeting. At the house. With me in attendance." He crushes her note between his fingers. "I shall rewrite the message and deliver it to the tavern myself this evening."

CHAPTER ELEVEN

There's a heaviness to Nathan today; Julia can sense it from the moment he steps into her shop. There are customers floating around between the shelves, picking up items to examine them before setting them back in other places. Julia knows this type of customer—the ones that are here to kill time as they wait for the rain to stop or the coach to arrive or the tide to fall. Knows they will leave without spending a penny.

She looks across the counter at Nathan. There's a new intensity to his blue eyes, and it makes her desperate to speak to him. But she knows she cannot do so with other people in the shop. At least, she cannot speak to him openly.

"Good afternoon, sir," she says to him brightly, avoiding Nathan's name in case Hugh, tucked away upstairs, should catch hold of it. "Feel free to look as you wish."

Nathan gives her a faint nod. "Thank you." He makes his way to the bookshelf, giving a wide berth to Minerva, who is stalking silently along the perimeter. He stands with his hands folded behind his back, eyes scanning the worn spines. He pulls out a title and flicks mindlessly through its pages.

Finally, the customers thank her and leave. Julia locks the door behind them. Nathan slides the book back onto the shelf as she comes close to him. She stops short of reaching for his hand as she longs to. She smells a faint hint of rosewater on him, and the cold, briny air.

"Are you safe?" he asks. "There's been no trouble from Holland?"

"No." Their voices seem to carry in the empty shop—carry all the way upstairs to where Hugh is hiding. Whatever Nathan has come here to say, Julia does not want her brother to hear it. She nods towards the cellar. "Down there," she whispers.

Nathan frowns. "Why?"

"Because it's safer. More private." Her voice comes out strained. The words sound too suspicious, or perhaps too intimate. She feels her cheeks colour violently. And she can't help darting a glance up towards the living quarters. She doesn't hear a sound from Hugh. But she knows he will be listening. If he has any sense that Nathan is here, he will try to catch a word from him, in an attempt to determine who the government spies might be. Julia will not give him the pleasure. Will not betray Nathan like that. At least not any more than she is betraying him already.

Nathan nods, not asking more questions. He follows her down the narrow stone staircase. Julia pushes open the door of the cellar and steps inside. She pulls the tinderbox from the pocket of her apron and lights the lamp. Orange light fills the space, falling over Hugh's bed in the centre of the room, blankets tossed messily across it. A look of confusion passes over Nathan's eyes.

"Is someone is staying down here?" he asks.

"I used to rent the room out to lodgers," says Julia. "For the extra money. I've not done it since the Rising began. Too dangerous." It's not a lie, she tells herself. Just a half-truth. But that does nothing to stop the tug of regret in her stomach. The room is too warm; smells cloying and inhabited. But Nathan says:

"I'm glad." He looks up to meet her eyes. "Why did you bring us down here now? You've never felt the need to do so before. And you've spoken to me about the Rising in the past."

Julia hesitates. "I'm coming to realise we need to be careful speaking of these things," she says. "Cordwell and Martin Macauley and the others that came to your house... They're fools, making their Jacobites sympathies so obvious, especially with the militia around. I'm sure it's only a matter of time before they'll be raiding houses and throwing people in prison like they're doing in Newcastle." She realises she is talking too quickly. These reasons, she supposes, are all valid. If not entirely the core truth of the matter.

Nathan nods.

"You did not come here just to ask about Holland, did you?" says Julia.

He sighs heavily. "No." He perches on the edge of the bed, curling his hands around his knees. "There's something I need to ask you. About the past."

And more of the story comes out. A lost letter; a privateer turned pirate; threats made against his family in the wake of his mother's betrayal of the Jacobites. More of the things Nathan Blake has been carrying on his shoulders since long before he came to Lindisfarne, Julia sees now.

"A letter?" she says. "That's what you've been doing in the house?" She dares to sit beside him on the bed. Is relieved when he does not shift away. He turns to face her, his knees inches from hers. Lamplight flickers against his shorn cheeks. Makes his blue eyes shine.

"My secrets seem so foolish now," he says. "But when I decided to keep them, I truly thought it was for the best."

Julia smiles wryly to herself. She understands that more than he could know.

The telling of this story, she realises, it seems to be loosening something inside him. Because as he has been speaking, his hand has drifted from his thigh to her own curled fingers, resting on the bed between them. His thumb traces light circles over her knuckles. Energy flickers through her.

"This man, John Graveney, he seems determined to punish us for the damage our mother inflicted on the Jacobite cause," Nathan says.

"I can understand that. The Jacobites are passionate men and women. They fail and they keep coming back. And they do not let go of grudges. I can see why this Graveney would do such a thing, especially now, in the midst of the Rising." She meets his eyes. "Not that I wish him to succeed, of course."

Nathan nods slowly. "I don't suppose your family knows anything of this letter? Your parents were on the island the same time as mine. You never heard them speak of it?"

"I'm sorry, no. I was only seven when Ma died. And Da, well… if he knows anything, I'd be the last person to know. I never heard him mention it when I was a child, and we barely speak these days. When

Bobby arrived, he was so ashamed he left Holy Island to get away from me. I went to see him yesterday to tell him about Michael. Didn't even ask me inside."

"I'm sorry." The disappointment in Nathan's eyes is poorly hidden.

A creak at the top of the stairs makes Julia's chest tighten. Nathan's eyes pull towards the sound.

"Is someone in the shop?" He stands from the bed. Julia bounds awkwardly in front of him and pulls open the cellar door. She scrambles up the stairs ahead of Nathan.

The shop is quiet, but she can sense Hugh is here. Can feel him breathing beneath the faint shift and crackle of the fire. In any case, she would have heard his footsteps if he had attempted to go back upstairs. Nathan strides purposefully between the shelves; opens the side door to peer out into the alley. Julia looks over the counter. Sees her brother crouched on the floor like a naughty child. She glares at him; receives a mocking smile in return.

"There's no one here," she says, trying to keep her voice level. She hurries across the shop towards Nathan, steering him away from the counter. She opens the side door again, scooping up Minerva before she dashes out into the lane. Nathan follows her into the alley, eying the cat warily. Julia laughs a little. "It's just a cat, Nathan. Not the devil's spawn."

He looks down into Minerva's golden eyes. "One and the same, if you ask me." He shakes his head. "Forgive me. I'm sure that thing's very dear to you."

Julia smiles. "*That thing* is, yes." She shoulders open the door and tips the cat back into the shop. Minerva stalks away with her tail in the air.

Julia turns back to face him. He reaches out tentatively, his fingers brushing lightly against hers. Wind tears through the alley, lifting the dark waves of hair from his neck. "I ought to get back," he says.

Julia nods. "Thank you for telling me all that you did. And I'm sorry I couldn't help you."

Nathan steps closer, making her breath catch. He presses his palm to her cheek, his other hand wrapping around her wrist. His skin feels warm against her own.

Julia hears her rapid breath; feels her chest straining against her stays. He tugs her closer. But as his nose grazes hers, he releases his grip on her suddenly. Steps away. The distance between them feels cavernous.

Nathan squeezes his eyes closed, shaking his head at himself. "I'm sorry," he mumbles. "I'm so sorry."

Julia pushes away her disappointment. "It's all right," she says gently. "Of course it's all right."

He swallows. "Thank you for being so patient with me."

Julia nods; gives him a faint smile. All that Nathan Blake is carrying. She is not sure if she is adding to it or taking it away.

Nathan murmurs his goodbye and Julia steps back inside. Closes her eyes for a moment. Her heart is fast. Unease, fear, and something else entirely. She locks the door behind her. Turns to see Hugh leaning against the counter, hands on his hips, shirtsleeves rolled up over his broad freckled forearms.

"This letter you were speaking of," he says. "I may know something that could help you."

Julia's stomach tightens. She had assumed that, hidden in the cellar, her and Nathan's voices were low enough to not be heard. Her brother has clearly become a master at catching other people's conversations. Had he been standing on the stairs with an ear to the door?

"There are rumours among the English Jacobites about the dissenter in the Whig party," he says. "I've heard men speak about him at a meeting in the Rose Tavern in Bamburgh. If those rumours came about because of this letter, it may well still exist."

Julia folds her arms. "Those rumours could have come from anywhere. Especially if there's any truth to them. This letter was written twenty years ago."

"True. But it seems your dear Mr Blake is in quite a situation. Is it not worth following a lead, however hazy?"

Julia strides upstairs to the living quarters in a desperate attempt to get Hugh out of the shop before anyone—especially Nathan—sees him. He follows her upstairs and sinks into a chair at the rickety wooden table.

She sits opposite him, toying with a half-drunk mug of tea left to grow cold in the middle of the table. "Why should I believe a word you're telling me?"

Hugh stretches his long legs out in front of him. "Is that where we've ended up? At complete distrust?"

"Can you blame me?"

He smiles wryly. "I suppose not. But I'm telling the truth about this."

For a long time, Julia doesn't speak. She suddenly remembers she left the lamp burning in the cellar. "Why?" she presses. "Why would you do this? Why help Nathan? You've made it more than clear what you think of him."

"Because I can tell you care about him."

She feels her cheeks heat. "Somehow that makes me even less likely to believe you."

Hugh leans back in his chair, surprise on his face, as though her words have struck him. Surely he cannot be surprised that there is little trust left between them. "I've never seen you like this around a man before," he says.

"Like what?" Her response comes out sharper than she intended.

He smiles, ignoring her brusqueness. "You let your guard down around him. As though for a moment, you realise you don't have to do everything under the sun all on your own."

Julia looks down. She hates that Hugh has seen all this. Hates it because it means he has been watching her and Nathan more closely than she realised. But she also hates it because she knows he is right. Ever since Bobby was born, she has carried an impossible weight on her shoulders. Not that she would change a moment with her son. But sometimes the strain of it is too much. There have been far too many nights that she has lain awake, doubting her ability to put a roof over her child's head. Far too many nights she has gone to bed hungry. Far too many nights when the fire has burnt out from lack of coal, her feet frozen inside wet stockings and shoes full of holes.

Since her father had cast her from his home; since Bobby was born and she had sworn to herself that she would make a good life for him, she has prided herself on her independence. But she cannot deny that sometimes, fleetingly, she wishes she had someone to share her troubles with. Someone who might ease the strain of this precarious, weighted life she has built.

It's ludicrous, of course, imagining herself up in Highfield House, building that life with Nathan. Nothing about the two of them align. He is rungs above her on the social ladder, and would surely support the king against the Jacobites if forced to make a choice. Besides, even now, with their distrust for one another fading and her heart and body alive for him, she is still keeping secrets that could turn him away from her forever.

But that does not stop her from wishing it. Or even daring to think it might be possible.

"Besides," Hugh goes on, "if I tell you what you wish to know about the letter, perhaps you might tell me what I want to know about the government spies."

This feels far more like the Hugh she knows. "I don't know who the government spies are," Julia snaps. "I already told you."

"You did." Hugh gives a short laugh. "But I know you're lying. I can only assume your Mr Blake knows who they are, given they were gallivanting around his house. And the two of you seem to be in the habit of sharing things with one another."

Julia says nothing. What her brother is asking—for her to betray Nathan's confidence by revealing Joseph Holland as a spy—is galling. But in a strange way, it makes her believe he might actually be telling the truth about the letter.

If they were to find the thing, against all odds, it would ease the strain on Nathan and his family. Get Henry Ward and his quartermaster out of their lives.

Julia wants desperately to trust her brother. But she knows that could turn out to be an enormous mistake.

"Do you really think me that kind of person?" Hugh says, as though reading her thoughts. "That I would deliberately put the man you care about in danger?"

"I do when that man is rumoured to be a government spy. You've made it perfectly clear what you think of him."

"Well." Hugh gets to his feet and takes the poker from up against the wall. He jabs at the dwindling fire in an attempt to coax it back to life. "In that case, I'm sorry. I didn't realise you saw me that way."

Julia gets to her feet. "I'm re-opening the shop," she says brusquely. "Don't come down there."

Hugh nods wordlessly. As she reaches the top of the stairs, he says, "They're meeting on Thursday at noon. The men I heard speak of the Whig dissenter. The Rose Tavern in Bamburgh. Perhaps they can tell you what you wish to know."

Julia doesn't reply, but his words keep circling through her head as she goes down to the cellar to blow out the lamp. As she returns to the shop and unlocks the front door. Minerva stalks silently out from between the shelves and Julia scoops her into her arms. She presses her cheek against the cat's silky fur.

She hates that she cannot trust her brother. But really, what else can be expected? They have always been a family of liars, of manipulators.

But was that genuineness in Hugh's eyes when he had promised he would not hurt Nathan? Would he truly lie and risk the safety of the man she has come to care for?

She desperately hopes the answer is no.

CHAPTER TWELVE

"Are you sure you'll be all right?" Finn asks, for at least the fifth time. He tosses the empty peat sacks into the boat, ready be filled by the farmers he is working for today. "I don't have to go, if you're unsure about being out here alone."

Eva stands on the jetty, shivering at a gust of icy wind. The sunrise is just peeking over the horizon, painting a corridor of gold light across the water. A thin line of smoke rises from the firebasket, its scent mingling with sea. "You do have to go," she says. "You've already told them you'll be there. Besides, we need to put food on the table." She looks at him pointedly. "Through honest means."

He grins. "I'd not dream of doing anything else."

Eva gives him a crooked smile. "I'm sure."

He holds up his hands in surrender. "I've not thieved so much as an apple in months," he says. "I swear it."

"Or a lump of coal?"

"Or a lump of coal."

She laces her hands through his and tugs him close. "In that case, you'd best get on. You don't want to be late." If she is honest with herself, there's a part of her that's nervous about being alone on Longstone. It's unease at Ward's nearness, yes, but it's also unease wrought by the island's deep isolation. That sense of being hemmed in by sea, with just the birds, the seals, the fish for company.

But there is money to be made and their lives to live. Besides, what

Ward would achieve by coming after her alone, Eva cannot fathom. The fear rooted inside her is for Finn's safety, not her own. She presses her cheek against his broad chest. Wraps her arms around his waist.

He looks down at her, and seems to catch something in her eyes. "Are you certain?" he asks again, a faint frown creasing his brow.

"Of course." She smiles, trying to force away her anxiousness. "Would you like to see me sail around the island once more, just so you can be absolutely, positively sure I can do it?"

He chuckles. "I trust you. As long as you feel comfortable taking the skiff out on your own if you need to leave for any reason." A sudden seriousness in his eyes. "If you see Ward's ship, get in the boat and go straight to your family's house. Or if you see anything else that makes you uncomfortable."

"I shall be fine," Eva assures him again. "Now go before you are late."

He tucks the edges of his scarf into his greatcoat then holds his lips to hers. "Get a little sleep."

Eva nods. With Finn off to work this morning, she had taken the watch since just after midnight, and her body is aching with tiredness. A few hours' sleep, she tells herself, then the day will be too full to spend any time or energy on thoughts of Ward and his crew. There's bread to make and bedsheets to wash, and water to be collected from the rainwater barrels behind the cottage. Then there is her needlework—mending and embroidery for mainlanders, met through the men on the farms. Doing her own part to put food on the table.

Earning coin with her own hands is strangely thrilling, she has realised. An upturning of her pre-emptively lived life in which her sole reason for being was producing Matthew Walton's children.

So yes, she tells herself again. Not a single moment to spend in fear of Henry Ward.

She stands on the jetty and watches as Finn pulls the longboat away from the island. Henry Ward's longboat, she thinks distantly. They had taken it from his ship the night he had tried to kill Finn. A few days ago, Finn had found it roped to the moorings at Lindisfarne, left there by Michael Mitchell on his way to re-join the rebel army.

Eva watches the boat disappear behind the scarps of the Pinnacles. She draws in a breath. Closes her eyes.

When she opens them, thick shards of sunlight are breaking through the clouds and turning the rockpools gold. And there is something magical about being alone on this island, she realises. As though she has opened her eyes to find herself in an otherworld. She finds herself walking the shallow crags of rock, peering into the pools to watch the miniature forests of green and yellow that dance in the low tide. Inhaling the sea salt and the tangible scent of cold. It feels almost as though she is experiencing it all for the first time.

Longstone is anything but silent. All around her is the constant lash of the sea, the chorus of birds and seals, the wind rattling the chain of the firebasket. And yet there's an impossible stillness here too; devoid of voices, of footsteps, of human breath beyond her own.

Twin feelings war inside her head: that she belongs out here in this cottage with Finn; and that the two of them have made their home in a place that was never meant for humanity. An intrusion in a wild place. To save lives—or is to atone for their own mistakes?

In the madness of the past weeks, Eva has barely had a chance to breathe, barely had a chance to look in detail at this life that has so unexpectedly become hers. She was never supposed to be a woman with callused hands and coal-streaked aprons, wearing soft and pliable jump stays that let her bend and crawl and haul firebaskets into the sky. Was never supposed to wear petticoats quilted against ocean air. And yet somehow, inexplicably, this is also exactly how she is supposed to be living. She longs to settle into this life without the threat of Ward and his crew. Longs to treasure this wild place without an undercurrent of fear.

The stillness is even more intense inside the cottage, with the sound of the sea muted. She rinses the breakfast plates in the trough, tucking them neatly away in the sideboard. Then she stumbles wearily into the bedroom. Unlaces her stays and climbs beneath the blankets Finn has left warm and rumpled.

Her mind races behind closed eyes. Because she can pretend all she likes that she and Finn are alone out here; that they have this island to themselves and the rest of the world is distant. But she knows it is all fantasy. Because not six miles away, Henry Ward's ship is lying at anchor, filled with men who wish to punish her family for her mother's crimes. Six days, Nathan had told her. Six days, and he will be forced to run. No—

five days, with the rising dawn.

Eva gives up on sleep.

She slips out of bed and wraps the blanket around her shoulders. With her shift bunched up in one hand, she teeters barefoot across the rocks and stands at the edge of the island. She sees the first vessels of morning dotted across the leathery, sun-streaked ocean, and they bring a tug of unease. Herring boats, she tells herself. Nothing more.

"Enough," she says out loud. Because she cannot build a life out here if she is to panic at every boat on the sea. She cannot settle. Cannot treasure. She reaches down and picks up two loose fragments of rock that are glittering like onyx on the edge of the pool. She carries them inside and sets them on the mantel between the lamp and old quadrant. She returns to the bedroom, tugging her stockings on over frozen feet. Draws closed the curtains and tucks herself beneath the bedclothes, in an attempt to make her wild place feel safe.

CHAPTER THIRTEEN

Harriet had assumed Edwin lying when he said he was going to leave the letter for Ward, inviting him to the house. But here she and her husband are in the parlour, waiting for the knock at the door.

Harriet has no idea if this is just a game. She doubts Edwin wrote the note to her father. Doubts he left it at the tavern for Ward to collect. All too easy, she knows, for them to wait out the hour, and then for Edwin to blame Ward's absence on his reluctance, or his busyness, or his failure to collect the message.

They sit in silence, side by side on the settle. The clock on the mantel ticks away the seconds. Harriet smooths her skirts, deliberate in not looking Edwin's way.

"I thought we might talk about things moving forward," he says finally.

"I thought we were here to speak with my father." She turns to face him. "Is this where you tell me you never sent the message?"

She sees Edwin's jaw clench. "I sent the message, Harriet. I cannot be held responsible if your father decides not to come."

She folds her hands. Shoots a surreptitious glance at the clock. At least if her father does not show himself, she can blame Edwin. Convince herself he is lying when he says he delivered the message. It's a far easier prospect to swallow than the alternative: that her father might not wish to spend time in her company.

"Very well," she says bitterly. "Speak to me about things moving forward. Speak to me about the wonderful life we are going to have once we return to London."

Edwin sighs. "You'd rather we be angry and miserable for the rest of our lives? Is that the kind of home you want our son to grow up in?"

"You destroyed my artwork," Harriet snaps. "How can I be anything but miserable when you have taken away the one thing that is important to me?"

She sees Edwin flinch at her choice of words, but he chooses not to comment. "Well," he says after a long silence, "perhaps once you prove yourself trustworthy, things can change. I have no desire to make you unhappy. I just wish for you to show some responsibility."

Harriet says nothing. Just stares down into her clasped hands. The appeal is a reasonable one; some part of her can see that. But there is another part that is preventing her from being reasonable. Some part that wants to retaliate; to be as difficult as possible. Her husband makes her this way, she knows. If she is to be treated like a child, so she will act as one. Or is it the other way around?

When the knock at the door comes, she is so flooded with relief she leaps instinctively to her feet. Edwin grabs her hand and tugs her back down to the settle. "Mrs Brodie will answer the door."

Harriet obeys—largely out of gratitude that Edwin had in fact delivered the message. It was not what she expected.

Her heart begins to pound when she hears her father's deep baritone in the entrance hall as he addresses the housekeeper. His footsteps echo down the hallway, growing louder as he approaches the parlour.

The door clicks open, and here is Henry Ward, hiding Mrs Brodie in his shadow.

Edwin stands. Offers him his hand. "Thank you for coming," he says, managing to sound remotely sincere. "My wife was very eager to speak with you."

Ward nods slowly, as though taking his time to determine the correct response to this. He eyes Edwin closely; shakes his hand with an expression that's impossible to read. Then, to Harriet's satisfaction, he turns away from her husband and looks squarely at her.

"Harriet." He nods in her direction. Lowers himself into the armchair.

She is disappointed, of course, at this sorry excuse for a greeting. Not that she has any intention of letting Edwin see that. She offers her father her most beatific smile. "Good morning. Thank you for coming." She has no idea how to address him. *Mr Ward* feels far too formal. *Father* feels impossible.

"Was there something in particular you wished to see me about?" Ward asks her.

"No," she admits. "I just… I rather hoped for the chance to speak with you. Get to know you a little better." She feels her cheeks flush. She can sense Edwin's eyes on her—and she is well aware she has never let him see this side of her before; this uncertain, needy side that craves validation. She can't bring herself to look at him.

Mrs Brodie reappears with a tea tray and sets it tentatively on the table. Her eyes dart to Ward, and Harriet can tell his presence has unsettled her. Is Mrs Brodie still shaken after the raid on the house? Or is it just the malaise of unease her father manages to inflict on people? She sets his teacup down on the side table beside the armchair and vanishes from the room.

Ward sits rigid in the chair, making no attempt at the tea. "Perhaps you might like to show me some of your work?" he says to Harriet. He clears his throat. "Your paintings?"

She feels a too-fleeting jolt of happiness. But, "I'm afraid I don't have any of my work here with me." She wonders if Ward can read the bone-breaking glare she gives to Edwin.

Her husband turns away from her cold eyes. Shifts uncomfortably.

"I've plenty of pieces in my workroom in London," Harriet presses on boldly. "When we return, I—"

"Nathan and I have made a number of changes to the house recently," Edwin cuts in. "I've replaced much of the old wainscoting here in the parlour. Painted a number of rooms. In addition to all the running repairs, of course. No doubt the place is quite different from what you remember."

What is he playing at? Harriet is sure the state of the house is the furthest thing from Henry Ward's mind. Edwin is keeping Ward away from their plans, she sees then. He does not want him to know they are planning to return to London. No doubt he fears Ward will alert his men. Send them after their family in a last desperate ploy for Abigail's letter.

She sips her tea with mildly trembling hands. She hates that Edwin has such distrust for her father. But really, what else can she expect?

"I see," Ward says thinly. "You must have some skills to have undertaken such a task yourself."

There's a difference to him today, Harriet notices. A difference from the bold, authoritative man he had been each time he had come to the house before. Each of those times, he had drawn everyone's attention. Turned heads. Incited fear.

Today, as he listens to Edwin rambling on about replacing cantilevers, Henry Ward does not feel bold and authoritative. At least, not to her. Today, he just feels like a normal man.

He is different, too, from the way he was when it was just the two of them alone in his cabin. He had seemed a little uncertain of himself then also—unbalanced by the discovery of her. But that day, she had at least had glimpses of genuineness. However fleeting and far between. But right now, the man her father really is has never felt so far away.

It's Edwin's presence, of course, that is changing things. Edwin, with his faux sincerity and rotting cantilevers. An irony, Harriet thinks, that her husband might conjure such unease in her father, rather than the other way around.

She had wanted to speak to Henry Ward again in the vain hope he might be more open with her. That he might let her beneath the surface and she might come to know who he really is. How hopeless that seems now.

She cannot force him to be more unguarded with her, of course. But she can be more unguarded with him. She can let him in, and hopefully encourage him to do the same. Even if that means letting Edwin see her for who she really is. Harriet pushes aside the dread that prospect brings her.

"I am very glad you're here," she blurts. "It means a lot to me."

A faint smile flickers on the edge of Ward's mouth, but it's an uncertain, transitory look.

"I would very much like to hear more about the time you spent with my mother," Harriet continues hopefully. "Did you come to the house a lot?"

Ward hesitates before speaking. Brings his teacup to his lips and takes a short sip. "As often as I could. My visits were sometimes months apart, thanks to my obligations during the war." He turns his gaze towards the window. "And your mother and I… I suppose we only really knew each other for a little under a year." He blows out a breath. Picks at the stitching on the arm of the chair. "I admit, it seems far longer."

Harriet smiles faintly. It pleases her that her mother might have made such an impact on her father. That Abigail Blake had proven impossible to forget.

Ward rubs a hand across his chin. His eyes have taken on a faraway look and Harriet wonders what he is thinking. Are his thoughts back in the past? In those months he had spent at Highfield House? Those months he had spent falling in love with her mother?

Harriet can see an ache in Ward's eyes. A reminder that whatever had once been between them, Abigail had fled the house so Henry Ward would not find out about his child. Harriet feels a faint satisfaction that they might be sitting here together; that she might be defying her mother like this. How might life have been different if she had grown up knowing her father?

Ward gets suddenly to his feet. "Forgive me," he says. "I shouldn't be here. I'm sorry."

"Don't be foolish," Harriet says desperately. "Of course you should be here. I…"

She gets to her feet, but he strides past her to the door of the parlour, making no more attempt at a farewell. Harriet turns hot eyes to Edwin, trying to manage a little rage at him. But as much as she tries to blame her husband for Henry Ward's leaving, she knows it's nothing more than hollow, misguided frustration.

Nathan is in his office reading through the deeds of the house when he hears Julia's voice. She's in the entrance hall, speaking with Mrs Brodie. His heart pounds—did anyone see her approaching the manor? He pushes the thought away. Surely now the spies have ceased to use this place, it's of no matter if Julia is seen here. Maybe his heart is pounding for an entirely different reason.

Nathan is well aware that, although he had told Julia almost the entire story about his mother's letter and the threats of Ward and his crew, he had neglected to tell her of John Graveney's ultimatum. Neglected to tell her that in five days' time, there is every chance he will be forced to run from Holy Island, just as his mother was. There is every chance he might never see her again.

He had left out this part of the story on purpose. He does not want Julia to see this fledgling thing between them as something that is about to die. He wants her to see it as something that is just beginning.

That's how he wants to see it too. However naïve and foolish that makes him.

He steps out of his office and makes his way down the stairs.

A faint smile flickers on Julia's lips at the sight of him. She is wrapped in her threadbare cloak, a blue shawl bundled at her neck. She takes off her bonnet and squeezes it between her hands. Shakes her head politely at the housekeeper when she offers to take it away.

Nathan thanks Mrs Brodie, and nods for Julia to join him in the parlour. He closes the door behind them.

"I need you to not ask questions," Julia says, before he can speak. Her eyes are down, her voice low. She sets her bonnet on the tea table and reaches for his hand. Nathan has the sense that she is doing it to test his trust in her. He nods slightly, urging her to continue.

"The dissenter your mother's letter speaks about. Someone has told me there's word of him among the Jacobites in Bamburgh. I know it's the smallest of chances, but it's possible these rumours came about because of the letter."

At once, Nathan's mind is racing, questioning where this information has come from. And also whether he dares to believe it. "Was it your father who told you this?"

"My father? No. I told you, we barely speak."

Nathan nods. He has been unable to shake the possibility that Julia's father might know something about the letter. Elias Mitchell had been an active Jacobite in the years Abigail had apparently been stealing from the cause. A likely candidate for someone who might have information about the letter and its whereabouts. But he trusts that Julia is telling the truth about barely speaking to him. She has always been brutally up front about her broken relations with her father. Where else the information might have come from, Nathan does not dare think about. He is coming to realise that the best way to deal with Julia, and the chaos she causes within him, is to ask as few questions as possible.

"I'm told these men are meeting in the Rose Tavern in Bamburgh on Thursday," she says. "Perhaps it's worth asking them some questions."

Nathan turns the thought over in his mind. He wants this scrap of hope. Needs it. The end of the week is approaching far too rapidly. He begins to pace in front of the simmering hearth. "I'll not ask questions," he promises. "Just tell me one thing: is this information I can trust?"

"I believe so, aye."

His heart is quick; always, his heart is quick around Julia—a product of his feelings for her, and the way she pushes at the edges of his fear. But right now, it is fast because he wants to believe this. Wants the chance of a future in which he is not left penniless by his mother's mistakes.

He wants the chance of a future with Julia Mitchell in it.

"Thursday," he repeats. "The Rose Tavern." And he finds himself agreeing.

CHAPTER FOURTEEN

"Look at you," says Julia that afternoon. "Willingly climbing into my boat without a look of blatant dread on your face."

"Oh, the blatant dread is still very much there," says Nathan. "I've just learnt to suppress it somewhat."

She smiles. "What is it you hate about the sea so much?" she asks, as if the wind weren't howling hard enough to strip a forest bare.

Nathan focuses on the Longstone firebasket out ahead. In the whitewash of daylight, the unlit basket is just a shape in the cloud, solid against the wild roll of the water. Julia's question is a complicated one, because there are far more things he does hate about the sea than those he doesn't. Prime among them is that hideous somersaulting of his stomach, and a sense of giving up control. "I suppose I feel less vulnerable with my feet on solid ground," he admits. "Comes with being a Londoner, I suppose."

"But you're not a Londoner," she reminds him. "This is where you come from."

"Yes. That's true." It's something Nathan barely acknowledges. He is not quite sure why. But he is dimly aware that he had not hated the sea as a child. He has faint memories of his father's fishing boat lying on the embankment outside Highfield House. Of being excited to scramble over the gunwale and watch the land grow distant. But Londoner or not, Nathan can't deny he feels far more comfortable without reams of ocean beneath him.

Julia's eyes glaze over as they approach the glistening crags of Longstone. "How is Harriet faring since Michael's death?" Her voice is suddenly soft.

"You've not spoken to her?"

Julia shakes her head, her face half hidden beneath the shadow of her bonnet. "It's petty of me, perhaps. But I'm not sure I could face her after… well… all that happened to my brother."

Nathan nods. He understands, though he is faintly regretful. He's sure Harriet would benefit from her friendship with Julia.

"She's… well, she's Harriet," he says uselessly. "To be honest, I often struggle to know what's going on in her head at all. But I'm sure she regrets what happened to Michael."

Julia nods. She eases the dory up against the Longstone jetty. The boat thuds softly into the worn wooden posts, and she winds the mooring ropes without speaking. Her eyes have darkened suddenly, as though her grief is once again fresh. The last time she had been out here, Nathan imagines, she had been coming to deliver the news of Michael's death to Angus. Coming to take him away to the mainland and send him off to London.

"I'm sorry," he says. "I shouldn't have asked you to bring me out here. I'm sure the place reminds you terribly of your brothers."

She gives him a small smile. "It's all right. I suspect you wouldn't have made it far without me."

He gives a gentle laugh. "Of that I can assure you." He clambers awkwardly from the boat and teeters across the slippery rock of the island.

Before they can make it up the front stairs, the door swings open and Eva steps out. She is without shoes, her hair hanging in a messy plait down her back, and her dark blue skirts streaked with flour that has escaped the confines of her apron.

Her eyes dart between Nathan and Julia. He can tell she is surprised to see them together. "Has something happened?" she asks. "I can only guess you'd not be jumping in a boat for a social call, Nathan."

He gives her a thin smile. "Everything is all right. Well. It's as good as can be expected. Given the circumstances."

Eva holds open the door as they make their way up the stairs and into the cottage. She eyes Julia with a mix of curiosity and wariness.

The house is warm, and fragrant with the smell of baking bread and woodsmoke. Wind whistles under the door, and makes the window frames creak. Eva has coated the entire table, and much of the floor in flour, a trail of white footprints leading to and from the door. A bread loaf sits cooling on a rack atop the sideboard, oddly shaped, but golden brown, and would smell delicious, if he didn't feel like he was about to lose his breakfast. Nathan glances around the tiny living space: navigation tools and rocks on the mantel, what looks to be a small net of some sort bundled into a corner. Kettle and cooking pot sitting on the hearth. He realises he is fascinated by this abrupt turn his sister's life has taken.

"Where is your husband?" he asks.

Eva reaches for a cloth and attempts to dust the flour from the table. "He has a day's farm work in Bamburgh. He'll be back this evening."

Nathan takes a step back to avoid the cloud of flour that is fluttering onto the floorboards. "I don't know how I feel about you being out here alone."

"It's a good thing you don't have a say in the matter then, isn't it."

He sees Julia cover a smile.

"There's no need to worry," says Eva. "If anything happens and I need to leave, I can manage the skiff on my own. Finn has made sure of that. Repeatedly."

"I see." Nathan pulls out a chair and wipes the flour off the seat before lowering himself onto it. Julia stays hovering a few yards back from the table.

"I've information on Mother's letter," Nathan says.

Eva's dark eyebrows rise. "What information?" The look she shoots Julia is more than a little suspicious.

Julia presses her lips into a thin line. "I shall be outside," she says. Before Nathan can protest, she throws open the door and disappears down the stairs.

Nathan turns to his sister. "Really?"

"I didn't say a word. She left of her own accord."

He shifts uncomfortably. "Make us some tea, will you? My stomach is rolling."

Eva takes the kettle from the hearth and hangs it on the hook above the fire. She turns back to face him. "What information do you have?"

Nathan hesitates. Is he being foolish by repeating what Julia told him about the letter? By allowing himself to believe it? Believe in her? Really, what choice does he have? They've gone far beyond the beginning of desperation.

More to the point, is he really going to let this hideous journey out here be for nothing? If he was going to have doubts, he might have had them before he left dry land.

He tells Eva. The talk of the dissenter. The meeting at the tavern in Bamburgh. He is dimly aware he is keeping his gaze turned downward, refusing to look her in the eye.

Eva goes to the sideboard and pulls out the teapot and tea tin. Nathan can practically see her thoughts whirring as she spoons the leaves into the pot. "This information came from Julia?"

"Yes."

"Then I—"

"I know what you're about to say," he cuts in. "But what choice do we have other than to trust her?"

Eva takes the kettle from the hook and fills the teapot. "Who told her?" she asks finally.

"I don't know," Nathan admits. "She wouldn't say."

Eva lets out her breath. "I am trying to trust her, Nathan," she says tautly. "For your sake. I really am. But she does not make it easy."

"I know," he admits. "But do you not think this is worth following up on? If it could put an end to all our trouble…"

"And what if it's a trap?" Eva demands, setting the kettle back on the hearth. "What if she's sending you into the path of more Jacobites who want to punish you for letting the government spies use the house?"

"Cordwell and Macauley found nothing. I've no reason to believe the Jacobites will be after us. Their failed raid on the house may well be the best thing that could have happened for us."

Eva sighs. She fills two cups and sets one in front of him. "You are going to go anyway, aren't you."

"Three cups," Nathan says tautly. He glances out the window at Julia, who is leaning up against the posts of the jetty, her eyes turned out to sea. Wind is blowing her cloak out behind her like a wave. "If you're going to cast her out of your house, the least you can do is offer her a cup of tea."

Eva sits and folds her hands in front of her on the table. Nathan can tell the third cup of tea is not going to be forthcoming.

"I am going to go anyway," he tells her. "I just thought you ought to know about this." He sips his tea. It's weak and tastes vaguely salty. Cheap stuff smuggled over from Guernsey, he guesses. He's seen it sold at Bamburgh market for pennies. "And I rather… Well… I hoped I might convince Finn to come with us."

Eva gives him hard eyes. "If you are so certain this is not a trap, why do you want Finn to go with you?"

He falters. Really, he had wondered that himself when he had asked Julia to bring him out here today. Had wondered that as he had watched Longstone emerge from the cloud. Had cursed himself for that faint doubt of Julia he is unable to wash away.

After Sarah had died, Nathan had not for a moment imagined ever finding someone else. As far as he was concerned, Sarah had been the only woman he would ever feel comfortable being around. The only woman he would ever want. Now she was gone, Theodora would be his everything. All he needed.

But he cannot deny those thoughts have changed since Julia has come into his life. He has fallen for her. Hard. He knows there is no point denying it, at least to himself. Perhaps he had fallen for her the moment he had first stepped into her curiosity shop and seen her bright smile light the shadows of the island.

But even beneath these most astounding of feelings, is that uncertainty he cannot break. Heaven knows he has tried hard enough. He knows he and Julia can have no future together if he cannot manage complete trust.

He has done his best to silence his doubt. To convince himself that asking Finn to come to Bamburgh is merely a matter of wanting extra support—rather than an extra pair of eyes on Julia. And a way of getting that support without being forced to asked Edwin, who will only berate him for his foolishness and tell him to pack his bags for London.

"These are unsettled times," he tells Eva, hoping he sounds somewhat convincing. "Safety in numbers and all that. Besides, I'm sure Finn is just as eager to be rid of Ward as I am."

"Why do you say that?" she asks defensively.

Nathan raises his eyebrows. "Are we not all eager to be rid of him?"

Eva sips her tea. She wraps her hands around the cup, as though trying to steady herself through its warmth. "I shall pass on your request," she says finally. "And I'm sure Finn will be happy to help you." She looks pointedly at Nathan over the rim of her cup. "But I'm coming too."

CHAPTER FIFTEEN

Traipsing out to Bamburgh to pick up the traces of a twenty-year-old piece of correspondence feels like a fool's errand. A thing of deep desperation. But that's where they're at now, isn't it? Deep desperation?

Besides, Finn is well aware of the whisper at the back of his mind—and, these days, more often at the front of his mind—that tells him he owes a debt to Nathan Blake for taking his brother. And—perhaps equally as unforgiveable in Nathan's mind—his sister.

Finn is still furious at Ward for refusing to fight John Graveney. If Ward was willing to take up arms and confront the men who are threatening his captaincy, they would all be free of this mess. Abigail Blake's letter could be packed off to the past—and so could Henry Ward, and all he represents. Finn knows the memories of his childhood on Ward's ship will never disappear completely. But surely they'll be less potent with his former captain gone.

Ward is more of a coward than Finn remembers. Has he always been like this? Has time and age weakened him? Or had Finn just idolised him so much as a child he'd been blind to his flaws? Seen him as a hero he was not?

Here they are in this shuddery rented wagon, with the sea rolling past on their left and the grey-stone maze of Bamburgh peeking over the horizon. Finn has taken up the reins, if for no other reason than to put Eva in the box seat beside him and stop her so obviously spouting her distrust of Julia Mitchell.

She glances over her shoulder to peek at Nathan and Julia inside the wagon. "What do you suppose they're talking about?"

"Well." He lowers his voice and leans in conspiratorially. "I'm fairly certain I heard her ask him if he thought it was going to rain. Can hardly believe the nerve of that lass."

Eva looks at him witheringly. "I'm glad you find all this amusing."

He laughs.

"Do you trust her?" she asks.

Finn smiles to himself. He's answered this question at least ten times. "She's given me no reason not to."

"Well, I suppose it was not your house she was hiding her brothers in."

"Aye, it was. I remember bloody Angus draining the last of my moonshine. On more than one occasion."

She laughs a little. "You know what I mean."

"What are you afraid she's going to do?" asks Finn, tugging on the reins to slow the horse as the path veers down a mud-caked hill. "All we're doing is asking a few questions. Questions I think we all know are going to come to nought."

Eva shoots another quick glance over her shoulder. "But where did the information about the letter come from in the first place? How are we expected to trust her if she cannot be honest with us?" She sighs. "I suppose I'm just worried about Nathan. He's been through so much. And for him to feel this way about someone, it is such a rare thing. It's taken him an age to trust her. If it turns out she's deceiving him, I cannot bear to think what it will do to him."

"Maybe the fact that he's taken an age to trust her means he's finally decided she's trustworthy," says Finn. "Your brother doesn't seem like the kind of man to leap into things without thinking."

Eva sighs. "I suppose you're right." She sounds more than a little begrudging.

He grins. Nudges her knee with his. "In that case, you might want to make your distrust for her a little less obvious."

The tavern Julia has directed them to is a dubious-looking place on the fringe of the anchorage, all dark windows and low awnings, and stone walls thick enough to keep secrets. Finn has heard of the place of course—the lads he works with on the farms are full of stories about the moonshine here that'll blow your head clean off—but he has always stayed away. Gunpowder moonshine or not, the Rose is known to be a Jacobite tavern, and the last thing he needs is to be caught here by the redcoats and locked up on suspicion of treason.

Julia climbs out of the wagon as Finn is tying the horse to a hitching post a safe distance from the building. Nathan follows close behind her.

"I ought to be the one to go inside," Julia says. "I can ask the barkeep if he knows anything of the letter."

"No." Nathan leaps in before Eva can get out whatever distrustful words Finn can see hovering on her lips. "Absolutely not. I did not intend for you to put yourself in danger on my account."

"There's nothing dangerous about asking a few questions. Besides," she lowers her eyes, "my family are known Jacobites. The barkeep will trust me."

"I'm coming with you, at least."

"Nathan." She looks at him pointedly. "They'll trust me. And they won't trust you. Everyone on Holy Island knows who you are. There's every chance you could be recognised here in Bamburgh too. Do you really think they'll take it well if you're seen to be asking about Jacobite secrets?" She buttons her cloak and pulls the hood up over her fiery hair. "The rest of you stay out here and keep watch for the army. And mind the wagon. I'm sure there are a few people inside who'd like to make off with a fine-looking horse like that one. Heard there's been a lot of thieving out this way lately."

Eva flashes Finn wide, desperate eyes. He can read the meaning in them: that there is no way in hell she trusts Julia enough to let her go off and ask questions on behalf of their family.

"I'll go with you," he says.

Julia presses her lips together and Finn knows she has caught on to his and Eva's wordless conversation. "Fine." She doesn't bother to protest.

Finn follows Julia towards the tavern, past a bank of old wooden houses that seem to be holding each other up.

"You shouldn't be here either," she says, not looking at him. "The people on Lindisfarne like to gossip. If any of them are here, they'll know you're married to one of the Blakes."

Finn sidesteps a mound of horse dung on the edge of the road. "I'll keep my distance. But Nathan's right—it's dangerous for you to be visiting the place on your own."

Julia snorts. "I'd thank you for your chivalry if it weren't so obvious your wife put you up to this."

Finn chuckles. "Eva's just concerned about her brother is all. She doesn't want to see him get hurt."

"Well, you can tell her that hurting Nathan is the last thing in the world I wish to do." Her voice wavers slightly, and Finn hears a deep sincerity.

"All right," he says. "Let's get in and out of here as quick as we can, aye? I don't fancy being here when the redcoats next pay this place a visit."

Julia nods. Shoves open the door. "Wait a minute before you follow me."

Finn watches through the grimy window as she makes her way into the tavern. Waits a moment before stepping inside.

The tavern is almost empty, with a few men clustered around a half-baked fire and a bored-looking young woman wiping out cups on the other side of the bar. The air is thick with the smell of woodsmoke and old, soured ale. Surely no place to collect information on a letter from the long-dead past.

Julia approaches the counter and speaks to the young woman. The woman nods, gestures to someone unseen. An older man shuffles in from another room. Julia leans over the bar to speak with him.

Finn takes a step closer, hoping to catch a piece of their conversation. He doesn't trust Julia Mitchell either, he realises. At least, not entirely. He can't tell if it's instinct, or if Eva has just gotten in his head.

He cannot hear what Julia is saying, but he sees her face fall. Sees her mouth a dejected thanks.

She sidles away from the bar. "The barkeep doesn't know anything of the letter," she murmurs. "But we ought to wait a while. The men I'm hoping to speak to, they ought to be here soon."

"How d'you know that?"

She doesn't answer. "Stay out of my way," she says, eyes darting towards the door as it creaks open, letting in two old men in tarred greatcoats. "If anyone recognises you as Eva's husband, they'll likely tell these people to keep their mouths shut."

Nathan can't see much from inside the wagon. The windows of the tavern are far too small and grimy to see through, and the wagon is too far away. Probably for the best, he tells himself. He is not sure he wants to watch Julia at work among the Jacobites. He is too nervous about her safety, he tells himself. Nothing more.

"All right." He slides out of the wagon and looks up at Eva. "Given you insisted on being here, you can come with me."

"Where are we going?"

He hesitates. "There's someone we need to speak to."

"I thought we were here to keep watch."

"We'll not be long. And this is very important. It could give us more of a lead on the letter than these men at the tavern."

Eva's eyes dart towards the crooked stone building. "What about the horse? Julia said there were thieves around."

"We shall have to take our chances. I'm not leaving you here alone."

He starts walking in the hope that Eva will follow. And that she won't prod at his ridiculously vague explanation of what they are doing. Of course, he has no such luck. She is full of questions Nathan responds to with stilted silence, until he steps into the post house and asks after the man he is seeking.

"Elias Mitchell?" Eva hisses, once Nathan has gathered directions to the man's house and emerged back onto the street where she is waiting. "Julia's father? Does she know you're planning to pay him a visit?"

"Of course not. She barely speaks to the man." Nathan keeps his head down, voice low. Shame prevents him from speaking any louder. He can't bring himself to look at Eva.

"So you are keeping things from her," she says. "Is that because you believe she is still keeping things from you?"

Nathan quickens his pace, irritated. "She's not keeping anything from me. And I'm only keeping this from her because I know things are difficult between her and her father. She'd not appreciate me speaking to him. But I need to. Elias Mitchell was part of the Jacobite movement when Mother was involved with them. There's a chance he may know something about the letter."

"I see." Eva nods.

Nathan raises his eyebrows. "Do I take it you actually think this a decent idea?"

She shrugs. "You've certainly had worse."

Nathan follows the directions he was given through the winding streets of Bamburgh. He feels horribly on edge as his footsteps clatter against the cobbles, past a boarded-up shopfront and a blood-splattered pillory. He knows this to be a Jacobite town, much of the land owned by Thomas Forster, a Jacobite commander. Knows the redcoats have had their eyes on the place since the Rising began.

He wonders, sometimes, how all this happened. Six months ago, he had been a flailing watch merchant, with nothing more interesting in his days than his sorry failures in his business. Sometimes this all feels as though he has stepped into someone else's life by mistake.

And yet, at the same time, buried deep, there's a distant sense of coming home. A home that is anything but easy. These months he has spent on Lindisfarne, breathing briny air and looking at the stars, have reminded him that this place, so long forgotten, has always been a part of him. Buried deep, yes. But perhaps beginning to make its way towards the surface.

He has seen it in Eva's eyes; that look that says, against all odds, that this is where she belongs. He wonders if there has ever been such a look in his own eyes. Is he carrying these same thoughts, so well hidden he can barely make them out? After all, he and Eva were born Northumbrian children, their nursery windows speckled with German Ocean salt. Is it so surprising they feel drawn back to the place?

There is more to it, of course. Because Nathan knows it is love that has made Eva plant her feet back in Northumbrian soil. And there's a part of him that's afraid he might be drawn here for the very same reason.

Either way, the thought of leaving—of being forced from Lindisfarne, just as his mother was—makes something ache inside him. When he had first been dragged up here by Henry Ward, all he wanted was to return to London. Thoughts of escape had never been far from his mind. But now, the thought leaves him feeling hollow. He knows how much Theodora loves it here, and in spite of everything, there's a part of him that comes alive when he steps out into the cold air of Emmanuel Head. A part of him that wants to spend his life peering at stars and auroras in the clear skies of Lindisfarne, unimpeded by London smog.

It's so unexpected he can barely wrap his mind around it.

He has still not said anything to Julia about his leaving. Doing so will make it too real. But he is well aware they are nearly out of time. The day after tomorrow, John Graveney and his men will be at the door. Leaving feels at once both inevitable and impossible.

Elias Mitchell's cottage is a grey and tilted stone hovel, a sea of brambles keeping visitors from the door. It's a sad and sagging place—or perhaps just made that way by Nathan's knowledge of Mitchell's family: one child lost forever, a daughter disowned, two sons gifted to the rebel army. Nathan feels a pang of regret. Mitchell has already lost so much to the Jacobite movement; surely he'll not help the children of the woman who had stolen from their cause—especially so soon after Michael's death.

But he has come this far. Risked this much. There is little point leaving now.

He steps onto the path, leaving Eva hovering beside the low stone fence. She wraps herself in her cloak.

"You go ahead and speak with him. I'll keep watch."

Nathan nods. He can tell she is reluctant to hear any more brutal truths about who their mother was. He is reluctant to do so too. But he knows it cannot be avoided.

Brambles on the edge of the path snag on his coat and breeches as he fights his way to the door. He knocks firmly. Footsteps sound through the house and the door swings open.

The man that stands in front of him is sharp-eyed and tall, with sallow cheeks beneath a fog of grey stubble. Nathan sees hints of Julia in his green eyes and pale, freckled skin, but there's a rigidity to him that is far removed from his daughter's brightness.

He puts a thick arm out across the doorway, as if to prevent Nathan from stepping inside. "Yes?" He looks him up and down.

Nathan swallows. "My name is Nathan Blake. My mother was Abigail Blake." He sees something pass across Mitchell's eyes.

"I don't think I want anything to do with the son of Abigail Blake."

"Why not?" he dares to ask. He knows the answer, of course. But he wants to hear it from the man's mouth. Needs confirmation that Henry Ward was not speaking in lies.

"Because your mother was a thief and a liar."

Expected or not, the words still strike a blow.

"I'm sorry for what my mother did," Nathan says. "I've only recently learnt of it. And now my family is in trouble because of her crimes."

Mitchell scratches his bristly chin. "Is that so?" His expression is unreadable.

"I wondered if you ever heard my mother speak of a letter," Nathan tries. Even as he speaks, he knows there is little point. Elias Mitchell had thrown his daughter into the street with a child growing inside her. He is clearly not a man prone to sympathy.

"Never heard her speak of a letter," he says brusquely. "But even if she did, I'd know better than to believe her."

Finn sits in the corner of the tavern, an untouched glass of ale on the table in front of him. From where he's sitting, he can see Julia pacing up and down in front of the bar. She has her gaze pinned to the door. Looks painfully obvious. Finn wants to tell her to at least buy herself a drink and stop looking so damn suspicious, but he knows she'll not welcome his intrusion. At least he can tell Eva that Julia is so terrible at this whole business, there's zero chance she's a Jacobite spy.

At a table a few yards away, pieces of conversation catch his attention: *treasure fleet* and *lost gold* and *New World*. He can't help being drawn to these stories of the sea. His years on the *Eagle* have left a deep-rooted mark upon him, in more ways than one. Not, of course, that he has any desire to climb aboard a ship again—least of all, Henry Ward's. That simple life beneath the Longstone light, that life he had once done everything to escape, is now the only existence he wants. Nonetheless, he can't help but be intrigued.

He slides onto the empty stool at the table the stories had flown from. Three men are sitting around it, capped heads bent towards each other. "This true?" he asks. "A treasure fleet's gone down?"

One man turns and scowls at the interruption. But another says, "So I hear." He chuckles. "Why? You thinking of going after it?"

Finn smiles thinly. "Nah. Just curious."

"Two Spanish fleets went down in a hurricane off the coast of Florida over the summer. More than a thousand dead. They was taking their gold and silver back to Spain. Now it's lying in the water, there for the taking. They say it's just washing up on the beaches. Anyone with two oars and a piece of driftwood is heading over there to see what they can find."

The door creaks open as the man speaks. Once, twice, three times. The tavern is filling slowly, Finn realises. Men in tartans. Men with Jacobite cockades pinned to their caps. Old men, mostly, a woman or two among them, the men of fighting age all off marching with the rebel army. Julia's eyes dart. Have the men she's been waiting for arrived? Does she even know who they are?

She makes her way to a cluster of people in the corner of the tavern. Finn keeps one eye on her, but can't help focusing on what the men at the table are telling him. *Lost treasure fleet* and *washing up on the beaches* has caused his mind to race. Because the wealth from these Spanish treasure ships, well that would surely outweigh whatever paltry sum the sale of a ruin like Highfield House would fetch.

"Army!" shouts a man at the window. Yells and thuds as people scramble to their feet. Stools thump to the ground, tin cups bouncing across the flagstones.

The door cracks open and soldiers charge inside. Four men; no, five. More outside, perhaps. Finn hears the crack of a pistol. Feels wood shards against his cheek as the bullet lodges in the rafters above his head. Gunpowder burns the air.

He grabs Julia's elbow and tugs her towards the door. Keeping to the edges of the tavern, he clambers over fallen chairs. Spills into the street with a tangle of men around him. He runs towards the wagon, looking over his shoulder to make sure Julia is following. He hears a window breaking inside the tavern. Hears a woman scream.

He lurches forward, panic jolting through him when he finds the wagon empty. The horse is thrashing against the hitching post, spooked by the sound of gunfire. Finn grapples with the reins, pressing a hand to the horse's neck in a desperate attempt to calm it.

He hears Eva call his name. She and Nathan burst from the tangle of streets and race towards the wagon.

"Where have you been?" Julia presses.

"We—"

"Militiamen were watching us," Nathan cuts in. "We thought it best to leave."

The look on Eva's face tells Finn her brother is lying. He doesn't push the issue. Not now, with bullets flying across the tavern. He scrambles into the box seat, reaching out a hand to help Eva up. She'll tell him where they've been later, he knows, once they're tucked away on Longstone and the rest of the world has fallen aside. And as for Nathan's reasons for lying to Julia, Finn is fairly sure that the less he knows, the better.

CHAPTER SIXTEEN

Julia finds Hugh in the cellar, dozing on the bed with his legs dangling off the mattress and one arm folded beneath his head. The room is hot, the air thick with the smell of her brother's pipe smoke and sweat. She yanks the blankets off him and shoves his shoulder hard. Hugh murmurs with shock as his eyes fly open.

"What in hell, Julia?"

"Get out," she demands.

He sits up, rubbing his eyes. "What?"

"I said, get out." This time, she will not let herself be swayed by him. This time, her anger is so vivid, so all-consuming that it washes away everything else her brother has done for her.

"Where exactly would you like me to go?" he asks, an amused smile flickering on his lips.

"I don't care. I don't want you here. I can't even look at you after what you did." She hears her voice rattle with emotion.

The amusement disappears from his eyes. "What are you on about?"

"Don't, Hugh. I've had enough of these games."

The bed creaks as he stands. He rubs blearily at his face. "I honestly don't know what you're talking about."

Julia closes her eyes. No. She won't let herself believe him. Won't let herself fall for this.

"Jul?" he says. "Is everything all right? Are you in danger?"

And that concern in his voice, it's so real, she finds herself saying, "I went to the Rose Tavern with Nathan today. At the very time you told me to go. Just as the redcoats turned up."

Something flickers across Hugh's eyes. "I hoped you wouldn't go with him."

"Why?" Julia hisses. "Because you led him into a trap? Because you hoped the redcoats would catch him?"

"Because it was dangerous," Hugh says tautly. "Can you really be surprised the army was watching? Bamburgh is a Jacobite town." He shakes his head. "Surely you can't be so naïve as to think that was my doing. How could I possibly know when the redcoats would turn up?"

"I don't know," she snaps. "I've no idea what you're involved in. I'd not put anything past you."

Hugh chuckles humourlessly. Shakes his head.

Julia had been terrified to climb back into the wagon with Nathan after the army had stormed the tavern. He would blame her, surely. Would demand to know where the information about the Rose Tavern had come from. Demand to know why she had led them into danger. And then things would fall, and splinter, and crumble beyond repair.

"I didn't know the army was going to show themselves," she had said, unable to look him in the eye. "I swear it."

"Of course you didn't. How could you?" Nathan reached across the bench seat and pressed a hand against her clasped fist, forcing her to look at him. "This was always going to be risky. That's why I did not want you to go in there in the first place. I'm just glad you're safe."

His words, Julia thinks now, they're so similar to Hugh's. Perhaps she is being unreasonable, blaming her brother for the army's appearance. But she'll not allow herself to be blinded by his games. Because at the back of her mind is the unsettling knowledge that Hugh has it in him to hurt others. He had pulled the trigger on a soldier—and who knows what else he has done?

Once, Hugh had been compassionate and kind. A loving husband and father. A loving brother. But with his wife and child in the earth, he has changed. His passion for this cause has taken over his decency.

Julia knows that in Hugh's eyes, he is doing nothing but good. Acting with honour to see the God-divined king upon the throne. And she fears that, for all his words about not putting the man she cares for in danger, he would not hesitate to put a bullet in Nathan's chest if he believed he was hampering the Jacobite cause. Would not hesitate to throw him into the path of the redcoats.

The knot in her stomach grows tighter. She ought to tell Nathan that Hugh is here. But all she can think about is how much will topple if she does so.

For the first time in her life, she is beginning to glimpse a future with a man, rather than just a half-remembered night of shame. She knows Nathan's trust in her is still flimsy; surely if he is to find out Hugh is here—that he has overheard his secrets, and that he is pressuring her for information on who the government spies are—it will shatter that trust for good.

"I had no idea the army was going to storm the tavern today," Hugh says. He sits back on the bed and reaches down to pull on his boots. "I'm your brother, Julia. I'd never put you in danger like that."

"But you would put someone in danger if they were suspected of spying for the government. Like Nathan Blake."

He holds her gaze. "Jul. I would *never* put you in danger. Even if you were gallivanting around the place with that dandy. I told you about the letter because I wanted to help him. Because I can tell how much he means to you."

She snorts. "You told me about the letter because you hoped I'd tell you who the government spies are."

"Well. That too." The smile returns to his lips. "You can't blame me for trying."

CHAPTER SEVENTEEN

Wrecked ships, sunken treasure, Floridian beaches glittering with gold.

Finn has slept little tonight, thoughts of what he learnt at the tavern circling through his head. He lies in bed in shifting darkness, the glow of the firebasket through the shutters painting stripes of orange light across the floor. He rolls onto Eva's side of the bed, soaking up the warmth she has left beneath the blankets.

He knows better than to believe these stories at face value. But if they are true, if these Spanish treasure ships really have gone down with their wealth littering the beaches, this is a precious piece of knowledge.

Even the smallest cut of such a haul would give Graveney and his supporters far more than they would gain from taking Highfield House from Nathan. And make a far better substitute for the immunity Ward has promised his crew.

Before he and Eva had returned to Longstone tonight, Finn had scrawled a note to Henry Ward; deposited it in the Lindisfarne tavern. Instructions for him to meet him there at noon tomorrow. He hopes he's not too late. He is well aware that tomorrow is Friday. Well aware that Nathan Blake is running out of time.

Finn slides out of bed, giving up on sleep. He is to take the watch in a few hours anyway, and would rather spend the night in Eva's company than tossing and turning in the darkness. When he steps out into the living area, he finds her at the table in a pool of lamplight, her dark head bent over her sewing. He watches her wordlessly for several moments, her needle darting in and out of the fabric, fingers flying. The floor creaks beneath him and she turns in surprise.

"What are you doing awake?" she asks. "It's barely midnight. I can stay up for a few more hours."

He makes his way over to her; wraps his arms around her from behind and presses his head into her neck. "I think I've slept all I'm going to tonight."

She reaches a hand up behind her to brush her fingers through his tangled brown hair. She holds up the shirt she is hemming. "Look how crooked this stitching is. Hope the fellow who owns it has poor eyesight."

Finn squints. It looks as straight as an arrow to him. "You're tired," he says, planting a kiss below her ear. "Rest."

Eva ties off her sewing and puts the shirt down on the table in front of her, but continues toying with a loose piece of thread. Finn uncorks the whisky bottle on the sideboard and sloshes a sizeable gulp into her teacup.

She smiles up at him. "I'm not sure that will help my crooked sewing."

"Probably not," he agrees. "But might help you relax a little."

"Mmm." She sounds unconvinced.

Finn nods at the cup. "Drink up." She takes an obedient mouthful.

He goes to the table and breaks a chunk from the bread loaf. Eats it at the window, looking out across the dark sea.

"Anyone there?" Eva asks edgily.

"Dark water. Seems even the herring fishermen are staying away." He wonders how many times tonight she has gone to the window to look for Ward's ship.

Finn turns away from the glass. He slides onto a chair at the table, deliberate in blocking Eva's view out the window. He stretches his legs out in front of him. "Where'd you and Nathan really go today?"

Eva takes another sip of her tea. "To speak with Elias Mitchell."

"Julia's father?"

"Estranged father," she says with a wry smile.

Finn chuckles. "I can see why Nathan dished out that load of rubbish about the militia."

"He hoped Mitchell might be able to tell us something about Mother's letter. Given he was active in the Jacobite cause when she was… well, involved with them."

"And?"

She shakes her head. "Nothing of any use. Just confirmation that Ward was telling the truth about everything Mother did." There's a heaviness to her voice. Finn presses a hand to her knee and squeezes gently.

"I so desperately wish I could speak to her," Eva murmurs. "Ask her why she did what she did. Ask her what really happened the night we fled."

Finn raises his eyebrows. "You don't think she fled because of Ward? Because she didn't want him to find out about Harriet?"

She fiddles with the hem of her sewing. "We left in the middle of the night. Why would she have done that? It does not make sense. There has to be more to it."

"Maybe Ward arrived unexpectedly," Finn suggests. "Maybe she saw him coming to the house and had no choice but to run before he found her. Maybe she worried that if he saw her, he'd know she was carrying his child."

Eva sighs. "Perhaps you're right. But there's no way we'll ever know for sure. I have to make peace with that." She looks past him, straining to see through the window.

It's doing her no good being out here, Finn can tell. He's sure she's thinking of nothing but Henry Ward and his connection to her family.

There's a part of him that wants to whisk her away from the island; take her someplace without an uninterrupted view of sea. But do that, and this uninterrupted view of sea turns dark. A treacherous passage of water likely to become a graveyard—and Finn knows neither he nor Eva could live with that on their conscience.

"These treasure ships," she says suddenly. "Do you really think they'll be enough to tempt Ward and Graveney away from Highfield House?"

"I don't know," Finn admits. "I hope so." He regrets telling her about the treasure ships; about his plan to meet Ward in the tavern tomorrow. He had done so in an attempt to give her a little hope and optimism. But he can tell it's just given her more to dwell on.

He reaches out and tucks a loose strand of hair behind her ear. "Get some sleep, Evie. Forget about Ward for a while. I can manage out here."

She hesitates. Looks out at the window again. "You'll tell me if you see anything out there?"

"If I see anything important, aye. But you need to rest. You've hardly slept in days."

She nods, getting wearily to her feet. "All right." She bends to kiss his lips and Finn feels a tug of desire. Considers tumbling her into the bedroom and making her forget about Ward in a completely different way. No. She needs to sleep. He squeezes her fingers and gives her a smile he hopes looks somewhat convincing. Eva takes another gulp of whisky-laced tea. She disappears into the bedroom on silent feet, closing the door behind her.

It's the stillest, deepest part of the night when Finn sees the lights bearing down on the island. He steps out of the cottage and peers across the water at the ship emerging from the dark. The firebasket gives out just enough light to tell him he will not have the luxury of speaking to Ward in the tavern this afternoon.

He waits on the jetty. Watches as a longboat is lowered from the *Eagle*. Watches as it approaches the island, oars sighing rhythmically through the water.

Ward is alone. Interesting, Finn thinks. When he has come for him in the past, he has always sent swathes of men to do his bidding. Finn is not sure if this solo visit makes him more or less wary.

For a second, he considers waking Eva. Considers keeping his promise to tell her of any news. He pushes the thought away quickly. Let her sleep. Let her have a few uninterrupted hours not filled with anxiety over Ward. She'll be furious if she finds out, of course. But it's a fury he's willing to carry.

Finn stands on the jetty with folded arms as Ward ties the longboat's hawser to the moorings. Climbs out with one step. He is dressed in a thick black greatcoat and cocked hat, a grey scarf bundled at his neck and a queue hanging in coils down his back.

"You couldn't wait a few more hours to speak to me?" Finn asks bitterly. His breath plumes out in a silver cloud before disappearing into the darkness.

"Waiting around for the days to pass will do no one any good." Ward glances down at his stolen longboat, roped to the other side of the jetty. "Glad you're making good use of my property." He begins to stride towards the cottage, but Finn grabs his shoulder, pulling him back.

"No. We can speak out here."

"Very well." Ward rubs his gloved hands together to warm them. "You have something to tell me, I assume? I hope you've finally come to your senses and will agree to come back to the *Eagle* with me."

"No, Ward. If you want that, you'll have to force me." And Finn knows, as he speaks, that there is every chance of that happening. Every chance of Eva waking up alone on the island, with no word of explanation from him. His stomach turns over at the thought.

Ward looks unsurprised. "Why did you wish to see me?"

And Finn tells him of the two lost Spanish treasure fleets; of the wealth now lying on the ocean floor. "Perhaps you can't offer your crew immunity," he says. "But surely the chance of enough wealth to see them through their lives is a fair exchange. It would restore their faith in you as captain, aye?"

Ward is silent for a long moment, eyes glazed over as he looks towards the dark shape of the *Eagle*. How close is he to losing his ship, Finn wonders? How many men would side with him if he found the courage to fight John Graveney?

"This could all just be hearsay," Ward says finally. "The ramblings of a few drunkards in a tavern."

"It could," Finn admits. "But is a prize like this not worth taking a gamble on? You find even a scrap of this haul and Graveney will have far more than he'd get from the sale of that ruined old house. Your captaincy would be secure again, and you'd have no need to fight for it."

Ward rubs his jaw. Finn can tell the idea has intrigued him. But he says, "Going after these ships is a risk. Two months to the New World, if we're lucky. And there's no certainty we'll find a thing. But the house is there for the taking." Before Finn can argue, Ward says, "You know that's how Graveney and his supporters will see it."

"And what about how you see it? You're the damn captain."

"And I'm doing my best to keep it that way." Ward digs his hands into the pockets of his coat, rounding his shoulders against the cold. Wind swirls off the sea, sending a volley of sparks fluttering down from the firebasket. "This is not just about the money," he says. "Graveney and his supporters are staunch Jacobites. They want the Blakes to pay for Abigail's crimes."

Finn lets out his breath. "You can't let him take the house. Eva's family would have nothing left to their name." He looks out at the lamplit ship, then back at Ward. "If you chose to fight Graveney, how many men would side with you? Half?"

Ward eyes him, and Finn doubts he is going to answer the question. But he says, "More, I should hope."

"Then why are you being such a damn coward?" The words fall out before Finn can stop them. He can tell there's a part of Ward that desperately wants to fight Graveney. But he's afraid of losing. Better to be captain merely in name, Finn supposes, than to fail trying to take back his power.

He is bitterly disappointed in Henry Ward. The very same way, he imagines, that Ward feels about him.

Ward chuckles dully. "I must say, your loyalty to the Blakes is quite something. Trying to make up for past mistakes, are you?"

"Does it not matter to you that it's your daughter's family Graveney is trying to steal from?" Finn demands, pushing past his question. "You're so determined to see me away from Eva because you think it's what Abigail would have wanted. But do you really think she'd expect this cowardice from you? You're just sitting by and letting these men take Highfield House."

"Abigail lied to me. Deceived me. I'm no longer so inclined to put my captaincy on the line for what she would have wanted."

Finn scrubs a hand across his eyes in frustration. "Then why in hell are you trying to force me from my wife?"

Ward takes a step closer. In the light of the firebasket, Finn can see the deep creases around his mouth and eyes. "I taught you many things when you were a lad," Ward says. "And one of them, I hope, was decency. Owning your mistakes."

And at once, Finn is a child again. He is huddling at the table in the *Eagle's* great cabin, listening to Ward's footsteps click back and forth across the floorboards in front of him. Listening to the captain berate him in that that steel-hard, expressionless voice. A scolding for losing his temper. For forgetting to scrub the back of the range. For sloppy handwriting. Oversleeping. *Aye, sir. Sorry, sir.*

Finn feels himself bow his head. Lower his eyes. The same reaction he'd had to Ward's reprimanding as a child.

"You're ingratiating yourself into the Blakes' lives," Ward continues, "all the while, lying to them about how their brother died."

"I've told them no lies."

"But no truths either."

Finn closes his eyes. He's right, of course. And this rationale, it's far worse than Ward trying to wrestle him away from Eva out of some long-ago loyalty to Abigail. It goes much deeper than that, Finn realises now. Perhaps it always has.

He looks at Ward squarely. "I am not going to leave Eva," he says. "Are you going to kill me for it? Because if you are, then just do it. Let's put an end to this." He hopes Ward can't hear the uncertainty in his voice. Finn is unsure what he is more afraid of: Ward putting a pistol to his chest and forcing him back aboard the ship, or Ward telling Nathan and Harriet how their brother died.

Ward holds his gaze for a long moment, and the tug of fear in Finn's stomach intensifies. Perhaps it's neither of these things he's so afraid of. Perhaps it's the possibility of his life ending tonight. Ward has tried to kill him before; under the rulings of the ship's articles, yes, but it proves he is not above such things. But somehow, Finn also senses that Ward will not do so again. Perhaps the act of keel-hauling the boy he had taken under his wing had been harder for Ward than he anticipated.

It's his history with Henry Ward that's saving him, Finn realises. It's those reading lessons, those open discussions about fear and courage, those nights spent on deck with a quadrant at his eye, learning to read the stars. Those scoldings at the table as Ward tried to turn him into a better man. He wonders how long such an amnesty will last.

"I'm not going to kill you, Finn," Ward says finally. "I'd not shoot you in front of your own home and leave your body for your wife to find. But my offer still stands. Come with me now and your crimes will be forgiven. I swear to you that I will never speak of them again."

"Come with you now? So I can be another body to help you fight Graveney? Is that what you mean?"

Ward says nothing. But Finn can tell by the look in his eyes that his guess is an accurate one. He would be valuable to Ward, yes. One more man to take his side; to help him secure his captaincy. Help rid him of John Graveney.

Finn lets out a desperate laugh. "I'm just one man, Ward. Do you really think having me fight for you will make a difference?"

"Every man counts."

Finn shakes his head. "I'm not coming with you. I'm not going to fight for you."

"Not even if it meant getting John Graveney away from your wife's family?" Ward looks at Finn for a long second, a faint smile flickering in the corner of his mouth. "It would seem as though we both want something from one another."

For a moment, time hollows and distorts, and Finn feels a falling sensation in his stomach. He swallows hard. "So if I re-join your crew, you'll fight Graveney and his men? Get them away from the Blakes?" The words feel impossibly heavy.

"I can't assure you we will be victorious. But I can assure you I will fight him."

No. He does not want to hear this.

But isn't this what he asked for? For Ward to fight for the Blakes? For Ward to turn on Graveney? Thoughts pound against his head. He feels hot and sick.

Ward's eyes spear him. "You have my word, Finn. You make your sacrifice, and in return, I will make mine."

The words strike him. Ward is a selfish coward, yes. But so, Finn realises, is he. He glances up at the firebasket. The flames have dwindled to a faint coppery glow and the basket needs refilling. The shadows across the island are becoming ink-dark. "I'm not going to leave Eva," he says again.

"Even if it meant helping her family?" Ward raises his eyebrows; a questioning, probing look Finn has seen from him all too many times. A look that makes him question himself. "Don't you owe them this?"

Finn feels painfully on edge as he goes to the shed for the coal. He refills the basket, then stands on the rim of the island, watching Ward's longboat glide back towards his ship.

You make your sacrifice, and in return, I will make mine.

Don't you owe them this?

He hates that Henry Ward's words always manage to work their way inside him. Right now, he knows they are having such an effect because they are right. Finn has kept secrets from the Blakes. Has sat around their table, has slept beneath their roof, made himself part of their family. All after taking their brother from them.

The realisation swings at him suddenly.

He cannot leave Eva. But he does need to tell her family the truth.

Telling them will give Henry Ward once less piece of ammunition against him. But that is not the argument that has him climbing into the longboat with the first blue light of dawn. It's the dull knowledge that Ward did teach him decency. And keeping this secret from Eva's family has not been the decent thing to do. He cannot change the past. But he can do the right thing now.

He rows away from the jetty before he can change his mind. Before Eva wakes and makes him doubt everything.

He hates that he is doing this without telling her. But Ward is right. He cannot sit around the table with the Blakes and pretend nothing had happened. Because yes, Henry Ward had taught him to be a better man than that.

He knows her family finding out the truth is the thing Eva fears the most. But he also knows Ward is right when he says the truth will not stay hidden forever. And Finn would rather they hear it from him.

CHAPTER EIGHTEEN

Nathan pokes at the fire in the parlour, willing the flimsy flames to warm the room. The house is full of blue shadow in the early morning, the walls radiating cold. Even Mrs Brodie has not shown herself yet.

He is not surprised his foolish venture to Bamburgh came to nothing. His mother's letter is from a past so distant that any knowledge of it can be based on no more than flimsy hearsay. He is just as unsurprised at Elias Mitchell's reaction to his turning up on his doorstep. He is just relieved Julia had not questioned his clumsy lie about being watched by the militia. He cannot bear to think how angry she would be if she knew he had been to see her father.

One day soon, he will stop lying to her. Once Henry Ward and his men are a memory, he will speak nothing but truths to Julia for the rest of his days.

But he is running out of time to make *the rest of his days* a reality. The six days Graveney had promised him are nearly over. And as much as it pains him, Nathan knows that is for the best. As he had lain sleepless in bed last night, he had stared down at Theodora in the truckle bed beside him and been hit with an enormous swell of guilt. Edwin is right—they need to get out of this house as soon as possible. Get their children to safety. Nothing else matters.

The knock at the door startles him. It's barely dawn—and these days, a knock at the door is rarely good news. He finds Finn on the doorstep, a look of deep unease in his eyes. Nathan's mind goes to freak waves and boating accidents, and all the other godawful things that might have happened to his sister out on Longstone.

"Has something happened?" he asks. "Eva, is she—"

"Eva's well," Finn cuts in. "But there's something I need to speak with you about." There's a desperate, lingering panic in his eyes; the same look Nathan is sure he himself has been wearing since Henry Ward first appeared on his doorstep. He nods, gesturing for Finn to enter.

Finn hesitates. He glances up at the bleak façade of the house, then digs his hands into the pockets of his greatcoat, his shoulders rounding. "Can we speak outside?"

Nathan has never seen him so uneasy. "As you wish." He takes his coat from the hook in the foyer and slides it on. Steps out of the house without a word and closes the door behind him.

Finn begins to pace, his boots sighing through the damp grass. His breath clouds, before disappearing into the pearly sunrise. "There's something I ought to tell you," he begins. "Something I regret not telling you earlier. It was wrong of me. But I've been too much of a coward to tell you the truth."

And Nathan understands, suddenly, the reason behind the panic in Finn's eyes. The desperation. The regret.

"I know about you and Oliver," he says.

Finn stops pacing. "What?" He hesitates. Opens his mouth to speak, then stops. "You recognised me?"

Nathan smiles wryly. "No." He wraps his arms around his body; shivers. "Ward told me before you and Eva married. He wanted me to put a stop to your wedding."

Finn stares at him. "But you didn't."

"No."

Ward had come to the house a few days before Eva's wedding, having overheard word in the village of her impending marriage. Told Nathan exactly who she planned to bring into the family.

Nathan knows he had not given Ward the response he was expecting. He had not gone tearing out to Longstone for revenge, or to drag Eva home. Perhaps that was what he ought to have done. Perhaps that was, as Ward had insisted, the right thing to do. The thing that Abigail would have wanted.

But Abigail is not here. The decision was not hers to make. And angry as Nathan was at Eva for bolting out to Longstone in the first place, somehow, it had felt wrong to deny her happiness on account of their cruel brother—even if it meant abandoning his last hopes of her marrying Matthew Walton. Nathan cares for his sister deeply. Is not sure he ever felt anything for Oliver other than fear.

Finn stands motionless for long moments, his gaze turned to the grey stone walls of the house's second storey. He knows the place perhaps better than anyone, Nathan thinks. Knows of the priest hole that had allowed him to hide, the passage in the wall that had given him an escape. He can only imagine the nerve it must have taken him to step back through the door again.

"Why?" Finn asks after a long silence. "Why allow Eva to marry me?"

"She loves you," Nathan says simply. "If she is able to look past what happened, then it seemed wrong for me to not do the same." He lets out a long breath, looking past Finn to the slate-grey roll of the sea. "I know what Oliver was like. And I saw what happened between the two of you that night. I know it was hardly a case of cold-blooded murder."

"That doesn't change what happened."

"No. That's true."

Finn looks at him for a long second. "Thank you."

Nathan nods. The muscles in his shoulders are tight, a dull coil of unease in his stomach. His body's eternal reaction to speaking of this piece of the past. In London, Oliver had been pushed to the back of his mind, the trauma he had inflicted along with it. Here in Highfield House, that past is harder to ignore. Still, he keeps the door to Oliver's old bedroom locked. Still, he can barely bring himself to step inside it. If by some miracle he finds a way to remain here on Lindisfarne, he will force himself to open that room up. Let the sea air blow through and take the memories with it.

"I wasn't sorry, you know," Nathan says suddenly. "About what happened to Oliver." The words spill. "At his burial, everyone approached me to tell me how sorry they were for my loss. And I realised I was glad he was gone." The moment he speaks, he feels his shoulders slump forward; feels that dread in his stomach begin to uncoil. This is a truth he has never admitted to. A truth he has been carrying somewhere hidden for the past twenty years. Speaking it makes him feel like a terrible person. But at the same time, it makes the weight on his shoulders grow a little lighter. Makes the memories of his brother lose their potency. He takes a long, slow breath, feeling the cold air fill his lungs, anchoring him to the present. For a long moment, neither of them speak, the wordlessness punctuated by the hush of the sea.

"I'm sorry," Finn says. "For not speaking to you about this much earlier."

Nathan smiles wryly. "I can understand why you didn't." He turns up his collar, huddling in on himself against the cold. "If I'm honest, I hoped it would be something this family would never speak of. Much like Oliver himself."

Finn's eyes turn downward. "Who else knows?"

"No one," says Nathan. "Just myself and Eva. What point would there be in telling anyone else?"

"What about Harriet?"

"It's best that she doesn't know," says Nathan. "Things are fragile enough between her and the rest of the family."

"I'm sure Ward will tell her if I don't."

Nathan shakes his head. "From what I can gather, Ward is not in the habit of sharing things with her. As much as she might wish otherwise."

Finn is silent for a long time, as though turning this information over in his head. There is something in his eyes that is not quite relief, not quite dread. No doubt he had expected to leave Highfield House with his secrets spilled; with the weight of them off his shoulders, but the consequences laid out in front of him. Nonetheless, Nathan is adamant that Harriet not know of this. He fears it would be the incision that would sever her from the rest of the family forever. She had never known Oliver, and the few times he has been mentioned in the past, they have always veered away from speaking of his true nature. His true death.

Succumbed to smallpox. Quick and unremarkable. Oliver Blake has become just an average boy who died an average death. Nathan knows Harriet will not see things the way he does.

"Has there been any sign of Ward these past few days?" Finn asks finally. "Or Graveney?"

Nathan is glad for the change of subject. Although the thought of Ward and Graveney is hardly more pleasant than the thought of his older brother. "No. I've not seen them since Graveney approached me in the village."

"What will you do?" asks Finn. "If he comes for the house?"

"*When* he comes for the house," Nathan says dully. "He told me I had six days. That was five days ago."

Finn nods. "What will you do?" he asks again.

"I will give it to him," says Nathan. "What else can I do? Edwin has offered to put Thea and me up for as long as we need it." Speaking the words aloud makes his shoulders sink forward. He will be penniless. Forced to rely on Edwin's charity until he can scrabble together some form of income. Once he is safely away from Lindisfarne, he can attempt to sell the house, of course, but he does not dare think about how long it will take to find someone willing to purchase such a faraway wreck. Rebuilding his business will be an impossibility with no money to his name. As will staying here on Lindisfarne to make a future with Julia.

He turns these thoughts over, feeling the weight of them.

"There may be another way," says Finn.

Nathan feels a faint flicker of hope. Pushes it aside before it can take root. "You know something of the letter?"

"No. But there's a chance Ward can give his crew the wealth they want, without taking the house from your family." And the story he tells is a fantastical one, filled with sunken ships and gold lost in New World hurricanes. True, Finn claims, at least as far as he can tell. Either way, it is a story Henry Ward believes.

"Ward came to Longstone last night," Finn says. "I told him about these ships. I could tell he was intrigued. He's afraid that if he doesn't give his crew the wealth and immunity he promised them, they'll overthrow him as captain. He thinks he has a chance of regaining the crew's trust if he takes them to Florida to salvage the gold. But he knows Graveney wants to stay and punish your family for what your ma did."

Nathan frowns. "How does any of this help me?"

"I'm not saying you ought to stay and fight Graveney," says Finn. "That's your choice to make. But Ward wants Graveney gone, and if he commits to going after these treasure ships, it'll likely give him fresh support from his crew. If you chose to stand up to Graveney, there's a chance Ward might support you."

The thought stays with him long after Finn leaves. Stays with him as he forces down breakfast with Theodora; as he pens his lacklustre responses to the watch manufacturers. And with it comes a strength he was not expecting.

Refuse to hand over the house. Stay and fight. It's not the kind of thing he has ever done in his life. But perhaps he has grown tired of being shaped by others' bidding.

Graveney will not kill him—the knowledge comes to him suddenly, in bright colours. It's a bold, brazen thought, but Nathan trusts it. He is the one who must sign over the deeds to Highfield House. If he is to die without doing so, the manor will pass into Theodora's dowry. For the place to be more to him than a pile of crumbling brick and stone, Graveney needs Nathan alive. It's an oddly empowering thought.

Over and over, Nathan has told himself he hates this house. Its poisonous past and its priest holes and passages. Hates it for the stress it has caused him; the sleepless nights. But he realises now he has been wrong. It is not hatred for the house at all. It is hatred for Ward and Graveney. And yes, for Oliver—because he may as well admit that now. Perhaps even for this darkest side of his mother and all the pain and stress her mistakes have caused him. This house, this island, salt-streaked and windblown, is not to blame.

Nathan realises then what he has known in the back of his mind for days: he is not going to give this house up. He is not going to flee like Abigail did. This is home. He is not going to give up on a future with Julia; a future of his own making.

He knows this is madness. But he also sees now what he had failed to see before: that he is not the only one who despises John Graveney.

There's a chance Henry Ward might support you.

"How big a chance?" he had asked Finn that morning.

"I can't be sure. It's a risk, for certain. But maybe one worth taking. Ward's afraid Graveney will mutiny. But if Graveney failed to get the letter, and failed to get the house from you, the men'd be unlikely to support him as captain. Especially if Ward's offering to take them to

Florida to salvage the treasure ships. There's every chance he might support you in order to make that a reality."

"Support me how?" Nathan asked, mind already beginning to run. "You think he and his supporters would fight Graveney on my behalf?"

"Maybe," said Finn. "He wants Graveney gone as much as you do."

A risk, for certain. But yes, Nathan thinks, it is a risk worth taking.

CHAPTER NINETEEN

"What do you mean you are staying?" Edwin demands later that morning. He paces in front of Nathan's desk, footsteps clopping against the floorboards. "Are you mad?"

"I need you to get Thomas and Thea out of the house," Nathan says, surprising himself with his calmness. "Harriet too."

"Don't be a fool," Edwin hisses. "I'm not leaving you alone to face these bastards. They're going to be on the doorstep tomorrow. And unless you have your mother's letter, or the deeds to the house for them, they'll likely put a bullet in your chest."

"I'm well aware of the situation." Nathan runs the soft end of a quill along his fingers. "But I'll not be facing Graveney alone. I'll have Ward's support." Edwin does not need to know that that support is no certain thing. Once Harriet and the children are out of the house, he will send for Ward and list all the reasons why he ought to raise arms against Graveney and get these men out of their lives.

In truth, Nathan would like to have Edwin here at the house with him, in case Ward's support falls through and Graveney appears on the doorstep as promised. Though he feels certain Graveney will achieve nothing from killing him, Nathan knows there is little chance of him coming out of this completely unscathed. If he could ever use a trigger-happy ally, it is now.

But he needs Theodora out of the house. Needs Edwin to take her back to London with Thomas and Harriet.

Edwin pulls the chair from the corner of the room and sinks into it. He leans forward on the desk, looking at Nathan intently. "Come back to London with us, Nate. Let Graveney have the house. Like I said, you and Thea can stay with us until you've found your feet again."

His patronising tone makes Nathan bristle. "No. Thank you for the offer. But I can't rely on your charity."

"Is accepting my charity worse than Theodora growing up as an orphan? Because that's where this is headed."

Nathan shakes his head. "Graveney won't kill me. He'll achieve nothing from that. He needs me alive to sign over the deeds to the house."

"And you don't think he can force you to do that?"

Nathan pushes away a swell of fear he can't bring himself to acknowledge. "He needs me alive," he says again.

Edwin rubs his eyes. "Ward has been doing Graveney's bidding for months, trying to get the letter from you. What makes you think he'll suddenly turn around and support you?"

"Finn tells me he has a way of gaining his crew's trust again. A way of giving them the wealth they want."

Edwin snorts. "I'm not sure I'd trust Finn any more than I'd trust Henry Ward. If his reputation is anything to go by, he's hardly the most honest of men."

Nathan doesn't speak at once. He is well aware that this is the height of foolishness. But something seems to have split open inside him—whether wrought by Julia, or by months of fear and threats, or by years of feeling weak and ineffective, he doesn't know. He only knows he cannot roll over like this.

"My mind is made up," he tells Edwin. "Will you take Harriet and the children back to London or not?"

Edwin sighs heavily. Gives Nathan a look full of disapproval. But he says, "Of course."

"It's looking like we've got more support coming from the south," says Hugh, leaning up against the stones of the fireplace and bringing his teacup to his lips.

Bobby looks up in interest from where he is sitting cross-legged on the settle.

"The Lancashire Catholics are ready to rise. About time, wouldn't you say, lad? Thought we'd never hear from the cowards."

Bobby nods enthusiastically. "About time, aye. The cowards."

"Stop it," Julia hisses at Hugh. "He doesn't need to hear all this." Once upon a time, she had loved how much Bobby idolised his uncle. Now it just makes her angry.

Hugh raises his eyebrows. "You going to raise him to support the Prussian, Jul?"

Julia fills a bowl of porridge for Bobby. Herds him to the table. "It's dangerous for him to know these things," she says, voice low. "If he said something to the wrong person…" She glances back over her shoulder at her son. His dark head is hunched over his bowl, and he's shovelling porridge into his mouth. He shows no inkling of having caught on to their conversation.

Julia takes two more bowls from the shelf. "It's already too much to ask to expect him to keep quiet about you being here. And now you expect him to keep quiet about the rebels' plans too?"

"I don't think you give the boy enough credit," says Hugh, folding his arms across his chest. "He knows these things are not to be spoken of openly."

Julia spoons porridge into the bowls, sloshing the colourless liquid over the side in her anger. "I know my son better than you do."

"Are you certain about that? I've been in his life since the day he was born. I'm the closest he's ever had to a father."

She grits her teeth. It's a razor-sharp barb, and entirely intentional. That reminder Hugh so often drops at her feet of all she owes him. She stands by the hearth and forces down a mouthful of porridge, not bothering to sit at the table. It sticks in her throat, made dry and tasteless by her complete lack of appetite.

She hears a knock at the side door. Glares at Hugh. "Not another word to Bobby about the Rising." She lifts her voice a little. "In fact, not another word from either of you. Could be anyone at the door. Understand, Bobby? Silence."

Her son nods obediently, flashing her a milk-smeared smile. Julia hurries downstairs, realising halfway to the door she has brought her porridge spoon with her. She flings it on the counter, cursing under her breath as it clatters to the floor.

When she opens the side door to find Nathan in the alley, it is all she can do not to sink into his arms.

"You look upset," he says. "Has something happened?" His voice drops. "Has Holland—"

"No." She steps out into the lane, pulling the door closed behind her. Shards of late-morning sun are struggling between the dark stone houses, but they're providing little warmth. Julia stands as close as possible to Nathan, without making contact with him. "Nothing's happened. There's been no sign of Holland. I've been doing my best to stay away from him."

"Good."

There's something different about Nathan today. A fresh blaze in his eyes. She is afraid of what might have caused it.

"May I come inside?" he asks. "There's something I wish to speak to you about."

Julia hesitates. Despite her warnings, she knows there's no way Hugh and Bobby will stay silent enough for her to invite Nathan into the shop. And she already knows Hugh is capable of eavesdropping into the cellar. "Bobby is still sleeping," she says, cursing herself for the lie. "If you don't mind, perhaps we could stay out here…"

"Of course." Nathan takes a step closer to her, his thighs brushing the soft swell of her skirts. "I've just come from the tavern," he says. "I've left word for Henry Ward asking for his help to get Graveney and his men out of our lives."

Julia frowns. "What are you talking about? Do you really imagine you can do such a thing?"

"I have to." Nathan reaches suddenly for her hands. Squeezes. "I am not going to let these men scare me from my home. I'll not be forced to flee like my mother did. This is where I want to be, Julia. Here on Lindisfarne. With you."

She feels a jolt in her chest. His words are so forthright, so open, they catch her by surprise. And there is joy at first; deep, searing joy, but beneath it, something far closer to dread. From what she has heard of this

Henry Ward, she hates the thought of Nathan's safety depending on his support.

And perhaps even more terrifyingly, how long will it be before Nathan learns what she is hiding? Can she get Hugh out of her house before Nathan discovers he is here? Before he learns what he has been trying to do?

Nathan falters. "Is that what you want? Have I been too forward?"

Julia dares a smile. Dares to feel a little of the happiness his words elicit. Dares to imagine that life of having someone by her side. "Of course that's what I want." She presses a light palm to his cheek. Feels the faint stubble beneath her fingertips. Feels his body shift with breath. After a moment, she pulls away. "But I'm worried for you. For your safety."

"These men won't hurt me," he says. "They need me alive."

"Are you certain of that?"

He gives her a faint smile; no, she reads in it. He is not certain. But he is doing it anyway.

Her stomach loops. A part of her wants to talk him out of it. But another part of her wants to support him unwaveringly. Wants every chance at making him stay.

"You are not going to change your mind about this, are you."

"No. I can't." He pulls her close. His fingers intertwine with hers, and he stands motionless for a moment, as though allowing himself to grow comfortable with the contact. His breath tickles her nose. "Edwin will take Harriet and the children off the island. But I can't run. I won't run."

There's a hardness to his voice Julia has not heard before. A new depth. A new resolve. It thrills her, frightens her—a deep concern for his safety.

"Be careful," she says, her voice catching. "Please be careful. If anything were to happen to you—" Before she can finish the sentence, he is kissing her hard. His lips are on hers before she can fully make sense of it, and she reaches out instinctively to grip the top of his arm. Desire uncoils from deep within her.

When he pulls away, his breath has quickened, his chest rising and falling beneath his greatcoat. She sees the flush of his cheeks, the heat in his eyes. *All right?*, she wants to ask—but she does not want to break the silence.

He gives her hand a final squeeze before stepping back and putting distance between them. "I shall be careful," he says. "I promise."

CHAPTER TWENTY

"No," says Harriet. "I'm not leaving." She is planted in the armchair in her workroom, watching with hard eyes as her husband paces the room. This is a stupid place for pacing, she thinks. Two steps across and two steps back.

"You cannot be serious," Edwin says. "All I've heard from you since we arrived here is how much you wish to be back in London."

"Things have changed," she snaps. Surely he can see that. Of course he can. He just doesn't care.

"I understand you have just met your father," he says tautly. "But he is the very reason we cannot stay in this place. For some ungodly reason, your brother is intent on fighting these *pirates*. Surely you can see that we cannot leave our son here."

"I am not afraid of the pirates," says Harriet. "My father will see to it that they do not hurt me. Or Thomas." Even as the words come out of her mouth, she can hear their naivety. They earn the snort from Edwin she expected.

"You barely know the man, Harriet. How can you make any such assurances? Besides, if Henry Ward truly does care for you, it will make you a target for the men he is to fight against."

If Henry Ward truly does care for you... She can hear the doubt in Edwin's voice. Or is that just her own uncertainty making itself known?

A return to London. For weeks, months, it was all she wanted. A thing she had longed for with every breath. But now she feels like she has little to return to. After her escape to Lesbury, Edwin will never allow her to see Isabelle, or any of the other artists in her circle. And she has no painting to lose herself in. What can London offer but bleak grey reminders of her every mistake?

Edwin had spoken of trying to resurrect things between them; trying to rebuild some sense of happiness in their lives. But how can she rebuild something that never existed?

She knows returning to the capital is inevitable. And really, she does not want to stay here on this scrap of an island any more than she wishes to return to that miserable London townhouse to be *wife* and *mother*. But she cannot leave yet. Not while she and her father still feel like strangers.

"Pack your things," Edwin says, turning towards the door without looking back at her. "We leave tonight."

Harriet waits. Listens to his footsteps echo down the passage, up the stairs. Waits until she hears the bedroom door thump shut. Then she takes her cloak and gloves from where she had tossed them on the table. Slips out through the kitchen into the vast expanse of white-haired dunes.

When Eva finishes Theodora's lessons, she makes her way upstairs to Nathan's study. Knocks lightly on the door.

The knowledge that Nathan might have known about Finn and Oliver, might have kept silent all this time, is astounding. When Finn had returned to Longstone this morning, he had told her everything. Told her of his need to unburden himself of the secret.

She understood. She is not angry; not really. Perhaps things would be different if not for this most unexpected of outcomes. But she understands the weight Finn has been carrying on his shoulders. For twenty years—and never more so in the months since they had met and married.

Finn had told her, too, of Henry Ward's visit to Longstone last night. About Ward's interest in the Spanish treasure ships. About the renewed possibility of Ward fighting Graveney. And Nathan's refusal to back down.

This is not the brother she knows.

For years, Eva has been nudging Nathan to stand up for himself, to show a little anger. But right here, right now? She knows well that he could die for it.

She finds him in his desk chair, poring over what look to be astronomical charts. She is not surprised. When he was younger, he had always sought solace in the sky when the real world was pressing down too heavily upon him.

He gives her a faint smile. Nods at her to enter.

She slides into the empty chair opposite the desk. She hardly knows where to begin. There is so much she needs to say.

"You knew," she says, "all this time, and you did not say anything?"

Nathan runs a finger across the star chart as though tracing a passage through the sky. After a moment, he says, "Oliver's death is not something I wish to speak about any more than I'm sure you and Finn do."

Eva looks him in the eye. "Thank you, Nathan. For not putting a stop to our wedding. I know you were well within your rights to do so. And I know how much you were counting on my marriage to Mr Walton."

Nathan leans back in his chair. Smiles wryly. "Agonising over your marriage to Walton seems rather trite now, I must say."

Eva holds the silence for a moment. "Is it true, then? You're considering standing against Graveney? Refusing to hand over the house?"

"I'm not considering it," says Nathan. "It's what I've decided to do. I'm sending Theodora back to London with Edwin and Harriet. And I've asked Henry Ward for his support."

Eva's stomach tightens. Some distant part of her had hoped her brother would see sense and change his mind. "These men are trained to fight, Nathan. How can you hope to defeat them?"

"Graveney will achieve nothing from my death. If he's to profit from this family, he needs me alive." His eyes draw downward, back to the tableau of stars. "I cannot just stand by and let these men take our family's home."

He's determined, Eva sees. For years, he had despised this house. Had done nothing but let it rot. But now there is no changing his mind. It is as though all the knocks of the past few years have collided to lead him to this.

"Is this because of Julia?" she asks.

Nathan is silent for a moment, as though debating whether to answer. "I've just had enough of acting on another's bidding."

Before Eva can respond, the door cracks open and Edwin charges inside. He is flustered with anger; red-cheeked and hot-eyed. Perhaps it's not anger, Eva thinks. Perhaps it's fear. Given all Nathan is risking, he would be right to feel it.

Edwin makes no attempt to acknowledge her. "I'm having Jenny take Thomas off the island," he tells Nathan. "Immediately. I've told her to take him to Bamburgh and find lodgings there until I come for them."

Nathan frowns. "What about Harriet?"

Edwin blows out a breath. "You tell me. She's taken herself off on another of her little runaway jaunts." He slams a fist into the wall, making the muscles in Eva's shoulders tighten. "I've been far too lenient with her. I thought that the best way to handle her. The best way to make her happy. But things can't go on like this. It's high time I treated her with a firmer hand." He glances then at Eva and she sees a flicker of regret in his eyes—regret, she assumes, that he had let her see his outburst.

For several moments, Nathan doesn't speak. "Perhaps now is not the time to be making such decisions," he says finally, with a calmness that is so uncharacteristic it makes something coil in Eva's stomach.

"I cannot wait for Harriet to show herself," Edwin says tautly. "Not when Graveney and his men could turn up at any moment."

"I agree," says Nathan evenly. "I don't want anyone in danger because of my decisions. Especially not the children. We'll manage Harriet when she decides to show herself." He presses his shoulders back, lifts his chin. "Have Jenny take Thea too."

Edwin nods. "All right. But she needs to be ready to leave in an hour so they can catch the low tide. I don't want my son spending another night in this house."

CHAPTER TWENTY-ONE

Theodora's tantrum is painfully predictable. "No!" she wails, as Nathan goes to the wardrobe and starts pulling out her clothes. "I don't want to go!" She flings herself onto his bed, blonde hair flying. "I want to stay here!"

"I'm sorry," Nathan tells her firmly, shoving her dresses and underskirts into a duffel bag. "But this is not up for negotiation. You're leaving and that's final."

She sits up on the bed and gives him defiant eyes. "No," she pouts. "I'm not leaving. I'm not."

Nathan sighs as he turns back to the wardrobe. How could he have imagined prising his family out of this damn house would be such a chore? He can feel his daughter wearing away the calmness he has been trying so hard to cultivate. He bends down to gather up a wrapping gown that has fallen to the floor of the wardrobe.

When he turns around, Theodora is no longer on the bed, her footsteps echoing down the staircase. He rubs his eyes. Drops the gown on the bed and hurries downstairs after her, shouting her name.

The front door is hanging open, empty dunes stretching out into a mist-streaked haze. "Theodora!" he barks. "Come back here at once!"

Eva appears at his shoulder from inside the house. She is wrapped in her bonnet and cloak, pulling on her gloves, as though she were about to leave.

"Help me look for Thea," he says tautly. "Check the outbuildings."

Eva disappears around the side of the house, leaving Nathan to charge over the grassy rise and fall of the dunes. He rushes past pools and rock stacks; peers inside Eva's boat that's moored high up on the beach. The tide is rising, pulling the fringe of the embankment beneath the surface.

He calls Thea's name, again, again. Is answered with nothing but the bawl of the gulls and the restless sigh of the sea. Needles of sunlight prick through the clouds.

He marches over the moorland in the direction of the village, anger and frustration building. Footsteps sigh through the wet grass towards him. He turns to see Eva running in his direction, skirts in her fist. It is only when he looks back at her and sees the manor like a doll's house on the horizon that he realises how far he has gone. How much time must have past.

"Edwin says Jenny and Thomas are leaving." Eva gulps down her breath. "He says they cannot wait any longer if they're to catch the tide."

Nathan closes his eyes. His anger at his daughter is starting to turn into something more pressing. Something veering closer to fear. He does not want Thea here at the house. Has never wanted her here at the house. And never less so than right now, with the threat of conflict so immediate. But he cannot expect Edwin to put his own child in danger.

"Tell him to go," he says to Eva. "Tell him to get Thomas to safety."

She hesitates a moment, concern darkening her eyes. Then she nods and turns back to the house. Nathan's regret lingers only a moment before it's pushed aside by a growing desperation to find Theodora.

He strides towards the village, calling for her, his voice disappearing into the vast top end of the island.

"I'm leaving." Hugh appears at the top of the cellar stairs with a pack on his back and his greatcoat buttoned to his chin. His fiery hair is tucked beneath his blue wool cap.

Julia feels a jolt in her chest. She looks up, drawn away from her account book lying open on the counter. This is what she wants, she reminds herself—for her dangerous brother to be gone. This is what she had longed for from the minute Hugh had come barging into her shop demanding shelter. So why does she feel such a pang of dread?

"Where?" she asks. "When?"

"I'm heading south to join the rebels. The Lancashire Catholics have twenty thousand men preparing to fight. It's time for me to join them. I'm going to be more use to the cause down there than I am up here, waiting for information on the spies that might never come."

Julia hesitates. Is this some kind of twisted game? Is he testing her, to see if she will give up Joseph Holland's name in exchange for him staying away from the army?

She won't do it, she tells herself firmly. She cannot put Nathan in danger like that. But nor can she bear the thought of losing another brother to the Jacobite cause.

"Please, Hugh," she hears herself say. "Don't. It's far too dangerous."

He chuckles. "Are you saying you want me to stay here?"

"I'm saying I don't want to lose you too." Her voice wavers and she feels a sharp pain in her throat.

His eyes soften, catching her off guard. For a moment, she sees the elder brother she had looked up to throughout her childhood. He reaches for her hand. "I have to go, Jul," he says gently. "You know that."

And perhaps this is not about trying to squeeze information out of her. Perhaps he really has decided he is better off out of Lindisfarne, fighting with the rebel army.

She shakes herself out of her sentimentality. He is right, of course. He does have to go. Not for the cause, but for Bobby's sake, and her own. They are in far too much danger with him beneath their roof. If he is to pay for his choices on some mud-streaked Lancashire battlefield, then so be it.

Movement on the street catches her eye, and she drops Hugh's hand hurriedly. Flashes him panicked eyes. He darts down into the cellar, closing the door behind him just as the door to the shop swings open. The bell jangles wildly.

She welcomes her customers—the elderly wives of two of the herring fishermen; does her best to look as though nothing is wrong. She tries to breathe. Of course Hugh leaving is the right thing. Of course this is what she wants. It's the only way for her and Bobby to be safe. She hears herself churn out rote answers the ladies' comments as they rifle though the shelves: *Yes, a lovely piece, isn't it. Sold to me from a woman up north. Yours for a shilling…*

She thanks them. Takes a moment to stand behind the counter and tuck the coins into her pocket book. The simple, everyday action feels jarring, somehow. As though day-to-day actions do not belong in this day. Her mind is racing with thoughts of Hugh's leaving; with Nathan's plan to confront Graveney. The writhing in her stomach seems to have become a constant fixture.

The bell above the door jangles again, making her look up. Julia freezes. And heat floods her body.

"Good afternoon, Mr Holland." She tries to keep her voice level. He's a boorish figure, seems to take up the whole doorway—though she feels fairly certain his size has been distorted by this sudden uptick in her fear. "Is there something I can help you with? Are you looking for anything in particular?" This is the best way forward, surely, to pretend this visit is nothing unusual. But it feels foolish. She knows, of course, that there is nothing routine about this visit. Joseph Holland has never come to her shop before. She cannot quite make sense of why he is here. She knows he has had his suspicions about her for many weeks—but what has brought him here now?

"Miss Mitchell." He nods brusquely. Does not answer her questions, just begins to stride wordlessly between the shelves. His footsteps are slow and rhythmic against the flagstones. Julia hears her pulse roaring in her ears. She hovers by the counter, uncertain of what to do.

Holland approaches the staircase. Nods towards the cellar. "Have you more wares down there?" And at once, Julia realises the reason for his visit. He has caught sight of Hugh, no doubt. In the street, perhaps. Or walking into her shop. Striding in through the front door like he hasn't a care in the world. No doubt Joseph Holland knows her brother is a wanted man. A Jacobite criminal.

No doubt he wants him punished.

"The cellar is private." She speaks loudly, clearly, in hope that her brother will catch her words. What Hugh can do about it, she has no thought. There is no way out of the cellar other than the stairs Holland is at the top of.

Holland looks down the dark throat of the staircase. Julia's heart thunders. What is he planning to do? He is clearly expecting to find her brother at the bottom of the stairs. Is he carrying a weapon in his pocket? Dizziness swings over her.

"I said, the cellar is private." She lurches towards Holland, in a desperate, thoughtless attempt to block his way. Her words come out too loud, too uneven. Before she can make sense of it, the cellar door blows open and Hugh is flying towards them. A pistol shot echoes in her ears. And Joseph Holland falls, suddenly, heavily, blood beading from the wound in his chest onto her cellar stairs.

CHAPTER TWENTY-TWO

"Is he the one?" asks Hugh. "The government spy? The one who was threatening you?" He tucks his pistol into the pocket of his coat. Clenches a fist to stop his hand from shaking.

Julia nods, hand clamped over her mouth. She can't pull her eyes from Holland's lifeless body. Blood is blooming in the centre of his chest, radiating steadily outwards. His glassy eyes bore into hers; steel-grey, she notices distantly, with flecks of midnight blue. The skin around them is paper-thin, almost translucent.

Bile rises in her throat.

"Can we expect anyone else?" asks Hugh.

"I don't think so. Nathan says the other spies are not from the island." The words spill out before she can hold them back.

"All right. Good." Hugh clambers over Holland's body to stand at the top of the stairs. "Help me get him down here."

"You can't keep him in the cellar." Julia's words come out sounding faintly hysterical.

"We'll get him out of the house," Hugh says firmly. "But we need to wait until dark." His voice sounds distant. Distorted. Julia feels panic weighing down on her. She presses a hand against the wall in a desperate attempt to steady herself.

"Come on, Julia." Hugh's impatience snaps her out of her haze. He leans down to take hold of Holland's shoulders. "Take his legs. I can't do this on my own."

Julia glances edgily out the window, then leans down and takes hold of Holland's boots. The mud on the soles is still cool and wet. It sticks to her fingers as she lurches down the steps beneath his weight. Blood on the cellar stairs, she thinks distantly. He has left his blood to stain her cellar stairs.

The distant jangle of the bell above the door makes her chest seize. In her panic, she had forgotten to lock the shop. She looks at Hugh with wide eyes.

"Go," he says, shoving the body into the cellar. "See who's up there. Keep them away from the stairs."

Julia stumbles dizzily back up to the shop. Blood on the stairs, yes. And on her shoes. And likely other places she has not even stopped to consider. She needs to get whoever is in the shop out of here as quickly as possible.

She stops abruptly when she sees Theodora Blake in the middle of the shop. She is without her bonnet or cloak, her blonde hair wild and her cheeks pink. She is crouching in front of the counter, stroking the cat, who has appeared from somewhere unknown.

"Theodora?" Julia manages. "What are you doing here? Are you alone?"

Theodora keeps stroking Minerva. "I want to see Bobby. And I want to stay here. Papa says I have to go away with Miss Jenny. Back to London. I hate London. I'm not going."

Julia blinks. "Bobby is at the dame school," she manages. She takes a step towards Theodora, blocking her view of the blood-spattered staircase. "Where's your father?"

She shrugs. "Don't know."

Julia reaches a hand towards Theodora's shoulder, but stops. She sees it then; the blood on her fingers. The crimson splatters on the edges of her apron. Has Theodora noticed?

Before Julia can follow that thought far, the door flies open and Nathan barrels inside. He grabs hold of his daughter, pulling her from the floor and wrapping his arms around her, even as he hurls out an avalanche of scolding.

He looks at Julia. And he sees it at once, she has no doubt. Sees the blood on her fingers. On her apron. Blooming across the top steps of the cellar. A fresh look of fear passes over his eyes.

"Theodora," he says stiffly, "go and look at the bookshelf for a moment. I'll not be long."

Chastened by his scolding, she slinks off towards the back corner of the shop.

Nathan looks up at Julia with expectant eyes. "What happened?" he murmurs. "Are you hurt?"

She shakes her head, unable to meet his gaze. She knows she needs to give him something; cannot just let him see all this without providing an explanation. But what explanation can she possibly give that will not implicate her brother? She knows that Nathan will not turn Hugh in; knows he would not do that to her. But she also knows that if Nathan finds out what she has been hiding, the fragile threads of trust between them will unravel completely.

"Nothing's happened," she hears herself say. "You just need to get Theodora home."

Nathan drops his voice even further. "Are you in trouble? Is someone here? Holland…" The intensity in his eyes makes her chest ache. Barely a whisper: "Nod your head if I'm right. If you need my help."

At the mention of Holland's name, Julia's stomach rolls. She wants nothing more than to throw herself at Nathan and tell him everything. But all she can think of is how wild with anger Hugh would be if she gave him away. And how thoroughly things with Nathan would be destroyed. She shakes her head. "There's no one here. Nothing's happened."

"Julia," he says. "Please." And she reads it all in Nathan's eyes: the disbelief that she might be keeping this from him. That after all they have managed to build, she might be keeping silent when there is blood splattered across her apron, shoes, stairs.

He reaches for her, then hesitates. Pulls away before he makes contact. Julia feels a deep pang of self-loathing. It's not his fear that is keeping him from touching her, she realises. It's his suspicion. The reality of it burns.

"Nothing?" Nathan says. "There is nothing you wish to tell me?" He holds her gaze for a long time; wordless, imploring.

"No." Julia's voice is trapped in her throat. "There is nothing I wish to tell you."

And almost as if it were a tangible thing, she feels Nathan's hard-fought trust in her shatter into pieces.

Nathan barely speaks on the way back to the house. He keeps his hand tight around Theodora's to prevent her from racing away again, and the rigid contact does little to slow the hammering in his chest.

He is far too angry at Theodora to conjure up any coherent sentence. And as for what he feels towards Julia, well, that's not quite anger. Closer to betrayal. Definitely bewilderment. And a sizeable helping of pain. He had thought they had managed to find trust for one another. Openness. Something that went far deeper than lies.

But then he thinks of his visit to Elias Mitchell. Thinks of *militiamen were watching us*. And he thinks of the blood on Julia's fingers. There has never been trust between them, he thinks. There has never been truth. Not really.

Perhaps, in standing up to John Graveney and his men, he is making the biggest mistake of his life. Because he knows that this decision to stay and fight, against every grain of sense in his body, is just as much about Julia as it is about him needing to take control of his own life. And perhaps Julia Mitchell has been the biggest mistake of all.

Blood on the cellar stairs. Blood on her apron. Blood on her hands.

Perhaps in the right situation, he could have looked past all of that. He knows the Rising, and their entanglement with Ward, has led them all to do things they would never have considered themselves capable of. But he cannot look past her silence, her secrets. How can they have any future together if she can look him in the eye and lie, with her fingers stained scarlet with blood?

A big part of him wants to go back to the curiosity shop. Wants assurances that she is safe. Wants to keep begging for answers. But he knows there is little point. He could see it in her eyes. Whatever she is keeping secret, she has no intention of sharing with him.

And so. Right now, he needs to turn his thoughts away from Julia, and towards getting his child safely off the island before men with pistols appear at his door. It's where his priorities always ought to have been.

How could he have let himself focus on anything else?

The tide is flooding the embankment, and he knows he is far too late to catch Jenny and Thomas. They will be tucked up safe in Bamburgh by now, away from the threat of John Graveney and his men.

Give in. The thought knocks against Nathan's head. *Give Graveney what he wants.*

But even in the face of Julia's silence, the prospect is sickening. He will not be forced from this house for the second time in his life. He will not be that man; constantly shaped by the wills of others.

As he approaches Emmanuel Head, he catches sight of Eva, still searching the rocky coastline on the eastern side of the island. At the sight of them, her shoulders sink in relief, and she strides over the uneven grass to catch them. And as far as Thea goes, he has one last option. Once last flimsy chance at keeping her safe.

"Go inside and fetch your cloak," Nathan tells his daughter sharply. "You're going to Longstone with your aunt."

CHAPTER TWENTY-THREE

Harriet has been waiting on the corner near the tavern for hours, and she is sure people are beginning to ask questions. Men are throwing looks her way as they enter the narrow street. She can just imagine what wild thoughts about her and her family are tearing through their heads.

The sun is beginning to sink. There is a deep chill on the air, darkness pushing out the crimson blaze at the bottom of the sky. Evening is drawing close, and she knows Edwin will be impatient to leave. Perhaps he will go without her. Is it foolish to hope she might be so lucky?

She huddles into her cloak, blowing against her gloved hands to warm them. Her stomach rumbles with emptiness. She peeks around the corner, watching a steady stream of men flow in and out of the tavern, in various states of disarray. No sign of her father yet. But he will come. She knows he will. Especially now, with so much conflict in the air, he will come here to collect any word from Highfield House.

It's almost night when she finally sees him. His head is down and he strides right past her, a deep frown of concentration creasing his brow. She watches him disappear into the tavern, then return moments later, tucking a folded note into the pocket of his justacorps. She steps around the corner and walks beside him as he cuts his way through the village.

Surprise flickers across his eyes at the sight of her. "Were you waiting for me?" he asks.

"Yes." She tugs her cloak tight around her body as wind whirls off the water. Above their heads, the first stars glitter in a brutally clear cobalt sky. "My husband wishes to take me back to London. He believes it is too dangerous here, given your men are after the house."

Ward doesn't look at her. "He is right. Especially given your brother has apparently decided to stay and fight."

"Stay and fight?" Harriet nods towards his coat pocket. "Is that what that note was about?"

Ward nods. He reaches into his pocket and hands her the page. She unfolds it curiously.

It's Nathan's handwriting, but the words do not sound like they come from her brother: *request assistance* and *confrontation* and *I intend to stand my ground.*

Harriet knows this is just bravado. Knows that if it comes down to it, and Graveney and his men appear on the doorstep with pistols waving, Nathan will crumble. He will hand over the deeds to the house and flee Holy Island with his shirttails flying.

Nonetheless, she is curious as to what her father sees in this.

"Are you going to help him?" she asks. "If Graveney and his men try to take the house by force, will you fight them?"

He looks at her sharply. "How do you know about Graveney?"

Irritation flickers through her at how similar he sounds to Edwin. "I listen," she says, forcing an airy tone into her voice.

Her father smiles wryly. "You eavesdrop."

Harriet shrugs, feigning nonchalance. She tries to look behind his eyes; tries to determine whether he is angry at her admission. She cannot read him, she realises dully. She has never been able to read him. She wonders if Henry Ward is always this adept at keeping his emotions hidden, or whether this is just a skill he has cultivated around her.

He stops walking and looks at her squarely. "What do you think I ought to do?"

Harriet feels something flip in her chest. She cannot remember the last time anyone asked her opinion on anything. Perhaps her father is just doing this to humour her. But she cannot quite make herself care.

She takes a moment to consider her answer. "I do not want my brother to die," she says. "And without the help of you and your loyal men, there is every chance he may."

Ward nods slowly. He begins to walk again, but doesn't speak. What is he thinking, Harriet wonders? There's a blankness to his eyes, and she cannot see behind them. She knows Ward's crew is divided. Knows he does not have the authority he once had. She also knows he is not about to admit this—especially not to her.

"Will you take me somewhere?" she asks suddenly. "On your ship?"

"I'm afraid that's not possible," Ward says stiffly. "I would not be able to ensure your safety."

"You took me aboard your ship before."

"Things have changed since then. Your brother has antagonised Mr Graveney by refusing to hand over the house. I'm afraid that would make you a target. Besides, there's little time for pleasure outings. I ought to pay your brother a visit. Discuss these dangerous plans of his."

Harriet nods, unsurprised, but faintly disappointed. She continues to trudge beside him as he leaves the village and steps out onto the path across the moorland. Wind skims through the grass, and in the fading light the dunes seem to ripple like water. Harriet teeters over the uneven ground, wishing she had thought to bring a lamp. She has been away from the house for far longer than she anticipated.

She glances at her father, willing him to offer her his arm. He continues to walk with his hands folded behind his back.

He glances at her curiously. "Where did you wish me to take you?" he asks, after several moments of silence.

Harriet considers the question. In truth, the request had been more about spending time with her father, and outrunning the evening so she would not be dragged away by Edwin. She had known it was unlikely to lead anywhere. But she says, "I should like to see the Farne Islands. I want to see where my sister lives."

Ward smiles wryly. "I imagine you'd be rather disappointed to see that miserable pebble your sister has made her home. As disappointed as you might be with her choice of husband."

Harriet laughs a little. "Well. I can't fathom why she would want to make her life out there. But she does seem to love her husband."

Ward frowns slightly and something passes across his eyes. He looks back at Harriet. "They've not told you, have they."

She raises her eyebrows. "Told me what?"

Ward digs his hands into the pockets of his coat and walks with his head down, a frown darkening his features. "About Finn Murray and your half-brother Oliver."

CHAPTER TWENTY-FOUR

Harriet has searched the house. Thrown open every unlocked door, charged into every room. There is no sign of her sister.

So Eva has left. Absconded back to Longstone to be with her wretched rogue of a husband. Harriet feels rage pounding behind her eyes.

Edwin's footsteps thump along behind her as she flies down the upstairs passageway. "Are you listening to a word I'm saying?"

He's rambling something about tides and wagons, she thinks. But no, she's not listening. All she can think about is the way her sister has betrayed the family. How could she knowingly marry the man who had taken their brother from them? How could she keep such a thing a secret? "Where is Eva?" she demands. "Has she left?"

"Yes, Harriet," Edwin says tautly. "She's left. And so has your son. I've had Jenny take him to Bamburgh. At least his nurse has some damn concern for his safety."

Harriet nods faintly. Supposes she ought to feel some guilt at this. But Thomas is safe in Bamburgh. What more could Edwin want? Surely he knows their son is better off in Jenny's care than her own.

She turns to face him in the gloom of the hallway. A single lamp flickers on the wall outside their bedroom, but it does little to light the house's long shadows. "I asked my father if he would commit to supporting Nathan," she says, forcing an evenness into her voice. "He told me he was undecided. He is downstairs speaking with Nathan now."

Edwin sighs. "I suspected as much. Nathan is a fool if he thinks he has any chance of succeeding." He throws open the door to their bedroom and grabs her smallest trunk from the floor. "Put your cloak back on. We're going to the harbour. Eva has taken Thea to Longstone to try and keep her safe. I'm sure they'll have you too."

"No." The word falls out before she is even aware of it. The thought of sailing out to that cursed island makes her blood hot. All Eva's talk about wanting Harriet in her life. All the while holding such a secret to her chest. Did she truly imagine the truth would never come out? That they might just carry on with their lives as though nothing had happened?

Harriet's anger at Nathan is just as blinding. Her father had told her he had gone to Nathan, telling him of all Finn had done. Imploring him to put a stop to Eva's wedding. How could Nathan have just sat back and watched her marry that bastard? How could he be so spineless?

"I'm not going to Longstone," she hisses.

Edwin rubs his eyes wearily. "Do you not understand what's happening, Harriet? Graveney told Nathan he has until tomorrow to hand over the deeds to the land. It's not safe for you to be here. And I don't want to see you in any more danger." He is trying to keep his rage down, Harriet notices. And for all his resentment, she can tell he still cares about her. She hates that this is the case. It makes her feel far too guilty. "Besides, you just told me you needed to see your sister."

"I am not going to Longstone," she says again. "Ever. I'd rather take my chances with Graveney and his men."

In the light of the firebasket, Theodora is prancing around the edges of the rockpools, squinting into their dark-gold surfaces, her doll tucked under her arm. She looks back at Eva and Finn, who sit watching her from the cottage steps. "I think I see a fish!" she announces.

Eva forces a smile. She shivers. The night is vividly starlit and bitterly cold.

"What were you thinking?" Finn whispers. "We can't keep her safe here. What if Ward comes again?"

"I had no choice. Nathan was desperate. It's far more dangerous for her to be in the house tonight." Eva shuffles across the cold stone of the step to press her body closer to Finn's. Nerves are roiling inside her. Before she had left the house, she had begged Nathan once more to reconsider standing up to Graveney. Her words had had no effect. "I'm so afraid for him," she admits.

Finn nods, not looking at her. He rakes a hand through the hair hanging loose on his shoulders. Scrubs a hand across his eyes. There's regret in him, Eva can tell. Though she cannot determine why.

She says, "What are you not telling me?"

Finn turns away from her for a moment. Lets out a breath. Finally, he looks back to face her. "It's my fault Nathan's decided to fight. I told him about the treasure ships." He sighs. "It was a mad thing to do. I wanted to help him, but I should have kept quiet. Because I know Ward's not going to support him."

The knot in Eva's stomach grows a little tighter. "How do you know that? Did Ward say something to you?"

Finn doesn't speak at once, his eyes fixed to Theodora as she bends to trail a hand through the rockpool.

"Finn," Eva pushes. "Tell me why."

He sighs. Rest his elbows on his knees and lowers his head, his hair falling forward over his face. "The night Ward came here to Longstone, he told me he'd only fight Graveney and his men if I agreed to re-join his crew. I told him I'd not do it." He glances at her, as though trying to gauge her reaction. Eva sees a wordless apology in his eyes.

She wraps her hand around his upper arm, pulling him closer. It feels as though she cannot get him near enough. "Why is he so desperate for you to re-join his crew? I know you know more than you are letting on."

He lets out a long breath. "He wants me away from you," he says bluntly. "Because he thinks that's what your ma would want. And he thinks it's the decent thing to do. He doesn't want you to spend your life with the man who killed your brother."

Eva feels a violent pain in her throat. She blinks back the tears that suddenly threaten behind her eyes. She thinks of Nathan, standing guard in that vast, creaking house. Counting blindly, foolishly, on Henry Ward's assistance. Assistance that will not come unless Finn agrees to leave her.

She had imagined being forced to make this choice between her husband and her family. But she had not imagined it would come like this.

"What did you tell Ward?" she asks, hearing the waver in her voice.

"I told him I wasn't going to leave you. But I don't know how Nathan will manage without Ward's help."

Eva swallows past the lump in her throat. "Nathan has made his own choices." She shifts on the step to meet Finn's eyes. "Henry Ward does not have the power to determine who I spend my life with." But even as she speaks, she recognises the cold reality of it: Henry Ward may well have the power to choose whether her brother lives or dies.

A wave swells over the edge of the island, catching the hems of Theodora's skirts. She yelps, and bounds away from the rockpool.

"Let's go inside," Eva tells her, climbing to her feet. She tries to inject a little brightness into her voice. "It's getting far too cold to be out here." She herds Theodora into the cottage, then turns back to Finn as he stands to join them. She catches his hand and tugs him close. "Please don't go with Ward. Whatever he thinks my mother would have wanted, and whatever he thinks is right, your place is here with me." She pulls the door closed behind them, muting the sound of the sea. Cannot shake the thought that she is sending Nathan to the gallows.

CHAPTER TWENTY-FIVE

"This is your final decision then?" Ward asks. The note Nathan had written him is sitting between them on the dining table. Nathan looks down at his own words: *request assistance… confrontation…* He feels oddly outside himself.

He sits rigid in the chair at the head of the table. His father's chair— no, *his* chair. "Yes," he says. "It is. I am not going to sit back and be forced from my home. If Graveney wants the house, he will have to fight me for it." He curls his hand around the arm of the chair. Despite all his self-encouragement, he is finding it hard to dig up the confidence he needs. "Can I count on your support?"

Ward leans back in the chair to Nathan's left. The vast wooden table stretches out before them, empty but for the misshapen scrap of the note, and a single spluttering candle. Nathan had sent Mrs Brodie back to the village earlier today. Had promised to fetch her again once the danger had passed. He had not let on that such a thing was no certainty. Couldn't bring himself to speak the words. In any case, he does not know how much his housekeeper is aware of, and he would prefer to keep as many of the details away from her as possible. The last thing this family needs is to be the topic of more rumours floating around the village.

Ward steeples his fingers. "Will it make a difference to what you do?"

Nathan knows it ought to. Without the support of Ward and his men, all he can hope for is for Graveney to see the pointlessness of putting a bullet in his chest. All of a sudden, his invincibility does not feel so secure. Refuse to hand over the house, and perhaps Graveney will kill him out of mere anger and frustration.

"I know you want Graveney gone," Nathan tells Ward. "I know you want the threat against your captaincy gone. And I know you want to leave Holy Island to hunt for these Spanish treasure ships."

Ward smiles wryly. "I see Finn Murray has been in your ear."

"I also know you loved my mother," Nathan says. "And I'm sorry for the way she betrayed you. But you know this is what she would want you to do."

Something passes across Ward's eyes and he swallows visibly. Tugs at his dark cravat.

Nathan leans forward, aware he has caught a hold of something. "Besides, this is not just for me. You want Graveney gone too. And surely you don't want his men coming here to the house, putting your own daughter at risk."

Ward clasps his hands in front of him on the table. He looks down into his folded fingers. Nathan wonders what he is thinking behind his deliberate façade of blankness. Of Abigail, surely. Of Harriet. At least, he hopes that's what he's thinking. Surely this is the only way to get Ward to do what he needs him to do.

For a long time, neither of them speak. Nathan can hear the distant tick of the clock on the mantel of the parlour. Hears heavy beams creak above his head. Ward stares into the flickering flame of the candle. In the dim light, his cheeks are shadowed, and he suddenly looks like an old man.

"You are right," he says finally. "I don't want my daughter at risk. And I do want to do what I think Abigail would have wanted, regardless of how she betrayed me."

Nathan shifts in his chair, the drum beat in his chest intensifying.

"Abigail would not have wanted Graveney in our daughter's life," Ward says. "But she did not want me in our daughter's life either. That's why I'm not going to help you fight Mr Graveney." Nathan opens his mouth to protest, but Ward raises a hand, silencing him before he can get a word out. "Your mother would not want you fighting. She would want you and your family out of this house. She would want you to get to safety.

You know she would."

"Graveney won't kill me," Nathan says, too desperately. "He needs me alive." The words come out softer than he hoped. He wonders if he is starting to doubt them.

"He does need you alive," Ward agrees. "But there's nothing to say he won't retaliate if you refuse to do what he is asking. And what about my men? What about me? Graveney does not need any of us alive. Are you willing to risk our deaths for your own cause?"

And for the first time, Nathan sees behind Henry Ward's eyes. He sees that there is fear in him, just as there is fear in himself. This refusal to fight, Nathan realises, it accounts to a failure for Henry Ward. That bold and daring privateering captain who had appeared at the house during Nathan's childhood, he is on the verge of losing his ship to stronger men. Perhaps there are more similarities between the two of them than Nathan had initially realised. Perhaps they are both just weak, unremarkable men, trying to cope as best they can with their failures.

"I'm sorry," says Ward. "I know this is not the answer you wished for. But I've made up my mind. I suggest you get out of this house as soon as possible. Leave now, while you still can."

"I can't leave. My daughter is out on Longstone. I'll not go without her."

"Get out of the house," Ward says again. "Find secure lodgings off the island tonight. You'll find someone to take you out to Longstone for your daughter in the morning. Leave in the dark so Graveney and his men can't see you from the ship. And take the deeds to the house with you. With luck, you can return here in a few years' time, if that is really what you wish to do."

Nathan feels something sink inside him. A sense of heavy resignation. He knows Ward is right. He is not the kind of man who fights. He is the kind of man who runs.

He cannot deny that Holy Island has cast its spell on him, with its pink light and rising waters. But he also knows it is Julia Mitchell who has done the most spell-casting. Heart-splitting Julia, with her gold-dust eyes and blood on her hands. Yes, he thinks. Running is the wise thing to do. Running. Hiding. Because really, if he is honest with himself, has he ever been destined for anything else?

CHAPTER TWENTY-SIX

They come almost as if he willed it. With Nathan Blake's daughter sleeping beneath their roof, there are lamps moving in the firelight. A longboat sliding soundlessly towards Longstone.

As if he willed it.

No—as if they have been watching. Watching the island, or watching Eva return from Lindisfarne with Theodora in the skiff, Finn doesn't know. Either way, it does not matter.

He stands on the jetty, watching the longboat approach. It is not fresh dread that he feels, because he has been expecting this. Has been carrying around this awful premonition since Nathan's daughter first stepped onto this island. She is currency, he thinks. She is the treasure that will make her father bend to John Graveney's will.

Ought he rush inside and wake Eva and Theodora? Hurry them into the skiff and try and escape? Try and weave through the reefs in the dark, with men on their tail? It's a suicidal mission—if it doesn't end with them all in Ward and Graveney's hands, it will end with them all at the bottom of the sea.

They are easy targets here; he always has been.

As the men draw closer to the firebasket, Finn sees their faces; hard, empty eyes. Eyes of men who are following orders. Ward is not among them—not that Finn expected him to be. He assumes this longboat of men left the *Eagle* on Graveney's bidding, without the captain's knowledge.

"Open up the house," says one man as he climbs from the boat. He holds a pistol out in front of him.

Finn plays things out in his head. Refuse and the man will surely pull the trigger. He suspects these men who sail under the black flag will have no issue with doing so. So, refuse and he will die. The men will step over his body and climb inside the house and they will find Eva and Theodora sleeping.

He goes silently to the cottage. Climbs the stairs, five men trailing. Pushes open the door.

The cottage is dark, lit only by the stripes of light the firebasket paints as it strains through the half-open shutters. Embers glow orange in the grate. The men follow Finn inside, the floorboards creaking beneath their weight.

"Why are you here?" he asks, though he doesn't need to. When the answer comes—"the girl"—it is both terrifying, and desperately predictable.

"Take me," he says. "I'm the one Ward wants." But even as he speaks, Finn knows this is not about Ward. Ward's control is slipping. These men are here at Graveney's bidding. And he himself is of little value to them.

He looks around him in the dim light for anything that could be used as a weapon. A fire poker, perhaps, but he is still outnumbered. And one blow is likely to be replied to with pistol fire. Eva will wake, will rush out here, and they will fire at her too.

And then they will take Theodora.

"I'll fetch her," says Finn.

One of the men follows him towards the bedroom. Finn steps inside the dark room, a pistol held between his shoulder blades. He sees the small shape of Theodora, curled up in bed beside Eva. Both are breathing deep and even with sleep. Finn leans down and scoops Theodora out of bed, his fingers brushing against Eva's. A bitter irony, he thinks, that tonight she has finally succumbed to sleep. Or maybe it's a blessing. Maybe she's safer this way.

He holds his breath. He knows how lightly she will be sleeping. Knows how easy it would be for her to wake up, panic, retaliate. How easy it would be for these men to fire their pistols.

Finn's heart lurches. Because he cannot let these men take Thea to the ship alone. His only choice is to go with her. And he knows that once Ward has him aboard the *Eagle*, he will not let him go.

He looks down at Eva, her dark hair spilling out across the sheets. He wants to wake her. Wants to explain. Wants to tell her he is sorry, and that he loves her, and that he will come back to her as soon as possible. But he cannot put her in danger like that. Not with these men clustered in the doorway, pistols moving in the darkness.

He takes Theodora's cloak from the end of the bed and wraps it around her, her stockinged feet dangling down past his hips. And he steps quietly from the bed, forcing himself to turn away from Eva.

He must go with the men. Must go to Ward's ship. And somehow, when all this is over, he will find his way back to his wife.

How he will do that, he cannot think about. Because if he thinks too hard on it, he will not do what needs to be done.

"I'm coming with you," he tells the men. "It's what your captain wants."

The men eye each other. Finn can see their indecision. Surely they must have foreseen this. Did they really imagine he might just stand back and watch them take a child from this island?

He wishes he had a chance to at least leave Eva a note. Telling her what has happened. Promising her he will return. He ought to have been more prepared. After all, he had seen this coming. But he just has to trust that she will understand. Surely once she sees Theodora gone, she will know.

He is walking towards the door before the men can argue. Before the need to turn back overwhelms him.

CHAPTER TWENTY-SEVEN

Theodora wakes when the longboat is surrounded by sea and the firebasket is little more than a glow on the horizon. She shifts on the bench beside Finn, where she is curled up beneath her dark blue cloak. She sits up suddenly. Her eyes widen as she takes in the men around her, the shifting longboat, the coal-dark water, as though struggling to make sense of whether she is still caught in a dream.

"Come here, Thea," Finn says, voice low. "Stay with me."

She shuffles across the bench so her shoulder presses against his side. For long moments, she doesn't speak, just alternates her gaze between him and the other men in the boat. None of them are looking at her, Finn realises. All of them have their eyes down, as though unable to look at what they have just been a part of. Finally, Theodora says, "Where are we going?"

"We're going to see the ship," Finn tells her.

"The ship outside my house?"

He nods.

"Why?"

"Because that's what these men want us to do."

There's a careful balance here. He needs Theodora to trust him. Doesn't want her to be afraid. Does he let her think he's the one behind this trip to the *Eagle*? The one responsible for tearing her out of bed in the middle of the night? Will that cause her to fear him? Or to trust that everything will be all right? He's not been in her life long enough for trust like that, Finn realises.

"Is it an adventurer's ship?" she asks, her voice still thick with confusion and sleep.

"Aye. Something like that." He glances back at the firebasket. It's beginning to burn out now. He ought to be out in the shed with a shovelful of coal.

That ache in his chest, he can't go near it. Not now, with Theodora here. He knows that once he is aboard the *Eagle*, it will be near impossible to leave. Ward will not allow him to escape a second time. The only way he will make it back to Eva is if Graveney succeeds in overthrowing Ward as captain. Finn can't bear to think what that would mean for the Blakes.

But he cannot think of Eva; cannot think of how she will react when she finds out he and Theodora are gone. All he can do right now is focus on keeping them both alive. On getting Thea back to her father.

They are on the ship too quickly, among shadows and dark wood and men moving in circles of lamplight. The *Eagle* feels old and worn, as though its best days are far behind it. How had he ever been awed by this ship, Finn wonders? How had he ever seen beauty in it? He is surprised he had ever been that naïve and foolish, even as a child.

Theodora looks around, wide-eyed, her stockinged feet silent as she crosses the tarred slats of the deck. She looks sickeningly out of place in her thin white nightgown, cloak wrapped around her shoulders and blonde hair tangled around her cheeks. Ghostly, almost. Finn can't tell if she's scared or intrigued. He keeps a firm hand around her wrist.

He sifts through the lamplight of the deck, searching for Ward. But it's an older man that comes towards them now—John Graveney, he expects. Finn does not remember Graveney from his time in Ward's crew. But he had seen this man arguing with Ward at the tavern on Lindisfarne several weeks ago—no doubt about Abigail Blake's cursed letter.

Graveney glances at Theodora; glares at Finn. He turns to the men who had brought them from Longstone. Speaks to them in inaudible words.

"I want to speak to the captain," Finn says tautly.

"This isn't the captain's business."

Finn grits his teeth. "Take the lass back to her father. You know he'll hand over the house in exchange for her safety."

"In good time." Graveney's voice is coarse and abrupt. "But let's give Nathan Blake time to discover his daughter missing."

Theodora takes a step towards Finn. He feels her shoulder press hard against his hip. Feels her hand clutch a fistful of his greatcoat. And yes, she is afraid now, he can tell. Perhaps made so by the mention of her father's name. He wraps an arm around her shoulder, trying to steady her. He feels her shivering hard.

"Take us below," he says. "It's far too cold for her to be out here in her nightclothes." Where in hell is Ward? Is he even aboard the ship?

Graveney calls to one of the men who had brought them from Longstone. Murmurs to him in words Finn cannot catch. But before the men can act, the saloon door blows open and Ward steps out onto deck. Surprise flickers across his eyes at the sight of Finn and Theodora. "What is this?" he demands. "Mr Graveney?"

Graveney doesn't respond. Just continues speaking to his men.

Finn meets Ward's eyes. "Take us below."

Ward nods silently. He calls across the deck to his steward, who gestures to Finn to follow him into the ship.

Finn glances back over his shoulder at Ward. He needs to speak with him urgently. Needs his help to get Theodora back to her father. But the captain is locked in a heated conversation with Graveney and his men.

Finn debates whether to stay on deck. No, he decides. He needs to get Theodora out of the cold, and he does not trust any of these men to be alone with her. He trails the steward down through the passages, stumbling as Theodora presses herself a little too close to his side.

There's a strange silence to the ship. Once, the *Eagle* had been full of shouted voices, banter, laughter. Now it's a place of whispers. Finn had not noticed it when last he was aboard. He'd been too preoccupied by the prospect of death—and by the prospect of Eva learning he had killed her brother. It's a silent kind of tension, wrought by a divided crew. A thread about to snap. He can only hope he is no longer aboard when it does.

The steward unlocks the door to the great cabin and steps aside, allowing Finn and Theodora entry.

"Tell Ward I need to speak with him urgently," says Finn. He hopes, as he speaks, that the steward is loyal to Ward. Hopes he is not another

Jacobite seeking to punish the Blakes for their mother's crimes.

The steward nods his grey head, giving nothing away. He pulls the door closed. Turns the key in the lock.

Finn glances around the great cabin. The air feels too thick, too close, too tainted with familiarity. The windows at the stern of the ship are boarded up, and the sight of it makes his chest ache. He knows this was Eva's doing; knows she had smashed the glass and leapt into the sea, risking her life so she might help him escape a keel-hauling—with the fresh truth of Oliver's death ringing in her ears.

Eva opens her eyes. It is dark—too dark. There is only ever this kind of darkness on Longstone when the rain is thrashing too hard for the firebasket to be lit. But she does not hear rain. Just the steady exhalation of the sea.

She reaches into the blackness for Theodora. At the feel of the empty bed, she lurches forward, scrambling for the tinderbox on the bedside table and calling Finn's name.

The silence is achingly deep. Her hand trembles as she lights the lamp and carries it into the living space. She calls for them again. Pans the lamp around the living area. There is the soup pot on the hook, the remains of supper growing cold. There are Theodora's black buckled shoes, lined up in front of the hearth to dry. Her doll lies abandoned on the table, eyes staring blankly into the darkness. Rocks and candles and twine on the mantel. Everything as they left it. No sign that anyone else has been here.

But Eva knows instinctively what has happened. Knows Finn was right to fear having Thea on the island with them. Knows that she had never truly been safe here. None of them have.

She rushes back to the bedroom and throws on her clothes and shoes. Grabs the lamp from the table and stumbles down the steps at the front of the cottage. Darkness consumes her, the meagre pool of lamplight powerless against the blackness of the island. Stars explode overhead, but the thin crescent moon provides little light. Just the faintest glow of orange from within the firebasket, a candle against an ocean of dark. All around her, she hears the restless sigh of the sea; hears the distant barking of seals. Hears her panicked breath rushing in her ears. Tonight, Longstone terrifies her.

She hurries out to the skiff and flings loose the mooring ropes. Forces aside the sudden fear of the dark, and everything that might lie beyond it.

CHAPTER TWENTY-EIGHT

There is not a cell in Julia's body that is surprised to be here, out on a dark ocean with her eldest brother, condemning Joseph Holland's body to the sea. Somehow, she has always known that having Hugh around her would lead her somewhere like this; deep into the heart of the Rising, where she never wanted to go.

She has fought it for so long; trying to keep Bobby blind and deaf to all that is happening; hiding her brothers' presence from everyone. Speaking in lies to a man who has made her feel the way no one has before. And for what? Bobby knows far too much. She surely has no way of ever rebuilding things with Nathan. And she literally has blood on her hands.

Julia had not said a word to her brother as they had carried Holland's body towards the anchorage, wrapped in hessian stolen from the fishermen's huts. Had not said a word to him as he had sailed them out here, to this gulf of dark water between Holy Island and the Farnes. Out here, Nathan had told her, Donald Macauley's body lies. And Joseph Holland is to meet the same fate.

Hugh piles stones into the hessian pall containing the body. Julia turns away, unable to watch. "All right," he mumbles. "It's ready. Help me."

Julia keeps her eyes averted. "Cover him. I don't want to see."

Hugh sighs. On the edge of her vision, she sees him folding the hessian back over Holland's face. When she dares to look back, his thick legs are still visible in their mud-caked boots. She closes her eyes and lifts the dead weight of Holland's legs. Together, she and Hugh slip the body over the gunwale. The boat tilts and Joseph Holland vanishes.

For several moments, they sit without speaking. Julia says a silent prayer for the dead man. With its mainsail furled, the dory is tugged along on the current, out in the direction of the Farnes. Julia squints. The Longstone firebasket is dark tonight. Everything is dark. She wonders if she ought to be concerned.

But then she sees light. The glow of a lamp on the sea. It's faint, candle-like, but drawing closer. Less than a mile away, perhaps. She panics. They cannot let themselves be seen. Never mind that Holland's body is sinking to the bottom; if she is caught out here so close to midnight with her criminal of a brother, they will be under no end of suspicion.

Hugh curses under his breath and lurches for the mainsail sheet. Tugs on the line to open the sail to the wind. Julia turns to look over her shoulder. The skiff is Finn Murray's, she thinks. She lifts the lamp; squints into the dark.

It's Eva at the tiller, alone in the boat without a cloak or bonnet, and flying out far too close to the reef. Julia can tell something is very wrong. She knows Eva is level-headed, sensible. An inexperienced sailor, she assumes, but still not the kind to behave so recklessly. Certainly not one to sail out here so late at night. Especially not alone.

"Get closer to her," Julia orders. "She's in trouble."

Hugh snorts. "We're not getting close to anyone. You don't think they'll have questions?"

"She'll not turn us in." Julia knows this with certainty. Distrusting of her or not, Eva will not turn her in for a crime she herself had committed. "Eva!" she calls. "Come about at once!"

Eva whirls around at the sound. She stumbles against the gunwale, but makes no attempt to back the mainsail and slow the boat. Julia tries to shove Hugh aside, elbowing her way towards the tiller.

Hugh curses under his breath. Something changes in his eyes—an acknowledgement, perhaps, that Julia is doing this with or without his consent, and that it will be easier if he plays along. He nudges her aside, taking the tiller.

The fishing boat flies over the swell, dark water sputtering up into Julia's eyes. She holds her breath as the dory careens out towards the reef. Lets out a sigh when Eva's boat begins to curve away from the Knavestone.

Hugh eases the dory up alongside Eva's skiff. The two small boats knock and grind together. Julia scrambles over the gunwale of the dory, landing heavily on her knees in the skiff.

"Are you all right?" she asks Eva, climbing to her feet.

Eva nods faintly, breathless.

Julia takes the tiller, easing the skiff into open water. She watches the lamp of Hugh's fishing boat fly off into the darkness. Watches her brother disappear with it. She swallows a swell of pain. Tries to make herself believe she will see him again. That one day soon, Hugh and Angus will be sitting at her supper table, telling Bobby about their enormous haul with the herring fleet. She can't make it feel like anything other than a lie.

Once they are clear of the reef, Julia looks back at Eva. "What's happened?"

Eva is huddled on the bench now, trembling, her eyes red and swollen. Her words are garbled with tears; hard to make out. Finn, she says; and Theodora; and, "We have to get to Ward's ship."

"No," Julia tells her, reining in her own panic. "That's madness. You know it is." And she steels herself against the tide of emotion that rises when she says, "We have to tell Nathan."

Nathan tells himself history is not repeating. Tells himself this is nothing like the circumstances in which he was forced from Highfield House as a child. This time, his leaving is a choice. A reluctant one, but an informed choice, nonetheless. He will leave the house, sensibly and safely, and attempt to sell the place from London.

The right thing to do. Because he is not the kind of man who fights. He is the man who had railed against his family coming here. Who had drowned in panic when Eva and Theodora had first appeared on the doorstep of Highfield House. He is the kind of prudent, rational man who is going to do everything he can to get his family to safety.

He throws his clothes into a duffel bag. Without a wagon, they will have no way of transporting their trunks into the village tonight, but at least he will not be reduced to running with nothing but the clothes on his back, like his mother was twenty years ago.

"You're making the right decision," Edwin says from the doorway.

Nathan can't look at him. Edwin is a reminder of the life he will be reduced to now. A life of pity and charity. For a moment, he understands his mother's need to break the law to ensure her family's security.

"Are you and Harriet ready to leave?" Nathan asks, not turning around.

"If I have to carry her out of here over my shoulder, then that's what I will do," Edwin says wryly. "I've locked her in the bedroom in the meantime. In case she has a thought to try to disappear again."

"Does she know her father has gone?" Nathan had watched Ward leave the house; knows he had done so without a word of farewell to his daughter. Had Ward simply decided things were easier that way? Or had he been so distracted by the conflict on his ship that it did not cross his mind to seek Harriet out?

He doubts it; suspects Ward's leaving had more to do with his knowledge that Abigail had never wanted him in their daughter's life. He knows Harriet would be devasted to learn of such a thing.

"I've not told her," says Edwin. "And perhaps it's best for her that I don't. Let her think I'm to blame for tearing her away from this place without the chance to see her father one last time. At this point, I don't think she can despise me much more."

Nathan turns to look at Edwin then; gives him sympathetic eyes. "Perhaps things will be different once you're back in London," he says. "Perhaps we can all begin to see clearly again."

Unbidden, his gaze drifts to the telescope Julia had given him, lying in its box on the bed. It would be foolish to take something so bulky with him, but he cannot bear the thought of leaving it behind.

He takes it to the window and pushes back the curtains. It is only when he brings the telescope to his eye that he realises he is using it to see Ward's ship.

No. He does not want this gift tainted by Henry Ward.

He places it back in its box. Considers shoving it in his duffel bag.

Leave it, he decides. For better or worse, when he runs from Holy Island, he will run from Julia too. And the only way he will survive that is if he does his best to forget her. If he's honest with himself, the two of them have never been destined for anything else.

Nathan buttons his bag. "I'll meet you downstairs shortly. Just give me a moment."

Edwin nods. Disappears from the doorway without another word.

Nathan feels a deep grief as he walks down the passage. It's a sadness he never imagined this house would be able to wrangle from him. This house has been in his family for five generations. He hates that it will be lost on his watch.

Maybe this was what had caused his mother to flee so abruptly—this reluctance to leave, even with the knowledge that she had no choice. Maybe hesitation had left her frozen, until Henry Ward's ship had appeared through the windows and she had run out of time.

He understands. Understands, now, the power this house has to creep beneath your skin. It's the windows that open onto the sea; the roll of the dunes on every side. The depth of the darkness when the lamps are dimmed and the universe unfolds above rows of smoke-stained chimneys.

He goes to his study. The room had belonged to his father, and his grandfather before that. He runs a hand over the smooth wood of the desk. Whoever buys this house will end up with all his family's belongings. He will have no chance to empty it. No chance to return. The deeds to the house will also give the new owners shelves of books his father had read, the dressing table with the mirror his mother had peered into so many times. Nathan can still picture Abigail sitting on her stool, running a brush through her long, dark hair. Pictures her eyes meeting his in the mirror when he would peer around the doorframe in an attempt to catch a glimpse of her.

All right, my love? he hears her say. *There's no need to hide.*

Despite his anger at his mother, the memory still feels precious.

He hates the thought of strangers walking through his family's past. Of them discarding the house's contents as meaningless junk. A strange thing, he thinks. Was that not exactly how he had viewed all this when he had first been forced up here by Henry Ward? Pieces of a life he had done his best to forget? He had been quick to bundle up all the moth-eaten clothes and tarnished jewellery and cart it off to the church's charity collection. Now everything feels impossibly valuable. He takes his father's penknife from the desk drawer. Tucks it into his pocket.

He steps from the study and closes the door behind him. Then he takes out the ring of keys and unlocks the door to Oliver's room. Steps inside.

The room is dark and cavernous, emptied of furniture when he had torn up the old floorboards while on a search for the letter. The dark is deep, but Nathan realises suddenly that the dread he has always felt in here is gone. Somehow, in the wake of admitting how he really felt about his brother's death, the room has lost its power. Become nothing but an empty shell. Hollow. Surrounded by empty walls.

A cruel irony, Nathan thinks, that he might have landed in such a place now, when he has no choice but to leave the house without looking back. As though Oliver is managing one last callousness, before Nathan lets him go entirely.

CHAPTER TWENTY-NINE

The door of the great cabin clicks open and Ward steps inside. Finn looks up at him from his seat at the table. A deep frown creases Ward's forehead, a look of unease in his eyes.

Finn nods towards the bed, where Theodora is curled up asleep beneath her cloak. "Was this your doing?" he demands.

"Of course not." Ward turns the key in the lock. "You know me better than that."

"But you just let your men row out to Longstone and take her from her bed?"

Ward fixes his gaze on Theodora. "I had no idea my men were on Longstone. I've been at the house. Trying to convince Nathan Blake to give up this foolish fight."

"I'm sure taking his daughter will do it."

Irritation flashes across Ward's eyes. "I told you, I had nothing to do with that."

"And yet it's got you what you want. Here I am, back on your ship, just as you wanted."

Ward slides off his coat and hangs it on the back of his desk chair. "It's the right thing to do, Finn. But I did not force you to do it."

"What choice did I have? You think I'd just let those bastards take Nathan's daughter?"

Ward smiles thinly. "Seems I did teach you a little decency after all." He goes to the cupboard beneath his desk and pulls out a bottle of whisky. Holds it up to Finn in offering.

"I'd rather keep a clear head, if it's all the same to you."

Ward ignores his sharpness. He fills a glass and sinks into his desk chair. "I had nothing to do with the men taking Nathan's daughter. I regret that that happened. I regret that my crew has become so lawless."

"You took a ship full of men from the Republic of Pirates. What did you imagine would happen?"

Ward doesn't respond. Finn watches as he brings his whisky glass to his lips. A faint tremor there. Ward is growing old, Finn realises. Weary. The captain he remembers would never have hidden away in his great cabin like this, while other men sought to take his ship. Sought to harm the family of the woman he loved.

Perhaps it's being around the Blakes that has made him so weary. Perhaps it's the knowledge of Harriet; the confirmation that Abigail had not loved him as he had loved her. This can come as no surprise, surely. Finn knows that, after the night Oliver died, Ward never saw Abigail again. How could he have imagined she did anything other than flee to escape him? Escape the poisonous influence of captain and crew.

And now what? Is Ward to sit back and let these men take as they wish from Abigail's family? There's a resignation in his eyes that suggests this is exactly what he plans to do. Once, Ward had told him that to spend a life at sea required nothing less than great passion for the cause. And Finn can sense that, as far is Ward is concerned, this passion is running thin.

But he thinks of the spark in his former captain's eyes when he told him of the Spanish treasure ships. That passion might be running thin, but it has not disappeared completely.

"Keep your word, Ward," Finn says finally. "I re-join your crew, you fight Graveney. Was that not the deal we made? Get Nathan's daughter home and get your men out of the Blakes' lives." These are dangerous words, Finn knows. Because he has no intention of staying here on the ship. He desperately hopes he can be back on Longstone before Eva even notices him gone. But with each passing minute, that is becoming less and less likely. Either way, he needs Ward to believe he is here to stay. Needs him to agree to this deal he had proposed.

"I told Nathan Blake to leave Holy Island," says Ward. "He has agreed."

"That's because he thinks his daughter is safe on Longstone," Finn hisses. He leans forward, smacking a hand into the table, a desperate attempt to spark Ward back to life. "You've always claimed to be a man of honour. You need to do as you promised. Fight these men." Finn watches the indecision pass over Ward's face. "Is this really what you want?" He gestures to Theodora. "To be the captain of a crew who stoops to such things?"

Ward takes another sip of whisky, hard eyes looking out across the cabin. Finn can tell this is not the first time he has considered such things. After a long time, he nods slowly. "You're right," he says. "This is not what I want. And regardless of your reasons, you are here as I wished. I know I cannot ask you to do what is right, if I do not do the same." He stands abruptly and clenches his jaw. Finn watches the muscles tick. "I shall tell my men to prepare for engagement."

Finn feels a tug of guilt. *I cannot ask you to do what is right.* He is deceiving Ward, there is no denying it. He is here on the ship now, just as Ward wished. But at the first opportunity, he will run back to his wife.

Ward goes to his desk drawer and produces a pistol. Sets it on the table in front of Finn, along with a handful of extra shot.

Finn glances down at it. He's not touched a weapon since he had sailed with Ward as a boy. Back then, he'd felt drunk on the power it gave him. Now, he wants nothing to do with the thing. Still, he can't deny that with the ship about to erupt, he feels a little safer with its cold metal between his fingers. He slides it into the pocket of his coat, along with the ammunition. Nods towards Theodora. "I'm taking her back to the house." Ward opens his mouth to speak, but Finn continues, "I gave you my word I'd stay. But you can't keep her here if you're about to open fire on these men. Once she's safely back at the house, I'll return."

Ward looks at him with doubtful eyes. He's right to, of course. Because Finn has no intention of returning. How he can he do anything but keep sailing on to Longstone and climb back into bed beside Eva?

But the thought is chased away by a sudden reality: escape from Ward again and he and Eva will continue to live with one eye on the horizon. They will continue to live in fear of stray bullets and lights on the sea. Eva will live at the window with her eyes on the water. She will spend her life sleepless; wondering, waiting, worrying. And it will only be a matter of time before Ward comes for them again.

He will come back to the ship, Finn realises suddenly. Ward will have what he wants.

He will come back, because he cannot do anything else. He cannot let Eva spend her life at that window, staring out over the sea. He cannot let her days and nights be consumed by worry. Cannot put her through any more of this unbearable anticipation.

He cannot condemn his wife to a life lived in fear.

The sudden reality of it makes his stomach lurch. His body turns hot, then cold and he grips the edge of the table to steady himself.

"My steward, Mr Slater, will go with you," Ward says pointedly. "See that you keep your word." He slides his justacorps back over his wiry shoulders. "I'll speak to my loyal men first. Then draw the rest of the crew up onto deck. Give you a chance to get the girl off the ship unnoticed. I'll have Slater ready the longboat."

Finn nods dizzily. Watches after Ward as he slips out of the cabin.

He waits. Listens. More voices. Footsteps. A muffled shout from somewhere far above. Everything seems distorted. Too loud. Too soft.

When he turns around, he sees Theodora standing a few yards behind him. The sight of her makes him start. He had not even heard her getting out of bed. She scrubs a hand across tired eyes.

"Are we still on the ship?" she asks blearily.

"Aye." Finn takes her cloak from the end of the bed and slings it over her shoulders. "But we're going to leave very soon, all right? So we've got to get ready."

Theodora looks up at him with wide blue eyes. She nods silently, fumbling with the buttons on her cloak. Finn makes his way across the cabin and presses an ear to the door. It's quiet in the passage now; he can hear the distant hum of voices from up on deck.

He touches the pocket of his coat, feeling for the pistol. Theodora hangs back, knotting her hands in her cloak. "Come on now," Finn says, voice low. "Quick as we can, aye?"

She nods. Hurries towards him, and reaches out to grip a fistful of his coat. Finn turns the key and steps out into the passage. And it's instinct guiding him, up this ladder, down that passage, past closed doors and groaning bulkheads. Because he remembers the hatch behind the mess tables that will take them out to the poop deck. Hopefully there he will find Slater and the longboat waiting.

He guides Theodora through the passage and up the ladder, reaching over her head to shove open the hatch. "Up here," he says. "Careful now. Hold on tight." She climbs slowly, feeling her way through the dark. He can make out little more than her fragile outline, moving steadily up the rungs, her nightgown glowing against the blackness. Finn scrambles up after her, squeezing his body through a hatch he last climbed through as an eleven-year-old child.

The deck is crowded and noisy, with men clustered towards the bow of the ship. Finn is dimly aware of Ward speaking heatedly to Graveney, but barely pays them attention. He cannot consider the prospect that this ship will be his life now. That these men are the people he will spend his every day and night with. All he can focus on is getting Theodora back to her father.

He cannot think of any of it. He just helps Theodora into the longboat and climbs in beside her, nodding to Ward's steward to row them back towards Highfield House.

CHAPTER THIRTY

Nathan hears a thunderous rap at the front door. He fears he is too late in leaving; fears Graveney and his men are here, a day early to catch him unaware. He snatches the deeds to the house from inside his bag before hurrying down the stairs. He had hoped to run without handing them over, but if he opens the door to waving pistols, he sees now that he will have no choice.

But when he pulls the door open, it is not Graveney or Ward, but Eva and Julia that fly inside, frantic and windblown, with wild hair and fear in their eyes. He cannot make sense of why they are here; why they are together; what he is supposed to feel in Julia's presence. And they are both talking at once, words so tangled Nathan can barely make them out. But: *Theodora* he hears; and *ship*. And every thought of fleeing suddenly vanishes from his mind.

From the water, the house looks as otherworldly and grim as it always has. A stone hulk against the emptiness of the dunes. Lamps are blazing in several of the windows, but they cast no more than meagre circles that do little to light its mass. At least, Finn thinks, when all this is over, he will never have to step inside the place again. The thought brings little comfort.

He feels his heart stutter. There's a boat on the embankment—his skiff. Eva must have brought it here when she discovered him and Theodora missing. He had hoped—naively, he sees now—that she would not get entangled in this. That she would sleep away the night, and know nothing of it until Theodora was safe and the *Eagle* was long gone. He cannot bring himself to think of what she had gone through, waking to find them gone, sailing in the darkness, drowning in panic.

He finds himself staring up at the windows, hoping for a glimpse of her. If Eva is here, Nathan must know that Ward's men have Theodora. What is he planning to do? Finn knows he has to get Thea back to her father before anyone acts rashly.

He tears his eyes away from the glass. If he sees Eva, he will never do what needs to be done.

He looks at Theodora. Her eyes are on the house, her small hands clasped tightly around the edge of the bench. She is gnawing on her lip, eyes wide and glistening. Finn turns to Slater. "When we get to shore, I need you to take Theodora back to the house."

"What about you?"

"I'll take the longboat around the point. Keep an eye on the ship."

Slater gives a humourless chuckle. "Sorry, lad. I've orders to keep an eye on you."

Finn scrubs a hand across his eyes. "Come on, man. Just do as I'm asking. Please. I'm just trying to stay the hell away from the house. I can't—" He stops abruptly. Refuses to speak of it. "Please just do it," he says again.

Slater lets out a sigh; glances back over his shoulder at the ship. Then he nods resignedly. A wave pushes the longboat closer to the beach and Slater clambers out, splashing softly into the dark water. He reaches over and lifts Theodora out of the boat. Finn hears her murmur. He can't look at her. Can't look at the house.

He shuffles onto the bench seat left empty by Slater and takes up the oars. He pulls the longboat around the point as quickly as he can, hiding the house from his line of sight.

A burst of gunfire. Finn whirls around to look back to the ship. He hears shouting drift across the water.

He pulls on the oars, further out to sea for a better look at the ship.

He sees lamps bobbing, tracing through the darkness. Men are pouring into the longboats from the *Eagle*, he realises. Boats are beginning to pull towards the house. His stomach plunges. Have Ward and his men been defeated? Has Graveney discovered Theodora is gone? Has he chosen to come for Nathan before he can run?

And he cannot hide, Finn realises. If Graveney and his men are coming to the house, he cannot just sit back and watch. Especially not now Eva is inside.

It was not clarity he was seeing with before, Nathan realises. Because he is seeing with clarity now. A singular focus. He must get Theodora out of the hands of these men. The house, the money, the letter—nothing else matters.

He hears pistol fire coming from the direction of the water. Cannot allow himself to think about what that might mean.

"Take me out to the ship," he says to Julia. "I know it's dangerous. But I wouldn't ask it—"

She nods before he can finish. She had prepared herself for such a request; he can tell by the hardness in her eyes. He murmurs his thanks.

On the edge of his vision, Nathan sees Edwin tucking his pistol into his pocket. He is grateful for the support.

"I'm coming with you," says Eva. "I have to find Finn."

Nathan throws open the door and steps out onto the dunes. There is no way, of course, that he is going to allow Eva to climb into that boat with them, but right now, he does not have the time to argue.

The sight before him turns his body hot, then cold. Longboats are cutting through the water towards the house. Lamps glowing, men shouting, shots flying. He hears a distant cry of pain.

A conflict between Ward's fractured crew, but Nathan knows this house—and his mother—is at the centre of it all.

There's a deep, boiling fear there, at his edges. But right now, all he can focus on is the tiny shape at the water's edge. His daughter, stumbling over the dunes in her nightgown, with a man by her side. Eva shoves her way past Nathan and rushes forward, letting out a stifled cry when she realises the man is not her husband.

Nathan flies towards Theodora, scooping her into his arms. Tears are flooding her face, falling harder with each echoed pistol shot. She clings to his neck, wraps her legs around his waist, buries her wet face against his neck. And for a moment, there is nothing beyond this; no men fighting, no boats approaching, just pure unbridled relief. Then the feel of her in his arms is too much, and dizziness threatens to overwhelm him. He sets Theodora down beside Eva. Tries to catch his breath. She wails harder at the loss of him.

"Take her upstairs," Nathan tells his sister. "Get her inside." His words come out in pieces: *the passage. Behind the priest hole. Oliver's room.*

Eva's arm goes thoughtlessly around Theodora's shoulders. But she starts to protest. "I can't. I have to—"

"Please, Eva. She's terrified." Nathan glances back over his shoulder at the approaching men. "We'll find Finn. I swear it."

Eva blinks back a fresh rush of tears. Another argument on her lips, then finally, a faint nod of acceptance. She hurries Theodora inside the house.

Nathan turns back to Julia. "Go with them." His voice is husky. "Get inside. Get to safety." She meets Nathan's eyes for a long moment, then follows Eva into the house without a word. Closes the door behind her.

Nathan reaches into his pocket, his fingers closing around the deeds of the house.

"Let's go," Edwin hisses, standing at his shoulder. "If we leave through the servants' entrance we can make it into the village—"

"It's too late to run." If they try to escape now, they will be easy targets out on the exposed dunes. Nathan knows he has to stay here with his house. Has to trust this place will protect them.

He curses Henry Ward for refusing to fight. Curses himself for refusing to run, until it was too late. And he curses his mother for not having the foresight to know where her crimes would lead.

But when he looks out to sea once more, Nathan realises he was wrong. Henry Ward is here among these men, a pistol in his hand, on his feet at the bow of one of the longboats. Shouting orders. Directing men. Fighting for them, as Abigail would have wanted.

But just like Nathan himself, Ward has made his choice far too late.

Because the first of the boats are sighing against the shore. Men leap out into the shallow water. And John Graveney strides steadily up the beach.

CHAPTER THIRTY-ONE

Eva rushes up the stairs, clutching Theodora's hand. Down the hall to the room at the end of the house.

The priest hole. The passage.

She has never seen them. Has only ever heard stories of them: Nathan crawling through the walls to find Julia's brothers hidden in the attic. Finn using the passage to escape, the night of Oliver's death.

The door creaks as she pushes against it, but it swings open willingly. Has she ever been inside this room before? The question is there dimly; poorly timed at the back of her mind. Certainly not since she had returned to Highfield House as an adult. As a child? Her memories of Oliver are fragile, built mostly on fear. She cannot imagine having willingly gone into his bedroom.

It's dark inside; feels airless, somehow. Eva imagines she can smell the decay of neglect, though she knows it can be nothing more than her own fear and racing imagination. Knows this was one of the first rooms Nathan and Edwin restored.

She hurries to the window and looks out. Lights on the water; boats moving through moonlight towards the house. Beside her, Theodora is sobbing messy tears, clutching at Eva's skirts, feet sliding over the floorboards in her dirty stockings.

Eva squints through the glass. There are men crossing the

embankment now, but she does not see Finn.

She swallows down a swell of grief and goes to the fireplace, a beastly black shape in the dark. Eva pushes against one wall panel, another, another; a desperate attempt to find the priest hole. And at once, her thoughts are back with Finn; with his panic, his fear, as he had scrambled to find the hiding place in the wall in the wake of Oliver's death. Her chest aches. And the house moves beneath her hands, the panel twisting open to reveal the hidden space behind.

Theodora's eyes widen. Her crying halts as she stares into the chasm inside the wall. Eva knows Nathan has always forbidden his daughter from coming into this room; has always kept it locked. Had he opened it just for this purpose, she wonders distantly? Had he seen this necessity coming?

Eva goads Theodora into the hiding place. Murmurs words of encouragement she cannot make herself feel. She pushes the wall panel closed, trapping her niece inside. Theodora pounds against the wall, howling out her protest. Eva feels a sharp pang of guilt. But she cannot stay here. She needs to find her husband.

Theodora's shrieks echo through the panelling as Eva hurries back to the window. It is still too dark to see much beyond inky shapes, but she sees the flashes of pistols, hears shots fly. Men on the dunes now too, coming towards the house. Coming *for* the house.

She hurries for the door. Turns at the sound of the priest hole groaning open. Theodora spills out and rushes towards her.

"Get back inside," Eva manages, but Thea is howling, hysterical, gasping for breath. Behind them, glass shatters, spraying into the dark room. A stray shot, sent from the beach, careening up into the house.

Eva stops herself on the way to the door. She cannot go out there now, not even to find Finn. Running into pistol fire and putting herself in danger will only cause more trouble for everyone.

She grabs Thea's hand and rushes back towards the priest hole, keeping low to avoid any more wayward shots. She pushes on the panel beside the fireplace and burrows into the wall, losing herself in the darkness within the innards of the house.

"Hold your fire." The order comes from Henry Ward; Nathan knows that voice all too well. This voice does not come from the fearful man who had sat at Nathan's dining table and told him to walk away. It comes from the man who had threatened him into returning to Lindisfarne, the man who had made him believe he held his life in his hands. Nathan wonders which version of Henry Ward is real.

And for all the conflict on that ship; for all the power that John Graveney seems to hold, Ward's words silence the fire. Men are still brandishing swords and pistols, but there's a sudden motionlessness. A held breath. The stillness that falls over the beach feels impossibly deep.

Nathan hears his pulse roaring in his ears. His legs feel weak beneath him, his vision pulsing at its edges. He is going to die—of that he is suddenly certain. Never mind that Graveney needs him alive. Never mind these deeds in his pocket, worthless without his signature and seal. To think that that would save him suddenly feels like the greatest of naiveties. Because Henry Ward may have rediscovered his authoritative voice, but Graveney is facing Nathan with a pistol in his hand, and the beach is already stained with blood. Men have fallen across the embankment, others slumped in the longboats.

To his left, Nathan catches sight of Finn, striding up the beach towards the house. Ward steps in front of him, presses a palm to his chest, holding him back.

Several of Graveney's men face Ward and his supporters, weapons held out in front of them. Silent; waiting for a signal to strike. And this held breath, Nathan realises, this fleeting peace, it's all for him. These men are waiting to see what he will do. Waiting to see if he will relinquish the house. If he will plunge his family deeper into poverty. If he will live his life at the will of another man.

"Mr Blake," says Graveney. "I trust you've made your decision."

My decision, yes. Relinquish the house. Plunge his family into poverty. Live by another man's bidding. But when he opens his mouth to answer, Nathan's rational thoughts disappear. In their place is that fierce single-mindedness that had consumed him with the news that Theodora had been taken. By the man that stands in front of him.

My decision. He reaches for the deeds, barely registering that it is not the paperwork he is pulling from his pocket, but his pistol. A singular focus. Clarity.

He hears the shot echo in the stillness. Barely realises he is the one to have pulled the trigger. And with a blissful sense of being outside himself, he watches Graveney fall.

CHAPTER THIRTY-TWO

Nathan waits for the responding shot. Waits to die. Because surely they will come for him now, these men who had rallied around Graveney; these fellow Jacobites who had helped him try to take the house. He feels himself being shoved backwards, pulled away from the conflict. Feels himself pitch sideways, stumbling against the damp earth of the dunes. Shots fly and swords collide. Nathan's thoughts are clattering too violently to make sense of who had pulled him out of the throng of men. Ward, perhaps? Or Finn? A stranger glad to see Graveney defeated? He cannot make sense of why he has been deemed worth saving.

His vision is swimming, his body hot. He can make sense of little beyond the humming in his ears and the lifeless body of John Graveney lying on the embankment. And the fact that Henry Ward is here, fighting, as Nathan had requested. He has no thought of what had made Ward change his mind. But right now, he has no thought of anything.

He crawls towards the house. Does not dare attempt to get inside, in case anyone tries to follow him. But he hunches behind the rise of a dune, hand clenched around his pistol. He knows there's little point—the barrel is empty; he has made his shot. And he may die for it yet. But somehow, he feels safer with the weapon in his hand. It makes him feel like something more than a man who runs.

Men fall, and shout, go loudly to their deaths; and after minutes, or hours, of distorted time, there is silence. Henry Ward marches across the beach. His deliberate stride suggests the blood splattered across his shirtsleeves is not his own. Victorious? Nathan supposes the fact he is alive would suggest as much. Ward reaches into his pocket and slides a fresh round of ammunition into his pistol. And for a moment, Henry Ward is the fearless adventurer Nathan had seen him as back when he was a boy. That mythical figure who had appeared sporadically at the house, as though he had been magicked in from an adventure tale.

"Take the fallen back to the ship," Nathan hears him say. "Prepare them for burial." Ward's gold-buttoned figure drifts in and out of focus.

Nathan turns his gaze to the sky. It's vividly clear tonight; an eruption of stars. *Pegasus, Sirius, Scorpius.* The constellations help him breathe.

His eyes draw downward to Graveney's body, lying a few yards away on a curve of a grassy dune. His chest is ink-dark with blood. The moon is too thin to light the details of his bearded face, and Nathan is glad for that reprieve. Easier to carry a death, he sees now, when the evidence is not so illuminated.

A close murmur snaps him out of his daze. To his side, he sees Edwin hunched over. Sees the hand clasped to his side. Sees the blood trickling out between his fingers, beading black on the grass of the dunes.

Finn's body is blazing. He has not come so close to conflict since he was Henry Ward's cabin boy, and as a child, he had had little sense of his own mortality. Now, he is surprised to find himself still living.

He hunches over, tries to catch his breath. Feels his boots sink into the pebbles of the beach. The pistol in his hand feels hot, though he does not remember firing. Cannot tell if the heat is just his imagination, or if he had pulled the trigger without being aware of it.

And fired at who, he finds himself wondering? A victory to Ward and the Blakes retain their home. A victory to Graveney and Finn has a path back to Eva. He knows it doesn't matter. His own undefined loyalty has had no bearing on anything.

He cannot help but be surprised that Ward has come out of this victorious. Alive. Or maybe he can. Maybe he had underestimated Ward.

Maybe the bold and forthright man Henry Ward had been twenty years ago is still in there somewhere.

Maybe the prospect of an undisputed captaincy has been enough to bring him to the surface.

Finn glances across the beach. Ward's back is turned, and he is locked in conversation with several of his men.

Now.

Finn lurches towards the house. He sees the irony in his desperate need to be inside that damn place. To walk that staircase again. To feel that worn banister beneath his hand. To stand in Oliver Blake's bedroom and see the monstrous fireplace looming before him.

Ward catches him on the fringe of the embankment. Takes a firm hold on his arm. "I kept my word, Finn. I expect you to do the same."

To hell with your word, he wants to say. What right does Henry Ward have to keep him from his wife?

But Ward looks into his eyes for a single, charged moment, and Finn sees it all.

He thinks of the broken windows in Ward's great cabin. Thinks how close he had been to losing Eva the night she had thrown herself into the sea to escape the ship. He thinks of her watching out the window for Ward on their wedding night; thinks of all her broken, anxious sleeps on Longstone, as she waits for that ship to reappear.

Is this truly the life you want for your wife?

She is better off without him; this Finn knows for certain. Safer without him. And in time, she will come to see that she is also happier without him.

At least he will leave knowing she is at Highfield House with her family, and not alone out on Longstone.

He pulls his arm from Ward's grip. But he can't take his eyes from the house. None of Graveney's men had made it inside, and Graveney himself is dead now. Eva will be safe in there.

But Finn knows she will come looking for him. She will climb into the skiff and sail out to Ward's ship, and she will put herself in danger again by trying to find him.

He cannot let that happen. Eva had almost died the last time she was on Ward's ship. He cannot let her sail out there a second time.

He strides across the embankment towards his skiff. Pulls the spare shot from his pocket and slides it into the pistol.

He holds his breath. Pushes aside his hesitation. This has to be done.

He fires into the hull of his boat. Wood splinters. And threads of dark water creep inside.

Finn closes his eyes for a second, trying to breathe. Then he shoves one of Ward's longboats out to sea and climbs inside, before he falters and changes his mind.

<h1 style="text-align:center">CHAPTER THIRTY-THREE</h1>

Inside the priest hole is dark, and dark, and dark. Eva hears Theodora's soft murmuring, hears her own rapid breathing, hears the creak of old boards above her head. She hears no more pistol fire.

She pushes on the wall panel and stumbles out into Oliver's empty bedroom. She hurries through the dark to the window, broken glass crunching beneath the soles of her shoes. Salty air gusts through the shattered pane, blowing her hair back from her face. Eva sees only in shadows and lamplight, but she can tell the shooting has stopped.

She sees men on the beach, milling about towards the boats. Henry Ward is there, but she cannot see Nathan, cannot see Finn. Does the fact that Ward is alive mean he has been victorious?

Either way, she can wait here no longer.

Finn must be out there. Either he had fought with Ward's men, or he is on the ship. The prospect of him being among the dead is one she cannot even bring herself to consider. And no matter what deal he had made with his former captain, Eva is not about to let him leave her. Who is Henry Ward to act as a judge upon their lives?

The skiff is still waiting on the embankment. She had made it aboard Ward's ship once before. And she will do so again.

She murmurs something to Thea that even she herself can barely make out, then she is flying down the staircase. She hears voices, murmuring, groaning, coming from the direction of the parlour, but she cannot find space to think about what this might mean. As she runs out of the house, she hears Nathan call her name from inside the parlour. Distant gratitude to hear he is alive, but she doesn't stop moving.

Outside the house, men are carrying lifeless bodies towards the longboats. Piling them into the boats like they are nothing more than sacks of wheat. Eva dares a glimpse at the dead men's faces. She can make out little in the darkness. But Finn is not among the dead, she tells herself. He cannot be. She will not even allow it to be a possibility.

She stumbles towards the skiff.

"Don't be foolish, Eva."

She whirls around at the sound of Ward's voice. Anger burns inside her. "Where is Finn?" she demands.

"He's returned to my ship."

Eva lurches forward, but Ward steps in front of her, blocking her way.

"Do you really think you can get out there without any of my men catching you?"

Fresh tears escape down her cheeks. "Why are you doing this to him?"

"I did not do anything. It was his own choice. He could have stayed on Longstone. He chose to come to the ship."

"Because your men took Theodora!"

"Because he knows this is what's best for you. And your family."

He is wrong, of course. Has always been wrong. About all of this. And if this is what Finn truly believes is best, then he is wrong too. This is not what is best for her. This is not what is best for her family. And this, Eva feels certain, is not what her mother would have wanted. Abigail would not have wanted this grief, this pain, this utter sense of loss for her daughter.

She stumbles across the embankment, her eyes not leaving the lamplit ship. Sailing out there alone, without Ward catching her, feels impossible. But she has to try. She needs to get to Finn. Needs to tell him he is making a mistake. Needs to tell him she would happily spend every night waiting for Ward to appear, if only he would come back to her.

She shoves hard against the skiff. Hears it groan and scrape against the pebbles of the embankment. She throws her weight against it again, but it refuses to be lifted by the tide.

She looks down. Sees the dark pool of sea gathering in the hull. Pain strikes her chest. Fury at Ward that makes her vision blur. Because this is his doing, surely. This is no accident. No wayward shot. This is his way of showing her he is in control.

She whirls around in search of him. Sees him march across the beach in the opposite direction, not looking back at her, as though she is not even worth another thought.

A soft knock at the bedroom door and Harriet stops pacing. She unwinds her fingers from her shawl.

"Why are you knocking?" she says bitterly. "It's hardly as though I can let you in." She hears the waver in her voice, wrought by the constant echo of pistol fire outside the house—and the utter helplessness of being locked in here like an animal.

For your safety, Edwin had claimed. She's no fool—she knows he had locked her up to keep her from running away again. Even the windows of her bedroom had kept her blind to all that was unfolding; looking out over the dunes behind the house, rather than out towards the sea.

The key turns in the lock. And it's Nathan that stands in the doorway. The coffee-brown waves of his hair hang loose on his shoulders, and there's a slightly wild look in his eyes. A hotness to his cheeks. And more there too—remorse, and regret, perhaps. Or is it pity?

"What happened?" Harriet asks.

He tells her in a soft, guilt-ridden voice about the bullet Edwin had taken to the side, about the way Julia had gone to the village for the barber surgeon. *We're doing everything we can*, he is saying; and *please try not to worry*.

Harriet listens with an odd sense of detachment. She waits for the horror she sees in Nathan's eyes to pass itself onto her. Instead, it seems to dissipate. "And my father?" she asks, her voice coming out far more level than she expected. "Is he still alive?"

"Yes."

"Was he hurt?"

"No. I don't believe so."

She hears herself murmur with relief. Feels the knot in her belly loosen an inch. Harriet smooths her skirts. "He fought Graveney and his men? As you asked him to?"

Nathan looks down. "Yes. He did."

There are things he is not telling her, Harriet is sure. She doesn't care. She is just grateful her father had helped her family. She wonders if her request for him to do so had had any influence on his decision.

"Where is Edwin?" she asks finally.

"In the parlour." Nathan looks up at her, his eyes alight with guilt. "The barber surgeon is with him."

She nods.

"We're doing all we can, Harriet," he says again, more feverishly this time. "With luck he will be all right."

She follows Nathan dutifully down the staircase. It's quiet downstairs now, apart from Edwin's muffled grunts sounding through the closed parlour door. The air is tinged with gunpowder and sea. Harriet stands with her back pressed to the wall of the hallway, staring at the parlour door.

What is it she ought to be feeling? Sadness? Anger? Relief? She can't tell. All she knows is that she ought to be feeling *something*. Something other than this emptiness.

No—emptiness; it's not right. It's just an absence of the things she ought to be feeling.

She turns at the sound of footsteps. Ward is standing in the entrance hall, looking like he belongs here. He is without his hat, a long strand of greying hair hanging loose from his queue. A spray of crimson paints the arm of his shirt, but she can tell by his movements that the blood does not belong to him. There's a glow in his eyes that Harriet has not seen before. A look that would make her afraid of him, if he weren't her father. Perhaps it makes her afraid anyway.

She swallows heavily. Nods towards the parlour. "Who did this to my husband?"

"I can't be certain. One of Mr Graveney's supporters, I assume. Retaliating in response to his death."

Harriet raises her eyebrows. "Edwin killed Mr Graveney?"

"No," says Ward. "Your brother did."

And of all the things that could have happened out there tonight, this is the outcome Harriet had least expected. She cannot imagine what might have driven Nathan to do such a thing. The last she had heard, he had had his bags packed and been ready to run.

"I'm sorry about your husband," says Ward.

Harriet doesn't reply. Possibly not trusting herself to make the correct reply; a reply that might suggest she has some humanity, some decency in her.

Footsteps clop across the parlour. Ward glances towards the sound, before turning back to her. "Harriet," he says, "may we speak in private?"

She nods. And she finds herself leading him down the passage to her workroom. She lights the lamp on the mantel and closes the door behind them.

Ward glances around the half-empty room. Harriet wishes she had her paintings in here to show him. Without them, the room feels impossibly bleak. Soulless. She and Ward face each other in the gloom. Neither attempt to sit.

"My crew and I are leaving," Ward says. "We've business in the New World."

The New World. Even with her limited knowledge, Harriet knows this is a dangerous, months-long journey. She feels something sink inside her.

"What kind of business?" she asks.

"Business that, with luck, will deliver my crew the wealth I promised them. The wealth they will not get from your family."

"I see." Harriet looks up at him hopefully. "When will I see you again?"

He is silent for a long moment, before turning away from her expectant eyes.

The realisation swings at her. "You're not coming back here, are you."

"No," he admits. "But surely you're not either. Do you not intend to return to London?"

Return to London? Is he truly speaking of such things when her husband may well be dying? Does he truly have no qualms about disappearing on her when she is on the verge of becoming a widow?

"You would leave me now?" she demands. "When my husband may well be on his death bed—at the hands of your own men?" Her words come out dripping with drama and childishness, but she doesn't care. At least Edwin's state has managed to conjure up some flicker of emotion in her. "Is that all I mean to you then? You'd rather chase gold than be a part of my life?"

She is just like him, she sees now. This is where her selfishness comes from. Her inhumanity. Her mother was right to leave him, she thinks. She was right to hide their child from him. Right to lie to her about who her father was.

Anger bubbles beneath her skin. It makes her hands clench into fists. Makes her want to strike him. She is seeing him for the first time: that man Eva and Finn had been so wary of. That man Nathan had fought to keep out of their lives. At first, she had assumed their fear came solely from their secrets, and the power Ward had to spill them all. But there is more to it, she sees now. Henry Ward is a man who will always put himself first. Even tonight, when he had risked his own life to rid them of Graveney, he had no doubt only done so because it would give him back a secure captaincy. "You're a selfish bastard," she hisses.

Ward's eyes flicker with surprise. "Harriet," he says. "Please calm yourself. There's no need for such hysteria."

She glares at him. She hates this façade of his she is unable to break through. Hates that she has no idea who he truly is. Does it even bother him a scrap that he is to sail out of his daughter's life, never to return? Did it ever even faze him to learn about her in the first place? Once, she had believed so. Now all she feels is doubt. Betrayal. A sense of being discarded. "How can I behave otherwise when you are acting with such selfishness and greed?"

"Is that why you think I'm doing this? Out of greed?"

"It's the truth, isn't it?"

Ward goes to the window for a moment and peers out onto the embankment. Harriet can see the faint glow of his ship just beyond the glass. After a moment, he turns back to face her. "Listen to me," he says slowly, carefully. "You know your mother never wanted you and I to be in each other's lives. And I'm choosing to respect her wishes." He sighs. "She was right to keep you from me. Look at all that has happened to your family with me in your lives." He glances down, and for the faintest of moments, she sees a genuineness in his expression. "In all honesty, I thought it best for both of us that I leave without a word. But then your husband was hurt, and I—"

"I don't care what Mother wanted!" Harriet cries, desperation welling inside her. "You cannot just disappear! I barely know you!"

Ward folds his arms and gives her hard eyes, forcing her into silence. "I care about you, Harriet," he says, his voice suddenly empty of emotion again. "But do not let yourself be fooled into thinking you have a say in what I do."

She presses her lips into a thin line. She had not grown up with any male figure in her life, beyond her older brother, less than a decade her senior. But with Henry Ward's eyes on her, scolding, scrutinising, she suddenly feels like a reprimanded child. And that is not a feeling she welcomes. She has enough of this from her husband.

She stares at her father for a long, wordless moment. She means nothing to him, she sees now. How can she? A man who cared for his daughter would never willingly cut himself from her life, regardless of what her mother would have wanted. She has been nothing to Henry Ward but a momentary interest.

"That's it, then?" she asks coldly.

"Well. I would hope we would manage an amicable goodbye." He reaches out a hand towards her, but she steps away. Ward swallows visibly, but holds her gaze. "Regardless of all that has happened, I am truly glad I came to know of you," he says.

Harriet grits her teeth. "I wish I could say the same."

CHAPTER THIRTY-FOUR

Finn watches from the deck of the *Eagle* as the longboats return. On the empty ship, the sigh of the sea against the hull is magnified, and he hears the ratlines clatter in the faint breeze. He stares down at the lifeless figures piled at the back of the longboats.

Now Ward has turned to piracy, Finn knows it will not be long until the rest of this crew follow these men into death. Whether his life will end on the gallows or with a bullet to the chest, he has no idea—but a life under the black flag is rarely a long one.

The ship begins to fill. The line of bodies at the gunwale grows. Finn looks past them to the glow of the lamps in Highfield House. Beyond the dark mass of Lindisfarne, the Longstone firebasket has burned itself out.

He watches Ward climb aboard the ship. Tries to force down a wash of hatred.

The remaining men gather around their captain. Forty souls left living; fifty, perhaps. Two thirds of the crew or more. The victory over Graveney has brought the unyielding look back to Ward's eyes. It's a look Finn remembers well.

"Mr Graveney is dead," Ward says. "And Abigail Blake's letter has not been found." He looks around the group, meeting the eyes of the crew. "I regret I cannot offer you the immunity I promised. But I intend to travel to the New World to uncover the cargo of two fleets of lost Spanish treasure ships. Anyone who does not wish to join us in Florida is free to leave now." His eyes meet Finn's pointedly, making it clear the offer does not extend to him.

Finn thinks of running, of jumping, of swimming back to shore. And he thinks of the pistol fire that will surely follow. Thinks of the men that will come to Highfield House, to Longstone, in search of him. Ward has kept his word. And now he needs to keep his.

When no one leaves the ship, Ward finds his navigator among the crowd. A course to the New World. It is suddenly hard to breathe.

"Prepare the dead for burial," Ward tells several of his men. "We will hold the service in the morning, once we are in deeper water." He turns towards the saloon.

Finn pushes through the cluster of men towards Ward, catching him before he steps inside. "I saw you go to the house," he pushes. "Did you see Eva? Is she safe?"

"She is," says Ward. "Safe with her family."

Finn nods. He knows he ought to be grateful for this—and in many ways, he is. But the pain of it is almost unbearable. She shouldn't be in that house with her family. She ought to be out on Longstone with him.

But the moment the thought comes to him, he catches its untruth. Eva is far better in the safety of her family than she has ever been with him. What has their life together ever offered her beyond danger and fear? What right did he have to make her his wife when he could not even give her a safe home?

Ward clamps a hand to Finn's shoulder. "Join me in the great cabin."

Right now, Henry Ward is the last person in the world he wants to be around. But he knows that steely tone in Ward's voice. Knows he does not have a choice in the matter.

Ward unlocks the door of the great cabin and steps inside, Finn following reluctantly. He opens the cupboard beneath his desk and produces the bottle of whisky he had been drinking from earlier. Fills two tin cups and hands one to Finn.

"Do you really imagine I want to drink with you right now?"

Ward ignores the question. He sits at the head of the table and brings his cup to his lips, staring up at Finn.

There is no other option but to sit. He does. And then he drinks. Just a mouthful. He knows he needs to keep a clear head around Ward now, in case he does something foolish. But he also needs something to calm that desperate ache in his chest.

The whisky only makes it worse.

"I'm sorry," Ward says after a moment.

Finn snorts. "No you're not."

"I am. I'm sorry that things came to this." Suddenly there's a distant look in his eyes. Finn wonders what he is thinking. Of Abigail? Of Harriet? "And I'm sorry I took you to Highfield House that night in the first place. I've always blamed myself in part for Oliver's death."

"Why?" Finn says gruffly. "You only took me there because I was unwell."

"No. That's not why I took you."

Finn frowns. "What are you talking about?"

Ward shakes his head. "It doesn't matter. It's all in the past."

Finn laughs coldly. All that has happened and Ward is still talking in riddles. He doesn't care. Whatever Ward's reasons, he cannot think on them. It will only lead him to madness. He gulps back another mouthful of whisky. "I need your word," he tells Ward, "that you will never go near Eva again. Or her family."

Ward nods, and Finn sees a sincerity in his eyes. "You have my word, Finn. You know you can trust me."

He nods. Because yes, in spite of everything, he knows that Ward is telling the truth. He is a man who does not lie. A man who sticks by his word. And despite the grief pressing down on him, that is some small consolation.

Ward meets his eyes. "You are doing the right thing, Finn."

He grits his teeth. The right thing? He is abandoning his wife mere weeks after they had married. But he also knows he has no choice.

He wishes he and Eva had the seemingly endless years he had once imagined they would have. Years in which he could ask for the answers to all the trivial things he is yet to learn about her. Whether she had slept well before she had begun to keep the light. Whether she has ever been to Scotland. Her favourite season. Cats or dogs.

But they do not have endless years. Or even a single trip around the sun. Not even another night of keeping the firebasket burning together.

But it's best this way. Eva is free of Ward now, and safe with her family.

He will give her back her unbroken nights' sleep. Will let that towering cottage on Longstone turn to a ruin, and the future he had imaged with Eva along with it.

Grief pushes at his chest. "Please," he says, swallowing past the pain in his throat, "we need to leave as soon as possible. If she can see the ship from the house, she'll try to come after me. I've damaged the skiff, but she'll find some way…"

Ward gives him the faintest of smiles. "She's a lot like her mother." He gets up and goes to the desk in the corner of the room. "My navigator is plotting our course as we speak. I'll give the men instructions to sail out of the bay in the meantime." He pulls a ream of papers from the desk drawer and tosses them on the table in front of Finn, placing a quill and inkpot beside them. Finn glances down at them. *Articles of the pirate vessel Eagle.*

Something turns over in his stomach.

Ward looks at him pointedly. A look that tells him to keep his word and sign his name. He leaves without speaking again.

Finn stares down at the articles. He uncorks the ink pot and dips in the quill. Tries to find the courage to put the nib to the page.

CHAPTER THIRTY-FIVE

Wartime now, thinks Harriet. And militiamen are everywhere. There are always soldiers in the streets, their eyes and ears open for Jacobite plans. They are easy to find in the alley outside the tavern—almost as easy as it had been to leave the house without anyone noticing.

Well, who was there to notice? Jenny and Thomas are away on Bamburgh; Nathan trying to pace away his guilt. Theodora, Harriet assumes, is still tucked away on Longstone with her secret-keeping aunt and uncle. And Edwin, well, he is alive, and she supposes there is gratitude there. But it's a shallow gratitude; overshadowed by the relief of how easy it was to slip out of the house and approach the authorities.

Harriet lifts her chin and strides up to the soldiers with as much deliberateness as she can manage. It's a difficult thing, given how much she is shaking. Shaking with grief, with anger, with a sense of betrayal. Shaking with the magnitude of all she is about to do. She barely notices when a raft of men spill out of the tavern towards her, hollering about *ladybirds* and *lift your skirts*. She just puts her head down and keeps walking.

She wishes she had never met Henry Ward. Wishes she had never gone searching for Samuel Blake's headstone. Wishes for her old ignorance.

For a while, being Ward's daughter had felt special. But that's not what she is. Not to him. She is nothing compared to an ocean of gold.

The two militiamen turn as she approaches.

"I've information," she tells them. Her voice trembles slightly. "About a pirate vessel leaving these waters. They took the cargo of the East India ship *Albion* off the coast of Nassau. And plenty more besides."

CHAPTER THIRTY-SIX

Harriet tries not to think about what she has done. She focuses on the soft sigh of her footsteps against the earth, the way the light of her lamp bounces over the dunes. The silver thread of moon in the clear sky overhead.

Reporting her father's ship is not bringing her the satisfaction she thought it would. Just a dull sense of self-loathing. And inevitability, perhaps. It feels as though this was always how things were destined to end between her and Henry Ward. After all, this was what her mother had wanted: for them to not be in each other's lives.

Since she had met her father, Harriet had been racked with anger at her mother. But now she has chosen Abigail's side.

Would her mother be proud of her for what she has done? Harriet wants to believe it. But she cannot quite see beyond the regret.

Movement on the embankment catches her eye. Harriet's heart flutters; she is on edge after all that has taken place tonight. It's her sister, she realises. And that fact does nothing to slow her racing heart.

At once, the thoughts of turning her father in are gone, burnt away by rage at Eva and all she had sought to keep from the family. She cannot make sense of why her sister is here—had Eva been here at the house the whole time Harriet had been locked away in her bedroom? Why is she not on Longstone with Theodora? Harriet pushes the questions away. She cannot make herself care about the details.

Eva is huddled on the water's edge, her knees pulled to her chest. She is staring blankly at her little boat. It seems to be languishing on the rim of the embankment, lame against the pull of the waves.

"What are you doing here?" Harriet hisses. "I thought you were on Longstone."

Eva doesn't answer. Her eyes are glassy and unfocused. Harriet wonders if her words have even registered.

After a long silence, Eva says, "Where have you been?"

Harriet's fingers tense around the handle of the lamp. She is not about to explain herself to Eva. Why should she? "Did you know it when you married him?" she demands suddenly. She holds out the lantern, spearing light into Eva's eyes.

Eva turns away. Her shoulders round and she hugs her knees tighter. Pieces of dark hair fall across her eyes. She doesn't look surprised. As though she has been waiting for this truth to find its way out. "Yes," she says finally. "I knew."

Her flat admission catches Harriet off guard. Something has happened, surely, but she cannot bring herself to care. "Did you really think you could go your entire life without any of us finding out?" she demands. "Or did you simply imagine we wouldn't care?"

Eva doesn't respond. Doesn't argue. Just rests her chin on her knees and continues staring out at the water. Darkness there now. For the first time in weeks, the bay is empty of Henry Ward's ship. Perhaps the *Eagle* has sailed far away, Harriet thinks. Perhaps the *Eagle* will not be caught. The thought feels naïve. Too hopeful. Or is it hopeless? She can't tell anymore.

"Oliver was a dangerous bully," Eva says finally. There is no fire to her words. None of the hostility Harriet was expecting. "Finn was just defending himself."

Harriet snorts. "Is that what you tell yourself to make it all right? Or is that what your husband tells you?"

Eva doesn't look at her. "You did not know Oliver. You do not know what he was like."

"And you did? How old were you when your husband killed our brother, Eva? Three? Four? Young enough for your memories to have turned into what you want them to be."

Eva looks at her squarely then, and Harriet sees her eyes are bloodshot and swollen with tears. The sight catches her off guard. Eva is rarely one for outward displays of emotion. "Well," she says finally. "You do not have to worry yourself over my husband any longer. He left. On your father's ship. Because he thought that was what was best for me."

Harriet's stomach falls. "On my father's ship?" she repeats. Her mouth turns dry and she feels her heart hammering against her ribs. But this is what Finn Murray deserves, isn't it? To hang at Execution Dock beside her father? Yes, she tells herself. What he deserves.

She can't quite make herself feel it. But what's done is done.

She swallows heavily. "I'm sorry, Eva," she says. Her voice comes out so soft she is not sure her sister even hears her. Without waiting for a response, she turns and makes her way inside the house.

CHAPTER THIRTY-SEVEN

When he wakes the next morning, Nathan's first thought is that he has killed a man.

His second thought is that Julia had not returned to the house after sending for the barber surgeon.

The barber surgeon's outlook, Nathan supposes, had been as good as he could have hoped for. Ball removed cleanly from flesh and muscle only. As yet no sign of infection.

The guilt of it is almost impossibly heavy on Nathan's shoulders. After all, Edwin had only been out there to support him. But Nathan cannot bring himself to regret the events of last night. Cannot bear to think what might have happened to Theodora if he and Edwin had fled from the house as they had planned.

When the sun has risen and the tide drained, Nathan takes Thea over to Bamburgh in a wagon and brings Jenny and Thomas back to the house. Fetches Mrs Brodie from the village. The house settles into a sluggish rhythm, with Edwin bleary with opium on the settle in the parlour, Harriet sitting dutifully at his side, and Eva locked away upstairs with her wordless grief.

And so. Edwin is alive, and Graveney is dead; and these things make it possible for Nathan's thoughts to veer towards Julia.

His heart is overbeating as he makes his way to the curiosity shop. And not in that dizzyingly pleasant way that being around her usually elicits. No, this time is far more laced with dread. A fear of what he might see when he steps through that door. Blood on her hands. Lies on her tongue. Nonetheless, he can't deny the pull to see her. To try and wrench an explanation out of her. Last night, he had believed his only choice was to flee Holy Island and never see her again. Now this chance to stay has been given to him, he knows he ought to be grateful. But he cannot quite make himself feel it.

He is not surprised to find the shop closed. How can Julia let customers inside with blood staining the stairs of the cellar? He knocks on the side door, caught between a desperate need to see her, and a deep desire to run away.

Julia opens the door without speaking. The shadows beneath her eyes suggest her night had been as sleepless as his.

"You thought it best to leave without a word last night?" he asks.

"Did you wish me to stay?"

He holds her gaze for a long second. Does not know the answer to that question.

Julia steps aside, gesturing for him to enter. Nathan expects to be led down to the cellar, or be herded into some lightless corner of the alley. But she leads him upstairs to her living quarters.

Nathan's gaze travels around the tiny space. A small round table is crammed up beside a threadbare settle, two bowls and teacups dumped into the trough by the hearth. Though the fire has burnt out, the room still carries its warmth, and the stale smell of burnt porridge. Two narrow beds stand side by side against the back wall, blankets tossed messily across them.

"I'm sorry," Julia says huskily. "It's a little small. And untidy." Nathan sees a flicker of shame in her eyes. A part of him wants to reach for her, pull her to him. Tell her she could live in a cow shed for all it bothers him. But right now, he cannot let that part of himself win. He has far too many questions that are in dire need of answers.

"You've never brought me up here before. Why now?" He wonders if it's some kind of peace offering. An attempt at letting him in, after all she has been keeping from him. Or maybe she has reached the point where she no longer cares. A point they can no longer come back from.

Julia doesn't answer. Doesn't sit, or offer him a chair. She just hovers by the table, picking at a scrap of dirt beneath her thumbnail.

"Joseph Holland was not in his cottage," Nathan says finally. He had gone to Holland's cottage on his way to the shop this morning, seeking confirmation of the suspicions he had begun to gather. Not that he had truly needed it.

"Is that some thinly veiled accusation, Nathan?" Something flickers behind Julia's eyes. "If there is something you wish to ask me, why not just do it?"

"I did that yesterday. And you refused to speak to me."

She lowers her eyes, her fleeting boldness disappearing. "How could I have spoken openly when your daughter was around?"

Nathan takes a step towards her. Softens his voice slightly. "My daughter is not here now."

For long moments, there is silence. Julia opens her mouth to speak, and then seems to change her mind. Nathan clenches his hands; wills her to talk to him. He is choosing to take her bringing him up here as a sign she wants to resurrect what was between them. He wants that too. Desperately. But they cannot resurrect anything with silence.

He tries to swallow his frustration. "Did Holland hurt you?" he asks finally.

Silence.

"Where is his body?"

"It's gone."

"Did you kill him?"

Julia looks up to meet his eyes. "Is that what you think me capable of?"

"No," Nathan says, without hesitation. "I don't." Thoughts of his own seconds behind the trigger flash through his mind. He had never imagined himself capable of killing another. Perhaps he is wrong about Julia too. "In any case, I know you are not capable of removing his body from your cellar all on your own." He looks at her squarely. "I assume from the blood on the stairs that that is where he ended up."

Julia doesn't respond.

And the removal of Joseph Holland's body, Nathan realises then, is just one in a long line of pieces that do not quite add up. Her reluctance to take him upstairs before now, her insistence on speaking in the cellar, the sound of hidden people moving around inside her shop. Pieces he has been doing his best to ignore, in favour of the way Julia makes him feel. He cannot be that naïve fool any longer.

"Who has been here?" he asks suddenly. "One of your brothers?"

His guess is not wrong; he can tell by the look in her eyes. He can see her thoughts churning, as though debating whether to be open with him. Is that really where they are at now? Have they ever been anywhere other than this?

Julia lets out a breath. She goes to look out the narrow window, keeping her back to Nathan. "Hugh returned to Lindisfarne not long after the siege at the castle," she says finally. "He told me I was to keep him at my shop, down in the cellar. I told him again and again that it wasn't safe. But he had no interest in hearing it. He said he needed to be on Holy Island to do his part for the cause."

"You were adamant that you would not let your brothers stay with you," Nathan says tautly. "Need I remind you, you hid them away in my attic. And then cast them off on Eva and Finn."

"I know. And I never wanted…" Julia trails off. Rubs her hand across her eyes. Finally, she turns to face him. "Hugh… He's different to Michael and Angus. He takes what he wants. Does not ask questions first." She sighs. "I wish I had the strength to tell him no. But I've always felt indebted to him, after all he did for me and Bobby. And he's a changed man now. Since his wife and son died, all he cares about is seeing the Rising succeed. He'll not listen to reason. And he doesn't care what anyone else wants. He wouldn't even let me tell Michael and Angus he was staying with me."

"You ought to have told me," Nathan says. "You know I would have supported you. I would not have told anyone he was here." He hears his voice harden. "Or did you not trust me enough to do that?"

Julia closes her eyes. Her silence is all the answer he needs.

"Well," he says tightly, "in that case, you ought to have kept your distance from me."

Tears slide off Julia's chin. "I could not do that either."

A chaos of emotions roils inside him. Nathan digs his hands into the pockets of his coat, so he will not be tempted to reach for her. "Did you tell your brother that Holland was spying for the government? I assume that's why he killed him."

"No." She looks at him squarely for the first time, her eyes dark and intent. "I swear it. Hugh tried to get the information out of me. But I refused to tell him. I knew it would put you in danger." She swallows heavily. "Holland came to the shop yesterday. Tried to force his way down into the cellar where Hugh was hiding. He must have seen him in the street, I suppose. Must have heard about the crimes he committed. Hugh fired at him the moment he saw him." She wipes her eyes with the back of her hand. "That's just the kind of man he is."

"Where is Hugh now?" Nathan asks.

"He left. Last night. He's gone to fight with the rebels in Lancashire."

Nathan nods. He sinks wearily into a chair at the table and stares into the unlit grate.

"What will you do?" Julia dares to ask. "Now Ward and his men are gone?"

Nathan doesn't answer. Doesn't have an answer. He feels stuck in limbo. He cannot leave Lindisfarne now, with Edwin in such a state, of course. But with luck, he will heal. He and Harriet will return to London with their son.

And then?

Nathan cannot deny that, in spite of everything, he has grown attached to the idea of staying here on Holy Island. Returning to London, and struggling to rebuild his business leaves him more hollow than he could ever have imagined when he had first been forced up here by Henry Ward.

A foolish thing, he knows, after all the distrust he has faced from the villagers. But with Holland's disappearance, rumours about the man will spread, and he will soon be revealed as the island's government informant. With luck, the suspicion will be lifted from Nathan's family.

Joseph Holland… Unsurprisingly, the thought leads him straight back to Julia. If he walks away from her now, with this thing in pieces, how will he ever pass her in the street? The village is too small to hold two people who can barely look each other in the eye.

He knows Theodora will be devastated if he tells her they are leaving. And he has no thought of what effect returning to London will have on her. Will she go back to her unsettled, fearful self, plagued by nightmares and haunted by the loss of her mother? Nathan would rather face Julia every day than put his child through that again.

He stands up from the table too abruptly. "Is there anything you need?" he asks, well aware he has not answered her question. "I want you to be safe."

Julia shakes her head. And as Nathan makes his way towards the stairwell, silence feels like the only fitting response.

CHAPTER THIRTY-EIGHT

Harriet listens to the raspy timbre of Edwin's breath. Inhalation. Exhalation. She watches his chest rise and fall beneath his thin linen shirt. She must be grateful he is living, because if she is not, well, what kind of person would that make her? She cannot bear to think on it.

Her eyes drift to the dark pearls of blood staining the fabric of the settle. There is something oddly fascinating about them. They feel so utterly out of place; a symbol of violence against the mundane bleakness of the parlour. In any case, focusing on the bloodstains, and on trying to force the gratitude of Edwin's survival, stops her from thinking about her father, and whether or not he is in the hands of the authorities now. And whether her sister's husband is in chains alongside him.

Harriet has no thought of whether the authorities have found her father's ship. Unlikely, she tells herself. Surely the militia's priorities will lie with the Rising, and they will have brushed away her report of pirates in the bay.

Wishful thinking. Harriet knows she was not imagining the hard look in the soldiers' eyes when she told them about the *Eagle's* attack on the East Indian trade ships. No doubt the authorities will derive as much pleasure from seeing pirates on the end of a rope as they would a band of Jacobite rebels.

And if this is the fate that is to befall Finn Murray, it is best that Eva does not know of it. Best she live ignorant, at least now, while she can. Best she hold onto her distant scrap of hope for his return for as long as possible.

Of course, if her husband is to be put to death, she will receive word of it. But she will never know that her sister had been the one to send the authorities after the ship. Harriet will make sure of that.

It has been two days since she went to the militia. Two days since she had confronted Eva about her husband's role in Oliver's death. They have not spoken a word to each other since. Worst of all, it is not even a malicious coldness. It is just emptiness on Eva's part. Deep guilt on Harriet's. Her vigil at this makeshift bedside of Edwin's is far more about avoiding her sister than it is about keeping watch over her husband.

Harriet hears the distant sound of voices outside the house. Hears a muffled scraping and crashing coming from the direction of the water. She cannot see out in that direction from the parlour.

With a distant kind of curiosity, she goes to her workroom and peeks out the window. Sees two of the herring fisherman on the embankment with Eva, hauling that sorry-looking boat of hers up out of the low tide.

Footsteps thump down the stairs and Nathan strides outside. "What is all this?" he asks.

Eva keeps her eyes on the boat. Harriet can just make out her words: "They've agreed to fix the skiff for me. I'm going home."

"Back to Longstone?"

"Yes."

Harriet is glad of it. Keeping her distance from her sister will be far easier, of course, with Eva marooning herself out on Longstone.

"Don't be foolish," Nathan says. "You cannot go out there alone. Please. Stay here with us."

Harriet holds her breath. Is relieved when Eva says, "No. I need to go back." As though it is not even a choice.

Harriet hurries back into the parlour before either of them catch her at the window. She returns to her chair at Edwin's side. Returns to watching his chest rise and fall.

It ought to be Eva that is feeling guilty, Harriet thinks. After all, she is the one who married the man who killed their brother. But she also knows that one word to her sister will send her tumbling down into this bottomless chasm of regret.

She stares at Edwin. His skin is pale, a sharp contrast to the dark hair that hangs limp and thready against his cheeks. A good chance of survival, the barber surgeon had said. Soon they will return to their house in London, with all their misery. She will be *wife* and *mother*, with her paintings burned, and there will be no escaping it all.

And if he doesn't survive? What would her life look like then? The townhouse would be hers, along with a comfortable settlement. No doubt she would be drawn back under Nathan's wing somewhat. But there are far worse fates. Nathan is soft and pliable. Far easier to manipulate than Edwin. He would put a paintbrush back in her hand, without demanding she behave herself first. He would allow her to see her artist friends. Perhaps allow her to travel to Paris with Isabelle.

Harriet is not even aware of having picked up the cushion. And she is watching from outside herself as she lifts it Edwin's face. Holds it to his mouth and nose. Gentle pressure at first, a faux thing, testing herself, imagining what the act would feel like. And then a little more pressure. A little more. Edwin's body twitches. He lets out an opium murmur, and the floor outside the parlour creaks. Harriet darts a glance over her shoulder, the cushion tumbling to the floor.

Theodora is standing in the doorway, motionless, watching. She holds Harriet's gaze for a long, wordless moment, her lips parted, her eyes wide and unreadable.

Harriet tries to smile. Her heart is speeding and her body is on fire. Her hands tremble with the realisation of what she had just tried to do. "Thea," she says, too brightly, "go and tell Mrs Brodie that Uncle Edwin would like some more water."

CHAPTER THIRTY-NINE

Over and over, Julia had told herself this would always be home. She had fought for it when her father had thrown her from his house—he had been the one to leave Lindisfarne, unable to bear the shame of her and her bastard child. She had held her ground. Fought for this place.

But she knows now that she was wrong when she claimed she would never leave. Because Lindisfarne has stopped feeling like home.

People are beginning to speak of Holland's disappearance. There are whispers about a man who lived alone; and those whispers, predictably, are leading to stories that he had been spying for the government.

Julia has not heard any suspicion cast in her direction. But that does not stop her from feeling guilty every time she passes another villager in the street. And it does not stop her from fearing that soon the suspicions will turn to her. All it would take is one glance at the blood she has been unable to fully remove from the cellar stairs, no matter how many times she scrubs them.

She stands in the middle of the curiosity shop. This life she had built from nothing. But she knows every time she hears the bell above the door ring now, she will think of Joseph Holland stepping inside. Will hear the echo of Hugh's pistol shot.

Worst of all, she knows she will think of Nathan. Of the way he had held her, kissed her, told her he planned to stay here and build a life with her. And she will think of the pleading look in his eyes when he had come to her shop the day of Holland's death. Will think of her own stony silence, and the unbearable look of hurt in Nathan's eyes.

Julia knows she cannot stay here. Her brothers have all left now, and she will follow them. Will leave no trace of her family on Lindisfarne, beyond her mother's grave. She cannot walk the streets with held breath every day, in fear of passing Nathan. Nor can she expect him to leave, given how hard he had fought for Highfield House.

She turns in a slow circle, taking in the cluttered shelves of her shop. The gold-embossed books, the gnarled and tarnished candleholders, the gaudy brass trinket boxes and that old pair of cavalier boots. Where to even begin packing up such a place? Is she to take these wares with her? Cart them across the country in an attempt to start again? Or just walk away, and leave this part of her life to be forgotten?

In the back corner of the shop, she finds an old wooden travelling trunk. She carries it over to the bookshelf. Begins to pull the titles from the shelf and place them inside. This, she supposes, is as a good a place to start as any.

Though he knows he should not be surprised to see it, the sight of Julia packing up the shop is a knife to the chest. Nathan has tried to stay away, but he keeps being drawn here. Cannot even make sense of why he has come here today. When he had left her yesterday, it had been clear there was to be no fixing things.

He knows the wisest thing is to walk away. Not ask questions. Accept that this is the way things are supposed to be.

He finds himself knocking anyway. Seeking what? Closure? An explanation that will make this make sense? Make it less painful, somehow? He doubts such a thing is possible.

Julia unlocks the door without a word.

"You are closing the shop?" he asks throatily.

"I'm leaving Holy Island."

Hearing her say it out loud makes his stomach fall. This is not the way things ought to be. Nathan knows how much she loves this place. He steps inside, closing the door behind him. "Because of Holland?"

Her eyes are glistening, but there is a hard look about her, as though she is refusing to let her emotions run away. "In part," she says. She swallows visibly. "In part, because of you."

Her honesty makes his chest ache. He stares at her for a long time. A part of him wants to beg her to reconsider. Cling to her. Keep her here. But something keeps him rooted in place. Something more than his fear.

"You know I'm right to do it," she says.

And he nods. "Let me be the one to leave," he says huskily. "This is your home. You told me once that you never wished to leave this place. I do not want you to do that on account of me."

"This is your home too," she says. "I know you forgot that for a time. But I think you have remembered it now." She lowers her eyes. Drops her voice. "It is best for me to leave. Before anyone begins to suspect I had anything to do with Holland's disappearance."

He reaches for her suddenly. Pulls her into him, feeling the warmth of her body against his own. Surely this has to count for something, the fact that he can hold her like this. Can feel his heart beating hard against his chest with something that is not fear or dread.

And yes, it does count for something. But it is not enough.

He closes his eyes for a moment, drinking in her nearness. When will he ever feel this again, he wonders? This need to be close to a woman. Perhaps never. But the two of them are an impossibility.

Julia pulls back and looks at him squarely. "I loved you," she says. "For what it's worth. I just want you to know that." She swallows visibly. "I love you."

"I loved you too," says Nathan. He cannot bring himself to consider whether he still does, after all this. Because if he reaches the wrong conclusion, he will try and make her stay.

"I'm sorry," he says.

Julia nods. "So am I. But this is how it is."

"Yes." He releases his grip on her. Clasps his hands together so he is not tempted to reach for her again. "It is."

Having no choice in the matter makes it easy to find courage. Harriet knows she cannot stay here, after all Theodora has seen; after all she has done to Eva. She cannot stay here and wait for Edwin to recover, for that colourless life in London to become a reality.

There's a simplicity to her leaving.

The deep darkness of the island is lit only with a single candle, and its light barely makes it to the corners of this vast, empty bedroom. There is something unnerving about being in this room alone so late at night. Something that makes her think of all the death and loss this house must have seen.

She slips her coin pouch inside her stays. It is still heavy with the money Michael Mitchell had paid her for her journey to Lesbury. It will be enough to get her off this island. Back to London. To Isabelle's garret in Lambeth.

Harriet knows Isabelle will keep a roof over her head for as long as she needs it. Until she finds a way to turn those coins into more. How she will do this, she cannot bear to think on. In her dreams, she does it by selling her artwork. In reality, she knows there are other horrors that are far more likely.

Still, she cannot stay. Simplicity.

She blows out the candle and feels her way through the blackness. She stands for a moment in the doorway, looking across to the nursery as her eyes adjust to the darkness.

This is the part of the equation that is not so simple. Or perhaps it is. Perhaps she just does not want to admit to that simplicity.

She touches the coins in her bodice. Enough to make it to London. But not enough to give a child a good life.

She pushes down anything that comes close to emotion. She does not open the nursery door. Does not peek inside at her sleeping son.

Edwin will recover, she tells herself. Thomas will have his father. And he is far better off without his mother. Always has been.

Simplicity.

With her bag on her shoulder, she walks down the stairs and out the door in the silence of the night, quietening the voice in her head that seeks to take away her courage.

CHAPTER FORTY

Longstone is where she needs to be. In spite of all she has lost, Eva has no choice but to be here. Because that firebasket must to come to life each night; must light the dark, to save lives.

It must be lit to atone for Oliver. To atone for Donald Macauley. And it must be lit because that is what Finn's father had wanted when he had built this place all those years ago, after his brothers had drowned on the Knavestone reef.

A thick autumn cold settles over the island, and Longstone becomes a place of silvery half-light. Eva goes to the mainland, to Lindisfarne, when she needs supplies: flour for bread, and vegetables for soup that all too often are left to curl and brown, neglected in the bottom of the sideboard. She mends hemlines and holes, exchanging them for coins that keep her fed and warm. She goes to Highfield House for Theodora's lessons; hears of Edwin's slow recovery, and Harriet's midnight escape. She sits through plea after plea from Nathan to return to the house and be with her family. Though she is thankful her brother is staying on Holy Island, she grows tired of refusing his requests. Begins to go to the house with less and less regularity, until Nathan gives up and sends his daughter to the dame school.

And as she exchanges words with the villagers, Eva hears things: hears of the Jacobite defeat in Lancashire; hears of the bloodshed on the heathland of Sherrifmuir. She feels the gloom fall over Lindisfarne when the troops return at the end of the campaign year, broken and defeated, and mourning the dead. She feels their heaviness and their grief, and she carries it back to her island.

Each night, as she lights the basket, she thinks of Finn. Wonders where the *Eagle* has taken him. She tries to hold on to that scrap of hope of seeing him again, but it feels so unlikely. So far away. She knows the *Eagle* is on its way to the New World, with nothing surrounding it but sea. No way off the ship. No way back to England.

No way back to her.

The emptiness is profound; deep and quiet and silver-grey. The nights are never-ending; and the day, when it comes, is pale and weak. She sleeps with the sparse hours of daylight. Rises with the night.

And that emptiness, it's almost unfathomable, given she has also become aware of the life she is carrying inside her. A profound un-emptiness in this face of this great hollow. But this is something she cannot acknowledge. Not yet, with the days growing shorter and the winter closing in. No, she thinks, she cannot even begin to contemplate that future when she will no longer be alone on her island. When this wild place will no longer just be hers. Because if she thinks of it, she will only manage fear and grief and loneliness; none of the happiness she wishes she could feel. Right now, it is easier to feel nothing at all.

Right now, she cannot think further than the next long firelit night that lies ahead.

News has reached them in the Marshalsea cell: Henry Ward has been taken to the Admiralty Court to face trial. The fall of a once-revered privateer. He will hang, of course; a warning to all those other privateers who have turned to piracy in the wake of this shallow European peace.

Ward's trial, Finn thinks, will be a spectacle. Not so much for the rabble he is locked in here with. Their trial will take place in two days' time—a foregone conclusion, he has no doubt. Each of these men had sailed from the Caribbean with Ward, lured by the promise of riches. And yet none of them have the pennies to do anything other than represent themselves. No choice but to put their own sorry defences before the court: stories of drunkenness, and regret, and lies of being taken from honest merchant ships by bloodthirsty pirates. Finn knows none of it will make a difference. In a few days' time, their bodies will be swinging over the Thames, to be washed by three tides of the river.

The cell is crammed with debtors and pirates, thick with the breath and grunts and snores of men. The stone floor is covered in straw. Buckets in corners and carpets of damp, foul-smelling muck. With a forgone trial laid out before him, Finn spends the nights with his knees hugged to his chest and an impossible weight bearing down on him. Floats in and out of hazy firelit dreams.

He hopes that somehow, Eva will learn what has happened to him. With his execution she will be free to marry again, free to start the life she ought to have been living. He longs to see her once more, if just for a moment. But even if he could somehow get word to her before he is to die, he would not want that for her. He does not want her last memories of their marriage to be of him climbing onto the scaffold.

Guards at the gate now. They unlock the door of the cell, the loud clatter pulling Finn from his thoughts.

He hears someone call his name. A guard, he realises. He can't make sense of it. Are they not all to go to trial together, this rabble of Henry Ward's? Perhaps he is delirious, his senses dulled by thirst, by fear, by grief.

He tries to stand anyway. His legs are weak and shaky from disuse, his calf aching dully behind the scar left by Martin Macauley's bullet.

With a vice-like grip around his arm, two guards lead him out of the cell, through narrow stone corridors with high peaked roofs. He shivers in the sudden cold. No one speaks.

They climb stairs. Walk more corridors. And a door is unlocked. A door to the outside world, Finn realises, as pale morning light trickles in, cold and smoky and stinking of the river. He gulps down the air as though it just rose off the sea.

"Henry Ward has confirmed you were a prisoner on the *Eagle*," says one guard. "He has confirmed your name was not on his pirates' articles."

And in his haze, and his grief, and his exhaustion, it takes Finn a moment to piece together these words. Takes a moment for him to understand that that foregone trial has fallen away. Takes a moment for him to realise he is free.

This is nothing but delirium, surely. How could it be anything else? But then Finn feels a silent laugh starting from deep within him, making his chest shake.

He thinks of sitting at the table in Ward's great cabin with the articles laid out in front of him, feeling the ship move, drawing him away from Eva. He thinks of the ink blots he had left on the articles, as his hand hovered over the page in indecision.

Thinks of the way he had tossed the quill aside at the shouts from the lookout—*enemy, three points to port…*

The prison gates clang open. Finn does not look back at the guards, or the sharp peaked roofs of the Marshalsea. Does not look back in case this is a dream, or the cruellest of tricks. How many men accused of piracy must have stood in the dock at the Admiralty Court and claimed they were forced aboard the ship? He supposes the words of the captain have far more weight than a desperate, accused nobody.

Finn knows he will not have the chance to thank Ward for this reprieve. And perhaps there's a part of him that does not even think he ought to be grateful. After all, Ward had been the one to force him onto the ship in the first place.

But he cannot help the lingering loyalty for the man who had once been like a father to him. For the man who had looked out for his safety; who had sought to allay his fears. For the man who had taught him a little decency. And he cannot help the lingering sadness that comes at the thought of Ward's approaching death.

It is a short walk from the prison to the river, through the winding cobbles of Southwark. The air is cold enough to make his breath plume, cold enough to coat the mud on the roadside with a thin layer of ice. Finn is dimly aware he ought to be freezing in just his shirtsleeves, but his pounding heart is making his body blaze.

Watermen's dinghies are tied up along the edge of the river, two small ketches moored alongside them. In the pink half-light of early morning, the river is coming to life, with a forest of masts already cluttering the water. Men shout to each other as they pile crates and barrels onto barges;

a waterman winds at his mooring ropes as two women in patched cloaks holler down at him from the bank.

But that sloop, over there, unattended and loosely tethered, that would be all too easy to climb into. All too easy to free from its moorings and take down the Thames towards the sea. Ocean-worthy, no, but he can cling to the coast; guide it carefully back towards Northumberland. Nurse it out the Farnes. Sleep beneath the upturned boat. Wash in the ocean. Pocket apples and bread loaves when no one is looking. Find a coat and hat left unguarded.

No more thieving, he had promised Eva. Not a single lump of coal. But he steps into the boat and grapples with the mooring ropes anyway, certain she will allow him this one last transgression.

CHAPTER FORTY-ONE

It's only when Finn sees the bonfires glittering on the hilltops that he realises he has sailed into Northumberland on midwinter's night. Fragrant ribbons of peat smoke thicken the air, and from the water, he sees the fireflies of torchlights as villagers march back to their homes. He thinks of childhood midwinters; traditions his Scottish-born mother had insisted on. Milk left on the hearth for the friendly spirits; iron hammers and axes beside it meant to keep the nasty ones away. Memories he has barely thought of in years.

Back when his mother was alive, the year's midnight had been his favourite time of year. But alone on Longstone with childhood far behind him, midwinter had been nothing but eternal cold and dark.

Tonight, though, there's a restless thumping in his chest, half excitement and half fear. He is just a handful of miles from Holy Island now.

Never in his life had he imagined the sight of Highfield House might bring him joy. He is craving it with every inch of his being. But beyond that desperate desire to return to the house is a fear of what he might find. He knows there's every chance Eva and her family may have returned to London. Knows he might have sailed right past them on his way back up the country. But he needs to try the house first. Needs to hope they have decided to stay in Northumberland, now Ward and Graveney are gone.

But then he sees a light he was not expecting to see. Out on his right, high in the sky. Guiding ships away from the Farnes, and the black crenelations of the Knavestone reef.

Finn hears his own exhalation, overcome with fresh emotion. He leans on the tiller, turning the boat out towards Longstone.

He thinks of Eva with ash on her hands. Thinks of her huddling over the lamp with her needle and thread, dark hair falling over her cheeks. Thinks of her decorating the cottage in flour as she wrangles out another half-moon of bread.

And he thinks of her standing at the window, looking out over the sea. Watching, waiting.

He had gone with Henry Ward so she might be saved from such a thing. So she might spend her nights with her eyes turned away from the ocean. But he sees now that he has been foolish. Sees he has only given her more reason for sleeplessness. More reason to keep her eyes on the sea.

As he gets closer, he sees her, dwarfed by the firebasket, illuminated by its light. He sees her fly down the stairs of the cottage, charge out onto the jetty. Sees her standing on tiptoe, trying to reach out to sea, a hand pressed to her mouth as though she is afraid to believe.

Finn wills the boat onward. Wills it faster. Wills it straighter. Feels waves of emotion tighten his throat.

When he had first climbed aboard Henry Ward's ship as a nine-year-old child, it had been with the hope that he would never see the tiny spit of Longstone again. But he has never been more grateful for the blaze of the beacon, bright against the darkness, guiding him home.

Edwin has not come after her; Harriet feels certain of that. If he wished it, he could find her here at Isabelle's garret with little difficulty. Perhaps he does not yet have the strength to come after her. Perhaps one day he will appear at the door. She knows it's a possibility. Nonetheless, with each day that passes without sight of him, the knot inside her loosens a little.

Harriet feels safe here in London. Sheltered. The only window in this attic room looks straight up into the sky—only the birds and the stars can see inside. Tucked away with her paints, with her easel, with this woman she cares for so deeply, Harriet is beginning to see flickers of light in the darkness.

She thinks often of her son. Argues with herself, berates herself, and repeatedly comes to the conclusion that she had done what was best for him. Perhaps it's just an excuse. But convincing herself of its truth is the only way she can carry the shame. The only way she can let this life she has longed for bring her any joy.

But today, that life is bringing her no comfort. Today the knot inside her is as tight as ever.

Harriet buttons her cloak. Pulls on her gloves. Forces down a fresh wellspring of regret.

"Shall I come with you?" Isabelle asks. Her voice is calm and gentle, and there's a part of Harriet that wants nothing more than her company.

But she shakes her head. This is something she needs to do alone. And perhaps there is a part of her that does not want Isabelle to see the guilt she carries. Sometimes faint, sometimes blazing.

She has begun to tell Isabelle about everything that happened on Lindisfarne. In pieces, only—it is far too much to spill everything at once. With each fragment of the story, Harriet feels herself unravelling, opening. Feels the glacier inside her beginning to thaw.

But she is not ready to speak about sending her own father to the gallows.

Isabelle had not judged her when she had admitted to leaving Thomas behind. Had not judged her when, in a half-whispered voice, Harriet had spoken of holding that cushion in her hands. That dizzying outside-herself moment of lifting it to Edwin's face. But condemning her own father? Harriet fears that Isabelle would not see past this.

She slips her coin pouch into her pocket and murmurs her goodbyes, keeping her head down so Isabelle cannot see her eyes.

Harriet climbs from the waterman's boat not far from the Tower. The streets are heaving; boats knocking up against each other along the water. A grand procession is to take place, she has overheard, from London

Bridge to Wapping, with the Marshall of the Admiralty carrying his silver oar. Her father, the condemned man, trailing behind. A final drink offered at the Turk's Head.

There's laughter in the air; raucous chatter, children running back and forth along the riverbank. It makes Harriet's skin prickle. Do none of these people understand that her father is to die? Sent to his death by his own jilted child?

Harriet pushes through the crowd. She fights the urge to turn back, and elbows her way past the wharves into Wapping. She follows the crowd past red brick towers, and warehouses echoing with thumps and voices. And she reaches Execution Dock; a floating pontoon just off shore, the noose swaying gently with the brown rise and fall of the river.

Harriet feels her stomach drop. Beneath her cloak and thick winter bodice, her skin is blazing.

She has never seen anyone put to death before. Has never seen the revelry in it; never understood why the end of life ought to be a source of entertainment. But she knows she needs to be here today. Knows this is her punishment. Once it is over and her father is gone, she will return to Isabelle and her painting and the quiet, sheltered garret with a view of the sky. She will try to remember that this life is making her happy.

The crowd chatters as it waits. Stories of hangings witnessed: men who took an age to die. Others whose bodies were rushed by the crowd, legs tugged downward to a quick and merciful death. Harriet's stomach turns over and she forces herself to breath.

The minutes tick towards twelve o'clock, beating away the seconds of her father's life. The knot in Harriet's stomach grows a little tighter. Will he see her here in the crowd? Will he know, somehow, that all this was her doing? That she, in a moment of unbridled childish rage, had sent the authorities after him? Had condemned him and his crew to their deaths?

Now she is off the island, calm and safe in Isabelle's company; now her decision to leave has been made and cannot be undone, Harriet is able to see with a little more clarity. She sees the foolishness, the childishness of her choice to turn her father in. And the regret is almost impossible to bear. Still, this is the choice she has made. And she must learn to carry it.

It is ten past the hour. Now twenty. With each distant rattle of cartwheels over the cobbles, the crowd turns as one. But the Admiral's procession does not appear. And the whispers are beginning. The rumours, the elaborate stories of last-minute pardons and jail breaks and escaped prisoners.

Harriet does not allow herself to believe them. Does not dare to, for fear of what this might mean for her, for her family. Does not dare to grapple with that flimsiest scrap of hope for a reprieve from the guilt that keeps her awake at night. Does not dare to imagine that her father, who had been privy to Jacobite secrets, might somehow have wrangled his way to freedom.

She does not allow herself to believe this, no. But that does nothing to change the empty swing of the hangman's noose, or the restless groans of the crowd. Does nothing to change the knowledge that her father will not cast a shadow over the Thames tonight.

ABOUT THE AUTHOR

A lover of old stuff, folk music, and ghost stories, Johanna Craven bases her books around little-known true events from the past. She divides her time between the UK and Australia, and can be very easily persuaded to tell you about the time she accidently swam with seals on Holy Island.

Find out more at www.johannacraven.com.